The Graphic Novel

Hansel and Gretel

retold by Donald Lemke

illustrated by Sean Dietrich

STONE ARCH BOOKS
www.stonearchbooks.com

Graphic Spin is published by Stone Arch Books,
A Capstone Imprint
1710 Roe Crest Drive
North Mankato, Minnesota 56003
www.capstonepub.com

Copyright © 2009 by Stone Arch Books

Library of Congress Cataloging-in-Publication Data
Lemke, Donald B.
    Hansel and Gretel: The Graphic Novel / retold by Donald Lemke; illustrated by Sean Dietrich.
    p. cm. — (Graphic Spin)
    ISBN 978-1-4342-0767-8 (library binding)
    ISBN 978-1-4342-0863-7 (pbk.)
    1. Graphic novels. [1. Graphic novels.] I. Dietrich, Sean, ill. II. Hansel and Gretel. English.
III. Title.
PZ7.7.L46Han 2009
741.5'973—dc22   2008006721

Summary: When their parents leave them in the forest, Hansel and Gretel must find their way home.
During their journey, they discover something better — a house made of sugary sweets! Too bad it's
owned by an evil, and hungry, old witch.

Art Director: Heather Kindseth
Graphic Designer: Kay Fraser / Brann Garvey

Librarian Reviewer
Katharine Kan
Graphic novel reviewer and Library Consultant, Panama City, FL
MLS in Library and Information Studies, University of Hawaii at Manoa, HI

Reading Consultant
Elizabeth Stedem
Educator/Consultant, Colorado Springs, CO
MA in Elementary Education, University of Denver, CO

Printed in the United States of America in Stevens Point, Wisconsin.
072013
007593R

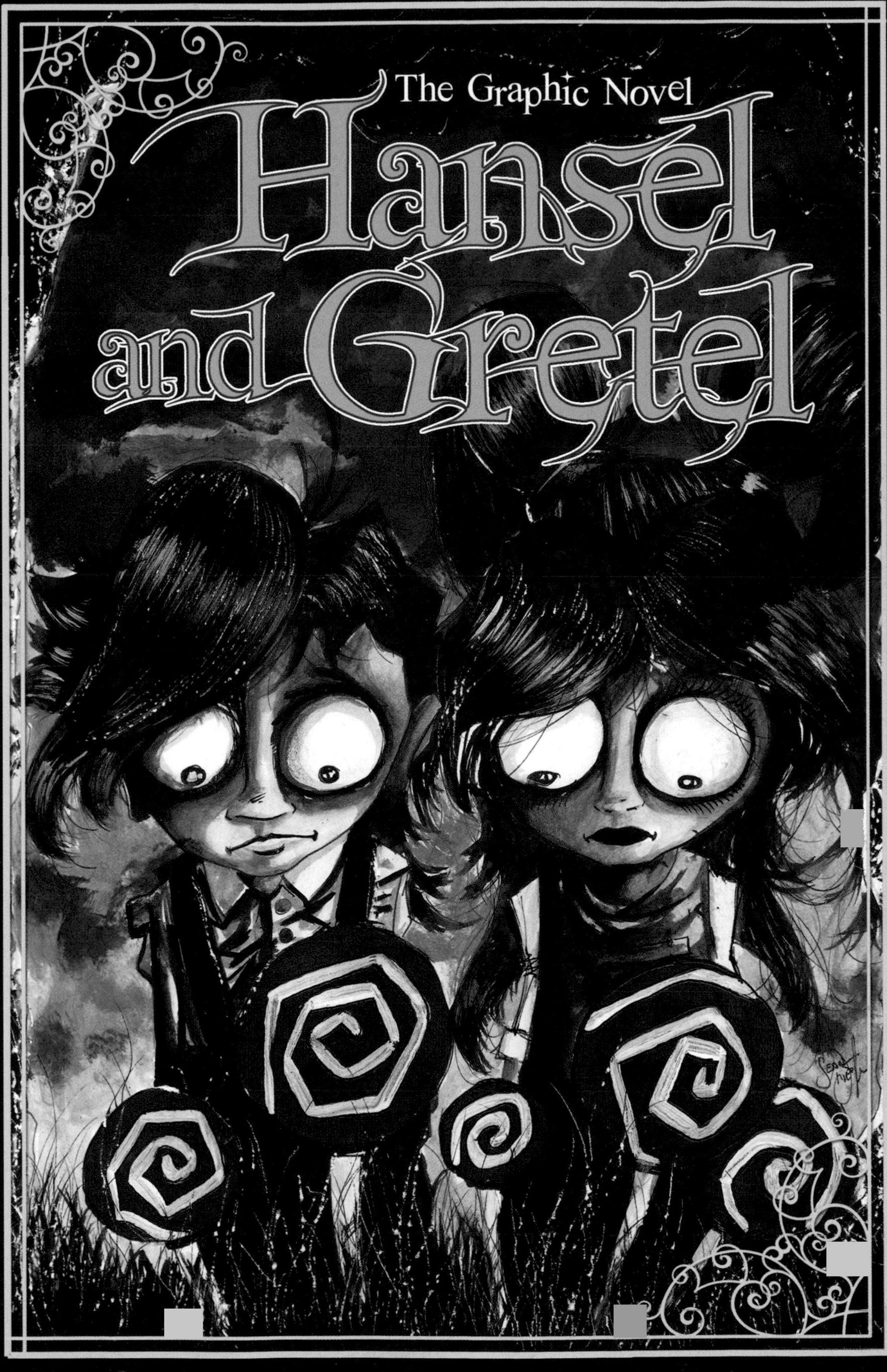
The Graphic Novel
Hansel and Gretel

Cast of Characters

The Father

Hansel

4

The Stepmother

The Old Woman

Gretel

On the edge of a great forest lived a woodcutter and his family.

The woodcutter made very little money, and his wife and children had very little food to eat.

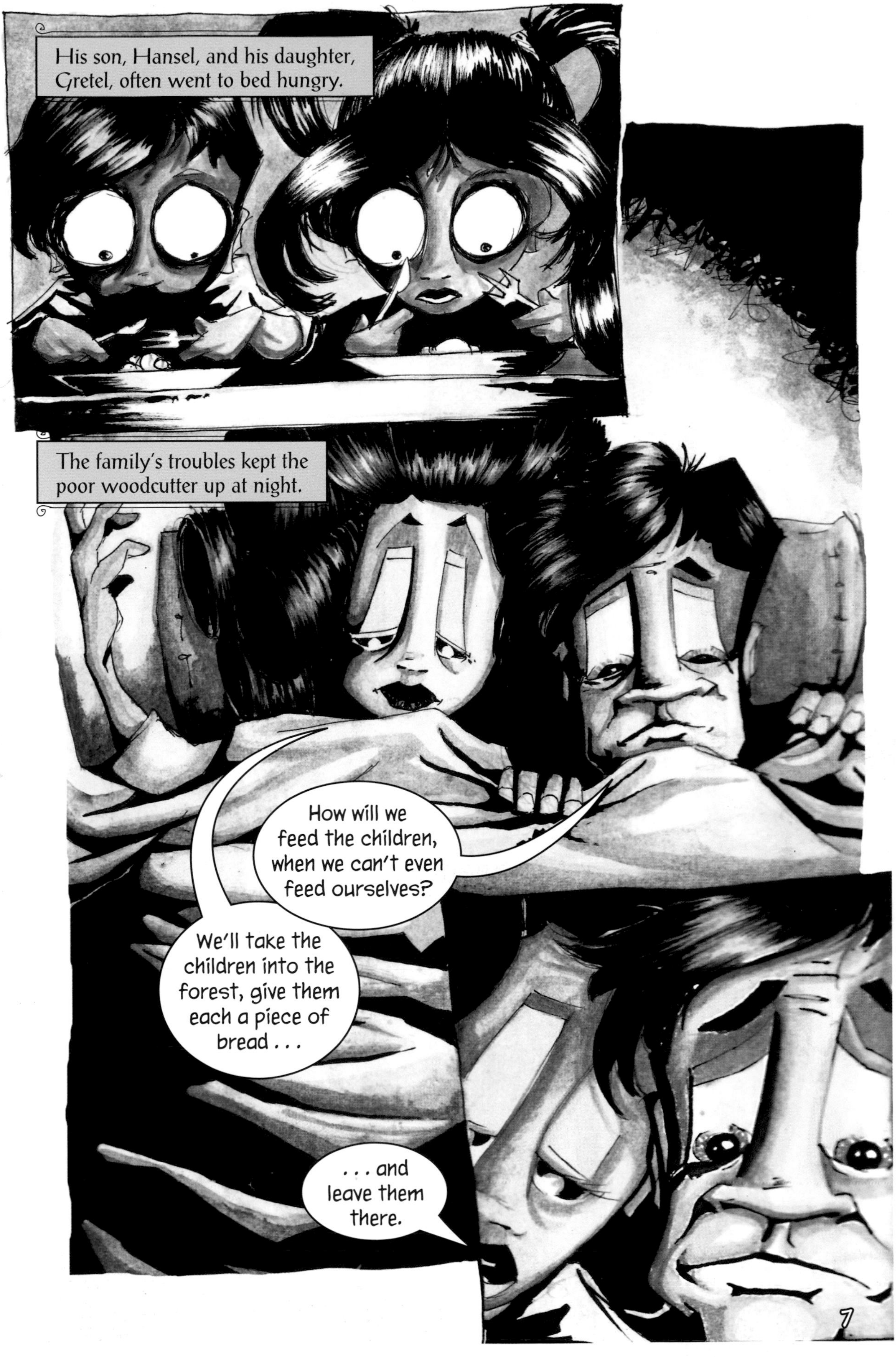

His son, Hansel, and his daughter, Gretel, often went to bed hungry.
The family's troubles kept the poor woodcutter up at night.
How will we feed the children, when we can't even feed ourselves?
We'll take the children into the forest, give them each a piece of bread . . .
. . . and leave them there.

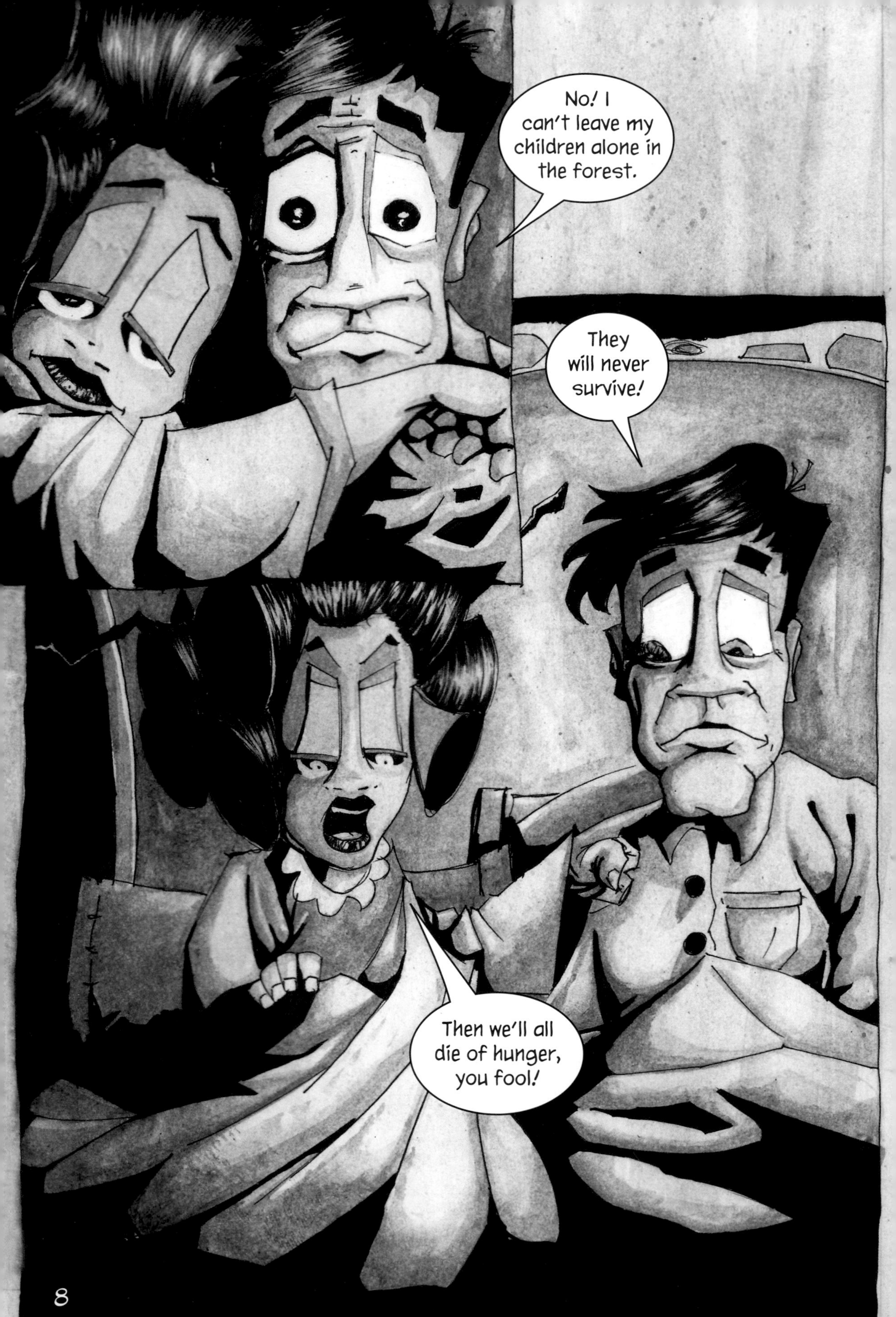
No! I can't leave my children alone in the forest.
They will never survive!
Then we'll all die of hunger, you fool!

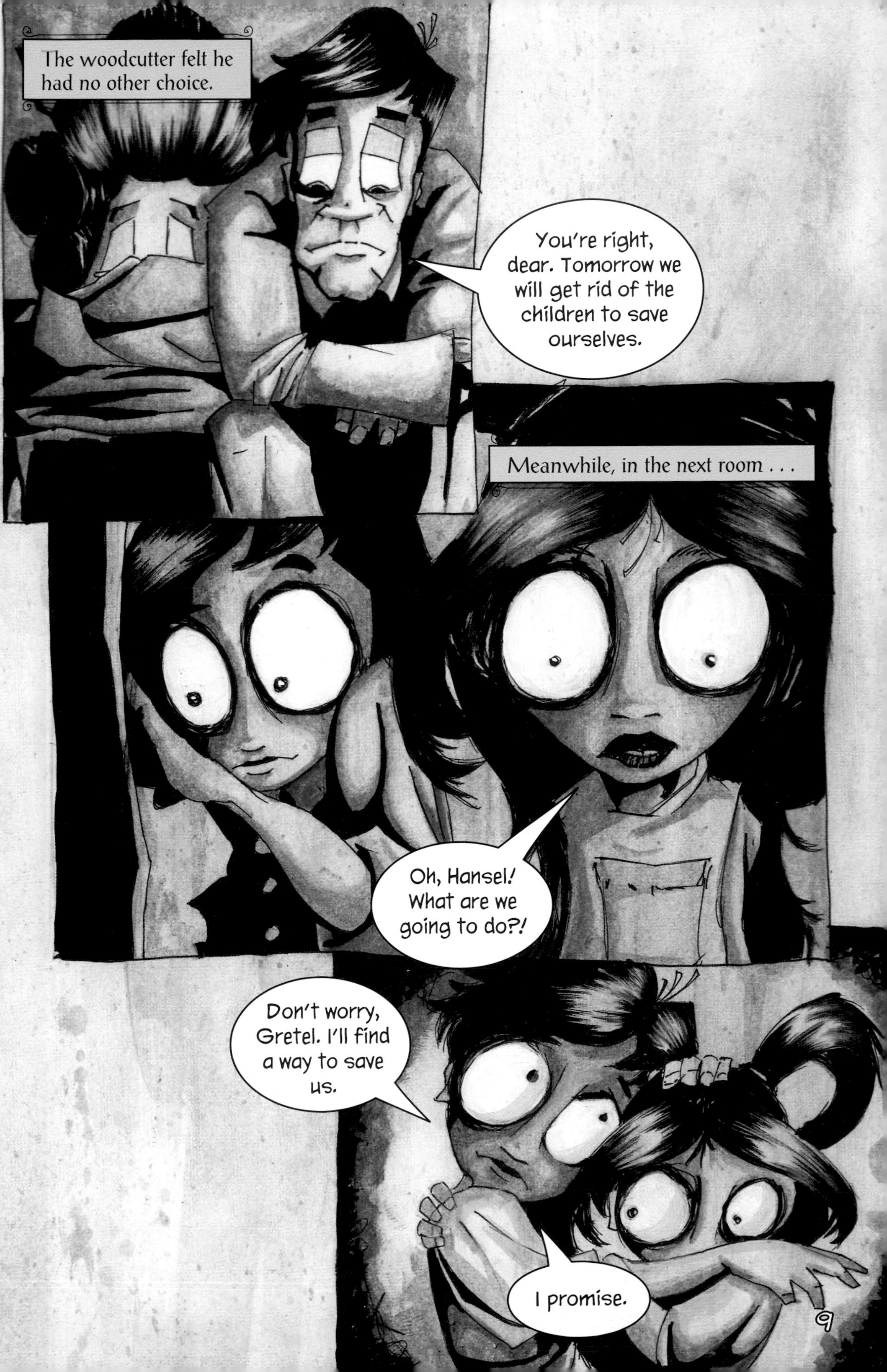
The woodcutter felt he had no other choice.
You're right, dear. Tomorrow we will get rid of the children to save ourselves.
Meanwhile, in the next room . . .
Oh, Hansel! What are we going to do?!
Don't worry, Gretel. I'll find a way to save us.
I promise.

Get up!

We're going into the forest to gather wood.

Here's a piece of bread for each of you. Don't eat it now.

You won't get anything else the rest of the day!

Yes, stepmother.

As they walked deeper into the forest . . .

What are you doing, Hansel?

That's the only thing we have to eat!

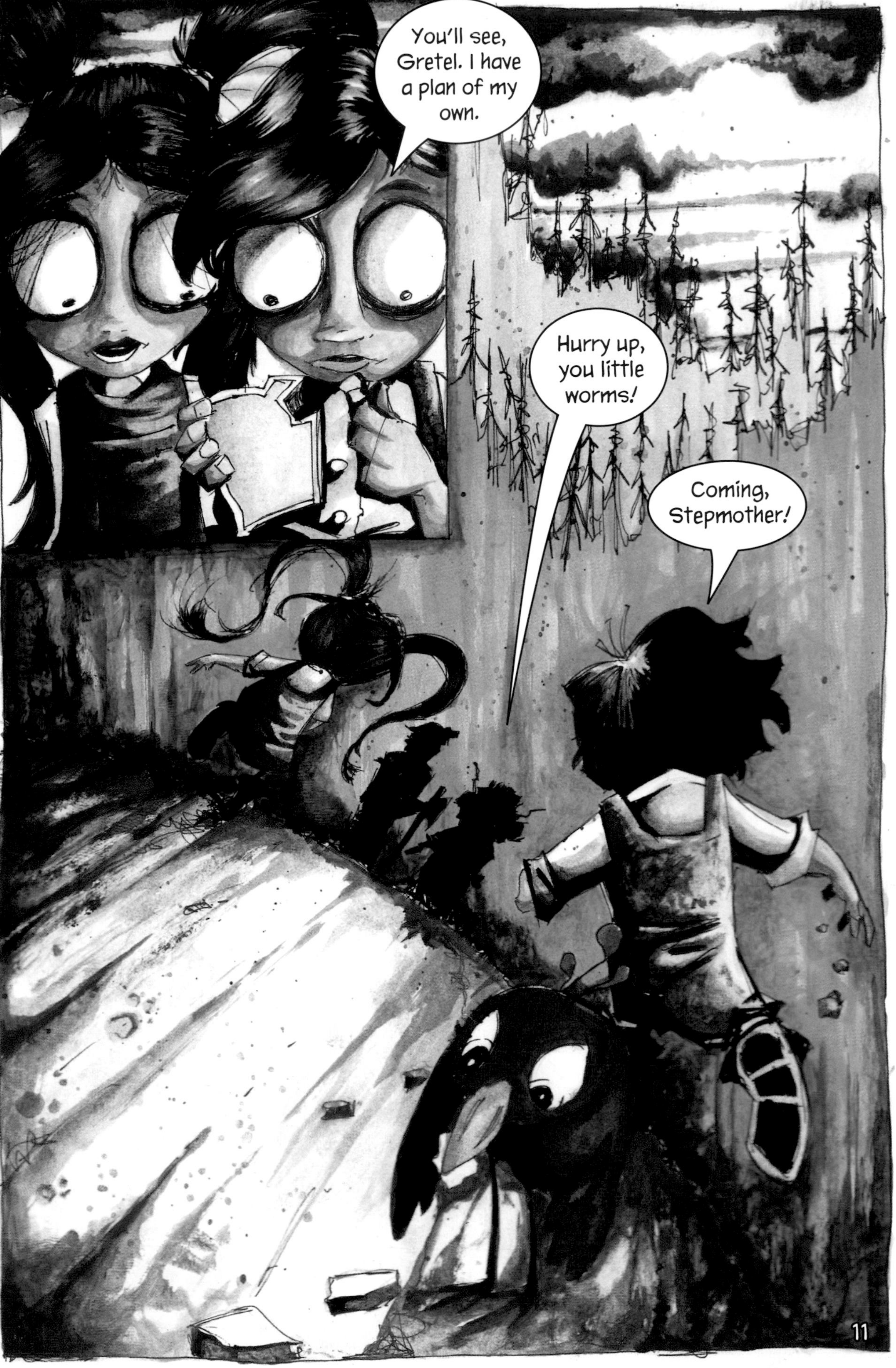
You'll see, Gretel. I have a plan of my own.
Hurry up, you little worms!
Coming, Stepmother!

A long walk later . . .
Stay here, children.
We'll come back when we're finished collecting wood.

Good-bye, my dearest children! I love you both very much.
Stop groveling, dear. We'll be back soon.

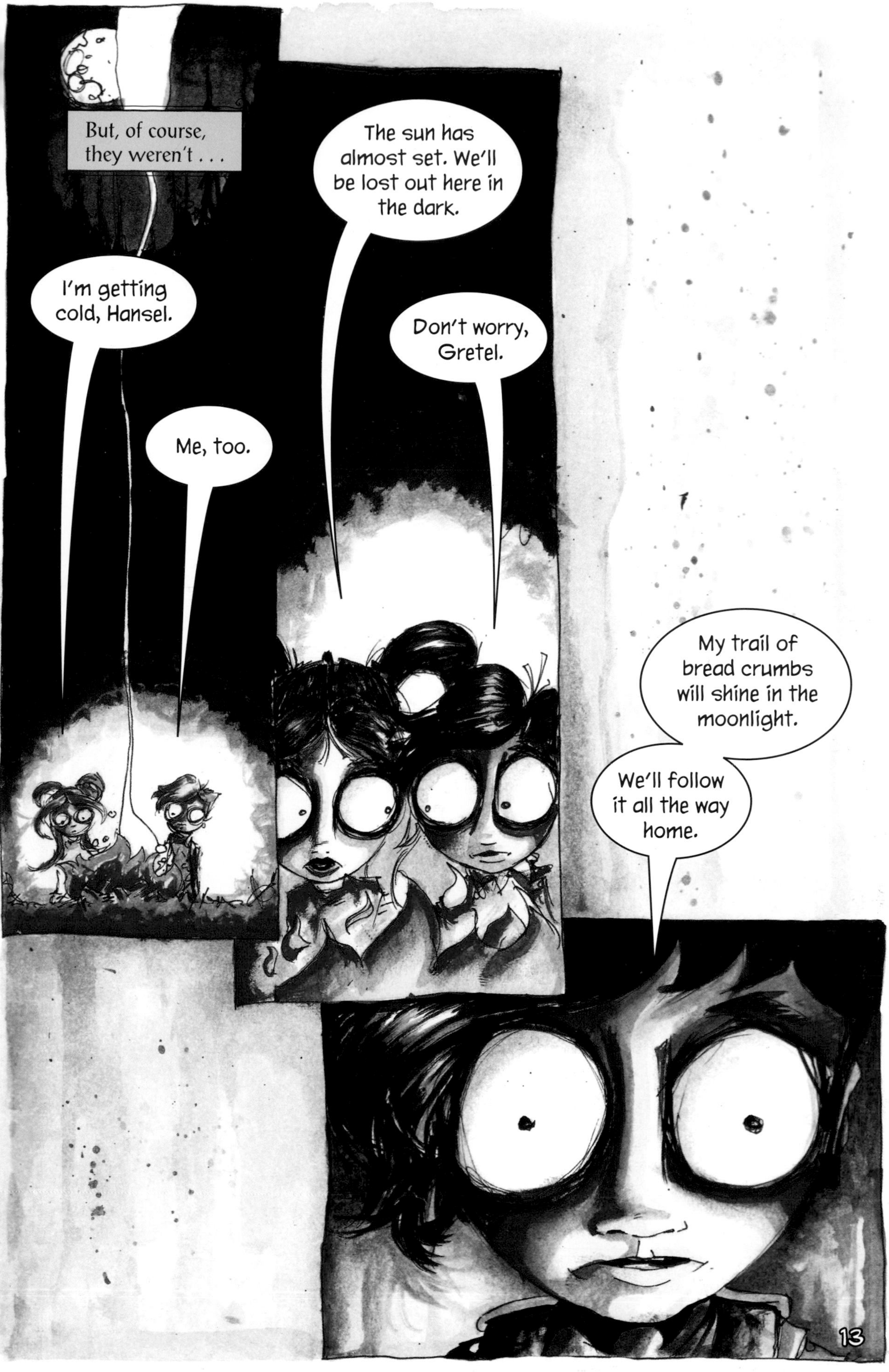

But, of course, they weren't . . .
I'm getting cold, Hansel.
Me, too.
The sun has almost set. We'll be lost out here in the dark.
Don't worry, Gretel.
My trail of bread crumbs will shine in the moonlight.
We'll follow it all the way home.

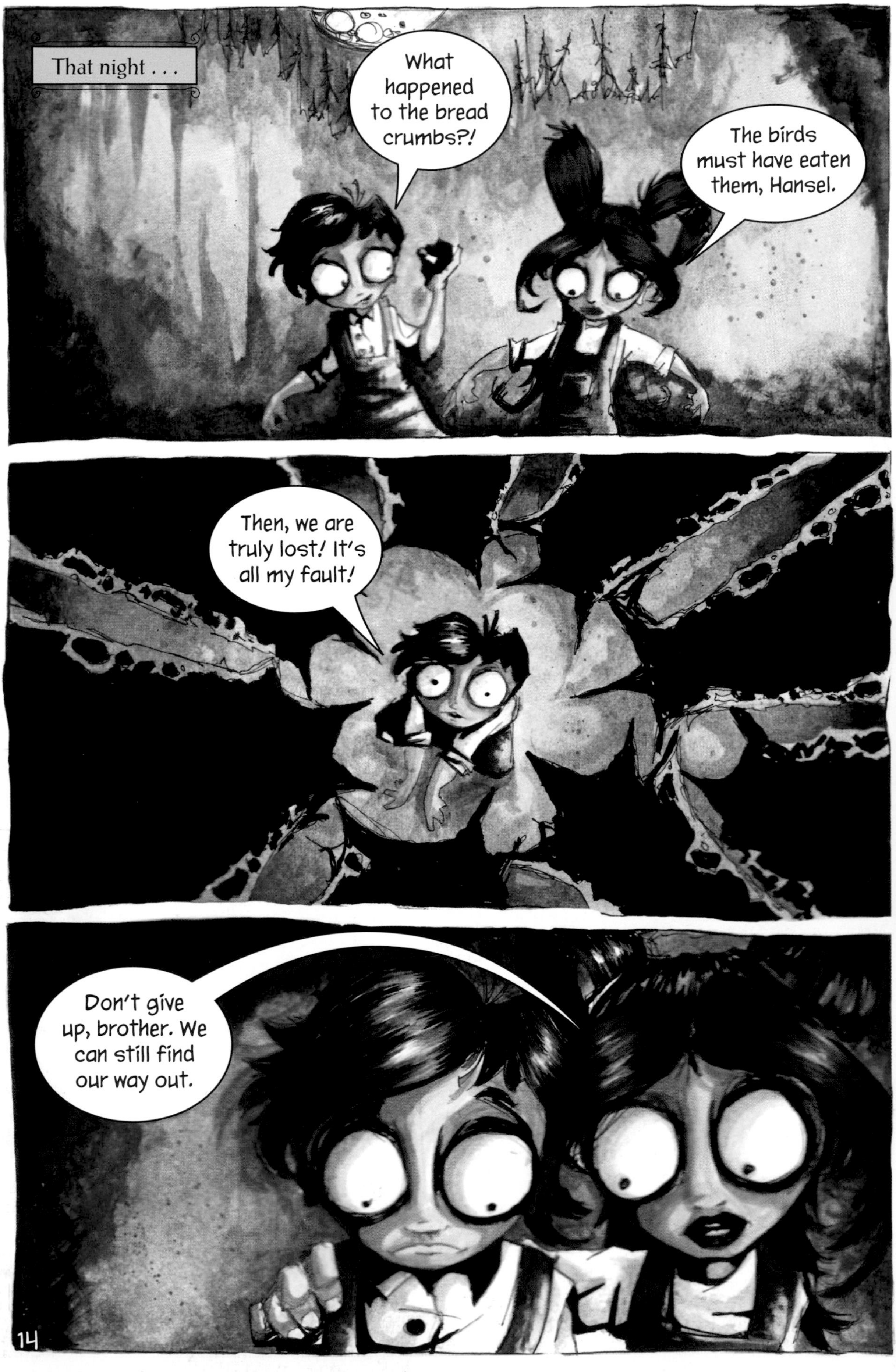
That night . . .
What happened to the bread crumbs?!
The birds must have eaten them, Hansel.
Then, we are truly lost! It's all my fault!
Don't give up, brother. We can still find our way out.

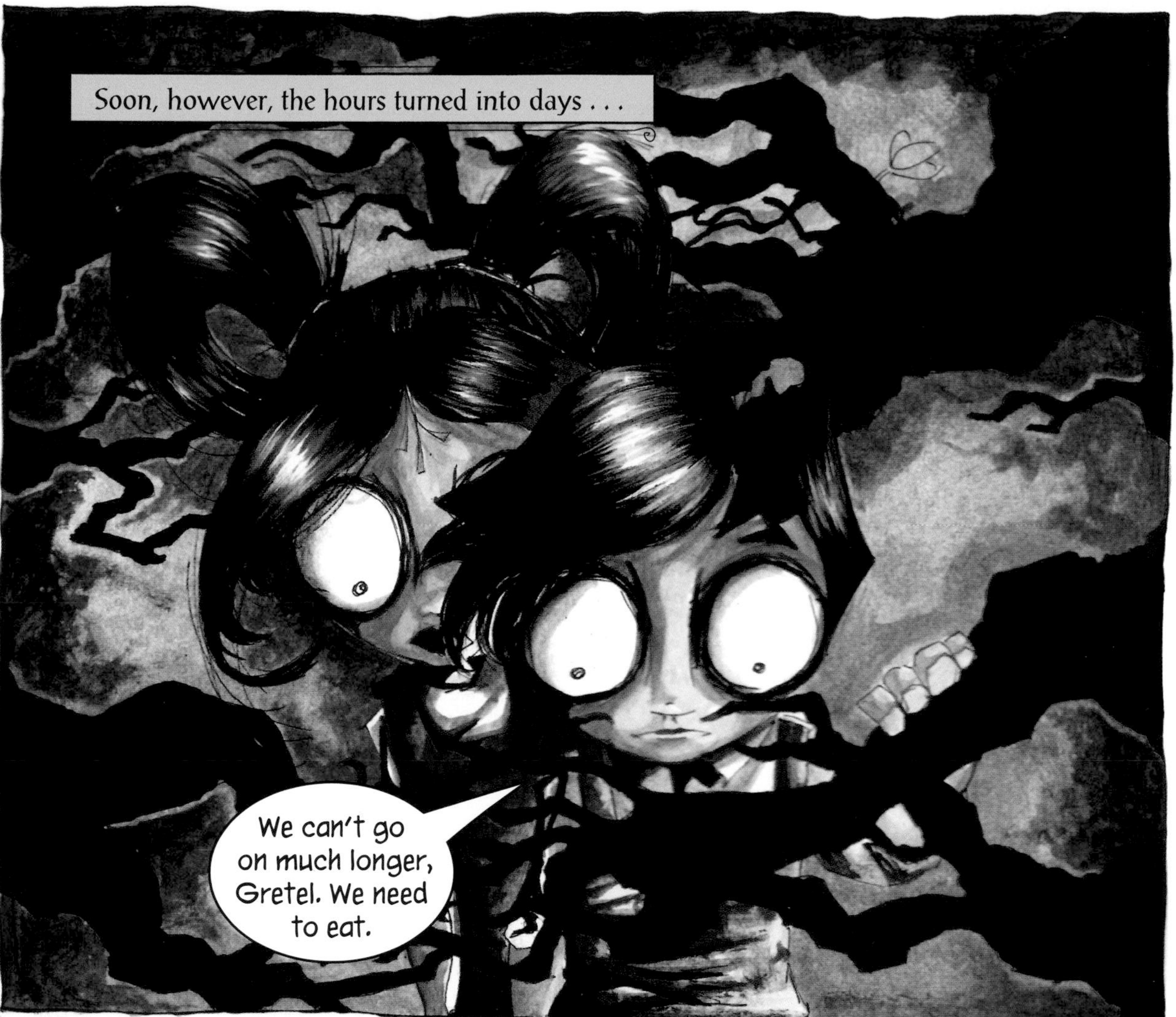
Soon, however, the hours turned into days . . .
We can't go on much longer, Gretel. We need to eat.

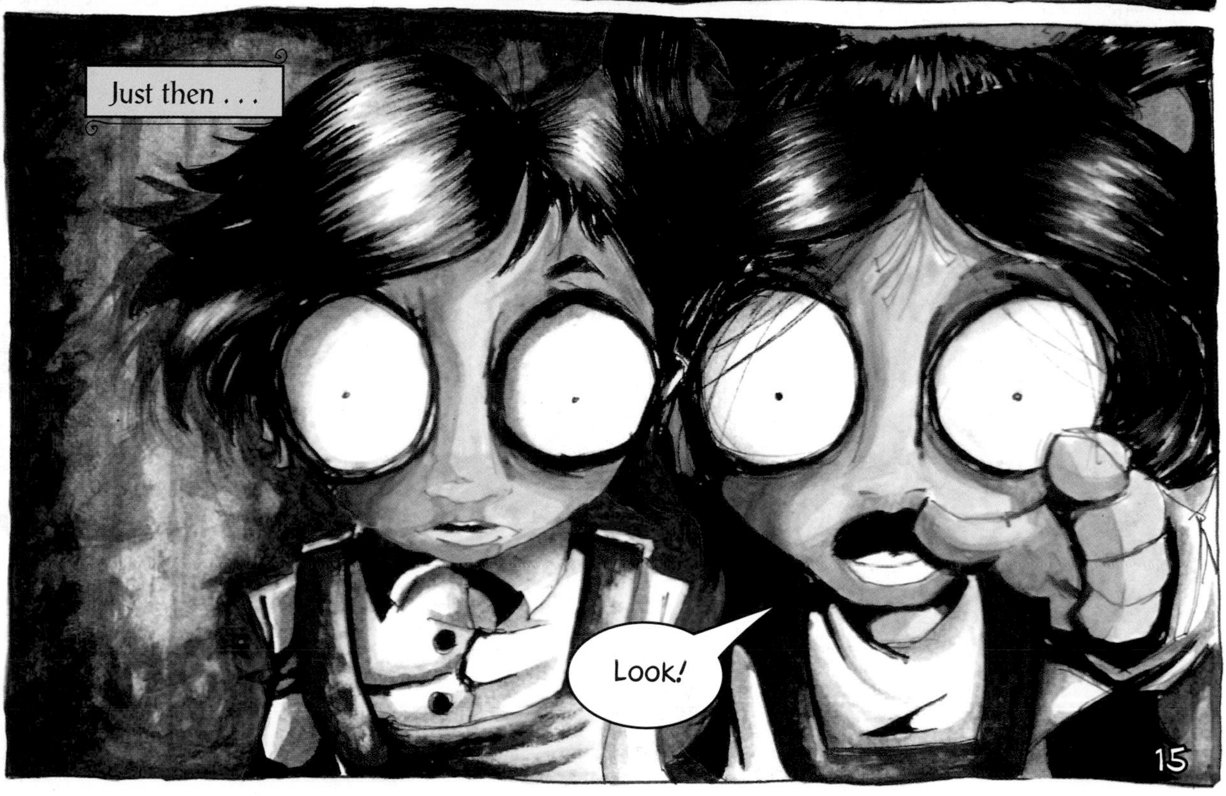
Just then . . .
Look!

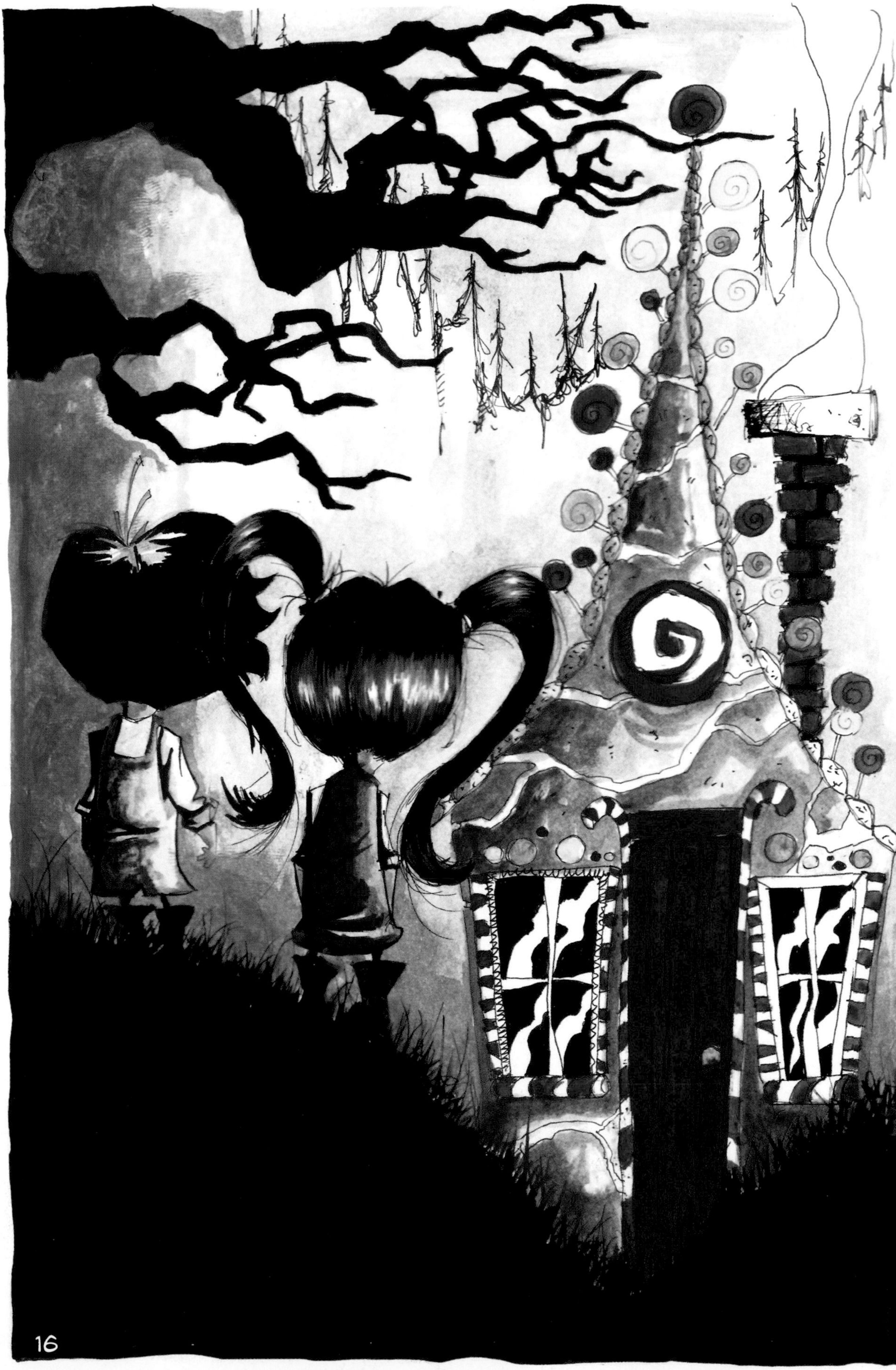

Look, Gretel, the walls are built with bread and cake!

The windows are made of sugar!

And it's all held together by sugary sweet frosting, Hansel!

Well, what are we waiting for?

17

You have to try the roof!

It tastes like a gooey, chocolate chip cookie.

Not until I'm finished with these shutters. They're sweeter than a lollipop!

Suddenly, a frightening voice interrupted their feast . . .

Nibble, nibble, like a mouse. Who is nibbling at my house?

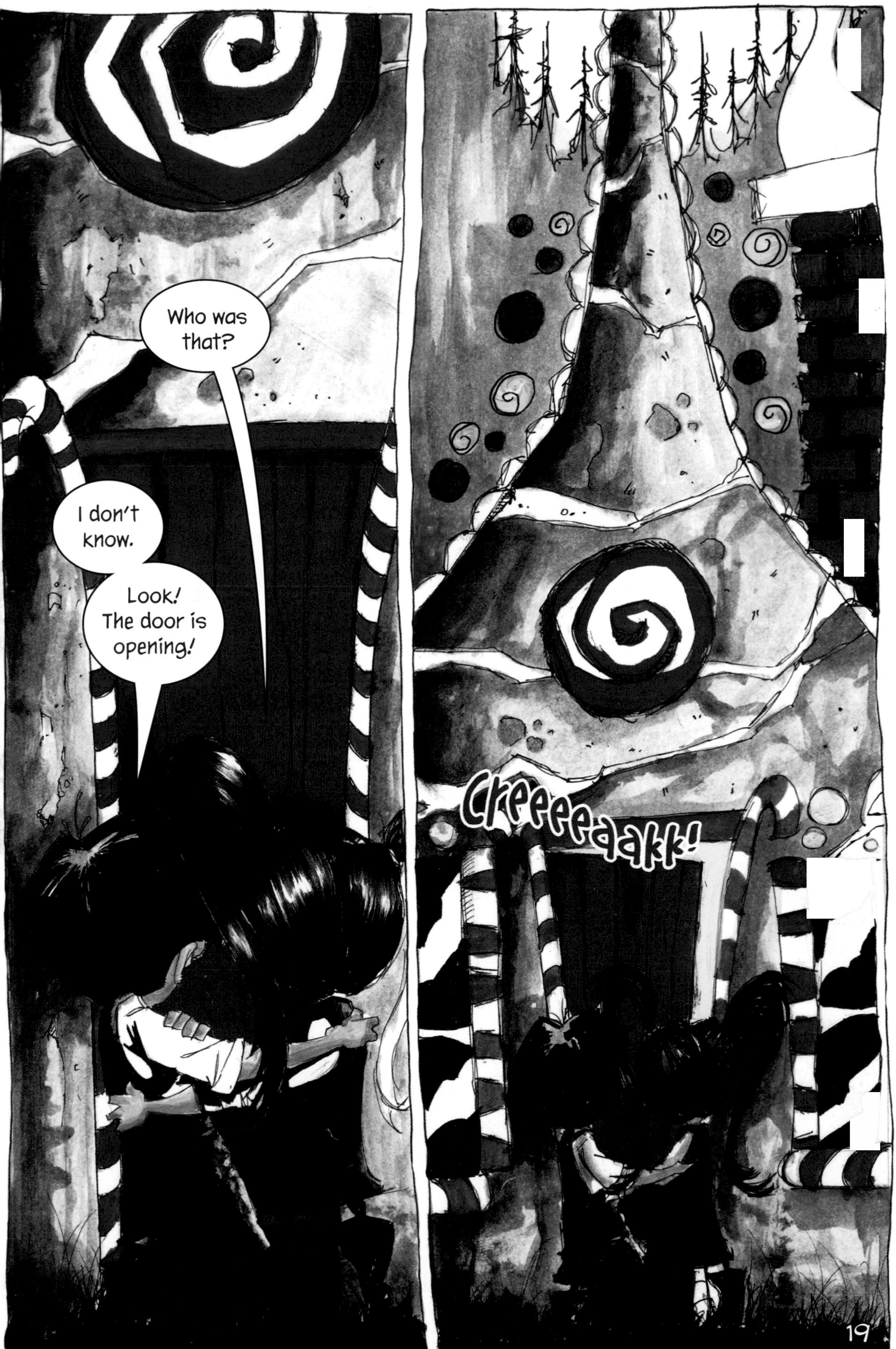
Who was that?
I don't know.
Look! The door is opening!
Creeeeaakk!

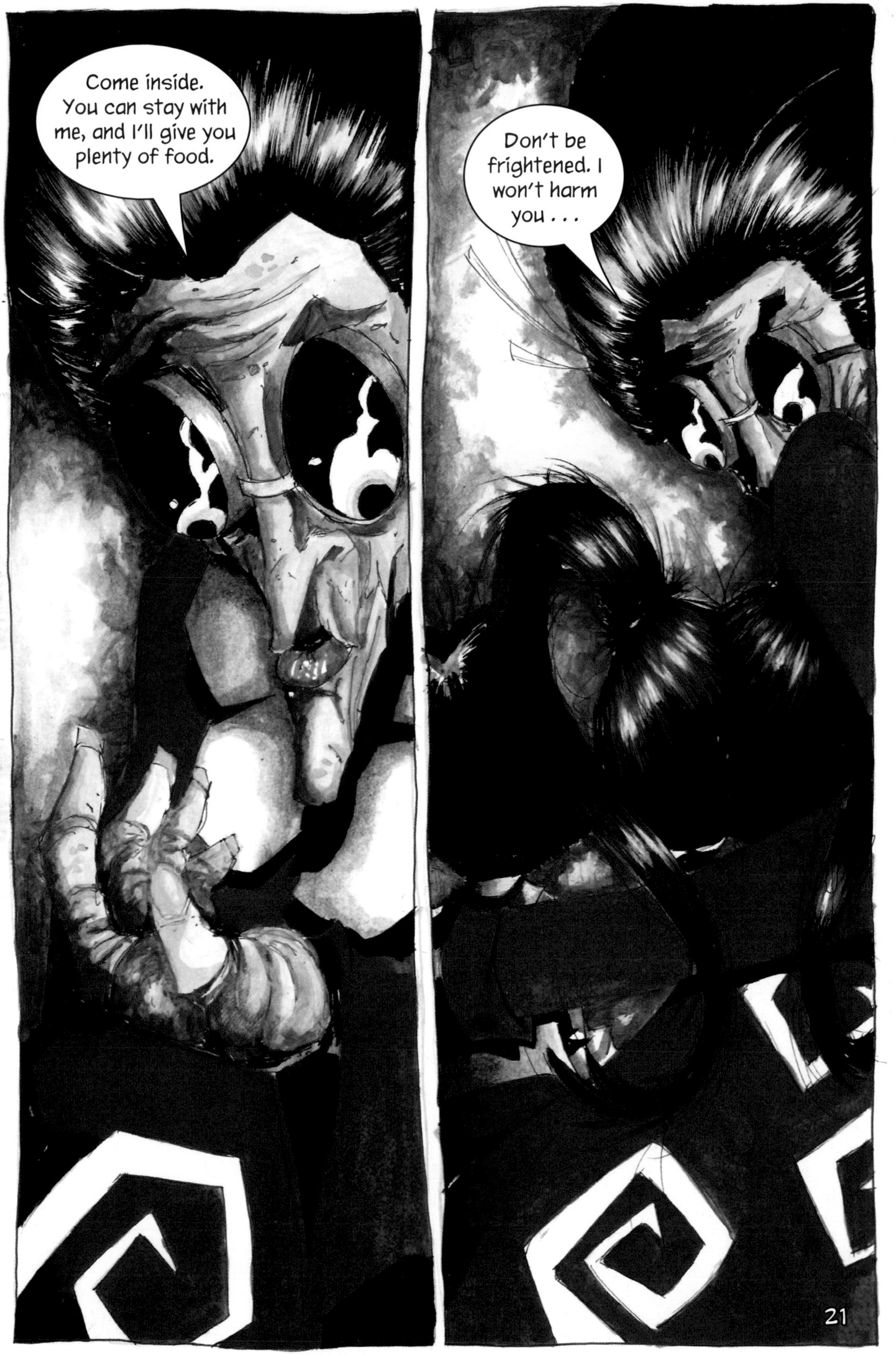
Come inside. You can stay with me, and I'll give you plenty of food.
Don't be frightened. I won't harm you . . .

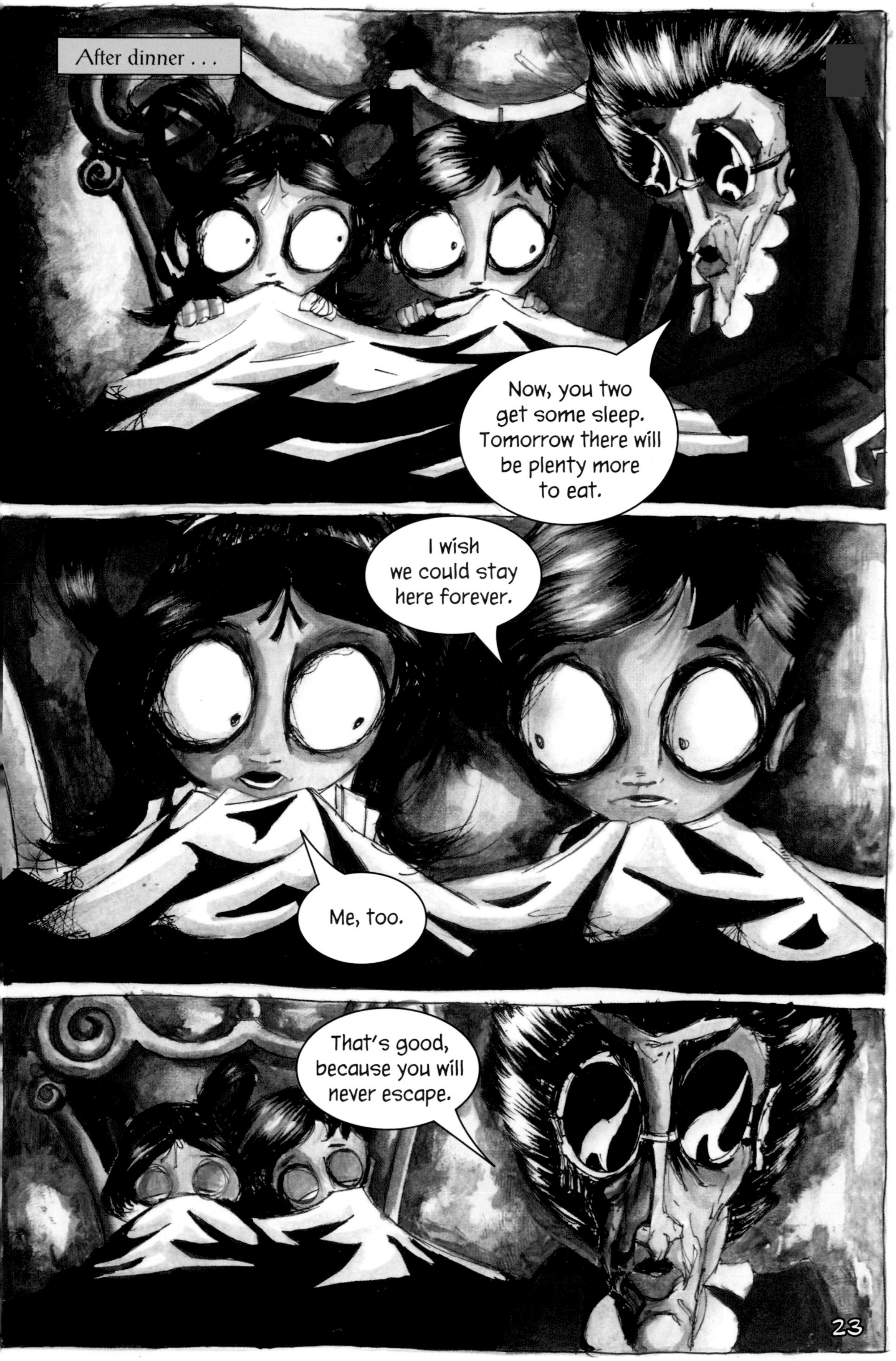
After dinner . . .
Now, you two get some sleep. Tomorrow there will be plenty more to eat.
I wish we could stay here forever.
Me, too.
That's good, because you will never escape.

The next morning . . .

Get up, you lazy child!

Ahh!

Where are you taking him?!

The old woman pulled Hansel into the barn.

Help! Let me out of here!

What have you done with my brother?!

I've locked him in the stables. He'll stay there until he's plump and fat.

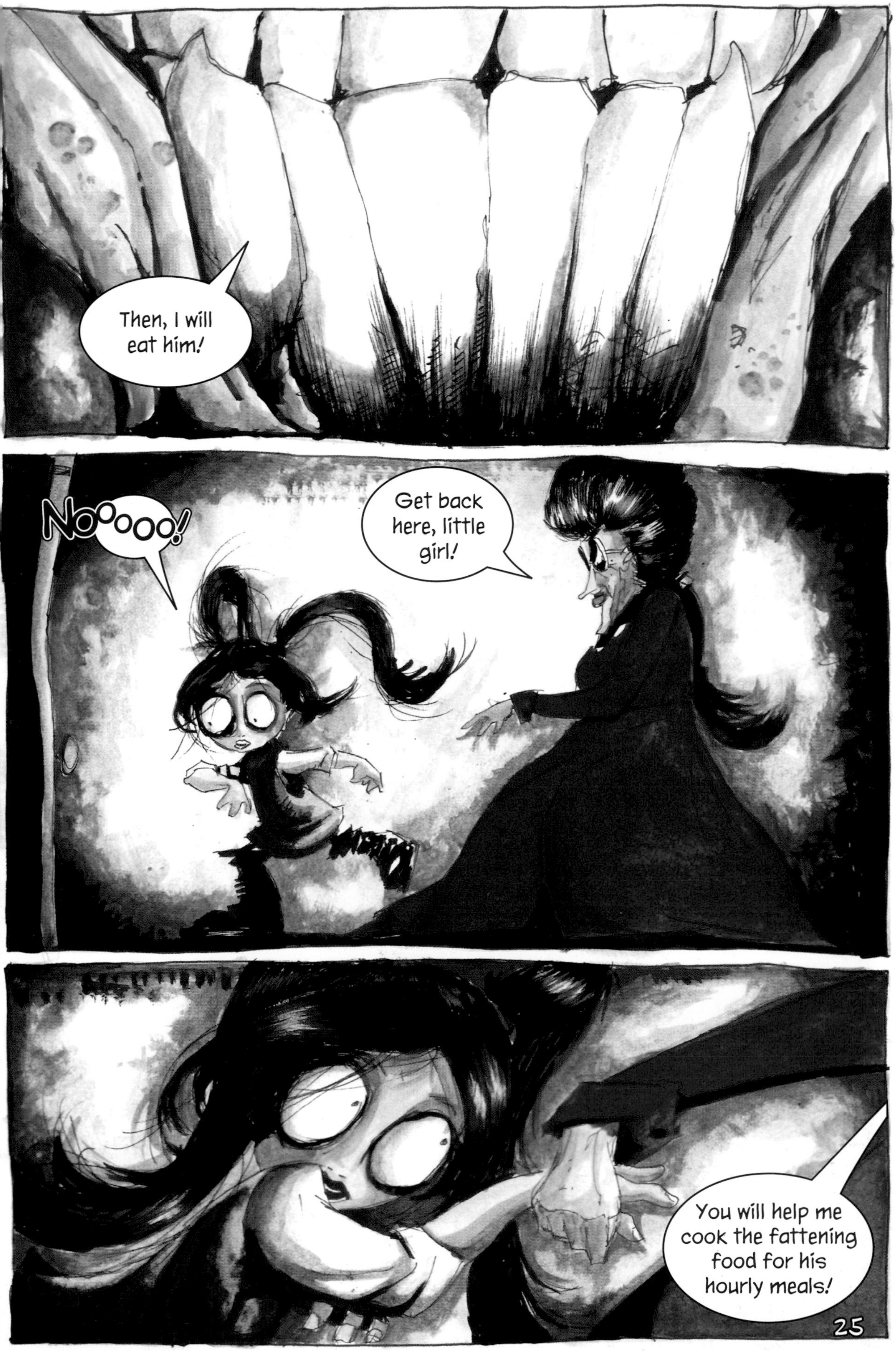
Then, I will eat him!
Get back here, little girl!
Noooooo!
You will help me cook the fattening food for his hourly meals!

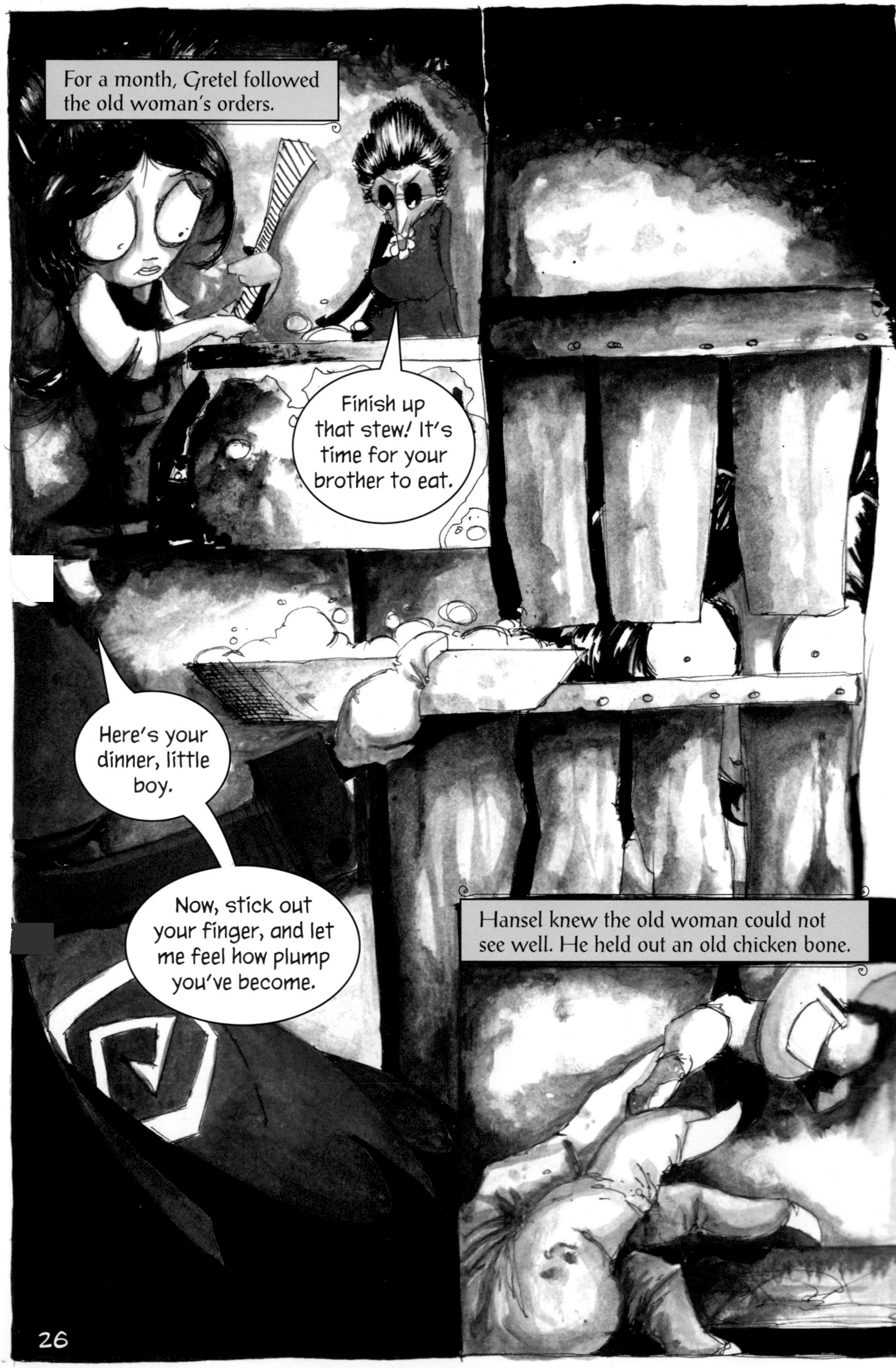
For a month, Gretel followed the old woman's orders.
Finish up that stew! It's time for your brother to eat.
Here's your dinner, little boy.
Now, stick out your finger, and let me feel how plump you've become.
Hansel knew the old woman could not see well. He held out an old chicken bone.

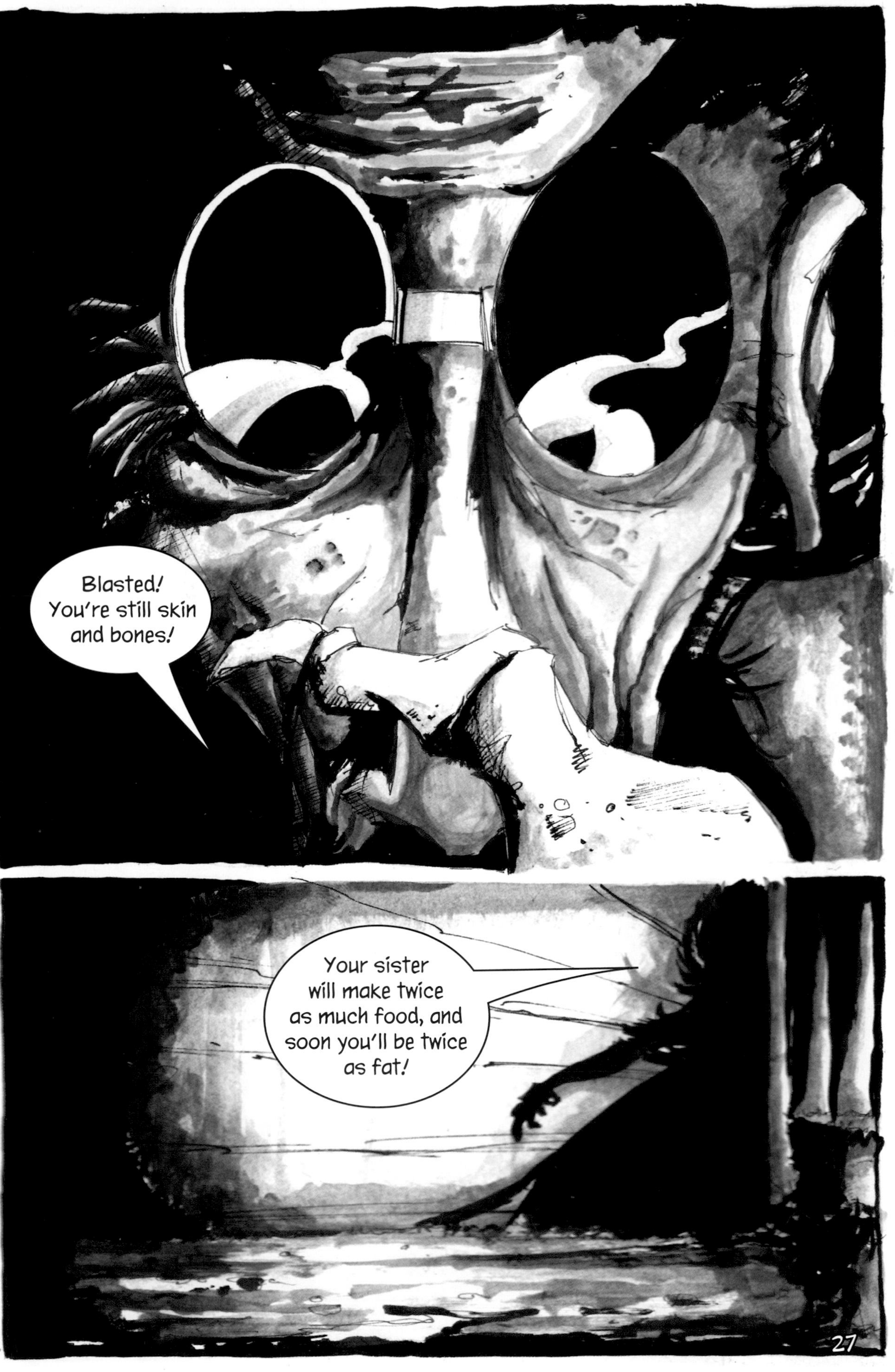
Blasted! You're still skin and bones!
Your sister will make twice as much food, and soon you'll be twice as fat!

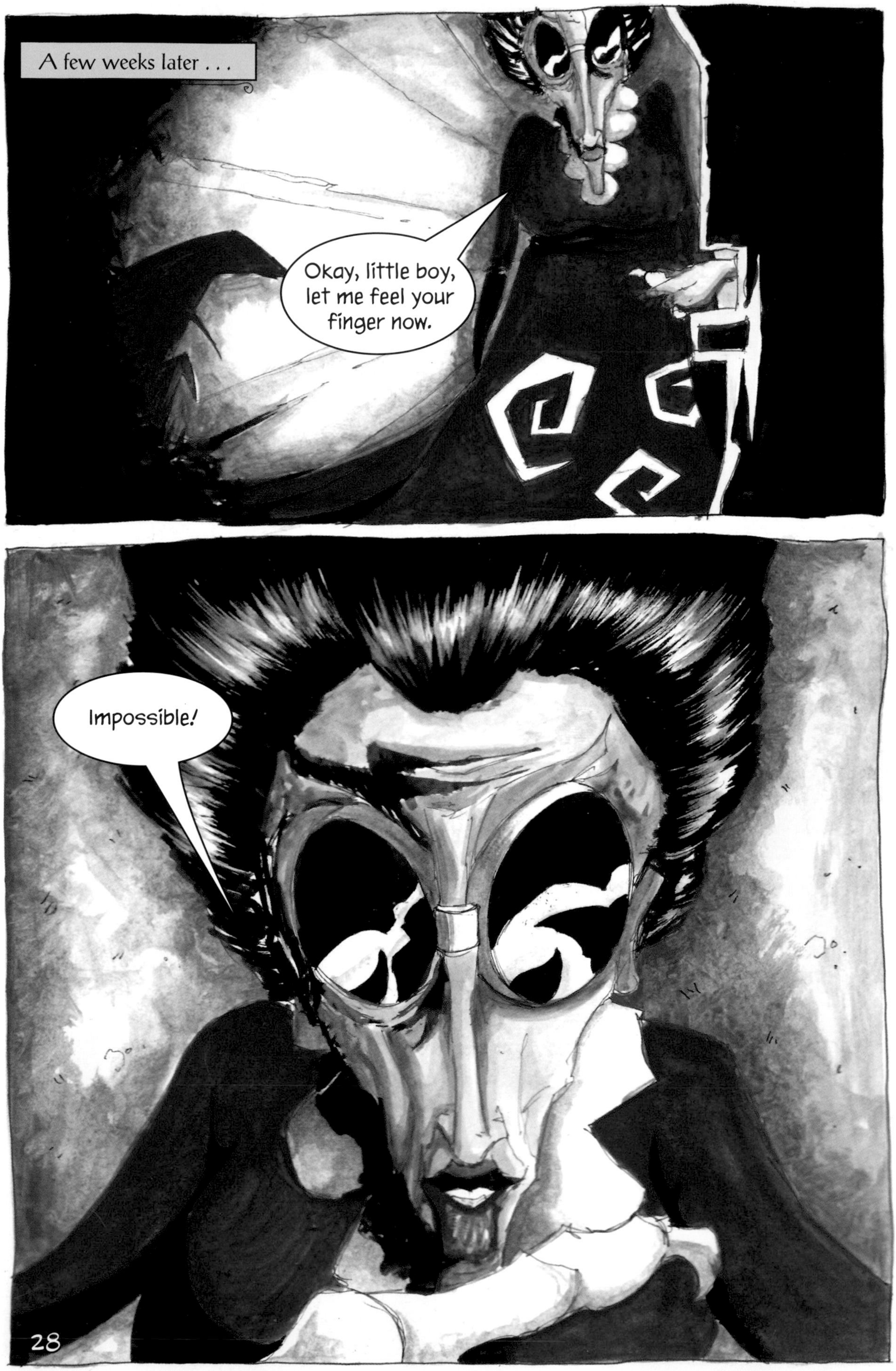
A few weeks later . . .
Okay, little boy, let me feel your finger now.
Impossible!

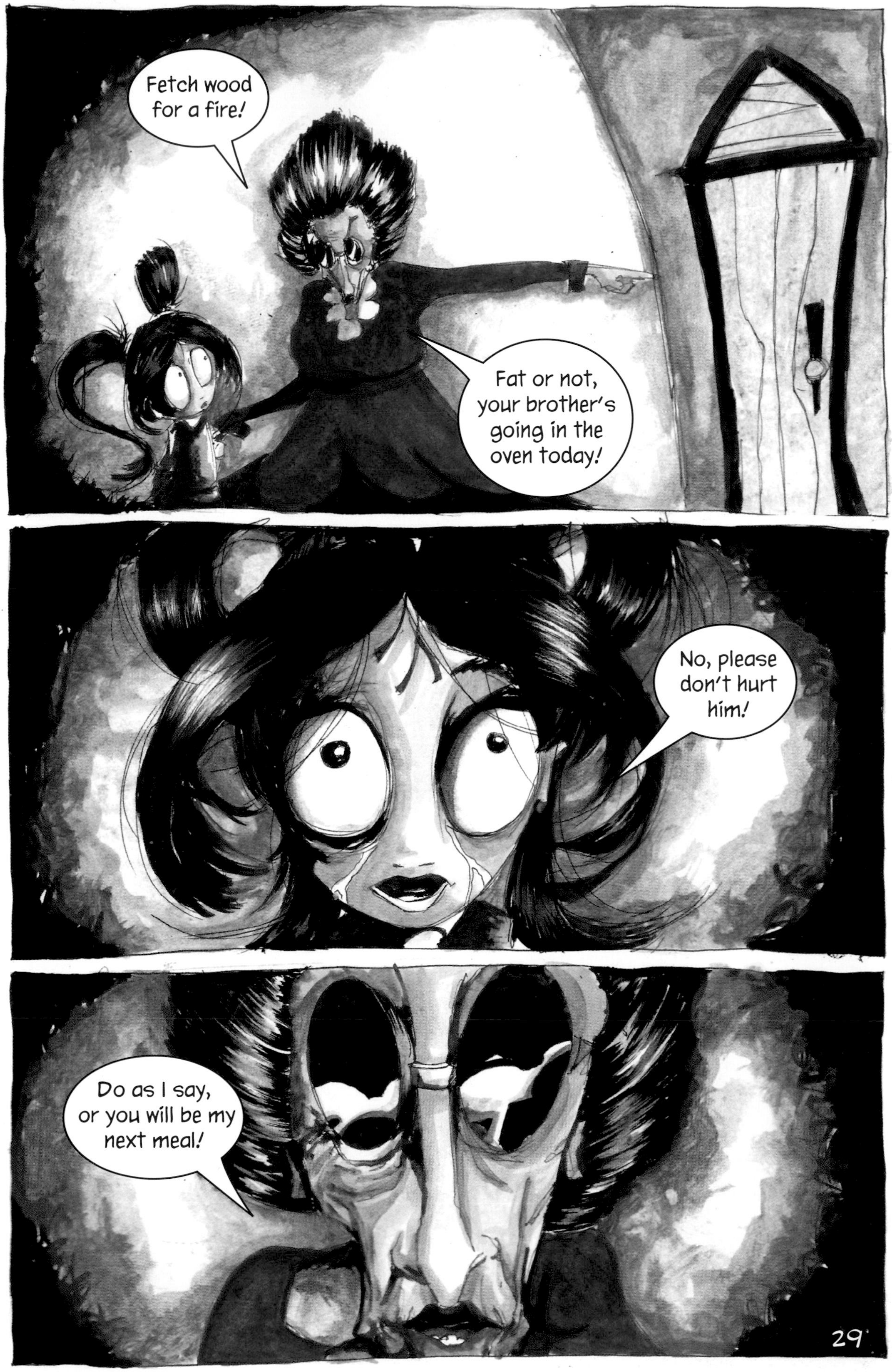
Fetch wood for a fire!
Fat or not, your brother's going in the oven today!
No, please don't hurt him!
Do as I say, or you will be my next meal!

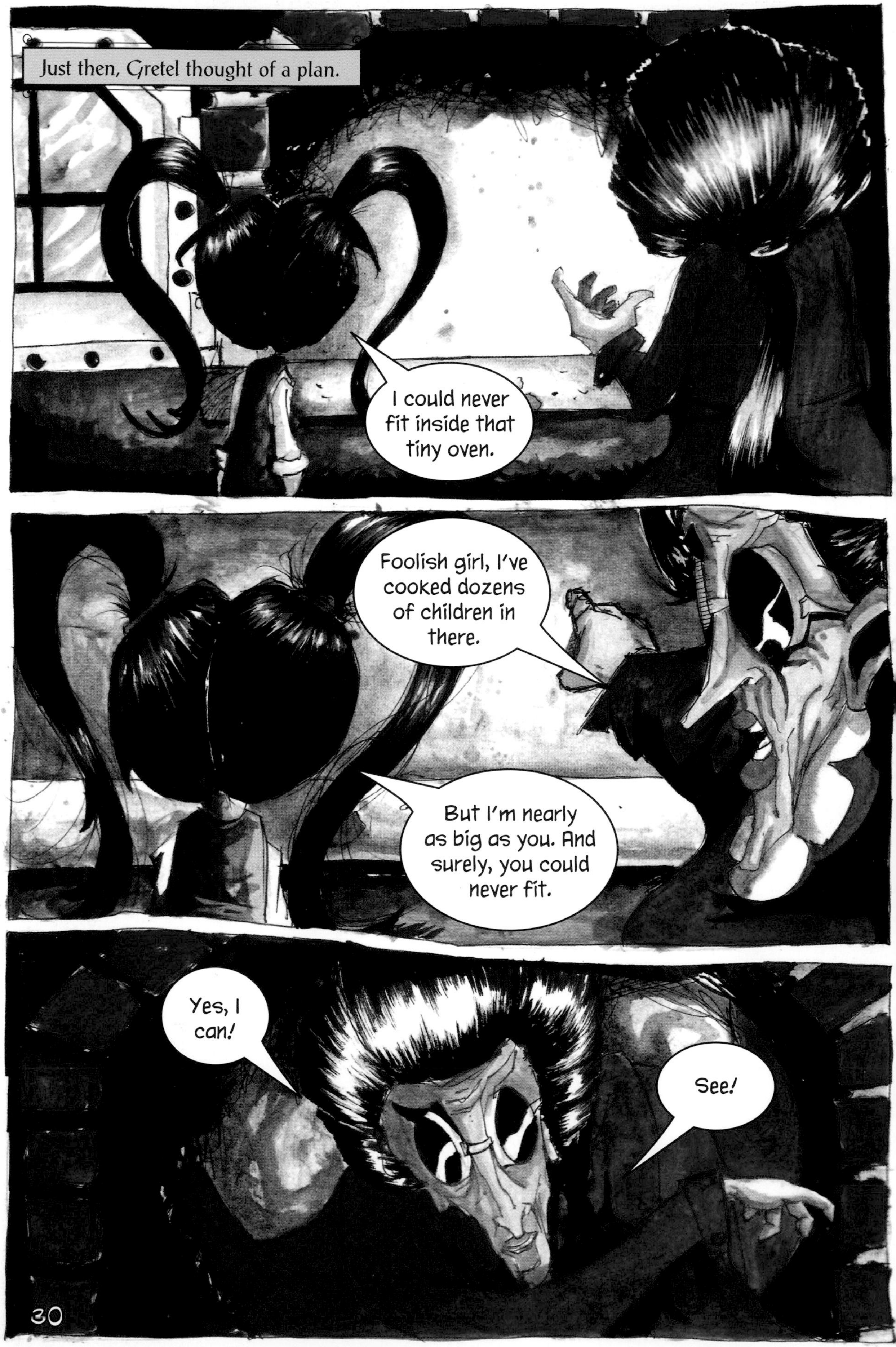
Just then, Gretel thought of a plan.
I could never fit inside that tiny oven.
Foolish girl, I've cooked dozens of children in there.
But I'm nearly as big as you. And surely, you could never fit.
Yes, I can!
See!

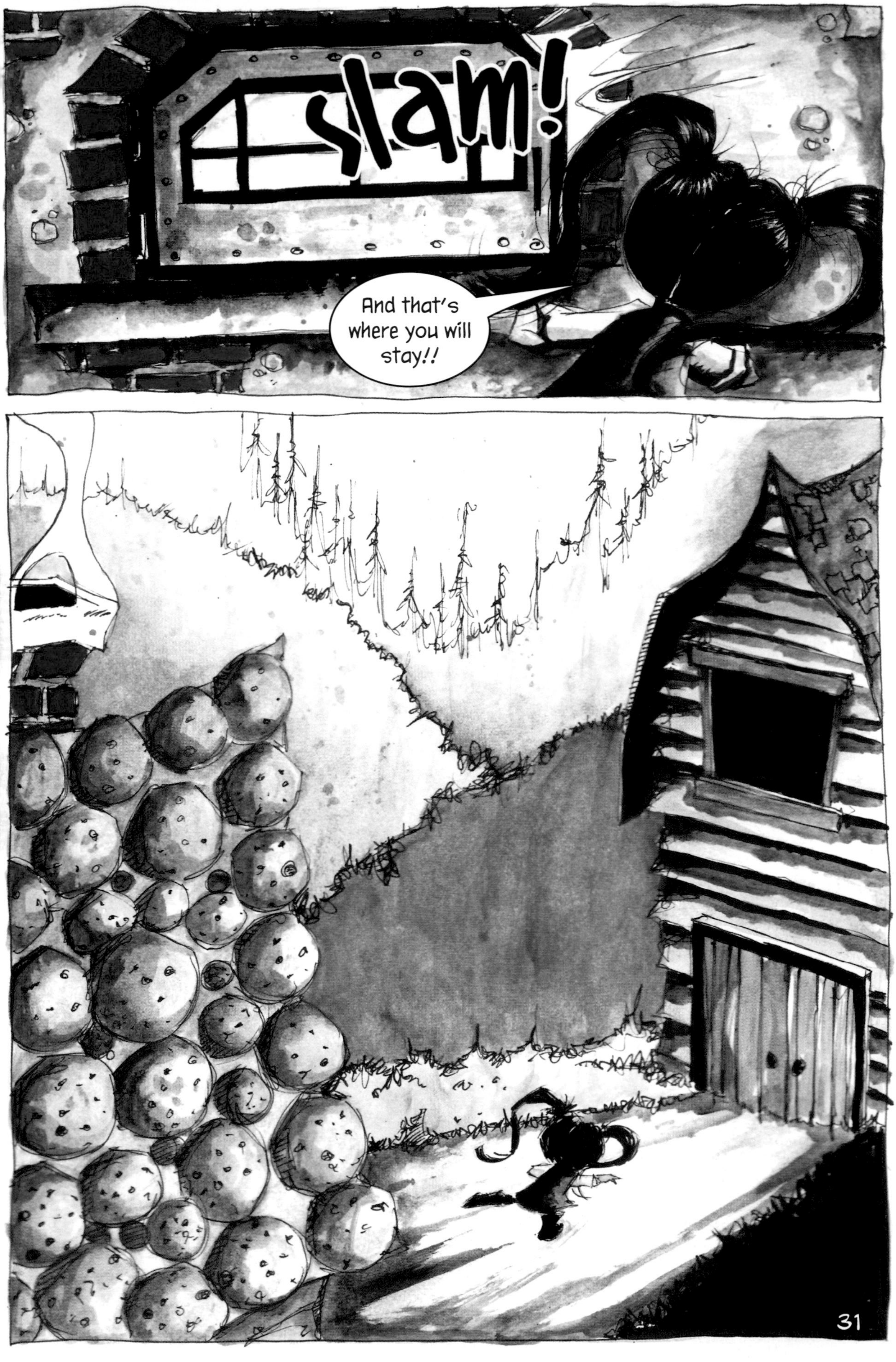
slam!
And that's where you will stay!!

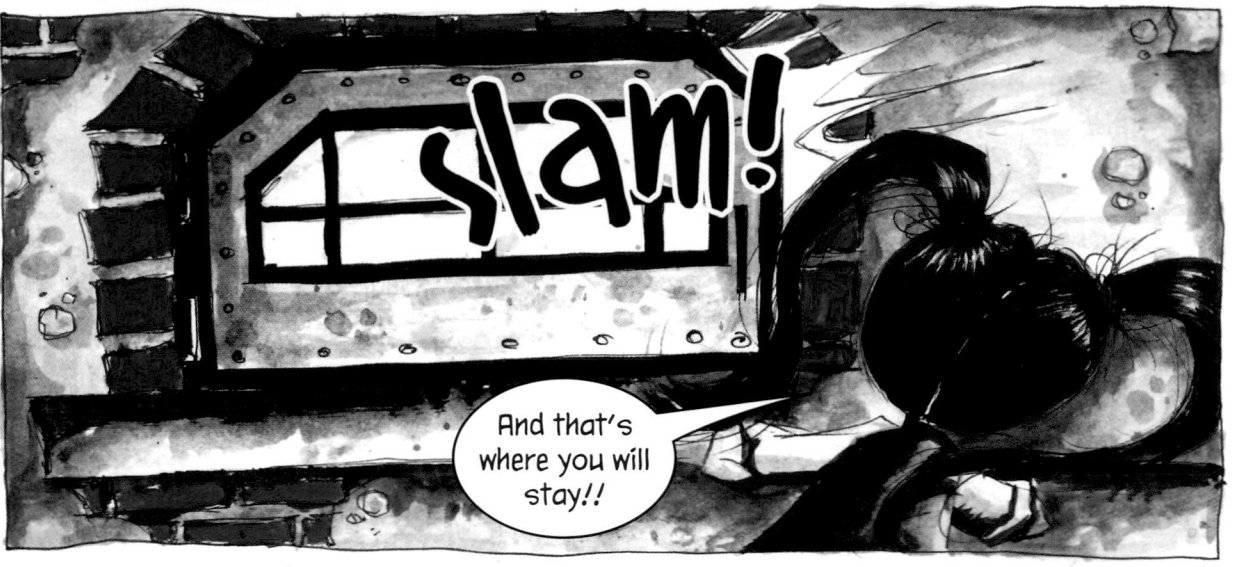

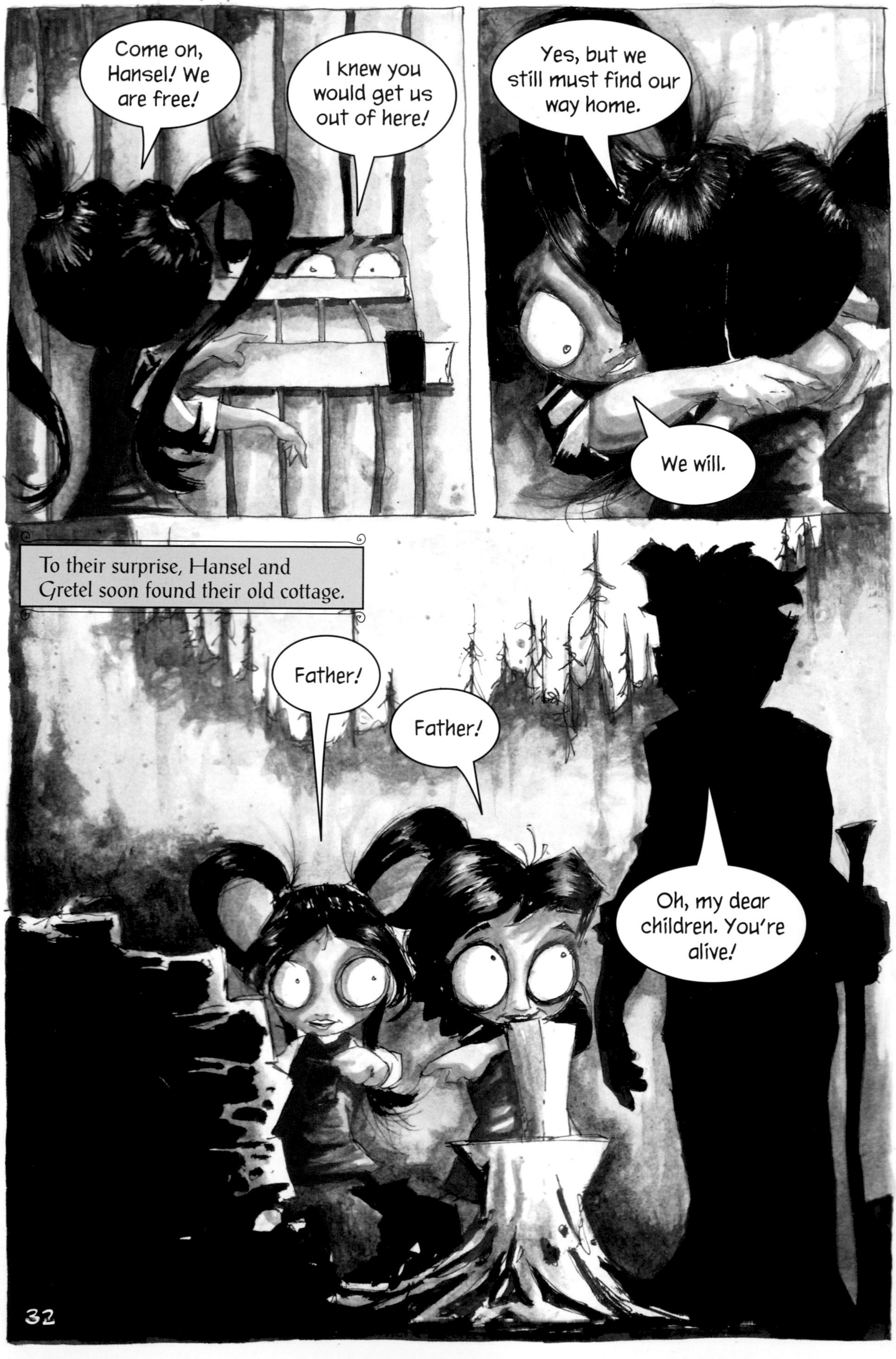
Come on, Hansel! We are free!
I knew you would get us out of here!
Yes, but we still must find our way home.
We will.
To their surprise, Hansel and Gretel soon found their old cottage.
Father!
Father!
Oh, my dear children. You're alive!

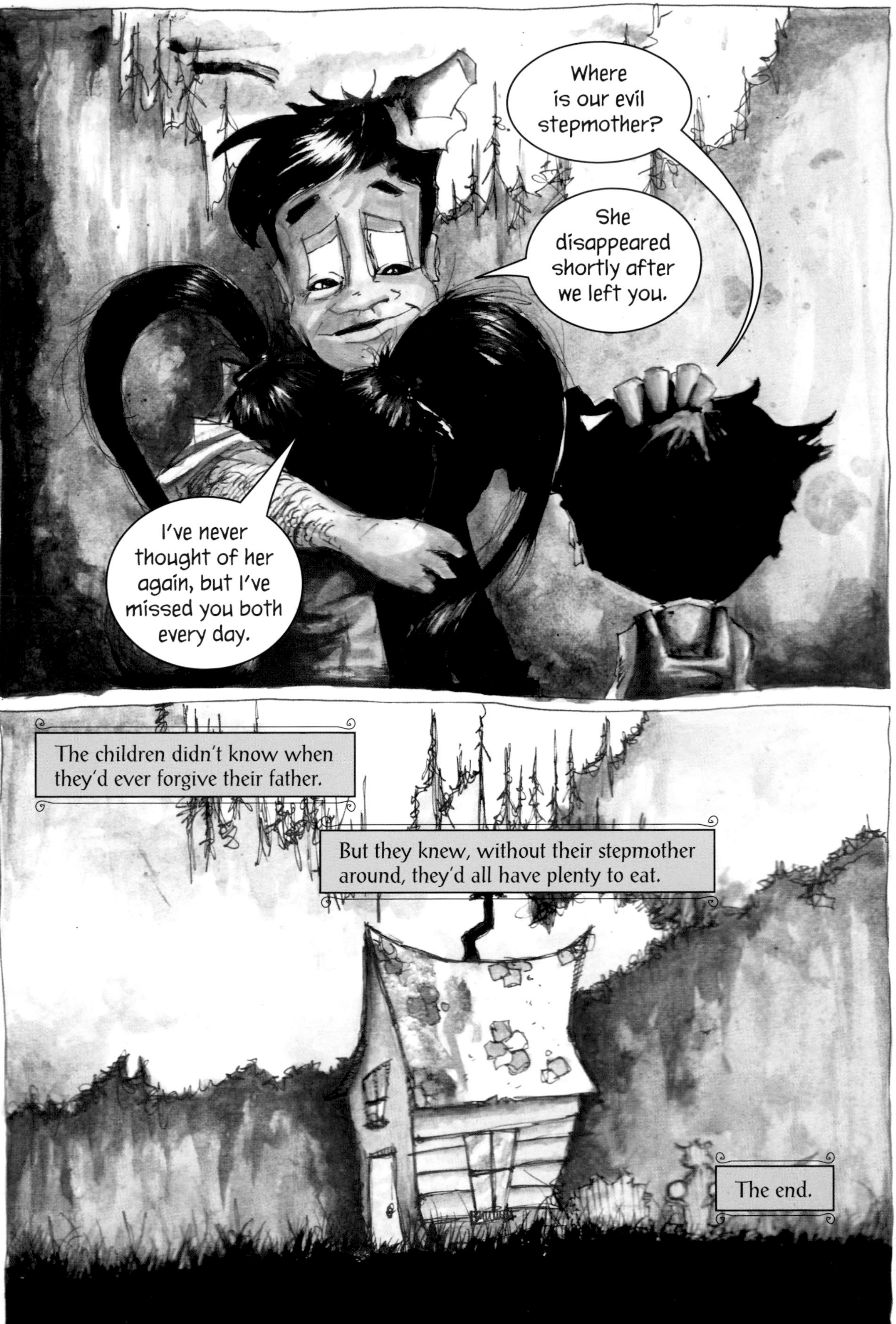
Where is our evil stepmother?
She disappeared shortly after we left you.
I've never thought of her again, but I've missed you both every day.
The children didn't know when they'd ever forgive their father.
But they knew, without their stepmother around, they'd all have plenty to eat.
The end.

About the Author

Growing up in a small Minnesota town, Donald Lemke kept himself busy reading anything from comic books to classic novels. Today, Lemke works as a children's book editor and pursues a master's degree in publishing from Hamline University in St. Paul, Minnesota. Lemke has written a variety of children's books and graphic novels. His ideas often come to him while running along the inspiring trails near his home.

About the Illustrator

Sean Dietrich was born in Baltimore, Maryland, and now lives in San Diego, California. He's been drawing since the age of 4. He had his first art show at the age of 6, self published his first comic book at 16, and has won more than 50 art awards throughout the years. When he's not drawing, Dietrich says he spends too much time in front of the TV playing video games.

Glossary

cottage (KOT-ij)—a small house

fattening (FAT-ten-ing)—feeding someone extra food to make him or her plump or fat

groveling (GROV-uhl-ing)—being unnaturally friendly or polite to someone

ma'am (MAM)—a formal title for a woman

nibble (NIB-uhl)—to take small, gentle bites of something

plump (PLUHMP)—somewhat fat or round in shape

shutters (SHUHT-urz)—movable window covers that help keep light out of a building

stable (STAY-buhl)—a building where horses or cattle are kept

stepmother (STEP-muhth-ur)—a woman who married a person's father that is not the person's birth mother

stew (STOO)—a dish made of meat or fish and vegetables cooked slowly in water

woodcutter (WOOD-kuht-ur)—someone who cuts down trees for firewood

The History of Hansel and Gretel

Like most fairy tales, the story of **Hansel and Gretel** is based on a long oral tradition. People in Europe and other places around the world often told stories of two children left in a dangerous forest. For hundreds of years, these imaginitive tales were passed from person to person and never written down.

In the early 1800s, brothers Jacob and Wilhelm Grimm started collecting many of these folktales. The Grimm brothers heard several of today's most famous stories including "Cinderella," "Snow White," and "Rapunzel." Scholars believe a woman named Henriette Dorothea Wild first told the Grimm brothers the story of **Hansel and Gretel**. They believe she heard the tale in the town of Cassel, Germany. In 1812, Jacob and Wilhelm Grimm published their book of collected stories called *Children's and Household Tales*.

Early versions of the **Hansel and Gretel** story were slightly different than today. The original story called the two children simply Little Brother and Little Sister. The Grimm brothers chose the names **Hansel and Gretel**. These were some of the most popular German names at the time.

Also in the original Hansel and Gretel fairy tale, the stepmother was the children's real mother. Jacob and Wilhelm Grimm decided an evil stepmother would be less likely to scare childhood readers.

Today, the Grimms' book of stories is known as *Grimm's Fairy Tales*. The book is still read by people around the world and has been translated into more than 160 different languages.

Discussion Questions

1. Why do you think the mean old lady's house was made of candy?

2. Hansel and Gretel's father left them in the forest. Do you think they should ever forgive him?

3. In some Hansel and Gretel stories, the stepmother turns out to be the mean old lady. Do you think the stepmother in this story could have also been the lady in the candy house? Why or why not?

Writing Prompts

1. Fairy tales are fantasy stories, often about wizards, goblins, giants, and fairies. Many fairy tales have a happy ending. Write your own fairy tale. Then, read it to a friend or family member.

2. Imagine you could build a house out of your favorite foods. Would your house have spaghetti carpet? How about cookies for doorknobs? Describe what your food house would look like.

3. Pretend you are the author and write a second part to the Hansel and Gretel story. Will Hansel and Gretel ever see their stepmother again? Will they forgive their father? You decide.

Internet Sites

The book may be over, but the adventure is just beginning.

Do you want to read more about the subjects or ideas in this book? Want to play cool games or watch videos about the authors who write these books? Then go to FactHound. At *www.facthound.com*, you'll be able to do all that, and more. The FactHound website can also send you to other safe Internet sites.

Check it out!

" Nibble, nibble, like a

Who is nibbling at my house?"

— the Witch

STONE ARCH BOOKS
Capstone Publishers • www.stonearchbooks.com
008-013 RL: 2.1 Guided Reading Level: I

ISBN 978-1-4342-0863-7

90000

The Scribbler's Guide
to
THE LAND OF MYTH
Mythic Motifs for Storytellers

Sarah Beach

THE SCRIBBLER'S GUIDE
TO THE LAND OF MYTH

Mythic Motifs for Storytellers

Sarah Beach

ISBN: 1-4196-9707-2

ISBN-13: 9781419697074

Visit www.booksurge.com to order additional copies.

For Dennis O'Neil

Sensei and Inspiration

TABLE OF CONTENTS

ACKNOWLEDGEMENTS

There are a lot of people I need to thank for their support over the years I worked on this project. Their interest often helped energize me to continue pushing on with the work I set before myself. Without their excitement in what I had to say, I would have felt I was doing this for an audience of one.

In particular, I need to thank Derrick Warfel for his early support. Jeff Pierson, Barbara Paul and Coleman Luck each gave me useful feedback that helped me find the right voice for this text. Coleman gets double thanks for challenging me to find a better handling of the issue of evil – he forced me to dig deeper. John Shepherd and Nancy Schraeder were early readers of the completed work, and their response was everything I hoped for. Erik Burnham, John Neal, Blake Snyder, Janet and Lee Batchler, all provided a supportive background that was very comforting. The regular posters on Chuck Dixon's Dixonverse message board get my thanks for some very useful discussions on what makes for a hero. David Bratman provided the keen eye for building the index. And thanks to my friend, Tim Tobolski for the cover art.

And then there are all those folks who listened with apparent fascination when I would be launched into talking about the project. Whether it was just courtesy or deep interest, their willingness to listen helped me articulate points that eventually went into the text. My thanks to them.

INTRODUCTION

How I Got Here

Once upon a time.... Isn't that the way stories begin? At some point something happens that moves us to tell a story. So let me tell you how this book came about.

I've always had a love of mythic stories. Something about them caught at my imagination, giving me joy. I was never sure what it was, for I was still young then, and uninfected by the rational thinking that fills our educational process. I read a story about the Hawaiian volcano goddess Pele, and some corner of me responded to her passionate violence. I read the tale of Odysseus and his desire to get home, and admired his wit and wily nature.

Years later, as a college student I studied literature, in order to learn how to write. Along the way, my love of mythology also prompted me to an even more serious study of that field. Those studies helped me find the key that explained my early love of mythic stories. Myth is the language of the human psyche. The stories of myth capture the drama of our inner soul searching, our journeys to understand ourselves and our world. As much as science details the mechanics of the universe and existence, it cannot answer a question like "what does this mean to me?" We may try as much as we can to be objective about human nature and how it functions, but we cannot escape the fact that our lives are subjective. We are not impersonal collectors of information, we are gatherers of interconnected experience. Things happen to us, which we give significance one way or another. I may know that objectively the sun is a star many, many times the size of our planet, burning basic gases and throwing out radiation and light. But some days, when the sky above me shines bright blue, ornamented with high piled clouds and the sun's glory gets captured in those rolls of white, I can easily imagine an awesome, powerful being sitting up there, fabulous and wonderful, just out of my sight. I can't help but think mythically. We all do it.

Given these human impulses, it helps a writer to become familiar with myths. The mythic significance of the world around us, and of our own actions, has not really changed down the eons of human existence. The story of Gilgamesh, the earliest known epic, can be read in translation today, and still be understood, because it is about being human. And yet, like all languages, myth does have its grammar.

So how do we, as storytellers, learn that grammar? For we really should learn it. Does it lie in becoming familiar with the multitude of stories from all the different cultures? Not really. Although such knowledge will give us access to many story plots and their endless variations, unless we understand the heart of the myth we are no better off than if we only knew one story. Until you know what is mythically hidden in the cloak of night, night will only be darkness in your tale, and it will tell your audience nothing deeper than the fact that the lights are out.

Through the years, I had begun collecting notes from many sources about the significances of myths and images. I would turn to these notes from time to time to check myself in my writing, to see if I was on the right track with a particular tale. But my notes were never all in one place, never organized in a fashion that would let me find just what I wanted when I wanted it. As knowledgeable as I was about myths and what many of them meant, some days when I was hashing over a rewrite, I longed for a road map through the land of myth. "I have this scene happening at night, but where the heck are my notes about what *night* can mean?" How I longed for a reference book that pulled these concepts together in such a way that I could easy find them. Volumes of mythology and encyclopedias and dictionaries of myth and folklore, though valuable, were not quite what I needed in molding my stories into even better shapes. What was needed, I felt, was a single volume which gathered things together in a way to help and inspire storytellers. The result of these considerations is in your hands.

Why You Need This Book

As I said, myth is the language of the human psyche. As storytellers, we want our work to touch the hearts of our audience. We want our stories to encourage, or alarm, or scare. We want our stories to challenge or inspire. We want, for whatever end, to reach that subjective core within the people receiving our story. To do that, we need to be grounded in the language of the subjective.

Many others have produced books about myth and psychology, about writers and myth. Many of them deal with the internal connection between the heart of the writer and the journey the story's hero ventures out upon. This is very true: every story is a reflection of the author's heart, in some fashion or other. If you, as a writer, do not understand that, you will probably miss many important elements in your own story. However, this book is not about the psychology of the writer and the writer's experience. It is about the experience you want to create in your audience.

This book is designed to give you the grammar of myth. It is designed to show you the variations in structure and significance. The more we know about the significance of an image or an action, the more we as writers will be able to make our stories touch the awesome power of myth. When a story resonates with a mythic tune, it stays with the audience longer. Is that not what we want to happen? This book will help you deepen the mythic significance of your stories.

How To Use This Book

The book has been ordered along the model of a travel guide. It was in part inspired by the fact that the first section was going to have to deal with the hero's journey motifs. But after starting out that way, it quickly became clear to me that this was exactly the sort of structure for the book that would be most useful.

For issues dealing with plot, explore the **GOING ON THE JOURNEY** section. Here you will find an examination of the elements of several journey motifs. The fact that there *are* several journey motifs will surprise many. In no way am I trying to imply that one motif is better than another. Indeed, in order to avoid the idea of outline-as-blueprint, the motifs from the different outlines have been gathered into one generalized form. There is some apparent repetition, but each discussion adds more to the understanding of a motif and how it can be used in a story. The reason the variations are included is because sometimes, when a writer is stuck, finding out that there is an alternative to a pattern can open whole new prospects, new landscapes. By comparing the different terminology used in the various outlines of the Hero's journey, we will broaden our awareness of possible story choices.

In the **TRANSPORTATION** section, we will look at the traditional divisions of drama. There is the Upturn of Comedy (meaning stories that move toward happy endings, not just stories that are funny), the Downturn of Tragedy, and what I call the Straight Through trip of Drama (where the story usually contains elements of both comedy and tragedy).

TIME OF TRAVEL considers the implications of the daily cycle as well as the yearly cycle. The significance of weather is also included in this section.

LOCAL RESIDENTS deals with character archetypes, not just in how they function in the plot, but what they are as people, in their relations to the hero and the rest of the characters in the story. Let me state at this point that aside from the sub-section that deals with imagery that is specific to males or females, the rest of the archetypes can be applied to either sex. In point of fact, a hero in a story may be either male or female. But I will use the term Hero to refer to the main character that you are sending out on a journey. Additionally, some of the character discussions have supplementary units, such as the exploration of Special Objects under the character heading of the Holy Ones.

From the character archetypes we then travel into **LANDSCAPE.** Here you will find contrasting elements grouped together: sky vs. earth, towers vs. caves, sea vs. land. Also under this heading, we will look at some other physical elements, such as fire and vegetation.

The last section, **THEME PARKS**, deals with what I call popular mythologies. By this I mean constructs which will sustain multiple visits, whether it is in the context of a television series, movie franchise, or on-going literary character.

In the text, to flesh out the concepts we will be looking at, you will find two things. The first is brief descriptions of myths that represent the element under consideration. These descriptions will be set off by indentations, and will appear in a different typeface.

> This combination of indentation and typeface will be used throughout for the description of the myth that applies at that point. After the myth itself has been described, the appearance of the text will be returned to normal.

The second item for fleshing out the discussion will be the inclusion of examples of the mythic elements as used in films. The use of film examples was chosen because movies (and television) have become the most powerful emotive medium available to storytellers.

Although I will not assume that you have seen all of the films, or remember all of the plot points, I will not be giving you complete descriptions of the plots. I plan only to describe the context of the particular mythic element under consideration. But I do hope the discussion will inspire you to check out the example. I want to assure you at this time that every single film that is cited has been specifically reviewed for this book. I have read some screenwriting books recently where it became obvious to me that the writer, in referring to a film, had not re-watched the film before writing about it, but instead commented on it only from memory. Reviewing the films has been a fascinating experience. I did not want to give you a catalogue of all the mythic elements in every film I mention, but it was fun to find other mythic elements at work in addition to the ones I planned to cite.

The text can be read straight through, or you can jump from point to point, whichever suits your purpose at the time. In the appendices, the various journey motifs and hierarchies will be listed for speedy reference.

Are you ready to set out on this journey? If so, then *Bon Voyage!*

PART ONE

GOING ON THE JOURNEY

Myths and legends endure because they spring from human nature, which doesn't change from age to age. The ancient stories tell us truths about what it means to be human, truths that only vary in incidentals through the eons. Usually the Hero in those stories heads out on a quest of some sort. More importantly, for storytellers to consider, is the fact that the ancient patterns of stories continue to echo in contemporary tales. For instance, take the story of the son who seeks revenge for his father's murder, and discovers his mother's lover is responsible. Is that the myth of Orestes, who discovered that his mother Clytemnestra and her lover killed his father Agamemnon when he returned from the Trojan War? Yes, it is. But it is also the basic outline of Shakespeare's *Hamlet*.

A storyteller doesn't have to know everything about myths to be a good storyteller. But knowing and being aware of mythic patterns can enrich the work of any writer. When we view the adventures of a particular Hero as a type of Journey, we can use the elements of a Journey or Quest outline to help shape our stories.

An outline of the events of the Hero's Journey, developed from studies of myth, serves as a useful tool for storytellers when structuring their tales, a sort of blueprint in building a story. There are a number of variations of the Hero's Journey, and no one variation is any better in a general sense than any other. In the appendices, you'll find several Journey outlines given separately from beginning to end. Here in the text we'll examine the specific elements of the different variations, gathered in a quasi-outline. Different points of view about an event can help you clarify what you might need at a particular point in your story. Studying the implications of terminology can open many doors for us into our stories.

The discussions are segmented into Beginning, Middle and End. (Screenwriters tend to think in terms of Acts 1, 2 and 3.) However we label the segments, the divisions are inherent in storytelling. The presentation of our Journey options comes in sections called **Setting Out**, **Quests and Conflicts** and **Coming Home**. In **Setting Out**, for instance, you will find discussions of the beginning sections of a Journey. The middle is covered in **Quests and Conflicts**, and likewise the endings are in **Coming Home**. Mythic motifs have a lot of flexibility to them. Elements can be shuffled around in sequence or left out altogether. The crucial thing for a storyteller is to know what the options *are*, so that you can make better choices for *your* story. Just as each storyteller is an unique individual, so too the needs of each story will be different. Follow the need of your story first, and some predetermined format second.

From time to time along the way, I will stop to ask you questions. The questions are geared toward helping you focus on your needs for your immediate story. They may not always apply to the work you have in hand. If they don't, move on. They'll be there when you do need them.

SECTION ONE: SETTING OUT

You get the ball rolling in this segment of the tale. There are many ways to get your story going. It may involve explaining your Hero's origins or it may be as basic as kicking him in the seat of the pants and getting him moving. Even if you begin with "once upon a time" what you say after that will be about something happening. Stories are about motion in time, pictures are about frozen instants. So get a move on.

Let's start with the basic territory of many stories. What do we need to consider here at the beginning of the tale? What things draw the audience into the story? What gets them engaged with the Hero, your main character?

Starting with the Ordinary World may seem like an over-obvious thing, but let's pause and consider it. The term Ordinary World can mean what is ordinary and known to the audience, or what is ordinary to your Hero. See? Already we have discovered two separate possibilities. The modern urban family setting of *Ordinary People* may be quite familiar and ordinary for the audience, but what about the context of *Star Wars* (1977)[1]? The opening of that film shows us a battle in space between ships not found in our real world. And once the audience is taken inside one of the ships, we also discover talking robots, called droids. We quickly realize this Ordinary World will be very different from ours.

As you can see, you need to establish the environment of your tale. It is a way of making the audience feel at home in your story's world. Whether you ease into the environment or plunge head first into it (as in *Star Wars*), your object should be to make the audience either comfortable or curious. If you want to alarm the audience right off the bat, the best way is to show them an Ordinary World that isn't behaving "right." But when all is said and done, we still come back to the point that you are showing the audience the Ordinary World that is the basis of your tale. Be sure you know what it looks like, and that you give the audience a full sense of it.

How you establish your Ordinary World tells the audience how to connect to the story and to your characters. *Clueless* (1995)[2] begins with a series of images of teen-aged girls laughing together in various situations. Then, as the voice-over begins, the images focus in on one particular girl, and we learn this high-schooler belongs to a well-off family. Even if few in the audience will live in such circumstances, they have had experience of teen-aged girls, either by having been one or by knowing one. In *His Girl Friday* (1940)[3] the busy newsroom tells us of the world we're venturing into, a fast paced, hectic place. As Hildy Johnson strides through the newsroom, everyone greets her warmly, letting us know she has been part of this world. Both of these films tell us stories set in arenas that the audience will find familiar. But what about unfamiliar settings?

Bringing the audience into an unfamiliar setting requires giving them cues about it. I mentioned that an Ordinary World that doesn't behave "right" can snag your audience. The film of *Harry Potter and the Sorcerer's Stone* (2001)[4] opens with the image of an ordinary modern street sign, which says "Privet Drive." Even the sight of an owl sitting on it doesn't seem too odd. However, the appearance of Dumbledore, in his long robe, long beard and pointed hat skews the Ordinary World into something a bit different. When Dumbledore puts out the street lights with a magical device, we know for sure this story arena is not quite what we'll find around the next corner.

Setting the context helps bring your audience into whatever your story's world is. In *The Fifth Element* (1997)[5], the very first images are of space, asteroids, and Earth seen from space. So the audience knows they are being given a different sort of approach to the story, especially when they see a spaceship approaching the planet. As the story begins, the prelude is set in 1914. The combination of period and odd looking aliens informs us that we are in for an off-beat story, a feeling continued once we jump into the future. The idiosyncratic tone introduced by the prelude lets the audience know that the rest of the tale will ride on a humorous course, however adventurous. This way of introducing the Ordinary World of the story also gives the audience an indication of how seriously (or not) they may view what follows.

When the Ordinary World of the story happens to be entirely different from our real world, you need to convey the basic nature of the setting. In the theatrical film version of *The Lord of the Rings: The Fellowship of the Ring* (2001)[6], from the beginning the audience knows they are entering a different place. The voice-over introducing the story tells us, "The world has changed." Those words set the story in a different world than the one we know. The presentation of the history of Middle-earth informs us of the stakes for the story that follows. That chore done, we meet our Hero, Frodo Baggins, sitting reading. It is when he meets Gandalf that we realize that even our main character is unlike anyone in our real world: he is half the size of an ordinary human. The little details gather together to settle us comfortably into this strange world.

Another story possibility comes in tales where the beginning setting will be totally changed by the adventures the Hero encounters on the Journey. While there are occasions when plunging right into the story is suitable, there are also times when you need to show the audience what the Hero will be leaving behind. For better or worse, once the Hero sets out on her Journey there will be no going back. Let us be clear: by "going back" I mean that *everything* returns to the way it was (which is different from "going home"). The Hero is inevitably going to be changed by the adventure, and that change will affect the Old World, making it something different. Thus, the audience needs to discover what the Old World looks like. For instance, in *Groundhog Day* (1993)[7], we are introduced to Phil Conners in his job of television weatherman. The audience learns that he is ill-tempered, egotistical and disrespectful toward his co-workers. All this will be changed by his adventure. But for the audience to value the change, they need to see what the Hero's Old World was like.

There is one further consideration in beginning your story.

What if you have more specialized needs for your story that the basic forms do not address? What if, for instance, you've got a story about a Hero of Destiny, rather than an Everyman Hero? There are patterns that can address these needs as well. Let us be quite clear that we are not discussing an Everyman. A Hero of Destiny usually has a special task to complete, something that she and no one else can do. When we are dealing with a Hero of Destiny, we have to give a bit more information about the Hero's origins. Why? It comes back to the matter of audience identification with the Hero. If you want the audience to care about a Hero that is different from them, special in some way, you need to give them an understanding of where that Hero has come from.

Now, some people consider the Hero of Destiny to be "above" us (that is, beyond the reach of an ordinary human). One way of responding to such a character is to say that since there is no possibility of achieving deeds like those of the Hero of Destiny, we are excused from acting like this Hero. We can absorb the story for the fun of it, going along for the ride. But another way of responding to the Hero of Destiny is to consider him as our substitute on the Journey. If we can accept that specialness of the Hero of Destiny, we acknowledge the possibility of such a specialness in ourselves. Such a Hero then becomes an ideal example of the type of person we might want to be, on a smaller scale.

How do you introduce this special nature of the Hero of Destiny? One way is to begin with the origins of this Hero, literally. You can show the Mysterious or Miraculous Birth of the Hero. Even if neither the storyteller nor the audience member has had a miraculous birth, do not dismiss this story option by thinking no one will be able to connect with such a Hero. Everyone desires to feel special in some way, and caring about a Hero born miraculously is one way of having that feeling. Also, do not undervalue the audience's ability to draw analogies. The audience may never be in the position to draw a magical sword from a stone, but they might someday find themselves as the person holding the answer to a small but sticky problem.

Continuing the introduction of the Hero of Destiny, consider the following elements: this Hero may have a Sequestered or Hidden Childhood (with Surrogate Parents), where the Hero's True Identity is Known Only to One. Because of the special nature of the Hero of Destiny, the audience may need to learn about the Hero's Education (with a Wise Teacher).

Now remember, we're still talking about the *beginning* section of your Hero's Journey. As you can see, in this type of story, the Ordinary World is of less initial importance than the Hero's origins. Often, the Ordinary World of this Journey is so ordinary to the audience it does not require much elaboration. Its main function is to show the background against which this Hero of Destiny will play out his story. By giving the Hero a Mysterious or Miraculous Birth, we are telling the audience that they can *expect* extraordinary things from this Hero.

Mythically, we can find models for this pattern in the stories of King Arthur and Moses.

Hero of Destiny - King Arthur[8] - Although the legend of Arthur was built up over time by several storytellers, it eventually settled into a generally accepted form. Uther Pendragon, a High King in early Britain, fell for Igrayne, the wife of the Duke of Cornwall. Whether it was love or lust, he wanted her. Cornwall, not exactly a dummy, realized Uther was encroaching and the two warlords went to battle with each other. Uther, however, had the magician Merlin on his side. He begged Merlin to make it possible for him to lie with Igrayne at least once (okay, that means he wanted to have sex with her). So, Merlin magically disguised Uther as the Duke, and when Cornwall was out of the castle one night, Uther went in and got what he wanted. Unfortunately, Cornwall was killed that night, so Igrayne suspected something was up. Uther married the now-pregnant widow.

By the time Igrayne's child was born, Uther had alienated most of the other warlords. Merlin confirmed to Uther and Igrayne that the child was indeed Uther's son. But he took the child away. Probably a good thing, since Uther's kingdom was collapsing.

Merlin hides the child, called Arthur, with an obscure knight, Sir Hector. The kid grows up as squire to Hector's son, Kay. But only Merlin knows just who Arthur is. Arthur learns his real identity and destiny as a result of the famous Sword in the Stone incident. He pulls the Sword out of the Stone - the *only* person who could do it - much to the chagrin of the realm's greatest knights. After all, here is this pipsqueak doing what none of them could do. And so his adventures begin, with Merlin acting as his teacher.

By detailing Arthur's origins, the storyteller gives the audience reasons for accepting Arthur's right to be king: he is his father's heir, he has learned how to serve, he will be taught by someone with special knowledge. Even if the audience has no expectation of winning a kingdom themselves, they are quite ready to identify with Arthur's career, viewing him as a model for lesser destinies.

It is worth noting, however, that although we usually equate hiding with obscurity (that is, being out of sight), it doesn't always have to be done that way. That is why the story of Moses is worth looking at in this context.

Hero of Destiny - Moses[9] - After the Hebrews had been living in the land of Egypt for several generations, the Pharaoh became concerned about this alien ethnic group in the middle of his kingdom. So he decided to oppress them. First he tried hard labor, but that didn't stop the growth of the community. So he ordered that all baby boys born to the Hebrews were to be killed. One inventive mother, however, hid her new-born in a basket and set the basket floating down the river. Her daughter, Miriam, surreptitiously followed the basket and saw the Pharaoh's daughter find the infant. Miriam then volunteered to help the princess find a nurse for the baby (choosing the child's real mother, of course). The princess called the baby Moses (the name means drawn out of water). The child grew up as a prince of Egypt. Yet, as a young adult, he was moved by seeing an Egyptian overseer beat a Hebrew, and he went to the rescue of the Hebrew, killing the overseer. Conflicted by his sympathies for the oppressed Hebrews and the Egyptian court culture he was raised in, he fled out into the desert of Midian. There, he had a close encounter of the divine kind: God made it clear that Moses was a Hebrew and was chosen by God to free the Hebrews from their slavery in Egypt.

So there you have it: Moses, as the culture hero of the Hebrews, was hidden in the rather public arena of the Egyptian court. Unlike Arthur, who grows up well away from the people he will later rule, Moses is pretty much front and center. As a prince of Egypt he was likely to have been in front of the eyes of the Hebrews. In this case, what is hidden is the true nature of the relationship between Moses and the Hebrews. *He* may not have been hidden, but the fact that he was one of them was obscured. The protection and preservation of his life indicates that he is headed toward something important. Yet, he's a Hero of Destiny who begins his adventure seeming to have screwed it up totally (killing someone not being the best of methods for becoming a hero).

Let's look at these two myths in the light of the details of the Hero of Destiny. The Mysterious/Miraculous birth – the magic used in Arthur's conception certainly would qualify as mysterious, while the fact that the infant Moses evaded the baby-killing order could be called miraculous. The Sequestered Childhood – Arthur lives as a type of servant with Sir Hector, while Moses is out of sight of his fellow Hebrews (as being a Hebrew, that is). It is worth noting that the word sequestered comes from a Latin term meaning to put in the hands of a trustee. Merlin trusts Sir Hector with the infant Arthur, just as the sympathy of the Egyptian princess for the "abandoned" infant wins the trust of Moses' sister. Then there's the element of the Child's Identity being Known only to One: Merlin knows and Miriam knows. We then have the Education with a Wise Teacher – Merlin teaches Arthur, and God (you want a wiser teacher than that?) teaches Moses. This education is likely to deal with the Hero's Special Duties and/or abilities, in effect, learning about himself. The Hero may have to face additional instruction farther along the road.

I won't labor the point by elaborating on the rest of the motif's elements with regard to these myths. Instead, consider what was made of these elements in a pair of films.

Excalibur (1981)[10] is an obvious choice at this point. Director John Boorman's film follows the events of Arthur's origins pretty closely. Yet the film also demonstrates the flexibility of these Journey motifs, since it presents some elements of the Journey motif in a different order than one may usually find them. In the film, Arthur arrives at the tournament as Kay's squire (still in the Sequestered Childhood). But instead of Completing his Education first, he faces his Call to Adventure: he pulls Excalibur out of the Stone. This act designates him as king. That is one heck of a Call to Adventure, going from knight's squire to king in one fell yank. Merlin then reveals Arthur's True Identity to the gathered knights. And *then* Merlin and Arthur go off into the woods to Complete Arthur's Education.

Another example shows up in the film *The Matrix* (1999)[11]. In this case, the mythic pattern appears not so much in the main character's *actual* history as in what the other characters *believe* about him. The story is set in a world run by a hidden computer, the Matrix, which tries to keep control of what the humans do and think. Creative, imaginative thinking is suppressed as much as possible because the computer can't control such non-linear responses - and its survival depends on control. That is the film's Ordinary World. Against this background, Neo has a personal birth history that is no different than anyone else's. Yet, Morpheus believes that Neo is the One, their Hero of Destiny. We follow the steps of the mythic pattern from the outside: whatever Neo's birth, something in his psychological make-up gives him Special Abilities (we see him creating outlaw computer programs early in the film). Morpheus believes, unshakably, that Neo is the One (the Hero's True Identity Known to One Person). Morpheus and his team introduce Neo to the realities of the Matrix (Completing his Education). They then explain what the One will need to be able to do (Revelation of Special Duty). Neo's training in how to be adaptable when they are in the Matrix brings us through the Development of his Special Powers.

Once you have set the stage for your story, the next elements are concerned with your Hero's relationship to whatever adventure you, the storyteller, will send him on. Something happens which triggers action by the Hero. You could call it the Point of Attack or the Call to Adventure. The Call to Adventure brings up a challenge aimed specifically at the Hero. It can be an invitation, a plea, or a choice which would obviously take the Hero away from his Ordinary World.

One of the things about the Call to Adventure is that it upsets what the Hero thinks is a good thing. For instance, in *His Girl Friday*, Hildy intends to leave the news business, and her recently divorced ex-husband Walter Burns, behind. But she arrives just when the newspaper is in the middle of covering a major story. Walter not only tries to talk her out of getting remarried, he also tries to get her back on the job.

Keeping in mind the fact that mythic motifs have a lot of flexibility to them, we should also note that you can jump into your story right at the Call to Adventure. To do so requires the storyteller to fill in any necessary information about the story's Ordinary World as things move along after that beginning. But to jump in feet first can be very effective. The 1986 film *Manhunter*[12], after giving us quick flashes of the crime, begins telling the story with a meeting between Will Graham and Jack Crawford, and the two are obviously not in agreement. Crawford wants something from Graham that Graham is not prepared to do. It's important enough for Crawford to say, "If you can't look any more, I understand." Graham is cynically skeptical of this understanding, replying, "Don't try to run a game down on me, Jack." Whatever the Adventure is, Graham has been invited to get involved, and that is almost the first thing the audience has learned.

Another way of triggering action from your Hero is to remove someone close to the Hero, a relative or close friend. The Hero's world can be disrupted by a Missing Relative. The absence may be voluntary or involuntary. When a character *chooses* to leave, it generates one sort of reaction in others, including the Hero. This includes the possibility of no reaction at all, when the assumption is made that the absence is part of the expected routine. But the point is showing the relationship between the Hero and the Absent Relative. An alternate version of this event focuses on the *absence* of the relative or friend (implying an effect on the Hero). Either way, the departure of someone disrupts the Hero's life. The difference shows up in the Hero's attitude and concern about the missing relative. A voluntary absence by the relative can leave a false sense of security in the Hero. The Hero may think the relative is off doing everything he or she intended. Then you have those occasions when the relative leaves and the Hero feels abandoned by this. Involuntary absences, of course, are very likely to churn up anxiety in your Hero, for something is certainly not as it ought to be.

In *The Lord of the Rings: The Fellowship of the Ring*, the voluntary absence of Bilbo Baggins, Frodo's uncle, precipitates crucial aspects of the Adventure. Certain things about Bilbo's attitude, especially those related to the Ring, raise questions and cause Gandalf to seek some answers. What the wizard discovers becomes the trigger for Frodo's adventures. Here we have a voluntary absence that initiates the adventure. An instance where the involuntary absence of a relative incites the action appears in *Indiana Jones and the Last Crusade* (1989)[13]. When Indiana learns that his father is missing, he immediately sets out to find the older Dr. Jones.

Calls to Adventure may be made to your Hero, but it is part of human nature to prefer to stick with the *status quo*. That is why the Refusal of the Call shows up so often in stories. "You want me to do *what*? You've got to be kidding! No way!" Enough people have experienced that resistance to change that this very human reaction will have the audience identifying with your Hero.

Of course, if you let your Hero get away with that stubborn response, you won't have a story. So you have to find something that will motivate her (that is, get her *moving*). But before *we* move on, remember this: the audience *wants* to identify with the Hero. If the Call is obviously important, something to which the audience is going to say "Well, of course someone has to do something about that," then your Hero's Refusal (whether voluntary or involuntary) has to be equally obvious. A simple "I don't want to do that" is going to alienate the audience. Unless you actually *want* your audience to view your Hero at this point as some sort of idiot, give her a good reason for Refusing the Call. And if needed, you can have someone encourage the Hero to take action.

Consider the possibilities of the Refusal. In *Braveheart* (1995)[14], William Wallace initially does not want to get involved with the Scottish resistance to the occupying English. He wants to resettle in his home village and live in peace and quiet. Of course, if he did so, there wouldn't be a story. The death of his wife Murron drives him to take up arms against the English.

Also, consider how much time you want to devote to the Refusal. Sometimes you may have a complicated process in getting past the Refusal. Other times you may want to zip ahead. We can easily imagine a sequence where the Hero's Call to Adventure, Reluctance, and Encouragement could be covered by as many sentences.

"Mike, you're the only one who can save the town from Crazy Larry."

"I can't stay, because Ma and Pa need me back on the farm tonight."

"I'm sorry, Mike, but Crazy Larry just killed them while burning the farmhouse."

Of course, that example is truly heavy-handed, but you get the idea. Call, Reluctance and Encouragement compacted together. Instead of three different scenes or events, these elements of the Journey motif can be treated as one event. You must decide what best suits your story.

One of the aspects that can be developed in the Call and Refusal sequence is direct conflict for the Hero. As you can see in the rough example, the Call to Adventure can include an actual Point of Attack, a threat to the Hero. The Point of Attack reminds us that the igniting event may be an assault, not just a Call. *Star Wars* provides both: Princess Leia's "Help me, Obi-Wan Kenobi" is the Call, but the deaths of Luke Skywalker's Aunt and Uncle provide the Point of Attack. Given this more active opposition to the Hero, this version of the Journey motif also allows for an Initial Struggle before Crossing the Threshold. Whether the Hero's struggle is with a foe, or well-wishers who want to keep her safe, or within the Hero herself, the step Across the Threshold may not come without some effort.

When your Hero moves beyond the Call to Adventure, she may meet a character who will provide crucial information for her, a Mentor. Or, Meeting the Mentor can provide the means of overcoming the Hero's reluctance to answer the Call. Mythically, there's a very good example for us to examine.

Mentor – In Homer's *The Odyssey*, Mentor, a resident of Ithaca, is first identified as a loyal friend to the missing Odysseus. Odysseus, the ruler of the island, has been gone twenty years – the first ten because of the Trojan War, the remaining ten due to a much-hindered journey home. In his absence, his son Telemachus has grown to be a youngster on the verge of manhood. Opportunists have taken up residence in Odysseus' great hall, hoping to get Penelope the queen (and Odysseus' wife) to marry one of them. One day, when Telemachus stands up and says he's going to sail away to look for news (at least) of his father, Mentor speaks up in support of him. Penelope's suitors don't think much of this suggestion: to them, Telemachus is still a kid and Mentor an old fool. Besides, they don't really want Odysseus to be found. The goddess Athena, however, thinks this is a terrific idea. She's fond of Odysseus and thinks the kid Telemachus has a lot of potential. So she disguises herself as Mentor and advises Telemachus on how to go about his search. As "Mentor" she travels with the young man, helping him find his way in the world beyond Ithaca.[15]

And there you have the origin of our term "mentor": a mentor is someone who behaves like Homer's Mentor (that is, the disguised Athena). A Mentor is ready to help the inexperienced Hero, with advice and information, and is often willing to travel with the wet-behind-the-ears adventurer.

Meeting the Mentor provokes an internal process in the Hero. The teachings of the Mentor cause the Hero to look within himself, to re-evaluate his connection to the world around him. We, like the Hero, recognize in ourselves the wisdom of the Mentor and thus accept it. Or we choose to resist the interference and reject it. But the reaction occurs inside us, and thus inside your Hero, hence "Internal".

So: your Hero is Refusing the Call to Adventure. The Mentor serves to help your Hero understand his place in the world, why he should Answer the Call, or how to go about Answering the Call (or any combination of those three possibilities).

One of the best known examples of a Mentor figure these days is that of Obi-Wan Kenobi in *Star Wars*. Ben (as Obi-Wan is also called) begins his job of mentoring Luke Skywalker by giving the young man his father's light saber. He tells Luke a bit of the history of the end of the Jedi Knights. But when he explicitly suggests that Luke should become a Jedi, Luke rejects it all (Refusal of the Call to Adventure). However, after Luke finds the bodies of his Aunt and Uncle, he returns to Ben committed to learning how to be a Jedi. Luke chooses the path of his Mentor.

Meeting the Mentor introduces a particular character (the Mentor) to help move the plot forward. An alternate variation of this Journey incident, the Supernatural Aid, covers a broader range of possibilities. Many of these possibilities involve exterior events, things that come to the Hero and change his external situation, rather than a Mentor changing his internal outlook. So, let's call it an external variation.

Supernatural Aid can mean many things. The word "supernatural" itself starts from a basic meaning of simply above the natural. In modern life, we tend to regard as natural just those things that science can explain. So anything that might fall beyond that line is supernatural. Whether one believes in a divinity or not, for the purposes of story, supernatural includes beings (or powers and energy sources) that are not necessarily physical, or even belonging to our dimensions (width, height, depth and time). It can be unaccountable and definitely beyond your Hero's ability to control. (That's another reason for calling it external.) But remember, whatever this supernatural thing or person is, it is there to *aid* the Hero. Let's look again at that bit from *The Odyssey*.

Athena as Supernatural Aid (and Mentor) – Athena was the Greek goddess of wisdom. To help Telemachus, she took on the disguise of Mentor, a friend of the youth's father. She was also a warrior-goddess who offered protection to various industries. She was the patron of architects, sculptors, spinners and weavers. A true "Working Girl" in the best of senses. It was a very big advantage to have Athena on your side.

If a goddess of wisdom isn't a Supernatural Aid, I don't know what is. For something to represent a Supernatural Aid then, it would need to possess qualities that are beyond the reach of your Hero (at least at this point in the Journey). If the Aid is going to be a person, it is very likely this person will be quite different from the people of your Hero's Ordinary World. If it is going to be an object, again, it will be something quite unlike anything the Hero has ever seen before. But this is not the only way you can look at the element of a Supernatural Aid. If we discount a manifested Supernatural Aid, what else can we use? You don't see Athena striding down Broadway in Manhattan very often. But most of us have experienced flashes of insight or wisdom that have felt as if they came from outside ourselves. As a storyteller, you are free to consider supernatural as nothing more exotic than a wisdom that is currently outside your Hero's nature.

Look again at the example of Obi-Wan Kenobi. Not only is he a physical presence in Luke's life, he has supernatural powers which he uses to help Luke. From Luke's point of view, Ben begins simply as a wise, older man who becomes his companion. After all, Luke is unconscious when Ben drives the Sand People away. But shortly after Luke asks to be trained as a Jedi, Obi-Wan demonstrates further supernatural abilities, by clouding the perceptions of the road-check Stormtroopers. With Ben's sacrifice on the Death Star, he at last blends into Luke's newly gained wisdom. If *Star Wars* were a realistic film, the promptings that later come to Luke in Ben's voice would be considered no more than consulting a memory of wisdom.

One way of enriching this phase of the Hero's Journey can be by showing the audience the Hero's Education or Initiation. Education can address things the Hero will need to know in order to complete his Journey. It is part of the power of stories in general and myths in particular that they can model on a grand scale courses of action and other choices ordinary humans may face. That is why the Hero's Education can often be fascinating for the audience: as the Hero learns, so does the audience. Education provides the Hero with the basics of his world. In *Iron Giant* (1999)[16], the boy Hogarth educates the Giant about what it means to be a Hero, especially a super-hero. He teaches the Giant about the sanctity of life, which will be an important factor later. In *The Mask of Zorro* (1998)[17] Don Diego trains Alejandro in the skills of sword fighting and personal combat. And then the education moves into even more difficult territory for the young ruffian, that of polished social skills.

An alternate to the Hero's Education can be the more specialized experience of Initiation. The terms education and initiation are not completely interchangeable. Education most often deals with the actual learning of things previously not known, information that could be of use to anyone. Initiation deals with an individual's relationship to society. In fact, it usually deals with a specific segment of society. The individual is instructed in the specialized knowledge of a particular arena. Beyond that, Initiation also carries with it what can be called religious overtones. At the very least, it indicates the Hero has a particular duty or task ahead of him.

To look back at *The Mask of Zorro*, once Diego has educated Alejandro in the physical and social skills he will need, he then initiates him into the finer details of being a folk hero, particularly the chores of gathering intelligence about the plans of their foes. In *Real Genius* (1985)[18], Mitch Taylor, the fifteen year old being admitted to college, is initiated into the laser project he will be working on by his teacher, Prof. Hathaway. To parallel that, he is initiated into college dorm-life by his roommate, and fellow genius, Chris Knight.

Something which combines aspects of the Call to Adventure and the Hero's Education, when dealing with a Hero of Destiny, is the Revelation of the Hero's Identity or Special Duty. One way of revealing or highlighting this extraordinary Call can be the use of a Divine Sign. A Sign provides a very particular type of Revelation. By including divine activity in the Hero's Journey (even if only as a sign), we heighten the impact, the specialness, of the Hero on the audience. In this case, it is not just a well respected figure pointing to the Hero, saying "He's the One" (as Morpheus does in *The Matrix*). A Divine Sign is something supernatural - perhaps even God - saying "This is the One."

Divine Sign - Jesus[19] - When John the Baptist went preaching repentance around Judea, near the river Jordan, Jesus joined the crowds listening to John. Now, this was before Jesus had begun his own ministry. John was baptizing people in the river Jordan

- that is, using the river water as a symbol of washing away the person's past misdeeds. Jesus joined those desiring baptism, and John balked at baptizing this man, whom he perceived as something special. Jesus insisted, John baptized him, and then it happened: the sky opened and a dove descended to Jesus. Since the dove is identified as the Spirit of God, it must have been spectacular looking. Then a voice sounded from above, saying "This is my beloved son, in whom I am well pleased."

Now, *that's* what you call a Divine Sign. The event occurs before the recipient embarks on his great adventure. It highlights for the audience the significance of what will follow and affirms the importance of the character they are looking at. Also it has a different intent than what we earlier called the Supernatural Aid. A Divine Sign doesn't necessarily involve an element of assistance or aid. And who knows? You might decide that it is a major problem for your Hero to be designated "the One".

And remember, this Divine Sign need not be explicitly supernatural. A good storyteller can introduce an event which focuses the attention upon the Hero in this special way. Early in *Dances With Wolves* (1990)[20], when Lt. Dunbar rides out into the open field, in a suicidal depression, he fully expects that the opposing Confederate forces will kill him. Yet, the Rebel shots entirely miss him. This inspires the Union forces to start shooting at the Confederates. All the while, Dunbar rides back and forth across the field, and he remains un-hit. This amazing circumstance attracts the attention of his commanding officer, which leads to special medical attention (an earlier, serious leg wound which could have led to an amputation is what provoked the suicidal impulse). For the audience, this event creates the feeling that Dunbar has been preserved for some special purpose.

Once we get beyond the possibilities of various types of Calls to Adventure (and the Hero's initial reaction to it) we can look at ways to prepare the Hero for his quest, Preparations that are more than just Education and Initiation.

An internalized, or spiritually influenced story may have the Hero Withdraw for a short period, especially if there is a need for Meditation. In the stories of great religious figures like Buddha and Jesus, the act of Withdrawal is a positive one. It can be a spiritual rite of passage, or a rebirth of the self. By withdrawing into the wilderness, or to a mountain or cave, the Hero moves inward on himself, encountering his soul as it really is, and possibly encountering the divine as well.

By facing the unknown (in himself, in God, or in the world) the Hero gains a degree of mastery over what he has encountered. And that mastery can be used to benefit the other people in the story. But this Withdrawal and internal confrontation definitely can involve physical and mental suffering. Without a doubt, the concept of losing one's self in order to find one's (true) self comes into play in this Withdrawal step.

The Withdrawal is a time of meditation and preparation for the path the Hero is about to follow. The Withdrawal of Jesus referred to happens after he is baptized (accepting the Call to Adventure), but before he begins his ministry (which would equate with the Hero's quest in other tales). Let's take a quick look at this Withdrawal.

Withdrawal – Jesus in the Desert[20] After he was baptized, but before he started preaching and teaching, Jesus withdrew from the social life of his country and went out into the desert. For forty days, he fasted and prayed. Basically, he was preparing himself for the chores he had ahead of him. At the end of this time, he had an encounter with the Devil, a testing of his character and resolution, as it were. Jesus comes through it and is now ready to begin his tasks.

As I said, the mastery or wisdom the Hero gains in this Withdrawal can be used to benefit the people around the Hero. The Hero can become a teacher or a shaman, able to convey to others what he has learned. We can see this pattern at work in Jesus' withdrawal into the desert. It is a changing point for the Hero, where he redefines himself.

In storytelling (especially in the visual forms of storytelling like film and television), the problem with Withdrawal and Meditation is the challenge to make it dramatic. However, it can be done. In *Lawrence of Arabia* (1962),[21] when Lawrence reaches Prince Feisal's camp in the Arabian Desert during World War I, the question is raised of how Feisal's troops can effectively be supplied by the British. The ideal solution, the taking of the small sea-port of Aqaba, seems impossible. Lawrence, who has been sent to Feisal merely to observe, must face his Call to Adventure. He must decide *if* he will become involved in Feisal's struggle against the Turks, then choose to what degree his involvement will rise, and finally determine how to solve the problem of the capture of Aqaba. After the initial discussion, Lawrence walks a short distance into the *desert,* and for a night and a day considers these things. He has Withdrawn - and before the quest has begun.

The storyteller also has the option of introducing complications for the Hero, things that may delay her before she sets out on her quest. For instance, the Hero might encounter a Prohibition (or Interdiction). And, of course, the Hero Breaks the Prohibition.

These events begin to test the nature of the Hero. The way in which the Hero faces a Prohibition or Interdiction will tell the audience a lot about the Hero's character. The words Interdiction and Prohibition have similar meanings. An *interdiction* is something spoken, like an order or a law. A *prohibition* can be something more physical, such as a barrier. Both can be regarded as a type of stop sign. Whichever form your stop sign is going to take, it will be by-passed in some fashion by your Hero. The stop sign, however, need not necessarily test your Hero's qualities or capabilities. It may, flat-out, be something blocking the way, stalling the forward movement of the Hero's Journey. In that case, what it will test is the Hero's determination to move forward on the quest.

Let's look at Telemachus again.

> **Prohibitions - Telemachus** - The young man's father is missing (the Missing Relative). Because of his youth, Telemachus has, before the story begins in *The Odyssey*, been restricted to the small island of Ithaca (the Old World). The suitors of Penelope, each of whom wants to wed her and become ruler, believe that the boy is too young and inexperienced to pull off a quest for his father. And of course, his mother would not want to risk losing him. But in spite of these obstacles (Interdictions and Prohibitions), Telemachus slips away to begin his search (Hero Sets Forth).

You can see in this mythic example the things that are trying to hold back the Hero.

What can these Prohibitions and Interdictions look like in your tale?

In *The Truman Show* (1998)[23], Truman Burbank copes with a psychologically induced Prohibition which keeps him in his home community. He's unaware that it is an artificial community, a massive stage set for the ultimate reality show, his life. All Truman knows is that he has a severe fear of bodies of water, and he lives on an island. His fear has kept him from leaving home. Even so, his desire to hunt for his true love prompts him to try and circumvent this prohibiting fear.

In *Monsters, Inc.* (2001)[24], the story itself is constructed around an Interdiction. The opening sequence shows us trainee Scarers learning the all important rule that human children should *not* ever enter Monstropolis, because "there's nothing more toxic or deadly than a human child." This Interdiction gets broken, and our heroes Sulley and Mike try to repair the apparent "damage."

These two examples are big obstacles. But your Interdiction or Prohibition need not be so large in your plotting. In *All the President's Men* (1976)[25], editor Ben Bradlee tells his reporters Bob Woodward and Carl Bernstein that they do not have enough support in their first Watergate story to link the burglary to the White House. This Interdiction makes the reporters delve deeper into the events, pushing the tale further ahead.

Remember, the Interdictions and Prohibitions are things your Hero has to circumvent, getting around them in some fashion that takes your Hero into new territory.

Another thing that can come into focus with these complications is the nature of the Hero's relationship to his family, his community and even his Opponent.

For instance, although it's possible that the Opponent has been present in the story before this point, during this Preparation stage you can have the Opponent start to create some problems for the Hero, by taking direct action. One version of this motif uses the term Victim in reference to the object of the Opponent's action, that is, someone possibly injured by the Villain. That term carries with it a sense of malice in action. But note also that it does not require that the Victim and the Hero be the same person. You have different possibilities *and* different relationships with either option. If the Victim *is* the Hero, the Hero and Villain oppose each other directly. If the Victim is *not* the Hero, but rather is someone close to the Hero, then the Hero's opposition to the Villain has a different tone to it.

This complication can be compacted into one simple, single action, a Successful Deception by the Enemy. The Opponent may seek some information and trick someone close to the Hero into revealing it. But an alternate variation includes some specific elements regarding the Villain's deception, which can flesh out your story possibilities. Let's look at them: the Villain attempts to possess something (or someone) as well as deceive someone. But also, the Victim, in some fashion or other, submits to the Villain's deception. This submission may be achieved any number of ways: fear, ignorance, indifference, pity, innocence. Regardless of the way the submission comes about, it has one consequence the Victim does not foresee: it somehow aids the Villain. Remember, as the storyteller, you have the option of making the Victim your Hero or only someone close to the Hero. If the Victim is the Hero, then this falling for the deception is going to shake the Hero's confidence (and she hasn't even set out on the Journey yet!). If the Victim is not the Hero, this weakness on the Victim's part (however it came about), will strain the Hero's relationship with the Victim.

In *Manhunter*, we see an instance where the Opponent (Lecter) seeks and gains information about Graham (Hero and Victim, in this case). Lecter circumvents the telephone security procedures in order to get Graham's home address from the office of Graham's friend Dr. Bloom, so that he can pass that information on to the killer Graham is hunting. This film actually shows us the Seeking of Information on two levels. Lecter seeks information in order to pass it onto Francis Dollarhyde, who wants information about the man hunting him. But in this instance, the only unwitting aid Graham gave to the Villain was that he told Lecter he was working with Dr. Bloom on the current case.

Occasions where the Opponent tries to possess the Victim or possessions of the Victim can be seen in *The Client* (1994)[26] and *Indiana Jones and the Last Crusade*. In *The Client*, various henchmen of the New Orleans mob figures try to make sure that young Mark Sway either keeps silent about the hidden body or comes into their hands. Avoiding these two possibilities moves the plot forward. In *Indiana Jones and the Last Crusade*, Elsa seeks to posses the diary containing all Dr. Jones' notes about the Holy Grail and its possible location.

Beyond the matter of specific examples, Disney's *Beauty and the Beast* (1991)[27] shows us several of the motifs working together. We begin in Belle's Ordinary World (the Old World). Her father Maurice sets off to take his invention to the fair (Relative Absents Himself). Maurice enters the Beast's castle (the Prohibition – it has, after all, been given a forbidding appearance). He sits in the Beast's chair (Breaking the Prohibition). Gaston tries to talk Belle into marrying him (Enemy Seeks Information). The Beast imprisons Maurice (Injury to Family). The horse comes home to Belle (Call to Adventure), and Belle goes to help her father (Hero Sets Forth). There is a secondary prohibition in this particular story, that enters a bit later. The Beast tells Belle to stay away from the West Wing of his castle. Belle breaks the prohibition, venturing into the Beast's own room. The consequence of this act is at first apparently negative, for she runs away from his anger. But note that I said apparently. In fact, this prohibition-breaking begins the process of improving the relationship between Belle and the Beast.

Another thing to consider about this particular story is that we have *two* characters filling the Opposition spot: the Beast and Gaston. Of course, that will change later in the story, but here at the beginning of the tale, in the Setting Out stage, as far as Belle is concerned they are both her Opponents. Once again, we see how flexible these story patterns can be.

We've looked at a number of ways of getting your Hero out the door. The possibilities that lie within the different elements can be mixed and matched to meet your story's needs. So now we can take a little breather and consider some things.

MUSINGS

> **The Muses** - The Nine Muses were daughters of Zeus, and they were the patronesses of the Arts. They hung out a lot with the god Apollo - the god of poetry (among other things) - and spent time dancing around the spring Hippocrene. The water of this fountain is called the source of poetic inspiration. (Are we sensing a theme here?)

The term muse in ordinary use means to think or ponder – and its origin is directly connected to the mythic Muses. We also use it to refer to inspiration in general. We like to think of the experience of inspiration as a gentle, warm rapturous one. On the other hand, we do have the phrase "the muse struck me."

From time to time along the way, I will suggest some Musings. I hope the questions will help you sort out elements of your story. But if they don't, it's all right. This isn't something where every cubby-hole has to be filled in.

Think about it:

* What kind of a Journey are you sending your Hero on?

* Is your Hero going to be a Hero of Destiny?

If so, what needs to be shown or explained about the Hero's origins, or his/her special powers and abilities?

* Are the Hero's family relationships going to be important motivating factors?

* Is the Hero's Opponent an important factor in the personal perspective of the Hero?

(The Opponent is always an important factor in the *plot*. I'm asking about the Hero's *relationship* to the Opponent.)

* Is the Hero eager to set out, or does he Refuse the Call? If he refuses, what people or events get him moving?

What Preparations does your Hero need to take?

SECTION TWO: QUEST AND CONFLICT

Very well then. We have begun our Journey. Our Hero has set off on the Adventure. What happens next? Where do we go from here? It has been said of story-telling: "First you get the Hero up a tree, then you throw stones at him, then you get him out of the tree." We're at the stone-throwing stage.

In this section we'll explore the possibilities for the middle of your story. This can be very important, as many storytellers often find themselves bogged down in the middle and a little bit at a loss as to how to get out of the quagmire.

Here come the stones! (With a little comfort thrown in.)

First off, it's at this point that the "journeying" really begins for your Hero. Crossing that first threshold sets your Hero out on a Journey of Arduous Tasks. You might as well face it now: there is not one version of the Hero's Journey that does not put the Hero through the wringer. That's the whole point of telling a story: the Hero is our surrogate. We test human nature (and thus ourselves) by telling stories of Heroes. We hope that we will be able to emulate their successes and avoid their failures. It doesn't matter whether you're telling the tale of an Everyman or a Hero of Destiny, the Hero is going to deal with problems. The only other things you need to consider in crossing this threshold is that if you are telling of the adventures of an exceptional character, the obstacles he has to face need to be a bit more difficult than "the usual."

Give a moment's consideration to the word arduous. It certainly means difficult, but its origin means erect, steep, laborious. If you thought the path was hard before, imagine it going up a steep wall. If you are puzzling over how to heighten the difficulties you want your Hero to face, give them a 90 degree turn upward and see what happens.

Okay, so we're clear about the idea of making things difficult for the Hero. But what specifically can be done? What will it look like? As the Hero sets out on her Quest or Adventure, she'll encounter Tests, Allies, and Enemies.

That sounds simple enough. Let's put it all under the microscope. Your Hero has crossed the threshold and set out on the Adventure. Immediately he finds out that things are not going to be easy. He encounters Tests. Now, the point of testing anything is to determine whether it is up to standard. We test children in school (supposedly) to determine if they have actually learned what they've been taught. We test new parts in an automobile to make sure they will function correctly. Also, you could say these events test your Hero's metal. Indeed, that phrase (testing your metal) comes from metallurgy, meaning to test the quality of the ore. After all, you don't want to mistake iron pyrite – also known as fool's gold – for the element Au (gold itself). Pure gold neither rusts nor corrodes, which helps explain why people prize it so. And you want to be sure you are working with gold. Don't short-change the audience in the Tests you lay out for your Hero. Choose Tests that will let him shine like gold, and the audience will value him more.

Allies are those people who join us in a cause, helping us achieve goals. Certainly, a Mentor would usually be classified as an Ally. But your Hero may need additional people to help him on his way. Think about who they might be and what help they will give. Enemies ... well, if you don't know what an enemy is, why are you telling stories?

However, these challenges do not come to us, or the Hero, in the safety of our homes. We have to escape the cocoon to find them. This stage, of finding Allies (and Enemies) and Testing, serves to reassure the Hero that she's on the right track (or warn her that she is not). She's moving out into the wide world to find whatever it is she needs to find. These elements of Tests, Allies and Enemies enrich the story and deepen the character for the audience. The three separate components are grouped together here, just as they might be grouped in your story. But they could also be separate stages. The Test might be given by an impersonal character in the tale, whose only purpose is to verify the Hero's qualifications. Indeed, the Test can also be an act or obstacle the Hero has to get past. When it comes to the other two factors, we certainly have every reason to expect that Allies and Enemies will fall into separate camps. They usually do. But what if they do not?

In *Indiana Jones and the Last Crusade*, these three elements (of Tests, Allies and Enemies) are combined, once again showing the flexibility of motifs. Indiana's Tests actually begin *before* he Answers the Call to Adventure. By translating the Latin text on the stone marker owned by Walter Donovan, and by revealing what he knows about the Grail lore, Indiana proves his competence for the quest. When Indy and Marcus Brody arrive in Venice, they meet Dr. Elsa Schneider, an apparent Ally. She leads them to the first serious Test: deciphering the significance of the Roman numerals in the notes belonging to Indy's father. Indy and Elsa continue following clues even when pursued by an apparent Enemy. As it turns out, Elsa is the character where these three elements combine. She holds the clue that sets Indy on his path, providing the first Test (the puzzle of the Roman numerals). She does help Indy (as an Ally) in these early stages of finding the second Grail marker and his missing father. But she is also an Enemy – as Indy discovers when he actually finds his father. It's an economical use of this motif.

Before we move on, let us consider one other thing. This can be the place where you first introduce the Enemy. If you don't use the earlier instance of the Opponent seeking information, this motif can be where your Enemy becomes active. This is a good moment for the Enemy to actively begin interfering with the Hero's actions. If you choose this option of not introducing the Opponent earlier, and the Enemy's involvement in the events is delayed, the Enemy is, for the audience, more emotionally removed from the Hero. The Opponent's presence, by itself, in the early stages of the adventure (especially in the Ordinary World of the Hero) does not insure that any emotional entanglements will be aroused in the audience. The audience responds to *interaction* between characters. It's your decision, as the storyteller, how and where you introduce the Enemy. Decide how interconnected you want your Hero and your Enemy to be, and weave that level into the story from the beginning.

Trials and Tests also help define what the Quest of your Hero is. On one hand, you may feel that the questing nature of the Journey seems obvious. But I'll pound the nail in once more: your Hero *seeks* something. Although stories have been told of characters meandering through a series of adventures, the most compelling stories come from a lack, where someone needs something. When a Hero feels that something is missing, be it an object, a person, or a state of being, we follow along in sympathy as that Hero goes out to fill that hole in her life.

Very well, then. The Hero is now off and running. He's encountered his first Tests upon the road. Perhaps those Tests reveal to him a need, something he has to delve into. In many stories this leads to experiences in closed places. You have a couple of options at this point.

Enclosed spaces like caves and the underground have a number of interesting implications for the audience. The first option is that of the Approach to the Inmost Cave. For now, let's just say that caves (or, in general, enclosed spaces) are places where the Hero goes for special knowledge. From the simple moment of just going within himself, to an actual descent into the bowels of the earth, in this motif, the Hero seeks to learn something. Also, note that the terminology here implies a voluntary action: the Hero *approaches* the cave.

Mythically speaking, there are two notable examples of this Approach. Both Odysseus and Aeneas in their adventures approach the underworld in order to gain special, needed knowledge.

Approaching the Underworld – Odysseus. Odysseus, in one of the numerous delays he encountered on his way home from the Trojan War, had a nice interlude with the sorceress Circe. When he finally decided that it was time for him and his men to head home, he asked Circe for directions. She told him that to get that information he would have to go to the house of Hades and ask the ghost of Teiresias. Now since Hades was the god of the Underworld, his home certainly has something of a cave-like nature to it. Although Homer doesn't explicitly describe the place as underground, it certainly has that connection and effect. Odysseus follows Circe's instructions for talking with a ghost, gets his information from Teiresias, and then takes the time to see other ghosts, many of them people who had died during his absence from home – including his mother.

In his underworld encounter Odysseus gains the specific special knowledge of how to get home and the actions he should avoid on that journey. But he also gains information about people from whom he has been separated by war and his strange journey. Virgil's hero, Aeneas, has a similar experience in *The Aeneid*.

Approaching the Underworld – Aeneas[1]. Aeneas, a Trojan who escaped with a band of followers from the destruction of Troy, reaches a point in his quest for a new home where he needs to get some special advice. He seeks out the Sibyl in her cave and she tells him that he's going to have to go deeper. In fact, he's going to have to visit the land of the dead to placate the spirit of a dead person (someone he'd once known). He undertakes this journey, does what is needed, and like Odysseus, hangs around to speak with other shades. There he is, the only *live* person in the Elysian Fields, having a chat with the shade of Anchises his father. Anchises gives the hero some detailed information about his future, information meant to help keep him on track.

Both of these heroes plunge into their descents voluntarily. They are nudged into these plunges by the needs of their situations, of course, but even so, they are still free to choose not to enter the underworld.

A straight-forward example of this voluntary descent into the earth occurs in the film *Raiders of the Lost Ark* (1981)[2]. In the film, Indiana Jones needs to find his way to the Well of Souls where the Ark of the Covenant has been hidden. To learn this location, Indy has to descend into the Map Room of the buried city of Tanis. He is lowered into the Room, armed with the real medallion of Ra and a staff of the correct height. With these instruments, Indy gains the special knowledge of how to locate the hidden Well of Souls.

For a less obvious, more realistic version of this motif, we can turn to the film *The Fugitive* (1993)[3]. In this film, Dr. Richard Kimble seeks to discover the real killer of his wife. Since he was convicted of her murder, it's obviously an important quest for him. He escapes from his jailers and returns to Chicago to begin his search. The one thing he knows about the assailant is that he is a one-armed man. Kimble takes a basement apartment to use as his base of operations. During his residence in this cave-like place he studies information about artificial arms of various sorts. While he dwells in this place, he also has a dream of his dead wife which includes visual information (or reminders, if you will) about the type of elbow joint the assailant's prosthetic limb had. When the police raid the house to arrest the landlady's drug-dealing son, the audience and Kimble are reminded that the underworld is not an entirely safe place. So, there you have his descent into the underworld, his gaining of special knowledge (and even conversing with the dead), and a reminder that this underworld is not where he should stay.

Events like these descents often appear as a prelude to the Hero's Supreme Ordeal, or the story's climax. Yet, both of the film examples I chose describe a preliminary sort of descent. In neither case does the Supreme Ordeal take place in these underworlds or immediately after the descents. Still, placing the climax of the story in a place resembling a cave can create a very powerful effect.

Consider, for instance, *The Silence of the Lambs* (1991)[4]. As the story nears its climax, FBI trainee agent Clarice Starling visits the house of Jame Gumb during her investigation of a serial killer. Clarice seeks information about the first victim. Gumb happens to be the killer and flees down into his labyrinthine basement, where his latest victim is imprisoned (but still alive). Clarice follows Gumb into this strange underworld. This is no longer just a descent in search of information, but also a descent to confront the Enemy. The experience is not only that of an underground place, but is intensified by darkness, when Gumb turns off the lights. Clarice must defeat her foe in an ultimate sort of underworld, cut off from the ordinary world and help, in complete darkness.

As you can see, an Approach to the Inmost Cave which leads into a Supreme Ordeal can create a very strong experience. But as previous examples show, it can also be very useful in earlier stages of the Journey. It depends entirely on how you want to shape your story. If that underground special knowledge is more useful to you at the earlier point in the story, put it there. If it has more power when leading to the Supreme Ordeal, use it at that point in your plot.

The Approach to the Inmost Cave is a voluntary experience on the part of the Hero. But what of an involuntary experience? The choice to visit an underworld can reflect an internal experience in your Hero. But when he is thrust into the enclosed space against his will, the causes are likely to be more externally driven. What happens to the Hero in this event can be called the Belly of the Whale experience.

The Belly of the Whale experience is less likely to feel like a positive event for the Hero, as the Hebrew tale of the prophet Jonah shows.

Belly of the Whale – Jonah[5]**.** Jonah's God calls him to go to the nation of his enemies, in Nineveh, to get them to repent (Call to Adventure). At first, Jonah refuses (Refusal of the Call). He sets out on a journey. Instead of going eastward to Nineveh as God told him to do, Jonah tries to get as far west as he can go. Out in the middle of the sea, with a terrible storm raging around them, the sailors find that they cannot move any closer to their goal.

Jonah admits to them that he's the cause and tells them to throw him overboard, which they do. *He* hopes to drown (some people will do *anything* rather than respond to the Call to Adventure), but instead a sea beast promptly swallows him. And there he stays, in that enclosed darkness for three days, until he says he will do the job.

Jonah's tale points out the difference between a Belly of the Whale experience and an Approach to the Inmost Cave. A Belly of the Whale experience tends to be involuntary. The experience can be linked to the great involuntary moments of the life-cycle: birth and death. After all, the image of the womb is very similar to that of the Whale's Belly. Also, as we see in Jonah's tale, the Hero may have failed to obey an Outside Authority. His defiance results in his imprisonment in the Belly of the Whale until he gives in to the Call to Adventure.

From being swallowed up by a fearsome unknown creature, the Hero goes through a transformation leading to an emergence, a rebirth. The involuntary aspect of this experience comes from the Hero's failure to conquer or conciliate the power of the Threshold Guardian he has confronted. Escape from the confinement comes only in his providing that acknowledgment or conciliation which the Hero failed to deliver earlier.

In addition to the difference between a voluntary and involuntary entrance into the enclosed space in these two Journey variations, we also have the difference between the seeking of special knowledge (implied in the Approach to the Inmost Cave) and an acceptance or acknowledgment of information being given to the Hero (as in the Belly of the Whale).

The implication of the forced confinement and acknowledgment of outside information belongs to stories of the Reluctant Hero. Unless you are telling a tale about an over-confident, pig-headed Hero who is sure he knows everything he needs to know. In fact, there are other variations on when you could apply the Belly of the Whale experience, and on whom you could inflict it.

Look back at the film *The Fugitive* again. In this movie, the Belly of the Whale experience is jumped to the climax of the tale (where it connects with the Supreme Ordeal motif). Yet, even though it comes at a later point in the structure of the story, it still retains the characteristics of the motif. It's found in the confrontational fight between Dr. Kimble and his dubious friend Dr. Nichols. When Kimble and Nichols fall into the elevator shaft and onto the elevator car, it promptly descends into the bowels of the hotel. So Kimble is taken into this enclosed place involuntarily. The hotel laundry where he ends up seems very cave-like, or womb-like. In order to gain release from this place, Kimble will have to stop Nichols and finally surrender to the Outside Authority, Marshal Gerard.

In addition to the flexibility of *where* you can place the motif, we have flexibility in which character can experience it. In *The Silence of the Lambs*, Clarice Starling makes a second visit to Hannibal Lecter, a notorious psychopathic serial killer, in the institution for the criminally insane where he is imprisoned. Her first visit had been (supposedly) to conduct a straightforward interview, but Lecter wasn't interested in responding. He did, however, hint that he possessed some special knowledge regarding another serial killer the FBI was trying to find. Clarice follows up this hint and discovers a severed head in storage unit. Her return visit to Lecter after finding the head represents for her a descent into the unknown, an Approach to the Inmost Cave. But the scene is also *Lecter's* Belly of the Whale experience.

How do you make an underground setting (like Lecter's cell) even more so? Turn out the lights and strip the prisoner's cell. The authorities do this to Lecter after Clarice's first visit. He had failed to Conciliate the Power earlier, by refusing to answer the FBI's questionnaire. His provoking his fellow prisoner Miggs to kill himself resulted in the removal of Lecter's few comforts. During Clarice's second visit, Lecter does two things which lead to the reward of having the lights turned on: he gives Clarice a towel (she's wet from rain), and he tells her the psychological key to the Buffalo Bill murders. So, in spite of his attempt at corrupting Clarice's relationship with her Mentor Jack Crawford by insinuating that a sexual interest exists between student and teacher, his positive actions result in the lights being turned on. Lecter offers Clarice a profile of the serial killer Buffalo Bill. This will eventually lead to Lecter's release from his Whale Belly.

This example from *The Silence of the Lambs* reminds us that the Hero isn't the only character in a tale making a Journey. Giving attention to the Journeys of other characters, especially that of the Opponent or Villain, can greatly enrich the story. One event can be two different things for two different characters. Clarice's second visit to Lecter may be *for her* an Approach to the Inmost Cave, where she seeks special knowledge, but the same event *for Lecter* is the occasion of his Conciliating the Power in his Belly of the Whale experience.

Jonah's release from the Belly of the Whale came by being vomited up onto dry land. However you choose to release your Hero from that experience, you next send him off down the Road of Trials. The Hero's goal may be, like Jonah, the land of his enemies, or it may, like the Yellow Brick Road in *The Wizard of Oz*, simply run *through* enemy territory. In either case, the Trials, like Tests, pare away the superfluous aspects of the Hero, sharpening his edges, testing his metal. However, each Trial should move the Hero further along the Road to his Goal. Nothing will disappoint an audience faster than Trials and events which add nothing to the story, which do not move the Hero closer to the Goal.

Once you have the Hero traveling the Road of Trials, he can Meet the Goddess. Make a note here that there can be a connection between the Goddess figure and Mother Figures. There is, of course, the good mother, who nourishes and comforts. Our first expectation will be that a divinity will be good, just as we expect mothers to be good. But there is also the bad mother.

Bad mothers come in several varieties. You can have the absent and unattainable mother, which your character fears and feels anger towards. There is also the hampering, forbidding mother, a constant frustration to your Hero. You can inflict your Hero with the type of mother who keeps her child bound to her, never letting the child (even as an adult) move away from her. And then you could have the bad mother reflected in Freud's Oedipus complex, the desired but taboo mother, who can be a lure to trouble. But remember, these are examples of *bad* mothers.

We will discuss Mother Figures more fully later. At this point, let's just consider those qualities of the good mother (nourishment and comfort) when they are given the extra voltage of divine power. The Hero has, by this point in the Journey, undergone some Trials and tribulations. So Meeting the Goddess in a positive mode can mean encountering a person or experience which refreshes and renews the Hero's sense of purpose. A negative encounter can challenge the Hero's resolution to continue the Journey.

Mythically we find a useful example of this element in *The Aeneid*.

> **Meeting the Goddess – Aeneas.** In *The Aeneid,* our hero, Aeneas, has escaped from the fall of Troy with some followers. After some hardships they land on the shores of North Africa. Aeneas goes ashore to hunt for some food, taking only one companion. He does that because he's depressed about the situation: he doesn't know where they are, they've lost part of their company, and he's not sure about his future. In the woods, the two men encounter a maiden who fills them in on the local situation. Aeneas suspects something's up about the girl, since she's so handy-dandy with information he needs. *He* thinks she's the goddess Diana. In fact, she's the goddess Venus in disguise - and she just happens to be his mother. She goes on to tell Aeneas that the company and ships he thought he'd lost at sea are actually now safe in Carthage. When the girl turns away to head off, *then* Aeneas recognizes his mother.

It isn't absolutely necessary that the goddess figure in this encounter be the mother of the Hero. It does add some umph to the emotional impact of the meeting, but the more important aspect is that the Hero gains some encouragement and important knowledge in the encounter. However, the conveyance of this knowledge doesn't have to be obvious: not every goddess figure has to pop in with a list of useful information and encouraging comments. She might be more enigmatic.

Consider this example: in *Ladyhawke* (1985)[6] as Phillipe the Mouse makes his escape from the city of Aquila, he evades the Bishop's guards and meets Etienne of Navarre. Until this meeting, everything has seemed like an ordinary medieval adventure. But Phillipe's first night in Navarre's company brings something else into the picture. The first time he encounters the eerily beautiful woman who has a strange bond with a wolf, the nature of the adventure changes. Even though the wolf has saved Phillipe from the murderous peasant who was about to kill him, Phillipe still thinks in ordinary terms. The woman (who remains unnamed in the story for some time) alarms the Mouse. He quickly realizes something strange, if not out-right magical, is at work. Later, when he takes Navarre's wounded hawk to the monk Imperius and finds (after sunset) the same woman wounded as the hawk was, he asks, "Are you flesh or are you spirit?" She answers: "I am sorrow." It's after this encounter that Imperius tells Phillipe the tale of Isabeau and Navarre and the true nature of the adventure unfolds. But, as is typical of a Meeting the Goddess event, Phillipe's first encounter with Isabeau changes his awareness of what is going on around him, and eventually changes his life's course.

Of course, a properly divine figure wouldn't absolutely have to be on the spot to make her power felt. The effect of her influence could touch characters by invoking her as much as meeting her face to face. An instance of this version can be found in *Terminator 2: Judgment Day* (1991)[7]. Young John Connor's meeting with the Terminator sent to protect him changes John's perception of reality. John had thought his mother Sarah a "total loser." Learning from the Terminator information that proves that Sarah was *not* crazy compels John to rescue her from the prison hospital. In reclaiming his mother, he accepts the future and the responsibilities she has always told him would be his. In this case, the presence of the Terminator, actual physical proof of the future Sarah had spoken of, invokes Sarah's power as the goddess figure at this moment. Sarah herself isn't present when John gains his new outlook, but all that she had conveyed to John comes into play.

The next event on the Journey can be the Performance of a Service. This frequently appears in fairy tales, where the Hero helps some seemingly innocuous person that turns out to be a king or a fairy godmother or some other person of power. However, in fairy tales, often the focus falls on the hidden power of the person helped (or *not* helped if you're telling an Anti-Hero story). But the intent of this motif, like that of the Tests in general, highlights a particular quality in the Hero himself.

An excellent example of this event comes in *The Fugitive*. After Kimble has gained the special knowledge he needs at the Cook County Hospital, a flurry of activity in the Emergency Room blocks his departure from the building. As he watches, he notes one particular injured boy and the fact that the emergency doctors have underestimated the boy's injuries. Kimble chooses to take the time to get the boy to a surgeon – an action that ends up saving the boy (although Kimble leaves before he knows that for certain). This action apparently has no connection to the rest of the plot – but that is only an appearance. It illuminates Kimble's character. And it has a consequence in the next motif in the Journey.

That motif is called Gaining an Aid. An alternate version of this motif refers to acquiring the Use of a Magical Agent. That agent might be an object or a person. And the term magical can imply something well outside the Hero's usual scope, be it supernatural or not. But the more general approach reminds us that aid may come to the Hero from surprising directions, more mundane than supernatural. And it comes to the Hero because of his act of helping someone earlier.

Turn back to *The Fugitive* again. Because Kimble Performed the Service of helping the injured boy in the Emergency Room, Marshal Sam Gerard begins to wonder about Kimble's guilt. In trying to answer the question of why Kimble was in that area of the hospital at all, the marshals are led to the clinic and labs for prosthetic limbs. This puts them directly on the trail of the real killer. They officially still follow this lead because it should show them where Kimble will go. However, because Kimble helped the injured boy, Gerard is drawn more and more to Kimble's side of the case, and to helping the fugitive doctor solve the problem of the murder of Kimble's wife.

Of course, the Hero's Path to his Goal can still have distracting encounters on it. One such encounter traditionally has been termed Woman as Temptress. You would have to be simple minded if you didn't see immediate possibilities in the idea of combining the two incidents (Meeting the Goddess and Woman as Temptress). However, the events have almost contradictory purposes. Meeting the Goddess, as we saw in the encounter between Aeneas and Venus (and which could also be connected to Athena's encounter with Telemachus in *The Odyssey*), serves the purpose of encouraging the Hero and giving him additional information. But a Temptress exists to be a diversion, something that can pull the Hero off his path. Although there are more aspects to Temptation that we'll go into later, at this point, we'll look at it in the narrow matter of relationships.

The traditional pattern for this stage has a Woman doing the tempting. Virgil delivers the archetype of the pattern in *The Aeneid*.

Woman as Temptress – Dido in *The Aeneid*. Just after Aeneas has been encouraged by his mother, he and his people visit the city of Carthage, to rest and relax. Queen Dido rules Carthage, and she and her people are devoted to the goddess Juno. Now, Juno doesn't like the Trojans (that is, Aeneas and his people) and doesn't want to see them raising up a new nation in Italy. However, she's not blind to the fact that Aeneas is attractive. Dido is a favorite of Juno's, and the queen had been widowed. So Juno decides that it would be a good thing for all concerned if Dido and Aeneas fall in love: then Aeneas would stay and keep Dido happy and Juno would never have to deal with those pesky opponents of her Carthage, the Romans (because Aeneas was destined to lay the foundations of the Roman race). Dido does indeed fall in love with Aeneas, and (to a degree) he with her. They have a wonderful interlude and it certainly tempts Aeneas to stay in the North African city. But Aeneas' destiny as the founder of a nation (the Roman one) gets in the way. Jove says that Aeneas has to shove off for Italy and the dutiful man reluctantly does so, leaving the grief-stricken Dido to kill herself.

All right now, class, remember: the purpose of the Temptress is to hinder the Hero.

Looking at *Indiana Jones and the Last Crusade*, we can see that although Elsa serves the function of an Ally in moving the plot forward, she also serves as Temptress to Indiana. He begins flirting with her the moment they meet, rather than focusing on either finding his father or sorting out what the elder Dr. Jones was working on. To be sure, those matters do resurface quickly. But Elsa succeeds in driving Indy's concern for his father from his mind at their first encounter. A later example of her diversionary powers occurs when they discover that their rooms have been searched. Indiana reveals that he has had the object of the search (his father's notebook) all along. Elsa accuses him of not trusting her, which leads quickly to a horizontal romantic interlude, once again deflecting Indy from the search for his father.

As I said, the power of the Temptress lies in relationships. But not all of these relationships need to have a sexual connotation. Any relational diversion would fit into this stage. Observe how in *Terminator 2: Judgment Day*, Sarah Connor moves from the Goddess function at one point in the story into Temptress, and without the sexual overtones. Sarah's complete focus on her mission (to destroy the formation of the Skynet computer), coupled with her emotionless demeanor, could tempt John into losing his empathy and care for human life. Her behavior declares that emotions must be sacrificed for survival. She is wrong, but given her powerful presence in John's life, her attitude could contaminate John's outlook. He resists the temptation to become like her, however.

So, the traditional view has been that women do the tempting. But actually, if a woman is the Hero in the story, then a man can indeed serve as the Tempter. It may be a less used pattern, but it works.

In *His Girl Friday*, Hildy Johnson arrives back at the newspaper offices of her ex-husband Walter Burns in order to tell him that she just became engaged to someone else, Bruce Baldwin, an insurance salesman. However, not only does Walter still love her, he's in the middle of a major news story and could well use Hildy's reporting skills. She agrees to cover the story. Yet, each time Hildy makes progress on the story, some incident involving Bruce (usually instigated by Walter) distracts her. It's clear to the audience that she belongs in the newspaper game, not married to an insurance salesman. Yet, Bruce's problems continue to tempt her to leave the reporting business. As the story progresses, however, Bruce's inability in dealing with the crises makes him less and less of a temptation to Hildy.

His Girl Friday is a rapid-fire comedy, so the Temptation aspect flies by speedily. A more leisurely and obvious presentation of Man as Tempter occurs in *Contact* (1997)[8]. In the film, the character of Palmer Joss functions as a Temptation to Ellie Arroway. His presence isn't just sexual temptation, but also a challenge to Ellie's point of view and to her sense of purpose. The first encounter between the two occurs just after Ellie arrives at Aricebo to begin her search for signals from space. Palmer's romancing of Ellie distracts her from her scientific endeavors. And his focus on his spiritual/religious experience challenges her rationally based outlook. However, Ellie evades Joss and they part ways.

He reenters her life at the time when Ellie presents the committee of the President's advisors with the blueprints of the alien machine. This creates emotional turmoil for Ellie just when she desires to be focused on the project of contact. When the machine is built and identified as a transport, Ellie becomes one of the candidates to make the journey. However, one of the judges of the candidates happens to be Joss, and his public question to her about belief in God results in her losing the position. This adds a quality of obstruction to the character's function as a Temptation, but this is not unusual. Temptations are often obstructions. And when, after the destruction of the first machine, Ellie prepares to make the journey in the second machine, Palmer appears again. He tells her that his opposition in the original selection process was actually motivated by personal reasons: he did not want her to go, leaving him. Again, this is an emotional Temptation, raising the possibility of drawing her away from the quest.

We see again the variety of ways this motif can be used in your Hero's Journey. It can be a simple event sequence, as in *Indiana Jones and the Last Crusade* where Elsa ceases to function as Temptress once her allegiance is revealed, or it can be an element that recurs at each crux point, as Palmer Joss does in Ellie's progress in *Contact*. Also, the Temptation can be fairly easily resisted by the Hero, the way John Connor does in *Terminator 2*, or it can be responded to, as Ellie responds to Palmer Joss. It all depends on the type of Temptation you the storyteller choose to inflict on your Hero, and the complexity of the relationship between the Hero and the person Tempting him or her.

Moving your story forward, the Hero makes Valiant Attempts at progress. These efforts could take your Hero into the Heart of the Enemy's Fortress, possibly even enduring the Supreme Ordeal. In this, you have two major conceptual units to fill out the middle section of your tale.

One new concept shows up in this option. It's the idea of the Hero actually following her quest into the Heart of the Enemy's Fortress. Other possibilities in the Journey might take the Hero through hostile territory (even territory controlled by the Opponent). But here we have the concept of the Hero actually making her way into the center of the Enemy's power. Think of all the challenges and drama that could come of that in your story. Indeed, if you choose to combine the Approach to the Enemy's Fortress with the Supreme Ordeal, you can have an intensely dramatic sequence. For instance, although there are many versions of the Sleeping Beauty legend, we can easily imagine a version where the task of the Hero hacking his way through the hedge of thorns is for the Prince both the Approach and the Ordeal – unless you consider kissing a beautiful girl and meeting her parents an ordeal. Take a good look at your own story – you may be able to heighten the drama by combining such elements.

If you wish to push your story beyond a mere confrontation in the Enemy's stronghold, you can send your Hero into even more extreme realms, Higher Planes or Dark Underworlds.

The Journey to a Higher Plane (or a Descent to Darkness) and Return introduces an element we have not encountered before. Up to now, we have seen Journeys that send the Hero into caves and undergrounds. Here, however, we have a movement to a Higher Plane.

Such a quest does resemble the underground visits to a degree, in that new knowledge can be gained in such a venture. But usually, knowledge on a Higher Plane is not so much hidden as it is difficult to get to.

We should note that the knowledge gained in an underground excursion is usually hidden or obscure knowledge, something specific the Hero needs. But a venture to a Higher Plane will likely bring about the acquisition of a broader outlook, an opening up of the Hero's perspective to things she had not considered before. In either case, whether the Hero goes up or down, she does return from that place with a newer sense of vision.

The return of the Hero from these different realms leads to Transformation. Journeys like these should transform the Hero, changing his outlook on life. I said earlier that any Journey will change the Hero, that things will not return to exactly the way they were before. This is the stage when that becomes clear. And it is not simply that the events have changed the Hero. The Hero also becomes conscious of the consequences of that change in himself.

The film *Contact* fills out these elements. The Arduous Tasks in Ellie's journey in *Contact* truly begin with the question of who shall be the one to use the alien transport. All her work up to this point has just been preliminary preparation. Dr. Drumlin goes from being her sometime boss and professional superior to being her rival for the chance to make the trip into the unknown. The interview process for that position hits hard on Ellie's (atheistic) straight scientific views. Also, the potential time lag of the journey (as far as the characters know) means that while Ellie is away, everyone that she knows on Earth will die. This strains her relationship with Palmer Joss. When the selection process passes over her, she has another hard thing to endure, watching her rival Drumlin take over the very thing she has dedicated her life to. The most arduous moment for her comes with the destruction of the first machine: it seems to be the end of all her aspirations.

In the film, we see the Journey to the Higher Plane (or Descent into the Dark) and Return, when a surprising turn of events allows Ellie to become the traveler in the (previously hidden) second machine. Her journey does indeed begin with a descent, literally a drop from a height. However, this same event transforms into an ascent into the cosmos. When Ellie releases herself from the chair (which had *not* been part of the original design), it vibrates itself into pieces. With the removal of this restriction, she receives a vision of a vast galaxy. For the audience, the image of the galaxy moves from this external view into Ellie's eye, signifying her inner consciousness, for the meaning of a Higher Plane is not simply a different physical level but an increased or expanded consciousness. With Ellie's awareness of the cosmos raised, she encounters an alien in the image of her father.

This meeting brings on a Transformation. Ellie's contact with the image of her father brings an emotional resolution to her sense of loss and guilt concerning her father's death. This reconciliation allows her then to deal with the alien in a more equitable fashion. She is given an affirmation of the existence of other intelligent life forms, and also an affirmation of human potential. These affirmations, combined with the disbelief she meets on her return, transform Ellie's understanding of what can only be called personal experience. Like

Palmer Joss' religious experience, she cannot provide objective evidence of her encounter, and yet she remains certain that she is not deluded in calling the event real.

A preliminary Transformation can lead to an Atonement With the Father. Ellie Arroway experiences something like an atonement. In some ways, this event can parallel a Supreme Ordeal. That should give you some idea of the emotional weight this occasion can have. Our in-depth discussion of Father Figures will come later. Here the significance lies in the authoritarian power that rests in a Father. Children, even adult children, can have a distorted understanding of the Father. This is especially true of relations between sons and fathers, but it can also be true of daughters and fathers.

Also, just as there are bad mothers, there can be bad fathers. The authoritarian power of the Father can transform him into an ogre in the Hero's eyes. That perception of the monolithic power of the Father, retained long after a character ought to have outgrown it, can keep the Hero from gaining a more balanced and realistic view of the Father, and, by extension, of the world the Father represents.

Sometimes a Father may indeed be an ogre, locked into his own view of things and not acknowledging the adulthood of the Hero. But just as often, it could be that it is the child who misperceives things. Basically, what the motif usually means is that (trite as it sounds) "Father Knows Best" and the sooner the Hero realizes that, the sooner he can cross into a truly adult outlook on the world. Let's delve further into the motif, making the assumption that the Father is in fact a good one. Certainly the clash between generations carries powerful drama, where the younger Heroes perceive the seasoned wisdom of the elders as merely stale experience - until the younger Heroes put it to the test. After which, a reconciliation between the generations is called for.

A growth of trust within the Hero becomes one of the key elements of this event, a trust in what the *ideal* of the Father is. As the Hero's eyes open to an adult awareness of the Father, he can have some faith that the Father is merciful and will act on that mercy. Thus the Hero can come to rely on the authority and understanding of the Father. However, this trust is not grounded on nothing.

By going through the painful process of coming to understand the Father's outlook, the Hero willingly accepts the pains of the process. Because, after all, his perception of the world has been changed as well, changed from a fearful dangerous place ruled by an ogre to a place washed with surprising joys, refreshed by a life-giving force. So, to reach this Atonement the Hero needs to gain understanding.

The word atonement carries such solemn implications, perhaps we should look at it more closely before pushing onward. For once, we have a word whose history is well rooted in the English language. It began by meaning to set or make at one. *At one* to *atone*. Yes, the first time I encountered the explanation, I thought it was too simple and cute. Therein lies its power.

To be at one with something means that the barriers and frictions that have kept two things separated have been removed. A unity has been achieved, usually through some effort. One of the definitions of atonement means to make a reconciliation for a wrong, a propitiation for an offense. Someone or something needs to be appeased. This motif indicates that the appeasement will have to be given to the Father (or a suitable substitute thereof).

Let's look first at a film where the interaction is indeed between a parent and child. *Indiana Jones and the Last Crusade* presents us with an estrangement between father and son, seen the first time we are aware of the senior Dr. Jones' presence. We don't see him, and he doesn't pay any attention to young Indy. Later in the film, when the adult son finds the father, they discover they have both enjoyed Elsa's favors. This further heightens the estrangement and rivalry between them. In rescuing Dr. Jones, Indy begins his Atonement with his father. In fact, this reconciliation drives the emotional force of the whole film, culminating in Indiana's bringing the healing power of the Grail to his wounded father. Dr. Jones acknowledges this reconciliation a t the climax. When his son starts to make the same mistake Elsa did of reaching for the Grail in the crevasse, Dr. Jones finally (and for the only time in the film) calls his son "Indiana," his son's preferred name. By this action, Dr. Jones accepts (and by implication approves of) the man his son has become.

This example shows that the reconciliation flows in both directions. It's not simply a matter of the younger generation accepting the wisdom of the older generation. It's also a matter of the older generation acknowledging that the junior one has crossed a threshold into adulthood. Nor does the interaction *have* to be between an actual father and son (or parent and child, to be less gender-specific).

In the film *Indian Summer* (1993)[9], we are shown a number of people returning to the camp they'd all attended as kids. It's a farewell gathering, of sorts, as the man who ran the camp, Uncle Lou, is about to retire. Jack Belston has returned to the camp to resolve his conflict with Uncle Lou. Twenty years before, he had taken and hidden Lou's boxing trophy in order to punish the older man for a perceived failure of principle. Jack now feels that his act of rebellion was too extreme. Lou, in turn, acknowledges to Jack that the younger Jack was correct in his criticism. Jack unearths the hidden trophy and returns it to Lou, signaling a healing in their relationship. The resolution of this healing, this atonement, is that Jack will step into Lou's role, running the camp and becoming a Father Figure to new generations of campers.

As with the Meeting the Goddess sequence, this motif results in a gaining of self-knowledge and awareness for your Hero. But there is a significant difference between the two events. In Meeting the Goddess, the knowledge and encouragement the Hero gains is *given* to him. In the Atonement With the Father, it must be labored for.

These two film examples fulfill our expectations of what should happen in this Atonement With the Father. But can you, as a storyteller, play against that expectation? Certainly.

We touched on the ogre aspect of the Father Figure. Usually, this is simply a matter of perspective, where a child views the discipline imposed by the father as harsh and cruel. When the child crosses the threshold into adulthood, he comes to understand the discipline and can thus reach an atonement with his father. But in *The Empire Strikes Back* (1980)[10], the Father Figure is shown to *truly* be an ogre. Of course, as the film begins, the real relationship between Luke Skywalker and Darth Vader is hidden. But Vader appears monstrous. He chokes two officers who fail him, killing them with his powers. His underlings freeze warily whenever he walks past them. In Cloud City, he threatens Lando when Calrissian objects to changes in their agreement. He puts Han into carbon freezing simply to test the equipment. For the audience, he becomes absolutely the *last* person in the galaxy that anyone would want as a father. He fights in a ruthless fashion, striking off Luke's hand (a very literal disarming). Yet in the next moment, he tells Luke that *he* is the young man's father.

In the motif, reaching an Atonement With the Father Figure leads into success in the Hero's quest. But Luke, here at this point in the larger saga of the *Star Wars* tale, cannot possibly make such an Atonement. Instead, he must completely reject the Father. Luke's jump into the core of Cloud City's structure provides that rejection. This anti-atonement allows Luke to move forward on his quest, but it also generates a darker tone in the story. The ogre has not been defeated (Vader continues in his position), the child has not accepted the father's discipline (Luke did not turn to the Dark Side of the Force), nor has the child actually crossed the threshold fully into the father's adult realm (Luke, although he acknowledges that Vader *is* his father, turns to his other Father Figure in Obi-Wan for answers). This creates in the audience a powerful emotional hook: since the Atonement was not reached, the audience feels that the story is incomplete.[11]

Avoiding the Atonement is an unusual way for the storyteller to handle this sequence. Avoidance extends the middle of the Hero's Journey, until the matter is resolved.

Getting past the Atonement gives the Hero the strength to face even more traumatic events. In particular, events we can call Death and the Scapegoat. We have brushed by the issue of Death in discussing the Inmost Cave, the Whale Belly and the Supreme Ordeal. Later we will put Death under the microscope. But here in the Journey section, Death signifies an element where the Hero must surrender some aspect of himself, from letting go of some cherished object all the way to the possibility of his own ceasing to exist. Death can be a powerful emotional moment for characters: everything is about to be lopped off. Never downplay the impact Death can have on the characters. The more realistically you render the characters' responses to Death, the more deeply you will engage the audience's emotions.

Let us now consider the motif of the Scapegoat. The term comes from an English Bible translator's (Tindale) attempt to convey a particular Jewish custom. On the Day of Atonement, two goats were selected as a sin-offering for the people. One was for the Lord, the other was let loose into the wilderness. In other worlds, it "scaped" (escaped). The concept of laying the sin (or blame) of things upon a representative is not limited to the Jewish tradition, however. Other cultures have contributed to the lore of scapegoating many different animals as well as humans. Especially humans.

In ancient Greece, a human scapegoat might be used to placate a god, to get rid of a plague or to avert some such disaster. In one particular ceremony in Athens, a man and a woman were chosen for this role. They would have a huge feast, after which the couple was led around the town while being beaten with green twigs (which have to have stung a lot). Then the couple was driven out of the city – and sometimes they were even stoned to death. This was done to protect the city for a year. The couple was chosen to represent all the possible bad things that might happen to the city. If the couple was gone, the bad things (hopefully) would be gone, too.

So the Scapegoat in a tale will probably be your Hero, who innocently gets stuck with the blame for other peoples' actions. Many stories have been built around this concept, wherein the Hero seeks to get out from under the blame and be reaccepted back into society. As a plot element, it can be as small as one moment where the Hero lets others put blame on him in order to protect another character. Unexpected and unjust scapegoating of the Hero engages the audience in their desire to have this wrong righted. An accepted scapegoating engages the audience's admiration for the Hero's generosity and nobility of carrying this burden. Either way, a Scapegoating incident can heighten the emotional level of a story.

A couple of examples can demonstrate the possibilities of the Scapegoat motif. One can be found in the television series *Star Trek: The Next Generation*. Another can be found in *Babylon5*.

In the episode "Sins of the Father," on *Star Trek: The Next Generation*[12], the Klingon Worf learns that his dead father is accused of treason to the Klingon Empire, as the result of a discovery of old records. Within the Klingon culture, the dishonor of a parent becomes the dishonor of the children. Worf and his brother Kurn attempt to clear their father's name, only to learn that the real traitor was the (now dead) patriarch of a politically powerful family. If Worf insists on exposing the truth, the conflict could throw the Klingon Empire into a chaotic civil war. To prevent that conflict, Worf chooses to accept Discommendation, a ritual Scapegoating which allows him to take all the dishonor onto himself, leaving his brother's name clear. In accepting the Scapegoating, particularly an unjust one, Worf displays a nobility of character.

Having a Hero accept and deal with an unjust Scapegoating can be very dramatic. But that is not the only way you can use the motif in your story. In "There All the Honor Lies," in the series *Babylon 5*[13], Captain Sheridan finds himself accused of murdering a Mimbari. When he tries to find out the truth of the murder, his investigation becomes blocked by Mimbari codes of honor, including a tradition of never lying. The frame tightens around him, a threat to his career, until he learns that Mimbari actually can (and do) lie, if it will save face for another. Once he learns this, Sheridan learns the truth of the plot against him. The dead Mimbari wanted to frame Sheridan in vengeance for actions in the past, during the Earth-Mimbari war. Because the actions of one can affect the reputations of his clan, Ambassador Delenn's aide Lennier, who was from the dead Mimbari's clan, could be disgraced if the full details of the plot are made public. Sheridan proposes to Delenn and the representative of the Earth government that they merely state publically that both governments are satisfied that the dead man attempted to frame Sheridan. The dead Mimbari's motives would be left a mystery, saving face for all concerned. In effect, the dead Mimbari becomes the Scapegoat of his own plot, carrying away from the community all the sins (the possible complications) of his own act.

Both examples show us the possible effect on communities if a Scapegoat does not carry the blame: civil war or renewed conflict between two starfaring races. The act of Scapegoating prevents that. It is a point you will want to consider if you choose to use the motif of a Scapegoat.

In moving toward the climatic confrontation, a Descent to the Underworld can follow the action of the previous events. We have had ventures into underworlds before. But in this context, on the heels of dealing with Death, the experience can have darker, deeper implications. Given the usual association of the Underworld with Death, we can hardly be surprised by the connection. The story possibilities can open up if we look at Scapegoating as a form of outlawing a character, setting the Hero outside the law and society. If the story shapes itself that way, all the possibilities of what the Underworld can mean come into play. In that context, the experience of the underworld can lead directly to the major conflict, or Battle.

The Battle represents the ultimate confrontation of the Hero's quest where the Hero comes face to face with his Opponent. The stakes of the Battle are directly related to whatever the Hero has been seeking. We are not talking about a simple action sequence, of conflict for the sake of conflict. The fight needs to be connected to the Hero's objectives.

One crucial element of the Battle is the Price that must be paid for success in the quest. An alternate terminology indicates that the Hero may be Branded or Wounded in some fashion at this point. But even if there is not a physical marking of the Hero, something must be paid out to achieve the goal. The possibilities are vast, ranging from loss of innocence to loss of life.

Again, the issue of value – to the characters and to the audience – comes into play. A cheap, easy victory only serves to irritate the audience. Indeed, a cheap Price devalues all the action that comes before it. But in addition to casting a light backward over the story, the Price can also shine forward into the Hero's future. The choice of what the Price will be can be very important for your story.

In *The Empire Strikes Back*, when Vader strikes off Luke's hand, we have a very explicit example of the Price, in this Wounding of the Hero. The loss of his hand is the Price Luke pays for gaining greater knowledge about himself and his quest. The aspect of Branding (or being marked as a type) will resurface for Luke in *The Return of the Jedi* (1983)[14] when he strikes off Vader's hand and discovers that it too (like his own replacement hand) was artificial. The sudden discovery of this parallel between himself and his father puts a damper on Luke's battle fury. (After all, he certainly doesn't want to become *like* Vader.) In these instances, we can see that the Wounding can be more than a simple passive marking of the Hero. Indeed, it can be something that will continue to affect the Hero in the future.

To further explore the effects of Luke's Wounding in the *Star Wars* saga, let's look closer at the course of events in *The Return of the Jedi*. We are reminded of Luke's Wound early in the film, during his fight with Jabba's warriors. A blaster shot rips through the artificial skin of Luke's hand, and after that scene, Luke wears a black glove on that hand. Later, at the moment he strikes off Vader's artificial hand, the Emperor tells Luke that Luke's hate has made him powerful, that he must fulfill his destiny and take his father's place at the

Emperor's side. The Emperor's words and the sight of the connections for Vader's artificial hand remind Luke of the Price he has already paid for self-knowledge. As a consequence of that reminder, he completely rejects the Emperor's promptings, and even tosses away his light saber. By this example, we can see that a Branding or Wounding may be both the Price of self-knowledge and the reminder *of* that same knowledge.

Discovering and accepting the Price of achieving the Hero's goal will lead directly to the Victory. Our word, victory, goes back to the Latin meaning to overcome, to conquer. Whatever your Hero has been battling, at this point he overcomes it (even if it is just himself). By viewing your Hero's objective in these terms of battle and conquest, you may find more dramatic ways of presenting his conflicts.

But what if your story doesn't call for an out-and-out battle? What will your ultimate conflict look like? Let us broaden our perspective by calling the event the Supreme Ordeal.

The origins of the word ordeal are grounded on meanings concerning a due or right part of something. As time built upon this, the meaning moved through to deal out and to give judgment ending with the definition we apply today: any extremely severe or trying test, experience, or trial.

Consider the original meaning. If the word first applied to a proper part of something, then now, in your tale, this Supreme Ordeal needs to be suited for your specific Hero. If your Hero's everyday world involves running around tunnels in near darkness, an underground climax will probably not have the desired effect on the audience. After all, if it is part of the Hero's Ordinary World, how can it be an extremely severe Test?

Basically, a Supreme Ordeal will be the worst possible thing that can happen to your Hero. But remember, what your Hero thinks is the worst possible thing and what *really* is the worst possible thing for him or her can be two entirely different things.

Look at George Bailey in *It's a Wonderful Life* (1946)[15]. George feels that he has sacrificed everything he wanted – college, travel, adventure – to sustain the Bailey Building & Loan. Serving that institution and the people it helps has tied him to a town that felt too small for him. When Uncle Billy loses the Building & Loan's cash, all of George's anger boils up, combined with his fear of losing everything. He frightens his family with his intense emotional upset. He goes to the man he despises most, Mr. Potter, who tells him he is worth more dead than alive. And George agrees, and so decides to kill himself. At this point, George thinks that the loss of all that he *has* (materially) is the worst thing that can happen to him. Yet once Clarence, his guardian angel, grants him his wish of seeing how things would have been without him, George is progressively rocked by how different the *people* are. The encounter that truly shatters him, which really *is* his Supreme Ordeal, comes in meeting Mary, a Mary who never knew or loved him. This Mary is very different from the luminous and loving girl he wed. This Mary is pale, pinched and frightened of everything, especially frightened of him. This revelation breaks George: he flees back to the bridge, crying out that he wants to go back, and he doesn't even care what will happen to him.

Coming through the Ordeal can lead to a transformation of the Hero, a change of a profound sort, an Apotheosis. This experience grows naturally out of the consequences of previous actions, such as achieving an at-one-ment with the Father Figure. If the Hero becomes at-one with the authority figure in his life, he can move on to becoming united with the world around him. The Hero moves closer to the divine realm. Indeed, that's what apotheosis means: to be made a god. The Hero, in passing through all his tests and ordeals has moved into a higher realm, something more than the ordinary.

A very archetypal version of this appears in *The Return of the Jedi*. When Vader rejects the Emperor, throwing away not only his master but also everything he had been for many, many years, he regains his identity as Anakin Skywalker. He sacrifices himself to save his son. When he takes off the Vader mask as he dies, he in effect reclaims his position as a Jedi. Luke gives his father's body to a funeral pyre (rather like a Viking funeral). The imagery of the film follows the flames upward into a star-filled night sky decorated with fireworks and then dissolves to several scenes of celebration. Then, as Luke rejoins his friends, he looks back to see the images of the Jedi Obi-Wan and Yoda. And then Anakin's image joins them: Anakin has achieved the Hero's Apotheosis as a reward for his sacrifice in saving Luke.

Not every Apotheosis need be so obvious. It may be as simple as your Hero being promoted into the position she's been hoping for, or at last rushing into that passionate kiss. (After all, haven't poets down the ages spoken of "finding heaven in True Love's arms"?) However you decide to present the Apotheosis motif at this point, the important aspect of it should be that your Hero has reached a new place, something better, higher than her starting point.

However, if you do not want to go so far as an Apotheosis, at least give your Hero a Reward. When your Hero faces and passes the Supreme Ordeal, he should receive a Reward. We think of rewards as prizes won at the end of a contest, or payment for solving/finding something ("reward for the capture of Nasty McKnee"). But the word began as meaning to look at, to regard. So this Reward can be as simple as your Hero being seen in a new light by his community.

For an example of this, let's delve into *It's a Wonderful Life* again. George's Reward for choosing life, no matter what the consequences, is his return to that life. He looks again at his town, at the people in it, and he rejoices in all of it. But that's not the end of the Reward: everyone (excepting Mr. Potter) pours in to give George money to help in the crisis, to cover the Building & Loan's loss. They do it because of who he is and what he has done for them. In a way, we could say that the townspeople look at George again. Even his younger brother returns home to proclaim George as "the richest man in town." And just to be sure we, the audience, don't miss what is being rewarded, Clarence's note to George in the angel's copy of *Tom Sawyer* says, "Remember, no man is a failure who has friends."

However you work out your Reward system for your Hero, remember that it has to address her Ordeal, that it has to reflect her character. If you have been showing the audience an un-materialistic Hero throughout the adventure, you cannot follow the intense emotional experience of the Ordeal with a Reward of money. Not only will it be irrelevant to your Hero, it will not satisfy the audience. Ending the adventure with the Hero kissing the girl in the story, especially when he hasn't shown much interest in her all along the way, won't charm the audience. That's hardly a Reward. Look at your Hero again, and Reward the person who is actually there.

Let me repeat the point. The Reward can be one of a multitude of things. The Boy gets the Girl (if he's been pursuing her). The Mystery is Solved. The Murderer is Caught. The Terrible Thing is Destroyed. Sometimes, as the saying goes, "Virtue is its own reward." The point is that for the audience, there's a *felt* resolution to the Ordeal, that the ending of the Ordeal has some stated significance. Withholding that resolution creates tension in the audience. When a storyteller withholds the resolution (or Reward) on purpose, he or she keeps the audience on the hook. The audience keeps waiting for the explanation of why things have occurred. If you hold back that resolution and reward in order to drive the audience into the Coming Home part of the tale, well and good. But if you simply just forgot or left it out thinking it unimportant, it can be a monstrously huge pot-hole on the road of the Hero's Journey. To a certain degree, you the storyteller need to remember that a Reward to the Hero also rewards the audience, for they have been identifying themselves with the Hero. In a way, what you do to the Hero, you do to the audience.

This brings us to the Ultimate Boon. Boon is a word that doesn't get a lot of use these days. It's defined as something to be thankful for, a blessing or benefit. Its origins actually trace back to an Old Norse word for prayer. So we could say that a Boon is something that has been prayed for, an outcome that someone greatly desired. In some ways, the distinction between a Reward and a Boon is that a Reward is usually specific to the Hero, while a Boon is something the Hero brings to others. Yes, it can benefit the Hero, but its effect extends beyond the Hero as well.

One of the simplest and most direct examples of a Boon comes in *Indiana Jones and the Last Crusade*. Indiana correctly finds the *real* Grail, and brings it to his wounded father. The Grail's healing power saves the life of Dr. Jones – definitely something Indy desired and was thankful for.

Indeed, a Boon is best presented in simplicity. It should be clear and obvious to the characters and audience that it *is* a benefit. Never underestimate the emotional satisfaction the audience can have at this moment.

And, of course, after Battle, after Ordeals, comes the Completion of the Quest. At this point the initial misfortune or lack, which set the Hero off on the quest in the first place, is liquidated. The problem that had set the Hero in motion flows away like water. The Hero has reached her Goal. The object of the quest now rests in her hands. The weapons can be laid down.

Meaning, we've reached the End of the Middle.

MUSINGS

The Muses are dancing around the spring of inspiration, laughing and playing. You, however, are hard at work. Your team is behind by three points. The bases are loaded, there are two outs, and two strikes against you already. It's the crucial moment of the ninth inning and with all your heart you want to whack that ball right out of the park and go prancing around the bases for the winning point.

A strong Middle to your story will win any audience.

Think about it:

*   What actually is the goal your Hero heads toward? Until you know this, none of the other questions can be answered in a meaningful way.

*   What Price will your Hero have to pay to achieve that goal? Does your Hero know the value of the Price from the beginning of the story or does he learn it as we go along?

*   What is the *worst possible thing* that can happen to your Hero? If you need to, draw up a list of possibilities for this. Go wild. You might be surprised at what you find.

*   What qualities (or objects) will the Hero need to complete his quest? Design your Tests and Trials to either show the Hero (and the audience) that he possesses those qualities, or to show the Hero how to acquire them.

*   Is your Hero *given* helpful information or does he have to *seek* it? And what kind of information is it? Is it special knowledge known only to a godlike few, or is it just difficult to find, requiring a steep climb?

*   Does your Hero need to go into the core of the Enemy's territory or fortress? What will this look like? What are the obstacles? What is gained by the action?

*   Do you plan on using the Scapegoat motif in your story? Who will be the Scapegoat? Is the ostracizing of the Scapegoat just or unjust? What community benefits from the use of the Scapegoat, and how is that benefit displayed?

*   How is your Hero changed by reaching the Goal? What Reward will be given to the Hero, and how does it reflect the Hero's qualities and goals? Does the Hero win a Boon for her community? What is the Boon, and how does it affect the community?

SECTION THREE: SIDE TRIPS

Before we set about returning the Hero to his home, let's look at some specialized Quest-Journeys.

The legends about King Arthur and his court brought storytellers the model for a very specialized type of quest for Heroes – the Grail Quest. The supernatural cup used by Jesus at the Last Supper was believed to give a great Boon to people, so of course, it was considered an object worth pursuing.

For storytellers, then, the Grail Quests provide models for Journeys with particular types of goals and relationships. These motifs can be used to shape either the middle course of your story, or the whole of it. There are three primal types of Grail Quest, each based on the character of one of Arthur's knights[1]. So, to begin with, let us get acquainted with those knights.

The Grail Knights – The chosen three Grail Knights are Gawain, Perceval and Galahad. Now, each of these knights was quite different in character. Gawain, in most all of his stories, is a hearty warrior, and a lusty man. He is easily romanced and easily drawn into battle. Perceval is a gentler soul, whose heart's desire is to be an excellent Knight of the Round Table. An idealist, he is also something of an innocent. Galahad is, of course, the Perfect Knight, pure in thought, word and deed, unlikely to be tempted to divert from his goal.

Now, in the legends, each of these three achieved the end of the Grail Quest in different ways.

The Grail Quests – Gawain followed the adventures of the Grail quest in an almost haphazard fashion. He never quite understood the significance of events in the quest, and at the end of it, only got a glimpse of the Grail before he returned home.

Perceval was a bit more aware of the meaning of the strange events of the quest, but he didn't always respond to them correctly. Still, he did take Communion from the Grail before he returned home empty-handed.

Galahad not only followed the path to the Grail with full understanding, he performed all of the services required of him. In the end, he stayed with the Grail and never returned to Arthur's court.

The knights' achievement of reaching the Grail is not the only important element in these stories. The other important aspect lies in the encounters these knights have with a wounded ruler, called the Fisher King.

The Fisher King – This wounded king can be healed only through the help of the Grail knight, the one seeking the Grail. The Land around the Fisher King's castle suffers from terrible conditions, paralleling the state of its ruler. However, when the wounded king is healed, the Waste Land which lies around the castle will become productive and fruitful again.[2]

The Land around the king reflects the ailing health of the king. How the Hero treats the king likewise has an effect on the Land. Later, we will look more closely at the nature of a Grail itself. For now, our focus lies on the interconnection between the Hero's quest and the environment (or community) around him.

Looking at your story, you may find that one of the Grail Quest motifs fits it quite well. This is particularly true if your Hero's quest directly benefits someone other than the Hero himself. We will look at each Quest outline in turn, examining the shapes they take. The outline presents the *traditional* form of that Quest. As always, how you the storyteller use the motif can vary widely.

Gawain's Quest

* *The Hero travels with an Unknown, who is on a quest*

* *The Unknown dies*

* *The Hero takes up the Unknown's quest*

* *The Land is wasted because of the Unknown's death*

* *The Hero fails to completely fulfill the task*

* *The Land is partially restored.*

As you can see, in Gawain's Quest, the Hero doesn't quite know what he has gotten himself into. He may be taking up someone's uncompleted job, without knowing the consequences of it. He may have to fumble his way through crucial elements of the Quest, and it is possible that he could fail to a degree because his knowledge of the Quest is incomplete. This sort of situation can be either highly comedic or deeply tragic, depending on the stakes you build into the story.

But lest you think the steps in the outline are cut in stone, let's take a look at a version of this Quest that does not play out disastrously.

In *The Fifth Element*, the young woman Leeloo fills the part of this Quest's Unknown. She literally falls into the company of Korben Dallas, by falling into his air taxi. Leeloo's quest is to collect the Four Stones of the Elements (those being Earth, Air, Water and Fire, not the chemical elements of the Periodic Table) and return with them to a temple in Egypt in order to activate the weapon which will drive off the approaching Great Evil. If she fails, the world will be destroyed. Korben, initially, has no interest in the quest. He is, however, extremely interested in Leeloo herself. Later in the story, Leeloo is wounded during the recovery of the Stones, her wound being more spiritual and emotional than physical. In her fragile emotional state, she slides toward giving up on life. The world will be devastated if she does. Korben, having taken up Leeloo's quest, gets her and the Stones to the temple. Although he can activate the Stones, Korben cannot, by himself, fulfill the task of the quest. So he has to give Leeloo the will to live and to complete the quest. By his doing so, the Great Evil is stopped and the world is saved.

The Fifth Element once again shows us how flexible mythic motifs can be. The Unknown does not necessarily have to die (as Leeloo does not). Incapacity of the Unknown can be achieved in many ways, so consider your options, from injury and imprisonment to death itself. Likewise, the Land around the Unknown, the Land that becomes wasted by the

Unknown's incapacity, can range from the whole world (as in *The Fifth Element*) down to a small family unit. It is your choice. The importance of the Land lies in the value you, the storyteller, invest in it. If you make it important to the audience it will not matter how large or small the Land is, only that it needs to be saved. In any case, the pattern of Gawain's Quest is that the Hero takes up someone else's task and brings it to partial or complete fulfillment.

In the Gawain Quest the Hero more or less stumbles into the adventure. In the Perceval Quest, he is noticeably more aware of the interconnected elements.

Perceval's Quest

* *The Hero knows the object of the quest*

* *The King ails and the Land ails*

* *The Hero must recognize what will heal the King*

* *If the King is not healed, the Land will be devastated.*

In this case, the Hero is the initial quester, unlike the Hero of the Gawain Quest. Also, the connection between the King's ailment and the sorry state of the Land is more explicit. However, the strongest difference between this Quest and the previous one lies in the Hero's awareness of what is needed in the quest. The fact that the Hero has to recognize what will heal the King means that on this quest, the Grail might not be something obvious. It means that although the Hero may know in a general sort of way what is required to bring healing, he might make a mistake of some sort when he encounters it. It adds another layer to the story, something that can touch deeper elements in the Hero's character.

The obvious example for this Quest comes in *Excalibur*. The film actually uses the Perceval Quest in its story. The knight chosen to exemplify this version of the adventure is, of course, Perceval. When the ailing Arthur sends out his knights to find the Grail, Perceval knows the object of the quest. The Grail can heal the king, and Perceval knows this. As Perceval rides out on the quest, he can see that the land ails just as the king does. Perceval clearly sees the oneness of the king and the land in both sickness and health. Remember, in this Quest, the Hero must recognize what will heal the king. At a point when the quest has greatly wearied Perceval, Morgana offers him false cups, false Grails. But he does not accept them. Morgana then hangs him in a tree and while there Perceval has a vision of the real Grail. Unfortunately, he cannot answer the Grail questions, "What is the secret of the Grail? Who does it serve?" (that is, he fails to recognize what is needed). After his failure, Perceval becomes even more sharply aware that if the king is not healed, the land will be devastated. Perceval humbles himself, keeps hope and gets a second chance at the Grail. This time he correctly identifies the secret of the Grail (that the land and the king are one), secures the Grail, and brings its healing to the ailing Arthur. Just as Arthur is healed, so too greenery and blossoms return to his land.

The Perceval Quest directly connects the Hero's actions to the healing of the king and the Land. The Galahad Quest separates the Hero's personal quest for the Grail from the need to heal king and Land, meaning that the story supports two purposeful through-lines.

Galahad Quest

* *The Hero is on a quest, for fulfillment of the self*

* *The Hero is destined to succeed in the difficult quest*

* *The Hero heals the ailing king before he completes his quest*

* *The Land is healed*

* *The Hero achieves the goal of his quest*

The film *My Favorite Year* (1982)[3] plays out its story according to the Galahad Quest. Let's consider its elements step by step.

The Hero is on a Quest for fulfillment of the self

Benjy Stone works as a freshman writer on Stan "King" Kaiser's television show, aspiring to a longer, established career as a writer. To show that he is at the beginning of his quest, we see that Benjy doesn't get much respect from his co-workers. Yet movie star Alan Swann compliments Benjy on the sketch the young man had written for Alan to guest-perform in. This reaffirms Benjy's potential for a successful career.

The Hero is destined to succeed in the difficult quest

The voice-over at the beginning of the film indicates that the narrator, Benjy, is looking back on past events. It implies that he succeeded in whatever adventure we are about to see: after all, he calls it "my favorite year." However, Benjy's "difficult quest" is not simply achieving his goal as a writer, it is getting Alan Swann to the end of the broadcast sober. The difficulty for Benjy lies in Swann's ability to absorb alcohol at the slightest provocation.

The Hero heals the ailing king before he completes the quest

Swann represents the ailing king. He's always late for something. He gets drunk easily. These things threaten the completion of that week's show (the Land), and by implication Benjy's future as a writer. In spite of the difficulties, when show day arrives Benjy has apparently gotten Swann past these problems. Then Swann discovers that the show is aired *live,* and he freaks out. The Land (the show) and the king (Swann) are suddenly in greater danger than they had been before. It's Benjy's angry statement to Alan, "All you end up doing is making anyone who cares for you unhappy," which starts the healing process of the Ailing King.

The Land is healed

Alan's ailment of being a drunk affects the possible outcome of the TV show. The movie star admits to Benjy that he is afraid: afraid of the audience, and afraid of what his young daughter thinks of him. This fear has driven him away from the TV show's stage. However, Benjy persuades Alan to take a chance. The young writer's ability with words comes into play, when he tells the actor, "You couldn't have convinced me the way you did unless somewhere in you, you had that courage. Nobody's that good an actor!" While Benjy conveys to Alan that his acting heroics must spring from some source in the man himself, mobsters are backstage beating up "King" Kaiser, thus threatening the show. When Alan sees the fighting on stage, he swings into action like the hero Benjy proclaimed him to be. Together, Alan and Kaiser defeat the mobsters and in the process, wow the in-studio audience.

The Hero achieves the goal of his quest

Benjy's idol *behaves* like a hero when it becomes necessary. Benjy's way with words convinces Alan, which implies success for Benjy's future as a writer.

As you can see, Benjy's personal quest of success as a writer could be pursued independently of keeping Alan sober and having the week's show be successful. But the way the story falls out, they *are* connected. And in a way, if Benjy failed to convince Alan that the actor did possess some heroic qualities, it's possible that in the long run he would fail as a writer. Inevitably, the Hero's quest for the Grail of his life will affect the characters around him.

Again, remember the flexibility available to you in using mythic motifs. A Grail Quest can shape the whole of your story (as it does in *The Fifth Element* and *My Favorite Year*), or it can shape part of the tale (as it does in *Excalibur*, providing a part of the Middle of that story). You have a choice on how completely you want it to inform your story.

MUSINGS

Sometimes you need to hack away all the details of your adventure in order to understand the shape of it. There may be a deal of blood shed in cutting to the bone, but once the skeleton is laid out, you have a better idea of what sort a creature (your tale) you've been battling.

Think about it:

* Will your Hero's quest greatly impact the community around him?

* If your Hero succeeds, will that bring a healing effect to a crucial figure?

* What are the stakes if the Hero fails?

If the failure affects only the Hero, you probably do not have a Grail Quest.

If the failure can devastate the Land of your story, you probably do have a Grail Quest.

* If you do have a Grail Quest, what sort of Grail Knight is your Hero? Is he worldly, innocent and naive, or pure in heart?

* But don't limit yourself to the formulas given here. Consider the possibilities of sending a worldly Gawain on a pure-hearted Galahad Quest. The tensions generated within a lusty, worldly character who must follow a pure and chaste course can be very dramatic.

* Lastly, of course, what is your Hero's Grail?

SECTION FOUR: COMING HOME

Many stories end with the achievement of the Quest, the resolution of the principle conflict, with the prize shining in the hand of the Hero. And if that is where you want to stop, then do so. But be aware that the Journey motifs also cover the types of things your Hero may face when she heads home. Even if the Hero has successfully endured the Supreme Ordeal, there may still be some things she has to face, some things she has to do.

One way you can handle this can be in grouping the beginning of the Hero's return with the major confrontation. This choice can convey that all the issues of the crisis need not be resolved before the Hero has seized the object of his quest. Indeed, if some elements find their completion while the Hero is being pursued on his way home, there may be a greater sense of organic unity to the story, rather than a feeling of mechanical clockwork. That said, the Road Back may seem like an obvious thing to include in your tale. After all, the Hero needs to return home, doesn't he? And although the Hero may not have to confront opposition in his return, the possibility of his revisiting his earlier battlegrounds can be of interest to the audience. By sending the Hero backwards over the territories of conflict, you can allow some reflection on the nature and value of the Tests and Trials the Hero encountered earlier. But whether the Road Back is straightforward and uncomplicated or whether it revisits and reevaluates previous events, the Road moves away from the intense moment of the Supreme Ordeal.

It makes sense that after the Hero completes his quest - after all those trials and tribulations, after the goal has been reached – the Hero wants to go home. It's a natural desire to head back to the safe harbor after a difficult, stormy voyage. Bringing your Hero home can be a satisfying experience for the audience. It allows them to see the Hero exercise the abilities he had gained in his quest. This is particularly important if your tale looks closely at the psychological effects of the quest on the Hero.

Once you decided to include this sequence in your tale, consider the things which can provide Hindrances to your Hero's trip home. As always, it makes the story tighter when these obstacles come from people and things the Hero encountered earlier. Did an action the Hero took in an earlier part of her quest set in motion a sequence of events that could end up blocking the Hero's path homeward? Or was there an encounter with someone who may have cause to resent the Hero? Perhaps the hindrance is an aspect of the Hero herself – an inflated ego as a result of succeeding in the quest can trip up many characters.

Whatever Hindrance you choose to use, the Hero can then encounter Help. This could be a reflection of the earlier step when the Hero Performed a Service. He can receive back help just as earlier he had provided help. In any case, the Help lets the Hero move forward toward home territory.

But what if, after coming through the Supreme Ordeal, the Hero does not want to go Home? What if, after securing the Ultimate Boon, the Hero would rather just stay put? Even though we usually expect the Hero to bring the Boon to his community, sometimes he refuses that responsibility. The Refusal of Return might be followed, or supplanted by the Magical Flight. In the Magical Flight, the Hero might receive divine assistance to begin moving toward Home. Or the Hero may be hindered by the Opponent's forces in pursuit. And the obstructions may be fantastic displays of the Opponent's powers (hence the use of the term magical). Indeed, by having the Opponent persist in pursuing the Hero even after the Hero has achieved the goal, you retroactively increase the audience's perception of the Opponent's power. "He doesn't know when to stop!"

If the Opponent's ability to cause great harm continues even after the Hero has achieved the Boon, the audience continues to root for the Hero to bring the Boon all the way home.

This complicated flight with its problems can then lead to the Rescue from Without. This Help can be something of a Supernatural Aid, a reflection of an earlier occurrence of Outside Assistance. If the Hero is stuck, the world may come and get him. In any case, the implication is that this rescue, or solution to a problem, comes from something *outside* the Hero. By that, I do not mean something totally disconnected from the Hero, something we had never seen in the story before. No, I just mean something or someone *in the story* that is beyond the Hero's internal power or understanding or grasp. Of course, in your story, this Rescue might vary from a simple nudge in the ribs to a complete and dramatic rescue from pending disaster.

Lest you think magical elements are required for this pattern (since there is that phrase, Magical Flight), consider the film *North by Northwest* (1959)[1]. In the film, two-thirds of the action focuses on Roger Thornhill's quest to find out who George Kaplan is and why all these nasty people are after Kaplan. But Thornhill's discovery of this information does not end the story. Instead, Roger learns that his adventures have put Eve Kendall in danger. In order to protect her, Roger goes along with a staged scene devised by the Professor to emphasize Eve's commitment to the Bad Guy Phillip Vandamm. His performance of this act provides the Boon to the community of the good guys in the story. However, Roger learns two things afterward that propel the adventure into the Coming Home steps. He learns that Eve will be staying with Vandamm, and that Vandamm is about to leave the country.

Concerning the *Refusal of Return*, after the staged shooting, the Professor intends to confine Roger in a hospital room "for the next couple of days." If it could have been practical, the Professor would probably have sent Roger home, in effect forcing a Return on the Hero. But Roger won't leave the matter alone: he values Eve more as a person than as an important American undercover agent. He chooses not to play the Professor's game.

Instead, he moves into the *Magical Flight*. Of course, since the film's setting lies in a realistic modern world, magic isn't really involved. Instead, Roger climbs out a window, along a ledge, through another room and escapes the area of the hospital by taxi. Since he achieves all this without being caught, observed or even hindered, it certainly rates as near-miraculous. Later, as Roger and Eve attempt their escape from Vandamm and his henchmen, their climb down the face of Mount Rushmore qualifies as a continuance of Roger's Magical Flight.

The Rescue from Without is the next step. In the film, Roger and Eve are in a precarious position on the face of Mount Rushmore. Roger tries to pull Eve up from a near-fall, but his grip on a ledge isn't very stable. The henchman Leonard appears, and rather than help, steps on Roger's fingers. He obviously intends that both Roger and Eve should fall to their deaths. Roger can do nothing to stop this. But suddenly, Leonard is shot. *The Rescue from Without* comes from the Professor and some law enforcement officers he has brought with him.

A Refusal to Return is just one way you can delay your Hero's return Home. Another Hindrance motif can be called the Unrecognized Victor. This possibility can spring from the fact that the "home folks" don't know what the Hero has gone through. You can play upon the audience's knowledge of all that the Hero has endured by using this motif. If the "home folks" regard the Hero in the same way they did before he set out on the quest, the audience's sympathy for the Hero is increased. Also, there is a new tension for the audience that will need to be resolved. The Hero has returned victorious in his quest, and we want that victory acknowledged.

An additional complication in this type of return can be the appearance of the Usurper. This will be someone who steals the focus from the Hero, someone who claims that the victory belongs to him and not to the Hero, someone who has laid claim to a place and/or power that is not properly his.

In the mythology of the Aztecs, there is a figure who models this usurpation.

The Usurper – Seven Macaw[2]**.** Seven Macaw, also called Vucub Caquix, was a monstrous bird deity at the time of the world's creation. At an early point in the creation process, Seven Macaw set himself up as a sun. He wasn't really the sun, because this was before the dawn of time. But Seven Macaw knew the sun would exist and how important it would be. He wanted to claim that importance for himself, so that *he* would have the worship and power that would properly belong to the real sun. He had to be killed before the creation of the world (including the creation of humans) could be finished.

Mythically speaking, there are few things more center stage than the Sun. Seven Macaw tries to snatch that place for himself, and has to be defeated before the *real* Sun takes its place.

The action of the Usurper both deflates the Hero's pride at her victory and increases the audience's desire for justice. We want to see the *real* victor acknowledged and recognized.

To achieve that comes the action of Providing Proof. In one version of the motif, this proof can come from a difficult task for the Hero to perform (something connected to the earlier quest).

In the film *Singing in the Rain* (1952)[3], the romance between Don Lockwood and Kathy Selden casts them jointly into the Hero position in the story. The progress of one is tied to the progress of the other. We learn that Lina Lamont's awful speaking voice threatens Don's career move from silent films to talkies. The threat equally affects Kathy. Cosmo Brown suggests using Kathy's voice in place of Lina's, and this saves Don's movie. Of course, Lina doesn't initially know of the substitution. With Kathy's voice performing Lina's lines, Don's film is a success. The elements of Unrecognized Victor and the Usurper run together here. Lina discovers the substitution and forbids the release of the information that Kathy supplied the voice. Additionally, by insisting that Kathy continue to provide her voice, Lina attempts to usurp Kathy's victory. However, Don finds a way to provide the proof that Kathy is the "real victor." When Lina is maneuvered into "singing" before a live audience, Kathy does the actual singing from behind a curtain. In the middle of the song, Don and Cosmo open the curtain behind Lina, revealing Kathy. Lina flees the stage, and Don identifies Kathy as the owner of the voice the audience had loved.

We can see in Don's action in the film a way of providing Recognition (for the Hero). The reality of who indeed was the victor becomes seen and known by the home folks. This recognition can come in many forms. Just as our society has many levels, so too can the recognition. You can show the audience that the Hero receives official recognition for his victory, but not the recognition of the story's general population. Or it can be done the opposite way.

The conclusion of the film *Contact* provides an example of this second variation. In the movie, when Ellie returns from her journey into the cosmos, she finds out that the facts (or the officially declared facts) indicate that nothing at all happened. She becomes the Unrecognized Victor. She finds that she has no support for her contention that she did indeed make the journey, contact an alien, and return. The Usurper in this case is the Presidential advisor Michael Kitz. After Ellie's apparently failed excursion, Kitz draws the focus of attention from Ellie to himself. He pushes an official investigation which implies that Ellie is either deluded or lying about her experience. Kitz's investigation also suggests that the whole matter of the signal from outer space and the construction of the machine was a hoax concocted by industrialist S.R. Hadden.

In *Contact*, the motif of Providing Proof is subverted. Where often the Hero *can* produce evidence the supports his claim, gaining him his proper recognition, in this film, such corroborating evidence is withheld from Ellie. However, the proof does exist. Although the authorities tell Ellie that the incident only lasted 45 seconds, the audience sees a conversation between Kitz and Presidential advisor Rachel Constantine where we learn that Ellie's equipment recorded 18 hours of static in that 45 second event. Although Ellie fails to gain official recognition of her experience in the machine, she leaves the hearing to discover that the general populace *does* accept her claims. The public recognition counterbalances (for the film's audience) the official denial of recognition.

One of the things your Hero might do after achieving some recognition is to create something important for his community. This would especially be the case if your character is a Hero of Destiny. This could be regarded as similar to the Hero bringing Home a Boon. In this case, the *Hero* creates something important. The focus falls upon the Hero's action rather than the benefit. Of course, the importance of what is created rests first with how important the characters in the story consider it to be, and secondly with how completely the audience accepts that valuation. Also, whatever it is that the Hero creates, it reaffirms his connection to the community that receives it, or to the whole of the human race. Creation is an act of choice, so this won't be something that automatically follows as a consequence to the Hero's adventure.

This act of creation also flows into the Conquest of Death and Ascent to Immortality. The two fit together in our intuitive response: if the Hero can defeat Death in some way, then she can gain immortality. It's that mortal/immortal combination, a sort of either/or switch. How you chose to present that can be as variable as human nature. First off, if you chose not to deal with *actual* death, then consider what will be the ultimate defeat for your Hero. There are so many options: failure in a sports competition, inability to solve a mystery, loss of love – not just the desired lover, but of the ability to even *feel* love. All these things, and many more, can be considered deaths. If you know what the death is that your Hero faces, you can more clearly design the appropriate conquest of death for your tale. Likewise, the type of Immortality your Hero rises to will depend on the type of death she has faced.

Dying and rising gods can be found around the world. By and large, they are vegetation deities, representing the cycle of harvest, planting and new growth. Even so, the return from the dark realm of Death touches at our elementary responses, our driving desire to stay alive. Two of the most famous representatives of this pattern are Osiris and Jesus.

Conquest of Death/Rising to Immortality – Osiris.

Osiris (the champion of good) and his wife Isis were the picture of happy lovers. But brother Set couldn't endure seeing them that way. So one day when the men went hunting together, Set killed his brother. Then he further indulged his nastiness by cutting Osiris' body into pieces and scattering them far and wide. When Isis found out about the murder, she hunted high and low and gathered the pieces together. She used her divine magic and brought her husband back to life. Of course, tradition has it that there was one part she couldn't find ... his (ahem) genitals. Something about the whole experience led Osiris to stay in the Underworld, so he became the Ruler of the Dead.

In Egyptian mythology, Osiris was the judge of the dead, largely because he had gone through and rose from the experience of Death himself. Yet, although he is a vegetation god, after he is brought back to life he doesn't have much to do with the living. The traditions about Jesus take a different tack.

Conquest of Death/Rising to Immortality – Jesus.

Because Jesus was something of an iconoclast in the eyes of the stiffer-minded community leaders, they arranged for him to be executed by the Romans. After the rather gruesome business of crucifixion, his body was hurriedly sealed up in a tomb. The Powers That Be were concerned that the body would be stolen – allowing his followers to claim he had risen from the dead. The authorities even put guards on the tomb. His followers, however, really thought he was dead. After the Sabbath, some of them went to treat the body more properly for its long-term burial. But hey! The guards were unconscious, the tomb unsealed and the body gone. Because they still thought he was dead, his followers didn't even recognize him at first when they saw him walking around.

Unlike the pattern for Osiris, the traditions related to Jesus indicated that the Hero after resurrection spent time in the land of the living, interacting with his community, providing them with a hope of something beyond the threshold of death before he went on into his Ascent to Immortality stage.

Let's see how this motif can work in a film. In *The Green Mile* (1999)[4], Death Row prison guard Paul Edgecomb learns that prisoner John Coffey has healing powers. Paul finds the combination of healer and convicted murderer strange and so begins a personal quest to understand how things came to this point. Along the way, Paul also learns that his friend's wife Melinda is dying from a brain tumor. Convinced that John will not run away, Paul takes John to his friend. This action could be death to Paul's career since his friend is also the Warden. However, John does indeed cure Melinda, and the Warden does not condemn Paul's action.

In this film, the Ascent to Immortality is separated from this action of Conquest of Death. The two are connected, but indirectly. The relatively inarticulate John conveys to Paul the truth about another prisoner by grasping Paul's hand. Evidently, along with the visionary explanation, some of John's healing power pours into Paul, with the result that Paul's life becomes extended to an extraordinary length. This film gives us a fairly literal interpretation of Ascent to Immortality. But you need not be that literal. Any achievement of the Hero's Special destiny could serve this purpose.

A Resurrection can be viewed as something different from a Conquest of Death. A Resurrection need not be just a matter of returning from the dead. The unexpected reappearance of the Hero in her home community may be regarded by the community as a "return from the dead." If, from the point of view of the Hero's Ordinary World, the Hero had ventured away into the unknown beyond their borders, they will be suitably amazed by the Hero's Return. Thus, the impact of "rising from the dead" is not so much how the *Hero* sees the results of her quest, but rather what those around her see and feel about the Return.

Another variation of the Resurrection motif can include the accompanying aspect of Rebirth. We did touch on this idea in discussing the escape from the Belly of the Whale earlier. But here we are looking at something that is much bigger on the story scale. In particular, we delve into the concept of renewal as a consequence of the re-rising. It would be a strange story indeed that showed a character *literally* being born again. On the other hand, we have all had experiences of refreshment and renewed energy in our lives after some sort of break. In one sense, this Rebirth can be the result of the newly gained self-knowledge your Hero has acquired during the Journey. Your Hero may have experienced such transforming events that she bursts out of the Descent to the Underworld a new person. Rebirth carries with it imagery of emergence from enclosed spaces – womb-like spaces – to new conditions. This can be either a major sequence in your story, or a repeated motif used to emphasize the growth of the Hero.

The Empire Strikes Back provides an example of multiple uses of the motif. Of course, for there to be a resurrection (which literally means to rise again) there must be a death of some sort, or at least a striking down. In the film, Luke actually goes through a series of deaths and resurrections, each moving him forward in his self-knowledge and quest. At the beginning of the film, a snow creature strikes down and wounds Luke. When the young man makes his escape, climbing *up* out of the cave, he collapses near death out on the ice field. In this threshold condition, he has a vision of Obi-Wan and is told to seek out the Jedi Master Yoda for instruction. Luke is rescued and treated, being reborn out of the Rebel's hospital healing tank. His next death/resurrection/rebirth sequence comes during his training with Yoda, and it is implied more than shown. When Luke descends into the place of the Dark Side of the Force, he faces a death of sorts when he strikes off the head of the figure of Vader and finds his own face behind the mask. His return to the surface represents the rebirth in this sequence. The event marks a dividing line between Luke's physical training and the more mental (or mystical or magical) training that follows it. The last of these sequences is Luke's jump into the core of Cloud City. He is reborn when he falls out of the chute on the city's exterior. This rebirth has brought him to a greater understanding of his own life and position in the course of events. He has learned a truth about his life that will shape his choices from that point on.

Continuing the rising motion from Resurrection and Rebirth we can travel right into the experiences of Ascension, Apotheosis and Atonement. Of course, we have met these elements before. You may ask why cover them again?

One factor of the earlier discussion considered Apotheosis was that it might appear in the middle section of your story. In that case, the Hero might achieve an Apotheosis after a serious confrontation, but before the major climax. And, in the process, then, learn something needed, something that enables her to face the conflict. Likewise, Apotheosis could be a Reward for successfully facing a challenge.

But here, when Apotheosis falls in the Coming Home section of your story, the implications can be even more dramatic, more emotionally powerful. When Apotheosis occurs near the end of your tale, the impact on your Hero (and hence on the audience) can strike very deep. Wherever you place the Apotheosis, in the middle or the end, before Atonement or after it, consider the type of effect you want it to have on your Hero and your audience.

That said, the myth of Prometheus can give us a model of the experience.

Apotheosis and Atonement – Prometheus. To punish Prometheus for stealing fire from the gods and giving it to humans, Zeus had the Titan chained on the peak of Mount Caucasus. Every day an eagle would come and feed on Prometheus' liver. Every night, because of the Titan's super-human origins, the liver grew back. Zeus left him there for a long time because Prometheus also had secret knowledge that affected Zeus' future and Prometheus wouldn't reveal it. To tell or not to tell: the question was eating away at Prometheus. Eventually, Hercules persuaded Zeus to release Prometheus and Zeus agreed, letting Prometheus into the community of the Olympian gods. Prometheus made his atonement by telling Zeus the secret: the sea goddess Thetis, whom Zeus had been pursuing romantically, was destined to give birth to a son who would be greater than his father. Zeus, relieved at his escape from disaster, backed off from his courtship and married Thetis off to a mortal.

Apotheosis can be an important element in your storytelling. It is not simply a Reward for the Hero's endeavors. It reflects the value a community puts on the Hero's actions. For humans, the gift of fire from Prometheus made him so important that he *had* to be the peer of the Olympian gods, even if he was not originally one of them. When storytellers fail to take into account the importance of addressing this perceived value aspect of the Hero's Journey, they can cripple the emotional power of the story. The reason is that the mythic pattern, the "historical" Hero rises out of the common mass and is taken up into the cosmos forever. The point is that in this action the attention of the audience is directed away from the mere actions of the Hero and is re-centered on the *significance* of the actions. The Apotheosis also leads to a more universal quality of the Hero's story. The outward motion to the cosmos means that the Hero and his actions (or at least the importance of them) are no longer limited by local concerns or claims. After all, if a myth is to speak to the inner life of anyone, it ought to belong to that eternal void or region that is beyond the ordinary.

Let me emphasize again the point that Apotheosis comes in the eyes of a community (be it within the story, or in the eyes of the audience). The significance of the Hero's actions makes him a World Hero, a universal model. Handling this aspect can be a delicate operation for storytellers.

In 1994, Paramount Pictures released *Star Trek: Generations*[5], with a story intended to bridge the gap between the original *Star Trek* characters and those of the later television series, *Star Trek: The Next Generation*. The story included a meeting between the legendary James T. Kirk and *Next Generation*'s Captain Jean-Luc Picard. The tale also brings us the moment of Kirk's death. In terms of the legend of Kirk and the plot of this film, Kirk's demise should be a moment of Apotheosis. Yet the story fails abysmally at presenting anything like that.

The film begins by telling the audience about the apparent demise of Kirk, in proper heroic fashion. He gives his life to save the *Enterprise-B* and the people being rescued by it from another ship in danger. A hole is punched in the ship, just where he was working, and his body was nowhere to be found. The emotional impact of this loss is conveyed by the sorrow of Kirk's companions Scott and Chekov.

Later in the film, Picard must stop the mad Dr. Soran from a course of action that will destroy the *Enterprise-E* and the population of a planet. To achieve this, Picard learns that his only possible ally is Kirk, who is not dead but rather transported into a sort of Never-never Land outside time.

This begins a reversal of the Apotheosis of Kirk. Whereas Apotheosis sends the Hero *outward* to the Void, beyond time, Picard's objective is to pull Kirk back *into* time. Kirk returns to a specific time and place. Additionally, although the process of Apotheosis moves the Hero away from fear and the limitations of time, Picard brings an anxiety about pending deaths and a time limit to their actions. As far as the matter of losing one's self in order to find one's self (also an element of Apotheosis), this is only vaguely hinted at in Kirk's discontent with retirement and the basic unreality of the Nexis (this Never-never Land). Kirk commits himself to the adventure "for the fun" of it.

By now, I hope you have gained a sense of how important it is to engage the audience in the story, to have them identify with the choices of the Hero. Yet here we are given an occasion where the Hero answers the call "for the fun of it." Not for the more immediately compelling reason of saving the lives of a crew and a planet's population (a population we *never* see, by the way). Picard does not emphasize that these victims actually figure into the picture. So we, the audience, are left unsatisfied by the image of Kirk going into action with a seemingly frivolous motivation. Picard harps on the matter of "making a difference" (a phrase with low-grade emotional force, unlike "save the world!"), but beyond the matter of stopping Soran, what that difference would look like is not spoken of *to Kirk* and barely shown to the audience.

Again, this is a point you the storyteller should make clear: *what are the stakes in the Hero's course of action?* It needs to be clear to the audience, and it needs to be clear to the Hero. Far more drama can be found in a character who knows, and knows deeply, what is at stake in his success or failure. Indeed, this had been one of the hallmarks of the character of Kirk in the original television series. This sort of knowledge drove some of Kirk's most impassioned speeches in the series. What are we given instead? A cool "make a difference" pep talk and a half-hearted choice to act "for the fun of it."

So much for the context of Kirk's death.

Let us now look at the death itself.

Does Kirk die in direct conflict with the villain? No. It is at best the third-hand result of an action by the villain, *and* accidental at that. Kirk had been on a metal bridge between two areas of rock. Soran shoots the bridge and it breaks. Kirk must jump from one portion of the bridge to another in order to secure a needed piece of equipment. He does so, using the device to turn off a screen/shield around a weapon Soran meant to use. While Picard disarms the weapon, the bridge fragment pulls from its moorings and falls — and Kirk falls with it.

Does Kirk save the day? Not really. In this case, he plays assistant to Picard, not lead Hero. Whatever off-screen maneuvering led to this decision, in terms of story, it was wrong. A Hero's death should be primal. We already knew that Picard would go on to other adventures, so there was no reason to insist that he have the primary position once Kirk committed to the adventure.

Do those who were saved know of Kirk's contribution? As far as we are told, they do not. We see that Picard buries Kirk and stands before the grave for a moment of silence. What we do *not* see is that Picard tells *anyone* how and by whom they were saved. Nor do we see any reason for Picard's choice of silence on the matter.

As a result, the whole adventure falls incredibly flat. With very little in direct confrontation between the villain and the Heroes, the members of the audience remain mere observers. Since Kirk never feels the emotional importance of the stakes, neither does the audience. Because Kirk's death is basically accidental — rather than inherently inevitable — it comes across with far less impact than it could, or should have.

Apotheosis hinges on the perception of a community. The community sees the actions of the Hero as having great value, and raises him up as an exemplar of behavior. The community can be the one within the story which benefits most from the Hero's actions. Or, the community can be the audience which observes the story unfold. In either case, the community must be emotionally engaged in the Hero *and* the choices he makes. *Star Trek: Generations* fails to deliver on any of these points.

I've elaborated on this because the death of Heroes is a tricky issue for storytellers. The heart of the matter lies in the essence of storytelling. It may be that in real life, heroic people do indeed die accidentally or inconsequentially. But when we turn to storytelling, we desire significance for a Hero's death. It should *mean* something. That is why Apotheosis provides satisfaction to the audience. It moves us toward the at-one-ment that ought to envelop the end of the Hero's Journey.

Let's look at an example that fulfills these expectations.

In the science fiction television series *Babylon 5,* creator J. Michael Straczynski ended the series with the Ascension and Apotheosis of the main character John Sheridan. The series' storyline had been constructed along the design of a Hero's Journey. In the course of that Journey, during his greatest contest, Sheridan had given his life in order to defeat the enemy and save several planetary systems. His Resurrection was the gift of the First One Lorien, an ancient alien of great power. But Sheridan's revived life had a limit of a mere 20 years' duration.

In the final episode, "Sleeping in Light" (1998)[6], Sheridan realizes his end is now at hand. His old friends gather together. In the course of the gathering, the audience receives reminders of all that Sheridan has achieved through the various things the friends focus on. This heightens our appreciation of those achievements because we are carried on the emotions of these characters. The solemnity of the impeding event gets emphasized by the characters' acknowledgment of the previous deaths of other friends. These sequences serve to convey to the audience the point that Sheridan is a worthy candidate for Apotheosis.

After he has made his goodbyes, Sheridan takes a ship out into space and goes to the place where he and his Alliance won their victory. There, as his life drains away, Lorien comes to him. Lorien and the other First Ones have been waiting for Sheridan. But in order for Sheridan to join them, he must let go of the life he has lived. As he does so, light fills the ship. Later, when the other characters find the ship, they discover all its entrances locked but Sheridan's body nowhere to be found.

Here is that element of Apotheosis of being taken into the Void. Indeed, the characters of Sheridan and his wife Delenn actually discuss the mythic impact of such a death. Sheridan, who had been a starship's captain, says that space is "where I belong." Also, he observes that by dying in space rather than on a particular planet, the various alien races who had become part of the Interstellar Alliance would certainly remember his death. The implication is that space belongs to all of them, whereas a planet-bound death would bind the memory of him too much to one place.

Since the character had been presented as someone bringing together very diverse peoples, a more appropriate ending would be difficult to construct. This one serves all the elements that it ought to serve: the character's value is affirmed, the achievement is acknowledged, the movement of his fate is outward to a boundless realm and not confined to a specific time and place, and it carries a sense of awesome mystery in it. The last element is not, of course, always necessary (especially if the Apotheosis you are delivering does not venture anywhere near actual death issues), but it adds a delicious flavor to the mix that audiences respond to (when it is well done).

Apotheosis can be particularly important in a story of a Hero of Destiny. The finale of the Hero's adventures needs to be on the same scale as the rest of the events. A larger than life Hero needs (and deserves) a larger than life finish, whether he dies or vanishes into the Great Unknown. You cannot backpedal at the end, if you have been racing intensely before that point. Such an action is far more likely to result in the collapse of bike and rider than it would in a spectacular finish.

That could be the end of your story, of course. The Apotheosis of your Hero, if spectacular enough, would be difficult to follow up. But if you do not choose to go that far, there are more events that can fill out your story.

This brings us to the Return with the Elixir, which reaffirms the Hero as a member of a community. He Returns with something that will benefit those around him. This is very similar to the Boon, so we'd better define what an elixir is, first.

A mundane definition of an elixir is a solution of water and alcohol which serves as a vehicle for medicinal substances – like cough syrup. That doesn't sound very mythic, does it? But the word also means something that can cure anything. That sounds more promising. The alchemists used the term to refer to a preparation which could transform base metals like lead or iron into gold. Ah, *there's* a bit of magic. But an Elixir of Life was also believed to be capable of restoring or prolonging life. Ah ha! Now we're cooking! Actually, as you can see by the range of definitions, you also have a range of possibilities for the potency (that is, power) of your Hero's elixir.

A mythic example of the Elixir appears in the story of Gilgamesh.

Elixir – Gilgamesh. In the Mesopotamian epic of Gilgamesh, the hero had a really close buddy named Enkidu. The two buds did everything together, to the point that the gods felt that Enkidu was keeping Gilgamesh from his duties. After all, Gilgamesh was the ruler of the land. So the gods decided that Enkidu had to die, and he did. This upset Gilgamesh so much that he went looking for the sage Ut-napishtim to find out how the old man became immortal. Eventually the Wise Man told Gilgamesh that the plant of immortality grew at the bottom of the sea. Gilgamesh dove in, snatched the plant and came up. He was hoping to both revive Enkidu and become immortal himself. However, on the way home, he took a break and set the plant down while he took a swim, and a serpent came along and ate it. So Gilgamesh didn't *successfully* return with the elixir, but he came close.

The film *The Matrix* gives us a good presentation of both a Resurrection and a Return with the Elixir. In the climax of the film, Neo undergoes a literal death and resurrection.

Killed within the computer generated world of the Matrix, his body shuts down. Trinity whispers to him that he *must* be the One, since she had been told she would love the One – and she loves him. She kisses him. Love and the kiss bring him back to life. Once alive again, Neo discovers that he possesses a complete understanding – and thus a complete control – of the Matrix. It can no longer kill him within the computer world, and he now can begin teaching others how to gain the knowledge he has. He returns with an Elixir of a new life for his fellow humans.

Again, do not feel as if you have to cover these matters in individually detailed incidents. Combining them into one compact sequence, say, of Climax - Resolution - Resurrection - Return with elixir could be all you need. Consider all possibilities. It is possible, for instance, that the Hero's Return may of itself be the Elixir to her community.

Stepping back and looking at events as a group can be very useful for the storyteller. There can be a danger for a storyteller in spending too much time crafting the individual elements of a story and too little time making sure the elements hold together. Our object in weaving a tale is to make it all of one piece, with the warp and weft of the fabric so tight it will not easily pull apart. Looking at your story against a cluster pattern of motifs can help keep the weaving tight.

With the last challenges faced, there only remains the last Crossing of a Threshold for your Hero, the steps that lead the character from the end of his Journey's Road and into his New World. Your story will show the audience the final Return. The effect of the Journey on your character will be seen, perhaps in that he has become a Master of Two Worlds (his old Original World and the New one, gained or created by his adventure). And with that Mastery, the Hero has gained a Freedom to live. This could be told with great grandeur and ceremony in your story, or it can be presented very compactly and economically. As an example of the compact option, look at the very ending of *North by Northwest*.

In the film, the motif elements are conveyed in short, tight images.

Crossing the Threshold – Roger labors to pull Eve up from the dangerous cliff, pulling her away from the threshold of death.

Return – The image dissolves directly into one of Roger laboring to pull Eve up into the upper bunk of a train compartment (very familiar territory for these characters by now).

Master of Two Worlds – We know, based on all we have seen of the characters before this point, that Roger successfully rules his Old World. Two words convey his New World: "Mrs. Thornhill."

Freedom to Live – a passionate kiss between two newly-weds goes a long way in assuring the audience the characters intend to live fully from this point on.

If the quick wrap-up doesn't satisfy what you want for your ending, then look at which elements you feel you need. Perhaps you feel a need to evaluate the whole Journey. In that case, the motifs of the Judgment of All and the presentation of the New World may fit your needs. By Judgment of All, I mean that all the major parties of the tale are sorted out: the good guys are rewarded and the bad guys are punished. This provides satisfaction to the audience, for they feel that everyone receives their just deserts. The New World gives the audience a glimpse of how the Hero's Journey has changed things – how the Hero has been changed and how his home community has been affected by his actions.

These last two elements are not absolutely necessary, of course. Leaving them out of the tale can give the audience something to speculate over afterwards. And although the audience desires the resolution of these questions, a storyteller's intentional refusal to address them can be powerful. If you want to push the audience into questioning the values and qualities that would be explored in these Stages, don't give them the answers. Instead of supplying *your* judgment of the characters, you can inspire the audience to do that work. However, you have to have given them enough material to work with: they have to be emotionally invested in the characters, the stakes have to have been clearly defined, and the opposing points of view have to have been carefully laid out.

After all the tests and adventures, at some point your tale will come to a resting place.

MUSINGS

As a storyteller, you want your tale to be a good strong lob over the net into the audience's court. A good story connects with the audience in such a way that they respond to each element of the adventure that you hit in their direction.

Think about it:

* After your Hero has completed his major conflict, fought his big battle, achieved his quest, is there anything more you want to say about him?

If not, *stop!* Don't feel that you have to take the story further just because the Return motifs exit. However, if you *do* have more to say....

* Was your Hero seeking an Elixir of some sort? If so, what sort of Elixir is it?

* Is your Hero reluctant to Return from her adventure? If so, what sort of nudging does she need to get moving?

* Does your Hero have to face some sort of Death? If so, what sort?

* What would constitute a Resurrection for your Hero?

* Is there a community depending on the Hero, looking up to him? Are they going to celebrate your Hero's victory?

* Is there a character who might Usurp your Hero's victory? If so, how and why?

If the Hero has to defeat a Usurper, what will constitute proof that the Hero is the actual victor?

SECTION FIVE: THE ANTI-HERO'S PATH

Most versions of the Hero's Journey have in mind a positive character as the main one. But what of those stories which have an Anti-Hero as their centerpiece? Such tales have been known to draw audiences as much as their positive counterparts. So what elements does a storyteller have to consider in shaping such a tale? There are not many guidelines available. So I have cobbled together such assistance as I could find.[1]

The Hero's Journey usually involves a story that tends to end on an upswing (which we'll look into more closely later). To shape a sequence of events that move toward ending on a downswing, and which takes its main character in that direction as well, requires looking at a sort of reverse of the more usual pattern, a sort of negative photograph of the motif.

If the Downswing Journey, the Anti-Hero's Journey, appears as the reverse of the Upswing Journey, what would constitute an opposite of it? Let's look at the pattern through the presentation of two well-known Anti-Hero stories. For the discussion that follows, the examples from the films will appear in different fonts. The film *Macbeth* (1971)[2] will be discussed in **boldface**. This Shakespearean tragedy is a straight-forward classical example of an Anti-Hero. The movie *Citizen Kane* (1941)[3] will be discussed in *italics*. Orson Welles' film is a classic in its own right, but it's also a more modern example of this Journey. Since in this case we are looking at the complete plot of two films, don't be dismayed by the length of the discussion.

The first division of the Downswing Journey covers the events that lead the Hero to become a Miser (and an Anti-Hero). In using the term Miser, I mean someone who clutches all things to himself, not just money. So we are about to learn how someone who probably started out open-handed became the opposite. The usual Hero's Journey tale starts with the events that unsettle the life of the Hero, with a State of Misfortune, some circumstance or problem that the Hero needs to address. That being so, the first sequence on the Downswing will be the opposite.

The State of Fortune

At the beginning, we will find our main character in some sort of good place. Either well off, loved or in some equally desirable condition. This will be a case where the audience would consider the initial World a desirable one.

In *Macbeth*, Macbeth has just been a victor in battle, and been rewarded with the title of Thane of Cawdor.

*In **Citizen Kane**, the young Charles Kane lives happily with his parents, even though they don't have much money.*

Unpreparedness

Where the usual Hero begins preparing for his quest and learning skills, the Downswing Hero suddenly encounters things he has no skills to deal with. He is *not* prepared to deal with the events of this stage of his Journey. This differs from the Tests and Trials we've met before. It should be something the Hero could not possibly have foreseen or expected.

Macbeth is surprised by the news from the witches that he will be "king hereafter," and he doesn't quite believe this information.

When his mother gains a fortune, young Kane's future is restructured without his being told. He doesn't understand why he has to leave his parents, and he doesn't want to go.

Losses and Hazards

On the Upswing, the Hero will receive incentives to move forward with the quest. But the Downswing Hero will suffer some losses and hazards. Things he values may be taken away from him. People and/or things that will obstruct his choices appear in the way. Whatever the element is, it encourages the Hero to focus inward on himself, rather than on his relationships with others.

For Macbeth, he finds his loss in the announcement that Malcolm will be King Duncan's heir, dashing the hopes that the witches raised in Macbeth. The hazard Macbeth faces is the taunting from Lady Macbeth that he is too timid to claim his future.

Kane's loss in leaving his parents and those happy days is symbolized by his abandoned sled. The hazard lies in the way Mr. Thatcher pushes the adult Kane to take charge of all his own business, even though Kane isn't interested.

Resistance

While the traditional Hero makes a commitment to his quest, the nascent Miser Hero resists moving forward. This Resistance may even be fed by the presence of Hinderers, who disrupt the main character's choices. There is a possibility, which you can hint at for the audience, that if this Hero on a Downswing had actually responded favorably to his Hinderers, things might not have turned out the way they will.

Macbeth's Resistance lies in his hesitation at the idea of killing Duncan. The Hinderers appear in the two servants sleeping in Duncan's room, and in the principles of Macbeth's friend Banquo, who refuses to take action to make the witches' prophecies come true.

Kane resists in his general dislike of "business." When he settles on newspaper publishing, he is obstructed by Thatcher's irritation and by the editor Mr. Carter's inability to adapt to Kane's methods.

Movement

Where in the usual Journey motif, the Hero makes plans and preparations before setting out, the Downswing Hero simply *moves*. He takes his most important steps toward his goal, and he may even think his goal is a good one.

Macbeth moves past his hesitation and toward Duncan's room to commit the murder.

Kane grandly declares he will "Tell the Truth" in his newspaper, and yet to his inner circle later jokes about not being expected to keep promises he has made.

These sequences have carried the story through the Setting Out section of the Journey. We are now ready for the serious stuff in the Anti-Hero's adventure.

Where the usual Hero tale involves the Hero's growth in character toward something more admirable, the Anti-Hero regresses.

Note the term regression. It's important. If you are using this motif, your character is moving away from something usually considered desirable. It is not necessarily a regression into a childish outlook. But the audience will probably view it as moving backwards.

The First Change

This is where the Upswing Hero faces the first hard reality of his quest. The opposite counterpart will also experience his First Change. Something in his personality is affected by the choice he has made in moving forward and we now get to look at the first manifestation of that change.

Macbeth finds murder very different from killing in battle. After killing Duncan, he quickly murders the two servants and glibly defends his action.

Kane marries the niece of the President, but the couple doesn't see much of each other.

In both of the film examples, the main characters have put on masks of sorts. Macbeth, previously honorable, not only murders the King but kills the servants in order to blame them for Duncan's death, claiming *they* had done the horrible deed. Kane's action is a less obvious one: he marries a young woman for the social prestige she can bring him (and his newspaper). These masks indicate that the characters have changed into something less honest that they were originally.

This change in the main character leads to the next stage.

The Anti-Hero is challenged

The parallel for the Anti-Hero to his positive opposite's experience of confrontation (or Trials and Tests) is that something, in some fashion, challenges the Miser. Some important figure, in the tale so far, questions the path the Anti-Hero has chosen, or represents a criticism of his choice. The challenger could be considered the voice of the audience, the person the audience is likely to identify with as the Anti-Hero moves more and more into darker territory.

Macbeth remembers the promise that Banquo's descendants will rule, and he takes this as a threat to himself.

Kane's wife Emily criticizes him. Kane is diverted from looking at things in storage from his mother's home (including the sled) by his first encounter with Susan.

Citizen Kane takes the challenge one step further than *Macbeth* does, by implying that if Kane had continued onward to look at his mother's things, he would have found the sled and been brought back from his inevitably tyrannical path . It's a point worth remembering when using this motif. Showing – or even just hinting – at the Might Have Been that would have made the main character return to an upward path enriches the story. It deepens the context the Anti-Hero moves through, and highlights for the audience yet again what the character has lost or is losing.

Which brings up the focus of the next stage.

The Victims

Letting the audience see how the Miser-Hero's actions affect various people increases the awareness of the character's increasing distance from the original State of Fortune. Someone is going to suffer directly as a result of the Miser's actions.

Macbeth orders the murders of Banquo and Banquo's son Fleance. The father and son are shown as a loving and loyal pair.

Kane's relationship with his wife and son is destroyed by his involvement with Susan and by the way he conducted his campaign for governor.

However, it is not enough to show the Victims and what happens to them. To fill out the portrait of the Anti-Hero, you need to show his reaction to them, or (more likely) his lack of reaction. Remember, the audience's emotional connection to the story grows through following the *interaction* of characters.

The Anti-Hero is indifferent to the Victims

In this type of story, the Anti-Hero's indifference demonstrates his remoteness from the general mass of people. He is less able to be touched in any fashion by those around him.

Although Banquo was a close friend, Macbeth displays no regret or other emotion when told Banquo is dead.

Kane thinks only of holding on to his political campaign, and that Emily is trying to "take the love of the people" from him. He doesn't see what he has done to Emily.

This stage allows the audience to see how the character has changed even further from the person they first met at the beginning of the story. By showing both the character's state at the beginning and this acquired lack of feeling, the audience can be touched by what is lost *within* the character. The audience can in effect grieve for a loss that the Miser himself would never even admit exists.

With the presentation of direct victims of the Anti-Hero, other characters become aware of the changed nature in main character. This leads to the next step.

Opposition

At this point in his quest, the traditional Hero takes action against his Opponent. But in the Downswing Journey, people move against the Anti-Hero himself. As his Miserly tendencies become more Tyrannical, people or events begin to trip him up. They express in action their response to what the Anti-Hero is becoming.

Macbeth worries about the escape of Fleance. Then the appearance of Banquo's ghost disrupts Macbeth's behavior in public.

Kane's affair with Susan becomes news and he loses the election. His best friend Leland wants to transfer away from Kane.

Faced with serious challenges, a positive Hero may discover that he has to give up or let go of something. But the Anti-Hero is considered a Miser for a reason, because the next stage in his Journey is called –

Refusal to Sacrifice

The Miserly Anti-Hero continues on, refusing to let go of those things he values, even though there may be a need to sacrifice something. This act of clutching things to himself can become a moment where the Anti-Hero actually defines himself.

Rather than repent, Macbeth becomes even more set in his ways, declaring, "For mine own good all causes shall give way."

Kane refuses to let go of his involvement with Susan. He tells Leland, "A toast, Jedidiah, to love on my terms. Those are the only terms anyone ever knows. His own."

The determination that the Miser displays in his refusal to sacrifice leads to the next event.

Crisis

By taking his stand the Anti-Hero then moves to prove he is right about his self declaration. This can spring from an awareness that he has placed himself outside the norm. He feels a need to show that he is right and that any critic is wrong.

Macbeth seeks reassurance from the witches. On one hand he is told to fear Macduff, while on the other he is told "None of woman born shall harm Macbeth."

Kane marries Susan and extravagantly promotes her career as an opera singer, even though she doesn't particularly want it. Kane fires Leland for telling the truth about her singing, even though Kane knows how bad it was.

This crisis moment leads to a major break between the main character and those close to him.

Separation

Because of the Anti-Hero's actions, people begin to put distance between themselves and him. In effect, they cannot follow him into the dark realm of his self-focus. Either they actively separate themselves from the Anti-Hero, or their psyche does that work.

Lady Macbeth's madness begins, and nobles start to flee from Macbeth's castle.

Leland and Kane are ended as friends, with Leland refusing the large severance check Kane gave him.

These events set the seal upon the Downswing Hero, transforming the character into something more than a Miser, transforming him into a Tyrant and Autocrat. The events that follow show how the Anti-Hero becomes more tyrannical.

Claiming a Prize

The first thing the Anti-Hero does in reaction to separation from those close to him is to lay claim to a prize of some sort. This public action serves to declare that he does not, in his own mind, need those he has been separated from.

Macbeth declares publically that no man born of woman shall be able to kill him.

Kane insists that Susan continue with her opera singing, even though she wants to quit.

Having begun with this sort of display, the Anti-Hero continues on this autocratic path.

Indulgence of Lust

One action alone has become insufficient for the Anti-Hero. He must assert his power in an elaborate fashion. But consider the possibility that lust in this case does not need to mean *sexual* lust. Anything this Tyrant has been desiring can be the subject of his lust.

Macbeth has all of Macduff's family killed.

Kane builds the fabulous and excessive Xanadu, and he keeps Susan there with him.

The Anti-Hero's Indulgence leads to the next step, a demonstration of this expanded self-perception.

Self-Aggrandizement

The Anti-Hero perceives himself as beyond the reach of others, and feels a need to show that to those around him. The self-aggrandizement will build upon his Indulgence of Lust.

Macbeth ridicules the approach of Malcolm's troops, and puts on his showy royal armor long before it is needed.

Kane "gives" Susan Xanadu, showing off the house to lots of guests. Yet Susan says "You never give me anything I really care about."

The great display leads us into the last section of this Anti-Hero Journey, that is, how this Despot is rewarded for his actions. The consequences of his choices become plain.

The Impossibility of Return

By this point our Anti-Hero has become so set in his ways that he cannot even imagine things being different. He has entirely lost sight of his original State of Fortune. But you, the storyteller, want to show that clearly to your audience. It probably will appear in losses your character will have.

Lady Macbeth dies (a probable suicide), and Macbeth is unmoved at losing her.

Susan leaves Kane, in spite of having a house full of guests. In attempting to promise to let her have her way, Kane says "You can't do this to me." He no longer understands what a relationship is.

The losses can precipitate the downward slide of the Anti-Hero.

The Fall

The Anti-Hero's Fall from his self-achieved heights comes quickly after we see how he cannot return to his starting point.

The "impossible" omen of his end that Macbeth was warned about happens – the "forest moves."

Kane violently destroys Susan's room.

Isolation

The fact that the Anti-Hero has driven everyone away from himself gets pointed out here.

Men flee Macbeth and his castle.

The huge staff of Xanadu are drawn by the noise of Kane's destruction of Susan's room, but none of them approach Kane when he leaves it.

Devastation

Everything the Anti-Hero has achieved or valued is brought low.

Fireballs land in Macbeth's castle, which has been emptied by fleeing defenders.

Kane dies.

No Home

Not only did the Anti-Hero reach a point where he could not return to his initial favorable state, his final state doesn't even resemble anything like a home (or any desirable world).

Macduff reveals he was not born as others are but rather "from his mother's womb untimely ripped," yet Macbeth will not yield. And so he dies.

With boxes and crates in Xanadu, the house is shown to be even less than a museum, and certainly not a home of any sort.

As always, this pattern need not be considered carved in stone. All motifs, even this of an Anti-Hero, have flexibility. The main thing the storyteller needs to remember is that the driving force of a Downswing Journey story moves in the opposite direction as that of the usual Hero's Journey.

MUSINGS

If you're going to tinker with the machinery of your story, it helps to know what type of machine you are working on. Make your adjustments carefully, and be sure you are turning your screws in the correct direction.

Think about it:

* Which path is your main character on, an Upswing Journey or the Downswing Journey?

* Are there Victims of the story's action? Who are they, and how does your character react to the Victims?

* If you are telling a Downswing story, what is the State of Fortune your Hero starts out in?

* What does the opposition to your Anti-Hero look like? What sort of people or obstructions get in his way?

* When your Miser refuses to sacrifice anything in his life, how does he declare that?

* How does your Anti-Hero show off how powerful and great he has become? What is his act of self-aggrandizement?

* What shows the audience that it is impossible for the Anti-Hero to return to his original State of Fortune?

* What is the least homelike ending you can find for your Anti-Hero?

PART TWO

TRANSPORTATION

TRANSPORTATION

The Journey motifs cover a lot of territory. However, aside from the differentiation between the Upside and Downside Passages, the Journey motifs do not address the actual type of dramatic tone your story might take. Just what sort of transportation are you going to use?

Ancient Greek drama, which was performed by actors wearing masks, gave us the two symbols for our choice of humors in drama – the Comedy and Tragedy masks. One shows a face laughing, while the other wails with grief. In general, we accept that these are the two types of stories: comedy and tragedy.

In many ways, our perception toward dramatic tone grows out of our way of looking at how Fortune (or luck or chance) figures in our lives. Humans have long felt that we do not have total control of our lives. Because of that, goddesses like the Roman Fortuna often show up in mythology.

> **Fortuna** – For the Romans, this goddess represented fate and all its unknown factors, the things one couldn't possibly anticipate. She was often shown standing on a ball or wheel. This was to indicate how speedily her favor toward someone could change (Have *you* tried standing on a ball lately?). She held a cornucopia filled with all sorts of wonderful things, and she would scatter these goodies about. She was also often presented as wearing a veil or a blindfold – which meant she wasn't really giving someone *special* attention if things went well.

Fortuna's presence eventually got upstaged by her wheel. Ah, yes, the Wheel of Fortune!

> **The Wheel of Fortune** – In the Middle Ages, the Wheel became a popular image for discussing the fate of one's life. If you grabbed hold of the Wheel at the right point, you could ride it upwards and away from the mire of life. However, you might also have the misfortune of riding the Wheel on its down turn, where you could be crushed by its rim as it rolled along.

The Wheel of Fortune elaborated the Masks of Drama. Comedy rode the Upturn of the Wheel and Tragedy rode the Downturn. Remember, Comedy does not necessarily mean *humor*. In dramatic terms, it was meant to signify stories that ended happily. Humor grows out of incongruity, when two things we do not generally put together are brought into a sudden conjunction. We laugh because our brains tell us "those don't go together." If the unusual conjunction continues to delight us, it is probably because we realize that *in that particular story*, the oddities actually *do* belong together. The specialized quality of incongruity is why it is very difficult to repeat the exact elements of one successful humorous tale in a sequel, or an imitation of the original story. The first time we heard a story about a housebound Dad, it was funny because it was a new combination. The next time, that situation is less inherently funny because it is no longer new or unexpected. The second time around, the story, if it wanted to be funny, would have to rely on the *characters* for the humor and not the *situation*.

The mechanisms of humor needed to be addressed before we actually discuss Comedy (or Upturn) stories. That is because it is possible to tell an Upturn story without loading it with "ha-ha" humor.

SECTION ONE: THE UPTURN STORY

Fortunes go up and down. If you, as the storyteller, know where your story is going to end, you have an idea of what sort of ride you want to give the audience. It has been observed that Comedy's plot has a U-shape, where the story sinks down into deep and often potentially tragic complications, and then swings toward a happy ending.[1]

The potentially tragic complications can enrich an Upturn tale. It can be very satisfying – if not exhilarating – for the audience to be plunged into the deepest "oh no!" state and then to be brought up out of it. But be careful that you chose the appropriate worst possible thing for your potential tragedy, *and* the right way to rise up out of that complication. Anything that reeks too much of *deus ex machina* ("the god in the machine" who makes everything okay in his one-and-only appearance in the story) frustrates the audience, for the simple reason that it comes into the story from outside. The solution to the problem in this type of story must already be within the story.

Let's look at the film *Grosse Pointe Blank* (1997)[2] for an example of how the ups and downs of the wheel work in what we call a Comedy. Martin Blank suffers a major discontent in his life. A very successful hit man, he's nagged by the prospect of his high school class's ten-year reunion and the chance of seeing the girl he left behind. The incongruity of a hitman at a school reunion provides the humor we expect from Comedy. Additionally, Martin's attempt to gain psychological counseling, in spite of the fact that his doctor fears him, brings more incongruity. These elements drive the laughter in this Comedy. But for the dramatic elements that contribute to this Upturn adventure, we need to look at other details.

To demonstrate that Martin begins on a downward swing of the Wheel of Fortune, we learn that while his colleague, the Grocer, wants to unionize the assassins, Martin doesn't want to join. His opposition to the Grocer prompts Grocer to set Martin up for a fall. Also, another assassin dogs Martin, trying to kill him. Beyond these professional problems, Martin discovers that his old home has been torn down and replaced by a convenience store, *and* that his mother has been institutionalized. Lastly, he finds that his old girlfriend, Debi, whom he literally left on her doorstep the night of their prom, is not going to make it easy for him to get back into her life.

Martin tries to put his life into an upturn, by *not* opening the briefing packet for his Detroit job and by working at reestablishing his relationship with Debi. He does fairly well at it, even though government agents and the assassin shadow him. But just when all looks well for him, especially with Debi, events go into a fast downturn. The assassin catches up with him at the high school reunion, and Martin has to kill him in order to save his own life. That might be a good thing, except that Debi sees him with the body and runs away. When Martin later tries to explain himself to Debi, a wonderful note of realism gets injected into the incongruous humor. Debi declares that killing is unacceptable. Even when he protests that he has lost his taste for the work, Debi tells Martin, "You don't get to have me." The Wheel of Fortune seems to have dumped Martin at the bottom of things.

But this story *is* a Comedy. How do the storytellers pull out of this realistic Downturn? Martin, thinking he has lost his New World, opens the job packet, and discovers his target is Debi's father, Mr. Newberry. Martin can now use his unacceptable skills to save Mr. Newberry's life, and win back Debi and his happy ending.

In this example, all the elements which add to the down spin, as well as make possible the upturn are inherent in the story. This organic unity brings satisfaction to the audience.

SECTION TWO: THE DOWNTURN STORY

We easily recognize the falling sensation that belongs to Tragedy. Very few people need complex explanations of it. Stories with unhappy endings are familiar aspects of storytelling landscapes. That useful U-shape of Comedy can literally be turned upside down for Tragedy. The action of the story can rise to a crisis, to a peripety (as one critic calls it), and then plunge downhill to catastrophe. The plunge can be precipitated by recognitions and exposures, all of which should be inevitable consequences of earlier actions by the characters.

Because of that rising action, in Tragedy the audience has the sensation of something desirable being snatched away. We ride the Wheel of Fortune on an upturn, reaching the top. We expect to keep going in that direction. Then, just as the Hero reaches out to grab the object of his quest, the Wheel turns further and the Hero (and the audience) plunges to earth. (Oh, and that is what peripety means, in case you were wondering: a reversal of intention, where the outcome the Hero intended becomes reversed for better or worse. It also depends on a recognition or discovery by the Hero that changes his outlook.)

It is worth taking some time here to discuss the difference between Tragedy and the Anti-Hero quest. Admittedly, both do qualify under the broader perspective of Unhappy Ending = Tragedy. Yet, there can be some important differences between the two.

As we saw in discussing the Downside Passage, the Hero of that type of Journey makes several very active choices which lead to the crash and burn ending. This isn't always true of a more standard type of Tragedy. In a non-Anti-Hero Tragedy, the circumstances (and possibly other characters) around the Hero tumble him down from the position of fortune. So, not every tragic Hero will become a Miser or Tyrant. When the circumstances bring the downfall of an appealing character, we the audience feel the Tragedy because we have been identifying *with* the Hero.

We are less likely to identify with an Anti-Hero, but even that is not impossible. A good storyteller will draw you into caring about an Anti-Hero and *then* reveal that you had mistaken the character's mind set. This can be quite powerful – as long as the audience, when looking back over the story can see that the character was consistent.

The film *American Beauty* (1999)[3] presents an interesting version of Tragedy. Now, Tragedy is not a particularly popular mode of storytelling in American films. That may be so because Americans tend to be optimistic or geared toward problem-solving. In some ways, the Anti-Hero may have more appeal for Americans because he exemplifies an individualistic Man Against Society stance. In any case, this film demonstrates one way of handling an audience aversion to Tragedy. First off, the film tells us at the very beginning that its main character, Lester Burnham, will die. *And* Lester's own voice conveys this news. This early revelation lures the audience into thinking that they will not be shocked by the unhappy ending. Secondly, when we first meet Lester, he is rather unappealing, both in the type of person he is at the beginning and in what it is that prompts him to change.

Lester, living a dull and constipated life, becomes inspired to change himself and break out of his rut by meeting his teen-aged daughter Jane's the best friend, Angela. Although his fascination with Angela skates the creepy edge of pedophilia, we can understand it. Lester cuts himself loose from his stultifying job (by the dubious means of extortion).

Both Lester's fixation on Angela and the means by which he exits his job cast him in an Anti-Hero light. However understandable these actions are in terms of human nature, they are not admirable qualities. Yet, we watch as Lester allows himself to start having fun and to begin to enjoy his life. Step by step, as he works his way toward self-fulfillment, he becomes more appealing. The audience progressively becomes more invested in Lester's changes. When he finally approaches his goal and is brought to a sudden realization of how inappropriate it would be to fulfill his fantasy, the audience is won over. We like him *because* of his realization.

But remember, this is a Tragedy. Lester's actions along the way have set in motion events which lead to the abrupt plunge downward to catastrophe. Thus, when he is shot at the end, the audience is shocked not because the death is a surprise, but because we don't want him to die. Our knowledge that he *will* die has been subverted by the way the story unfolds.

As I observed, Lester demonstrates many elements of an Anti-Hero. A Tragedy with a more ordinary Hero is Shakespeare's *Hamlet*. Franco Zeffirelli's version of *Hamlet* (1990)[4] plays to our expectations of a Hero in that Mel Gibson is cast as Hamlet. The actor's resume of previous heroic parts becomes mixed with the presentation of the character of Hamlet. From the beginning of the film, things are clearly not on an upturn for the Prince of Denmark. His father the King has just died, and his uncle Claudius has claimed the crown. Hamlet isn't happy about that, nor about the fact that his mother Gertrude quickly remarries – to his uncle. Then he learns that his father's Ghost has been seen by guards during the night. He cannot escape the situation because the king and queen insist that he remain at Elsinore. All of these things ride on a downturn of Fortune's Wheel.

When the Ghost tells Hamlet that Claudius murdered him, the Prince finds an upturn of sorts: he now knows the truth of the things he had only suspected; and he is given a goal, that of avenging his father. Fortune, however, has other plans for him. The luck she strews for him is less than good: his stalled romance with Ophelia gets entangled in the machinations of Claudius, and his every movement is shadowed by two old school chums set to spy on him.

Even so, Hamlet uses a play to test Claudius' guilt and he is overjoyed at the result. Claudius' actions speak loudly of culpability. But before Hamlet can take advantage of this upturn, he's dumped down again. He kills Polonius by accident. Claudius sends Hamlet to England, to be killed there (Downturn). Hamlet escapes that trap (Upturn). He returns home to find Ophelia dead (Downturn). He is apparently accepted back to court (Upturn). But Polonius' son Laertes plots with Claudius to kill Hamlet – and they succeed. That Hamlet achieves his vengeance of killing Claudius cannot lift him away from the terrible down-spin of death.

Tragedy and Comedy have been the primary divisions of drama for ages. Yet a third option exists, widely in use, particularly in America.

SECTION THREE: THE STRAIGHT-THROUGH STORY

As I observed, the traditional divisions of drama have been the Ups of Comedy and the Downs of Tragedy. However, we can find a third variation. This third option combines elements of both the Upturn and the Downturn. I call it the Straight-Through Story.

A Straight-Through tale usually has three threads woven through its plot. One thread has elements of an Upturn Journey, and one which covers Downturn territory. The third and anchoring thread travels straight through the events. The anchoring thread maintains a level of equilibrium from its beginning to end. These threads combine to weave a fabric that contains many of the cathartic elements of Tragedy with some feel-good elements of Comedy. However, the overall tone of a Straight-Through story tends to be very serious.

In *All the President's Men* (1976)[5], we find the combination of up and down cycles that make for the Straight Through Drama. In this story there are three lines affected by the turns of the Wheel of Fortune. The reporters themselves represent the first line. By this, I mean who they are *as* reporters. The story they investigate (the Watergate break-in and its repercussions) is the second line. The last line springs from the national circumstances of Nixon, his campaign, and the cover-up.

The reporters Bob Woodward and Carl Bernstein, for all the adventures of their investigation, at the end of the story are not personally very far removed from where they began. They started as hungry reporters and ended still doing the same job. They haven't advanced out of their Old World into a New World. This core stability in the anchoring line of the story defines the Straight Through Drama.

The line for their investigation of the Watergate break-in goes through a number of ups and downs. Each time Woodward and Bernstein advance, it becomes harder for them to learn more. Each revelation provokes a tighter closing of ranks among the people the reporters need to speak to. Yet, for each slight downturn, they gradually gain more information, moving their news story into an upturn on the Wheel of Fortune. Their crowning achievement comes when their investigation leads them to top presidential advisors. Thus the arc for the reporters' news story is the upturn of the happy ending.

But this movie also has the counterweight of a tragic line. The fact that the news story Woodward and Bernstein follow leads to the resignation of a President has all the solemnity of the downturn of tragedy. The Republican workers the reporters interview indicate that they are being intimidated by their superiors, the involvement of more and more prominent figures in the cover-up, the discovery that the dubious activities originated in the White House - each of these steps plunges this element of the tale lower.

Thus, the Upturn line of the news story and the Downturn line of the national circumstance are both anchored on the through-line of the reporters. It is this even-keeled line which allows the audience to navigate the tensions created by the two opposing lines. We can safely feel appalled at the tragedy of the national arc, *and* elated by the success of the news arc because we travel with, identify with, two characters who make the journey without great changes in themselves.

In *All the President's Men*, the mix of Upturn and Downturn builds a sense of high drama. It also generates the feeling for the audience that the story might go in either direction. (Never mind that we already know how *history* went. Here we are talking about the effect of the storytelling.) That pending uncertainty of whether the story will have an Upturn aspect to it in any way can have a great deal of power over the audience, even to the point of bringing them to easily accept tragic aspects in the story line.

The film *Chinatown* (1974)[6] gives us another example of the Straight Through story. Just as in *All the President's Men*, the up and down turns of Fortune's Wheel can be followed in three lines in this story. The anchoring through-line belongs to Jake Gittes. The other two lines are those of Jake's investigation and of Evelyn Mulwray.

Jake's investigation goes through a series of ups and downs. He is hired to find out if Hollis Mulwray is having an affair. Jake gathers information that (apparently) confirms this (Upturn). Then Jake learns that the woman who hired him was *not* Mrs. Mulwray and that he will be sued (crashing Downturn). This revelation calls into question everything he had learned about Mulwray earlier. Determined to find out the truth behind the set-up, Jake begins all over again (for his own satisfaction). This time the pathway becomes decorated with threats, assaults and deaths (more Downturns). Even so, Jake moves the investigation forward and discovers why someone wanted Mulwray investigated – and later, murdered. For all the violence, because the investigation succeeds in reaching its goal, the storyline for the investigation has an over-all Upturn arc.

Evelyn's story line, by contrast, has an over-all Downturn arc. Mysterious and reticent, Evelyn endures Downturns, first in the scandal Jake's initial investigation ignites, and then in the death of her husband. When she takes an active step in helping Jake's investigation (when she helps him at the nursing home they visit), her life rides an Upturn. Her participation in the investigation leads to a romantic involvement with Jake – the one warm relationship in the whole story. Yet, even that quickly goes into a Downturn when Jake discovers her secrets. He dislikes being lied to, and nearly reveals her to the police who want to arrest her. As her secrets are exposed, her storyline spins quickly to a tragic finale.

Jake's through line anchors the contrasting arcs of the investigation and Evelyn. None of the events drastically change his Ordinary World – his life as a private investigator. The police threaten to have his investigator's license pulled (Downturn) and he becomes involved with Evelyn (Upturn). But in the end the cops leave him alone (Upturn), while he loses Evelyn (Downturn). However, even that loss of Evelyn is mitigated in its impact:

to protect her, Jake resolves to let her go. He even works to make her escape possible. So, emotionally, Jake has disconnected from Evelyn by the time she meets her fate. He regrets her death, certainly. But in the long run, his World has not been greatly changed by the events.

As we can see by these two examples, the Straight Through drama seems to run counter to almost everything we found in the conclusions of the various Journey motifs. With the Straight Through story we are far less likely to see large differences between the Hero's original world or arena as found at the beginning and his world at the end of the story. If your Hero moves by the Straight Through transportation, we probably will not see anything like an apotheosis. The impact of this type of tale apparently falls more on something the Hero is doing or working on, and less on transforming the character of the Hero. In making these distinctions, however, I do not mean to imply that the Hero does not change in his character at all. After all, at the end of the tale in *Chinatown*, Jake is a "sadder but wiser man". And the reporters in *All the President's Men* have improved their skills at their job. These are both changes to the character, growth that the audience can expect to see. But as I said, the *circumstances* of the Hero from beginning to end show considerably less change.

This Straight Through type of story is a more complex form to deal with. For its best effect, the storyteller needs to decide which line will anchor the story, and make sure that in spite of its ups and downs it begins and ends at fairly even or balanced points. Then both the Upturn and Downturn lines need to be properly shaped. If one thread will have something like a happy ending, then the other thread ought to have the falling ending of a tragedy arc. Additionally, the success of the Upturn line has to precipitate the crisis or affect the events of the Downturn line. The two turning lines must be interconnected.

As a side note to this discussion, we could look at the history of the making of *Chinatown*. The additional commentary materials available on the DVD release of the film provide some interesting points. Writer Robert Towne wanted Jake to get the girl (i.e., Evelyn) in the end, but director Roman Polanski said that no, the girl had to die. When we look at this film against the Straight Through structure, we can see why. If Jake succeeds in his investigation *and* achieves a happy ending in his relationship with Evelyn, the whole tone of the film would be changed. Indeed, the audience's expectation with an ending like that would be to also see a greater change in Jake's character as a consequence of everything he goes through. But that would require changing details throughout the *whole* of the story. If the only difference between the film as released and the story as Towne originally wanted it were the nature of the final scene, it is likely the success of the film would have been quite different. To have all aspects of the story move to an Upturn ending, and yet to lack the major internal growth in the central character that should accompany such a story, would result in a story that the audience would find shallow.

The texture provided by the contrasting Upturn and Downturn arcs enables us to accept stories wherein the Hero merely becomes a bit wiser.

MUSINGS

When you hit the road with your story, you need to be clear about the type of baggage you're going to travel with. If you want to go swiftly and lightly, you pack one way. If you're contemplating a long, serious trip, you're likely to want heavy baggage. And if you are going to be all business about it, you have to mix and match how you pack, to make sure you take everything you need.

Think about it:

* What kind of a story are you telling? Is everything working toward the happy ending of Comedy? Or is everything falling toward Tragedy's complete Downturn? Or is your story the hybrid of the Straight Through Drama?

* If you are writing for the Upturn story, what is the worst possible thing that can happen to your Hero? What would make your story a Tragedy (if you were going to leave it there)? Don't pull any punches, for the deeper our awareness of the potential Tragedy, the greater our elation when we get the happy ending.

* If you are writing for the Downturn story, what is the ultimate success your Hero could gain? What shining, wonderful thing does your Hero is reach for throughout the story?

Be sure to convey to the audience how desirable this goal is: how it will fulfill a great desire in the Hero, or correct a great wrong in the world. Thus when it is snatched away from the Hero – or he falls away from it – we grieve for the loss.

* If you are tackling a Straight Through story, do you know what the three threads of your tale are?

What is your anchor line? Remember that there is likely to be little change from the beginning context of this line to the end context.

What is your Upturn line? What element is likely to follow the arc of Comedy, including that moment when everything about it looks like it will fail?

What is your Downturn line? What element of your story has the potential for Tragedy, especially in having that moment of almost winning something wonderful to lose it in the next breath?

How does the success of your Upturn line affect the fall in your Downturn line? In what ways are the two lines interconnected?

PART THREE

TIME OF TRAVEL

TIME OF TRAVEL

When we plan a trip in the real world, we take into consideration the season, the likely weather, and even the time of day we will be traveling. These are practical considerations. Would anyone in their right mind be planning a ski trip in southern California for, say, late July? (It would be a very unusual year if they were.) Does it matter if we arrive at our destination in the dead of night? Well, if we have to find our own way in unknown territory, we probably would prefer to arrive in daylight.

So, just as there are considerations of time and season in our real world endeavors, so too are there parallel considerations in our storytelling. The human psyche responds to day and night, the seasons, and to weather in various ways. Knowing what traditional significances accompany these factors can enrich your storytelling. You can beef up an expectation or play against an expectation. But don't assume that the audience has *no* expectation of the imagery of time. Even if the symbolism we are about to discuss does not really apply to your story, be aware that the audience might subconsciously be bringing these expectations with them. By knowing how the audience may perceive these elements, you as the storyteller can encourage or subvert how the audience responds to them in your story.

SECTION ONE: 24 HOURS

The cycle of day and night is a basic function of our lives. Just like breathing in and out, the alteration of day and night fits into our bodies' rhythms. There are the simple differences between day and night, light and darkness. Beyond that we have distinctions between the sun and the moon, and those powerful threshold images of dawn and dusk. We will consider each of these in turn.

Day versus Night

One of our primary associations with day and night is the simple fact that, for most of us, we go about our activities in the daylight and take our rest at night. We consider this not only proper, but necessary. Even our mythic perceptions include this expectation.

Day and Night – Australian Aborigines. The aborigines of Australia believed that in the beginning, the Sun didn't need any rest. Because of that, the day went on and on until the humans became exhausted. The god Norralie took pity on the humans and cast a spell over the Sun. He made the Sun descend from the sky and refresh its fires on a regular basis. This allowed the humans a time of rest.[1]

This is the ultimate in the cry of "Give me a break!" We know we need rest and we accept that the night time is the right time for that rest. So, one of the first things an audience might expect is that characters ought to be resting at night. When they don't, we know that something is going on.

But rest and activity are not the only things we expect of daylight and darkness. This is where we look at what some of the more traditional mythic figures do and mean. Let's start with Apollo.

Sun God in Day – Apollo. Apollo was a really ancient sun god. In this case, ancient in the sense that he goes back a *long* time in history. By no means was he seen as an old man. Always youthful and handsome, he seemed the perfection of physical beauty. He was the god of poetry, music, archery, prophecy and the art of healing. He was considered wise and just. So reasonable a god was he that we have an adjective named for him: Apollonian. That means to be serene, calm or well-balanced, even poised and disciplined.

How's them apples from Apollo? We subconsciously think of daytime as the realm of reason, of thought. Maybe because of the simple fact that the human creature can *see* well in light and cannot do so in darkness. We feel that to see a thing is to know it, at least in a basic way. Thus, our expectation of daylight events is that they will be understandable – subject to Apollo, if you will.

What happens when night falls, then? Mythically, things get darker.

Night – Nyx. The Greek goddess Nyx personifies the night. In some cases, this primordial goddess wears a dark star-spangled gown. This may seem rather tame for someone who is the essence of night, but when we start to look at her family, we discover interesting things. First off, she's the daughter of Chaos (that's pretty turbulent). Then we've got her children: Oizys (distress), Apate (deceit), Hypnos (sleep), Nemesis (we'll meet her again), and Thanatos (death – who we'll also get to know better later).[2]

Nyx's family relations convey how disturbing we find night to be. In contrast to the wisdom and justice of Apollo, we find personifications of distress and deceit. Countering the discipline and order of Apollo, we have this daughter of Chaos (for I think we'd be safe in saying "like father, like daughter" in this case).

The Greeks presented the negative elements of night more by implication than by direct example. They made Night young and beautiful, but gave her children some rather unpleasant aspects. The Hindus were more explicit about the undesirable nature of darkness.

Darkness – Nirrti. A destructive goddess of darkness, Nirrti has a generally malignant aspect. Pain, misfortune and death are associated with her. She lives in the land of the dead. And, of course, she wears dark clothes.

Obviously, we humans don't think that night time or darkness is exactly a good thing. Because we cannot *see* in the dark, everything that treads the borders of the unknown ends up belonging to the dark. Night and darkness can hide so much that the deities of that time period can become powerful information brokers. If the information we seek doesn't obviously fall into the realm of reason and order, perhaps the rulers of night can tell us what we want to know.

For this reason (and we'll go into some more reasons when we discuss the Moon), the night becomes the time of hidden knowledge. Non-logical thinking, even insanity, finds a natural setting in night and darkness. Indeed, when someone has gone off their rocker, we often say that their mind is dark. But not just madness makes its home in the night: magic and mystery, because they are part of the unknown, also easily put on the cloak of night.

These mysterious powers, which lie beyond reason, convey special types of knowledge that the Apollonian daylight cannot bring to the Hero. Leaps of faith, things beyond logic, mysteries beyond reason are at home in the night life with all the terrible children of Nyx – which is probably why they are as warily regarded as deceit and death are.

But how, you ask, do we apply to stories our awareness of what day and night can mean? I'm glad you asked.

Let's look back at the film *Ladyhawke*. The fairy-tale atmosphere of Isabeau and Navarre's transformations dwells on the different worlds of day and night. Navarre, human by day, moves in a straightforward manner. There is little sense of the magical about him or his attitude. Even the fact that he travels with a hawk is not particularly upsetting, for such birds were regularly used in hunting in the medieval period. Indeed, Navarre is something of a medieval rationalist. However, when night falls and it is Isabeau's turn to be human, everything is laden with a mysterious atmosphere. She is an unusual woman, fierce and yet ethereal. She travels with a wolf, a supposedly wild and alarming creature, untamed. And she, the human of the night, accepts the magic and the need to act on faith, rather than rely only on reason.

It is at night that Phillipe learns the history of the lovers, for this is both hidden knowledge and something that does not fit the rational world of day. Night, as I said, is a time of magic and faith, which is why Navarre, who is locked into daytime, has such a hard time accepting the plan Imperious has devised to end the curse on the lovers, for the plan seems magical and unreasonable. Only when Navarre sees the wounds his wolf-self inflicted on Phillipe does he acknowledge the need to attempt the monk's plan. He still doesn't *believe*, but he is willing to act on the plan. Likewise, only when the solar eclipse begins, and he *sees* the proof of "a day without night, a night without day" does he at last believe.

Another factor in the contrast of day versus night lies in the contrast between reason and emotion. The realm of emotions, perhaps because of their unaccountable nature, is identified with night. The contrasts of day/reason with night/emotion can be used to emphasize elements in a story.

An example of this reason versus emotion contrast can be found in *Lawrence of Arabia*. Of course, the matter of day versus night is tempered in this film by some basic practical facts: battle sequences are going to happen in daylight. So, although we cannot evaluate *every* scene by these implications, there are some notable sequences addressed by this motif.

Lawrence's involvement in the Arab cause is a highly emotional one for him. Yet Lawrence's meetings with General Allenby about continuing his connection with the Arabs all occur at daytime. In each meeting, Lawrence's reluctance to continue is overcome. Allenby persuades him to stick with the Arab campaign. These daylight scenes represent the realm of reason exerting its control over Lawrence.

These daytime sequences hardly bring us any surprises. The night scenes, however, with their connotations of hidden knowledge and emotions, prove to be very interesting. Ali asks Lawrence about his family history at night (both an emotional subject and something Lawrence has kept hidden to a degree). When Ali learns that Lawrence has no formal ties to others, he declares that Lawrence can choose his own name (i.e., his destiny). This certainly has mystical overtones. Later, the night before the assault on Aqaba, Lawrence is forced to make a judgment (a rational solution) on a matter that carries an emotional punch for him. The man Casim whom he had rescued from the desert had killed a man from another tribe. To prevent further bloodshed between the tribes, Lawrence must execute Casim. The conflict of the rational with the emotional needs takes a terrible toll on Lawrence. The weight of the irrational aspects of night color that event.

Again later, it is night when Lawrence suggests going into the Turkish held town of Dara. Ali advises against this irrational sortie. Lawrence goes anyway, venturing into the unknown, and the excursion has disastrous consequences: primarily Lawrence's capture while in disguise and the terrible beating he endures. In many ways, the night is not Lawrence's proper realm. Its secrets and non-rational elements provide very little help to him.

So far we have seen day and night with the rational contrasted by the mystical and mysterious (*Ladyhawke*), and with the rational contrasted by the irrational and emotional (in *Lawrence of Arabia*).

If day is the realm of reason, order, and intellectual pursuit of obvious facts, then night is the realm of intuition, chaos, ventures into the unknown, and hidden knowledge. *The Silence of the Lambs* lays out these distinctions all the way through its story. The elements of rational day contrast the night of hidden information.

DAY: Clarice's first visit to Lecter: she thinks it is entirely an intellectual pursuit of factual information.

DAY: Clarice deduces the location of Lecter's storage unit - a rational activity.

NIGHT: Clarice ventures into the realm of the unknown by visiting the storage unit. She finds the severed head there, which only raises more questions.

NIGHT: Clarice makes her second visit to Lecter, where he begins to give her insights into the "Buffalo Bill" murders (hidden knowledge).

NIGHT: "Buffalo Bill" snatches his next victim (chaos striking).

DAY: Clarice goes to the autopsy of the most recently found victim - calling for rational observation and deduction.

NIGHT: Clarice tells Crawford that his treatment of her in front of others matters, which is more a matter of intuitive interaction than something obviously rational.

NIGHT: Clarice goes to the museum to learn about the moth (special or hidden knowledge).

NIGHT: (IMPLIED) We see "Buffalo Bill's" hide out, a chaotic, virtually insane realm.

DAY: News of the kidnapping is broadcast – straight factual information.

DAY: The offer to Lecter for his help on the "Buffalo Bill" murders, which leads to the beginning of Quid Pro Quo (a rational exchange of information).

DAY: (IMPLIED) Dr. Chilton mocks Lecter for believing Clarice and her offer, and offers him an alternate deal (revealing a truth).

NIGHT: Lecter is moved to Memphis (putting this agent of chaos in motion).

NIGHT: Clarice visits Lecter in Memphis and reveals her secret; Lecter returns her case file to her and hints that he has given her information (hidden knowledge in both cases).

NIGHT: Lecter escapes – being insane in his own special way, night *is* his realm.

NIGHT: Clarice reviews the case file (intuition), and works out the meaning of Lecter's note (hidden knowledge).

DAY: Clarice reinvestigates the first victim (bringing more facts to light).

DAY: Clarice confronts the killer (underground, but letting the light of reason and law into his dark realm).

The back and forth of day and night in this film perfectly suits its events. Events that should occur in the rational light of day do so. Events that would be boosted by the non-rational emphasis of night receive that boost. This appropriate use of day and night, of light and dark proves to be entirely satisfying for the audience. None of our subconscious expectations about the two time periods are disrupted, which allows us to ride the flow of the story without hitting rough water. However, that is not the only way the elements of day and night can be used.

In *The Birds* (1963)[3] our expectations are played upon, expectations concerning the reasonableness of day and the ominous factors of night. We begin in daylight hours, when Melanie Daniels meets Mitch Brenner. Their interaction leads Melanie to follow Mitch to his hometown of Bodega Bay. All the action seems to be setting a course for a mild romantic story, when a dive-bombing bird strikes Melanie on the head. Although the locals comment briefly on this unusual bird behavior, the story settles back to an expected pattern.

Melanie decides to stay overnight in Bodega Bay. Some minor elements add to the suspense: Mitch's mother Lydia learns that her chickens are not the only ones acting strangely; when Melanie leaves the Brenner place after dinner, Mitch notes an unusual number of birds sitting on the power lines; and at Annie Hayworth's home, in spite of the light of a full moon, a bird crashes into the front door. Individually, none of these incidents is particularly scary. Even taken together, they are not very alarming.

Now that our expectations of safe day and slightly sinister night have been set up in the film, the tables are turned on the audience. Young Cathy's birthday party is attacked by gulls. The scene is both unexpected and alarming. Birds physically attack children, burst balloons, cluster on people, pecking at them. Our adrenalin gets pumped up, yet we get no explanation for the event, leaving the audience as confused as the characters. The next night sequence consists of small birds coming down the chimney and into the Brenner house. Although this night invasion startles us, none of the characters is physically hurt by it. The suspense builds from two sources: the fact that the seemingly innocuous birds are attacking humans, and that daylight might be a more dangerous time than night.

The remainder of the film plays this out, with the attack on the schoolchildren leading into the all-out assault on the town. The fact that it happens in daylight, and therefore the characters can *see* the assault, gets everyone's adrenalin rushing. The following long sequence of Melanie and the Brenners waiting through the night plays on the power of the unseen. Aside from bird beaks and one or two birds working their way through shutters, it is the *sound* of the birds, not the *sight* of them which terrifies us.

Although the traditionally alarming aspects of night get used in this film, in the end, it is the daylight sequences which stay with us more. Because these daytime scenes play against our expectation that daytime is a safe time, the bird attacks mesmerize us. We don't want to believe it, but there it is. Instead of the unknown being acceptable because it comes at night, we are shown a daytime unknown (*why* the birds are massing and attacking). And reason (a function of daylight, remember) can find no cause or explanation for the birds' behavior, so we leave the film with a delicious feeling of unbalance.

Light and darkness, day and night, these are the primal elements we have looked at so far. But they are not the last of things to consider. There still are those bright objects in the sky to look at (and I'm not talking about stars).

Sun versus Moon

The alternation of light and darkness comes from the daily cycle of the sun. The rotation of the earth brings each location into the direct beams of solar radiation on a regular basis, and then into shadow. The Sun makes a powerful impact on our awareness. And even though the Moon gives off no light of its own, its reflecting brightness, particularly during night, affects our thinking as well.

Many cultures describe the Sun and Moon as the eyes of a supreme being. We look up at the Sun and Moon, and they look down on us. Either as the eyes of a god or as divinities in themselves, we tend to think of them watching us. From that point, the human imagination moves on to interaction between humans and these celestial beings. Generally, the Sun, with its regular rising and setting, comes to represent constancy (among other things). The Moon, however, gets treated differently. We learn in school that the light of the Moon changes because as the Moon orbits the Earth, it passes into the shadow the Earth casts out into space. We may *know* this basic fact, but what we *see* is a Moon that keeps changing its face.

Because the Moon goes through these changes, the dramatic possibilities it represents are stronger than those of the Sun. The constant regular Sun comes and goes and returns. But the Moon changes visibly, and in fact disappears entirely, only to reappear again after three dark nights. In many primitive cultures, the disappearance of the Moon became linked with the first man who died. But because the Moon reappears after its darkness, death came to mean not extinction, but a change to a new kind of life. The cycle of life became linked to the cycle of the Moon. And the myths tied to the Moon include stories of death and resurrection, of the land of the dead, of fertility and birth, of initiation and magic.

Now that we've made ourselves aware that the Sun and Moon *have* mythic power, let's look at them more closely.

Sun – Ra. The primary Egyptian solar god is Ra, whose name probably signifies Creator. Since it is the power of the Sun which draws up vegetation, it makes sense to equate the Sun with creativity. Ra is also the sovereign lord of the sky. From our point of view here on earth, no other source of light can supersede the Sun's, so by rights, it can claim lordship. Additionally, the Egyptians taught that Ra was born each morning as a baby, grew to manhood in mid-day and afterwards fell into a decline, to die at night as an old man.

It is fun to find that the Sun's course can parallel the changes of a human lifetime. We'll look at the specific moments of Sunrise and Sunset in a bit. But in the meantime, it is worth considering that the passage of the Sun can convey a sense of aging to your audience. It can be a useful shorthand for a storyteller, telling the audience how you want them to look at the life of the characters you show them. Before we move on to the Moon, let's also look some more at the Sun's power of creation. More than just bringing a new day, when the Sun rises, it pours greatly needed energy down on the life-forms of planet Earth. Photosynthesis allows plants to live, processing sunlight. That's a creative aspect of the Sun. From drawing vegetative life up out of the ground to drawing works of art out of human soil, the Sun symbolizes all of creation.

Because of the Moon's changing face, more variety can be found in lunar mythology. One scholar calls some of the myths of the Moon more dramatic than tales of the Sun. Dramatic or not, we're going to discover some fascinating lunar aspects.

The Moon – Thoth. The Egyptian moon god Thoth measured out time, dividing it into months, seasons and years. Clocking the moon was the most obvious of his regulative duties, which included all calculations and annotations. He was the patron of science and literature, wisdom and invention. He invented all the arts and sciences, but most especially the art and/or science of *writing*.

I can hear you asking how a deity connected with night (as a Moon god is likely to be) becomes the patron of science. After all, haven't we established that night-time is unreasonable, irrational? Well, yes we have. And that is exactly the point. Look again: Thoth is marking out the changes of the Moon, bringing its apparent inconstancy into the realm of the rational. It's a sort of threshold activity, taking the tools of rationality (found, perhaps, in the *light* of the Moon) and bringing order to something that seems erratic. Thus you have Thoth as the patron of invention. For invention involves a leap of intuition (a quality of darkness and night) shaped by order and mechanics (qualities of light and day).

It is from this background that we draw images of mad scientists working in the dark of night. These insane inventors are trying (in their own minds) to draw something new out of the realm of darkness and into the light of day. Victor Frankenstein and all his literary and cinematic descendants are, basically, trying to be like Thoth, trying to make something ordered out of the irrational chaos of the dark. This is also why such characters never see or realize that those around them think these scientists are crazy. When a character believes he is engaged in a rational pursuit, he won't be aware if or when he himself crosses over into irrational territory.

We have a hard time imagining a wacko scientist working by day or a serious scientist working at night (unless he or she is an astronomer). That problem comes from the forceful implications of day and night. But as we see in the figure of Thoth, we do find it natural for innovators and mad scientists to work at night, by the light of the Moon. You, the storyteller, can take these expectations into account as you plan your story. Should you desire to emphasize the aspect of the irrational, even the insane, in the activities of your innovator character, then letting him work *only* at night will tell your audience a great deal. But equally effective would be a choice to play against the audience's expectation. Remember how effectively Hitchcock played against our expectations of daylight in *The Birds*.

As common as images of mad scientists in moonlight are images of lovers in moonlight. A mythic figure for this aspect of the Moon is the goddess Selene.

The Moon – Selene. The goddess Selene was shown as a beautiful young woman with a very white face. Her moon rays fall on people like kisses, for Selene was famous for her countless love affairs. This romantic history reflects the fickleness of the Moon's shape. Just as the lit shape of the Moon changes, so too did most of Selene's love affairs.

Storytellers should consider more aspects of moonlight than its romantic aura. The possibilities of playing upon the fickle nature of the Moon's cycle get used far less than the enticing mood of love is used. Too often the only image of the Moon that gets used in a story is that of the full Moon. Following that come images of the night sky with *no* Moon present. Yet, the audience would respond to waxing and waning Moon-shapes, since those images not only appear regularly in our sky but also can represent inconstant relationships.

Indeed, the changing face of the Moon gave rise to a tradition of equating its cycle with stages in a woman's life. Various goddesses come to be associated with specific phases, but we'll just look at the overall pattern.

The Moon – The Triune Goddess. *The Waxing Moon:* as the Moon grows out of its dark phase, it is equated with the Maiden aspect – youthful and maturing. The Maiden represents energy, vitality and freedom. *The Full Moon:* the complete wholeness of the full Moon is represented by the Mother (or Matron) aspect, ripe and full of power, strength and passion. *The Waning Moon:* as the full Moon melts away, the Crone becomes its representative figure. She rules over a time of wisdom and psychic ability, a time of banishing and reversing things.

You can see here how the phases of the Moon can be used to underscore growth in a character – particularly a female character. Or a particular phase of the Moon can be used to represent one of the qualities associated with that aspect. The point is that a Moon in the sky does not always have to be a full Moon. Look beyond the obvious image, the easy image, and consider what it is you want your story to be conveying. Then choose the lunar face that best suits what you are doing.

One last element of the lunar cycle remains to be considered: the dark of the Moon.

The Moon – Hecate. Hecate, a Greek goddess, is said to appear "when the ebony moon shines." In case that doesn't register, that means during the dark phase of the Moon. She is a goddess of the crossroads, and came to be considered the goddess of witchcraft and/or evil.

Hecate's connection with witchcraft and evil makes sense to us when we look back at the implications of darkness. The unknown knowledge that lurks in the darkness thus comes under Hecate's dominion. But we also find that here, when the Moon's light has melted away and the night is at its darkest, as goddess of crossroads, Hecate can represent the choices we make. After all, when two paths cross, the traveler has three new directions to choose from (assuming he does not go back the way he came). All paths lead off into the unknown. So, this Moon phase can indicate a time of choice for your character, or a time of venturing out into new and/or unknown territory.

After going into all of this, I will mention again the power that we have, as storytellers, to play against the expectations of the audience. When we know how an image is likely to strike the audience, we can build conditions to work against the anticipated response. As an example of this, I will mention that in the Arctic regions, everything we have discussed so far is actually reversed. In the Arctic, mythic language indicates that the *Sun* is feminine and the *Moon* is male.

Moon and Sun – Arctic Reversal. In many regions of the far North, the myths declare that the Moon is male and the Sun female (the reverse of the role assignment made by the rest of the World). For more southern cultures, the softness of the Moon's light, and (where they are aware of the fact) its passiveness in reflecting the light of the Sun, cast the Moon in the feminine role. But in the Arctic, the difference in power (light) between the two is less evident. The Sun disappears for much of the year. Even when it *is* high in the sky, it doesn't have the same scorching force as it does in Southern latitudes. But the Moon in the Arctic winter can stay risen for long periods of time, its half-light intensified by the reflective surface of ice and snow.[4]

Whether or not the Sun or Moon is male or female in the mythic outlook seems in part to be connected to the perception of which celestial light is more reliable. Alas for the chauvinism of the ages, the feminine aspect gets stuck carrying the load of being unreliable or changeable. In the Arctic, we see that the Sun's absence of half a year means it's a less reliable source of light. So, all the activities which rely on light shift to the domain of the Moon.

Between light and dark, day and night, Sun and Moon, we have found quite a variety of meanings. Instinct might lead you to the beginnings of one of these options. But by knowing the outlook that lies behind each option, you can punch up the impact of your imagery. Either building on the audience expectation or playing against it.

Let me emphasize that in playing *to* the subconscious audience expectations of an image, you are not being less creative as a storyteller. Look back again at the discussion of *The Silence of the Lambs*. Scenes dealing with facts, rational matters, deduction, and order were set in day. The scenes dealing with intuition, chaos, irrationality occurred at night. *Because* these scenes were set in their appropriate time period, and because the usage of day and night was consistent throughout the film, the audience was swept along. In a film whose subject matter promised to be very disturbing, anything that helped it keep its shape became important.

That said, I'll also repeat my observation that power can spring from working against expectation. When the audience is caught in the sensation of "No, it should not be this way," you have a potent tool in your hand.

For instance, we would expect that a tale of intrigue and deception to have plenty of dark, night sequences (all that hidden knowledge, after all). But the film *White Nights* (1985)[5] takes place during the arctic summer, when the sun does not set. The title refers to the fact that even the night hours are lit by the beams of the sun. The creative aspect of the sun finds representation in the realm of dance, the context of the story. A Russian dancer, Nikolai Rodchenko, who had defected from the Soviet Union eight years earlier, is among the passengers on board a plane forced to land in the Soviet Union. His resistance to the intrigues of Colonel Chaiko and his maneuvers to escape the control of the Soviet officials are all played out against the long, unbroken daylight. The light of the sun, and the truth it requires, provides a fascinating, unexpected background for intrigue. Intrigue usually falls into the realm of night, where elements of hidden knowledge and deceit are common. But in *White Nights*, aside from the early lie Chaiko tells the Americans about Nikolai's condition, everyone basically tells the truth. Virtually all the deception in the greater part of the story consists of people *evading* giving answers: there are very few out-and-out lies.

By contrast, the one actual night sequence – that is, one that occurs in the dark – is heavy with hidden information. Raymond Greenwood, who helped Nikolai make his escape, has remained in the power of the Soviet officials. Chaiko conveys Raymond to a mysterious location, not answering any of Raymond's questions about where they are going or what happened to Nikolai and to Raymond's wife Darya. Chaiko even goes so far as to speak the second explicit lie of the film. He says to Raymond, "Funny the Americans didn't want you any more than we did." It's worth noting that in this film, in this darkness sequence, not even the moon appears. This movie plays out all of its intrigues in the openness of light, creating a fresh experience for the audience.

There is one other thing about the Moon that can be of use to storytellers, and that is the list of the names of the Full Moons. Because in primitive – or agricultural – societies the light of the Full Moon can extend the day's activity. Thus the names tend to reflect what happens in the world under that Full Moon.

January	Moon After Yule	(Yule time is the darkest time of the year, the longest night, and so the light of the Full Moon is very important.)
February	Snow Moon	(In many locations, the later end of Winter brings many wet snowfalls.)
March	Sap Moon	(The warming after the worst of Winter marks the time when the sap in trees rises again after being fairly dormant during the cold. In Maple trees in particular, there is sugar in the sap of late winter, so the trees are tapped in order to make syrup.)
April	Grass Moon	(Spring showers bring the first shoots of vegetation, and grasses are among the earliest to push their way up.)
May	Planting Moon	(Do you need an explanation of this? This Moon gives more light to the process of getting the seeds in the ground.)
June	Honey Moon	(Ah ha! Now you know the origin of the term for the after-wedding trip. June, because it often brings a break in farming activity, traditionally became a good time to attend to such personal business as getting married. And why "honey"? After collecting the pollen from the blooming flowers of May, June tends to be one of the most productive times of the year for honeybees.)
July	Thunder Moon	(The heat of the middle of Summer tends to generate turbulent weather fronts, especially the crashing thunderstorms.)
August	Grain Moon	(The plants that were planted in May have now grown to fruition. The fresh, mature grain can ripple like the sea under the light of this Moon.)

September	Fruit Moon	(In September, many fruit trees become loaded with the mature fruit.)
October	Hunter's Moon	(The Autumn season brings the migration of many birds, the first of the hunter's prey.)
September or October	Harvest Moon	(The Harvest Moon is the Full Moon closest to the Autumn equinox on September 21. It could be either in late September or early October. It is, of course, the Moon under which the last of the harvest is brought in.)
November	Frosty Moon	(The first serious frosts harden the ground as Winter approaches)
December	Moon Before Yule[6]	

Of final note is what people call the Blue Moon. This has come to be used for those infrequent occasions when one calendar month has two Full Moons in it. The second one becomes called a Blue Moon.

If you thought we had reached the end of discussing day and night images, you've forgotten two that are, in many ways, the most powerful elements of the 24 hour cycle: sunrise and sunset.

Sunrise, Sunset

Threshold moments of any sort are very powerful occasions. We hover between one state and another, watching a new condition asserting itself. As we go through our existence, the most visual and immediate image we have of this transformational tension comes from seeing the sun rise above or fall below the horizon. With the motion of the sun across our landscape, we can see the world transformed, for good or for ill.

On the ominous side, and for the rise of the sun no less, we have this from the Aztecs:

Sunrise – Morning Star. The Aztecs named the Morning Star Tlahuicalpantecuhtli, and he was an aspect of Quetzacoatl. This celestial object was the planet Venus as it appears before sunrise. They considered that period just before dawn an inauspicious time. Tlahuicalpantecuhtli was a fierce deity whose anger could be terrible.

This fierce god captures our sense of insecurity at what a new day might bring. Without certain knowledge of what lies before us, humans by nature become anxious. Any figure having power over that moment thus gains power over us.

Yet anxious uncertainty is not the only thing associated with sunrise. In fact, far more common these days is a sense of promise regarding what will come after sunrise.

> **Sunrise – Khepri.** The Egyptian scarab god Khepri presided over the sunrise. He represents He Who Becomes. The Egyptians compared the rising sun to the scarab beetle, believing that it emerged from its own substance and was reborn of itself. Thus Khepri was the god of life's transformations, a cycle the Egyptians thought was ever renewing.

Dawn and dusk are often treated as siblings, for the two threshold occasions are very similar.

> **Dawn and Dusk – The Zorya.** In Slavic mythology two daughters of the Sun, Zorya Utrennyaya and Zorya Vechernyaya are in charge of the gates of the Sun's celestial palace. Zorya Utrennyaya (the Aurora of the Morning) opens the gates when the Sun sets out on his journey. Zorya Vechernyaya (the Aurora of the Evening) closes the gates when the Sun comes home at night. In a later myth, with a third sister of Midnight, the sisters guard a wild dog chained to the Little Bear constellation. If the dog gets loose, it will eat the world.

Here we have sunrise and sunset doing guard duty in a couple of ways. In the first, they serve the life-giving power of the Sun by overseeing its appearance and withdrawal. In the second, they watch over a force belonging to the darkness (it is part of the *night* sky, remember) that could destroy the earth.

The connection with the setting of the sun and death has a long history. Losing the light of the sky, and the bright blood red color of sunset that bleeds away as dusk grows have contributed greatly to this conceptual joining. Yet, even as the sun goes down, human nature looks forward to its next appearance, leading to an expectation of resurrection.

Sunset – Osiris. The Egyptian god Osiris has a strong connection specifically with the setting sun. Set, in the guise of the dragon Apep – the force of darkness or chaos – kills Osiris, who after being brought back to life becomes the god of the dead.

Death becomes easily linked with sunset. But other undesirable things also become related to the sinking sun.

Sunset – Sundogs. A sundog is a parhelion, or a bright spot on a solar halo. Usually there are two or more seen on opposite sides of the sun in the sky. For the Bella Coola Indians of British Columbia, Alqol ti Manl t'aix is the sundog to the west of the sun. When it drops down to the earth (as it would at sunset), it causes epidemics.

The gathering of unknown, and therefore unwanted, forces with the coming of sunset puts a chill on our expectations of the image.

As you can see, these threshold moments can cover a range of emotional expectation. For the ominous aspect of sunset, we can look to the closing of *The Silence of the Lambs*. After Lecter makes his taunting call to Clarice at her graduation, he saunters off into the gathering dusk – into the unknown, the hidden. He's free in the night realm of the irrational. We could even view him as a deadly walking epidemic, like the Bella Coola's sundog – bright but alarming. The unknown prospects and changes that sunrise (or sunset) can bring are also seen in the final images of *Shane* (1953)[7]. Shane's confrontation with Jack Wilson at the tavern takes place at night, in the hours of disorder. And when the fight is over, Shane rides off into that darkness, leaving young Joey Starrett calling after him, calling him to remain. Our awareness that the next sunrise will bring good things for the Starretts is mixed with our uncertainty about the wounded Shane's future.

A more explicit linking of sunset and victory comes at the very end of *Indiana Jones and the Last Crusade*, where our heroes ride out of the canyon and straight into the sunset. They have achieved their quest and the sun goes down on their success, marking the end of the journey and (with the coming of night) a promise of rest. Rest of another sort, the rest of death, receives a sunset expression in *Excalibur*. Arthur is mortally wounded at sunset. In fact, the sun is shown as blood red. The mystical aspects of sunset, especially that of venturing into the unknown, appear with the mysterious ship which carries Arthur's body off into the sunset. Arthur's ideal kingdom has failed (for the time being), but is he actually dead? The land beyond the sunset hides Arthur's fate, while the sunset itself emphasizes the sense of ending.

By contrast, the final episode of *Babylon 5*, "Sleeping in Light," plays against our expectation of equating death and finality with sun*set*. Instead, the element of sun*rise* is carefully woven in. I need to emphasize that point: the use of sun*rise* with the death of Sheridan is not sprung on the audience at the last minute. The imagery builds up to it in the episode.

First, as he feels his death approaching, Sheridan chooses to rise early to watch the sun come up. For the last 19 years, as leader of the Interstellar Alliance, he has been living on his wife's home planet, but he has never taken the time to watch the sun rise there. Now he does so, and the audience watches the warm golden light grown on the faces of this loving couple. Secondly, Sheridan speaks of how when he was growing up, his family would go for wandering Sunday drives. And the day he knows to be his last is a *Sun*day. The third and most important element comes with his actual death. As he dies and light fills his ship, Sheridan says, "Well, look at that. Sun's coming up."

Each of these elements speaks to the symbolism of hope that gets carried in the sun imagery. Indeed, more than hope rises with the sun. Dawn also brings with it the reminders of return and renewal. So fittingly, the last image of the series emphasizes the return and renewal of all that the character of Sheridan symbolized – idealism, community, compassion, principle. In that last image, Delenn sits watching and reaching toward a sunrise, while a voice-over says, "As for Delenn.... Every morning for as long as she lived, Delenn got up before dawn and watched the sun come up."

From dawn to dusk and into the night we have covered the particular mythic elements we respond to. But I haven't focused much on another way we regard these patterns. Very often we draw a parallel between the progress of day and the progress of a person's life. But the passage of daylight is not the only motif we link to the human lifespan.

The British folk-rock band Steeleye Span recorded a traditional ballad which conveys these linkages.

When the dawn of the day is a-breaking

When life beckons you to awakening

When spring is in the air

And the world is fresh and fair

When the dawn of the day is a-breaking

When the noon of the day is a-brightening

When the height of the sky is a-lightening

Your laughter and your tears

Are the summer of your years

When the noon of the day is a-brightening

When the dusk of the day is a-darkening

When the evening star is starting

In the autumn of your days

Walk gently in your ways

When the dusk of the day is a-darkening

When the end of the day is a-falling

When nighttime's rest is a-calling

You can hear the winter horn

On the lover at home

When the end of the day is a-falling[8]

And thus with the turn of the seasons we move from time of day to time of year.

SECTION TWO: THE SEASONS

Many myths were born in order to explain the hows and whys of the world around us. Because these explanations sprang from human hearts and imaginations they still communicate how we *feel* about things, even if we recognize the truth of the scientific explanations.

The courses of the seasons are no different in this regard than the nature of the sun. Just as we have learned that the sun is a huge mass of exploding gasses, we have learned that the seasons depend on the tilt of our planet's axis and the globe's proximity to the sun's energy. Yet these science facts do not convey our emotional experience of the seasons, how we feel about the world as Autumn changes into Winter and Spring bursts out of the seemingly dead earth. So, even though we no longer need myths to explain the How and Why of the seasons, they can still effectively convey the What of our feelings about the annual cycle.

Perhaps the most famous of the myths about the seasons is that of Hades and Persephone.

Seasons – Hades and Persephone. Persephone was the lovely daughter of the goddess Demeter (whose charge was over growing things). Persephone was so lovely that Hades, the god of the underworld, wanted her. Zeus, not bothering to tell Demeter, told Hades he could have the maiden. She was out gathering flowers, the earth opened up, and Hades snatched her away into his kingdom. Demeter went looking all over the earth for her daughter. Finally Hermes told her about the deal Zeus had made. Demeter was furious. She left Olympus and refused to do her job. Pretty soon, plants stopped growing and there was nothing to harvest. By the time Zeus agreed to give Persephone back to her mother, the earth had gotten barren. Meanwhile, down in the underworld, Persephone had been holding out against Hades. She was a sunshine girl and didn't care for his dark kingdom. She wouldn't even eat the food he gave her – mainly because if she did eat the fruit her captor gave her she would be obliged to stay with him. Still... she was down there a long time and even immortals get hungry. By the time Zeus sent an order that she was to return to her mother, it was revealed that she had nibbled on four pomegranate seeds. Now if you've ever seen a pomegranate and its seeds, you'd know that there's not much there. But Hades insisted that the rules be applied and that he would get to keep Persephone. This put Zeus between the proverbial rock and hard place. Traditions couldn't easily be flouted, after all, but on the other hand, Demeter's anger was creating famine in the world. So he compromised. For four months of the year (to account for those nibbled seeds), Persephone would live in the underworld with Hades. The rest of the year, she would return to her mother, and the earth would be fruitful. Thus as the time comes for Persephone to go to Hades, things die off (Autumn). While she lives in the underworld, the upper world is barren (Winter). When she returns to her mother, new life bursts forth (Spring). And the happy days she spends with her mother in the upper world promote growth and harvest (Summer).

The myth, of course, comes from a part of the world where there are notable distinctions between the seasons. Yet even in parts of the world where the seasons locally are not as distinct from each other, all humans recognize the impact of the four season cycle and respond to it.

Because we inevitably connect the freshness of Spring with the beginnings of life, we'll start our discussions with that season.

Spring

Spring, like dawn, brings us stories of birth. Tales of beginnings seem ideally suited to the season of Spring. We find myths about the birth of the Hero set in Spring, myths of revival and resurrection. Stories of creation or the defeat of the powers of darkness (or Winter or death) rise in our minds with Spring. Spring provides the bright setting for new adventures and the celebration of life. Whatever was barren and lifeless, whatever was in need of healing, when brought into the context of Spring such things find renewal.

The film adaptation of *The Secret Garden* (1993)[1] presents us with a whole population (with few exceptions) of characters who are in need of the renewal of Spring. Ten year old Mary Lennox, orphaned by the deaths of her neglectful parents, comes in Winter to live at the isolated manor of her uncle (her mother's brother-in-law), Lord Craven. The house is dark and gloomy. Indeed, when she explores it, Mary comments that the house seemed dead. Due to her negligent upbringing, Mary herself has a sour temperament. Lord Craven, who has a hunched back, lost his wife in childbirth, and he has mourned her ever since. His son Colin, who had been very sickly as a child, has been coddled by a fearful staff, all of whom (father, son *and* staff) believe the boy will die. In fact, Colin has hardly ever been out of his bed, and he does not walk. The house and the residents desperately need the awakening of Spring.

All the trappings of Winter are seen in Mary's arrival at the manor. And not simply because the season *is* Winter. Gloom hovers over the house, the colors are dark, and there is a coldness to the way Mrs. Medlock, the housekeeper, treats Mary. Isolation also figures into the environment, for not only is Mary left to her own devices, she is not told she even *has* a cousin. She discovers the ten year old Colin by herself.

Outside this house, Mary discovers a walled up, neglected garden. She is led to it by a cheery robin (a bird notoriously associated with Spring). In the garden, she finds a plant sending up new green shoots, the one bright, new green growth in the seemingly dead garden. It becomes her mission to bring the garden back to life. She gains help in this from the knowledgeable Dickon. Her industry in the garden parallels the growth of her relationship with Colin. She sees no reason to treat him softly, and her blunt temper challenges him to question his own belief in his supposed feeble health and pending death.

Just as Spring brings growth and bloom to the garden, so too does it transform Colin. With Colin's improved health, the absent Lord Craven is drawn back to his home to discover life and love again. Mary grows less sour, Colin grows strong and the dim manor takes on life again. The story is the epitome of a Spring tale: revival and resurrection, a defeat of darkness, and a happy ending.

As you can see, Spring is almost the easiest of mythic images to draw upon. How can we not respond to the wonder of fresh green vegetation bravely pushing its way into the dark, cold winter world? Yet how often do storytellers overlook the simple connections that could be made in using Spring imagery?

Spring is merely the beginning of the cycle of seasons, however. All that newborn vegetation will grow and flourish under the Summer sun.

Summer

The warmth of the Summer season brings us optimistic stories, stories of triumph. It is the season for apotheosis and the sacred marriage. When all the world around us is peacefully growing toward harvest, we think that we might be entering into Paradise. In the rich season between the labor and beginnings of Spring and the labor and winding down of Autumn, Summer holds the ideal moment for wishes and wish-fulfillment. When the growing world soaks in nourishment, doing the quiet work to prepare for harvest, we can easily believe that anything is possible. We expect happy endings and comedy (of the laughter provoking sort) in the sun drenched days of Summer.

In *American Graffiti* (1973)[2], several of the Summer elements come into play. The story is set at the end of summer, the last night in town for two high school graduates who are college-bound. Although the story is episodic, in following the courses of several different characters, each thread demonstrates a characteristic of a Summer story. Comedy, Wish Fulfillment, the Sacred Marriage, and Adventure and Apotheosis each are handled in separate threads.

Comedy occurs in the thread concerning the mismatched pair of John and Carol. John, a couple of years older than the high school graduates, owns the coolest car in town. He cruises the town, looking for a girl to be his companion for the evening, and through a quick conversation at a stop light acquires Carol, an under-aged teen. He is embarrassed to be seen with the girl (since her age could get him into trouble), while she wants her friends to see her with John. This incongruous pair ends up having a pleasant evening together. He takes her to a junkyard and entertains her with stories of the crashes represented by some of the wrecked cars. Later, the two gleefully play a prank on a car full of girls.

The excursions of Terry "the Toad" Fields give us Summer's element of Wish Fulfillment. The most unlikely young man in town receives the loan of his friend Steve's car, a considerable leap up the status symbol ladder from his little scooter. He unexpectedly gains the company of the pretty Debbie. He then gets to show how grown up he is by securing some hard liquor and getting drunk with Debbie. Hardly model behavior, perhaps, but everything Toad had dreamed about and never gotten before.

The Sacred Marriage of Summer finds its representatives in Steve and his girlfriend Laurie. For their friends, Steve and Laurie are the definition of what a couple is. But for the two themselves, this night becomes a crux point. Steve, about to leave town for college, wants them to try dating other people. Laurie, on the other hand, doesn't even want him to go. The course of their perambulations go through several ups and downs, ending with Steve's resolution *not* to leave town for college, but rather do his studies locally so he can stay near Laurie.

The movements of Steve's friend Curt give us Summer's Adventure and Apotheosis. Curt seems to drift through the night, unsure of what he will do with his future. The Blonde in the T-Bird flits across his vision, punctuating his adventures. He falls in with some local gang members, and they make him accompany them on some escapades. In stepping outside his usually good guy role, Curt gains self assurance. Whereas he began the evening unsure that he wanted to leave his hometown, by the next dawn he can confidently board the airplane which will carry him up and away into the wider world.

American Graffiti uses the Summer motif elements in an episodic fashion. And certainly when you have several potential elements to deal with, assigning one element to one story thread is a pragmatic solution. Focusing diverse Summer elements into one story line, however, is equally effective.

The film *Field of Dreams* (1989)[3] weaves together three of the Summer story components. Youth, fruitfulness and especially wish-fulfillment all shape this story.

Throughout the story, as Ray Kinsella pursues his adventures, he tells various people things about his childhood and his relationship with his father. The sunshine on the green baseball diamond he creates out of his cornfield warms those memories. He can even begin to articulate what drove him away from his father: "I never forgave him for getting old." As Ray connects with Terence Mann and (the ghost of) Doc Graham each reveals how the dreams of their youth are connected to baseball. Even young Karin Kinsella, Ray's daughter, takes to the joy of watching the game. Of all the characters in the story, Ray's brother-in-law Mark most seems to have lost any connection to the youthful joy in baseball. All he can see is the waste of planting acreage. Literally, that is all he can see, for he does not see the ghost players hitting balls on the diamond.

Mark's inability to see the players is in fact connected to the matter of fruitfulness in this story. Throughout the tale, his refrain "You're going to lose the farm" interferes with the wonder of Ray's quest. The contrast between Mark and Ray could rest on the question of whose outlook is more fruitful. Certainly, if Mark had his way, the baseball field would be returned to planting, more corn would be grown (that's fruitful) which would bring in more money (that's fruitful). But does Mark's way represent the *best* type of fruitfulness? By following his inexplicable promptings, Ray reconnects with a joy from childhood, returning delight to a life that was beginning to be closed off and dour (that's fruitful), to regain a pleasure in the act of living. If anything, this story captures the idea behind the saying, "What does it profit a man if he gain the whole world and lose his soul?" By following the mysterious urgings, by exploring old dreams and wishes, Ray's existence takes on a new life, with the fruit of new friendships.

Indeed, deep woven in this tale is the matter of wish fulfillment. At each step along the way, wishes and dreams are explored. Mann wishes he had Ray's passion, and by catching a ride on Ray's quest Mann moves closer to his own wish for involvement in baseball. Ray's inquiry into what Doc Graham wished for brings the young Archie Graham to Iowa. Archie's presence reminds Ray of his own father's dreams of playing professional baseball – and it also means that Doc is at hand to save Karin's life at a crucial point. Through all these adventures, wishes are fulfilled, dreams are actualized, and Ray's life becomes richer. Yet as the story seems to draw to its end, when Mann is given the chance to go off the field with the players, Ray discovers he still lacks something. He doesn't quite know what it is (although the audience has actually heard him speak of it throughout the story). But before Shoeless Joe leaves the field, he repeats the sentence that had set Ray on his quest: "If you build it, he will come." The answer comes when Ray recognizes the image of his father as a young man. The answer to his question, the fulfillment of his wish – to play catch with his father.

If a storyteller intends to use a particular season throughout the whole of a tale, the story will be considerably enriched if the aspects of that season affect all the elements of the story. When the various threads of a story reflect the symbolic power of the season, this underlying mythic glue can hold them together. Consider again *American Graffiti*. Taken separately the various plot lines don't have any necessary connection to each other. But two things are used to keep them together. One is the fact that the various characters are presented as friends with each other. We, the audience, therefore easily accept that their lives will interconnect. The other thing contributing to the unity of the story is that each thread reflects an aspect of a Summer story. The first is a connection we see, the second a connection we *feel*.

Likewise, *Field of Dreams* conveys an overwhelming sense of Summer. So much so that it is easy to forget that the story does *not* take place all in one Summer. After Ray builds his field and has gained a sense of satisfaction in doing that well, *nothing happens*. Two visuals tell us of the long wait he endures until the next Summer. They are (1) a shot of snow falling on the diamond and bleachers on a dim winter day and (2) Ray looking out at the baseball field while in the background the family is celebrating Christmas amidst holiday decorations. Only after this brief pause in the story, with its apparent death of Ray's inspiration, do we return to the question of the fruitfulness and fertility of Ray's Summer quest.

Drenching the story's setting with the effects and significances of a particular season is one way of emphasizing the events of that story. For instance, the ripe fertility of Summer's sticky heat provides the context for *Cat on a Hot Tin Roof* (1958)[4]. Rampant fecundity finds expression in the relationship of Gooper and Mae, with their five children and Mae's pregnant condition. Yet for all this apparent fertility, the marriage of Gooper and Mae seems unappealing and their children barely human. Indeed, Maggie frequently refers to the children as "no neck monsters."

But the intent of the tale focuses on Big Daddy's impending death, and the barren state of affairs between Maggie and Brick. The Summer context thrusts these two story elements into our attention, because they run counter to the implications of the season. Throughout the story, both the knowledge that Big Daddy is dying and his apparent inability to truly deal with *life* rather than *things* press against the Summer expectation of life and fruitfulness. The same is true of the relationship between Brick and Maggie. This tension between our underlying expectation and what we are given in the story holds us to the end, in spite of the fact that the characters are not exactly appealing.

I've mentioned before how effective a story can be in touching its audience when the storyteller plays against the audience's expectations. In *Cat on a Hot Tin Roof*, Summer's expectations are thwarted. On the one hand we are given the vacuous fertility of Gooper and Mae (two people difficult to like) and on the other we see the passionate isolation of Brick and Maggie (a couple you cannot feel indifferent towards). Engage the audience in this way, by running counter to what they anticipate, and the audience will do half the storytelling labor for you. Plow your story field well, sew your story seeds carefully and you can reap a rich harvest of audience involvement.

And with that, let us look at the season of harvest, Autumn.

Autumn

Autumn brings two important aspects with it. The positive aspect is that of the harvest. The negative aspect is that of the dying seasons and the coming of the apparent barrenness of winter.

Harvest is a time of labor. The relaxed days of the youthful Summer season are over and the farmers must cut and gather the produce. Autumn becomes a time of threshold crossing, in particular that of leaving behind the playfulness of youth and taking up the more serious duties of adulthood.

Indeed, perhaps more than other seasons, Autumn has a right to be called the Season of the Threshold. We use the word threshold these days to indicate the entrance of a building. Or in the context of entering or beginning something new. But the word's origins are connected to harvest activities. In ancient times threshing often involved trampling or treading on harvested grain, in order to break the seed coverings away from the meaty part of the grain. Frequently this activity took place in the yard in front of the farmer's home. Thus this almost violent activity was needed to uncover the truly valuable fruit of the Summer growing season.

The darker aspect of Autumn is that of the death phase. Autumn brings us myths of falling and defeat, of the dying god. Autumn myths are often of violent death and sacrifice and isolation, particularly of the Hero. In areas away from the tropics, such motifs are accompanied by the imagery of the world itself, as tree leaves turn brown and fall to the ground, leaving stark bare branches against darkening skies.

As you can see, Autumn holds rich story possibilities. Whether facing death itself or simply a major change in how a character has been living her life, Autumn can provide a setting that speaks to the audience about these things. How completely you use that imagery, and how far into the positive or negative aspects you go depends entirely on the type of story you wish to tell.

An example of the positive side of Autumn can be found in the film *Indian Summer*. The name itself keys us to the autumnal setting, for Indian Summer is that short time between the end of the high heated days of Summer and the empty, chilling days of full-blown Autumn. Indian Summer stands as a threshold between the carefree youth of Summer and the more adult aspects of life, the harvest of Autumn. The season reflects where each of the characters in the film are in their lives. Each is either still caught in their Summer mode or they do not know how to move forward as adults.

The plot of the film is simple: a group of childhood friends, now in their thirties, reunite at their old camp with "Uncle" Lou, who has run the camp for over thirty years and who is about to retire.

Jamie Ross seems never to have grown up at all. He likes to play, especially with his 21 year old fiancée, Gwen. Whenever Gwen (who *is* moving toward true adulthood) raises questions about their future, about settling down, Jamie's response is "I like my life." Matthew Berman, an artist, has been in business with his cousin Brad, designing sporty clothes. But he isn't happy. And his unhappiness disrupts his relationship with his wife Kelly. Brad has been totally given over to business. He has a difficult time getting into the fun of this reunion. He also spends a great deal of time marveling at how small everything in the camp is. Jack Belston has returned to resolve an issue with Uncle Lou.

By briefly reviving their childhood in remembering Summers past, each character is enabled to cross the threshold into Autumn, allowing them to harvest the fruits of their youth. Matthew rediscovers his love of art and chooses to leave his business partnership with Brad. Brad acknowledges that he is now grown up and can both have fun and continue in business on his own. Jack and Lou reconcile, and Jack chooses to take on the running of the camp.

As this story shows us, however, even the positive side of Autumn involves endings. These characters must end or let go of one thing in their lives in order to cross that threshold into something new in their lives. There is no escaping the element of endings in an Autumn tale. And the negative side of Autumn magnifies that element. The colder winds of the Autumn blow chilly emotions our way.

The Tim Burton film *Sleepy Hollow* (1999)[5] plays upon these darker aspects of Autumn. Here, the tone of tragedy sounds in the actions of violent death and isolation of the Hero.

From the beginning of the film, the dark season of Autumn is highlighted, with images of dry leaves trashing the ground and hanging like rags in trees. Also, the presence of that famous American autumn squash, the pumpkin, punctuates the dark tones with splashes of orange. The carved jack-o-lantern face of the first pumpkin we see inevitably generates a connection in the minds of the audience with the Autumn celebration of Halloween – and its connection to the dead.

There is no mistaking the violent death present in this story. Cutting off people's heads cannot be seen gently by the audience. Indeed, the film shows us the terror of the characters at this event, both the victims and the community alarmed by the events.

Into this autumnal setting of violent death comes our isolated Hero, Constable Icabod Crane. Crane's isolation grows out of his obstinate fixation on using scientific forensic procedures in an era that does not (yet) understand them. He is very much the odd-man-out professionally, and he continues as such when he reaches the town of Sleep Hollow to investigate the deaths. As a scientific rationalist he remains isolated in this community that easily accepts the supernatural aspects of the events they endure.

Visually, the film holds to the darker nature of Autumn, washing the screen with somber tones as long as Crane marches his way through the grim adventure. However, once he has succeeded in his quest – and won the fair lady of the tale – Crane's return to his starting point of New York City comes in brighter, sunnier, warmer autumn colors. Crane steps across a threshold when he gets out of his carriage in the city during a gentle snowfall. The horrors of violent Autumn are left behind as he moves into a new maturity in his life.

The dark, violent mode of Autumn acquired a particular mythic image which brought a sense of desperation to people – the myth of the Wild Hunt.

Autumn – The Wild Hunt. The dark cold nights of Autumn became the chosen time for the Wild Hunt. Unlike the boldly sporty hunting activity of humans riding over fields hunting wild animals, this Hunt sought after the humans themselves. Various ominous figures were named leader of the Wild Hunt, including the Devil himself. This fearsome figure with his clamoring host and noisy hell-hounds was said to be hunting the damned souls. But it was also said that for someone to see the Wild Hunt riding it was at best bad luck and at worst, death. Prudent, cautious men – if they chanced to be out of doors at such times – would fling themselves face down on the earth as the Hunt passed overhead.

Now, while it is possible that this mythic imagery was inspired by the clamor of wild geese flying across the stark night sky of Autumn, the myth also carries the terror we feel when faced with drastic change. How we have our Hero face this ominous harbinger of Autumn can help define the character strengths of our Hero.

The Wild Hunt dramatizes the darker nature of Autumn, thrusting it into action. The Headless Horseman of *Sleepy Hollow* serves as a prime example of the terror the Hunt can bring. Almost all of those who see the Horseman die, Crane being an exception. However, since his early encounter with the Horseman happens when he has fallen to the ground, he comes through safely. Later in the story, we learn that the Horseman goes after specific victims. He is quite literally, *hunting* them. The film effectively invokes the sense of doom connected with the presence of the Wild Hunt.

Eventually, the Autumn wind blows until it whistles through the barren branches of trees. The Sun spends little time in the sky. The days grow cold. Autumn departs, giving way to the season of Winter.

Winter

Our imaginations need not stretch very far to discover that Winter is the season of darkness. Guilt by association brings us myths of dissolution, of the triumph of the powers of darkness, and of the return of chaos. Winter is the season most associated with the ultimate defeat of Heroes, the ending of gods and the destruction of worlds. If an Autumn tale brings shadows of such things, the Winter tale pushes them to their most extreme form. If you want to find a suitable season for the worst aspects of human nature, what better choice can a storyteller make than the cold-hearted season of Winter? It's a harsh season, and ends up being represented by rough mythological personalities.

Winter – Skadi. Skadi (who gave her name to Scandinavia) was a Norse mountain goddess. Associated with winter, she was frequently out tramping in snow and hunting animals using a bow and arrows. For a time she was married to the god Njord, a sea god who represents the fertility of springtime. But they had irreconcilable differences and the marriage fell apart. Cold hearted and predatory, she was not someone who was sought out much.

So, what can a storyteller make of this harsh season? It is associated with darkness because the days are short. It is associated with dead emotions for we draw parallels between cold weather and cold hearts. But let's consider some examples.

Although the story of *It's a Wonderful Life* covers the whole of George Bailey's life and all its seasons, the crucial season in the tale is Winter. In the cold of Winter, the day before Christmas, close to the shortest day of the year and the longest night, George goes through his crisis. George fears he will lose everything. He contemplates suicide in the dark of that cold night. And the crucial question throughout is whether he will chose life and look forward to Spring's rebirth.

Indeed, the aspect of looking forward toward a season change is often a factor in Winter stories. In *Groundhog Day*, weatherman Phil Connors must participate in the small-town hoopla of Groundhog Day, against his will. Cynical, self-centered and cold-hearted, Phil has no real interest in the proceedings. He doesn't care about the folklore of a groundhog predicting a possible early Spring. In fact, he is barely interested in actual weather conditions, missing information about an impending blizzard. And because Phil doesn't look for Spring, or pay attention to the dangers of continuing Winter (the blizzard), he finds himself stuck in an endlessly repeating cycle of this threshold day.

But look beyond the simple factor of the weather of a season. A season can provide a *thematic* basis for a story. The connotations of a season that we have looked at can underpin a tale as effectively as direct imagery can.

For example, Laurence Olivier's television production of *King Lear* (1984)[6] demonstrates the thematic elements of Winter, even though the seasonal weather itself doesn't affect the drama. At the very beginning, Lear refers to his "dark purpose" in dividing the kingdom. This division will plunge the kingdom into chaos even though Lear thinks otherwise. So, here very speedily at the beginning, we find the Winter elements of darkness and chaos invoked.[7]

The wintery aspect of dissolution also plays a major part in this story. Lear dissolves the unity of his kingdom. He also dissolves his relationship with his daughter Cordelia when she cannot verbally gush out her love for him. Gloucester's illegitimate son Edmund brings about the dissolution of his father's relationship with his legitimate half-brother Edgar. Indeed, Edmund's very existence implies a dissolution of Gloucester's own marital relationship. The ill treatment of Lear by his daughters Goneril and Regan springs from a dissolution of their filial duty and respect. All of which contributes to the dissolution of Lear's mental capacities.

The story plunges toward the end of the world as the characters have known it, where darkness triumphs (for when Cordelia returns with troops to rescue her father she is defeated, and is killed). The old age of the central character reflects the barren nature of Winter. We do not, in this story, see any promise of renewal.

As you can see, we find in *King Lear* that a story can be a Winter tale without showing us any of the physical manifestations of the season. This is part of the power of the symbolic language of myth. The thematic elements can call up a sense of the season, if those elements work strongly together.

Multiple Seasons

However, although I have focused on each season in turn, as storytellers we need to remember that the seasons flow from one into another. The cycle has a regular pattern. The symbolic implications of one season and the questions they might raise in your story may find their answers in the season that follows. Although remaining with one season can give a powerful background to your story, the change of seasons can also be used by storytellers.

You've Got Mail (1998)[8] covers three seasons, Autumn, Winter and Spring. The film begins in Autumn, with Joe Fox and Kathleen Kelly corresponding anonymously by e-mail, behind the screennames of NY152 and Shopgirl. The Autumn season signals impending endings, changes. As Joe Fox is about to open a super-bookstore near Kathleen's children's book shop we can quickly deduce that her business will probably end. But as both characters are in established relationships, we can expect those to end as well. Indeed, during Winter, those relationships break up. Kathleen's business closes. The Winter-death claims everything, it seems. NY152 apparently fails to meet Shopgirl, putting the e-mail relationship at hazard. And Joe, meeting Kathleen face to face in a café, gets tromped on by her hostility. Winter holds no hope. Spring, however, is a different matter altogether. Seeds buried and dead in Winter stir to life. Joe begins a new type of relationship with Kathleen in the Spring. He meets her face to face as a friend, using his e-mail persona of NY152 as a foil. And because Spring is the season of hope, beginnings and growth, we expect this relationship to succeed. It does, and we are satisfied. These particular seasons provide an ideal backdrop to the story. It would probably have charmed us in any season. But the fact that Kathleen's time of greatest aloneness falls at the darkest, coldest time of the year adds to the impact. It would not feel the same if it fell at the Summer solstice, in warmth and sunshine.

Being conscious of the implications of the time settings of our stories can help us enrich our tales. When we are conscious of the traditional associations of time of day or time of year, we can look for those aspects of our adventure that can be enhanced by stronger temporal connections. Which brings me to another aspect of the calendar, holidays.

SECTION THREE: HOLIDAYS

I'm not going to elaborate at length about specific holidays. There are whole books which discuss the folklore and traditions of various world holidays.[1] It is a rich and fascinating subject.

The point I want to make is that as storytellers we should be careful about how we handle holidays. Whether or not a particular holiday figures in our personal calendar of celebration doesn't usually matter to the story we tell. By that I mean a Jewish or Islamic writer might include Christmas celebrations in a story set during Winter, because that fits with who the characters *in the story* are. There is nothing in the world to prevent *any* storyteller from including *any* holiday in a tale. Nothing, that is, except ignorance.

There is nothing worse for the audience than encountering a story with a holiday in it where it is clear that the storyteller had no understanding of the nature of that holiday. How many mangled Christmas stories have been sent out into the world? Mangled, because the storyteller didn't understand the deeper meanings that make it a special day.

It doesn't matter whether the holiday is Christmas, Ramadan or the Japanese Festival of the Chrysanthemum. If you include a particular holiday in your story, be sure you understand the thematic implications of that holiday. This applies to the smaller – and seemingly sillier – ones as well as the major holidays.

For instance, *Groundhog Day* was built around the American folklore and traditions of February 2. The tradition states that if the groundhog emerges on the morning of February 2 and sees his shadow, there would be six more weeks of Winter. On one hand, it is a silly holiday, for the Spring equinox (and the beginning of Spring) will indeed fall six weeks after February 2. On the other hand, the celebration of Groundhog Day represents the anticipation and desire for Spring. For the purposes of the story, the whole process of determining when Winter will end ties to the heart of the story: when will Phil start to be human, start to warm up.

The filmmakers of *Groundhog Day* understood the impulses and themes attached to the holiday. And this holiday is one of the lighter ones to be found on a calendar of holidays. What can we find if the holiday is one of the majors?

Christmas provides the holiday backdrop for *It's a Wonderful Life*. A holiday that celebrates the coming of hope at the darkest time of the year ideally suits this story of a man who has lost all hope in his life. Additionally, the Christmas custom of giving gifts to others underlies George's actions throughout the story: he gives his savings to his brother for college, he gives his honeymoon money to uphold the Building and Loan during a bank run. He gives and gives to others. The pay-off for this comes when the community gives back to him – at Christmas.

The important thing to remember about holidays is that their origins have meanings. They are significant for particular reasons. A little bit of research on your part can uncover those reasons. You can then decide on how much impact the thematic core of the holiday has on your story. But let me urge you *not* to rely on how a holiday has been used in some other story. Many holidays come with a rich spectrum of meanings, and a specific story may only deal with one portion of that spectrum. And that portion may not suit the needs of your story. For instance, if all you know of Christmas is what you learned in the film *It's a Wonderful Life*, you will be missing quite a few important issues, and your use of the holiday will feel artificial to the audience.

As a last word, always treat the holiday you are using in your story with respect. However obscure it may be, there may be someone out there in your audience to whom the holiday is important. This does not mean that all your characters need to take the holiday seriously. As we have seen, in *Groundhog Day*, Phil Connors considers the holiday not merely silly but also beneath his notice. Yet the filmmakers treat the local customs and traditions of the holiday with a gentle respect. This gives the holiday setting greater depth, which the audience appreciates.

As I said, the calendar is chock-full of holidays and celebrations of all sorts. A little bit of research can give you ideas of what a particular holiday means. It is then up to you as the storyteller to decide how important that meaning can be to your tale.

SECTION FOUR: WEATHER

Our planet Earth is a dynamic engine, with atmospheric changes created by time of day or time of year. Weather ends up being frequently connected with time and/or place. Because some weather effects are definitely connected to seasons, we will look at them here, rather than in connection with **LANDSCAPE**.

STORMS

In general, storms are likely to be the greatest powerful force of nature that most people encounter. And because they are beyond our control they have always been regarded as either the personification of divinity or the manifestation of the acts of gods. If you overlook the mythic implications of weather, you short-change the environment of your tale. Weather in your story need not be merely incidental set dressing. It can enrich the context and underscore theme, as long as you, the storyteller, are aware of the implications.

However strange it may seem, a storm god could be regarded with something approaching affection. Such a one was the Norse god Thor.

> **Storms – Thor.** Thor was presented as a large, hearty strong man, a solid, not-to-clever fellow. He drove across the sky in a huge chariot, and thunder was the rumbling of the chariot's wheels. But for all his hearty-ness, Thor had a temper, and his eyes would flash red and fierce with lightning. He had power over storms, so farmers called on him for rain for their crops, and sailors called on him to hold off storms at sea.[1]

As you can see, Thor's power can be exercised either positively or negatively. And also, the presence of a storm isn't necessarily a bad thing. For farmers, at the right time of the year, a storm can be a benefit. Either way, what is unmistakable about storms is their power.

If the too hearty image of Thor doesn't convey a sense of power for you, then consider the Caribbean and Central American storm god Hurakan.

> **Storms – Hurakan.** Hurakan was a creator god and master of storms who unleashed the deluge which wiped out the unsatisfactory first race of humans. Frequently regarded as a demon, he ruled weather in all its manifestations, but especially tempests, rain, lightning bolts, thunder, and sheet lightning. He was a sky god of whirling ferocity, for indeed, our word hurricane comes from his name. But he was more than simply dangerous, for he had an additional name of Heart of Sky.

As with Thor, Hurakan's second name reminds us of the real complexity of power. It is never simple. Beyond the raging torrents of a hurricane storm, hidden in the center of that whirling devastation there is the still heart of calm, strange, eerie and beautiful.

It is very easy for us to focus on the negative effects of storms, especially when we tell stories. They can be such effective physical hindrances to the progress of your Hero. And they can symbolically underscore moments of chaos and destruction. But if you stop there, and never consider the deeper meanings possible in storm imagery, you could very easily short-change your story.

Consider the use of a storm in the film *The Matrix*. When Morpheus' team picks up Neo in their car, it is at night and there is a rainstorm about them. The storm rumbles ominously. Usually this would be a negative omen, but we could question that interpretation in this film. The rumbles certainly make us uncertain about the good intentions of the team. But there is a positive virtue hiding in the heart of this encounter – Neo's chance at freedom. Morpheus gives Neo a choice of pills (which, since they are only virtual inside the Matrix, are actually just symbols for his choice). Thunder rolls as Neo takes the pill leading to freedom from the Matrix – power is about to be exercised.

The storm underscores the importance of Neo's choice. It invokes the mastery over his existence inside the Matrix which he is about to acquire. In a way, by the end of the film, Neo will gain a type of god-like power over the computer construct (while outside the Matrix he can go on being "just a guy"), much the same way Thor exercises power over storms.

The specific manifestations of storms also carry particular implications for storytelling. So, let us look at them more closely.

LIGHTNING

The exchange of electrical charges between ground and sky, especially when seen against the darkness of a night sky provides one of nature's more startling spectacles. Lightning bolts falling from the heavens alarm us, for we cannot predict where they will strike. Yet, their apparent limitation to a specific location, rather than scorching a broad territory, makes the strike-point seem to be an intentional target.

The variations of how we read the fall of a lightning bolt give us many interesting possibilities.

Lightning – Hurakan. One of Hurakan's primary manifestations was as lightning. He was called the One-footed God. That did not mean that he was crippled. That one foot, that one leg (the bent form of lightning), was Hurakan stomping his foot down from his heavenly realm. That certainly seems ominous and deadly. Except that the god of maize was born from the point where Hurakan's foot first plunged into the earth.

Once again we have an example of something dangerous having the potential to bring about something good. Yet beyond this, we humans also have the tendency to regard the fall of lightning as a warning. The Etruscans even had this systematized.

Lightning – Etruscan Jupiter. The Etruscans' version of Jupiter possessed three thunderbolts. The first one he could hurl down on humans as a warning, whenever he wanted to do so. His second bolt was not merely a warning. Some scholars call it premonitory, which meant that it not only warned about things to come but promised divine attention to the human's actions. But to throw that bolt, Jupiter had to get the permission of twelve other gods, which meant there was nothing fickle about its fall. The third bolt was the one that punished. But Jupiter could only release that one with the consent of some superior or hidden gods.

The progress from warning to punishment echoes our desire for a rational order to the universe. Even if we do not understand the purposes of those divine thunderbolt throwers, we imagine that they have reasons. Yet, we do also acknowledge that there can be an arbitrary destructive element to lightning. The African goddess Tsetse embodies that hateful mischief.

Lightning – Tsetse. Tsetse was such a trouble-maker that the creator god Bumba chased her up into the sky. Even so, Tsetse sometimes leaps down and strikes the earth, causing damage. You will notice that the name of this troublesome goddess is the same as the fly which carries the Sleeping Sickness, a disease that devastates cattle herds and threatens human health in Africa. Now, whether the fly was named for the goddess, or the goddess was named for the fly, you have some idea of how unfavorably Tsetse the goddess was regarded.

These then are some of the implications of lightning. Consider them when you use lightning in your storytelling, for your audience may be drawing upon these implications. After all, lightning is frequently used as visual punctuation in thrillers and horror films. So much so that it has become a cliché: suspense builds, the characters make a discovery, someone makes a warning statement and bang! lightning flashes outside the windows. Of course, the lightning flash became a cliché because the mythic references have remained so primal and obvious to us. It is powerful, it is dangerous, it comes from the sky outside our realm of control.

The film *Phenomenon* (1996)[2] makes use of the lightning imagery in a broader way, however. On the evening of his 37th birthday, ordinary George Malley happens to be outside alone. He sees what seems to be a ball of light falling out of the sky like lightning. It smacks him and he falls to the ground.

From that point on, George is changed – not so much in terms of character but rather in terms of ability. He suddenly understands chess as he never did before, he reads voluminously, begins inventing things, learns languages at an incredible rate. He becomes sensitive to sub-harmonic waves prior to an earthquake, and he develops telekinetic powers.

However, this seemingly divine gift carries some negative consequences. George's neighbors become wary and fearful of him. The government wants to use him and his abilities. When George is knocked down by a mob at a public function, he sees another ball of lightning falling on him. Waking up in the hospital, he learns that he has a brain tumor which is killing him.

George's friend Doc suggests that all the abilities George has demonstrated are a consequence of the tumor, including the light bolts which George saw, and which (apparently) no one else saw. This organic explanation isn't completely persuasive to the audience, however. And the reason springs from the imagery used in the storytelling.

The filmmakers may have intended the causes of George's abilities to be organic. Before the first incident, at George's birthday party, Doc (who has known George since childhood) says that George has potential, that "George Malley has something extra to offer this world." Later, when the tumor is discovered, Doc tells George that he has been using far more of his brain than has ever been observed in any other subject. And George himself at one point makes a soft-pedaled comment about how the potential to do what he does is in all humans. It is perhaps these elements in the story that led one reviewer[3] to comment, "Similarities between George's powers and the alleged benefits of Travolta's religion, Scientology, led to charges that the film was veiled pro-Scientology propaganda."

If the filmmakers did intend for George's abilities to be organic (that is, part of George's actual, if untapped, potential), if they did indeed want to imply this potential resides in all of us, their use of the bolts of light undercut that intention. The script implies that these two blobs of light were actually subjective hallucinations caused by George's tumor. But because the image is there on the screen, the bolt from the sky is *objective* for the audience. Because George is the only character present in the scene of the first occurrence, the audience has no measuring stick other than George concerning the reality of the light. Later, characters speculate about what George has described, but none of them were present at the event.

This lack of a secondary character to question the objectivity of George's experience leaves the audience open to respond to the image however they choose. And that response will be colored by the mythic implications of lightning. Lightning comes from the gods: therefore, the cause of George's abilities is external to himself, regardless of potential. Lightning is both a warning and a possible troublemaker: therefore, we are not surprised at the problems George's abilities bring to him, both with his neighbors and with the government officials. Lightning is fickle: therefore, the second bolt becomes the warning of the end of the adventure. By the time an objective explanation is given for George's abilities, our mythic responses have entrenched themselves in our imaginations, in effect over-riding the explanation.

Never underestimate the power of an image. Because, in the context of a story, it is never "just" an image. It is a key unlocking a horde of implications. If you do not want those implications to flood into your story, either do not use the image, or be certain that you have characters present who define the image/experience in the manner you want the audience to define it.

THUNDER

Very rarely do we see lightning without hearing the roll of thunder. They make an exciting sensory one-two punch. However, we frequently hear thunder without ever seeing that traveling electric blast called lightning. And thunder, too, has its own impact in storytelling.

Thunder – To the Isoko of Africa, their Supreme Being shows his anger through thunder. Some thunder gods are benevolent, punishing evil-doers. Heno, of the Iroquois, was considered beneficent when he brought clouds and rain to cool and refresh the earth – but his thunder was punitive. Boza, of Ethiopia, was responsible for regulating social and moral conduct, so we can easily imagine that his thunder was a sign of judgement. But the storm goddess Dobeiba from South America, vented her anger in lightning and thunder, while Chemen of Malaya caused thunder with a spinning top. Chemen's thunderbolts, capriciously thrown off the whirling top, caused death and illness.

As you can see, thunder can evoke a full spectrum of responses, from the positive to the negative. Because that spectrum exists, pay attention to what reaction you might be generating in your audience. Be consistent with the particular story you are telling as to what you want thunder to mean. Most of the time, storytellers stick to a middle ground and use thunder to merely signal a warning, creating an ominous atmosphere. But you could also have it serve as a favorable sign for your Good Guys and a threat of punishment for your Bad Guys.

In the film *Shane,* when "Stonewall" Frank Torrey goes into town alone, with the innocent intent of getting a drink, thunder rumbles ominously. The ranchers (the Bad Guys) taunt him, and eventually kill him, all to the background roll of distant thunder. We never see the rain fall, but we hear the heavens grumbling about what is happening. And Torrey's death leads toward the final confrontation between Shane and Wilson, of good versus evil.

RAIN

Thunder and lightning are usually accompanied by rain. Now, it's obvious that rain is frequently used for the setting of sad stories. That's the power of analogy: we compare the falling of raindrops with the falling of tears. Very few people need to have that imagery explained to them. There are, however, some other simple implications that come with rain, particularly that of washing things clean or washing away bad stuff.

> **Rain** – The Hindu god Parjanya was a god of gentle rain, the sort that softly feeds vegetation, encouraging them to bring forth fruit. The Aztec Tlatoc was also a fertility rain god, but he was possibly a bit more intense and fierce than Parjanya. After all, children were sacrificed to him, in order that he would bring the rain which would end the dry season. The Shinto Kamo-Wake-Ikazuchi was a rain god, overseeing thunder, storm and rain.

Very few mythologies that deal with storms and rain overlook the fact that water is very crucial to life. Plants need it to grow. Humans need it to survive. Additionally, many mythologies draw an analogy between the appearance and effect of rain and the appearance and effect of semen. Although we shall consider this further later, here I will just observe that the male sky rains its fluids down on the female earth, generating new life. In our modern, urbanized, nearly demythologized life, we may forget the sexual and fertility connotations of rain, but they still remain and still affect our imaginations.

When weather enters the story in the film *Pleasantville* (1998)[4] we certainly have an instance of thunder and lightning signaling important events. Especially on the cataclysmic evening when the rain comes. The torrential rainfall marks key emotional moments in the life of Pleasantville. While the rain falls, Betty has her portrait painted by Bill, and she gets kissed by him. While the rain falls, David-as-Bud kisses Margaret at Lovers' Lane, and he then reassures the other teens that there is nothing to fear in the rain. While the rain falls, George (Betty's husband) wanders through his empty home and then seeks out his fellow bowlers. The life-giving fertility of the rain affects all who experience it, except David (who still views Pleasantville as unreal) and George (who is still set in the pattern of the black and white Pleasantville). David, at least, is puzzled by the fact that *he* remains in black and white when everything around him flows into color.

The fertility of the rain wakens new life in the town of Pleasantville. Its power runs through its liquid form. But what happens when it takes on its other seasonal form, when it becomes ice and snow?

ICE AND SNOW

Although the weather elements of ice and snow do carry many of the connotations of the season of Winter, they can also do work of their own. Of course, some aspects of these chilly events are obvious: cold, the freezing solid of fluids, the physical obstacles and dangers they can create. Certainly metaphors built on these things appear in our language use – cold hearts, blizzards of activity, skating on thin ice. We recognize the real conditions and also the implications they can have as representational imagery. But we can explore these elements more deeply.

Ice and Snow – Cailleach Bheur was a Celtic goddess of Winter. Annually, on October 31, she would be reborn into the world, bringing snow with her until the goddess Brigit would depose her in the spring. Cailleach Bheur was depicted as a blue-faced hag. Nong was a god of Winter and cold weather from the region of Afghanistan. He lived in a glacier, cracked ice, and could be seen in the meltwater. He was perceived as a misogynist and was often depicted as a wooden effigy, though apparently the form was not clearly human. Windigo, an Eskimo ice god was a terrible being formed of ice as a skeleton. He symbolized the starvation of Winter and he was a cannibal. And a human could be turned into a windigo like the god through possession.

There are, of course, many other such mythic figures who represent such features. But these three can give you an idea of the things that ice and snow can represent.

If you have ever been out in the cold of a snowy Winter, you know how the tips of your fingers can turn blue if exposed for a long time. Just like Cailleach Bheur's face. Because less hot blood is carried to the extremities, the blue coloring of the veins predominates, as does the cold touch of lowered body temperature. So someone identified with snow will probably have a cold touch.

Nong actually lives in the ice, and he can crack it as well. He reminds us of how brittle cold things can be. Breakable and fragile, ice can also be alarming. But is it human? We're not sure about that. When you chose to identify something or someone with ice, these things can come into play.

The Windigo takes the alarming aspects of ice even further. Starvation can be a powerful image. But starvation to the degree that you would consume other people? That could be terrifying to confront in a story. What could be worse? Why not the ability to turn other people into such a creature.

As you can see, ice and snow bring additional power to stories. Don't overlook how they can affect the characterization and theme of your tale.

As an example, let us consider *Smilla's Sense of Snow* (1997)[5]. This film provides us with several manifestations of various aspects of ice and snow.

The cold blue face of Cailleach Bheur shows up in the opening images of the film. The vast arctic ice fields caught in a cold blue light are accompanied by the sound of wind. The blue makes us feel cold, as it is unrelieved by even the yellow of sunlight. Smilla Jasperson reflects this harshness in her character. She is coldly harsh to her neighbor when she returns from seeing young Isaiah's body in the morgue. We see this unyielding coldness in Smilla again at the end of the story as she watches Tork Hviid struggle in the icy water before he sinks to his death.

Smilla's chosen isolation easily exemplifies Nong the ice cracker. We first see Smilla as she studies ice. Even as she remembers her first encounter with Isaiah, we see that Smilla wants to be alone. Just as Nong is misanthropic, so is Smilla. She tries to avoid becoming involved with her neighbor, telling him, "I try to be rough all over." When the authorities review her personal history, they label her a troublemaker and someone who has never fit in. The woodenness and questionable humanity of Nong are expressed in Smilla's own lack of self-definition. At one point, young Isaiah asks her, "Do you know who you are?" and she answers "No."

We find touches of the Windigo in Smilla's character, particularly in the harshness she displays toward Benja. Admittedly, Benja likes Smilla even less than Smilla likes her father's partner. Still, Smilla's cold rudeness rakes Benja.

For all these traits, Smilla is driven by a cold passion. It is not a sentimental emotion that compels her to pursue her investigation into Isaiah's death. Because of her intellectual knowledge about snow, and her knowledge of the boy's fear of heights, she questions the official statement that he was playing on the roof of the apartment building before falling to his death. Her cold intellect keeps her from being diverted by emotion. To emphasize the importance of intellect in Smilla's life (and to show that she *is* human) we see her come alive and sparkling as she describes her love of mathematics. Vividly, we see a passion quite different than the usually steamy emotion.

Weather can be so much more than set dressing in your story. Take advantage of the human impulse to draw analogies between a character and her surroundings. Wind, rain, ice, snow. Think of the qualities of each and how those qualities might be reflected in your stories. Take advantage of them and draw the audience along with you in the direction you want them to go. Be aware of where the imagery might take the audience and decide if that will affect the meanings you want to convey. If there is any possibility that your imagery could take the audience someplace other than where you want them (as seems to be the case with *Phenomenon*), find a way to address that in the story.

Before we leave the weather of the Land of Myth behind, there is one thing that often comes after the storm.

THE RAINBOW

In the real world, the appearance of the rainbow is perhaps one of the most delightful and unexpected consequences of weather. Science can explain how that glorious arc appears in the sky, why it seems to reach from earth to heaven. Knowing those facts could make it easy for us to predict the appearance of a rainbow, to know where to look for it. Even so, it remains a surprising pleasure to us when it appears.

Mythically, the rainbow showers us with several possible meanings.

> **Rainbow – Noah.** The world had gotten to be a pretty sorry place, so God decided to start again. He had Noah construct an ark (a large boat) wherein to save the animals of the world. Rain fell, night and day, for over a month. Then the ark floated on the flood for several days. When finally a dove brought a branch back to Noah, showing that dry land had reappeared, God put a rainbow in the sky. The rainbow signified a promise between God and humanity, between God and every living creature, that he would not flood the world ever again. The rainbow was to signify that promise and interaction between the divine and mundane.[6]

From the promise of interconnectedness, the rainbow also extends itself as a bridge between two realms.

Rainbow – Bifrost. The Norse rainbow bridge Bifrost reaches from Midgard, the earth of humanity, to the heavenly setting of Asgard, the realm of the gods. Supposedly the bridge was made of fire, air and water, all elements unlike the gravity-bound earth.

More than a bridge to heaven, a rainbow also brings messages down from heaven to earth.

Rainbow – Iris. The Greek goddess Iris rode the many-colored stream of the rainbow down from the heavens to bring messages from Zeus.

Whichever variation might affect your use of the imagery, be aware of how much it can convey. For some reason, rainbows don't often appear in films, but they can convey a great deal.

Although the actual *image* of a rainbow is not present in *The Wizard of Oz* (1939)[7], the concept of the rainbow is powerfully evoked by the song, "Over the Rainbow."[8] Visually, we have a black and white context with an appealing young heroine, Dorothy longing for a special place "beyond the rainbow." The elements of a promise of good things and a bridge to a divine realm play into our response to the longing that the song conveys. Thus, when Dorothy (and the audience) lands on the other side of the storm, the revelation of color provides a pleasing shock. Suddenly, all the colors of the rainbow fill the picture before us and we are quite pleased to say "we're not in Kansas anymore."

But just to touch base with a film that actually does have a rainbow in it, look at *Pleasantville*. The rainbow shows up over the town the morning after the great rainfall. It signals the promise of good things to come for the citizens of the town.

Come rain or come shine, weather and its effects can add symbolic energy to your story. In addition to the excitement weather can bring as plot elements and obstacles, it also reeks with mythic power which you should not overlook.

MUSINGS

When you set out on your story's trip, the time-setting at which you begin and travel through can affect the meanings the audience draws from the tale. Whether you prepare for rain or excess sun, be aware of what can be conveyed by the time and weather in the story.

Think about it:

* What events do you have set during the daytime? What sequences fall during the night?

Do your daytime sequences play to or against the mythic elements of day? How much do your nighttime sequences play to or against the meanings coming from night?

How many of your daytime sequences actually have to happen in the day? Can setting the scene in a different time of day change the audience expectation of what is happening? Remember that subverting the audience's underlying expectation can be as engaging as playing to their expectation.

* Are the sun and/or moon important images in your story?

* If you are using the sun as an image, do other aspects of the story reflect the meanings of sun-imagery?

* If you are using the moon as an important image in your tale, have you looked beyond the shape of the full moon? Would another part of the lunar cycle bring more meaning to your story? Take advantage of the different stages of the moon.

* What time of year does your story take place in? Spring? Summer? Autumn? Winter?

* If the actual season doesn't matter to the story, does the thematic significance of one of the seasons fit your theme? If so, which season? Would including the imagery of that season add energy to your story?

* Is there a holiday which figures in your story? If so, which holiday?

Have you done a little research on what that holiday represents? Does the meaning of the holiday emphasize or distract the audience's attention to your theme?

* Is weather important to your plot? Will the mythic implications of weather add to or detract from your theme? Would adding a particular type of weather to your story bring deeper meaning or greater thematic significance to your tale?

PART FOUR

LOCAL RESIDENTS

LOCAL RESIDENTS

One pleasurable aspect of traveling into new territory lies in the chance to meet new people. The same holds true in storytelling. The audience takes pleasure in meeting new characters in stories. When it comes to mythic patterns, there are archetypal characters.

Now, the word archetype gets tossed around a lot. Its roots lie in the Greek language, and it means original pattern. So what we are talking about are the basic shapes characters may take, or the principal foundation they might be built upon. The seven traditional character archetypes will be discussed in the Day Laborers section. But first we'll want to consider something even more basic in your characters: their sex.

SECTION ONE: SEX (OR GENDER)

Biologically speaking, every human being on the planet is either a male or a female. That's just the way the human creature is constructed. Each sex has a specialized role in the propagation of the species, and so certain specific functions in the raising of offspring are traditionally assigned to one sex rather than the other.

That being said, it's of course proper to note that *these* days some aspects of life that used to be entirely the purview of one sex (such as Males being the Warriors) can actually be performed by the other sex (even nurturing can be taken on by Males, if not the actual act of childbirth). I want to be clear on that point, because in the discussions that follow, I want it understood that these descriptions are not exclusive. By that I mean that even though we will discuss being a Warrior as a stage in a Male's life pattern, individual women are not excluded from being Warriors. Likewise, in discussing the role of Nurturer as part of the pattern of a Female's life, I'm not trying to say men cannot do that job. These are the *basic* models, the original patterns we will be looking at. There will always be exceptions and variations. *Of course* there will be variations: that's why we are storytellers.

The world is filled with these two types of humans. According to Genesis, it has been so by design, from the beginning.

Man and Woman – Genesis. During creation, God chose to populate the world. He created humanity in his image (though what image means is subject to much theological debate). And he decided that this creature would come in two forms: male and female. They would have dominion over all the other creatures of the world, and they would be partners to each other.[1]

So here we are with two aspects of humanity. But what are the special qualities of being Male or Female? We will consider the journey of a man and a woman in six stages each. I've adapted these stages discussed from some psychological studies[2] for use in our explorations. And although generally speaking a person would move progressively through each stage during his or her life, in actuality, someone might skip over a stage, be locked in one specific stage, or be a mixture of a couple of stages. And when it comes to storytelling, you may find that your character is firmly rooted in one specific stage, regardless of his or her age.

Now that we've gotten these preliminary matters out of the way, let's get down to the specifics.

MALE

The six stages in a Male's life are the Noble Savage, the Phallic Man, the Warrior, the Wounded Male, the Mature Ruler, and the Sage.

The Noble Savage

I will admit up front that I am being a bit ironic in the title of this stage of life, especially in using the word noble. This stage is a primal one, the first experiences of life. Childhood usually occupies this stage. The most significant thing about the person in this stage is that he's very self-centered. The Noble Savage has little or no socialization, and isn't even conscious of being self-centered. It's natural to him, a matter of course. He does, however, have a sense of needing to belong, to at least have a mother to nurture him to some degree.

The nobility of this stage lies in the enthusiasm the creature has for life. Un-pessimistic, un-oppressed, the Noble Savage is full of life and energy. The savagery springs from the lack of socialization. Sometimes capable of great good, the Noble Savage is equally capable of terrible destruction. Without the guidelines of socialization, the Noble Savage will startle those around him.

A forceful mythic example of the Noble Savage comes from the earliest existing epic, *Gilgamesh.*

> **Noble Savage – Enkidu.** Enkidu, Gilgamesh's best pal, was molded out of clay by the gods and given something of the image and essence of a sky god and a war god. That combination seems to have made him both rather turbulent and ungrounded. He's the prototype of the natural or wild man who lives among the animals.

Some of the best examples of the Noble Savage appeared in literature and became favorites of filmmakers.

In the early years of the twentieth century, the writer Edgar Rice Burroughs brought forth his character Tarzan. Tarzan, actually the orphaned infant son of English parents, was raised by "great apes" (Burroughs' term) without seeing another human until he was nearly adult. Tarzan's choices were based on what he needed to survive, and what was needed to protect those he cared about. If those needs were served by the death of other animals (or even, later, other humans), Tarzan had no qualms in killing. As he became socialized, he gradually accepted Society's rules prohibiting murder, but even so, killing in self-defense or defending his loved ones was a logical action to him.[3]

In Disney's animated *Tarzan* (1999)[4], Tarzan, before he meets other humans, does not register things as being right or wrong. He lives in the self-centered existence of the child, which does not take into account the opinions or emotions of others. Because he still responds only to the promptings of his own emotions, Tarzan disobeys Kerchak's order to stay away from the humans. Indeed, when Jane says she will have to leave because she has not seen any gorillas, Tarzan leads her to the family group of the apes. This disobedience, this disregard of the wisdom of others, endangers the gorillas. Tarzan had acted on his own desires, rather than any principle. In fact, he does not seem to recognize the principles which lie behind Kerchak's prohibition. By the end of the tale, however, he has come to understand the leader's responsibility to the group and he grows out of the Noble Savage stage.

Like all Disney animated features, *Tarzan* shows a lighter, brighter presentation of the Noble Savage. A darker take on this stage appears in the live action adaptation *Greystoke* (1984)[5]. *Greystoke* follows the Tarzan legend fairly closely, so again, an ape foster-mother raises the orphaned child. Until he becomes an adult he knows nothing of humans. So we can easily imagine someone who has spent all of his life up to that point in the first stage of a man's journey.

When Tarzan rescues the Frenchman d'Arnot, he begins to learn the language of humans. He also learns to see that he is not like the apes he has lived with. As a consequence, the Noble Savage's emotional need for belonging propels Tarzan to go into civilization with d'Arnot.

In his reclaimed identity of John Clayton, Tarzan moves into a society that we see in its worst light: stubbornness, bigotry, and cruelty are all around him. As a Noble Savage, Tarzan/John's emotions quickly drive him into conflict with civilization. He fights the whites he sees beating a black boy. In England, on his grandfather's estate, when he sees the estate idiot being abused, he drops a rock on the abuser's automobile and then indicates in the manner of the apes that the idiot is under his protection.

At each turn in the story, his emotions drive Tarzan/John into action. The story elements are stacked against any of the other aspects of civilization. The audience is shown such a dismal picture of humanity that they agree with all of John's actions, even down to his rejection of civilization. This film ignores the responsibilities that accompany John's inheritance, such as the fact that many people depend on the Earl of Greystoke (which he becomes) for their livelihoods. The reason for ignoring these aspects of the inheritance is that to acknowledge them would require moving Tarzan out of the stage of the Noble Savage and into the next ones. And these storytellers didn't want to do that.

The Noble Savage is driven by his own needs and emotions. The claims of others have no effect. Not even the romantic attachment of love holds this Noble Savage within the boundaries of civilization. Tarzan sacrifices his love for Jane in order to return to the jungle.

The character of Tarzan (as written by Edgar Rice Burroughs) carries a lot of nobility, not just of birth but also in his personal qualities. We can easily identify him as a Noble Savage. The second literary character that conveys the elements of the Noble Savage is that of J.M. Barrie's Peter Pan. Peter very quickly became an archetype after Barrie introduced him to the world. Possessing some of the qualities of the spritely figure of Puck mixed with some of the endearing characteristics of childhood, Peter Pan is an apparently less violent version of the Noble Savage than Tarzan.

Disney's version of *Peter Pan* (1953)[6] makes a point early on that Peter Pan represents an early stage in a Male's life. The narrator says that Mrs. Darling believed that Peter was "the spirit of youth." When Peter arrives on the scene, hunting his missing shadow, we see quite clearly his self-centeredness. Typical of his youthfulness, he isn't even conscious of his egotism. He tells Wendy that he comes to hear the stories she tells. She observes that her stories are all about him – and that, of course, is why he likes them.

Peter takes for granted that he will be the center of attention. This frustrates all the girls around him. Tinker Bell is jealous of Wendy. The mermaids are jealous of Wendy. Wendy is jealous of Tiger Lily. And Peter notices none of this. His attention always rests only on what interests *him*. When he and Wendy go to Skull Rock, where Captain Hook means to leave Tiger Lily, Peter gets caught up in showing off to Wendy by teasing Hook. Thus, he forgets that the Indian princess needs to be rescued and must be reminded by Wendy. And when he rescues Tiger Lily, he forgets Wendy.

Peter is irritated toward the end of the film by the Lost Boys' fascination with the concept of a mother. But his irritation springs from the fact that he isn't the center of attention at that moment. Wendy's decision to return home and grow up disappoints him. But he goes along with it and takes the Darling children back to their home.

The Disney version ends with this mild and contented home. The children have had their adventure and have returned to the real world, and all is pleasant and happy. The musical stage version (1955)[7], however, ends with the bittersweet turn that J.M. Barrie felt to be important. In the show's epilogue, once again the nursery windows spring open and Peter Pan flies in. But Peter still has no interest in grown-ups and so rejects the adult Wendy in favor of her daughter Jane. The underlying cruelty of the rejection of the grown Wendy is not disguised. Peter's self-centeredness is complete. It's because he's unaware of it, and that as a child it's still reasonable that he should remain unaware, that saves him from being rejected by the audience for his insensitivity. Were he an adult, the audience would not accept it. But he is, forever, Peter Pan, the boy who "won't grow up."

When a storyteller chooses to use the Noble Savage in shaping a character, there are some crucial things to consider. First off, will the character be an adult or a child? The audience will give a child considerably more leeway in behavior – especially self-centered behavior – than they will an adult. If you choose to present an adult Noble Savage, if you want the audience to like him, you had better build a good reason for his lack of socialization and his disconnection from other humans. Tarzan was raised in the jungle and never met another human until he was an adult. What's your excuse?

Of course, if you don't mind that the audience dislikes the character, then you needn't explain his lapses. The not-so-Noble Savage could make for a good villain, after all. Self-centered, motivated only by his own wants and needs, forgetful of others and their feelings, but perhaps tainted by an unconscious need to belong to *something* – all these elements can be seen in many a villain that has passed before an audience.

As I said, for the purposes of your story, you may root your character firmly in the soil of one particular stage. Or, like a vine, you may have him be in the process of crossing the threshold from one stage to another. You may even (if you have a lot of space and time) want to show the progress of your character through each stage in turn. You're the storyteller. The choice is yours.

That being said, we can move on to the next stage in a Male's life.

The Phallic Man

This stage in a Male's life (like its counterpart in the Female's Journey, the Young Woman) focuses on the innate *sexual* energy of humanity. Not merely about the indulgence of sexual activity, this stage also provides the arena for the learning of relationship that would be necessary for that indulgence. Not that men always realize the importance of relationship in the satisfaction of sexual urges (okay, remember this is a woman speaking).

In spite of the amount of commentary that exists on the sexual indulgences of men, the power that women can exert over men in the sexual arena is often underestimated. Men are known to sacrifice their careers, reputations and marriages for the physical pleasure women can give. But make no mistake: the pleasure is far more than sexual. The relationship needs of the Phallic Man, of affirmation, acceptance, and praise, when they are fed and energized during intercourse, also contribute to the pleasure felt. Indeed, that neediness should not be overlooked when working with a character in this stage. Frequently, we will find a character in this stage also displaying at least some of the self-centered qualities of the Noble Savage.

In terms of finding a legendary representative of this stage, we need look no further than Samson.

Phallic Man – Samson. Samson was raised to be a leader and strong man for his people, the Israelites, but he had an unfortunate tendency to fall for pretty women. And too frequently, they were Philistine women, nominally the foes of his own people. He saw a pretty Philistine girl and had his parents arrange a wedding for him. But the girl's people used her against him, attacking the Israelites, so he gave her to a friend of his. He even ventured into Gaza (deep in Philistine territory) and had a fling with a prostitute. And then, of course, there was Delilah, who used his sexual interest in her to weasel the secret of his powerful strength out of him. She betrayed him to the Philistines, who captured, blinded and imprisoned Samson. He managed to pull down the house on the Philistine leaders, but it cost him his life.[8]

It's typical of this stage that by giving into his sexual urges, the Male frequently lands in trouble. Letting his physical impulses lead his actions can distract him from important issues he should be dealing with or from potential environmental dangers.

One of the best known exemplars of this behavior can be found in the character of James Bond, particularly in the film *Goldfinger* (1964)[9]. Now Bond of course, is something of a mixture of the Phallic Man and the Warrior. But we could say that the Phallic Man stage gets a degree of focus in this story, even to the extent of getting the man in trouble.

In the opening sequence, James Bond delays his departure from the locale of his mission in order to have a last rendezvous with a tavern dancer. Yet, she's setting him up for an attack. Again, when he has been told to observe Auric Goldfinger in Florida, he romances Jill Masterson, Goldfinger's female companion. This not only focuses Goldfinger's attention on Bond, but it also gets Jill killed. Jill's death makes Bond more committed to his pursuit of Goldfinger, however.

In following Goldfinger to Europe, Bond again gets momentarily distracted by a pretty woman in a convertible when she passes him on the road. He has to remind himself to be disciplined. But when a rifle shot of hers hits near him, he does pursue the woman. She tells him her name is Tilly Soames, but she's actually Jill's sister. She attempts to sneak onto Goldfinger's property intending to kill him. Bond stops her, but in doing so sets off an alarm, leading to Tilly's death and Bond's capture.

So far, each of Bond's attempts at romancing have not only been bad for the woman (Jill and Tilly are dead, and the dancer was beaten up), but have endangered Bond himself. When he encounters Pussy Galore, he tries charming her, but she stays cool. It takes some time, but eventually he does win her over, with the result that she helps him in foiling Goldfinger's plot.

For Bond, in this film, his sexual activities frequently endanger him. But they also (more than his effectiveness as a Warrior) win him crucial help from Pussy, without which he would have failed.

Moving beyond the stage of indulging in procreative urges, we come to the other notoriously masculine stage.

The Warrior

The Warrior Stage reflects the Male's greater participation in the society around him. However, that involvement appears in a specialized fashion. For the Warrior also *competes* with his peers. Warriors compete to be the best, the biggest, the toughest, the richest, the smartest, the most well-known. Their call to battle frequently gets expressed by killing the competition, combating the opposing viewpoints, fighting their declared enemies and even sometimes their own marriages and families. Perhaps the battling spirit was born in the desire to protect the Male's own territory and family. Yet that fighting spirit can rise without those causes as well.

When we tell stories about Warriors out on the battlefield, we can easily identify them. But what sort of things can we expect when we place a Warrior in a non-lethal environment? The Warrior spirit fills athletics, and finds expression in business. And even though in the general course of events we prefer a society with a low level of violence, there are occasions when we need the Warrior. The question is not so much whether the Warrior *ought* to be in our society, but rather what does the Warrior fight for? Does he fight for a righteous cause? Or does he just fight? Are his opponents legitimate foes, or does he just destroy everyone within weapon's range? Likewise, story potential lurks in the Male character who is thwarted in expressing the Warrior Stage in his life. But, storytellers should be careful not to devalue the nature of the Warrior.

The positive aspects of the Warrior are in his strength, his urge to be the best, to fight against defeat. We could say that the sexual energy of the Phallic Stage grows outward, to be spent in more vocational pursuits. For, as I said, the Warrior fights in more arenas than just that of the battlefield. Yet, to a certain degree, although a Warrior usually fights *for* a society, he's often separated *from* that community.

What can Warriors look like in stories? Mythically, we can find an example for the Warrior in the figure of Achilles.

The Warrior – Achilles. Achilles is, in many ways, the prototype for the Warrior, a hero in battle and a symbol of the fighting man. But the frequent fate of a Warrior is to die in battle. Knowing that, his mother Thetis did two things to try and protect him. When he was a baby, she dipped him in the supernatural river Styx, making him invulnerable (except for his heel, where she held him). Later when the Trojan War began, she knew how likely it was that he would die an early death. So she sent him away and had the youth disguised as a girl, and hid him among a gaggle of young females. The Greek leaders came looking for the boy and couldn't find him. However, the wily Odysseus (he's always called that) suspected something, for he had some swords and shields placed in among a vast display of feminine finery. He then collared Achilles when it turned out the youth was the only one of the girls interested in the weaponry. Achilles went off to war and became the mightiest of the Greek heroes, undefeated in battle (well, except for that arrow-in-the-heel incident).

Like all good archetypes, Achilles demonstrates an attraction to the tools and accoutrements of this stage. He's drawn to weapons, he fights undefeated. He's the ultimate warrior in many ways.

That's the archetype. But when *we* tell stories of Warriors, what might our characters look like?

Consider the film *Shane*: Shane's a Warrior. He does want to move out of that gunfighter lifestyle, especially when he encounters the farming settlers. He's content to help farmer Joe Starrett. As a Warrior, Shane has been separated from being involved in community life. The Starretts offer an opportunity to make a connection with people. But Shane can't ignore the conflict between the farmers and the ranchers. He can clearly see that the farmers are not equipped to fight these battles. When the ranchers hire gunfighter Jack Wilson (the other true Warrior in the story), Shane knows he can no longer stay out of the fight.

Shane demonstrates for us a case of where a Warrior was certainly needed to fight a battle. What can we look for when we place a Warrior in a slightly less obvious situation?

In *Lethal Weapon* (1987)[10], Martin Riggs has transferred his focus as a Warrior from the military to his job as an L.A. cop. Although suicidal over the death of his wife, his commitment to the war on crime keeps him from taking his own life. Part of Riggs' melancholy springs from his inability to see his life in other terms (or other stages). He says to his partner, Roger Murtaugh, of his training as a sharpshooter in the military at age 19, "It's the only thing I was ever good at." In spite of this self-perception on Riggs' part, the audience can see that he actually is a pretty good detective. Even so, it's his skills as a Warrior that free him and Murtaugh from the Bad Guys, leading to the successful end of their case.

Warriors need a cause to fight for. It's what they exist for. If they are removed from their cause, their purpose in life, and are not given or do not acquire access to another stage in a masculine journey, they become drifting modules of violence. The gunslinger Wilson in *Shane* is just such a purposeless warrior, and Shane himself runs the risk of becoming like that. Riggs in *Lethal Weapon* finds a new outlet for his Warrior energy. These Warriors can both find righteous causes to fight for and can conceive of another way of life for themselves. That's one option you have as a storyteller.

But we can also show the audience a character so locked into the Warrior mode that he cannot imagine another way of looking at his life.

The science fiction film *Soldier* (1998)[11] puts forward a very focused portrait of such a Warrior. The beginning of the film introduces the concept of a Warrior selected and trained from birth to be the ultimate fighter. In this case, we see that the chosen children are raised to unquestioningly kill the competition, opposing viewpoints, and their declared enemies. The main character, Sergeant Todd has survived many battles, and the story begins its main action when he is declared obsolete.

Colonel Mekum brings a new group of soldiers to Captain Church. These fighters haven't just been *raised* to be soldiers, they have been *bred* for it. To demonstrate the superiority of the new soldiers, Todd is pitted against Caine 607. Although Todd wounds Caine in one eye, Todd is defeated. Apparently killed by a fall, Todd's body is dumped on a barren planet used as an inter-stellar trash heap.

But Todd is not dead. Shipwrecked colonists discover him, and they take him in and nurse him back to health. Within this community of families and warm emotion, the emptiness of the pure Warrior gets highlighted. Without being preached at, the matter of fighting for the right things gets dramatized. As Todd watches these families, seeing their lives in context, he has flashbacks to occasions when he, the ultimate Warrior, killed civilians who got in the way of the fight.

When Mekum chooses this planet as a training ground for his new soldiers, the colonists are put in danger. The military thinks that the planet is uninhabited, and that any personnel encountered can thus be regarded as hostiles. By being amongst the colonists, Todd gains a cause to fight for. Instead of just following his orders, Todd now fights for a right thing. His newly awakened emotions will lead him into a new stage of life (but that doesn't figure in this story).

Todd represents a Warrior who gains both a new cause to fight for and a vision of another sort of existence. But what does a Warrior look like when he has forgotten that there anything more to life, a Warrior who will fight without a cause? We caught a glimpse of such a character in the figure of Wilson in *Shane*. But in *The Jackal* (1997)[12], we are presented with a fuller picture of such a complete Warrior. The Jackal carefully prepares his weapons and equipment. He prepares for contingencies – as seen in the way he tests and times how long it would take him to wash a layer of paint off his van. Isabella, one of the few people who have ever seen his face, observes, "This man was ice, no feeling. Nothing." His one consistent quality is his focus as an assassin. He apparently has nothing else in his life. No cause to fight for, not even revenge. Although he has crossed paths with Declan Mulqueen before, he displays no feeling about that. He merely uses his knowledge of Declan's passions to manipulate his opponent.

Warriors can be exciting and inspiring figures in stories. Whether they are fighting actual battles or figurative ones in sports or business, the Warrior's willingness to face and deal with conflict stirs us. And yet they can also be dangerous and frightening in their focus. When they fight for a worthy cause, we need them and praise them, but when they fight for *no* cause, we fear their destructiveness and shun them from our society.

These are the possibilities in using the Warrior in stories. As the storyteller, you need to know what cause your Warrior may be fighting for and whether or not he can look beyond this stage. For, after all, we still have some stages in the Masculine Journey to consider.

The Wounded Male

The woundedness of the Male grows out of his life experiences. Although some Males do suffer drastic injuries (physical, emotional and psychological) in childhood and youth, woundedness generally is more manifested in adulthood. That is, the effect of being wounded becomes clear in the adult, regardless of when the important wounding occurred.

Likewise, passing through this Stage is normal, almost to be expected, in life. We are more likely to be suspicious of someone who has not suffered wounds. The experience of profound loss and alienation emphasizes the connectedness of the individual to the community. When a character lives with a deep seated wound to his soul, he's very conscious that he's disconnected from those around him. Yet even in that awareness lies a knowledge that he *ought* to be connected. He's out of place, "out of joint" as Hamlet says.

The wounding usually comes upon the Male when he's not prepared for it, and it strikes deeply to the core of his being. How the man deals with the wounding can lead to many different stories. For one of the things we should be aware of, as storytellers, is that objectively speaking, wounds can be healed. By that, I do not mean that they are erased or made as if they had never been. Rather, the wounds heal, the person continues able to function, though he often carries a scar of the wound. But all kinds of stories lie behind a character's choice regarding healing: will he accept healing? will he seek healing? will he recognize that which *can* heal him? does he *want* to be healed? All these choices offer you many possible turns to your stories.

For a model from myth, we can consider Osiris again.

The Wounded Male – Osiris. You will recall that Set envied and hated his brother Osiris so much that he attacked and killed Osiris. But this wasn't enough for Set: he chopped up his brother's body and scattered it across the landscape. Isis brought healing to her husband, by gathering his pieces together again and bringing him back to life. Yet, the wounds of the assault stayed with Osiris, for he had been betrayed and killed by his own brother. And also, even though she had done her best, Isis could not find that crucial bodily part of his reproductive organ. As he was divine, this loss did not affect his ability to father a child with Isis after his resurrection. Even so, that physical loss remained.

The story of Osiris reminds us that we are not talking about incidental breaks and cuts, the ordinary injuries of life. We are talking about a wounding that goes to the core of the man, his most important relationships, his self identity.

In the film *The Fisher King* (1991)[13], both Parry and Jack Lucas are wounded men. Jack's lack of social sensitivity pushes one of his radio listeners into an act of violence which results in the death of Parry's wife. The event knocks both of their lives off track. Jack, shocked at what his words caused, sinks into depression, losing his job. Parry sinks into a crazed and homeless insanity colored by Arthurian legends. Both these men need healing, and their adventures together lead them toward it.

The wounds of those two characters are quite evident to the audience. But not all wounds need to be so obvious.

As we said, woundedness need not be just a physical aspect of a character. Any serious event in a character's life can lead to this powerful wound. In *The Quiet Man* (1952)[14], when we first see Sean Thornton as he arrives in Innisfree, Ireland from America, he hardly seems wounded at all. Yet, it quickly becomes apparent that he does not want to talk about what prompted him to return to his birthplace in Ireland. Michaleen Flynn describes Sean as "a nice, peace lovin' man come home to Ireland to forget his troubles." For quite some time, we do not know just what Sean's "troubles" are, but we certainly do see the effect of them. Sean refuses to get into fights. No matter what provocation Will Danaher puts forward, Sean restrains himself – even when Will refuses to let Sean court his sister, Mary Kate.

Sean does not deal well with this new wound (the thwarting of his courtship). Father Lonergan speaks of the appearance of Sean's anger: "Sean with a face as dark as the black hunter he rode. A fine ill-tempered pair they were." Yet, even after achieving his desire in wedding Mary Kate, the deeper, older wound remains. When we finally learn the cause of his wound, that he killed another boxer with a blow during a match, his reluctance to fight gains a greater dimension. At the time of this revelation, Sean says, "All I know is that I can't fight or won't fight unless I'm mad enough to kill." What makes this revelation even more poignant is that the fight Sean now faces is with his own brother-in-law. He believes that he cannot fight unless he is "mad enough to kill" and he does not want to be in that mental place, nor, in fact, does he want to kill Will. The healing of his wound lies in his finding a way to fight without indulging in a lust to kill. Until he does so, his responses to events are crippled.

The wounding a Male can suffer can affect major portions of his life. And it's entirely possible that you would find the elements of this Stage mixed with those of another Stage. But should he successfully deal with his wounding and be ready to move onward, the Male will gain in maturity. It adds a richness and depth to a character that can be useful to the storyteller. And that maturity will assist in giving the character leadership skills. Which leads us to the next Stage.

The Mature Ruler

Gaining maturity gives a man a greater understanding of himself as an individual. Since he has survived being conscious of his alienation from the community, he can appreciate what makes himself unique. He knows his own strengths and weaknesses and can return to dealing with relationships enriched by his self-knowledge. He brings an understanding to his interactions that draws people to him. Because he has endured being wounded, he's also not as susceptible to outside influences. He's not as driven by his own emotions as the Noble Savage is. Nor is he diverted by his physical responses and need to be admired the way the Phallic Man can be. Although he may recognize the need for a particular fight, he himself no longer *needs* to fight. Instead, he can extend his wisdom to those around himself, guiding and shaping their courses. In a word, he can *rule*.

For a mythic model of this, look at King Arthur.

The Mature Ruler – King Arthur. Arthur shows us the ideal of a good ruler and leader. He belongs to a type called a World Restorer, someone who binds up the wounds of internal strife, defeats barbarians, destroys enemies and restores peace. These are all things Arthur did fairly quickly, after he pulled that sword from the stone. The land had been in conflict and turmoil ever since the death of Uther. Arthur pulled the warlords together under his leadership. They drove out marauding barbarians and settled down into a well ordered life under his rulership. The kingdom had many years of peace under his wise guidance.

Let us be clear that the leadership of the Mature Ruler is not one imposed by force. Rather it's won by the ability the Mature Ruler has in understanding the problems and outlooks of those around him, and in his ability to generate solutions for those problems.

We have defined the Mature Ruler as someone who's independent of outside considerations or influences. But as an example, I draw your attention to George Bailey of *It's a Wonderful Life*. As we see George's life unfold, time after time he sets aside his own plans and desires in order to serve the Bailey Building and Loan, and his community. Is this independence?

But look closer. In one of the earliest episodes we see of George, he thinks for himself and doesn't automatically do what the grown-ups tell him to do. This particular incident concerns the pharmacist Mr. Gower for whom George works.

The boy sees the telegram informing Mr. Gower that his son has died. So George knows Mr. Gower is upset. He observes that Mr. Gower, in his emotional turmoil, has mistakenly included a poisonous ingredient in some medicine for an ailing child. By asserting himself, George prevents Gower's mistake from having a tragic effect.

At each point as the story moves forward, when the continuance of the Bailey Building and Loan lays a claim on George, *he* makes the choice to stay with it, even though the people around him expect him to leave – to go to college, to go on his honeymoon.

If the Mature Ruler is known by his relationships, then it's very easy to see in this film that George and not Mr. Potter is that Ruler. The ending demonstrates the power of George's relationships, whereas elsewhere in the film it's said of Potter that he hates everyone.

As for the wounded aspect of the Mature Ruler, every dream George gives up creates a wound. But let us remember that wounds do not have to be crippling or never-healing. The experience of being wounded may not be forgotten, as George never forgets his lost dream of travel and adventure. But the wound can be healed, as Mary's love for George and his for her provides that healing. George holds in his hands the lives of many of the people of Bedford Falls and by his decisions he can improve or ruin their futures. And *that* is the power of a Ruler.

When you tell stories involving a Mature Ruler, these are the things that undergird his nature. He has insight into the needs of those around him, seeing solutions they do not. His leadership springs from his understanding of other people. This can be a powerful element in a tale, as long as the storyteller understands what makes the Mature Ruler work. After all, you don't want a character intended to be wise and discerning to come across as weak and foolish.

What more can a man look for in his life? What further Stage can we expect to find in the life Journey of a Male?

The Sage

Don't think of the Sage as some senile oldster planted in a rocking chair, who adds very little to the life around him. No, the Sage is a man who has reached a point where he has gained a sense of fulfillment. He has also gained a sense of connectedness with all of life. His participation in society shows up more in his willingness to share with others the wisdom of his experience than in any impulse to order the comings and goings of others. It's the Sage who guides others in maintaining and reconciling their relationships, by providing advice and counsel. And yes, we do have an expectation that a Sage will be an *older* man. Society expects younger men to be filling the jobs of Warriors and Rulers. And besides, it takes years to acquire the wisdom and insight expected of a Sage.

Where can we look for a legendary model of this wisdom-holder? Why, to Solomon, of course.

The Sage – Solomon. According to the legend, God gave Solomon the choice of anything he wanted. And although this son of King David was young and just newly come to his throne, Solomon asked for wisdom. This pleased God very much and so he gave Solomon a lot of it. Solomon's wisdom gave him the ability to find solutions that others couldn't even imagine when faced with problems. He became famous for his talent for discernment and judgment, which he used to benefit his people. In fact, he became so famous that the Queen of Sheba came visiting to find out if he was for real.

You will notice that the mythic model for the Sage was not an *old* man. Because I want us all to remember just how flexible these things can be. What's important is that we understand the *nature* of the motif.

Sages very easily fill the roles of Mentors in stories. After all, they are the ones with the knowledge to help the Hero.

In *Star Wars*, you could say that Obi-Wan's position as a Sage is debatable. Luke calls Ben a "strange old hermit." Uncle Owen says "that wizard's just a crazy old man." Whose evaluation are we supposed to trust? Neither of them is quite on the mark. However, remember that a Sage is someone who has achieved a sense of being connected to all of life. Ben demonstrates his "at-oneness" with the universe when he feels the destruction of Alderaan. The Sage aspect of his persona shows up in his willingness to extend the benefit of his wisdom and experience to Han. It's Obi-Wan, after all, who identifies the single fighter they encounter in Alderaan space as an Imperial fighter and the small moon that they see as a space station.

While Obi-Wan demonstrates the Sage as something of a Hermit (something we'll examine more closely later), we can also find a Sage fulfilling a more public role. In *Excalibur*, Merlin figures as a Sage in his at-oneness with the land. In his "connection to all" he sees the possibility for good in a child of Uther and Igrayne. But although he seems a bit like a Hermit at times, Merlin also remains at Arthur's court, available to anyone who chooses to take advantage of his wisdom.

As I observed, Sages very easily can play the part of Mentors in stories. But you might want to consider other possibilities for using the Sage. Remember, the strengths of this Stage are the knowledge gained from experience and the man's connectedness to the world around him.

Do all Sages have to be old? Not really. A storyteller should explore *all* possibilities. But remember what the qualities are that place a character in this Stage and not some other one.

These then are the Stages of a Male's Journey through life. He progresses from the self-centeredness of the Noble Savage, through the Stages of Phallic Man, Warrior, Wounded Man and Mature Ruler, all the while growing toward the community-mindedness of the Sage. We have looked at these aspects primarily in their positive light. But by stretching the imagination, a storyteller can conceive of what the negative image of a particular stage might look like. The key is to have a definition of something, in order to say "what if a character were *not* this way?"

But now that we have run through the Stages of the Male, let us consider those of his counterpart.

FEMALE

The six Stages in a Female's life are the Flower Child, the Young Woman, the Nurturer, the Wounded Woman, the Relational Woman, and the Woman of Strength.

The Flower Child

Like her Male counterpart, the Noble Savage, the Flower Child, at the beginning of her life's Journey, is self-centered and driven by her own emotions. She's not socialized, not really conscious of the community around her except as it affects her. Her own pleasures and needs occupy most of her attention. She can be open and honest and innocent, simply because she has not experienced much of life at all.

Mythically, Persephone gives us a model for this Stage.

Flower Child – Persephone. Persephone, the daughter of Demeter, was so lovely that even as a child everyone who saw her loved her. Fittingly, for the child of an agriculture goddess, she loved gathering flowers. For all her loveliness, she had not reached the point in her life where she was looking for relationships beyond the one with her mother. Indeed, when Hades snatched her, Persephone pined to return to her mother.

We expect to see this Stage manifested in the young. We don't expect to see it as the Female gets older. And yet, there are some interesting possibilities for stories in this Stage.

Consider the film *Hope Floats* (1998)[15]. The young daughter Bernice lives at an elemental level. The events in her life are in *her* life. She cannot see beyond how things touch her life. This is appropriate for a child. She does not understand the true nature of the adult relationships around her. She only sees them in how they affect herself.

As a contrast, we are a bit surprised to see that Bernice's mother Birdee also demonstrates traits of the Flower Child. However, in Birdee's case it's more because she has to go back to her beginnings and relearn some crucial things. When Birdee's marriage to Bill Pruitt falls apart, Birdee returns to her hometown and moves in with her own mother. In her hurt, Birdee reverts to the self-centered emotionalism of the Flower Child. Before she can once more move forward with her life, Birdee has to become reacquainted with her own wants, needs and desires. Once she does that she can engage in stronger, more secure relationships.

As you can see by *Hope Floats*, although the Flower Child Stage is typical of childhood, placing an adult in that Stage can be interesting. But be sure that you, the storyteller, know the reasons why the adult Female may have either remained stuck in that Stage or may have reverted to it. After all, the audience has a certain expectation that characters are moving toward growing up and gaining a greater maturity in their relationships.

And as the Flower Child begins focusing on relationships with others, the Female crosses into the next Stage, that of the Young Woman.

The Young Woman

The Female enters the Stage of the Young Woman as she becomes aware of her effect on others. As she grows conscious of the power of her beauty and how it can draw relationships to her, she also becomes conscious of the fact that she lives in a community that does not necessarily revolve around herself. While she enjoys the love and attention that comes to her, she also becomes aware of the relationships of other people.

There's no better mythic model of this Stage than Aphrodite.

The Young Woman – Aphrodite. As the Greek goddess of love, Aphrodite was very much into the activity of promoting amorous relationships between people. She was, herself, the most beautiful of the goddesses and she liked to indulge in love affairs.

You might imagine that the goddess of love ought to represent a more mature Stage of life. But, even though love and the pleasure of being loved can come to someone at any point in her life, it's the youthful joy in the experience that best represents it.

In film, *Clueless* perfectly captures this. From its beginning, the film shows us a portrait of a character crossing the threshold from the Flower Child Stage into that of the Young Woman. Our first encounter with Cher is of her primping for the day. Although her own pleasure in her looks is of some importance to her, so too is the way others will regard her appearance.

Cher's aspect as a Flower Child shows up in her disregard for things around her, like flower pots on curbs and stop signs. She's self-centered and wrapped up in her own feelings. She even displays scorn for her relationship with Josh at the beginning.

However, as the story progresses, her interactions with Josh prompt Cher to start looking outside herself, to begin to actually pay attention to the people around her. When she finds herself no longer the center of attention, she starts to consider just what makes a better person (and, by implication, someone people are drawn to). With these changes, Cher grows in her identity as a Young Woman. She no longer takes for granted that she *will* be the center of attention. Instead, she becomes more concerned about *how* people – and in particular, Josh – regard her.

During the course of the film, we watch as Cher transforms from the self-involved Flower Child to a Young Woman just becoming conscious of the excitement and pleasure of relationships, and of her own powers in attracting and building a romantic relationship.

The transformation of a character from Flower Child to Young Woman is just one story possibility. Of course, many stories have been written featuring a Young Woman in the fullness of this Stage. Love, sexual attraction and the beginning of intense relationships are the usual story-ground for the Young Woman. However, there's no rule against your trying to find other arenas and other types of stories for her.

In the meantime, let us move onward to the next Stage in a Female's Journey.

The Nurturer

This Stage in a Female's life obviously reflects a basic biological function. Females give birth to children and provide the first nourishment to the infant. Yet, even if a woman doesn't bear children, there are aspects of this Stage which become reflected in a woman's life. For one of the consequences of this Stage is that the initial relationships that the Young Woman began in part in her own self-interest now grow outward to others around her. The impulse to provide care, nurturing and comfort to others characterizes a woman in this Stage.

As always in any motif, we look primarily at the positive ideal. Of course, negative examples exist. As storytellers, we would be foolish not to recognize the possibilities lying in the counter image. But the clearest way of showing the negative is to know the nature of the positive example.

That said, let us consider some mythic examples of the Nurturer.

The Nurturer – Demeter and Ceres. Demeter was the Greek goddess of nature and agriculture. An Earth Mother type, in fact. We've already seen how determined she was when her daughter was snatched. She left everything, including her primary job of helping plants grow, to search for her child. And she intimidated even Zeus with her determination. Ceres, the Roman version of Demeter, also specializes in encouraging the growth of food stuffs. After all, her name gave us the word cereal.

We are certainly used to the appearance of mothers in stories. For at rock bottom, that's what a Nurturer is. And we will look more closely at Mother Figures in the **PARENTS** Section. Yet the aspect of Nurturer can have a broader domain than basic parental duties, even though most Nurturers appear as a woman exercising the duties of a Mother.

When the film *Baby Boom* (1987)[16] begins, we see J.C. Wiatt as a very successful business woman. She revels in her nickname the Tiger Lady. She talks fast and in abbreviations. She moves through her world unencumbered by formal attachments. When offered the chance at becoming a partner in the firm, she speedily dismisses her boss's concern that trivial things like marriage and family would ever distract her. She says, almost proudly, that she's "not really great with living things." If anything, at the beginning of the story, J.C. could be called an anti-Nurturer.

Of course, since J.C. starts out as the least likely example of a nurturing female, in good storytelling fashion she's immediately confronted with being the sole guardian and provider for a baby girl, the orphaned child of a distant cousin. She tries to get out of the job, but can't bear to leave baby Elizabeth with the unfeeling prospective adoptive parents. Her role as a Nurturer begins to awaken. She struggles to learn how to take care of the child. And as she becomes more involved with the process, business passes her by and she's squeezed out of a major deal she had set up. She leaves the job and New York City, and moves to a farm in Vermont.

J.C.'s nurturing ability continues to grow in the new location. Life in the country, with maintaining an old farmhouse, turns out to be more expensive and more work than she had anticipated. Out of boredom, she turns her excess apples into applesauce (from a recipe she created for Elizabeth). Out of financial necessity, she starts selling the applesauce. Her business sense kicks back in and she builds a business making gourmet baby food. With this extension from her immediate nurturing of Elizabeth, she moves outward to nurturing others. First off, she's making *baby food*. That's an obvious nurturing. But beyond that, as the business grows, she gains employees. As the business moves beyond applesauce, her company helps the local economy, by becoming a purchaser of the local farm goods. All of these can be seen as nurturing functions. By the end of the film, J.C. has become content with this new life. She passes on the big deal of selling her company to a large corporation. Not only has she learned to nurture others, she has learned what nourishes herself.

Is there more to a Female's life than what we have seen so far? Certainly. Although most stories don't look beyond these initial Stages, there remains plenty of unmined material to consider.

The Wounded Woman

As with the Male, so too with the Female can we expect to find a Stage of wounding in a woman's life. The causes of wounding can be as varied for a woman as they are for a man. Unmet needs, broken relationships, unexpected tragic events can all leave deep wounds in a woman. An important aspect in dealing with this woundedness is that the woman take ownership of her injury. Acknowledging the hurt can lead to healing, while denying it or holding on to it can lead to even greater pain. Going through the Wounded Stage gives a character a chance to either withdraw from society, losing herself in her pain and hurt, or to reach outward toward healing and reintegration with society.

Perhaps the most dramatic mythic example of this Stage is that of Medea.

The Wounded Woman – Medea. Medea, a young woman who possessed considerable magical skill, fell for the adventurer Jason. For love of Jason, Medea betrayed her father and helped Jason steal the Golden Fleece. Pursued by her father, she then killed her own brother and cut him into pieces, knowing her father would stop to pick up his dismembered son. Thus, Jason and Medea got clean away. The lovers were happy together for enough time to become parents to two young sons. However there must have been something alarming about the formidable Medea, for Jason eventually abandoned her. Officially for political reasons, but also probably because she was a younger, prettier model, Jason married the princess Glauca. Medea didn't take this well. She sent Glauca a beautiful dress the girl was certain to wear at her wedding. The dress was poisoned and killed the girl in front of everyone at the ceremony. In the meantime, Medea had killed her children by Jason and had fled.

As you can see, a Wounded Woman who can't find healing can be a terrible thing to encounter. The impulse to destroy and to bring others into the realm of pain she lives with can rip to shreds all sorts of relationships around her. Unless the Female can absorb the experience of being injured, find healing and move beyond the boundaries of pain, she will become like a black hole in space, pulling all into her nothingness and destroying them.

Sarah Connor in *Terminator 2: Judgment Day* shows us a Wounded Woman in very real danger of becoming like Medea. When we first see her in the film, she's working out in her cell in the hospital for the criminally insane. Her doctor believes she suffers from dangerous delusions, and her son considers her "a total loser." She's denied the thing she most wants, to see her son. She has been very wounded by her concern for her son's future, a future she has reason to believe will be very dangerous. She has the unmet needs, the broken relationships and the unexpected tragic events (John's father, whom she loved, was killed before the boy was born) that define the Wounded Woman.

When she escapes with the help of her son and the Terminator, she withdraws into herself, seemingly unresponsive to her son's attempts to reach out to her. Her deep woundedness drives her anger and makes her almost as deadly as the T-1000 sent to kill her son. If she stayed in that attitude for long, she would end up driving John away from herself. As it is, she almost succeeds in that when she goes to kill Miles Dyson. Dyson is the programmer who designs the future computer system that is Sarah's ultimate enemy. But the sight of Dyson and his family cowering before her fury breaks through her defenses. She at last lets herself *feel* her wounds. And when she realizes her son has followed her to stop her from killing, she finally says, "I love you, John. I always have." From this point on, Sarah becomes a partner with others in trying to solve the problems coming at them.

A different handling of a Wounded Woman can be found in the character of Reggie Love in the film *The Client*. As a divorced woman, Reggie carries the wound of an ended marriage and the loss of custody of her children. Signs of the wound show when Dianne Sway asks Reggie if she has kids: Reggie avoids the question. She bristles when Roy Foltrigg mentions that she has been treated for drug and alcohol abuse. Even though she has gotten past that particular experience, everything that contributed to it still affects her.

An interesting aspect of the use of woundedness in this film comes when Reggie reveals to Mark Sway the details behind her divorce, drinking and drug abuse. Her vulnerability and hurt win over the young client. By showing Mark her injury, she gains his trust. In this story, woundedness actually becomes an asset for the character.

As you can see by these examples, many story possibilities lie within the character of the Wounded Woman. Whether you want your story to be at Medea's end of the spectrum, running rampant with destruction, or at Reggie's end, using the acceptance of the wounds as a strength, the richness a wounded past can bring to a character should not be overlooked.

That said, let us continue onward to the last two aspects of the Female's Journey through life, first with the Relational Woman.

The Relational Woman

The Relational Woman is one who has reached a Stage of being connected with the people around her. And not simply because she's frequently found in family relationships. Rather, all her life experiences to this point have brought her to the realization that all life is connected. Her abilities in forming relationships have gained ascendency, as she also has gained skills in encouraging others in their lives. She does, however, have to learn how to balance the outward activities of relationships with the inward need to be true to herself as an individual. The positive, or ideal, form of this Stage is *not* a woman who makes herself into nothing in order to serve the needs of others. Rather, as she becomes more herself, she grows in her ability to help others. The negative side of this can be that the woman allows other people to define who she is, or that she so devotes herself to others' needs she has no sense of herself.

For a long time, storytellers have short-changed the possibilities in the Stages of a Female's life. Yet, when we start to look beyond the prospect of female characters being either love objects or mothers, we find that there can be as much variety in stories about women as there are in stories about men.

If we want a mythic model for this Stage, Demeter again can help us.

The Relational Woman – Demeter. Among other things, Demeter was a goddess of civilization. And of course, civilization is founded on the ability of humans to relate to each other in an ordered fashion. As a goddess of agriculture, she taught the wild nomadic mortals how to plant and reap. With the settled life, tied to one locale by their crops, the mortals also learned to build lasting relationships with each other.

Demeter, of course, demonstrates this Stage on the grandest scale, pulling people together into civilization. But let's consider a few films for examples of the Relational Woman at work in a smaller perspective.

In *His Girl Friday*, when Hildy arrives at Walter's office, she's attempting to establish a new context for her life. Up to this point, her life had been defined as Walter's reporter/editor and wife. When that apparently did not work out, she found a new definition in being the prospective wife of insurance-salesman Bruce. But, she has been finding her identity in the context of those around her. This plays to her weaker side, in that she is *letting* the others define her, rather than *finding* herself in the nature of her interactions with others. But gradually, her nature as a reporter, and her ability to draw a story out of people, asserts itself. It's her relational skills which enable her to pull a deeper story out of the prisoner, Earl, than any other reporter got.

Hildy is a woman finding her way into a new Stage of life. Another variation on that appears in *Erin Brockovich* (2000)[17]. The character of Erin in the film can be prickly and uncompromising. For instance, she likes the way she dresses and sees no reason to change simply to make *other* people comfortable or to fulfill their expectations of what she should be like. She also shows many of the traits we would expect to find in an Wounded Woman. Yet, she's also an excellent example of a Relational Woman. In the particular situation the film shows us, Erin succeeds because of her relationships with the people she meets. The townspeople of Hinkley, especially Donna Jensen, respond to her and follow her lead because she gives them each respect, and because she cares about them personally, not just about "the cause." This relational connection is so powerful that Erin succeeds in getting *all* of the plaintiffs in their case to agree to the binding arbitration.

Just as Erin moves from Wounded to Relational Woman, many other stories deal with this transformation. It can be a rich ground for growing stories.

The First Wives Club (1996)[18] also shows us three characters in that transition from being Wounded Women to being Relational Women. As friends in college, Elise, Brenda and Annie had been very close. But time and their lives have taken them away from each other. When the story begins, they each are also in the process of being divorced – definitely, they are wounded. The story asks the question of how they will respond to this wounding.

At first they have to cope with the fact that in general, society has a limited perception of what a woman can be and do. As Elise, the actress, says, "There are only three ages for women in Hollywood. Babe, District Attorney, and Driving Miss Daisy." Even so, the trio find a way to move beyond their woundedness. As they find a way to exact some judgment and justice from their ex-husbands, they expand their outlook to the possibilities in helping other women.

In re-establishing their friendship, the women move from injured isolation into relational strength. Their mutual support allows each to step into new territory. It requires work and honesty between them to maintain the relationships, but in the end, they achieve their goals.

Finding strength through companionship and relationships isn't the end of a Woman's Journey, however. There remains one Stage that can bring us more storytelling material.

The Woman of Strength

Similar to the Sage Stage in the Masculine Journey, the Stage of the Woman of Strength exemplifies maturity and wisdom in the growth of a female character. There's power in a Female who has gained this Stage, for she has mastered many skills. She continues to maintain a connection to the society around her, frequently addressing the needs of the community. But unlike the Relational Woman, her strength does not begin with her relationships. Rather it springs from deep inside herself. Thus, even though she may be an active participant in the society around her, she has no need to lean on anyone.

Mythically, Penelope exhibits the characteristics of the Woman of Strength.

Woman of Strength – Penelope. Penelope was the wife of the wandering Odysseus. In spite of having a slew of unwanted suitors hanging around her palace, Penelope spent the better part of twenty years ruling the island of Ithaca and raising her son all by herself. She held off the suitors for several years with a clever trick. She told them she couldn't consider choosing a new husband until she had finished weaving a funeral shroud for her father-in-law. So she spent a portion of the day weaving, and a portion of the night taking out the weaving. Eventually, the trick was found out, but by that time, Odysseus had returned. But even then, her cautious nature devised a test to make sure this raggedy arrival was indeed her husband and not an imposter. For nearly twenty years she had kept all men out of her bedchamber. So, to test this man claiming to be the returned Odysseus, she told him he could move their bed outside the room for the night. Odysseus exploded furiously, demanding to know who had messed with his bed. Because, you see, he had built the bed into a large tree that grew inside the house – and the bed could not be moved at all. By this clever test, Penelope made certain she'd got the right man back.

Cleverness, endurance, patience, wisdom. All these are qualities we can find in a Woman of Strength. How else can we identify her in a story?

Look back at *His Girl Friday*. Hildy moves from being just a Relational Woman to being a Woman of Strength in the course of the film. While all the other reporters in the prison press room know that Hildy is a reporter through and through, Hildy has to discover this in herself. As she does so, her awareness of the greater social implications of the news story grows. She has it in her power not only to save a man's life but also to more thoroughly expose official corruption. And she means to use that power.

(The film does date itself at the very end with Hildy's weepy uncertainty as to whether Walter really will choose to remarry her. It was, after all, 1940. A more recent film would not quite so undercut Hildy's discovery of her own strengths by giving her such an emotionally dependant finish. Certainly, a romantic partnership is a good thing, but these days we tend to find extreme emotional dependence between adults distasteful.)

However, let's not make the mistake of thinking that the Woman of Strength has things easy. We've seen before that a character can combine aspects of two different Stages. Reggie Love in *The Client* is another of those who present such a combination. In addition to showing aspects of the Wounded Woman, Reggie demonstrates a character who grows in the Woman of Strength nature. The way other characters treat her also show the difficulties a Woman of Strength can face. At her first appearance in the story, Mark mistakes her for a secretary. When he learns that *she* is the lawyer, he resists the idea that she could be the right one for him. But she does convince him.

Mark isn't the only person to discount Reggie's ability and focus as a lawyer. When Reggie walks into the first meeting with the Federal attorneys (all men), Roy Foltrigg makes an attempt to distract her with blatant flattery: "You're going to have to forgive us, Miz Love. How could anyone mistake you for a lawyer?" Reggie ignores the ploy and plows forward, pinning the male lawyers for their various legal infractions in trying to intimidate Mark into giving them the information they want. Even when Roy puts Reggie at a disadvantage by knowing more about Mark's movements than she did, she holds her ground – she challenges the means by which Mark's fingerprints and blood type were obtained.

At the later point in the story when the Federal attorneys force a hearing before a judge in order to compel Mark to tell them what they want to know, Roy again tries to distract Reggie with flattery. Reggie attempts to delay any forced revelation from Mark by requesting that the hearing be moved from Memphis to New Orleans. Roy, on the other hand, wants *no* delay. The exchanges between them escalate, and then Roy suddenly throws out the comment, "That's a pretty suit, *cher*." Reggie doesn't miss a beat with her reply: "Drop dead, Roy." She has become more certain of her ability to cope and stand her ground. Appeals to vanity that might succeed in distracting a Young Woman can be easily deflected by a Woman of Strength who can remain focused on her purpose. And indeed, Reggie becomes so settled into the aspect of the Woman of Strength that she can face down the killer and then come out victorious in one last battle with Roy.

Now, although we would usually expect a Woman of Strength to be an older woman, let us remember that keyword I have mentioned several times: *flexibility.* As storytellers, we can enrich our tales by looking beyond the usual expectations.

As an example, consider the character of FBI Special Agent Dana Scully in the television series *The X-Files*.[19] She gives us an excellent portrait of the Woman of Strength, especially since it does not carry the impression that only old women could be found in this Stage. Scully's competence and clarity are evident from the beginning of the series.

In the Pilot episode, Scully has been an FBI agent for 2 years. Her competence appears early, for she's well informed about the reputations of her colleagues, particularly that of Fox Mulder. When she's told to work with Mulder and write reports on the validity of his work, she flat out asks if she is to debunk his work. The official response that she "make the proper scientific analysis" suits her temperament of seeking the truth of things.

Challenges to her integrity do not shake Scully. When the distrustful Mulder challenges her purpose in working with him, she declares, "I'm here to solve this case, Mulder. I want the truth!" Unfortunately, things do not go well for the investigators. Witnesses are killed or uncommunicative, their evidence and notes are destroyed by fire. When Scully makes her report on this case, Section Chief Blevins tells her that her report isn't supported scientifically. Rather than cower before this official disapproval, Scully pulls out of her pocket the one piece of physical evidence left, a strange device she had found in the nasal cavity of a corpse. In spite of the opposition faced, Scully had remained focused on her quest for scientific truth.

In a later episode, "Clyde Bruckman's Final Repose," it's Scully's ability to keep focused on plain essential facts that leads to the solution of the case. In the swirl of distracting events revolving around psychic phenomena and fortune-tellers, Scully continues to note and subconsciously compile factual data. One of the strengths of this particular script is that it does not detail the mechanism of detection, although it very carefully represents the elements. One factor is that of the tendency of some serial killers to observe the official investigation of their crimes. Thus, in this case, when a victim's body is found, Scully turns and scans the faces in the watching crowd. Present each time (except for the last) is the face of the man the audience knows to be the killer. Other small details of ordinary physical evidence combine in Scully's mind, and she recognizes their connection to the face that's missing. She *apparently* makes a leap of intuition, but her recognition of the killer is actually solidly grounded in plain facts. Once she pulls those facts together, she proceeds with dispatch and a clear decisive manner. The unusual circumstances in this story do not distract Scully from her strengths, her ability at rational, scientific deduction.

In the episode "Chinga," Scully's strength is demonstrated in an alternate fashion. In this case, her strength lies in her willingness to consider supernatural phenomena as causing the strange events she encounters. Although she continues to eliminate the ordinary possibilities with her usual rational focus, she also reviews the supernatural possibilities with a clear-eyed consideration. Unlike the locals who respond fearfully, with alarm, to the supernatural, Scully, in accepting it as a legitimate possibility, evaluates the potential danger and narrows the hunt down to the correct target. Again, it's her focus and surety in herself which brings her through this case.

Scully's unusual only because women of her relative youth are rarely presented as Women of Strength. Yet her intellect and wisdom about human nature support her in her career as a scientific investigator. Additionally, Scully has frequently been presented as emotionally vulnerable, in that her experiences *do* affect her personally. However, and I cannot stress this too much, Scully's vulnerability is never presented as a weakness. Too often, whether the character is Male or Female, the correlation is made that emotional vulnerability equals weakness of character. But Scully, with her character strength, demonstrates that "vulnerability equals weakness" need not be an inevitable choice in storytelling. Instead, she solidly exemplifies the attraction an emotionally open (that is, vulnerable, rather than enclosed in a shell) character can have for an audience, especially when also shown as being strong in other areas.

Each of these characters shows us the variety of ways a Woman of Strength can be presented in a story. Your character may be just finding her way into this Stage of life, or she may already be a Woman of Strength as the story begins. If nothing else, you should now be aware that the stages in a Female's life give you more options than "Babe, District Attorney and Driving Miss Daisy."

MUSINGS

You want to make a splash with your characters. You want to drench the audience with a strong sense of who the Hero is as a person, and the first thing the audience will notice is whether the Hero is Male or Female. You can sprinkle demonstrations of the nature of your Hero's character throughout the story, but it helps knowing where your Hero *is* on his or her Journey before you begin.

Think about it:

*   Is your Hero Male or Female? Is that an absolute necessity for the story? What if the character were of the opposite sex?

*   Of your Male characters, do you know what Stage each one is at?

*   Of your Female characters, do you know what Stage each one of them is at?

*   Is your Hero completely in one Stage, or does he or she combine elements of two Stages?

*   Warriors are traditionally Male and Nurturers are traditionally Female: if you have one or the other of these in your story, have you considered reversing the traditional assignments?

*   Whichever Stage your character is in, what does the negative version of that look like? Would it be useful to introduce the negative possibilities into your story?

*   Is your character stuck in one Stage when he or she should be moving on to the next one? What keeps your character from moving forward? What kind of transformation is needed to help the character move forward to a new Stage?

*   If your Hero is wounded, how is he or she responding to the wound? What does the Hero need to heal the wound? Does the Hero deal positively or negatively with being wounded?

SECTION TWO – NEEDS

Before we move on to the various archetypes the characters can appear as, let's look at another element of a character's context. I'm talking about the basic *Need* of the character. (Capitalizing a word helps us focus on it). Now, by basic Need I don't mean what a *character* thinks he or she needs. Rather, I mean an internal Need that drives the character.

In the 1950s, psychologist Abraham Maslow tried to synthesize a large body of research on human motivation into a useful system.[1] Maslow felt there was a progress up a pyramid of needs from basic survival needs toward more personal ones. Although most research since then indicates Maslow's theory was too simplistic, and that people do not necessarily progress up the pyramid in any particular sequence, for *storytellers*, Maslow's hierarchy can be a useful tool.

When the storyteller understands the nature of the Hero's core Need, it can be a great help in shaping the tale. But many storytellers find themselves stuck when someone asks "What does the character need?" That stickiness usually comes from being much too close to the story. It also comes from not having a useful vocabulary to apply to this question of Need. Well, now you will have such a vocabulary.

First I'll give you the list of Needs, from the most basic (the bottom of the pyramid) to the more specific (the upper reaches of the structure). Then we'll consider each Need in turn, and in depth.

1: Survival

2: Safety and Security

3: Love and Belonging

4: Esteem and Self-respect

5: To Know and Understand

6: Aesthetic

7: Self-Actualization

As you can see, a certain logic does underlie this catalogue of Needs. And as we continue the discussion you'll find how we can look at stories as dealing with these Needs.

1:   Survival

Simple basic survival needs are easy to understand. The need for food and shelter cannot be more basic. Without food, our bodies very quickly give out. Without shelter, the elements of the world (all that weather we met earlier, for instance) can injure and even destroy our bodies. The need to stay alive has driven many stories.

In *The Edge* (1997)[2], the weary-looking Charles Morse enters the story seemingly a man with *no* needs. A billionaire with a beautiful wife, Mickey, he absorbs information like a sponge. Mickey says "Charles knows everything." He denies this, saying that he only retains facts, adding "But putting them to any useful purpose is another matter." Since he apparently needs nothing, he obviously wonders about the usefulness of not only his knowledge, but of himself as well.

However, a string of circumstances lead to a plane crash which strands Charles in the Alaskan wilderness with photographer Robert "Bob" Green. Charles suspects (correctly) that Bob's having an affair with his wife and indeed is plotting to kill him. Suddenly thrust into a situation where all his advantages have been stripped away, Charles, with his reservoir of facts, comes alive. His need to survive has gotten a severe kick in the seat of his pants. He discovers that he does not want to die, that the world around him is fascinating and beautiful (and dangerous), and that all those bits of information he has retained actually can be useful. Bob, on the other hand, has a hard time handling their situation. After one particular setback, he rants at Charles for being able to cope: "But get you in an emergency and you bloom!" That's an accusation from someone who has placed his own comfort above his survival. Because Bob, so thoroughly urbanized, cannot recognize the importance of the Need to survive, he grows dull and doomed. By contrast, as Charles grows more and more competent in basic survival, his sense of life and his desire for a full life also grows.

Charles went back to the basics in this story, learning how to meet the most essential Needs of life. But what follows once those basic Needs are met? What next becomes the focusing drive in a character?

2:   Safety and Security

Once a character knows he has the means to survive, the next thing that may preoccupy him is making sure he can hold onto the food and shelter. A desire to be certain of not just the next meal, but of the next several meals, can fuel a character's passion. Likewise, the sense of having a place of one's own, of being assured of a roof over the head, can root a tale, anchoring the story in whatever emotional tempests you intend to inflict on the audience. For remember, the audience usually plugs into the emotions of the central character of a story. Wherever the character goes, the audience goes with him.

In *Gone With the Wind* (1939)[3], Scarlett O'Hara presents a subtle portrait of this Need as a driving force. While the story focuses primary attention on Scarlett's fixation on Ashley

Wilkes, underneath that we see time and again Scarlett's insecurity. Her home of Tara serves as the primary symbol of security. When things become most difficult for Scarlett in Atlanta, it is to Tara that she returns. When Melanie Wilkes dies, and Scarlett realizes that she truly loves Rhett and not Ashley, it is to Tara she returns after Rhett leaves her.

Two scenes in particular underscore this Need as the driving force in Scarlett. The first comes when she has been stripped of virtually everything that made her feel safe. She has come home to Tara, to find it devastated. In addition to being responsible for the ailing Melanie and her infant son, Scarlett finds her sisters weak from recent illness, her mother dead and her father broken. Nothing seems secure in this place. Yet, taking her stand on her home ground, she declares, "As God is my witness, they're not going to lick me.... If I have to lie, steal, cheat or kill. I'll never be hungry again." From that point on, she makes choices that are grounded almost entirely on building security, which she equates with having money. She marries Frank Kennedy, who was sweetly smitten with her sister, in order to save Tara.

When Frank is killed, Scarlett has grown enough in character to regret what she did to him. Even so, after she (finally) marries Rhett, her Need for the assurance of security reasserts itself. In the second scene that openly focuses on this Need of hers, Scarlett has a bad dream. She dreams of being cold and hungry, and she wonders if she will ever dream of being warm and safe. Rhett speculates that she'll stop having the bad dream when she at last feels safe, and he promises to give her that safety. Of course, as we can see in the story's end, the reality is more that she will stop having the bad dream when she stops needing safety and security more than she needs love.

These first two Needs have something of a primordial nature to them. They are also basically situational Needs, dealing with a person's circumstances. The next two are relational Needs, dealing with a person's interaction with others.

3:   *Love and Belonging*

The desire to be loved and to have a sense of belonging represents key parts of human nature. With that sense of belonging also goes the desire to express the love that you feel for others. Although the search to find someone who will love the Hero has driven many a story, don't overlook the story possibilities in a Hero who wants to express the love he or she feels. Likewise, the quest to belong to a community, to a circle of friends or to a family can have rich story potential.

In the film *Notting Hill* (1999)[4], both William Thacker and Anna Scott hunger to love and be loved, and to find a sense of belonging. William, abandoned by his first wife and striving to make a go of a bookstore specializing in travel books, has an emotional gap in his life. Anna, a hugely successful movie star, believes that her career will inevitably cut her off from anything approaching a normal life. Yet William finds it very easy to give himself to Anna. But that openness also makes him very vulnerable to the hurts her professional world can inflict. On Anna's side of the picture, she finds that she longs for the easy acceptance and camaraderie she finds amongst William's friends. And to make sure that the audience believes these two belong together, we are shown that while Anna gives William great delight and joy, he gives her understanding, support and encouragement (such as running lines with her and suggesting she tackle Henry James). In both of their lives, the other areas of Need seem to be quite adequately addressed, allowing the story to focus on the longing for a home place and sheltering love.

4:   *Esteem and Self-Respect*

The Need for Esteem and Self-Respect differs from the Need for Love. Although in some ways to be loved does mean to be esteemed – that is, to be highly regarded and considered of value – the two are not necessarily the same. It is possible for one person to love another, and yet not esteem them very much. And vice versa: not every person you esteem is someone you love. These distinctions can be important coloration in storytelling. Likewise, characters who have a driving Need for Esteem and Self-Respect can bring us some challenging tales.

The film *Thelma & Louise* (1991)[5] shows us two women very much in need of some esteem and self-respect. Louise Sawyer, a short-order waitress, feels the need to get away for a short vacation. And she wants the company of her best friend Thelma Dickinson, a housewife whose husband Darryl treats her more as slave-labor than domestic partner. Louise's relationship with her boyfriend Jimmy frustrates her, especially given his frequent absences. Neither of these women are much esteemed, and they don't seem to have much in their lives that gives them self-respect.

Thelma, in particular, once she is away from her oppressive home atmosphere, rushes to the opposite extreme of wanting to indulge herself in excess. When Thelma's self-indulgence leads to Louise killing a would-be rapist, the two are cast headlong into a situation beyond anything they ever imagined.

Louise, certain that neither of them would be believed about the facts of the shooting, forces the pair into flight. This lack of belief in their own credibility, this lack of self-esteem and self-respect is the core cause of all that follows.

Both women struggle with their fear of not knowing what to do next. They have little background experience or knowledge to draw upon to help them solve their problems. And their continuing expectation of being disbelieved pushes them further and further away from a solution that would allow them to return to society.

In the most off-beat development, Thelma solves the pair's money problems by committing a robbery in the manner of the hitchhiker J.D. During the course of a night's romp, J.D. had described his methods to Thelma. After he absconds with their money, Thelma uses his technique to get some cash. This event thrills her, not just from the adrenaline rush of committing a robbery, but also because, for once, she does something competently, without Darryl's impatient disrespect filling the air.

The fact that these women find a value for themselves by the means of criminal activity adds a bitter undercurrent to the story. Hal Slocum, the cop pursuing them, does give them respect, and indeed would have believed them about the shooting. Yet that esteem proves insufficient by the time he is finally able to speak with Louise. All that the women can see in the prospect of surrender is an even greater confinement of life than they had known before they set out on their adventure. Having no other resources of character to draw upon, Thelma and Louise choose to die free rather than live confined in any fashion.

When this film was released, it was a novelty, in that it featured female characters in what was essentially an action-adventure. That alone makes it notable. But step back and consider the issue at hand. These two characters certainly had a Need for esteem and self-respect. Is this Need met in the story? In a backhanded way, yes. But the story leaves us disquieted because their self-respect is founded on such dubious ground. Being able to commit crimes is not a trait most people want to put on their resume. Especially since the cops are quickly on the trail of the criminals. But there can be no mistaking that this Need is the one that drives this particular story. Throughout the tale, the matter of disrespect exhibited toward women in general, and toward Thelma and Louise in particular, gets highlighted.

I've spent some time on this analysis since the Need for esteem and self-respect can be crucial in some stories. The storyteller ought to understand the distinctions between a need to be loved and a need to be esteemed. A knowledge that oneself is loved does not satisfy (or at least not completely) a need to know that one is valued. A lot of potential story material lies in these distinctions. Think of all the conflict that can arise when a supporting character mistakes the Hero's Need for esteem and self-respect for a Need to feel loved. Resentment and misunderstanding can add fuel to small emotional fires in the story.

These two Needs have been concerned with relational contexts. The remaining ones are what could be called more personal Needs, those Needs that are internal to the person.

5:   *To Know and Understand*

Without a doubt, this Need is the one that usually drives detective and mystery stories. It also drives stories of scientific research and exploration. Because it is personal to the Hero, other characters might not have the same imperative for discovery – which gives you conflict potential. Of course, as the storyteller, you have to create obstacles that impede the search for knowledge. And the best way to do that is to withhold the knowledge.

A prime example of both the Need and obstruction by withholding can be seen in the film *The Maltese Falcon* (1941)[6]. The action is set in motion when a woman hires Sam Spade and Miles Archer to find her sister and a man named Thursby. It's evident the men don't totally believe her story, and they have reason. Archer gets killed following Thursby, plunging Spade into a tangled plot. Not long after that first murder, Thursby gets killed, and the police obviously suspect that Spade is responsible for both deaths. As Sam pushes into his investigation of the mystery, his secretary Effie tells him, "You always think that you know what you're doing. But you're too slick for your own good." In this case, the fact that Sam knows so little becomes his biggest danger.

Sam reconnects with the mystery woman, who admits her real name is Brigid O'Shaughnessy. She asks for his help, but he insists, "I gotta know what it's all about." In spite of his assertion, she does *not* tell him what it's all about. As the story progresses, little bits of information pop up, for each person refuses to tell all that he or she does know. Sam has to persist, for until he unravels the whole plot, he cannot determine who actually killed his partner (and thus prevent the police from arresting *him* for the murders). That basic Need to know feeds his Need to understand what all the deadly maneuvering is actually about.

The Need to know and understand seems pretty straight-forward when we look into it. The next Need seems less obvious.

6: Aesthetic

I suppose we should begin by defining what aesthetics means. A basic definition indicates that aesthetics is the study of the mind and emotions in relation to the sense of beauty. The word is most often connected with the Fine Arts, for the arts are the human expression of our response to beauty. A further definition of aesthetic says it is concerned with pure emotion and sensation as opposed to pure intellectuality. This Need springs from a human sense of being (or desire to be) connected with something greater than the self, especially something of beauty or emotional power.

Inevitably, stories of artists, musicians, writers and dancers plug into this Need. So many things can hinder the fulfillment of the Need (especially a lack in the more basic Needs).

In *White Nights*, Nikolai Rodchenko exemplifies the Aesthetic Need. For Nikolai, dancing is everything. The back story of the film indicates that he had defected from the Soviet Union to America, in order to have greater artistic freedom. Early in the relationship between Nikolai and Raymond, when the men clash over whether or not America is good, Raymond accuses Nikolai of just running away "to where the pay's better." Chaiko tries to persuade Nikolai to rejoin the Kirov (and *not* try to return to the West) by catering to his ego. He says, "If you return, you'll be respected as a cultural hero." He adds a jab by telling Nikolai that the dancer is "only a fad" in the West.

When Nikolai meets his former dance partner (and ex-lover) Galina Ivanova, his personal drive (or need) comes into greater focus. She has toed the Soviet line since Nikolai's defection, and has risen to head the Kirov ballet company. She accuses Nikolai of selfishness in making his defection. He responds by saying, "I was choking here." A later conversation between the pair highlights this issue. Although Galina listens to music of an outlawed folk singer, and studies costume designs for an Evening of Balanchine, Nikolai observes that things have not changed in the Soviet Union. They had been talking about dancing a program of Balanchine choreography eight years before, and while she is *still* dreaming of doing so, he *has* done so. He then makes a key statement which demonstrates this Need: "I'm not a hero. I'm just a dancer. It's all I can do. It's what I live for. But they will never let me dance for myself here."

As we can see in this example, an Aesthetic Need can put the Hero in conflict with the society around him. The last Need can, in effect, put the Hero in conflict with himself.

7: *Self-actualization*

This term comes to us from the language of Psychology. A basic definition (such handy things, dictionaries!) describes it as the achievement of one's full potential through creativity, independence, spontaneity, and a grasp of the real world. But as storytellers, we need to look more closely at this. A Hero in Need of Self-actualization pursues the need regardless of whether or not the actions will be recognized or acknowledged. This takes it beyond the Aesthetic Need. For the Aesthetic Need still has a connection to a social context, since the appreciation of beauty and the communication of that appreciation implies at least one other person around. But Self-actualization is the most internal of the Needs.

If Self-actualization means doing something regardless of whether or not anyone will know of the action, then Susan "Soosh" Teague in *Changing Habits* (1997)[7] fits the bill as a model for this Need. Even though Soosh appears to be someone struggling with the most basic needs, in fact, her greatest need is to express herself. Certainly, Soosh has a number of emotional issues to deal with, but the way she does so is both artistic and solitary. She works to express herself for herself alone. She finds a neglected space in the basement of the convent where she is staying, and she proceeds to paint a mural on its wall, a mural about the key aspects of her life. Soosh does her artwork in private, indeed, in secret. She does not do it for public acknowledgment or praise. She does not do it to gain parental approval. In fact, given that she is very alienated from her painter father, it's interesting that her Need for self-expression – Self-actualization – manifests itself in painting. In any case, Soosh's need to express her own nature drives the rest of the action in the story, from her falling in love with the art supply store owner, Felix, whom she's been stealing supplies from, to reconciling with her father.

Dramatizing a Need for Self-actualization may not be the easiest storytelling choice, but it isn't impossible. But it certainly means that the storyteller must know far more about the Hero's psychological history than the character knows.

MUSINGS

In shaping your story you want to hit the bull's-eye when it comes to identifying the driving Need. When you know what you're aiming at, it is much easier to focus on the target. When you're not sure about your target, your shot might go anywhere. And let's remember that hitting the bull's-eye gets you more points than hitting any of the outer rings does.

Think about it:

*   Do you know what the core Need of your Hero is?

If the Need is not personal to the Hero (as it rarely is for someone like James Bond, for instance), what Need of society does the Hero serve?

*   The core Need in a story is usually reflected in other elements in the tale: Does your story contain that same reflection?

How many ways can the Need be expressed in your story? How many of those ways are useful to your storytelling? Choose the best ones.

*   What sorts of things can thwart or prevent the satisfaction of the Need? Are you using them in the story? Do you have a character who represents that opposition?

Can or do any of your Hero's allies contribute knowingly or unknowingly to that opposition?

*   If the core Need is Survival, what things threaten the Hero's survival? What does your Hero need (in terms of specifics from air to breathe all the way through food and shelter) to survive?

What things can prevent your Hero from gaining what is needed to survive?

*   If the core Need is Safety and Security, what things threaten that? What does the Hero need to acquire that safety and security?

What things can prevent your Hero from achieving the goal of being safe and secure?

*   If the core Need is Love and Belonging, what – and who – stands between your Hero and that goal? What sort of relationship will fulfill this Need?

If Belonging is an important factor, especially Belonging to a group or community, have you made that group appealing to the audience? Remember, the audience identifies with the Hero, so make the relationships appealing and engaging.

And, as always, what character, event, or object has the power to prevent or destroy the fulfillment of this Need?

* If Esteem and Self-respect make up the core Need for your story, have you shown the audience how the Hero lacks these qualities?

In what specific way does your Hero lack this sense of being valued? Have you shown the daily context the Hero lives in which contributes to the Need?

What does the Hero need to learn in order to gain Esteem and Self-respect?

Do the changes in outlook have to be those of the Hero alone, or will other characters have to change as well? If so, how, and what will trigger those changes? Do other elements of the story reflect this core Need?

What can prevent this Need from being fulfilled?

* If the core Need is to Know and Understand, how well have you worked out just what the Ultimate Knowledge for your story will be?

Who or what has the key to the knowledge? Does one person or object have *all* the information, or do several people each have differing bits?

What are the stakes for your Hero if he or she does *not* gain the knowledge? Have you made the stakes clear to the audience?

What can keep your Hero from gaining the Knowledge and Understanding?

* If the core Need is Aesthetic, how is this expressed?

Have you made it clear to the audience how crucial the Need is for your Hero?

What stands in the way of your Hero fulfilling this Need? Is it society, physical constraints, or family and friends around the Hero?

What happens to your Hero if the Need is not fulfilled? Is *that* clear to the audience?

* If Self-actualization is the core Need, have you chosen a dramatic way of presenting the internal quest of your Hero? Have you fully prepared your Hero's history, so that you-the-storyteller know what the Hero does not know about him- or herself?

By what means does your Hero get to know him- or herself? What events, characters or places can provoke revelations for the Hero?

What can prevent your Hero from achieving self-fulfillment?

If you find that multiple Needs are pulling at your story, which one is the most important? Prioritize the Needs, putting the one that *absolutely* must be fulfilled in the story in the number one position.

Use secondary Needs to add color to your story, to add conflict. But do not let them overrun the primary Need.

SECTION THREE – DAY LABORERS

There are seven traditional character Archetypes for stories. They describe functions a character may have in the story, in helping the plot to move along. They can also just be a definition of what the character is as a whole. By that I mean that a character can be a Trickster or a Threshold Guardian at a specific point in the story, or he can be that Archetype throughout the whole of the story. It's your choice to make as the storyteller. As long as you know what you are doing with the Archetype, *and you are doing it deliberately,* no one can tell you that you did it the wrong way. My whole object is to help you understand the nature of the Archetype so that you can make well-informed story choices.

I'll repeat myself about the use of these Archetypes: a character may exhibit the traits of a particular Archetype for a specific instance or purpose in the plot of the story, or may exhibit those traits all the way through. Neither choice is more correct than the other. It all depends on the story you want to tell.

As for the seven Archetypes, they are the Hero, the Mentor, the Threshold Guardian, the Herald, the Shapeshifter, the Shadow and the Trickster.

The Hero

Do we need to discuss the Hero much? Actually, we *do* need to spend a little time on this Archetype, as there are layers of usage for the term.

On the very simplest level of usage, the Hero is the central character of your story. And of course, as I said at the beginning of our adventure, the Hero can be either male or female. Yes, there is the term heroine for application to a female character. But unfortunately, the word has too often been applied to a female sidekick or supporting character of a story. So rather than conjure up such images, let us simply agree that the Hero can be either male or female.

The next level up in usage is of a character in a positive light. This is where the term Anti-Hero comes into play. Generally speaking, if you want the audience to identify with the central character you call him or her the Hero. But if you do not want the audience to identify with the central character, if you want to hold up the character as someone people do *not* want to be like, you call the character an Anti-Hero.

The next step up is the Hero as the Extraordinary Example. In some ways this character is someone the audience *wants* to be like, but has no expectation of ever being called upon to perform in a similar manner. An outgrowth of this definition of the Hero is the comic book Superhero. Nobody expects to have the powers of Superman, for instance. But these Extraordinary Examples and Superheroes exemplify the ultimate ideals we have. They are the extreme description of some particular quality we do admire.

Why should we care about Heroes, at whatever level of meaning we use that term?

The Hero serves as the audience's Avatar in the story. The audience wants to identify with the Hero, to feel the emotions the Hero feels, to learn the same lessons, have the same adventures – all at one step removed. Also, the Hero represents the ideals of the audience. When the Hero behaves well, wisely and with compassion, we in the audience want to believe that we too will be capable of acting in a similar manner. That, after all, is what it means to be a positive role model. Do not underestimate that desire on the audience's part. Nothing can lose an audience faster than to follow the adventures of a Hero they do not find credible. If the character is stupider than he or she ought to be, the storyteller had better have a very solid reason for it. You don't want to have the audience feeling contempt for your characters. Hate the villains, yes. Fear the cruel characters, yes. Dislike or be chilled by your Anti-Heroes, yes. But feel contempt for the Hero? No. That feeling disengages the audience from the story when your whole object should be to have them absorbed in the tale.

But for the rest of our discussions, let us understand that the Hero is your main character, and that you want the audience to identify with the Hero in a positive fashion.

That said, let us move on to considering the other traditional Archetypes.

The Mentor

The Mentor frequently has very specific duties in the plot of your story. We looked at those duties during the Journey motif discussions. But here we want to explore what the Mentor is like *as a character*.

In some ways, the Mentor resembles the Sage in the Stages of the Male. And that's why Mentors frequently appear in stories as older men or women. The acquired knowledge and experience of a Sage can certainly supply the needs of a Mentor assisting a Hero.

Let's remind ourselves of the mythic model of the Mentor – good old Mentor himself.

Mentor – In *The Odyssey*. Mentor was a citizen of Ithaca who had been a friend to Odysseus himself. When Telemachus stood up to the overbearing suitors of his mother, Mentor spoke out in support of the youth. Athena thought so well of both of them that she took on the guise of Mentor in order to give Telemachus good advice and counsel as he went on his adventure.

It's the giving of advice and counsel that defines a character as a Mentor. The Mentor is geared toward shaping and guiding another character, teaching and leading that character into a new (and usually specific) arena of life. And, as always, this can take many forms.

The particular job of Mentor involves initiating the Hero into a new realm of experience. The Mentor's task usually encompasses giving the Hero particular information, rather than guiding the entirety of the Hero's life. Still, there is obviously an overlap between many Mentors and the functions of a Father Figure (which will be dealt with later).

Such an overlap shows up in *Star Wars*. Ben begins mentoring Luke by giving the young man his father's light saber. This opens the prospect of Luke becoming a Jedi. The initiation continues as Ben tells Luke of the history of the end of the Jedi Knights. Once Luke does choose the path of his Mentor, Ben begins to reveal the more supernatural abilities of the Jedi.

Obi-Wan represents the Mentor who instructs the Hero in a specialized area of activity (in this case, that of a Jedi Knight). Broadening that, we can easily see that any teacher also can appear in this role.

Indeed, when a story takes place at a school, we frequently find teachers filling the role of Mentor to young Heroes. *Dead Poets Society* (1989)[1] certainly fits that pattern. In a way, the character of John Keating almost becomes elevated to being the Hero of the story. The young students, particularly Neil Perry and Todd Anderson, become inspired and stimulated by Mr. Keating. Although both youths struggle with conformity to parental expectations, they each in their way respond to the world Keating opens to them.

The course of the story leads inevitably to the crash of Keating's nonconformity with the school's rigid structure and belief that the parents are right. Keating has already shown the boys that at times, the individual cannot defeat the social structures. So his dismissal from his position has, in a way, been foreshadowed for the audience.

The film delicately balances the focus between the boys (the actual central characters of the story) and Keating (when Robin Williams' performance becomes an attention magnet). Although the story is about the changes the students go through because of this teacher, the teacher himself must be shown as equally fascinating to the audience. Thus we have a tale where the Mentor's profile rises considerably higher than that of a merely supporting position.

Although Mentors are significant as teachers, and thus we expect them to be more knowledgeable than the Hero (at the very least), that does not mean they need be perfect. Indeed, if you choose to make your Mentor figure more of a central character, instead of a supporting one, the less perfect they are at their job, the more interesting they are.

"What's that?" you say. "A Mentor as a *central* character? You mean, a Mentor can be a *Hero* of a story?"

Oh, yes. Remember, storytelling is about flexibility. New stories lurk behind everything, and it only requires a "What if–?" to draw them out. *What if a Mentor figure was the Hero of a story?*

In the film version of *My Fair Lady* (1964)[2], we can see that Professor Henry Higgins has some failings both as a Hero and as a Mentor. That this tale falls into the category of Mentor-as-Hero can be seen in the fact that if Higgins did not take on the task of mentoring Eliza, the story would not exist. Thus, Higgins sets about the business of teaching Eliza how to speak well. He also attempts to teach her social graces, but as he has none himself that task falls to the secondary Mentor figure of Colonel Pickering. The progress of the plot shows us an intriguing storytelling twist: when the pupil has grown beyond the need of a Mentor, what happens to the relationship? *My Fair Lady*, in fact, leaves that issue somewhat unresolved, giving the audience something to speculate about.

Higgins, as a teacher, is an obvious example of Mentor-as-Hero. Is it possible to be less obvious, and still have a Mentor figure also serving as the Hero?

Lawrence in *Lawrence of Arabia* presents us with the further possibilities of this option. Ideally, Lawrence is Mentor to Feisal and Ali. Part of his job is to introduce Feisal to modern warfare. Likewise, as Mentor to Ali, he demonstrates the possibilities that lie beyond Arab tradition. Indeed, Ali, after watching Lawrence maneuvering the Arabs and British, begins to study politics. Ali observes to the American reporter about this, "I have a good teacher."

However, after his encounter with the Turkish Bey, Lawrence wants to abandon his role. He is persuaded not to do so. But in returning to the Arabs, Lawrence no longer acts as Mentor but rather as a Hero pursuing his own glory and destiny. In doing this, he begins to alienate the people around him. The result is that when the Arabs reach Damascus, Lawrence cannot sort out the tribal enmities nor the Arabs' lack of technical knowledge. The Arabs give up and leave the city.

Lawrence of Arabia shows us what can happen when a Mentor steps outside his role. That should inspire you with the possibilities that can lie in moving beyond the traditional appearances of an Archetype. A Mentor need not be only an element of the plot, serving only plot necessities. As long as you remember what qualities make up a Mentor figure, you can explore the options of using that figure in any way in the story. Likewise, remember that a Mentor need not be an older man. The Mentor need not be *older* (look at Lawrence, a young man) nor even a *man*. Consider all you options, explore all the possibilities, look for the unexpected.

The Threshold Guardian

The Threshold Guardian quite obviously fits into the plot of a story at stages of testing and/or obstruction. And we meet them quite frequently in everyday life. Company managers who conduct employment interviews, security guards at notable locations, the representative of the Department of Motor Vehicles who conducts your driving test, all these are Guardians of various Thresholds.

You will recall from our earlier discussion just what a threshold is. Concerning entrance to the threshing floor during the threshing, you wouldn't want someone blindly or carelessly stepping out on the grain. But on a more basic level, you don't want Just Anyone walking into your home. Thus is born the concept of a threshold guardian.

If you think the occupation of Threshold Guardian would be too humble for a mythic figure, you haven't met Janus or Charon or Cerberus.

Threshold Guardian – Janus. Janus, a Roman god, was the god of all doorways. His domain went from important doorways like the public gates of a city through which roads passed all the way down to the smallest entrance into the humblest dwelling. Two of his signs were also tools of his trade: the key to open and close the door, and the stick used by porters to drive away people who had no right to cross the threshold. Pictures of him often have two faces: this is so he could watch over the inside *and* the outside of the house at the same time. You had to pass Janus coming in *and* going out. As a threshold god, Janus was also a god of beginnings, so he became a promoter of all initiative. Each beginning requires stepping out across a threshold, so it makes sense that Janus oversaw them.

As you can see by this description, Janus wasn't particularly threatening – unless you were trying to get into some place you shouldn't be. Keep that in mind when you use a Threshold Guardian in your story. The Guardian doesn't necessarily have to be unsympathetic toward the Hero.

However, if you want a model for a cranky Threshold Guardian, you can find it in Charon.

Threshold Guardian – Charon. One of the children of Night (his father was Erebus, who was Darkness personified), Charon was the ferryman of the Greek Underworld. His was a necessary job, since the only way you could get to the Elysian Fields in the realm of Hades was to cross the rivers Acheron and Styx. If Charon wasn't bribed with a small coin, the cranky old man would drive off the intruder and shove off from the shore. That would leave the spirit of the dead person wandering haplessly on the shores of the netherworld rivers, in a sort of limbo.

Here we have a case of having to appease the Threshold Guardian in some way. And if he isn't satisfied with your offering, you could be stuck in an undesirable place.

Just to round out our examples of Threshold Guardians, let's look at Cerberus.

> **Threshold Guardian – Cerberus.** Cerberus was the Hound of the Underworld, and a pretty frightening creature at that. After all, how would you like to encounter a beast with not one, not two, but *three* vicious, snarling heads? (The noise alone when he *was* upset must have been ear-busting.) His primary job was to keep the living from sneaking into Hades' kingdom. However, there *was* a way to get past him: he could be calmed by music or by offerings of food.

Here's that fearsome Threshold Guardian that we usually expect. It's the huge dog sitting in a yard just the other side of the gate, the great-granddaddy of the dogs who harass mail carriers. And of course, he's considerably less reasonable than either Charon or Janus.

When bringing a Threshold Guardian into your story, consider which sort will be the most interesting. A Threshold Guardian doing his job challenges whoever might want to cross his threshold. Still, a Hero can get past him. Janus can be convinced that you actually do have a right to enter, Charon can be bribed, and even Cerberus has a weakness for music and food. Consider these things when involving this Archetype in your story.

An expanded example of a Threshold Guardian shows up in the film *An Officer and a Gentlemen* (1982)[3]. For Zack Mayo, getting through the officer training course for the Navy flight school is the only way he can see to reach a better life. But to achieve that goal, he has to satisfy the judgment of Sergeant Foley. Foley, thus, is the Threshold Guardian in Zack's quest. As Foley says, "A flight education is worth one million dollars – but *first*, you got to get past *me*." When Foley discovers Zack's hustling stash, he makes it clear that he wants Zack to quit. Zack refuses, and so Foley pushes the young man even harder. When Zack's buddy Sid commits suicide, *then* Zack wants to quit. But by this time, Foley has come to think well of the recruit, so he provokes Zack into a one-on-one fighting match. After Foley finally floors Zack, he then says the recruit can choose to quit if he wants. Foley, as a Threshold Guardian, oversees passages in either direction: he makes it difficult for the recruits to become Qualified for flight training, but he also makes it difficult for a

Qualified candidate (like Zack) to abandon the quest and cross back over the Threshold. In the end, of course, Zack continues onward, but Foley has done his job.

From considering the Archetype who guards thresholds, let's now look at an Archetype who often has to *cross* those Thresholds.

The Herald

A Herald, particularly in medieval courts, was someone who made announcements and carried messages from a ruler. The term thus grew to mean any person or thing who indicates or announces the approach of something (especially something important).

Having said that, we can now consider the Archetype within stories. Since the Herald's function is to bring information and knowledge, you should realize that there are many ways you can use the functions of the Herald. From reporters on TVs or radios in the background to babbling neighbors, many incidental characters in a story can function as Heralds.

We can find mythic models of the Herald in both Norse mythology and in Greek mythology.

Herald – Norse. The god Odin had two ravens, Huginn and Muninn, that he'd send out into the world every day. Each evening they would come back to him, sit on his shoulders and tell him of the things that were moving out there. This was one way Odin gained advance knowledge of events, before anyone else among the gods learned of them.

Odin's ravens primarily brought news to the god. But our Greek example frequently carried messages *from* the gods.

Herald – Greek. One of the chores for the fleet-footed (that's why he has wings on his sandals) Hermes was that of carrying messages for Zeus. One well-known example of this job occurs in *The Odyssey*. The nymph Calypso had been holding that wily wanderer Odysseus at her romantic hideaway from several years. After Athena convinced Zeus that it was time to send Odysseus home, Zeus sent Hermes to tell Calypso to let Odysseus leave. This wasn't exactly happy news for Calypso, since she was rather smitten with Odysseus, but when the message comes from Zeus, what's a girl to do? She let him go.

As we can see by the example from *The Odyssey*, sometimes the news the Herald brings isn't going to be good news.

Whether the information the Herald brings represents the Call to Adventure, or other points in the plot where the Hero needs information, it makes for better storytelling when the Herald is integrated into the story. The more important the information, the more the Herald ought to be connected to the whole of the story. I'm not saying that you could not have a Herald appear out of the blue, drop a bomb of major information, and then disappear forever. In stories, anything ought to be possible. However, if you do use the Herald that way, there should be some major repercussions not just from the information but also from the Herald's appearance.

On the simplest level of being a Herald, R2-D2 in *Star Wars*, like Odin's ravens brings news of the world (and the Rebellion) to Luke and Obi-Wan. R2-D2, of course, has important news, but in terms of using the Archetype, it's an uncomplicated appearance. A more complex use of the Herald appears in *The Hunt for Red October* (1990)[4].

In the film, Jack Ryan starts out in a Herald function. He flies from London to the States (even though he hates flying) to bring some disturbing information to Admiral Greer at the CIA. Jack's information concerns a new Soviet submarine, the *Red October*. In proper fashion for a Herald, Jack carries this information about the approach of something, something very important.

What's unusual in this tale is that not only is Jack the Hero of the story, but also his job as Herald continues beyond the initial presentation of information about the sub. He serves as Herald when he gives a briefing on the submarine to the National Security Advisor, Jeffrey Pelt. After that meeting, Pelt decides that the fleet ships in the Atlantic have to be informed of the progressing events outside the normal communication channels, and he sends Jack (a Herald once again). While at sea, when Jack realizes part of how Captain Ramius plans to conduct his defection, he has to carry this information to the American submarine that has been tracking the *Red October*. Time and again, in addition to his story activities as the Hero, Jack also serves the function of Herald to other important characters in the tale, bringing them crucial information.

The Shapeshifter

The Shapeshifter is a special figure from folklore. Sometimes evil and sometimes not, Shapeshifters often are keepers of special information. But whether the Shapeshifter is a positive or negative player in the story, the Shapeshifter's changeability creates a problem for those around him. As we go through life, we rely on consistency in the people around us. When that consistency disappears, things become unbalanced. Of course, in storytelling, that unbalance can be a very useful thing, for conflict and drama can spring out of it.

Certainly the Shapeshifter's changeability can cause problems. Likewise, getting information *out* of the Shapeshifter challenges the Hero. Usually, this character displays reluctance at giving up his information. So how do you get this information? Well, one way is to take a lesson from our mythic example.

Shapeshifter – Proteus. Proteus is a wise figure in Greek mythology, who could see into the future and who spoke the truth. The problem was that he wouldn't speak oracularly unless he was forced to do so. And even when someone grabbed hold of him to try and make him tell their fortunes, he'd try anything he could to get away. And since Proteus could change his form at will, he wasn't easy to hold on to. He might turn himself into something small and wiggle out of your grasp, or he might turn himself into something ferocious and scare you into letting go. The trick was to hold on until Proteus gave up and talked. By the way, his name gave us the adjective protean meaning something that can take many forms.

So, one way to get the crucial information out of a Shapeshifter is to hold on for dear life until they give in. A second way of dealing with a Shapeshifter shows up in folklore, and that is to become a Shapeshifter as well, matching change for change. Of course, at the heart of this method remains persistent determination, to not give up until the desired information comes out. Thus, the way to fight a Shapeshifter, or to get information from one, is to either become a Shapeshifter or to be absolutely steadfast.

Again, although this Archetype frequently makes a limited appearance in a story, for the purposes of the plot, there are other storytelling options. The 1999 film *Entrapment*[5] broadens the scope of what a storyteller can do with a Shapeshifting figure. The main character, Virginia "Gin" Baker first appears to the audience as an insurance investigator who specializes in high-priced theft cases. She wants to go after an infamous thief, Robert "Mac" MacDougal. However, we soon learn that Gin herself is a thief, and that she wants Mac's help on some big job. So, that's one shape-shift we see her perform.

Yet, just when we've adjusted to the idea of Gin-as-thief, she checks in with her boss, Hector Cruz at the insurance company. In addition to Gin's switching back and forth, we discover that Mac, who seemed to be falling for her, in fact distrusts her enough to listen in on her phone conversation with Hector. And a conversation between Mac and his equipment supplier Thibadeaux hints that Mac has a hidden agenda in working with Gin. So Mac also changes shape in front of our eyes.

Even Thibadeaux is not what he seems. He *appears* to be just Mac's technology supplier. In fact, he's an FBI agent who has been tracking Gin's criminal activities and is using Mac to trap Gin. At the finale of the film, he reveals this official identity to Hector, and these two law and order representatives apparently reel in the two thieves. But Gin's escape has been engineered by Mac – the person who seemed to betray her. Gin's escape prompts Hector's departure. Then we see Mac give Thibadeaux some valuable computer chips, and Thibadeaux lets Mac go. This action leaves the audience wondering just how above board Thibadeaux is – for he has changed *his* shape again.

In the midst of all these Shapeshifters, Hector remains constant. But in this case, with so many transformations happening around him, he's also the one character who doesn't win anything. The others have been too slippery for him. Hector doesn't hold on long enough.

For a pursuer who *does* persist, let's look at the film *Black Widow* (1986)[6]. As the film opens, we watch the Widow, called Catherine at this point come home to the news that her husband has died. The settings tell us that considerable wealth is involved. And when the Widow pours out the brandy in a sink, the audience realizes that she caused her husband's death. That she is a Shapeshifter becomes clear when we see her next: with an entirely different appearance, attitude and name, she's married to a Texas toy mogul.

When the Texas husband dies, an investigator in the Justice Department, Alex Barnes suspects he was killed, and that the death connects to the one that opened the story. While Alex gathers information and pictures and studies them, the Widow studies rare coins and Indians of the Pacific Northwest in order to move in on her next target, William Macauley. The Widow has again changed her appearance, attitude and name, in order to win her way into Macauley's life.

While the Widow constantly hunts for the next man in her life, Alex, surrounded by male co-workers who are interested in her, lives a solitary life. The Widow's appearance changes often, while for most of the film Alex has a consistent casual appearance. They are both hunters, however. And Alex hunts the Widow.

When Macauley dies and his widow – our Widow – disappears, Alex becomes even more determined to catch this killer. Her boss, Bruce, is reluctant to send her out into the field. She has been an office-bound data analyst and is unprepared (in his judgment) for the potential dangers. Alex is so determined to pursue this killer that she quits her job. She has reason to suspect that the Widow has moved to Hawaii and she means to follow the woman there. When Bruce visits her before she leaves for the islands, they discuss the case. Bruce doubts Alex can succeed. Alex says, "You want to catch her, you gotta think like her."

In Hawaii, where the women finally meet, Alex also begins to change how she presents herself. By this time, the Widow knows that she is being pursued for her murders and that Alex is the pursuer. By the end of the film, Alex has, in a way, demonstrated both methods of catching a Shapeshifter: she puts on the changeability to keep up with the Widow, while retaining in her core that unswerving resolution to bring a murderer to justice.

One of the pleasures in being a storyteller is the opportunity to explore the possibilities that Archetypes and motifs present. One aspect of that involves delving into the consequences of a character appearing as an Archetype.

In the film *Braveheart*, Robert the Bruce fills the role of a Shapeshifter. When we first see him, he is playing politics and maneuvering to accommodate the English King Edward's initial plans for Scotland. Indeed, his leprous father advises him to play a two-sided game. As a consequence, the Bruce cannot maintain a steady presentation of himself.

Yet, when Wallace earnestly urges the Bruce to *lead*, Robert begins to consider real, honest leadership (inspired, of course, by what he sees in Wallace). Young Bruce wants to believe Wallace's declaration that he (Bruce) is strong. But as the battle of Falkirk approaches, Bruce heeds his father's urgings to play it safe and side with Edward. Wallace's unchanging nature has a strong hold on Bruce, for after his betrayal of Wallace's forces, Robert wanders the battlefield taking in the price of his own shapeshifting. He returns to his father to proclaim his last change, that he wants to be like Wallace: "I want to *believe* ... as he does." To emphasize the point, he declares, "I will never be on the wrong side again."

Wallace's unyielding determination took hold of the Bruce's heart and brought an end to his shapeshifting. *Braveheart* would have been quite a different story if Wallace had used the other method of dealing with the Shapeshifter. As the storyteller you will need to consider the options for the Hero. The method the Hero chooses to use with the Shapeshifter can have serious implications on how the audience perceives her character. The flexibility of changing shapes along with the primary Shapeshifter has to be weighed against the power of an immovable determination.

The Shadow

Frequently, the term Shadow gets used for the villain of a story, for whatever negative presence might be present in the tale. It can be a useful shorthand, but it also diverts us from other possibilities in the Archetype. For just this reason, I sought some additional Archetypes to expand our creative vocabulary. For what could be called an absolute villain, there is the Corrupter figure, which we'll discuss later. In the meantime, let's throw some light on the Shadow.

In the physical world around us, shadows are cast when light falls on an object. There is a connection between the shadow and the object that casts it. The same holds true for the Shadow Archetype, particularly in psychology. The Shadow represents what a person rejects in him- or herself. Aspects and traits that you reject in yourself become part and parcel of your Shadow. Most of us reject unpleasant and undesirable qualities, which is why Shadow figures do often play villain roles.

Inevitably our mythic model is one of those unpleasant types.

Shadow – Set. The Egyptian god Set is the perpetual adversary of his brother Osiris. Where Osiris is the god of fertile vegetation, Set is the lord of the arid, barren desert. The Egyptians considered Osiris the source of life and blessing. As his Shadow, Set was thus the source of destruction and perversity.

Let's look at some examples of Shadow figures to get a better idea of how to use the Archetype.

In one analysis of *The Silence of the Lambs*, Hannibal Lecter has been called Clarice's Shadow Mentor. The conjunction of the terms indicates the limitations of the short list of Archetypes. Whose Shadow *is* Lecter? Ideally, if the villain of a tale is a Shadow, he should be the *Hero's* Shadow. Of course, given all I have said about the flexibility of all these motifs, I can't claim that rule is chiseled in rock. But the implication in the analysis cited is that Lecter is *Clarice's* Shadow. If that were so, why include the term Mentor? Actually, it's the use of that term which points us to the character casting this shadow into the story. If Lecter is a Shadow, he would have to be Crawford's not Clarice's. While Crawford initiates Clarice into the realm of law and order, Lecter attempts to initiate her into the realm of chaos and disorder.

The film *Wall Street* (1987)[7] offers us a more intriguing use of the Shadow Archetype. Especially when we look beyond automatically equating the Shadow with the villain of the story. Who is the Shadow here, I ask you? Most people would point (automatically) at Gordon Gekko, since he pretty much fits the bill for the Bad Guy. But if he *is* a Shadow, whose shadow is he?

Let's begin with our Hero, young Bud Fox. Ambitious, materialistic, impatient and rather selfish – these are qualities Bud actually *shares* with Gekko. And since the Shadow represents the negative of the figure it relates to, Gekko doesn't actually fit as Bud's negation. In fact, the *real* Shadow to Bud is *not* Gekko, but rather Bud's father, Carl Fox. Carl is content in his work, unimpressed by money, very patient and generous. These are all qualities Bud has pushed away from himself. Likewise, if Gekko is a Shadow of anyone, he is a Shadow of *Carl*, not Bud. For Gekko is everything Carl has rejected.

The truly interesting twist, however, comes near the end of the film. Bud, after realizing that Gekko means to break up the company Carl works for, arranges for Gekkos' rival Sir Larry to outmaneuver Gekko in the purchase of Bluestar Airlines. When Bud meets with Gekko afterwards, having done, in essence, the opposite of what Gekko would do, Gekko says, "You could have been one of the great ones, Buddy. I look at you, I see myself." Of course, Bud has just done what Gekko would reject doing. It seems that by the end of the film, Bud is Gekko's Shadow. This triangular action of casting Shadows makes for some interesting storytelling.

As I said, a Shadow Archetype ought to be related to another figure in the story, usually by displaying qualities that are the opposite of the principal character or in representing things that character has rejected. If your villain doesn't fit this pattern, don't panic. There are other ways of handling villains. Just remember that Shadow figures have a stronger direct connection to the principle character than other Archetypes (in some ways, closer even than the Mentor).

The Trickster

The Trickster has a very rich tradition in the folklore of the world. Tricksters are frequently smaller creatures who find ways of besting larger adversaries. Because of this "underdog defeats big bully" aspect to the Trickster, such characters have become culture heroes in many places. Culture Hero means that a culture views the actions as being highly significant in the formation of their life or society.

Additional aspects of the Trickster Archetype are that the Trickster can be greedy, erotic, imitative. A Trickster can be stupid or pretentious or deceitful. Then there is the matter of his trickery itself. It can take many forms, but a frequent result is that the Trickster himself gets caught in his own web of deceit.

Tricksters can contribute comedy to tales, for they are often the character who deflates over-expanded egos, who pops balloons unexpectedly. That's the positive side of the picture. The negative side is that the Trickster can also frequently be on the side of evil. This could be so because the Trickster is genuinely destructive (or evil) *or* it may be because the Trickster has simply decided to be contrary. In one sense, the only consistent thing you can expect from a Trickster is that he or she will be, well, inconsistent.

Two Tricksters found in mythologies are Maui and Loki.

Trickster – Maui. The Polynesian god Maui was very much a Trickster hero. He had all the qualities of being a rebel, a seducer and iconoclast. Perhaps his contrary behavior began with his entrance into the world. Premature when his mother had a miscarriage, Maui was wrapped up in a lock of his mother's hair and thrown into the sea. So little respected or valued at his birth, he reciprocated by returning disrespect to all order. Even so, he had a certain fondness for humans, as he slowed down the passage of the sun so humans would have more time to do things.

Maui had a rather positive effect in many of his deeds. Loki is another story altogether.

Trickster – Loki. Loki lived among the Norse gods, the Aesir, but he wasn't one of them. In fact, his parents belonged to the race of giants, who were often opposed by the Aesir. He pulled tricks on Thor (who was not noted for quick wits). He would occasionally do some service for the gods. But under it all, he plotted against them. He caused the death of Balder the god of light. See, Balder was the most handsome and best loved of the gods, and everything in the world had promised not to hurt him, so Balder was apparently invulnerable. But Loki, by prying around, discovered that the insignificant mistletoe had not been asked to make this promise. One evening he encouraged the gods to have some fun by throwing things at Balder and watching them fall short. Everyone played, except Balder's blind brother Hoder. To help him

join in the fun, Loki gave Hoder something to throw at Balder —
the mistletoe. To everyone's astonishment (except Loki's), the twig
killed Balder. The gods punished Loki for this, imprisoning him
where a giant snake's venom would drop on his forehead.

Loki's fate demonstrates that matter of the Trickster's pranks rebounding on him. Of course, Loki is an extreme example of the pattern. Yet, you might want to keep this aspect of the Trickster in mind when having your comic sidekick deflate the egos of those around him.

In any case, an excellent example of the Trickster at work shows up in the film *The Mask* (1994)[8]. If ever there was a small creature beset by larger adversaries, Stanley Ipkiss is such a creature. We watch as a female co-worker at the bank takes advantage of Stanley's good nature and cons him out of hard-to-get concert tickets. This incident, falling early in the film quickly defines Stanley's character for the audience. A beautiful customer, Tina chooses to speak with Stanley about opening an account for no other reason than that his desk gives her hidden camera a good line-of-sight into the bank vault. Stanley's mechanics scam him on car repairs. Indeed, the loaner car they give Stanley is the ultimate in automotive lemons: it breaks down on a bridge. In fact, it literally falls apart. On the verge of jumping into the river, Stanley spots what he believes to be a body, but is actually the magical Mask (which later in the film is identified as the Mask of Loki).

Once the Mask falls into Stanley's hands, Trickster aspects take over the story. Tricksters are greedy, and so Stanley as the Mask robs the bank (just before a gang of robbers try to do so). Tricksters demonstrate erotic tendencies, and so does Stanley-Mask at a nightclub, going ga-ga over Tina. Stanley-Mask works a humorous revenge on the greedy mechanics. He also diverts the police who are out to capture him by enticing them into a huge street-dance number. We are given plenty of instances of the playful, deflating aspect of the Trickster at work.

The climax of the film, however, covers the matter of how difficult it is to control a Trickster. Bad Guy Dorian, realizing that the Mask bestows powers on the person wearing it, takes the Mask from Stanley. But (because the film *is* a comedy) all the consequences of the acts of Stanley-Mask end up falling on Dorian-Mask – from all the general chaos down to the bank robbery. It is certainly a version of the tricks of the Trickster (Stanley-Mask) backfiring on the prankster (in the form of Dorian-Mask).

These seven Archetypes serve some basic storytelling needs. They frequently address crucial plot points. And of course they can be used much more extensively than as mere prods to the story's action. However, they also function in very broad strokes, when you may want a tighter focus in describing your characters. Consider the description of Hannibal Lecter as a Shadow Mentor. Can we find some way to fine-tune our outlook? I think so, and I'll introduce them in the next section.

MUSINGS

In stepping up to the tee in presenting your story, you want your stroke to drive the ball all the way down the fairway to the green. Choosing the right clubs for the various situations is part of the game. The club you use from the tee is not likely to be the same club you would use in a sand trap or on the green putting toward the cup. Each club has its use, and the player who uses them most effectively finishes the course with the best score.

Think about it:

* The Day Laborer Archetypes serve functions in the plot. Do you know what functions various characters perform in your story?

* Which character is the Hero in your story?

Before you start laughing at this question, look at your plot again. Which character makes the most choices, drives the story forward? Which character will the audience most connect with?

If you discover that the character you originally thought was the main character is not the one driving the story forward or making the dramatic choices, you need to rethink your approach. Either refocus the story on the character who *is* driving the action, or replot the story to beef up the character *you* want to be the central one.

* Do you have a Mentor in your story?

Does your Hero *need* a Mentor? If not, do not concoct one, for the character would serve no purpose in the story.

If your Hero *does* need a Mentor, what is the special knowledge the Mentor is there to convey? How do you establish your Mentor's credentials for the job?

Does your Hero accept the guidance of the Mentor easily, or does she resent the Mentor as interfering?

* Do you have a Threshold Guardian obstructing the Hero's progress?

What is the threshold the Hero needs to cross? What sorts of things could keep him from crossing it?

What sort of authority does the Guardian have over the Threshold?

What things could appease, placate, or bribe the Guardian?

* Do you need a Herald in your story?

If you do, what information does your Herald bring, and who does he bring it to?

Does your Herald have a one shot function, or does he have ongoing duties?

Can one of your characters function as the Herald for a single point and then go on to do other things in the story?

* Do you have a Shapeshifter in your story?

If you do, does the Shapeshifter have crucial knowledge that the Hero needs?

Is your Shapeshifter a help to your Hero or a hindrance?

Is your Shapeshifter in opposition to the Hero? If so, how will your Hero fight the Shapeshifter? Will the Hero remain resolute and unchanging, or will the Hero become a Shapeshifter as well?

* Do you have a Shadow figure in your story?

What are the qualities your character rejects in herself? In whom do those qualities appear? What is the relationship between the character and the Shadow?

Is the Shadow figure a negative version of the principal character, or a positive version?

Is the Shadow cast by someone other than the Hero? If so, by whom? And what is that character's relationship to the Hero?

* Do you have a Trickster in your story?

Is your Trickster a principal character or a sidekick?

What does the Trickster react against?

Who does the Trickster deflate?

Do any of the Trickster's pranks backfire on him? In what way?

As always, stretch your mind to consider fresh ways of using these Archetypes. If you can see a way of playing *against* an Archetype which will strengthen your story, by all means, use it.

SECTION FOUR – PROFESSIONAL SPECIALISTS

I have often been frustrated by the fact that the seven traditional Archetypes did not always help me understand the specifics of a character (either one of my own creation or one in someone else's story). After looking at lists of character types with labels like Cop and Librarian, which seemed far too specific and limiting, I found a grouping that seemed very useful. A combination of social functions and character qualities, they can help us define how characters influence and shape certain stories. I call this group the Professional Specialists. They are not meant to replace the traditional Archetypes, but rather to supplement them. Indeed, you will also find some subdivisions with certain of these Archetypes, which will elaborate specific aspects of the Archetype.

So, without further ado, let us meet these storytelling friends.

The Innocent or Fool

Before you wrinkle your brow, I'd better explain the use of the term Fool. I don't mean someone who is a complete idiot, or a madman. Well, actually, those definitions might apply if you want to tell a story about such characters. But I'm focused more on the blithe, careless type of character who will step out into anything without thinking. You may prefer to use the term Innocent.

However, Innocent also needs some definition. At its Latin source, the word refers to someone who does not do injury. General definitions of the term will get you descriptions like free of evil or pure or unoffending. Frequently, those who would be called innocent are also inexperienced in the ways of the world. But if there's one thing you need to be clear on, that is that *innocent* is not necessarily the same as *ignorant*.

Your Fools and Innocents are the sort of Hero often found in Fish-Out-of-Water type stories. He's the type of character whose eyes become opened to the world as he goes along. She's the sort who gains an education as the story progresses. A certain lack of self-awareness frequently marks the Innocent or Fool. He might not be aware that he is either destined to be, or is growing into, a very real Hero, of the type people admire. Also, because this Hero usually lacks experience of the world at large, he may be more idealistic than those around him.

Out of the mists of legend, we can find this model in Perceval.

The Innocent – Perceval. Perceval starts out with a mother who doesn't want him to know anything of knighthood (a boy could get killed, after all). But once he saw some knights, it was all he wanted to be. So off he went to Camelot. Pretty much the country bumpkin, he slowly learns his lessons about being a knight and a hero – the hard way. Perceval makes major mistakes as he goes along (due to pure inexperience), and has to endure the knowledge that he goofed. However, he does do well, becoming one of a very few knights who do find the Holy Grail.

Although none of us would want to admit to being as inexperienced about life as the typical Innocent in a story, we still find something appealing in the Archetype. For the audience, the experience of following the adventures of an Innocent can be refreshing. The wonder with which the Innocent views the world can charm, and the idealism the Innocent carries can pleasantly infect the audience. And these pleasurable sensations should not be overlooked by a storyteller. But examples will help to explain this.

At the very beginning of *The Truman Show,* Christof admits that the world Truman Burbank resides in is counterfeit. But, he insists, "There's nothing fake about Truman himself." Christof, the creator and producer of the 24 hour, continuous television show about Truman's life, has controlled Truman's knowledge entirely. *Everyone* around Truman knows the reality, only Truman is kept ignorant. He blithely goes through his life, and charms the world's watchers with his sunny disposition. Yet, underneath it all, Truman wants to get away from his home and go in search of his one true love, Sylvia. She was an actress who was supposed to be a mere background player in the show of Truman's life, but whom Truman was attracted to and fell in love with, in an all too brief relationship.

Yet Truman's ignorance of the reality of his world cannot in the end overpower his intelligence. When bits of his world start behaving strangely – such as a spotlight falling out of an apparently empty sky, or people sitting casually in chairs behind what should have been elevator doors – Truman doesn't ignore them, nor is he satisfied with the explanations showered on him by the people around him. The realities of human nature assert themselves in Truman's mind, leading him to question everything in his life. He realizes that his wife Meryl doesn't love him, and so he wonders why he's being pushed toward paternity.

Truman is a fish out of real water, who wants to get into the swim of things. He wants to shape his own life. The flow of the story shows us this Innocent growing in self-awareness until he reaches the point where he can take his life choices out of the hands of those who have kept him ignorant of reality.

Truman is an Innocent who has been purposefully *kept* in that state. Sarah Connor in *The Terminator* (1984)[1] gives us an ordinary example of the Innocent Archetype. She initially displays a degree of ineptitude for life in general: she's not a particularly good waitress (from what we see), and she gets dumped by her date via an answering machine message (he doesn't even bother to do it face to face). She certainly doesn't seem competent to deal with things in an ordinary way, let alone the life and death conflict that descends upon her. When Kyle Reese tells her that she is legendary (as in hugely admired rather than fictional) in the future, she emotionally tries to reject this destiny. First, she says disbelievingly, "You're talking about things I haven't done yet in the past tense!" A moment later, frustrated by her own sense of inadequacy in the face of this destiny, she exclaims, "Do I look like the mother of the future? Am I tough? Organized? I can't even balance my checkbook!" The emotional storm builds to an angry declaration: "I didn't ask for this honor, and I don't want it! Any of it!"

Still, let us be clear that the innocence and lack of preparation that signifies this Archetype does not mean that the character needs to be dumb. When Sarah realizes she may be the target of the killer (before she has even met Reese and his explanations), she tries to call both the police and her roommate. She does not make the mistake of brushing aside the implied danger to herself. And when Reese initially explains the nature of the Terminator, she rightfully says, "Look, I'm not stupid, you know. They cannot make things like that yet." As events progress, she does learn to deal with them, to the point that she at last *does* stop the Terminator. The drama lies in her progress from the charming haphazard incompetent of the beginning to the stern, determined fighter of the end.

It is the Innocents (or Fools) of the world who blithely venture out into the world without planning and preparation. They are very likely to develop into some other type of character during the course of their Journey (as Sarah moves from Innocent to Warrior). But whatever direction you choose to move your story, if you use the Innocent, always be aware of the qualities of the Archetype.

The Transformer

The Transformer Archetype is one who changes things around herself. By that I mean that her job *and* her personality are such that people and things cannot remain *status quo* in her presence. It's this Archetype that gives us the healers and magicians in stories. It's their *job* to change things. But beyond that, it should be part of their personality. A Transformer cannot help but cause change.

Now change can be a good thing or a bad thing. This is where your storytelling options come into play. Do things change for the better around your character? Or do they change for the worse? Most of the time this Archetype appears with positive results, but you don't always have to follow that pattern.

Just to help us get rolling in considering this Archetype, let's look at a couple of myths.

The Transformer – Isis. In addition to transforming Osiris from the dead back into the living, Isis assisted her husband in his work of civilizing Egypt (transforming the people and lands from wildness to culture). She taught women to grind grain (transforming basic grasses into bread). She taught people to spin flax and weave cloth (transforming plant fibers into graceful garments). She also instituted the practice of marriage (transforming independent indulgences into a committed domestic life). So, it makes sense that she was also the goddess of medicine (transforming illness into health).

Another example of a Transformer comes to us from Greek myth.

The Transformer – Asclepius. Asclepius, a son of the god Apollo, was taught the art of healing by the centaur Chiron. He learned his lessons so well that eventually he could raise the dead back to life. Zeus, concerned by the idea that mere humans might become immortal, zapped Asclepius with a thunderbolt, killing him. Then Zeus changed his mind and transformed the dead man into a minor god whose job was overseeing medicine and healing.

Changing things, especially changing for the better (or attempting to do that), can be a very dramatic undertaking in stories. Transforming the world is a challenging goal, since, by and large, the world does not want to be changed. If you plan on using the Transformer Archetype in a story, be very conscious of all that will resist the Transformer's influence.

By definition, doctors are Transformers. They attempt to transform disease into health. In the film *Patch Adams* (1998)[2], Hunter Adams has a burning desire to be a doctor who treats people, rather than just the disease (which is how he perceives the attitude of the medical establishment). By acting on his desire, he transforms the *outlook* of what it means to be a doctor. This commitment to never losing sight of the person in the patient makes him outstanding among his fellow students. It also leads Carin to tell him that she sees lives transformed around him (as she herself is).

Changing a state of health can be an obvious factor in the appearance of a Transformer in a story. But you can expand your usage beyond that. We can find an example of a first level type of expansion in *Outbreak* (1995)[3]. Sam Daniels is a doctor, a military doctor engaged in research. He hasn't actually been treating patients. His just-divorced ex-wife Robby is also a doctor. She's chosen to go to work for the CDC, where she *will* be helping patients. Sam needs to transform his work orientation. He does so by trying to deal with the deadly virus which has stricken a town, helping the people who may die from the illness. He also needs to transform his relationship with his ex-wife, to learn to communicate how *alive* his feelings for her really are.

Beyond changing himself, the Transformer reaches out to those around him. In *The Green Mile*, John Coffey, with his healing powers, is obviously a Transformer. He heals Paul Edgecomb and transforms the guard's life. He heals Melinda, the Warden's wife and restores peace to that household. But for all his powers, he cannot significantly change either the guard Percy Wetmore or the killer "Wild Bill" Wharton.

By now you should be able to see the obvious elements of the Transformer when it comes to characters that are healers. But is that all that can be done with the Archetype? Nope. Not by a long shot. Let me give you a couple more examples to demonstrate this point.

In *Erin Brockovich*, Erin presents us with an unlikely Transformer. Her forceful personality at first glance seems to be one that would cause people to resist her. Yet, influenced by her persuasion, Ed Masry pursues the legal case against PG&E beyond the edges of his own doubt, changing both his attitude about the case and his attitude about himself. Erin reveals the truth about the water supply to Donna Jensen and transforms that woman's understanding of the ailments she and her family have suffered. Erin transforms the lives of the people of Hinkley by fighting their battles. Along the way, Erin transforms herself from a struggling single mother with no apparent skills into an intelligent, thorough and capable investigator.

In *Norma Rae* (1979)[4] we have the presentation of another Transformer who is *not* a doctor. Norma Rae works in a clothing mill, in the small Southern backwater of Henleyville. When we first meet her, her life is obviously not in the best of states. We see her waiting at a motel for a married man she's having an affair with. And when she tells him she's going to stop seeing him because it doesn't make her feel good, he hits her. As far as he is concerned, she exists to make *him* feel good. Yet, Norma Rae remains determined to change this aspect of her life.

When Reuben Warshowsky comes to town to convince the mill workers to unionize, everyone treats him warily, even Norma Rae. However, we have already seen that she has made small attempts to try and better things at the mill. Management offers her a promotion to the position of spot checker, which she takes because she needs the pay raise. But this position cuts her off from her friends, and rather than lose her friends she gives up the promotion.

Norma Rae knows she needs to change her life. She tells Reuben, "One of these days I'm going to get myself all together." Having dumped the married man, Norma Rae finds herself being courted by regular nice guy Sonny Webster, and marrying him. But even while her personal relationships become "all together," she begins to become more interested in the union matters.

Norma Rae's knowledge of her neighbors and her own persistence transform the attitudes of her co-workers. Overcoming both racial bigotry and suspicion of outsiders, she leads her peers toward a vision of better working conditions. Even though she loses her job in the process, she inspires the mill workers with the idea that they *can* change things.

These last two examples demonstrate how you can use the Transformer Archetype in stories in ways other than as a doctor. Any character who sets out to change things around himself could be a Transformer. Any crusader advocating a cause to better the world could be a Transformer.

However, remember to consider the possibilities in the negative version of the Archetype. A Transformer whose changes go all wrong, or someone who seeks to petrify the world around him – each can give you stories. Don't overlook the story possibilities you may find in a Transformer who fails in her goal.

The Ruler

Leadership and a ruling authority are qualities that belong to this Archetype. When we considered the Mature Ruler in the Journey of the **MALE**, we were looking at a Stage of life experience. Here, we want to explore the Ruler as a job.

To rule over something means to have authority over how activities are conducted in your domain. The Ruler decides how things will be put in order, to whom jobs will be delegated, how long some event will continue. But the implications of having a Ruler are not only the commanding presence of that character, but also that there are people to be ruled. A Ruler without subjects is a character in an empty job. The fact that rulership does include these secondary characters brings in more story options. Do the subjects follow the Ruler voluntarily? Has the Ruler earned the respect of the subjects, or are they obliged to obey the orders of a Ruler they know nothing of? Any one of these choices can take your tale into fresh territory.

A legendary ruling personality can be found in King David.

> **The Ruler – King David.** David became king of Judah (and later of Israel also) after many years of establishing himself as a leader. For several years before David came to the throne, while King Saul basically regarded David as an outlaw, men would leave their homes to join David. When David did become king, he built and secured his kingdom, ruling well (except for mishandling his own children – but that's a different matter). Men willingly followed his orders, even if they did not understand his intentions.

Do all Rulers, then, govern countries? No. Wherever someone has to exercise authority, you have a situation where the Ruler Archetype can come into play.

In *All the President's Men*, the character of Ben Bradlee functions as a Ruler. When Woodward and Bernstein submit their first major story on the Watergate break-in, they had mentioned the White House in the story. Bradlee deletes the mention. They hadn't sufficiently supported their assertion that the White House was involved. "You haven't got it," he tells them. He trims the story, making it less specific. Afterwards, Woodward acknowledges that the ruling was just. As the film's tale moves forward, it is Bradlee who keeps it on track by asking "Where's the goddamn story?" His insistence that the reporters discover "what it is all about" drives them forward. As the overseer of their actions, Bradlee establishes the ground rules for Woodward and Bernstein. He also stands by them when they come under fire, providing them with the support they need to do their job.

Bradlee's support of his reporters reminds us of another aspect of the Ruler. A Ruler not only enjoys the privilege of giving orders and overseeing actions, but also has the responsibility of supporting his underlings as they do their jobs and of giving them some protection in order that they may complete their chores.

Negative versions of the Ruler are easy to imagine, and of course many stories make use of that alternate of the Archetype. Tyrants to be overthrown, weak Rulers who lose their domains – every version of a Bad Ruler has been seen in story at one time or another. But what happens to your story if you have a situation that calls for a Ruler and you put *no one* in that place? How will your characters cope without a Ruler? And what sort of circumstances led to there being no Ruler? Even in a complete democracy, *someone* has to take charge. Vacuums (where a crucial spot is empty) and conflicts (when more than one person vies for that crucial spot) both can generate story energy.

The Holy One

This Archetype is one that most people shy away from discussing, since they want to avoid treading on other people's religious toes. And for a similar reason, I chose not to call the Archetype the Priest, as that would have focused attention more on someone's religious practices. I am not trying to make any judgment about anyone's preference when it comes to the practice of their belief system. Rather, I want to deal with an outlook that's part of human nature, when it contemplates its relationship to all of creation.

That said, the first task in exploring this Archetype is to discuss what it means to call something holy or sacred. Holy means that something is connected to a divine power, or at least something that is regarded as worthy of veneration. Sacred means much the same thing, coming from a word meaning to consecrate or dedicate something to special service, usually to a deity. Holiness also implies a degree of perfection (if perfection can show gradation).

Whether or not you believe in a god is beside the point. Human nature looks toward an ideal, and gives respect to those things that become most like that ideal. When we start broadening our perspectives, we find that many things in the world deserve to be treated with high levels of respect. And as we come to that realization, we also find that some individuals have chosen to dedicate themselves to the service of a particular ideal. They become, in effect, priests to that ideal. And as a consequence of their dedication to this service, these servants, these priests, take on some of the holiness of the ideal they serve. That is why I chose to call them the Holy Ones.

As I said, these Holy Ones serve their particular ideal. In doing so, it's likely that certain rituals develop in that service. Likewise, there will be occasions where an established Holy One may be called upon to initiate a novice into the rituals, arts and practice of their particular service.

Although there are a few mythic figures whose purpose is oversight of holy things, in this case, the historical Vestal Virgins of ancient Rome make the most useful example of this Archetype.

The Holy One – Vestal Virgins. The Vestals were priestesses dedicated to the service of the goddess Vesta. Vesta was the goddess of the hearth and home. The importance of the home was a very big deal to the Romans, and violations of it (from housebreaking to adultery) were affronts not just on a social level, but also on a religious one. So the temple of Vesta, where her holy flame was kept burning at all times, was a very special place for the Romans. Candidates for her service were between 6 and 10 years old, of Italian birth, and nearly perfect in mind and body. If the young girl was accepted, she spent 10 years training. When she became a priestess, she vowed to live celibate. Then she spent 10 years in service – watching and keeping the sacred fire, bringing water each day from the fountain Egeria, being custodian to the sacred Palladium from Troy. For the next 10 years, she trained and instructed novices. After 30 years of service, she could then leave the temple if she wanted to retire. She could even marry if she chose. If she wanted to stay she could, serving the other Vestal Virgins. The veneration of the Vestal Virgins also affected the society around them. At public events, Vestals were given seats of honor. In courts of law a Vestal was not required to swear to tell the truth, since her simple word was considered sufficient. She could pardon criminals if she met them on the street, even if the criminal was on his way to execution. It was a capital offense to even insult a Vestal – the violator was beaten to death. And if a Vestal violated her vows while serving as priestess, she was stripped of her sacred dress and sealed in an underground vault with a bed, bread, wine, water, oil and a lighted lamp and she was left to die. This method was used so that no one's hand was responsible for the death of even a dishonored Vestal. So seriously did all Romans take this service that reportedly in the thousand years the office of Vestal Virgin existed, only 18 girls were punished for violating their vows.

As you can see, for the Romans the sanctity of the goddess and what she represented was extended to her servants. And so it is with all Holy Ones, all figures who serve something set aside as being special, important and worthy of respect.

I've dwelt on this at length because I want to make it clear that although this Archetype certainly *does* parallel the job description of clergy of any organized religious faith, it can also be applied to *any* character who approaches his or her job with this special attitude. Let me show you some examples.

In many ways, Clarice Starling figures as a priestess in *The Silence of the Lambs*. In her backstory, as a youngster she had attempted to rescue lambs from slaughter. This act, more than following the model of her father, brought her to a law-enforcement career. In this case, the holy thing is life itself, and her job is the reverence and service of life. Her job preserves the safety of those still living and respects the lives of those who are murdered. This includes acting as their instrument of retribution. Consider the sequence where the body from the river is examined. The male investigators are all focused on getting on with business. The local state troopers, who actually have no function in the pending examination, are shooed off by Clarice. She does it by invoking respect for the victim, very much in the manner of a priest about to conduct holy business. It's notable that the troopers do not argue with her. Her authority at that moment comes from her dedication as a servant of life and its law-enforcement and not from any authority delegated to her by her supervisor, Crawford. Indeed, when she tells Lecter about the lamb incident, her whole-hearted service to life comes through in her statement, "If I could save just *one*."

As a side matter, since we usually consider priestly figures to be celibate (after all, they *have* dedicated themselves completely to something – like the Vestal Virgins), this is why Clarice's flirtation with the bug specialist in the story feels irrelevant. We don't take the flirtation seriously because it does not touch her holy cause. Yes, it *is* present to remind us that Clarice is not, in fact, a nun. But it also does not resonate as anything serious for her on an emotional or commitment level.

Another example of the Archetype at work appears in *The Green Mile*. The guards Paul Edgecomb and Brutus "Brutal" Howell serve as priests to the ultimate threshold, Death. They follow their rituals, doing their job, helping prisoners over that final threshold with as much dignity and calm as they can. They even have a temple of sorts, for the electric chair, Old Sparky, sits in the execution room looking very much like an altar in a chapel. The guards insist that the experience be treated with respect, which is one of the reasons why Percy's behavior is unacceptable. To emphasize the priestly function, when John Coffey's execution comes, Paul asks if he wants a priest. John says no, but that *Paul* could say a prayer if he wanted. Paul has acted very much as a servant of something holy, and John recognizes that.

As you can see, neither of these examples are what we would initially consider priestlike. Clarice is a criminal investigator. Paul is a prison guard. But both bring a priestly outlook to the pursuit of their jobs. As a storyteller, consider the possibilities in endowing your Hero or another character with this consecrated attitude. The artist who serves Art, even more than expressing his own Aesthetic Need. The builder who insists on exactitude in construction and will not even consider cutting corners. The doctor whose god is medicine (rather than the health of her patients). The scientist who serves the pursuit of knowledge in face of the fears of the general populace. You have a whole spectrum of possibilities to draw upon, from the Hero who rightly serves a worthy ideal, all the way to a character who serves the *wrong* ideal or who is not temperamentally suited to be in such dedicated service at all.

Indeed, now that I have mentioned the matter of being temperamentally suited, let me explore a side issue here. We often speak of the spiritual side of a character. But we also tend to be indistinct in what we mean by that. For the purposes of storytelling, let's define the spirit as the animating quality in a human, that something extra that goes beyond the merely biological functioning of the organism. Additionally, being spiritual means having a sense of connection to the world around us.

Once we have defined this as a legitimate aspect of a character, we can also evaluate the *quality* of a character's connection to other people and the universe in general.

M. Scott Peck has developed a means of defining a person's spiritual development.[5] I've adapted it for use in shaping characters for stories.

Spiritual Development

There are four Stages in the evaluation of a character's spiritual development and sense of connection to all of creation. They are ordered from least connected to most connected. I've called them the Bottom Stage, the Falling Stage, the Threshold Stage and the Rising Stage.

1:   The Bottom Stage

A character in this Stage tends to be antisocial. His self-esteem is the most important thing to him, even beyond society's approval. As a result, he will be utterly unprincipled. The lack of any sense of connection to the rest of the world means that rules have no meaning for this character. Above all else, that means the Bottom character lies whenever it suits him. Truth doesn't matter in and of itself, only what *he* regards as important. Although he (or she) may be capable of pretending to be loving, in reality all relationships will be self-serving. Indeed, that driving force of self-service gives a Bottom character considerable skill in manipulating others. Nothing can govern this character except his own will. Pursuing his ambition is the only discipline he will recognize.

Mythically we can see this attitude in Loki.

The Bottom Stage of Spirit – Loki. Loki was always very conscious that he lived among a bunch of gods with who he had no real connection. And although he enjoyed the freedom that living with the Aesir gave him, he also did everything he could to destroy them. Indeed, in many ways, he brought about the death of Balder simply for his own amusement. By being of occasional service to the Aesir, he could pretend to be less malicious than he actually was.

Lest you think that a character in this Stage will be rough and unpleasant to encounter, consider Hannibal Lecter in *The Silence of the Lambs*. We can clearly see examples of this Stage in Lecter's behavior. Self-esteem is important to Lecter. He condemns rude behavior, priding himself on his courtesy (toward Clarice, if no one else). When Clarice discusses the taking of trophies by serial killers, he points out that he did not do so. Clarice's clear insight, "No. You ate yours," strikes a blow to his self-esteem. He doesn't like being categorized. He is unprincipled: he uses the kidnapping of the Senator's daughter as a means to his escape. He gives false (or at least intentionally cryptic) information to further this end. He doesn't care about the missing girl's fate. He manipulates Dr. Chilton and then the Senator. He disciplines himself from the moment Chilton disrupts Crawford and Clarice's plan, all toward the moment when he can escape. As for being governed only by his own will, we see that at the end: he tells Clarice she has nothing to fear from him. "The world is more interesting with you in it." It is his own interest in her that eliminates her as a possible victim. She has value to *him*, which determines his choice. It is not Clarice's own abilities, or her value in the broader world. He won't be deterred by law, or any other consideration. It is just *his* choice.

Obviously, storytellers tend to cast characters who dwell at the bottom of the ladder of spiritual development in roles of villains. After all, storytelling is a social activity and so it becomes difficult to find ways to consider the anti-social personality in a positive light. However, if you do find a way to create such a character, by all means do so. You will have added something new and fresh to the storytelling repertoire. That said, let's move on to the next Stage.

2:   The Falling Stage

A character in this Stage will have a love of formality. The rules and rituals of society will be important to her. Indeed, she will rely almost entirely on the institutions she participates in. By that, I mean that those institutions will define the character's perceptions. So utterly will the character rely on the *forms* of the institution, its laws and rituals, that she will overlook the *intention* of the institution, its purpose for existing. Possibly she will even overlook the purpose of the rituals she clings to. Because of this dependency on the forms, she will become upset if the rituals and rules are changed or disrupted on her. If she is conscious of a divinity, that divinity will be external to her perceptions. She will not conceive of a direct contact with god or the rest of the universe. By her lights, it is the rules of society that make possible any sort of human interaction.

Looking for this sort of attitude in myths, we can find Athena giving us a good example.

The Falling Stage of Spirit – Athena. In general, Athena is the goddess of wisdom and behaves well and with wit. But even she had her lapses. Especially where the matter of reverence for the gods was concerned (and, it should be added, pride in her own skills). Among all her other activities, Athena was an excellent weaver. At the highest levels, to the Greeks, this meant not just the ability to make a fine piece of cloth. It meant being able to weave in images which told stories – what we now call tapestries. Now, there was a mortal woman, Arachne, who was such a good weaver, people thought she'd been taught by Athena. Arachne denied this and challenged the goddess to a contest. The invitation annoyed Athena, but she accepted it. Athena's tapestry was a beautiful depiction of great acts by the gods. Arachne's, however, was a clever and amusing (and disrespectful) depiction of the amorous antics of the gods. The content infuriated Athena, as did the fact that Arachne's workmanship was indeed excellent, at the very least on a par with her own. She destroyed the tapestry and loom. Terrified by the wrath of the goddess, Arachne tried to hang herself. But Athena changed her into a spider instead.

Arachne rattled Athena's cage in the matter of proper respect toward the gods. Rather than let the apparent disrespect stand, Athena destroyed the work and the worker.

This reaction is something you need to consider in dealing with characters at this stage. I'll discuss this further after we've finished looking at all four stages. But for now, just consider the matter that for a character who lives by forms and rituals of an institution, any questioning or breaking of those rules can, at the least, rock the foundations of his existence.

In the television series *M.A.S.H.*[6], the character of Major Frank Burns clearly exemplifies this dependence on formal structures. Although he, like the central character Hawkeye Pierce, is not Regular Army, he cannot conceive of stepping outside the Army regulations. The needs of the patients do not touch him. So well known is this trait, that when in one episode ("Operation Noselift") Hawkeye decides to help a depressed private have his huge schnozz trimmed (an unauthorized surgery), Hawkeye also has to plot a way of distracting Frank, first from the surgery itself and then from the actual patient.

Indeed, Hawkeye's propensity for circumventing the rules and regulations leads Frank, on at least two occasions, to bring charges against the non-conforming doctor. In "House Arrest," when Hawkeye accidentally hits Frank, Major Burns files charges against Captain Pierce. On a later occasion ("The Novocain Mutiny"), when Frank, in the absence of Colonel Potter, is made temporary C.O., the Major has Hawkeye brought up on charges of mutiny for various infractions.

Frank Burns demonstrates the use of a character in this Stage of Spiritual Development in comedy. And of course, much humor can be had confounding a by-the-book character. But there is also a negative side to this type of outlook, and we can see it at work in General McClintock in *Outbreak*. McClintock has been overseeing the secret programs dealing with biological warfare. Even in the face of the outbreak of the deadly disease, he sticks by the book of his agenda: protecting the secret of the development of viral weaponry. He remains unmoved, even after the anti-bodies for the virus mutation have been discovered. Unlike the White House advisor who insists that everyone be aware of the residents of the town they are about to destroy (because of the viral outbreak) as individual citizens, specific people, the General does not consider the citizens at all. They are, in his mind, less valuable than keeping the secret of the development of the virus.

Neither Burns nor McClintock is intended to be much of a positive portrait. Yet individuals in this Stage can provide storytellers with opportunities for more complex characters than either of the first two examples.

In *The Bounty* (1984)[7], the portrait presented by Lieutenant Bligh shows a far from simple man. A career naval officer, when he receives the commission of taking the *Bounty* to Tahiti to get breadfruit plants, he chooses his *civilian* friend Fletcher Christian to fill a key officer's position, that of Master's Mate. That choice shows a certain flexibility in Bligh's thinking (at least at the beginning of the adventure). Yet, his facial expressions during the ship's celebration of crossing the equator make it obvious that the raucous party unsettles him. One part of his mind acknowledges the need in the crewmen for such ritualized disorder on occasion, but it clearly makes him uncomfortable. An episode involving gagging two sailors for several hours as a punishment for talking back to an officer further demonstrates Bligh's reliance on a set order. When Christian asks to end the punishment, Bligh accompanies his permission with a pleased soliloquy on the need for discipline in the Royal Navy.

Bligh's downfall in dealing with his crew lies in his inability to distinguish between his *personal* need for complete order and the effective use of order and conformity in unusual circumstances. He cannot cope on a middle ground. And when he realizes that his friend Christian has become powerfully attracted to the life in Tahiti – and to the King's daughter Mauatua – his ordered perception of the world is shaken. Bligh attempts to force Christian back into conforming to his perception of how the world should be, ignoring Christian's distress at leaving Mauatua. Bligh's insensitivity precipitates the mutiny.

Oddly enough, however, the very attitude of living by-the-book which led to Bligh being cast adrift in a launch is the attitude that allows him to successfully cross a huge expanse of ocean in that launch and reach safety, without losing any of his fellow castaways. Bligh demonstrates the curious ambiguity of this Stage – how the rigid mentality of depending on institutions can in one situation be disastrous, while in another can be very effective in a positive way.

One consequence of relying so much on institutionalized rules and rituals is a certain blindness to the broader picture. This blindness can easily be seen in *The Bridge on the River Kwai* (1957)[8]. From his first appearance in the film, Colonel Nicholson clearly demonstrates the qualities of someone committed to an institution. A career Army officer, he marches his raggedy troops into the Japanese prisoner of war camp to the beat of a jaunty tune. He is so very much a by-the-book man that he carries a copy of the Geneva Conventions' rules for the treatment of prisoners. He even chastises the Japanese Colonel Saito for his non-compliance with those rules, such as Saito's threat to use the officers and sick men in manual labor.

But Nicholson's regimented approach to things has some drawbacks. He tells the American Shears that since his regiment had been *ordered* by the British to surrender, any attempt by his men to escape might be construed as an illegal action. In taking this position he overlooks the positive psychological element of hope, of giving the men something to look forward to in planning an escape.

To counteract the loss of the hope of escape and to instill a sense of order in his men, Nicholson decides to tackle the job of building the Japanese a *proper* bridge over the Kwai. Up to this point, the prisoners had engaged in the passive sabotage of shoddy workmanship. Additionally, the design and location of the bridge the Japanese planned would almost have assured its collapse with the passage of the first train. But once Nicholson latches onto the idea of building a bridge that could last and be useful for hundreds of years, he becomes totally committed to building the best bridge possible. He ignores the Medical Officer Clifton's concern that by building the bridge so effectively the prisoners would actually be *aiding* the enemy.

Nothing of the bigger picture occurs to Nicholson at all. He had been so focused on the goal of building a good bridge for the sake of glory and the morale of his men, that he even ends up actually doing what Saito had only threatened to do: he puts the officers and sick men to manual labor. Only when he sees the returned Shears (who was believed to be dead) trying to complete the sabotage, does Nicholson realize how his commitment to strict routine had endangered the larger aims of the Allied war effort.

If a character in the Falling Stage of Spiritual development can be shaken by the disregard or questioning of his rules, what about the character who raises those questions? We'll find that character in the next Stage.

3:   The Threshold Stage

Since we've discussed thresholds in other situations, you should have some idea of their significance. When we consider a character who is in a threshold state in his being, we usually find a vibrant character. He will definitely be an *individual,* with a sense of his distinctiveness. He will also be something of a skeptic, questioning the existence of set forms and rules. His questions probe the purpose and value of things, for the character in this Stage is after the truth. He will be committed to his relationships and causes, for he has become connected to the wider community. Along with his greater involvement in and engagement with the society he lives in, this character is also likely to be probing his relationship to the universe and the divine. Since this character has fewer fears of those things which don't conform to rules, he's also likely to be more loving toward those around him.

Reaching out from myth, we find that Prometheus fits this picture.

The Threshold Stage of Spirit – Prometheus. Prometheus, one of the Titans, didn't agree with the rules the Olympians laid down for mortal men. The first quibble was over the matter of sacrifices to the gods. Prometheus felt that the gods had no need to take the entirety of a sacrificed animal from the mortals (who needed the food as the gods did not). So he made a deal with Zeus. He prepared two types of offerings for Zeus, and Zeus would choose one of them as the proper form of sacrifice for the mortals to give the gods. The first offering looked solid and juicy, while the second one looked like ooky innards. So Zeus chose the first offering. Well, the reason it looked solid and juicy was because it consisted of the bones and fat from the sacrificed animal – and that's *all* it was. Prometheus had hidden the meat of the animal inside the stomach sac. All the "good stuff" was in the second offering. Zeus was so furious at this trick, he ruled that the secrets of fire be kept from mortals. (That way, they would be totally dependent on the gods.) Prometheus, who happened to love humankind, wasn't going to sit still for that. He stole fire from the gods and brought it to the mortals. He taught them how to use it, to cook food and to work metals. All in all, Prometheus questioned many of the rules Zeus considered very important.

Questioning set forms and procedures, *and* acting on his convictions could be considered the hallmarks of this character. For storytellers, that means a very active character, and one likely to be disruptive for those around him.

In the film *Real Genius*, Chris Knight represents this level of development. Chris displays an irreverence toward authority, questioning – through his actions – the seriousness with which all around him conduct their studies. His involvement in society stands out in the way he organizes some fun breaks for his fellow students, such as the ice party in the dorm and a pool party in an auditorium. He is a truth seeker under his frivolous behavior, as seen in his concern for Mitch's obsession with his studies. He warns Mitch that the younger student runs the risk of cracking, the way Lazlo Hollyfeld did (a psychological truth). Later, when the students realize that Professor Hathaway had a particular use intended for their laser experiments, Chris leads the way in finding out the truth.

Where Chris displays the qualities of this Stage in a humorous context, Clarice in *The Silence of the Lambs* exhibits the traits in a more serious context. She is very much an individual, mostly seen as a loner (in fact, we first meet her in the film out on the obstacle course alone). Her involvement in society shows up in her friendship with Ardelia Mapp. Clarice questions set forms: she asks Crawford if she was sent to Lecter in order to get help on the "Buffalo Bill" murders. By doing so she asserts her independence, not accepting what her Mentor teaches her without question. That Clarice is a truth seeker should be obvious by her choice of profession. However, it's also emphasized in her first meeting with Crawford: he says he gave her an A in the course he taught at U.Va. She corrects him with the truth: he gave her an A–.

Clarice, however, is also growing toward the next Stage of Spiritual Development. As she pulls together the facts of the case, combining them with what she has been learning from Lecter, she begins to see more of the unity of the events. She also grows more comfortable with Lecter's cryptic comments. But she is, as yet, only touching that next Stage (being still on the threshold, as it were).

Characters in this threshold state have a powerful attraction for storytellers. After all, since the characters are on a threshold, they might go in either direction. They might move toward the security of living by-the-book in the Falling Stage. Or they might move toward the unrestricted conditions of the next Stage.

4:   The Rising Stage

A character in the Rising Stage displays mystical qualities. Since this character has gained a sense of a broader, deeper connection to the rest of the universe, he also has a more communal bond to his society. This character will see a cohesion beneath the surface of things. Because he has less need to rely on formal structures, has less fear of non-conformity, he will enjoy paradoxes. That is, he isn't likely to be disturbed by a paradox in circumstances, and indeed may enjoy speaking in terms of paradox. This character will love to solve mysteries, but he also knows he's not likely to find *all* the answers. He can be comfortable with mystery and unexplained circumstances.

Legend gives us an example of someone in this stage in the figure of Galahad.

The Rising Stage of Spirit – Galahad. Galahad as the best knight in the world represents the ideals of his world. But more than his prowess as a knight, his perfection of character and spiritual development are what help him succeed in the Grail

Quest. Because he was more receptive to unusual phenomena, he could better respond to the strange challenges of the quest.

That greater sense of connection to the universe tends to make characters of this Stage very suitable for the job of Mentor. But whether you use this Stage to describe the Mentor or not, it gives you an opportunity to add some complexity to your cast of characters. A little bit of well chosen ambiguity increases the depth of your story.

For example, Merlin in *Excalibur* sees cohesion beneath the surface of events. His sense of the oneness of the land enables his ability to see into the future. Continuing with the qualities of this Stage, Merlin also likes to speak in terms of paradox. Of himself he says, "I have walked my way since the beginning of time." It's a nice line, but can it be true, even of a wizard? A paradox.

Now that we've explored the four Stages of Spiritual Development, let's look back at Athena's reaction to Arachne's irreverence. One of the key elements about the interaction of characters in the various stages is that those on the lower Stages tend to feel threatened by those on higher Stages of Spiritual Development. The important aspect of this is that this threat is more likely to be perceived than it is actual. The simplest example would be the threat the non-conformist seems to be to the ordered universe of the well-regimented mind. Likewise the communally minded character of one of the upper Stages may seem threatening to the utter self-centeredness of the Bottom dweller.

Look again at *M.A.S.H.* Because Frank Burns cannot cope with disregard of rules, he demonstrates the fear that someone on a lower Stage has of someone on a higher one. Is Hawkeye in fact a threat to Frank? Only to Frank's dignity. But Frank sees Hawkeye's skeptical and nonconforming attitudes as a threat. Likewise, in *The Bounty*, Bligh does not know how to deal with Christian. The ease with which Christian took to the alien culture of Tahiti unsettles Bligh, just as Christian's ability to comply with orders later disturbs Bligh. Christian never comments on Bligh's orders, and when he finally does come to Bligh to warn him of the possibility of mutiny, he does it as a friend (the personal connection). Bligh rejects the warning, perhaps because Christian did not do it by-the-book as an officer (the institutional way). In *The Silence of the Lambs*, Clarice's tendency to question Lecter's pronouncements makes her a challenge to him. Although we could say that Lecter does not see others as a threat to *him*, only to his freedom, he does call Clarice after his escape. And although that call apparently is for the purpose of telling her that she is not in danger from him, its purpose is to disarm her. Her understanding and insight make her one of the few people who actually *could* be a threat to him.

Before we leave the matter of the Holy Ones altogether, there remains one additional arena to consider, and that is the matter of Special Objects.

Special Objects

Because of their association with something considered holy, some objects take on aspects of that holiness. It is as if they absorb some of the divine power. The book containing the communications of the divinity. The largest tree in the area, representing an ongoing fertility in the region. The specially provided sword which protects the realm. The grail that offers healing.

When it comes to telling your story, you need to pay attention to any Special Objects you introduce. The reason is that there tend to be three major types of Objects and they do different things in stories. They evoke very different responses in the audience. So you need to understand what it is you have in your hands.

1:   Swords and Spears

These weapons symbolize power – power to protect or destroy. Inevitably, because mythic thinking links objects of similar shapes, swords and spears are identified with the male sex organ. Beyond that, the presence of weapons of violence acknowledges the necessity of confrontational action. Additionally, because they are cutting weapons, they also bring division, or the potential for division, with them. That dividing power can be a positive thing, separating what is good from what is bad. But the dividing power can also be a negative thing, cutting apart that which should be unified. The Sword itself is neither good nor evil – how it is used determines its place on the good/evil scale.

Excalibur is, of course, one such very special Sword. Early in the film *Excalibur,* its purpose is declared as "to heal, not to hack." This gives it something of an unusual quality as a Sword. It is certainly a Sword of Power, and the symbol of the power of the king. It embodies the ideal of "one land, one king." When Arthur drives the sword into the ground between the sleeping lovers Guinevere and Lancelot, he begins the course that leads to the ailment of himself and the land. Lancelot knows what it means, crying "The king without a sword! The land without a king!" But just as Arthur's thrusting the sword between the lovers divides them from each other, this use of it also divides him from his sense of unity to the land. Indeed, all around the king, the land and people become divided from each other, making them easy prey for Morgana.

Excalibur shows us the use of a Sword gone astray. What about objects that unify rather than divide?

2:   Grails

The Grail brought healing and wholeness to those who found it. Like the Elixir of the quest, it represents a positive boon to the community. It has the power to draw people together in a positive way. This leads to Grail objects being almost universally positive motifs in stories. As with the Sword, physical resemblance leads to Grails being categorized as feminine. Which is also why they usually carry nurturing powers, from being a cornucopia of plenty to the provider of ultimate refreshment. However, more often than not, it is a Grail's healing power which figures in stories, especially when the object is *the* Grail.

In *The Fisher King*, we have an object that is designated as the Grail. Parry had identified a particular chalice (a trophy in a rich man's house) as the Holy Grail. He has, basically, chosen *that* chalice to be sacred. In this particular story the chalice does not manifest a supernatural healing power. Instead, Parry's belief in it endows it with psychological healing power, drawing Parry out of his catatonia.

By contrast, in *Excalibur*, the Grail specifically and supernaturally has the power to heal the king, and thus the land. The action of the Grail is presented in a fairly straightforward fashion, without much elaboration.

In *Indiana Jones and the Last Crusade*, the Grail is described as bestowing the gift of youth, of giving eternal life. The villain of the story understands this to mean immortality, that is, deathlessness. Yet along the way, hints are given that the villain is mistaken. At one point it is said, "The search for the cup of Christ is the search for the divine in all of us." At another point, one of the protectors of the Grail asks Indiana, "Why do you seek the cup of Christ? Is it for *his* glory or for yours?" Indy's response is that he is *not* seeking the Grail, only his father. His unselfish motives allow him to win his way past the guardians. Later, a guardian tells the Bad Guys, "For the unrighteous, the cup of life holds everlasting damnation."

Underlying all of these references is the attitude that the Grail *enhances* what is *good* in life, while destroying what is not. Its healing qualities are, of course, crucial to the plot, as Indy uses the Grail to save his father's life.

As you can see, Swords and Grails actually do have functions in the story. Additionally, they have value for the audience, for the audience agrees with the value of the object in and of itself. By that I mean that however the object is presented in the story, the audience sees and agrees that *even if it were not a story,* this object would be a good thing to have around. There is, however, a third sort of object in stories, which director Alfred Hitchcock labeled the McGuffin.

3: The McGuffin

Hitchcock frequently used McGuffins (and yes, it is also spelled MacGuffin and maguffin) in his films. Other storytellers quickly recognized its usefulness in tales. Hitchcock's explanation was that a McGuffin was a plot element which "must seem to be of vital importance to the characters" even though its specific identity is unimportant, at least to the audience. The crucial aspect of using a McGuffin in a story is that it be very important *to the characters*. The audience is frequently willing to go along on a ride, chasing after some object, as long as they can see that the object has major importance or value to the characters. Even if the storyteller never reveals *what* the object really is to the audience, if they are convinced by the earnestness of the characters, the audience won't complain.

Early in the film *Ronin* (1998)[9], the Irish woman Deirdre briefs the team of mercenaries she has hired on what their mission is: they are to snatch a metal case. The American, Sam, asks what's in the case, but Deirdre doesn't answer his question. A bit later, Deirdre tells the team that an international bidding war is going on for the case. Again, Sam asks what's in it. This time, he tries to convey that he does have a need to know the contents: is it explosive, how much does it weigh, what safety issues are related to the content? Again, Deirdre does not give him an answer. When the team moves from Paris to Nice, Sam asks once more what is inside the case. This time Deirdre responds by saying, "Something we're paying you for." This repetition about the case serves to emphasize that the object is important for Deirdre and the people she represents.

When the story moves forward and the team snatches the case, we learn that people are willing to kill to get the case. This increases its significance for the characters, but we, the audience, continue to be uninformed as to what the contents are. When Gregor betrays the team, disappearing with the real case while leaving the team with a bomb, the desire of all the players to get the case is pumped up even further. We watch the Russians and the Irish trying to out-maneuver each other, while the remaining mercenaries, Sam and Vincent, try to reclaim the case as well. The various conflicting elements come crashing together in the end, but the audience *never* learns what is in the case.

This is a classic McGuffin: we are shown emphatically that the case is very important to a number of the film's characters. And yet, it fits Hitchcock's definition, in that the contents of the case are actually immaterial to the audience. The case is important to the audience because it is important to the characters. In the end, however, the story is not about what the object actually *means* to the characters (or the audience). Frankly, it is a plot device, to show off the natures of the characters. Neither a Grail nor a Sword, its importance is in its existence but not in its essence – in what it means to the characters, not in what it means to the audience.

Ronin dealt with one very specific object as McGuffin. In *North by Northwest*, Hitchcock runs through a *sequence* of McGuffins. The first one is the mysterious Mr. Kaplan, whom everyone seeks and no one sees. But even though the audience learns fairly early that there is no Kaplan, Roger continues to search for him. The storytellers divert the audience from worrying about the Kaplan McGuffin by informing us that the Good Guys have an undercover agent amongst Vandamm's people. Because the character who *is* the agent is not identified for a while, the agent becomes McGuffin #2. By the time both Roger and the audience have caught up with the information that Eve is the agent, the Professor has introduced the matter of Vandamm's trading in secret intelligence, McGuffin #3. The overlap of concern for one McGuffin with the introduction of the next keeps the audience engaged. Do we ever learn (and do we even care) *what* secret information Vandamm has acquired? No. Does it matter? Not in the least. What carries us forward is the concern the *characters* have for these matters. Telling us that the secrets are atom bomb secrets, or the timetable for an invasion of an unfriendly nation might up the emotional intensity a bit. But since the story *itself* isn't about these issues, such specificity would only succeed in distracting us from the story (and possibly dating it as well).

So, again, when the object itself does not bring an inherent contribution to the story, it will be a McGuffin.

When it comes to Special Objects in your story you need to consider which category your object falls into. This is important because not only can there be subtle but important differences in how the characters regard the object, but also in how the *audience* regards the object. And each option evokes different types of feelings. You do not want to mistake a Grail for a Sword or a Sword for a Grail. Or either for a McGuffin. I must emphasize this, Swords and Grails provoke very different feelings in the audience.

Let me give you an example of what kinds of problems can spring from misidentification of the Special Objects.

In his novel *Raise the Titanic*,[10] Clive Cussler makes a point of emphasizing that the byzanium ore his hero hunts for can only be used in a defensive system, that it would be of no value in a weapons system. When the system (called the Sicilian Project) is initially explained to Admiral Sandecker, he exclaims, "The ultimate weapon!" The explainer responds, "The Sicilian Project is not a weapon. It is purely a scientific method of protecting our country." Later in the story, when the Russians are attempting to get their hands on the ore, the Russian Prevlov argues their rights. Dirk Pitt refuses to cave into the demands.

> "If it were a work of historical art, a national treasure, my State Department would no doubt see it off on the next ship back to Murmansk. But not when it's the prime ingredient for a strategic weapon. If our roles were reversed, Prevlov, you wouldn't give it away – any more than we would."

> "Then it must be destroyed."

> "You're wrong. A weapon that does not take lives, but simply protects them, must never be destroyed."

Cussler may have used the word "weapon" here, but it is quite clear that his intention is to create a *Grail*, something that will be a boon, a benefit to Society. He has credible characters denying that the system would be at all effective as a Sword. By making this distinction, by making the object of the quest a Grail, he allows the audience to root whole-heartedly for the heroes to find the byzanium. The audience agrees with the value Dirk assigns to the ore, and thus we accept the cost (in battles fought and money spent) involved in the quest.

When the 1980 film version of the book came out[11], it became apparent that this difference between Grails and Swords was overlooked. Perhaps the filmmakers believed they were being more realistic in the choices they made.

As in the book, the extremely rare byzanium is the key to the development of the ultimate defense system. As one character says, with this system, "We could make nuclear warfare obsolete." The context of the story sets it in the late days of the cold war between Soviet Russia and the United States, so the appeal of such a defensive weapon can easily be understood by the audience. But the character raises the question of using the byzanium in an offensive weapon. Raises the question, yes, but never really addresses it.

When the information of the Sicilian Project and the salvage of the *Titanic* (the Heroes believe the crucial ore to be in the hold of the ship) gets leaked to the press, Sandecker is asked about using the byzanium for the most powerful bombs ever. He doesn't answer this question. Later, when they discover that the ore is not in the *Titanic's* vault, Sandecker admits to Gene Seagram, the scientist who developed the Sicilian Project, that he didn't think they could have tagged the byzanium for defensive use only. This not only rattles Dr. Seagram, it rattles the audience, particularly when he continues, "Somewhere in the world ... they're figuring out a way to build a byzanium bomb." The filmmakers totally change our perception of Sandecker's character with this next statement: "If it didn't work defensively, if someone was going to build a byzanium bomb, I wanted it to be us."

Whammo! In one fell swoop, the filmmakers turned a Grail into a Sword, and the audience is not really prepared for this. The background of the story does not provide a sense of urgency that would cause us to accept the need for such an offensive weapon. Nothing in the film story came near to generating the sense of necessity that, for instance, the circumstances of World War II did in the creation of the atom bomb.

Seagram's reaction to Sandecker's statement is "If I felt the way Sandecker does, I wouldn't have started the damn project in the first place." The audience's reaction is more likely to be "If I felt the way Sandecker does, I wouldn't have wasted my time on this stupid movie."

The crux of the problem here is the value the audience places on the goal of the quest. If the audience is convinced of the great need for the weapon, for the Sword, they will be content with the quest for that weapon. But in the film, the goal has been presented to the audience as something benign, both by statement – "the ultimate defense system" – and by characters' attitudes – Seagram's purpose in development and Dirk Pitt's drive to find the byzanium. To suddenly tell the audience that not only could the goal of the quest be made into an offensive weapon, but that one of the key characters (Sandecker, whom we thought shared the vision of the Grail) actually expected (and perhaps even wanted) it to become a Sword, throws everything off track. Sandecker is not the person we thought him to be. And the value of the goal has been changed – and not for the better. Plop, flop.

Again, I don't want to imply that Swords only have a negative value in storytelling. That is not the case. But I do want to drive home the point that Swords have a *different* value for the audience than Grails. They are *not* interchangeable.

Would it be possible to pull the kind of switch that the film of *Raise the Titanic* did poorly? Yes, it can be possible. A good storyteller, armed with a clear understanding of the nature of Swords and Grails, might be able to do it. Flexibility *is* our watchword after all. Let's consider one more example then.

The animated film *The Iron Giant* shows us an imaginative twist on the types of Special Objects. A giant robot from outer space – the title Iron Giant – crashes to earth near a little town in Maine. Because of the crash, he cannot remember anything about himself. As he is befriended by the boy Hogarth, the Giant learns from the boy. One of the things Hogarth tells him is that he (the Giant) is *good*, not evil. Later, when this odd pair of buddies see a deer killed by hunters, they discuss death and the immortality of souls. And Hogarth tells the Giant that since the Giant has feelings, he has a soul.

All this sets up the question of what the Giant was constructed to do in the first place. When he automatically starts blasting at the toy gun Hogarth points at him, we see that he was probably built as a weapon. Indeed, he may have been the offensive weapon the paranoid government man Kent Mansley believes him to be. But the Giant's blasting turns out to be in *reaction* to a perceived threat, a defensive action. Whether because it was part of his purpose all along or whether it is due to Hogarth's influence, the Giant does not want to hurt people. And he becomes willing to sacrifice himself to save others.

On its simplest terms, this story is about a Sword that wants to be a Grail. There is a great deal of sweetness to that desire, without being at all corny. And we find considerable value in the transformation from offensive weapon to protector. It works here because the storytellers knew exactly what they were doing, and laid solid ground work for it.

The primary consideration in dealing with aspects of the Holy Ones is that of value. A storyteller who shrugs off such considerations deprives his tale of some broad, rich vistas. And as you have seen, these Archetypes are not the sole property of religious concerns. Many aspects of ordinary life can be treated as something holy. Consider the story possibilities that the Archetype can bring to your work.

Let's now move on to further Archetypes.

Lovers

First and foremost, the Archetype of the Lovers is about relationship. A lover who doesn't love someone else will be a pretty pointless character. If you put forward a character as a lover, be sure you know which character will be the partner.

Maybe we should clarify what love is first, though. We're not talking about sexual lust here, although physical attraction certainly plays a part in the relationship. Likewise, there's more to love than that rush of positive emotions one person can have for another. Love is more than emotion. Love also involves the choice of two people to make a commitment to each other. Ideally, love is a partnership.

For a mythic model, we may as well go back to "the beginning."

> **Lovers – Adam and Eve.** Back when God created all the creatures, he happened to make *one* human. But God very quickly decided that this creature needed a partner, so he made it fall asleep. Pulling out a rib, God formed the second human as a female, letting the sleeper be the male. The male was named Adam and the female was named Eve. Companions and helpers to each other, they were supposed to enjoy their lives in the Garden of Eden. Unfortunately, that little snake incident disrupted those plans.

As storytellers, *perfectly matched* Lovers aren't always the most interesting choice: where's the drama between people who mesh well? If you want to tell a story about characters who *are* suited for each other, the most interesting choice would be to put them in circumstances that keep them apart. Another option would be to have two characters who have to learn how to be good partners. Two characters who are mismatched in any way carry a load of drama from the first moment.

The most important thing in telling a story about Lovers is to make the relationship compelling for the audience. If you are inclined to tell a positive story, the object should be to make the audience want this couple come together. If you want to tell a more negative tale, show us how ill suited the couple is, in spite of their attraction to each other.

If Adam and Eve are the most obvious mythic example for lovers, the most obvious *story* example is, of course, Romeo and Juliet.

In his 1968 film version of *Romeo and Juliet*,[12] director Franco Zeffirelli makes it clear that this tale of young love is set against a backdrop of much violence. The opening images are of intense fighting in the streets. Yet in the midst of this, young Romeo Montague has kept out of the brawling – mainly because he's pining for a girl who pays no attention to him. To lighten his mood, his friends, led by Mercutio, talk him into crashing a huge party thrown by the Capulets (the rival family with whom the Montagues have been brawling). Just as he looks for the lady he's been pining for, his eyes land on young Juliet, and his world changes. But additionally, when Juliet sees *him,* she pays attention, which leads to their first conversation and then to their first kiss.

The relationship between Romeo and Juliet is certainly one of young passion. Yet it also demonstrates a commitment in the face of some very serious hindrances. The enmity between their families means they're unlikely to get support from their relatives. And then comes the test of Tybalt's death. Romeo regrets the death, Juliet is shocked by it. Yet when Juliet's Nurse condemns Romeo for the death, Juliet chastises her for criticizing Juliet's husband. And when the Nurse tells Juliet to go ahead with the marriage her parents have arranged to another young man, Juliet realizes she is on her own in keeping faith with Romeo.

Remaining faithful to the loved one, even onto death, is part of what makes the tale of Romeo and Juliet such a classic example of lovers and their commitment to each other. It's the ideal of what that relationship should look like, for the emotional content at the very least.

For an example of Lovers without so much of the influence of young love, consider *Ladyhawke.* Isabeau of Anjou and Etienne of Navarre appear as completely committed lovers. Even though they are separated by another's curse, they remain partnered. Isabeau as the hawk stays close to Navarre, whereas he as the wolf is never far from the lady. To reinforce our sense of how joined these lovers are, Navarre tells Phillipe that hawks and wolves mate for life, and that the Bishop (who cast the curse) didn't even leave them that. That is, there's no animal frolicking for the pair. It's absolute physical and emotional chastity for them: "always together, eternally apart." Until the curse is broken, which it is.

The partnership of lovers can be shaped in many ways, and you need to consider all the possibilities. Are they partners because they share the exact same interests and professions? Or are they partners because their interests and abilities complement each other?

Also, when shaping stories, you can explore the options of mismatched pairs. You can have a couple who seem wildly unsuited for each other, and yet whose love and concern for each other gets expressed at every turn. In the other direction, you may have a couple that appears to be perfectly matched partners that fail the crucial tests of attention and commitment. Once you understand the balanced partnership of the ideal relationship of lovers, you can explore all the less perfect possibilities. Whether you want the audience to root for the couple to come together or whether you want the opposite, be aware of what the ideal would look like.

From the intensely social Archetype of the Lovers, let's consider the solitary opposite.

The Hermit

As I said, the Lovers are very social. To love someone else requires that you be around and interacting with that other person. The Hermit, by contrast, does the opposite.

Now, the reasons behind why a character would chose to withdraw from social interaction can be quite varied. Some have religious reasons – wanting to draw nearer to their god. Some have emotional reasons – withdrawing from contacts that have created great pain. Whatever the reason for the isolation, one thing that stands out is the separation from society. The Hermit may be regarded by those who are in community as being a reject or an outcast. He may be considered a madman or a holy man. It is the disconnection which marks the Archetype.

We can see this separation modeled in Jesus.

The Hermit – Jesus. After he goes through the very social experience of being baptized by John, right there in the middle of a crowd, with some dazzling divine special effects, Jesus heads out into the wilderness, alone. He had a purpose, in wanting to meditate about what he was going to do next, but the fact is, he went out there alone. Totally cut off from society. And even after he came back and began traveling around with his followers, he would occasionally go off by himself for a time.

There is a very strong tendency in storytelling to endow Hermits with special knowledge. Perhaps it is because we suspect that anyone who can survive on his own, without other people, has mastered something special in the arts of life. That is why the Hermit frequently becomes a crucial source of information in stories.

In the film *Real Genius*, Lazlo Hollyfeld plays the part of a Hermit. He withdrew from society when he learned his scientific discoveries were being used in weapons. He chose to live hidden away in the steam tunnels of the school's campus. Yet, when Chris and Mitch succeed in their laser experiment, Lazlo brings the wisdom of his experience to them. He warns them that Hathaway may have done to them the same thing *he* experienced. And then he follows that warning with advice and assistance in the retribution they plot.

As you can see, Lazlo demonstrates that aspect of providing special wisdom and knowledge. And that is a typical use of the Archetype. But remember that you can take advantage of those expectations that the audience has. Consider your options and what your story needs, you may find that countering the expectations will make your tale richer.

The Hanged Man

This Archetype deals with a particular type of wounding. Now, in the sections on the Male and Female Journeys, we looked at what wounding can do to the character's psyche. One of the important things in that consideration was that the wounding could happen in many different ways. With *this* Archetype, however, we are concerned with a very specific sort of event. Whereas with the Wounded Male and Wounded Woman the wounding might be accidental or incidental, in this case there is a very intentional aspect to it.

It could be that your Hero chooses to suffer an injury in order to gain special knowledge, or in order to benefit someone the Hero is protecting. The event could symbolize a character's change from being focused on materialistic things to moving into spiritual concerns, or from dwelling on mundane matters to much more cosmic issues. Of course, this change in outlook gets manifested by suffering and possibly sacrifice. We will look at Sacrifice more closely later. But here we want to consider what the experience of being wounded can bring to the character himself.

A mythic model of the Hanged Man Archetype is Odin.

The Hanged Man – Odin. The Norse god Odin spent a lot of time thinking about the future, since he knew the Aesir would face a terrible battle. Now, the god Mimir watched over a fountain that contained, even flowed with, all wisdom and knowledge. Odin wanted to drink of this water, but he had to pay a price for it: he had to give up one of his eyes. So Odin did that, and took his drink. On another occasion, because he felt it was important that he meet that last battle with vigor and youth, rather than the decrepitude of age (for the Norse gods were not perpetually youthful), Odin hung on the World-Tree Yggdrasil for nine nights. He did this to fulfill a magical rite which would rejuvenate him. Not only was he hanging there in the branches, he was also wounded by his own spear. Apparently, the experience was worth it, for when he finally did drop to the ground he was youthful once more.

The Hanged Man motif represents something beyond the basic element of woundedness. This Archetype combines the wounding with purpose. It may be a matter of sacrifice, but it includes an aspect of gaining knowledge as a result of the wounding. The tales of Odin illustrate this.

A film example of the Archetype can be found in *The Vikings* (1958)[13]. In the story, there are two incidents of wounding, one which represents this motif and one which does not.

The first occasion of wounding is when Einar is blinded in one eye by a hawk. He's been abusing the young hero, the slave Eric, and Eric set his hawk at Einar. This incident does not fit the Hanged Man type of wounding, for the only knowledge Einar gains from the incident is of the steel in Eric's character.

It's the later incident in the story that touches on this motif. In that instance, Eric has escaped from the Vikings and made his way to the English kingdom. He turns over his captive – the Viking leader, Ragnar – to the English. Aella, the English ruler orders that Ragnar be thrown bound into a pit of hungry wolves. For Ragnar, as a believer in Odin, this would be an honorless death. Eric, raised with the same beliefs, knows this. Yet Eric cuts Ragnar's bonds and gives him the sword, so that Ragnar could die with sword in hand, fighting, making him eligible to enter Valhalla. For this action, Aella cuts off Eric's hand.

The loss of Eric's hand is the important wounding. Through his choice and his acceptance of the punishment, Eric gains an understanding of honor, of leadership, and of compassion for an apparent enemy, all qualities which will later help him to be a strong king.

Back when we were considering the elements of the Journey motif, we looked at the matter of the Price the Hero must pay in order to achieve the victory in her quest. This Archetype in many ways fits hand in hand with that plot element. Of course, the wounding that *you* consider important might not occur at the climactic battle (it doesn't happen at that point in *The Vikings*). But wherever you place the wounding, and whatever type of wound you design it to be, you will want the experience to have a strong resonance in the audience. Stupid accidents will not win much sympathy from the audience.

If enduring a wound involves crossing a threshold, our next Archetype involves the ultimate threshold – Death.

Death

Whether you use the Death Archetype in your story as a character or as an event, always understand that you are dealing with one of the most emotionally intense issues your character – and your audience – will face. The "other side of Death" remains the great unknown territory. Belief systems may shape your concepts of what comes after the end of material life. But *factual* knowledge remains minimal. As a result, Death brings with it a great deal of uncertainty.

In addition to the matter of what a character facing Death may feel, you also have the reactions of the people around the dying person. Because humans live in community, the death of one person inevitably has an effect on others. Some will feel the death as an intense loss of a crucial part of their lives. Others might feel that the death of a specific person would be greatly desired. But at whichever end of the spectrum you place a character's death, it should never be a totally casual event. Remember that (in the ordinary course of events) the dead person was important to *someone*. Of course, you might see some story possibilities in writing about a character whose demise touches no one. But again, in doing so, you need to be conscious of the fact that the audience will want to know *why* no one cares that the person died.

When thinking mythically, the human psyche has a difficult time conceiving of Death as a total cessation, of complete annihilation. Perhaps we are subtly but powerfully affected by the constant recycling of the world around us. We exhale carbon dioxide, which plants convert back into the oxygen we need. Wind and weather and water grind down the mountains, and the sediment becomes deposited elsewhere, building up new land. Water evaporates from lake surfaces, travels through the air, becomes precipitation falling to earth and it either nourishes the plant life or flows together eventually forming new lakes. Round and round, we see these cycles. So, mythically, we tend to look at Death as an opportunity for transformation.

Thus, when we look for mythic figures dealing with Death, we find imagery that is less than horrific.

Death – The Hero Twins of Central America. Hunahpu and Xbalanque were twin brothers who set out to avenge the deaths of their father and uncle at the hands of the evil lords of Xibalba (malevolent Underworld gods). The Xibalbans put them through terrible ordeals, and it wasn't enough for the brothers to survive – they had to out and out *win* their contests. Ultimately, they were charged with attempting to annihilate the Lords One and Seven Death – meaning they had to overcome death itself. Of course, the Xibalbans didn't expect the boys to succeed. When the brothers *did* succeed, the Xibalbans were terrified, expecting to be executed themselves. Instead, the Twins agreed to spare them as long as they stopped demanding human sacrifice. In getting the Xibalbans to agree, the brothers cleared the path of death for humans, so that it would lead to the Upper World rather than the malevolent clutches of the Underworld gods.

The Greeks also seemed to regard Death with some mildness.

Death – Thanatos. Thanatos was the Greek god of death. He was the brother of Hypnos, the god of sleep. And although there is something a little bit fearful about death, Thanatos was commonly seen as a bringer of comfort. He was frequently pictured in an un-sinister appearance – that of a winged spirit.

As you can see, Death is a complex subject for storytelling. You have the dying character's fear of the unknown. You have the sense of loss in those around the dying character. You have the possibility of transformation that Death could bring. However you deal with it, don't belittle it. Remember it is a serious issue to your audience.

Without a doubt, the film *The Green Mile*, set in the death row of a prison deals with the issue of death. There is some speculation on the part of the characters as to what may lie beyond this ultimate threshold. And Melinda, the Warden's wife, suffers under a "sentence of death" from a tumor. But for the most part, the film concerns itself with the facing of and approach to death. Death gets regarded with due seriousness by all the characters – except the two we are clearly intended to dislike: Percy and "Wild Bill."

Another consideration of Death issues comes in *The Sixth Sense* (1999)[14]. The advertising tagline for *The Sixth Sense* made it clear to the audience that death was central to the story: "I see dead people." Young Cole Sear suffers a great deal of anxiety, and Malcolm Crowe, child psychologist, sets out to help the boy. Cole fears the dead people he sees, understandably so: they're scary to look at, frequently angry and demanding – and he *knows* they are dead. That last fact plays to the simple human reaction to encountering death – we fear becoming like the dead.

One would think that Cole, when asked what he wants, would say that he wants these ghosts to go away. But Cole has apparently lived with this ability all his short life. Instead, he says, "I don't want to be scared any more." Basically, Cole needs to move from one state (being scared) to another (being without fear). Which means crossing a threshold. Thresholds, as I've said, are part of Death imagery, the crossing from one form of being into another. Thus, this story takes place in autumn, the season for such matters. And Malcolm works to help Cole make that transformation. Of course, one of the satisfying elements of this story is that Malcolm also needs help to cross a threshold, and that Cole provides that help.

One of the crucial aspects about the use of death in this story lies in how it plays against the expectation of death as an ending. The ghosts seem to expect that death is an end, and so become stuck at that point. The solution comes in recognizing death as a threshold.

Now, whether or not you believe in some sort of continuance after death, you need to be aware that most of the audience will respond to the concept. Whether as a matter of intellectual or religious explanation or simply as a mythic (and intuitive or emotional) response, Death as a threshold has considerable power and should not be overlooked by a storyteller.

Indeed, how characters respond to Death (or any traumatic change) can carry a lot of drama. That being so, let's consider those reactions.

Stages of Grief

Since the early 1970s, studies in the reactions of terminally ill patients when they learned their prognosis led to considerations of the stages of grief. And originally the term grief was not used. Instead it was called the Stages of Receiving Catastrophic News[15]. "Receiving catastrophic news" considerably broadens our perception of what conditions can precipitate these feelings.

Grief is a term we tend to associate with major loss, certainly death, but also other losses. But catastrophic news need not be *loss*. Anything that traumatically changes the conditions of life could qualify as catastrophic. As a storyteller, you need to keep those possibilities in mind as you shape the events your characters will face. Even an apparently *good* change, *because* it is a change, may trigger these reactions in your characters.

And just what *are* these reactions? The actual number of Stages varies, depending on the writer discussing the matter. But a basic synthesis will give us the following list:

Denial

Anger

Survival

Awakening

Bargaining

Depression

Acceptance

Forgiveness

Transformation

Denial. We all can recognize the "this can't be right" reaction. We've all felt it in varying degrees, from the surprised "That's unbelievable," to the furiously defiant "I *don't believe it!*" The point is that the character resists the drastic change (death, illness, moving away) on the most primal level. And you can handle this in your story with a lot of options –

will it be obvious to the audience that the change is inevitable, or will they at first believe with the character that whatever the news is, it is not true? But remember, denial is about a big "No." It does not mean that what the character says "no" to is actually true. Consider all your options. You can find a lot of drama in this reaction.

Anger. We'll look more specifically at special aspects of **ANGER** in the next section. But in this context, we just want to consider the emotional reaction in itself. The feeling of anger springs from a sense of imbalance, that the structure of things has been improperly disturbed. In particular, the feeling that the change has *destroyed* a perfect balance, that whatever has been lost or taken away will cause the collapse of that perfect balance or structure. The emotional reaction is hot and intense, and so will often override reason. When you use this in your story, think about what it is your character will consider most important to the stability of his or her life. If that is shaken or threatened or destroyed by events in your story, you have a ripe dramatic breeding ground, for your character just might explode.

Survival. Here comes the "batten down the hatches" reaction. That determination to dig in the heels, and hang on in spite of all the terrible stuff going on. Now, on the one hand, this reaction can be an admirable thing. On the other, the Survival instinct can be the child of Denial. It's the Survival impulse that generates comments like "I'll come through this in spite of all the evidence to the contrary." Survival, when embraced, brings a lot of energy to a character. Even if the character is indeed doomed to experience the traumatic change he is facing, this determination to survive can push the character forward in action.

Awakening. When we've cramped the nerves of an arm, the return of sensation brings with it a pricking feeling, tingling in a way that isn't exactly pleasing. Likewise, when a character begins to awaken to the reality of the catastrophic change before her, there will likely be unpleasant pricking in the intellect and emotions. Reality and delusion are sparking in the brain, and reality starts to win out. Awakening creates discordant feelings for the character, because it undercuts the emotional intensity of either anger or the survival impulse. Yes, recognizing truth is a good thing in the objective sense. But subjectively, it may not be pleasant at all. It can be unsettling, even confusing.

Bargaining. Of course, once a character realizes the truth that the major drastic change cannot be diverted, he may still try to avert the disaster from himself. "If I do *this*, can you keep *that* from happening?" Indeed, if Survival is the child of Denial, the Bargaining is the child of Survival. Yet, included in this feeling is the willingness to *sacrifice* something to hold off the pending disaster. What is your character willing to give up to avoid the fate falling on him? Indeed, this moment of bargaining can reveal much about your character and what he values. And there is high drama indeed in a character who sacrifices something or someone of value to avert something everyone can see is inevitable.

Depression. Inevitably, when bargaining fails and reality is faced, emotional energy drains away. When a character feels that nothing can be done, she'll feel like doing nothing. Lethargy and inaction mark this condition. For storytelling, you might think it difficult to dramatize a character in depression. But think of it this way, a depressed character will be a drag for all those around her, slowing down action. The contrast between the depressed character and the others can generate some conflict.

Acceptance. Eventually, it is possible that your traumatized character can reach a point of acceptance. There is more to acceptance than just finally acknowledging the truth of a situation. Acceptance also means letting the change come into the character's thinking and outlook. Instead of being something kept outside, the pending change is let inside the character's personal barriers. By stopping trying to fight the traumatic change, the emotional energy the character had been spending on resistance can now be spent on other things. When it comes to drama, in the story, this change in the character can surprise those around him.

Forgiveness. Forgiveness could be called the child of Acceptance. The difference between the two is that forgiveness comes from a sense of being injured. Certainly if the catastrophic change your character faces was caused by someone else, forgiveness can flow between them. But if the trauma is not caused by another character? Perhaps the forgiveness would be expressed in a re-establishment of your character's relationship with his god, or just with the community around him.

Transformation. When a character has come to terms with her traumatic change, she may change the way she goes about her life. Things that used to be important may be less so now. Things that she might not have cared about much before may become very important. This can be very effective and moving in your story. Whatever the drastic event is that affects your character, consider what the before and after may look like.

Although our intuition can see a progress through these stages, in reality, a person doesn't necessarily have to go through all these stages. Nor is it set in stone that a person would even progress from one stage to another. A particular person might jump over a stage, or skip several stages. He might even stay stuck on *one* stage. Using a wide variety of possibilities will keep your story fresh, and much less predictable.

In the film *Groundhog Day*, the stages of grief are treated as a progression, with moments where Phil's activities reflect each stage. *Denial*: Phil doesn't believe what is happening on the first repeat of his day. When the second repeat begins, he just wants to rush though the day, as it has no importance to him (after all, not only does he dislike the whole broo-ha-ha of the festivities, this is his third time going through it). When *anger* kicks in, he wonders why *he* got stuck in this never-ending day. He then decides that if there is no tomorrow, he can do whatever he wants, taking his resentment out on the community of Punxatawny. His interest in Rita resurfaces and he begins a type of *bargaining*, as he spends each day's rotation by trying to learn more and more what would appeal to her. In spite of what he learns, he fails at winning her, which leads into *depression*, where Phil becomes lethargic and suicidal. This fails him, bringing him at last to *acceptance*, where he goes through the days helping those he is able to help, stepping outside of himself and his own predicament.[16]

As you can see by this example, the traumatic event your character faces need not be death. Any drastic change can trigger these reactions.

There are mythic models for changes.

Changes – Khepri. Khepri was the Egyptian god of transformation, of the changes life goes through. His name signifies "he who becomes," implying change. He was represented by the rising sun, reborn each day.

Khepri's changes were those of renewal. The changes of Proteus were somewhat different.

Changes – Proteus. Proteus didn't like giving up his oracular secrets. So to get away from those who tried to get something out of him, he would change his shape. A lion, a dragon, a bull, a hawk — anything to alarm and intimidate the person who tried to capture him.

However you want to use change in your story, remember that your characters *will* be affected by it one way or another. From small changes to large ones, from changes that transform lives to changes that are geared to escape, from turning a corner to death itself, change can be a powerful dramatic tool.

MUSINGS

When it comes time to get down to business, be sure you have all your data collected. In making a deal with your audience, you have to be prepared to deliver on what you promise them. Deliver on your contract, and the audience will return as your customer. Remember the bottom line.

Think about it:

* Do you have a character who is either an Innocent or a Fool? Is your Hero a fish-out-of-water, or really without knowledge?

What knowledge or event would cause your character to stop being either Innocent or Fool?

* Is one of your characters a Transformer? What conditions will he change? Does she need changing herself?

How is your Hero's transforming power expressed? What events or experiences demonstrate his ability to transform things?

* Is one of your characters a Ruler? Do we see her giving order to the lives of those around her? How is his leadership demonstrated?

Is your character a good Ruler or a bad one?

Does your Ruler start out holding authority or does he have to win it? If he has to win that authority, do we see him do it? If your Ruler already has authority, is it challenged in any way? Is your Ruler in any danger of losing her authority?

* Do any of your characters function as a Holy One?

If so, what does your character serve? What activity, attitude or object is holy, and how does your Hero relate to it?

If a job has a priest-like function, what are the daily rituals that go with it? Do your characters take the job seriously, with the proper respect? Or does any one of them demonstrate disrespect? If so, how?

* Do you know which Stage of Spiritual Development your character belongs to?

Do you have a character in the Bottom Stage? How does that attitude show up in your character's behavior?

Do you have a character in the Falling Stage? What are the structures, institutions or rules that shape your character's life? What consequences does your character believe will fall if things are not done by-the-book?

Is one of your characters in the Threshold Stage? What rules and behaviors does your character question? In which direction will your character's choice lead him? Will he become more by-the-book? Or will he move into the next Stage?

Is one of your characters in the Rising Stage? How is that exhibited? What things does your character see that others do not?

If you have characters at different levels of Spiritual Development, how does the one at the lower level regard the one at the higher level? Remember, those at lower levels usually feel threatened by those at higher levels. How is this manifested in your characters?

* Do you have any Special Objects involved in your tale? Is it a Sword, a Grail, or a McGuffin?

If the object is a Sword, how do you demonstrate its power? Is it a good thing or a bad thing? Who wants it?

If the object is a Grail, have you clearly explained how it benefits people? Who wants it, and why? Do they want it for good reasons or bad reasons?

If your object is a McGuffin, have you made it clear how important the object is to the characters?

Remember: do not mistake a Grail for a Sword, or a Sword for a Grail – unless you want to use that difference for a point (look back at *Iron Giant*).

* Do you have Lovers in your story? Are they well matched partners or mismatched partners? What obstacles lie in the way of their being together? How have you conveyed that these two people *do* belong together?

* Do you have a Hermit in your tale? Why has she withdrawn from Society? What special knowledge has he gained in his isolation?

* Do you have a Hanged Man in your midst? What type of wound does your character suffer? What does your character gain from the experience?

* Does Death enter into your story? Either literal Death or the figurative Death of a drastic change?

How do your characters react to this Death?

What aspects of grieving do your characters feel?

Do your characters stay in one stage of grief, or do they move from one stage to another?

If the Death is figurative, what kind of change do your characters face? Is it a change that transforms, or is it change for escape?

SECTION FIVE – GOOD VERSUS EVIL

Aside from certain instances that usually have negative presentations (such as the Archetypes of the Shadow, the Bottom Stage of Spiritual Development), I've worked to indicate that most Archetypes can be used in either negative or positive modes. What I want to present here in this Section are Archetypes and issues that *do* have specific connotations on the Good/Evil scale.

Our perception of Good and Evil frequently begins with relativistic evaluations. If a character belongs to a community, certain qualities definitely have value toward maintaining the relationships of that community, while other qualities can be disruptive. And we usually label the first Good and the second ones Bad. Yet, even beyond these relative social values, there are absolute qualities of Good or Evil. A community might consider something Good which is, in fact, Evil. We only need to look back a moderately short time in history to find a prime example of this attitude in action. The Nazis of Germany in the 1930s and '40s accepted as a community value the idea that the extermination of certain races (Gypsies and Jews) was good. And yet, most people now will agree that it was an appalling attitude.

There does come a point at which we draw absolute distinctions between Good and Evil.

So, having accepted that there *are* absolutes of Good and Evil, how do we navigate our way (and the paths of our characters) between them?

In some eras of history, Good and Evil have been treated as equal forces, dual powers (hence the term dualism). Yet if Good and Evil are seen as opposite ends of a horizontal scale, we're still at a loss as to how to describe one as preferable to the other. If Good and Evil are equal, what's the point in choosing one over the other? And yet, we *do* say Good is more desirable than Evil. How do we get around this?

If we turn that horizontal scale (which makes dualism seem obvious) to the vertical, we get an answer. Think of a rope, anchored in Absolute Good and which hangs downward from that point. Your Hero, your community, your story may be at any point on that rope. But now we have the beginning of a way to describe why being Good is hard work (climbing that rope) or why Evil seems to cover more territory (the lower reaches of the rope sway much more than the upper ones), or is easier to do (gravity pulls you down the rope).

This isn't intended to be a comprehensive discussion of Good and Evil. The example just given is only a starting place for considering these elements. And it's only intended to give you an imaginative vocabulary for dealing with the issues in your story. But don't make the mistake of thinking that Good or Evil are irrelevant in storytelling. They're the primary ground of drama, the most certain battlefield a storyteller could want.

So let's look a bit closer.

EVIL

Let's get the bad news out of the way first.

What we really want to know is just what Evil looks like.

Many philosophers and thinkers have hunted for a satisfying definition of Evil. One says that Evil is that which harms others. Yet, a rock falling from a cliff can harm someone: is this Evil? If someone intentionally pushes the rock, yes. If it fell naturally, it's unfortunate, but not Evil. Another writer defines Evil as that which causes suffering. But some natural processes, such as teething in children, cause suffering and yet are not Evil.

This brings us to the awareness that Evil lies within people. Firstly, Evil starts with the *intention* of a character. And certainly, if a character intends harm and suffering, we can call the character Evil. But is that the end of the situation? No. For there can also be situations where a character does not *intend* Evil, and yet the consequences of his actions cause harm and suffering. If your character completely ignores the consequences of what she says and how she acts, can she be totally free of Evil? When shaping the nature of your Bad Guys, consider the whole range of possibilities in the combination of intention and consequences. For indeed, many an interesting villain thinks he's doing something good.

For the ultimate Bad Guy, there's the *character* Archetype of the Corrupter.

The Corrupter

The Corrupter is, without a doubt, a Devil figure. This character destroys whatever he decides to destroy, without regard to the value that object or person may have for the rest of society. Basically, this character would demonstrate the ultimate selfishness and self-centeredness. It has been said that Evil is a parasite on what is Good. It's also been said that Evil isn't particularly creative, being unable to originate something new. Rather, Evil (and the Evil Character) deforms things that exist. As I said when discussing the Shadow, when using a shorter list of Archetypes, the Shadow would handle many of these functions. But, a Shadow has a relationship or connection to another figure (besides not necessarily being negative). A Corrupter need not have a direct relationship or connection to another character in your story.

Several mythic figures can give us examples of this type.

The Corrupter – Loki. Loki's name meant allure or fire – an interesting mixture of qualities, individually somewhat positive but when combined, unsettling. And unsettling was exactly what Loki was. He constantly subverted the order of Asgard. Sometimes he was just making mischief, mocking the gods (especially Thor). But other times he had a definite darker intent, as when he brought about the death of Balder.

Loki may have engaged in some playful humorous activity. Our next contestant, however, had only one object in mind.

The Corrupter – The Eden Serpent. In Eden, where Adam and Eve were living in perfect harmony, the Serpent decided to mess up the good vibrations. He urged Eve to give the Forbidden Fruit a try. At first, Eve dutifully said that God had told them not to eat the fruit, lest they die. The Serpent said, "Nah, that's not going to happen. What's he going to do? Zap you with a lightning bolt? He just doesn't want you to know what Good and Evil are." "Evil? What's that?" "Eat the fruit," said the Serpent. "Then you'll find out." She picked a fruit and the Serpent slunk away. Sure enough, once she ate the fruit, Eve realized the mistake. There was no going back once she knew right from wrong. Disobedience was not the same as obedience. Well, misery loves company, so she got Adam to eat some of the fruit too. When God found out, he first grabbed the Serpent. "You've really messed up the picture here. Your reward will be to slither around on your belly. And of course, the children of Adam and Eve are going to hate you from now on, because you got them kicked out of a cushy spot." Because, of course, God couldn't let Adam and Eve (now imperfect) stay in that perfect place, Eden. And, oh yeah, they did end up dying out there in the harsh nasty world, so God's prohibition "on pain of death" turned out to be true as well.

As a final example of the Corrupter, let's look at Set.

The Corrupter – Set. Set lived in eternal opposition to what was good. He absolutely could not stand it. He actively opposed all the good that Osiris would do, trying to destroy whatever he could. He wanted to make everything dark and dead.

The signature of this Corrupter or Devil-figure lies entirely in the impulse to destroy things around the character. As we saw earlier, a Shadow figure need not necessarily be destructive. But a Corrupter always will be, to one degree or another.

There can be no mistaking Lecter's aspect as the Corrupter in *The Silence of the Lambs*. His history labels him as such a Devil. So also does his appearance in the film. Anthony Hopkins has said (in an interview with James Lipton for the Actors Studio) that, if anything, he modeled his attitude for the role on that of a cat. However, the final effect of the slicked down appearance, unblinking gaze and hyper-controlled movement seems more that of a snake than a cat. And ever since the tale of the Garden of Eden, snakes have been associated with the Devil. (Of course, as it happens, cats have been long connected with the Devil as well, so either animal image works.) Yet, Lecter also proves his devilishness in his actions as a Corrupter. He tries to corrupt Clarice's relationship with her Mentor Crawford, by urging speculation about possible sexual interest. He does corrupt Crawford and Clarice's quest for information by mutely encouraging Dr. Chilton's interference.

Although we have looked at Gordon Gekko in *Wall Street* as a Shadow figure, a better typing for him would be as a Corrupter. He embodies everything that the ambitious Bud wants to be, in terms of power, money and lifestyle. Yet, the audience sees very quickly that Gekko is not a pleasant person. On the phone to one of his henchmen, he says, "Rip their fucking throats out." There's no mistaking his ruthlessness. Yet, he can be charming.

As a reward for Bud's first successful dealing, Gekko treats Bud to an expensive lunch, recommends his personal tailor, and later sends a high class call girl to Bud for a night of entertainment. But once Bud has acquired a taste for the lifestyle Gekko can offer, Gekko also makes it clear that the price is ruthless participation – in particular, illegal insider information. Additionally, Gekko makes it clear that feelings have no place in his world – and yet, it's obvious that Gekko knows how to play upon Bud's feelings.

Gekko pushes Bud's ambition and desire for wealth. He entices Bud with glimpses into his own money-dripping lifestyle. He puts interior decorator Darien in Bud's path and encourages Bud to pursue her (and she's a girl with expensive tastes). All this temptation, and Bud doesn't resist it in the least.

Only a Corrupter, a Devil-figure, would put forward the following litany as a positive dictum: "Greed ... is good. Greed is right. Greed works." Countering this, in addition to the character qualities Bud's father exhibits, is Lou Mannheim, who does not respond to Bud's hustling brokerage deals. He tells Bud that there are no shortcuts, and "The main thing about money, Bud, it makes you do things you don't want to do."

As if to chart Bud's response to the corrupting influence of Gekko, Bud's morning exchanges with the receptionist Carolyn are very telling. At the opening, she asks how he's doing. He responds, "Great. Doin' any better, it'd be a sin." The morning after his first dubious (in ethical matters) success, he answers her query with, "Any better and I'd be guilty." But this time, she shoots back, "You were never that innocent." And most tellingly, the morning after he has countered Gekko and saved Bluestar, he enters and tells her, "There's justice in the world." There is indeed, and it awaits him in his office. The Federal authorities arrest him for illegal actions he committed on Gekko's behalf.

It's a strength of this story that it shows the consequence of submitting to the enticements of a Corrupter. Even though Bud has repented of his illegal actions, and made a certain degree of reparation, he still cannot avoid all of the inevitable consequences.

Lecter and Gekko both are rather obvious negative figures. A less obvious one is that of Christof in *The Truman Show*. Christof undoubtedly regards himself as a Father Figure to Truman, for he has overseen every event of Truman's life, from birth onward. Yet, in reality, he has no relationship *with* Truman. His moments of tenderness toward Truman are not expressed to Truman himself, but rather the *image* of Truman on a screen.

Indeed, Christof has corrupted and thwarted Truman the person at every turn in Truman's life. He removed Truman's true love Sylvia, because his own plans were for Meryl to wed Truman. To prevent Truman from desiring to leave his island home, Christof creates a phobia of water in Truman. He does this by "writing the father out of the show," giving the father character an apparent death at sea in a storm when Truman was young. All that mattered to Christof was that Truman have a built-in reason to stay put. Christof totally disregarded the extreme emotional trauma this event would create in Truman. Likewise, the whole push for Truman and Meryl to have a child happens because *Christof* decided it should happen. When Meryl breaks down under the weight of Truman's suspicions, Christof's intentions remain intact. He'll introduce a new romantic interest, for he's still determined that the first on-air conception will take place. Remaining submerged in the storytelling is the fact that, basically, Christof expects the actress to prostitute herself for the sake of his show.

In the end, Christof's attempts to control his piece of entertainment are thwarted by Truman's pure-hearted focus. Truman wants to go search for his true love Sylvia, no matter what he has to face (including his water phobia). Christof corrupted most of the actors who participated in Truman's *faux* world, giving them places on the most popular television show in the world. But he had no real control over Truman's heart and mind. And once Truman leaves the set for the real world, Christof loses that worldwide audience he had sucked into his voyeuristic program.

If a Corrupter seeks to draw others away from the good and balanced things in life, just what are these vices that get talked about so much?

The Seven Deadly Sins

First off, the term sin springs from a Latin word simply meaning guilty. In Old English, the word had a general sense of being an offense, wrong-doing, or a misdeed. Having said that, if you don't want to deal with the concept of a sin being an offense against divine law, you can skip it. It may be enough that it disrupts the social order. If you do deal with the religious aspects, treat them seriously. Otherwise, you run the risk of making your characters look stupid.

With that out of the way, let's look at that list of the Seven Deadly Sins. The traditionally seen sins are sloth, gluttony, envy, covetousness, lust, anger and pride. We'll consider each in turn, so that we can have a better grasp of the possibilities for our character's behavior.

Sloth. We're not talking about a tree-dwelling mammal of the Americas, here. Rather, it's a good old English (literally, Old English) word that means slow. The modern definition means a habitual disinclination to exertion, or indolence, or plain old laziness. Now, when no one else is involved, it probably doesn't matter how quickly a character gets around to doing something in particular. But in a community, when a character drags his feet in attending to something, the results can be disastrous. The character may be late in delivering important medicine. Or may be too late to prevent some disaster.

In *Hamlet*, this flaw shows up in the Prince's indecision. He cannot bring himself to take action, because he dwells too much on the consequences to himself and those around him. The goal set for him was simple enough: avenge his father's murder on Claudius. But Hamlet's concern for his mother, his tangled feelings for Ophelia, his intellectual caution all hinder him. So he does little. And then gets mad at himself for his inaction. His lack of direct movement toward his goal allows all the other elements to combine for his downfall, both emotionally and physically.

Gluttony. Although these days we do speak of someone as a glutton for punishment, we don't otherwise deal much with this offense. It meant the excessive consumption of food and drink. Of course, with our plentiful supplies of these items it's difficult to see this sin as a social disorder. We are much more inclined to view it as a personal problem. Back in earlier ages, when food was in shorter supply, the person who gulped down huge amounts definitely was a problem. Yet, even now, you could certainly use a character's fixation on consuming food as a trigger for conflict with those around him. From the amount of time spent eating to the problems a glutton could cause in a situation with limited supplies, you might be surprised at the drama you could generate from issues about food.

When you start applying that desire to consume more and more to things other than food, you will see the birth of *greed* in your character. Certainly, envy and covetousness figure into greed, but the driving motivation behind that subdivision of sin springs from gluttony. It lies in the sense that what the character already has will never be enough. More and more and more must get collected, consumed, gathered or otherwise brought into the character's possession. When the storyteller stops looking at gluttony as being just about food, and starts considering it as the desire to consume *anything,* all sorts of possibilities will start opening up.

Envy. Envy is a discontent provoked by seeing others possessing things one wants for oneself. "I want one" is a common enough response, and of course modern advertising plays on that feeling. We all want to have good and pleasurable things in our lives. But when a character becomes fixated on all the things she *doesn't* have in her life, she can throw her interactions with others into disorder. The drive to acquire all those desired objects can disrupt more truly important activities. And too, spending time being overly conscious of the fact that someone else has something you want doesn't help your relationship with the other person.

Covetousness. To covet means to want what someone else has, without regard to the rights of the other person. Rather than simply wanting something *like* what another has (as is the case with envy), when a character *covets* something, he wants the exact thing that the other person has. ("I don't want a car *like* Charlie's, I want *Charlie's* car.") It doesn't take much thinking to recognize how very disruptive covetousness can be. Beginning with plain theft, covetousness can grow to a consuming impulse that can be deadly.

If envy springs from a discontent provoked by seeing others having things one wants for oneself, then we can see Tom Ripley affected by this feeling from the very beginning of *The Talented Mr. Ripley* (1999)[1]. In the opening scene, Tom plays the piano accompanying a singer at an upscale party in an apartment overlooking Central Park in New York. Tom has borrowed a jacket for the occasion, and the jacket had a Princeton badge on it. Mr. Greenleaf mistakes Tom for a Princeton student, a possible classmate of his son. Tom doesn't correct the mistake, because he's just had a glimpse of a world he wants to enter. He continues to play upon this misperception when Mr. Greenleaf asks Tom to travel to Europe to try to persuade his wayward son Dickie to return home. When Tom encounters Dickie, he envies the easy, careless life Dickie leads. The young men strike up a friendship and Dickie persuades Tom to use the expense money Mr. Greenleaf sends Tom for the recreation of both of them. Of course, because of his envy, Tom actually doesn't need much persuading. Dickie goes along with the thin explanation that he knew Tom at Princeton, even though he doubts it. For the present, Tom amuses him and also provides funds for his entertainments.

But Tom's envy of Dickie's lifestyle moves very easily into coveting it. In this case, it isn't a matter of Tom wanting to live *like* Dickie. No, he wants *Dickie's* life. Tom looks through Dickie's things. He practices imitating the way Dickie speaks. He even tries on Dickie's clothes. When Dickie catches him at this last intrusion, Tom quickly says he was just "fooling around." But as Tom's fascination with Dickie grows, Dickie's amusement in Tom cools off. Just as Dickie begins to pull away from their relationship, Tom declares, "I've gotten to like everything about the way you live. It's one big love affair." This unsettles Dickie, leading him to tell Tom, "You can be a leech. It's boring. You can be quite boring." The young men come to blows, and Tom kills Dickie.

Suddenly, the story pushes forward into the ultimate fulfillment of a covetous desire. Tom takes Dickie's life. Not just in the sense of having killed Dickie, but also in the sense of taking over Dickie's social identity. The two young men were similar enough in appearance that Tom can get away with using Dickie's identification.

The disastrous consequences of envy and covetousness get played out in this story. Tom's killing of Dickie leads to additional murders, committed to cover up the first death. Tom throws chaos into the lives of Dickie's father and fiancée Marge. By indulging his envy and his covetous desires, Tom becomes an unpleasant destructive force in the world.

Lust. Associated primarily with the matter of sexual attraction, lust is an intense desire or appetite. Indeed, it's an overwhelming passion to possess the object of desire. It shows up in a phrase like "a lust for power." The examples of stories that are driven by lust are so many, I won't even single out a particular one. All the storyteller needs to remember about lust is how disruptive it can be. When it is a sexual lust, it can shatter marriages when it intrudes. It can derail careers by diverting a character's attention from the job. And fulfilling that lust can become so important to the character that *anything* that becomes an obstacle or thwarts movement toward the object can become a trigger for violence. There's nothing gentle or kind about lust. Just because the object of the lust may indeed be a good or beautiful thing, that doesn't ultimately justify the lust. This gives a storyteller plenty of explosive material to deal with. Is a character deluding herself, trying to explain her lust for power as simply wanting the fruits of her labor? Does a character try to convince himself that his lust for a married woman is actually love? Lust becomes the crux of so many stories because it creates such a volatile environment.

Anger. Anger can be a tricky emotion. It begins as a strong feeling of dislike aroused by a wrong. Any unbalancing of order can provoke anger, especially when the unbalancing happens unexpectedly. "So, where's the sin in that?" we ask. "Isn't there such a thing as righteous anger?" Yes, there is. The danger in anger lies in what a character does with the anger and where the anger takes her.

Righteous anger focuses on proper balance. It's more concerned with what's appropriate for the whole of the community. It doesn't dwell on any sense of personal injury. Of course, that doesn't mean that reacting to an offense against personal integrity is inappropriate. The actions taken by a character feeling a righteous anger should focus on restoring proper order both socially and personally.

In the film *Clear and Present Danger* (1994)[2], anger triggers much of the action. When a Colombian drug cartel kills a close friend of President Bennett along with the man's family, the President's anger at the murders leads him to surreptitiously authorize an illegal covert action against the drug lords. In the meantime, Jack Ryan steps into the position of an acting director of the CIA when Adm. Greer becomes ill. Jack appears before a Congressional oversight committee requesting funds, and in the process gives his word that the funds would *not* be used for covert American troops in Colombia.

The events which the President's anger sets in motion lead to Jack discovering that others have made a liar out of him. Of course, this angers *him*. But what angers Jack even more is the discovery that as presidential Advisor James Cutter and Jack's co-director Ritter closed down their illegal operation, they left the American commandos in Colombia. Indeed, Cutter betrays the commandos to Felix Cortez, one of the drug lords, as part of a trade-off. Cortez will take over the cartel and cut back the amount of drugs coming to the United States. But Cortez wants the commandos. Without blinking Cutter gives them up. Jack discovers this and confronts Ritter about Ritter's part in the events. Ritter belittles Jack's outrage over the events, implying that everything is relative ("shades of grey"). But Jack insists that it's about right and wrong.

The importance of right and wrong over the injury to one's integrity or feelings distinguishes righteous anger from sinful anger. And that judgment scale also shapes the actions that are inspired by righteous anger. Where the President's anger led him to agree to illegal actions, Jack's anger leads him to first remedy the other's error (by rescuing the remaining commandos and bringing them home), and then exposing the whole covert operation (regardless of what it might cost him). Indeed, righteous anger willingly accepts the consequences for actions moved by it (as Jack is willing to face death in the rescue, and possible professional suicide in exposing the actions of the President, Cutter and Ritter).

By contrast, at every turn, the President tries to sidestep the consequences of his angry choices.

The key thing about righteous anger is that it knows when to stop. The character does not allow the intense passion to run amuck. The sinful type of anger burns so fiercely that it runs to destructive hatred. When anger becomes blind to the big picture and can only think of destroying the object of the anger, you know we've crossed into the danger zone.

The War of the Roses (1989)[3] shows us a couple whose unexpressed anger with each other escalates to destructive hatred. Although Barbara and Oliver meet in a cute fashion – on a rainy day at an auction – they compete in bidding for a carved ivory figure. She wins the bidding, but he's the one that knows its true monetary value. She bought it because she likes it, he wanted it because it was valuable. Although the couple starts out in love with each other, this basic difference in approach continues to run through their relationship, gradually giving birth to anger.

Simple disregard feeds the growing anger between the spouses. Barbara obviously thinks Oliver works too much – which seems to be true, since we see him working even on Christmas Eve. Yet she's still attentive to his likes, buying him a Morgan car that he's always wanted. As he rises in his career as a lawyer, she continues to shape and furnish their home environment to his desires and expectations. However, she's the one who finds their lovely house, and she wanted it because she liked it.

By the time their children head out for college, Barbara has served Oliver's career and been disregarded as a person for a long time. When she announces that she wants to start a catering business, Oliver's displeased, asking why his income isn't enough. When Barbara asks him to look over a contract for her, he forgets about it. When she reminds him of it (the evening before she is supposed to sign it), he barely gives it attention, and then uses the contract as a fly-swatter.

From this point on, the anger between the two surfaces, progressing in actions and comments. She wants to be free of him, and he refuses to let go of any of his possessions, particularly not the house. The hatred between them blossoms into destruction and violence.

And, lastly of the Deadly Sins, we have Pride.

Pride. Pride is perhaps not too well understood these days. We are so concerned with self-esteem and learning to value our achievements, that we do not consider the dangers of excessively high self-evaluation. Until, of course, it hits us in the face. When we suddenly encounter someone who believes he can get away with anything, we are sharply reminded of the dangers of pride. Each of the qualities known as the Deadly Sins involves a self-absorption that's indifferent to other people, and pride represents the ultimate of that attitude. Pride leads a character to separate herself from those around her, in her mind elevating her far above others.

In the film *Citizen Kane*, Kane's pride lies in his inability to connect with the people around him. He starts out idealistically determined to help "the underprivileged" (although he apparently knows no one of that class). But soon, his choices are not about what's good for the poor, but rather are completely ruled by *his* will. He's absolutely sure that he's in the right. His sense of purpose and self-identity is so great, he cannot imagine anything running counter to it (let alone the possibility that a criticism might be accurate). His determination to make Susan an opera star, when she's merely someone with a mildly pleasant singing voice, demonstrates his pride: what is his, what belongs to him must be the grandest thing possible, for anything less diminishes him. When Susan leaves him, he can only see how the event affects *him* ("You can't do this to me!").

If the Seven Deadly Sins are the primary negative attitudes humans can have, what about how a character might come to be *in* those attitudes? Of course, *choosing* a course of action is the primary mover. But we can find a couple of nudgers in the actions of Temptation and Betrayal.

Temptation

Temptation (beyond the matter of sexual temptation) appeals to a genuine need or desire in your Hero. After all, you can hardly be tempted by something that doesn't interest you. A secondary consideration about temptation is that the bait that's dangled in front of the Hero might not be, in itself, a bad thing. *But* it may be that the approach to and/or taking of the bait is not the right thing for the character to do at that point in the story. Or the *means* by which the Hero could reach it, at this point, are inappropriate. Indeed, the phrase "the ends justify the means" is itself a temptation. Some things the Hero may not have *at this time* or *by this path*. It's not that the object itself is forbidden, but rather that it has to be approached in a particular fashion.

As an example: your Hero has fallen in love with the girl next door, Rosalie Morgan. Her parents like the Hero, but they don't want their daughter to become engaged or get married until after her 18th birthday, four months away. So your Hero sees Rosalie standing in her back yard in the sun, looking wonderful. *Temptation Alert!* Your Hero has two options. He can wave at Rosalie and talk with her, secure in the knowledge that in four months everything will work out. *Or*, he can jump the fence, destroy Mrs. Morgan's flower beds, grab Rosalie (possibly frightening her) and run off with what he wants.

That's the point about temptation: that giving into it can be destructive. Not necessarily to the Hero at that immediate point, but certainly to relationships, property and others' emotions. Innocent or harmless temptation doesn't really exist, at least not when it succeeds. When the Hero resists the temptation, only *then* could it be considered harmless.

Temptation comes in various degrees, as can be seen in some myths.

Temptation – Tantalus. Tantalus got in bad with the Olympian gods – he'd stolen Zeus' favorite golden dog, and snatched some of the gods' ambrosia and nectar and given it to mortals. But worst of all, he killed his son and served him up to the gods as food. He got a pretty severe punishment in Hades: he was confined in a river in the Underworld. Nearby was a tree branch laden with plump, juicy fruit. But every time he reached for one, the branch rose up away, out of his reach. When he would try to bend down to get a sip of the sparkling water he stood in, the water would sink away from him, out of reach. He wasn't able to either eat or drink. To make the situation even more uncomfortable, a huge stone hung over his head, ready to fall at any moment.

This little story of punishment gives us that first tickling degree of temptation, caught in the word tantalizing. Such temptations – possibly even something we need – sit right there, almost in our grasp. But it always shies away when we reach for it.

As storytellers, we can find plenty of food for drama in the prospect of *almost* having something in our hands. It teases characters, possibly provoking inappropriate action. The flirting appearance and withdrawal of something desired or needed can increase a character's emotional tension with each incident. Also, one character can use things to tantalize another as a punishment, or a torment. But as you can see, the objects used ought to be something the victim needs or wants.

Temptation also tries to circumvent rational thinking. Indeed, the Greek myth of Pandora describes just that point.

Temptation – Pandora. Zeus was greatly irritated by all the things Prometheus did, circumventing the rules for mortals that Zeus had laid down. He finally decided that something needed to be done to distract Prometheus. So he had Hephaestus the smith fashion the most beautiful woman ever. The woman was endowed with gifts from the gods – beauty, grace, a wonderful voice. And Zeus gave her an elegant container (but told her not to open it). Then Zeus called Prometheus. So Prometheus came visiting with his brother Epimetheus. Zeus brought out Pandora (whose name means all-endowed) and said she'd been created as a bride for Prometheus. She was breathtaking and Prometheus thought about it. After all, his name meant fore-thinking. He decided that no matter how wonderful she was, a gift from Zeus was probably a problem. He decided to pass on the matrimony. Epimetheus (a bit slower than his brother – after all, his name meant after-thinking) said "*I'll take her.*" So Pandora married Epimetheus. They were fairly happy together. Of course, there was that container Zeus gave Pandora.

Since insatiable curiosity was one of the qualities Pandora had been given, she eventually opened the container, springing Zeus' booby-trap. Inside, Zeus had packed it with all the possible evils for humankind he could think of. They went zipping out into the world. One last thing was left behind for the married couple to keep – hope.

There are a couple of levels of temptation wrapped up in this story. There's the temptation Pandora herself represents for Prometheus. Companionship with beauty can be enticing. But for Prometheus, he also had to consider the source of all this wonderfulness. He just didn't trust Zeus – obviously, with reason.

That, of course, is one thing to consider in telling your tale. Where does the temptation come from? What sort of relationship does your character have with the source of the temptation? And is your character going to think about the offering (like Prometheus), or will your character fall for the temptation like a ton of bricks (as Epimetheus does)? There's a secondary level of temptation in the story, of course. It's that container (or box or jar or whatever) that Zeus gave Pandora. There it was, a beautiful thing she was told not to open. Insatiable curiosity battled it out with obedience, and curiosity won. Those released evils represent the hidden dangers that are wrapped up in temptations your character faces. If something tempts your character, there's bound to be some sort of problem lying in the core.

It's an issue you need to think about in shaping your story. Since temptation is all about what's inappropriate for a character at that time and place, you need to know what the problems are that will be released if your character opens that box. Whatever tempts your character needs to be appealing, but will probably bring problems with it if your character gives into the impulse to take the tempting item.

Of course, the biggest model of temptation was when the Devil tried tempting Jesus.

Temptation – Jesus. After his baptism, Jesus went out into the wilderness to meditate about what he was going to do next. He was out there for forty days and nights, fasting. By the end of that time, he was hungry. So up pops Satan and he says, "Hey, if you're such a big deal, the son of God, you could command these stones to become bread." After all, Jesus *was* hungry. But he said, "Man does not live by bread alone." Satan didn't appreciate having scripture thrown at him, especially since he was trying to get Jesus to use power the wrong way. So he upped the stakes and took his victim to the top of the temple. He said, "Come on, show us what you can do! Since you love quoting scripture, let me remind you that it's written that 'He will give his angels charge over you.' You could throw yourself down from here, and the angels would bear you up." Jesus just said, "You should not tempt God." Satan was really put out by that, so he took Jesus to the top of a mountain and showed him all the countries of the world, all their riches and power and glory. And he said, "Look at this! I'll give it *all* to you, every bit of it – *if* you bow down and worship me." Jesus just said, "Go away. Worship belongs to God, not you." So Satan left him.

In this story, each temptation is about using power in an inappropriate way. Of course, Satan certainly implies that Jesus *does* have the power to do what he's urging. Jesus looks beyond the immediate situation in resisting these temptations.

The first temptation was about using something special for a mundane matter. It's true, Jesus was hungry. But to transform matter to satisfy hunger immediately – well, it's rather like using a blowtorch to kill a fly. It'll work, sure, but the consequence could be toasting the environment. The second temptation is to use power to show off. After all, the temple was located at the highest spot in the city of Jerusalem. A pretty spectacular location to start with. So we're talking about an event that would attract *a lot* of attention if he'd done it. Again, it's about the inappropriate response to a situation. Satan wants Jesus to *show* he's got the power. Apparently, Jesus was quite content merely *knowing* he had the power: he didn't need to show anyone anything. The last temptation begs a lot of questions: Satan says he'll give Jesus the whole world in exchange for some worship. So Satan's asking for something that belongs to someone else (that is, the worship) in exchange for something *he says* he can give (the world). I don't know about you, but when someone offers me the world, I wonder if it's his to give.

Now, if you're thinking that you are not planning to tell stories about any sort of divine Hero, and so you're wondering how this last example will apply, hold on. Let's look some more at the issues at hand.

First off, there's the temptation to satisfy one's immediate needs *immediately*. Just because your character is hungry, you're not planning to have her snatch the nearest sandwich from the nearest kid, are you? Just because someone has the power to do something – especially if it's immediately satisfying – that doesn't mean that would be the best use of the power. Yet, in stories, there can be plenty of opportunities where you can show your characters facing this possibility. They need not have an outside tempter nudging them into inappropriate action. They might consider doing that stone-to-bread transformation all on their own. After all, if no one's watching, who's to know it even happened? Well, *the character* would know. By giving into the impulse to satisfy the immediate desire or need *simply because he can do it*, the character has changed the way he looks at himself and his powers and abilities. When someone decides he *will not* wait for something because he can *take* it immediately, he's likely to stop paying attention to the issue when he's with other people. And that's not good. Using a power inappropriately in private can lead to using it that way in public – without regard to other people. These are all things that can enrich your story, depending on how you decide to have your character respond to that temptation.

The second temptation starts out seeming to be about showing off. "Come on, show us what you can do!" That's a taunt that has launched many a misadventure in stories. And it gets used a lot because it works. The taunt pricks the pride of your character. And of course, the ordinary human wants to prove he *can* do something. But beyond that aspect, the ridicule also implies that your character *can't* do the deed. This plays upon the character's sense of self. Does your character trust her abilities? Does she really need to show off to everyone else? Or is it enough to know she can do what's necessary *when* it's necessary? What would happen if your character *did* give into the temptation? How does that change the way people regard him? And what kind of difficulties will come from it?

That last temptation may seem like something that won't happen too often. But consider again. Tempters promise characters the world pretty frequently. It may be a limited world, but for the character being tempted it can mean a lot. All the power of a company may be offered to the rising young executive. The audience will eventually want to know if the tempter really does have the power to bestow what he's offering. And also, just what does he ask for in return? Most likely, it's going to be something your character cannot give, because it belongs to someone else. Does the matter seem too cosmic to apply to your little story? How about this simple scenario: a female executive will give her married male colleague power in their company if he'll just have sex with her. First off, she's asking for something that belongs to someone else (since the man has made a promise of sexual fidelity to his wife). And secondly, even if she has the power to elevate her colleague's position in the company, that doesn't mean she can command the rest of the workers to respect his authority in the new position. In which case, it was a fairly empty offer to start with, even though it seemed big.

The use of temptation in a story can add a lot of resonance for the audience, especially if you have been careful to make the temptation suited for your character. When the offer is an easy way to a goal, you need to show the audience what it may cost your Hero if he chooses that path.

The Emperor in *The Return of the Jedi* tempts Luke by playing upon Luke's feelings for his friends, while harping on the inevitable defeat of the Rebel Alliance. The Emperor alternately urges Luke to give into his anger and try to strike him, and then to join him because the Rebels are doomed. Although these promptings do put stress on Luke, they do not quite tempt him to abandon his principles. No, Luke's temptation buttons lie in his anger. When the Emperor has the incomplete Death Star fire upon the Rebel fleet, Luke angrily snatches up his light saber. Vader easily stops Luke's blow from reaching the Emperor. Now, Luke has been made to act against his principles. He's shown he could do it, except, of course, he wasn't able to *complete* it. When the Emperor calls the fighting between Luke and Vader "good," Luke again backs off. He tries to recover his ground, asserting he will not fight Vader. His combat moves become entirely defensive, until once again his anger buttons are pushed. The sheer act of indulging in anger, however, isn't what tempts Luke. Only when Vader, after reading Luke's thought about his sister, says,

"If you will not turn to the Dark Side, perhaps she will," does Luke completely give into his anger. The temptation for Luke lies in using his anger as *a means to an end*. The whole point of Luke's training has been that the ends do not justify the means, and that the easy way leads to the Dark Side. The trigger for the temptation is of course Luke's wholehearted commitment to Leia and his friends, whom he had been unwilling to sacrifice earlier. Giving in to his anger, using it as a means to destroy Vader and the Emperor and thus, supposedly, protecting his friends, will *not* get Luke to a better place.

Whatever you do when you introduce temptation into your story, don't do it cheaply. Pull out all the stops. Up the stakes. Go for broke. Casual temptation only flattens out the impact of a story. But a temptation that reaches (either quietly or with a big bang) all the way into the core of your character will hold the audience very well.

Betrayal

The last factor we need to look at in this section is the matter of betrayal. Betrayal represents the ultimate corruption of a relationship. If there is trust between people, betrayal breaks that trust and reliance. It means shirking on the responsibilities of a relationship, whatever the nature of that relationship may be. But it isn't a matter of simple deception. For when one person begins a relationship with intentional deception, in a basic sense, he never really *established* a real relationship.

Betrayal involves the corruption of a real, valued relationship. That's why it can have such power in a story. The breaking of such bonds can generate intense feelings.

The classic example of betrayal is that of Judas.

Betrayal – Judas. Judas had been one of the most trusted members of the inner circle of followers of Jesus. The group trusted him so much that they made him their treasurer. Since he handled the money, that means he's the one that made sure they had their groceries and that everyone got enough. He must have done a pretty good job. But underneath all that trustworthiness, something must have bugged him, because he was also stealing from them. And when the local authorities let it be known they'd pay to get information on how to get their hands on that pesky preacher Jesus, Judas turned up on their doorstep. Maybe he just hoped to push Jesus into starting a revolt. Whatever his reasons, he knew the authorities wanted to kill his friend. Even so, he agreed to lead the guards to Jesus. On top of that, he told them that the guy they wanted was the one he'd greet with the kiss of friendship. And he went through with the deal. However, when he saw his friend beaten and whipped, he was horrified by what he'd done. But it was too late then.

Judas. Judas kiss. It's become the most notorious betrayal story. In the accounts, the fact that it shocked the others in the group shows up in how little they want to talk about the man. All the good feeling (and there must have been *some*) that used to exist toward Judas disappeared with his act. And that's what can happen with betrayal. The Betrayer may lose far more than she possibly imagined. However compartmentalized she may think her life is, each part connects to other parts. When one section gets ripped out, everything else becomes distorted.

It's crucial for the storyteller to remember that betrayal depends on a real, valuable relationship. If you're going to include this type of incident in your story, you need to take time to build up the importance of the relationship. Thus when the betrayal comes, it should rattle both your character *and* the audience.

An excellent presentation of betrayal shows up in the film *Braveheart*. After their victory at the battle of Sterling, the Scottish nobles wrangle over which claimant to the throne of Scotland should become king. When Wallace leaves this chaos, Robert the Bruce follows him. Wallace encourages Bruce to assume the leadership. His earnestness surprises Bruce and unsettles him. While Wallace's affirmation of strength in Bruce warms the younger man, he cannot resist the cold pragmatism of his father, who urges him to side with the English. The emotional power poured into the encounters between the two men (Wallace and the Bruce) compels the audience to root for Bruce to side with Wallace. Thus, as the Scots are being defeated at Falkirk, the sudden revelation to Wallace (and the audience) that Bruce has not merely joined the English, but has been at the side of the enemy King Edward, stuns. The betrayal, of the cause and of himself, by someone in whom he has wholeheartedly invested himself, incapacitates the wounded Wallace. All his willpower runs out of him at that instant. The true beauty of this moment in this film is that we, the audience, see a betrayal and the reaction to it without an instant reversion into revenge. Wallace collapses, and Bruce is horrified by what he has done to the other man by betraying him.

As you can see, the Vices are grounded on warping relationships or things that might otherwise be good. Likewise, you can see that the disruption of social connections leads to negative consequences. What about the positive qualities of life?

GOOD

Some people claim that writing Good (as in virtuous) characters is boring. But how can *any* aspect of human nature be boring for a storyteller? And certainly, there can be plenty of drama in a character holding on to a virtue in the face of temptation, or in spite of heightened emotions, especially anger. In reality, writing a believable good character is a challenge, hence the impulse in the writer to avoid doing that work. Besides, flawed characters are all the rage these days.

Perhaps the difficulty in writing virtuous characters lies in a lack of understanding of what qualities actually *are* virtues. What do these things look like? What are the consequences of them? How can they be challenged or shaken? We're going to explore these issues in this next section.

Good carries with it the sense of completeness. Things that are not fractured, but rather, whole. If Evil devalues everything around it, then Good lifts up and prizes all that it can, whatever is worthy of that attention.

And the principal character Archetype that represents this is the Savior.

Savior

The opposite of a Corrupter is a Savior. Now of course, frequently in stories a Hero will play the part of a Savior for other characters. Such a context lies behind the concepts of the Boon or the Elixir. But in this discussion we want to consider more closely the elements that are specific to the Archetype of the Savior.

The simplest level of being a Savior consists of someone pulling another away from a disaster. That action indicates a value in the endangered character. The Savior's willingness to act also plays an important part in the event. So there's a first clue as well: being a Savior is a voluntary action. A Savior has made a *choice* to act. Certainly, a storyteller can come up with occasions where one character manages to save others without being aware of the rescue. Indeed, you can introduce a great deal of irony in such a situation. For even if those rescued consider the Hero a Savior, if the Hero didn't know about the danger, he'll probably feel unworthy of the title.

At the other end of the spectrum, we have the Savior who gives up her life to accomplish the rescue. We'll be considering the specifics of **SACRIFICE** later. But right now, let's just take it in the context of saving others. This ultimate action helps us focus on the essential quality of being a Savior.

It has been said that a Savior cannot save himself. Now, that statement does not mean that a Savior will inevitably die in the act of saving others (although that fate does indeed happen a lot). Rather, it means that a Savior cannot consider his own survival as he goes into action. That's because saving others goes beyond shielding and protecting the victim. Those aspects may be part of the action, but not the totality of it. Instead of simply holding off the impending doom, the Savior manages to deflect, defuse or otherwise remove the threatening disaster.

There is a story that shows a Savior in action.

The Savior – Jesus. One day as Jesus was walking through a town, he encountered a mob of men about to stone a woman. She'd been caught in an act of adultery and stoning was the punishment laid down by ancient law. For some reason, the mob was quite determined to go ahead with the punishment (once again, like the punishment of dishonored Vestal Virgins, stoning meant that none of them would have her blood on their hands). Jesus decided to intervene. He stepped between the woman and the mob. By interfering with what was considered a proper punishment, he could have been killed along with the woman (that was part of the law, too). Even so, he put himself between the woman and the impending doom and accepted that he might be stoned himself for doing that. He turned aside the danger by challenging the mob. He said that the person among them who was without sin should cast the first stone. Maybe it was a bit of a trick question. You see, according to Hebrew law, the *witnesses* of the crime were supposed to cast the first stones. *And,* for it to be considered a crime at all, there had to be *two* witnesses. But to catch the woman *in the act* of adultery, they, umm, sort of had to burst into the bedroom in the middle of the act (and why, one wonders, wasn't her partner in crime also about to be stoned?). So these guys weren't exactly blameless in character. Caught out, they all slunk away into the shadows. Left alone, Jesus told the woman to go home and change her habits.

There you have that action of stepping between the victim and doom, becoming possibly subject to the doom. It makes the action something more than protection. The danger to the Savior needs to be as real as it is for the victim. That increases the impact the event will have on the audience – particularly if they are conscious of the degree of danger for the victim in the first place. That danger also distinguishes a Savior from a Protector – Protectors may not be in any special danger from the threatening doom (for instance, will an ordinary bullet be any threat to Superman?). Keep that factor in mind when you use this Archetype. When the audience knows that both the victim and the Savior are in danger, their emotions are doubly engaged in the event. And if it's necessary for the Savior to lose her life while doing her job, you can generate a lot of emotion in the audience. As long as the audience agrees that the potential victim is worth saving. You *can* play with that value, as long as the *Savior* has reasons for saving the unworthy. But you can't ignore how the audience will regard the event.

In *The Terminator*, Reese certainly plays the part of protector of Sarah. His whole mission centers on protecting the young woman from the cyborg. But when the story moves to its climactic action, Reese also moves into the role of Savior. As the pair flee through the factory pursued by the stripped-down robot, Reese steps between Sarah and the Terminator. He uses the last of their homemade bombs to blow the robot to pieces. When he took this action, he knew he would probably not survive the blast. Yet it was what he needed to do in order to save Sarah. The fact that a portion of the robot still pursues Sarah is irrelevant to the nature of Reese's action: he's diminished the Terminator's effectiveness, so that Sarah could deal with it. He saved her.

Having looked at our ultimate Good Guy, what about those qualities called virtues?

The Seven Virtues

Over the ages, as the model of the Seven Deadly Sins took shape, people also drew up a list of Virtues, positive qualities, that counterbalanced the Vices. Four of the qualities – justice, prudence (or judgment), fortitude (or strength) and temperance – were collected by classical writers and thinkers. These were joined with three other Virtues, love, faith and hope. Each of these qualities embodies a positive response to the world around a person, including valuing the interconnectedness of various segments of life.

Love. This goes beyond a mere swelling positive emotional (or romantic) feeling. In this case, we're talking about a valuing of something and someone outside the self. That assignment of value also means that the value isn't dependant on the character (i.e., the person *feeling* the love) himself. Love ends up being the expression of the character's valuing of the other, without expecting something in return.

There are also some qualities that grow out of love that a storyteller should keep in mind. For instance, there's mercy. Mercy springs from the value your Hero sees in *all* life. It's a choice to withhold devastating consequences from falling on the Hero's opponent. Or not carrying out a justly leveled punishment. Mercy expresses the *Hero's* values, and *not* necessarily the worthiness of the person receiving the mercy. The difference between the worthiness (or rather *un*-worthiness) of the recipient and the amount of mercy shown to him can create intriguing drama in your story.

Compassion and empathy also spring from a character's love for others. After all, love is an *outward* movement of feeling from the character. Although it's a wonderful thing to receive love, the Virtue expresses the outward direction of positive actions. In stories, we'll see love in actions of characters which support others, which lift up others, which shelter and protect others. As a storyteller, you have unending possibilities of demonstrating love in action. A whole range of possible connections spreads from the love between two people all the way to a broad love for others (which could lead a character to give up his life for those others).

Faith. This term gets used most frequently in connection with religious belief. But a storyteller shouldn't let himself be limited by that. In fact, to have faith in something means to have confidence or trust in a person or thing. For instance, any storyteller will have faith in his ability to communicate. Someone crossing a bridge may have faith in the skills of the engineer of the bridge. We usually do have faith in things that can be tried, tested and proved. Yet humans often also place that trust and fidelity called faith in things that cannot be based on proof. Even aside from the matter of religious faith, humans place their faith on other people's character. We frequently rely on someone being consistently dependable. We say "I have faith in you."

As a storyteller you can take advantage of our impulse to have faith in people or things. Is the object of your character's faith reliable? If your character has faith in something she cannot prove, how do those around her react to that? Is your character's faith challenged or belittled? Is your character's faith strong enough to withstand battering?

Again, it doesn't matter *what* your character has faith in. It *does* matter how well you convince the audience that your character isn't an idiot for having faith in whatever the object/person is. Whether the object of faith is God or flubber, let your character's conviction be honest and genuine. The minute the audience senses that the storyteller thinks the character is an idiot for having faith in something in particular, the audience will back off from the character.

Now, if you *do* want to hold up a character's faith as ridiculous, be sure of what you are doing. Any errors of fact or information on your part will undercut your intention. Accusations of bias will fly your way. If you want to make sure that the audience knows that the character's belief that he can fly is a delusion, you need to demonstrate your grasp of the laws of gravity and aerodynamics. And then hope that your character (or audience member) hasn't been working with experiments on anti-gravity magnetic fields.

Still, having faith in something *is* a Virtue. The character looks beyond the self, values something that (most likely) the audience can see is worthy of being valued, is indeed reliable and trust-worthy. Having faith in something or someone gives a character a support to his strength, reinforcing him and increasing his ability to withstand oppression and abuse.

In *The Return of the Jedi*, Luke looks beyond himself to the virtues of the Jedi Knights. As the story moves forward, we see Luke acting on this faith. His faith rests in the nature of being a Jedi Knight. His first communication in the film, his message to Jabba, includes the statement that he is a Jedi Knight. The significance of that calling (or at least what it means to Luke) underlies his discussions with Yoda and Obi-Wan about his father. Luke insists that his father still has good in him, but Ben flatly says that Vader is evil. When Luke declares that he can't kill his own father, Ben indicates that if Luke doesn't, they (the Rebellion) are lost.

Yoda also warns Luke (again) that giving into anger, fear and oppression lead to the Dark Side of the Force. And, he adds ominously, that giving into the Dark Side will forever affect Luke's destiny. Yet, when Luke does face his father, he continues to assert that there is good in the older man. Vader denies it, insisting that he must obey his master, the Emperor. Apparently, Vader believes his choice of the Dark Side is irrevocable (as it seems Yoda believes). "It is too late for me, son," Vader says to Luke. "Then my father is truly dead," responds Luke.

In spite of this statement, when Luke pulls himself back from the brink of killing Vader in anger, his declaration to the Emperor tells us the basis of his faith. "I'll never turn to the Dark Side. You've failed, your highness. I am a Jedi, like my father before me." The Emperor responds, "So be it – *Jedi*." In using that title, the Emperor acknowledges the Jedi qualities.

Luke had in fact begun down the path to the Dark Side. Yet he pulled himself back from it by remembering the nature and qualities of a Jedi Knight. The principles of the Jedi sustain Luke's faith. But more than that, Luke claims those qualities for his father ("like my father before me"), in spite of all evidence to the contrary. Luke's faith, in the end, proves to be well founded, for the elder Skywalker does act on those principles in order to save his son, returning to his Jedi training and faith.

Vader gives us the picture of someone reclaiming his faith. The *loss* of faith obviously has figured in many stories. From loss of faith in a deity down to loss of faith in one's own talents and abilities. Artists who feel they've lost their touch, musicians who've lost heart in their music, detectives who feel they can no longer do their jobs – all these and many more have stumbled their way through stories.

Hope. Hope is a feeling that something desired will indeed be had, or that a desired outcome of events will indeed come to pass, or that current circumstances (possibly bad ones) will turn out for the best in the end. It can mean to look forward with desire and a reasonable confidence. Or even more simply, it means to believe, or desire, or trust in something positive.

Many people treat hope as if it were the same thing as not being cynical. However cynicism usually focuses on expectations about human nature. The worst actions of his fellow humans never surprise the cynic. But if something other than human nature grounds the hope, why, it would be possible to have a character who is a hopeful cynic. Consider the possibilities that lie in your choice of focus for your character's hope. If the hope is grounded in something unexpected, or intangible, your character may be able to hold onto it in spite of great trials.

Likewise, give some thought to what might shake your character's hope. Challenges to the foundation of hope, and how the character responds to challenges, can provide the means to show the personal qualities in the character, or even provoke growth. (And, of course, those challenges can be emotional and dramatic.)

While we're looking at challenges to hope, let's give some thought to the negative counterpart – despair. Despair overruns a character when the circumstances seem to become too much for the character to cope with. Discouragement can lead a character to give up on her endeavors. And that can create all sorts of problems in the story (problems in this case meaning drama, conflict – exactly what you want in a story). So don't overlook what you can add to your tale by exploring what can happen when your character *loses* hope.

The 1960 Disney version of *Pollyanna*[4] gives us a portrait of hope, and its power. When the recently orphaned Pollyanna Whittier arrives in the small town of Harrington, to live with her rich aunt Polly Harrington, her ugly dress proclaims the limited circumstances the child has known all her life until that moment. And yet she maintains a positive outlook on all that comes her way, something she had learned from her missionary father. By contrast, her Aunt Polly maintains a cold, controlled facade, which cracks slightly at the warm kiss goodnight which Pollyanna gives her on their first night together.

Pollyanna's hopefulness, her looking for the positive, appears in her reaction to the room her Aunt gives her in the big house. Instead of one of the large, unused bedrooms on the same floor as her Aunt's bedroom, Pollyanna receives a small room up in the attic. Even the sour housemaid Angelica expresses some disapproval of this choice: "Not much of a room, is it?" Pollyanna, however, says, "But it's my own, anyway. I'm glad of that."

As she becomes acquainted with the townspeople, Pollyanna's persistence with what she calls the Glad Game amuses the adults, who cynically underrate its power. The ill-tempered Mrs. Snow, an apparently house-bound invalid who constantly talks of her impending death, runs smack up against the strength of the young girl's hope. The pair had struck up an unlikely friendship. Yet, when Pollyanna visits the older woman, intending to recruit her help for a charity bazaar, she finds Mrs. Snow selecting her coffin. Pollyanna's rare anger surfaces. "A person shouldn't think about dying so much. I don't *want* you to die." The adults make dismissive noises at what they see as childish inexperience (forgetting she was recently orphaned). "You should be glad you don't need these horrid old coffins," cries Pollyanna. "You ought to forget about dying and be glad you're living!" She then says she doesn't want to see Mrs. Snow anymore and leaves. The older woman loses interest in her attitude of illness, and changes.

Pollyanna's hopeful attitude, looking to see the best in others, affects all those she encounters. Her attitude inspires them to start trying to live up to her expectations.

And then Pollyanna falls from the tree outside her room, paralyzing her legs. It's one trauma too many for the young girl, and she loses her optimism. Dr. Chilton, who wants to take her to the city for surgery expresses concern about her attitude. After all, depression would not be a good condition when facing an operation. "What that child needs is a good shot in the arm of hope," he says. The good shot comes in the forms of the townspeople, all of whom have been touched and changed by *her* hopeful outlook.

As you can see in this example, hope is something more than an blind, naive optimism. In looking for the best in any situation, the power of hope can reach beyond the character who expresses it.

These three Virtues cover very broad territory. In their basic aspects, most people have no problem recognizing them. The remaining four are perhaps (in this day and age) more subtle. But they frequently show up in stories in some fashion or other. Understanding them as specific qualities will help you use them more effectively in your own tales.

Strength (or Fortitude). This Virtue seems simple enough to understand. Strength gets displayed in the ability to endure, to stand up to assault, to be reliable. From physical strength to an adamantine toughness of will, strength in one character or another supplies an anchor to many stories.

Strength is also a quality that draws other people to the person who possesses it. The Strong Man becomes an anchor or shield for others.

Mythically, we can see this quality at work in Hercules.

Strength – Hercules. Hercules was the half-mortal son of Zeus, and was regarded as the greatest hero of the Greeks. One of the benefits of his parentage was that he had supernormal strength. In spite of personal troubles and the animosity of Hera pursuing him, as Hercules went through his adventures, he frequently earned the admiration of the people he helped. His ability to withstand and endure some incredible challenges demonstrate that quality of Strength.

Hercules certainly captures the image of physical strength. But by stretching the imagination a bit, we can conceive of strength in non-physical areas. A strong intellect which can withstand attempts to brainwash or baffle. A strong sense of compassion that persists in the face of cruelty. Find some element that can be made unshakable in your Hero – and then set all sorts of forces against that quality in the Hero. Moving from obvious physical strength to strength in other aspects can intrigue the audience.

For instance, consider what happens to Arnold Schwarzenegger's character Dutch Schaeffer in the film *Predator* (1987)[5]. First off, casting Schwarzenegger in a role almost automatically conveys the implication of strength. Dutch and his men are career soldiers, so we don't think of *any* of them as weak. What takes Dutch's team beyond the realm of strictly being Warriors is Dutch's statement about the types of missions the team accepts: "We're a rescue team, not assassins." This mission statement gives a positive connotation to the team's existence. We can easily approve of them as rescuers, and can, with them, resent that they are misused by Dillon. We consider this attitude on their part as a strength.

When the Predator starts hunting the team, we get caught up by the drama of strong rescuers who are unable to rescue themselves. But as the situation grows more and more threatening, we see that mere physical strength does not carry the day. The team members, and even Dillon, grow fearful and susceptible to panic. But Dutch's strength of character and his focus on survival anchor the others, holding off disaster longer than the Predator expects. It's not just Dutch's physical prowess that lets him survive the Predator: it's his strong determination and adaptability.

In *The Green Mile*, Brutus "Brutal" Howell conveys in his nickname the implication of strength – in fact, a strength that can be ruthless. Even though the massive presence of John Coffey overshadows him physically, his steadfast nature supports Paul Edgecomb throughout. That Paul attracts the loyalty of such a strong character enriches what the audience sees in Paul.

You, the storyteller, need to consider that point. What if the character who embodies strength in your tale is *not* the Hero, but rather one of the supporting characters? Such a shift allows a greater degree of vulnerability in the Hero, while still providing an anchor or support where it's needed. It also means that your Hero could be learning to be strong from the example of the supporting character. Indeed, when you can create a learning curve for your Hero (no matter what the subject being learned), you increase the amount of involvement the audience will have with the Hero (always a good thing).

Temperance. These days, the term temperance is most associated with the drinking of alcohol. Or rather, the *not* drinking of alcohol. The Temperance Movement in American history strove to get people to *stop* drinking (they were concerned about the problems drunkenness creates, both in the destructive behavior toward others by the drunk, and the damage to the drunk's own health). But that's a very limited understanding of what temperance can mean.

Basically, what the word means is moderation, self-restraint and self-control. Looked at that way, it's easy to see how this quality can be of value. Especially if the story around the temperate character whirls with passion and imbalance. As with strength, temperance can become an anchor or linchpin that keeps the action from spinning away into chaos. That still, calm center gives the audience breathing space.

For instance, in Zeffirelli's *Hamlet*, Horatio provides a counterweight to Hamlet. The Prince can go off on wild tangents, but the quiet, steady Horatio keeps him anchored. When the Ghost first appears to Hamlet, Horatio tries to hold back the Prince, warning him not to rush after the apparition. After Hamlet has spoken with the Ghost, his bursting energy runs into Horatio's reasoned caution. "These are wild and whirling words," says Horatio. Hamlet instantly latches onto that temperate remark, and decides to use his own *in*temperance as a disguise. Horatio's calmness and reason at all times contrast with the turmoil of Hamlet's own emotions and thoughts.

It's crucial that storytellers not overlook the value temperance can bring to a story. This overlooked Virtue can become very important to the action. In *Lethal Weapon*, Roger Murtaugh provides a balance to Martin Riggs' over-the-top behavior. Because Murtaugh confronts Riggs' suicidal impulses, he provokes Riggs into backing away from those same impulses. He also gets through Riggs' defenses by apologizing for some harsh comments and by thanking Riggs for saving his life. After that, he overcomes Riggs' psychological defenses by ignoring them. This approach provides Riggs with a more balanced context for life, an outlook his own isolated existence had previously lacked (and which Riggs actually finds attractive).

The last two Virtues are similar to each other. Justice and Judgment will often travel hand in hand. But they are distinct, and we will look at them that way.

Justice. Justice is the quality of being fair. It's all about being balanced in the approach to what is right. Justice weighs things and determines the nature of what's under consideration.

Mythically, the Greek goddess Nemesis personified justice.

Justice – Nemesis. Nemesis was a daughter of Night, and as such was regarded warily. Indeed, to the ordinary mortal she was a bit terrifying. Nemesis was responsible for seeing that order was maintained, so she wasn't concerned about the emotions of people. She was concerned with equilibrium. She rewarded virtue and punished wickedness. Indeed, she pursued those who were putting the order of the world out of balance. Her ruthlessness in that pursuit eventually led to her being regarded as a negative aspect (after all, these days we use the term nemesis to mean an implacable foe). But in reality she was always only concerned about maintaining balance and order. If virtue was neglected, she made sure it was acknowledged. If wickedness was rampant, she made sure it was suppressed.

Nemesis captures the reason why justice can be a seemingly harsh virtue. It isn't concerned about the emotions of characters. Instead, it focuses on restoring and maintaining the order of life. In general, justice doesn't care about mitigating circumstances that mercy might take into account. Mitigation isn't part of the territory justice patrols.

In *The Fugitive*, the character of Sam Gerard serves as a figure of justice. In the early part of his quest, Gerard is only concerned with the strict limits of his job, bringing in the escaped fugitives. The whys of the prisoners' convictions do not matter to him. The escape throws things out of balance and it's his job to put them back in order. So, when he encounters Kimble in the tunnels of the dam, and Kimble says "I didn't kill my wife," Gerard only responds "I don't care." The issue of Kimble's guilt or innocence isn't his job.

However, as he continues to do his job of pursuing Kimble, Gerard becomes puzzled by the doctor's actions. They don't seem to balance out the way he expects. Why does Kimble waste precious time helping an injured boy? Why does Kimble seriously search for a one-armed man? In seeking answers to these questions, Gerard's sense of justice begins to over-ride his simple duty to his job. The closer he gets to Kimble, the more certain he becomes that the doctor is not guilty and that someone else is. Thus, he can do his job at the end by taking Kimble into custody, while making sure that, based on information he has uncovered, justice will now be properly meted out to innocent and guilty alike. The fact that Kimble, as the outlaw, accepts Gerard's acknowledgment of who the real culprits are indicates that Gerard is the figure holding the sword of justice – and that Kimble trusts justice.

Judgment or Prudence. Judgment and Justice are close siblings, but they are not precisely the same. Indeed, where justice evaluates objects, judgment (or prudence) decides what to do about the object. A dictionary describes judgment as the ability to form an opinion objectively and wisely. Prudence is defined as caution in practical matters, with a secondary definition of foresight. These definitions help us get a grasp on the concept of judgment and the sort of character who would embody it. That quality of foresight lets us know that this judgmental character will consider how present actions may impact the future. Where justice will lay out that this one and that one are right and wrong, or good and bad, judgment will look at them and say, "That may be so, but we cannot take action at this time." Of course, judgment could also say, "In that case, A goes here and B goes there." The Judge determines what action will be taken.

> **Judgment – Samuel.** In ancient Israel, Samuel was a Judge, which meant he went around the countryside, hearing disputes and sorting them out. As a servant of his God, he also carried out judgments that God himself had leveled. For instance, as King Saul was laboring to establish secure boundaries for the kingdom of Israel, God sent him to fight the Amalekites who were encroaching from the south. God ruled that no property or hostages should be brought back and that the Amalekite leader should be killed. A little consideration will show the pragmatic nature of these orders (since the Amalekites might want their stuff back). Yet, Saul after defeating the Amalekites got greedy for their property. He also struck up a sort of buddy relationship with the Amalekite king Agag – and brought Agag north as a prisoner. When Samuel learned this, he had to go to Saul. Samuel had to carry out God's judgment and execute Agag (for after all, a live king as hostage would soon encourage his people to invade Israel). But also, Samuel had to level a judgment on Saul. Fond as he was of Saul (and he was very fond of the king), the plain truth was that Saul frequently failed to follow God's orders. So, Samuel told Saul that his days as king were numbered.

The story of Samuel shows us the Judge delivering the judgment. As you can see, it isn't always a pleasant experience for the Judge. But it has to be done.

Another story shows us a more familiar perspective of judgment.

> **Judgment – The Last Judgment.** Jesus told a story about the Last Judgment, where people would be divided into two groups. They would be judged according to their behavior in life, on how well they treated their fellow humans. And the group judged

favorable would enter the presence of God while the other group would be banished to the outer darkness, far from God.

In this tale, we find the expected sorting out that we associate with judgment.

Let me elaborate on this again: the job of justice is to bring things into balance, to determine the correct weight of events and people. (That's why the figure of justice uses a scale to weigh things.) Justice knows the weights of right and wrong and identifies which one's at hand ("Is this thing correctly identified as right or wrong?"). Judgment decides what to do with the sorted items, people or actions.

In the film *Absence of Malice* (1981)[6], the Justice Department representative James Wells sweeps in at the conclusion to make judgments of the behavior of the various other characters. He conducts an informal (but on the record) hearing about the events which led to a newspaper story claiming that D.A. James Quinn had accepted a bribe from Michael Gallagher. Wells allows Justice investigator Elliot Rosen to question Gallagher, but unfortunately for Rosen, all of Gallagher's responses are innocuous and non-evasive. In the course of trying to explain why he believed Gallagher was behaving illegally, Rosen reveals that he himself is guilty of breaking the law by authorizing illegal phone taps. Wells' questions to reporter Megan Carter also make it clear that Rosen used her for his own ends. After sorting through everyone's behavior, Wells makes a judgment that Gallagher has done nothing illegal. He does suspect that Gallagher maneuvered the others into acting foolishly, but Wells exercises some prudence by not putting the question forward on the record.

Wells informs Megan that she had been used to publish inaccurate information (which ends up costing her job). He tells Quinn that the controversy has unfortunately damaged the D.A.'s credibility, and that not only has Quinn's campaign for elective office been severely crippled, but also that he recommends that Quinn resign as D.A. (which Quinn regretfully agrees to do). Lastly, Wells turns to Rosen. Rosen says that he won't resign, apparently thinking that he will not be judged for his illegal actions. Instead, Wells reminds Rosen that *he* hired the younger man: Rosen gets fired.

Wells weighs all the actions and hands out judgments. He exercises prudence in not overdoing any of his actions. But his judgments *are* final. They are not to be bargained with. His judgments bring the conclusion of all the tangled activity.

These seven aspects are what anchor all the other shades of virtue or goodness. By understanding what goes into giving a character a virtuous outlook, the storyteller will find greater story possibilities. When you know what a character's primary virtue is, you can more easily create opposition to him.

MUSINGS

When you throw out at the audience the idea that a character is good or evil, you want to be sure that the edges of your idea are sharp enough to stick in the target. A little time with the whetstone of contemplation will make the cutting edge as clean as possible. Then, once you have the nature of the character balanced and ready, you can aim for maximum impact on the audience, and let fly.

Think about it:

*   Just how bad is your villain? Is she an all-out Corrupter, or is there a limit to how far she will go to achieve her ends?

What aspect in your Hero is the villain trying to corrupt?

*   Which of the Seven Deadly Sins plays the strongest part in your story?

*   If Sloth or Laziness figures most strongly as the flaw disrupting the Hero's Journey, how is it manifested?

How is the Hero tempted to delay action? What excuses or reasons does he have for staying put? What problems arise out of the character being stuck in the mud?

*   Is Gluttony the flaw that most affects your tale?

Does someone in your story have an excessive desire for some commodity (food, things and such)? Does that desire disrupt the access of other characters to the commodity? What does the character neglect while trying to satisfy this desire?

*   Does Envy affect any of your characters?

Who feels the Envy? Which character is being Envied and why?

Have you shown the audience enough of what the Envious character's life is like so that they understand *why* he Envies someone else?

*   Do any of your characters Covet what another has? What is the relationship between the two characters? What is the object that is Coveted? Who does it belong to?

What are the consequences of the character snatching what he Covets?

Is the character aware of crossing from Envy to Covetousness?

*   Are any of your characters consumed by Lust?

How does the Lust disrupt the lives of the characters? Is the Lust out in the open, or is it hidden? Is the Lust indulged or satisfied, or is it left un-satiated? Remember that an unsatisfied Lust can drive drama.

* Has Anger been set off in any of your characters?

What triggers the Anger?

Is your character able to keep the reaction within the boundaries of Righteous Anger? What will happen if the character gives into *unrighteous* Anger? What unwise actions, rash choices spring from the character's Anger?

* Are any of your characters afflicted with Pride?

How does it show up in their actions and the way they treat other people?

* Are any of your characters going to be faced with Temptation?

What Tempts your character and why? What happens if your character gives in to the Temptation? What will be lost?

What happens if your character resists the Temptation? What will be gained by that?

* Does Betrayal figure in your story at any point?

What character betrays which other character? What is the relationship between the two characters?

Why does the character Betray the other? How is the Betrayed character affected by the action? What happens to the Betrayer after the event?

* Does your Hero (or any other character) have to play the role of Savior?

Who needs to be saved? What threatens them? Is the Hero seriously in danger when she steps between the victim and doom? Does your Savior succeed in this action?

If the Savior succeeds, does she do it without suffering the full effect of the doom? If the Savior succeeds, but does suffer the full effect of the doom, how does this affect the other characters?

* What is the strongest Virtue in your story?

Which character manifests the Virtue most clearly?

* If Love is your story's strongest Virtue, which character manifests it the most? What is the greatest threat to it? Which character is most opposed to the Virtue, and why?

*   If the strongest Virtue in your story is Faith, which character manifests it?

What is the object of the Hero's/character's Faith? How do other characters regard your Hero's Faith? Is the character justified in her Faith, or not? How do you demonstrate that? What challenges your character's Faith? How?

*   If Hope serves as the strongest Virtue in the story, what is hoped for? Who manifests this Hope?

Will the audience be convinced that what is Hoped for is worthy of the attention? What threatens Hope in your story? What will happen if the character loses Hope?

*   If Strength or Fortitude is the most important Virtue in your story, which character plays that part? How is the Strength demonstrated? What challenges or threatens your Strong character?

*   If Temperance is important is your tale, which character fulfills that role?

What is the *in*temperance or wildness that your character serves to moderate? How is that other character's chaotic behavior manifested, and how does your Temperate one react to it? Can anything shake the Temperance? If so, how?

*   Does the mantle of Justice rest on one of your characters?

What imbalance is he addressing? How does he go about sorting out things? What are the rights and wrongs that your character has to weigh?

*   Do you have a character who manifests Judgment? Who will she be Judging?

What are the Prudent evaluations your character has to make? Is your character comfortable making the Judgments or does he have a problem pronouncing the Judgments?

SECTION SIX – PARENTS

Parents or parental figures often enter into stories. Mentors in stories are frequently Father Figures. That Goddess we met in the Journey motifs often represents a Mother Figure (indeed, if you'll recall, the mythic example for that motif *was* the Hero's mother). If the figures themselves are not present in the story, then maybe your Hero (or some other character) needs to deal with issues that spring from her relationship with either or both parents.

In discussing parental figures in stories, we storytellers need to understand how to step outside our own psychological issues regarding our own parents. Frequently a writer can get trapped into writing about a parental figure according to his own experience (good or bad) – *and* thinking that everyone else shares that outlook. Parental figures in stories can be incredibly powerful, and a storyteller ignores that power at his peril. An unbalanced approach to them will unsettle the audience, and not in the way you *want* to unsettle them. It's one thing to choose to present a bad parental figure for a specific story, and it's something else entirely to present all parental figures in a bad light.

Some people contend that adulthood consists in reaching a point where the Hero no longer has a need of a parental figure. Some claim that when an individual can assert autonomy from a parental figure, that individual has at last grown up. But is this really true? If it were true, why do adult artists still seek the response of those they respect? What do people look for in that action? The desire for affirmation (from some sort of authority figure) remains.

Although I have tried to avoid overloading these discussions with psychological theories, some issues require a consideration of psychology. And the issue of parental figures is one of them. That said, I'll observe that I believe the assertion of autonomy that many applaud is, in fact, *not* a growing beyond the need of what one gets from a parental figure. Rather, I think what some call autonomy is in fact a recognition that the specific parental figure in one's life does not or will not perform a crucial function. With that recognition follows either a self-affirmation (basically, the Hero doing the work of the parental figure for himself) or the discovery and/or choosing of another character who will actually perform the needed function.

That word function is a very important one in considering parental figures. For parents *do* have a function in a person's life and development. Parental figures exist to bring a character to a fully rounded and completed humanity, not just to bring about the biological creation of life. And since, ideally, humans continue to grow and expand their psyches to the end of their lives, there can always be a use for Mother and Father Figures, regardless of the age of the character.

Stories leave plenty of space for a wide variety of relationships between child and parent figure. There are the flat-out rebellions against the parent, rebellion for no other reason than rebellion. Or there can be rebellion because the parental figure dwells too much on one function, while ignoring a more necessary one. Or the child may rebel on principles, because he disagrees with the standards of the parent. Likewise, the failures of the parental figure can provide obstacles and hindrances to the progress of the child. The failure of a parental figure to either allow the child to cross a particular threshold of development, or to recognize that the child has in fact crossed that threshold has driven many stories. Likewise, stories about the child who clings too long to one particular aspect of the parent can easily be found.

The presence of a parental figure in a story both serves as a reflection on various qualities in the Hero, and as a key relationship for the Hero. The two characters ought to interact in the story, so that the audience can *see* these qualities. As with the discussions of the stories of the Male and Female Journeys, this look at the functions of the Mother and Father Figures does not mean that a male cannot fulfill the Mother's functions, nor that a female cannot fulfill a Father's. All such things are flexible. We are just separating them into their most recognizable forms. There's no such thing as simplicity in the twists and turns of human interactions. And that's why there are so many stories to tell.

THE FATHER FIGURE

As I observed earlier, the Father Figure is often identified with Mentor Figures. Their functions do indeed overlap. But a Father Figure has additional aspects to it, so let us build our model.

The first element we can look for in a Father Figure is that of a Protector. Inevitably, we expect that the father will provide a safe haven for the child, warding off invasion, fighting off threats. The Father Figure provides a shield, often standing between the Hero-as-child and anything that might disrupt the child's growth. Battles the child cannot fight are fought by the Father Figure, until such time as the child is ready to take on the confrontations of the world.

Secondly, the Father Figure is indeed a Mentor. He generally trains and prepares the child to take up his own tasks and battles. The Father Figure provides the information the child needs to move forward in life.

The third function of a Father Figure is that of Priest. He initiates the child in each special stage of life. Indeed, this is one of the most emotionally powerful functions of the Father Figure. Here lies the source of a character's desire for parental approval. For in the priestly function, the Father Figure determines that the child is ready to cross a major threshold of life, and additionally blesses the child after he does cross the threshold. When the child moves into a new stage of life, or a new arena of activity, it's the Father

Figure who, in effect, says "Welcome, and congratulations. You are now a peer (my equal) in this realm." Of course, the Father Figure may also be a master of other and/or higher realms, but within the boundaries of the particular new arena, he now views the child as a peer.

This aspect of a Father Figure generates the highest percentage of stories, because of the emotional dynamite tied to the functions. When the Father Figure withholds approval or blessing from a Hero, conflict rises up. The audience becomes engaged, especially when we can see that the Hero has indeed fulfilled the conditions required by this stage of his progress. But equally dramatic are those occasions when a character seeks to force a blessing from the Father Figure that is neither earned nor deserved.

These interactions play into the fourth element of a Father Figure: his function as a Judge. As such, the Father Figure weighs all performance and declares things good or bad, according to his standards. This specifically concerns (in the ideal form) a character's *actions*, and not the character himself. However, there's no escaping the fact that the accumulation of acts and deeds will reflect a character's nature. The judgment, however, comes in spite of the Father Figure's emotional connection with the child. Our impulse may be to disbelieve the "this hurts me more than it does you" type of statement, and yet, with a close look at the nature of a Father Figure, we can see that it might be possible. If the Father Figure's function of Judge wars with his function of Protector, we can find great emotional drama in a story. There's the conflict *within* the Father Figure, between two clashing functions, and then there's the collision between the Hero and the Father Figure.

The last function of the Father Figure is that of Ruler. In this mode, the Father Figure presents the standards and rules that are being applied to the child. In this mode, he determines and orders the progress of the child, making clear his expectations of behavior or achievement.

When, as storytellers, we look at these elements that make the Father Figure different from a Mentor, we can see all sorts of exciting story possibilities. What if a Hero looks to the Father Figure for one function, when what he needs is another, such as looking for the Protector, when what he really needs is a Judge? Or what if a Father Figure clings to one aspect of his job and refuses to perform another? Father Figures who insist on being Rulers but never perform as Priests have long been popular in stories.

Odin serves as one mythic model for a Father.

Father Figure – Odin. One of Odin's names was Allfather. By our standards, he wasn't a particularly cuddly father though. His concern about trying to prevent the fall of the gods tended to make him rather harsh (that Protector mode in overdrive). He was the one who laid out the rules for human society.

The harshness that can come from a Father Figure shows up in Odin. And that harshness can figure in stories as often as the softer aspects of the role do. But understanding the specific elements of the Father Figure can help us clarify *when* in a story the emotionally charged relationship of child and parental figure comes into play.

For instance, for most of the film *The Silence of the Lambs*, Jack Crawford acts as Clarice's Mentor. He initiates her into the special activities of the Behavioral Sciences division of the FBI. He oversees her investigations. When he sends her to Lecter the first time, he warns her *not* to tell Lecter anything personal (knowledge is power, after all). These are all functions of a Mentor. But by the end of the film, Crawford's relationship with Clarice changes slightly. Throughout the film, there had been no physical contact between Crawford and Clarice. But as she exits Jame Gumb's house, Crawford puts an arm around her shoulder, shielding her from the news reporters on the scene. With that protective move, Crawford steps from Mentor to Father Figure, a change affirmed at the graduation of the FBI candidates. Once again, he touches Clarice, shaking her hand. He bestows the paternal blessing on Clarice's crossing this threshold of life by telling her, "Your father would be proud." With this touch and comment, Crawford reveals for the first time that he knows anything of Clarice's personal history (other than recalling her as a student at U.Va.). The character of Crawford in this story demonstrates how easily a Mentor figure in a tale can shift into being a Father Figure.

Where in *The Silence of the Lambs*, the Hero's father only appears in the flashbacks of Clarice's memory, in *Indiana Jones and the Last Crusade* the Hero's father actually appears in the story. In the prologue of the film, young Indy races home to seek his father's advice. But in this, the audience's introduction to the senior Dr. Jones, we do not even see him and apparently he doesn't even look up at his son's precipitous entrance. This is a remote, distant father.

As the story progresses, the adult Indy is frequently made to seem juvenile in his father's presence. Dr. Jones (Sr.) persists in calling his son "Junior." Each time Indy gloats – or at least rejoices – in an achievement during their escape from the Nazis' castle, he finds his father glaring at him and he is chastened. At almost every turn, Dr. Jones by word and look criticizes and judges Indiana's actions. The one occasion during the escape where Dr. Jones takes pleasure in Indy's actions comes when Indiana snatches a flag pole and levels it at an oncoming opponent. The resemblance of the opposing motorcycles to charging knights catches the attention of the medievalist in Dr. Jones: it's the one thing with reference to *his* area of specialty.

The underlying element in all this, is that Indiana is *still*, even as an adult, striving to please his father, striving to win the approval and blessing that is the father's job to bestow. When Indiana disappears in the crash of the tank, Dr. Jones suddenly realizes how distant and uncommunicative he had been. He realizes that he had not done his job as a father.

To take a step further away from an actual child and father relationship, let's consider a story where an unrelated character takes on the mantle. In *Indian Summer*, Uncle Lou represents a very obvious Father Figure to the returning adult campers. In this role, it's his job to affirm the growth of the campers and give them his blessing to cross the threshold into a fuller adulthood. He reassures Jennifer that she is a woman of value, addressing her insecurity in still being single. He gently encourages Kelly to confront her husband Matthew. He helps Beth resolve her grieving period for her husband's death, enabling her to begin a relationship with Jack. *Indian Summer* displays the Father Figure at work in a gentle and sweet context.

For a more challenging use of the Father Figure, we can look at the character of Robert McCall in the television series *The Equalizer*.[1] The series plays to the audience's impulse to turn to a Father Figure for solutions to problems or shelter from troubles. Although it could have been simplistic about that matter, the show generally handled things in a more sophisticated way.

In the "Lady Cop" episode, Officer Sandra Stahl seeks McCall's help in dealing with her corrupt partner Nick Braxton and his two buddies. Initially, she had sought advice from her own ex-cop father, but he only recommended that she say nothing and transfer away from the dirty trio. Failing to get that parental blessing for crossing the threshold into being a good cop, she turns to McCall to fill the gap. When they first meet, Officer Stahl says she would not testify against the trio. But when Braxton ups the stakes by killing a bum with her gun, McCall, the Father Figure as Mentor, forces her to acknowledge that she *will* have to testify against fellow cops.

In "Reign of Terror," McCall finds himself in the awkward position of being asked to help the doctor of a street clinic, a woman who doesn't want his help. Dr. Elly Watson objects to the use of violence – especially the use of guns – in dealing with the street gang threatening her clinic. McCall assesses the gang as being very dangerous, and that to confront them unarmed would be an act of folly. Logic tells him to walk away from the situation. But his Father Figure role of Protector leads him to do what he can to help Dr. Watson according to her guidelines – no guns.

A more enriched consideration of the Father Figure appears in the "Prisoners of Conscience" episode. In this case, Father Figures are important in two plot-lines.

In the plot-line of McCall's client, we have Waldo Jarrell, a writing teacher who had been jailed and black-balled during the Hollywood Red Scare. He has developed considerable affection for his student Antonio Cruz, an immigrant from Chile. When Antonio is snatched by mysterious men, Waldo seeks McCall's help. Antonio, it turns out, may have information about rebel leaders in his homeland and his captors plan to torture him for that information. This reminds Waldo too uncomfortably of his own past. As Waldo waits while McCall works, he reveals his parental feelings toward Antonio. He later demonstrates the Father Figure's Protector side by willingly walking into the hands of Antonio's captors, so that he can bring help to the young man.

The second plot-line dealing with Father Figures appears when McCall learns that Antonio's captor is none other than Randall Payne, the man who murdered McCall's own father. This news calls up a jumble of feelings for McCall: revenge toward Payne, and also some anger toward his own father for unresolved issues. About those issues, McCall tells his colleague Control, "The trouble is there was so much left unsaid between us." In relating his father's history, McCall concludes, "He felt he had something to prove to his family, to himself ... to his son. It made him a damn good soldier – and a damn bad father." McCall's internal conflict on these issues causes his memory to conjure up a ghost image of his father. McCall bitterly confesses, "It seems to me that I've been chasing your ghost half my life. Neglecting my family, as you neglected us. Every time I look into the mirror, I see you." The ghost merely responds, "A soldier has to accept responsibility for his own actions. Robert, you have no one to blame but yourself." Here, we have the Father Figure not merely acknowledging that the child has crossed a crucial threshold and become his peer, but also reminding the child of the responsibilities of this realm of life. After that reminder, McCall seeks out a direct confrontation with Payne. Everyone expects McCall to fulfill his revenge in that confrontation – it's understandable. But when the moment comes, when McCall finally does fire the gun – he shoots to one side, refusing to murder the other man. Instead, he acts on the principles his father held to, principles that led Payne to murder Capt. McCall in the first place. Payne says, "You're just like him, after all." It's the affirmation a child quests for. "Yes," responds McCall with a labored smile. When Control questions McCall about why he did not kill Payne, McCall answers, "I'm just doing what my father would have done." The child has recognized and accepted the standards of the Father Figure.

This particular episode should remind us storytellers of the fact that parental issues do not grow weaker or fade away, simply because a character grows older. The quest for affirmation, in particular, can affect anyone at any time in his life. Perhaps the error that some storytellers make is to assume that these needs of the child (even in an adult character) are actually *childish* (as in, immature), and therefore somehow ridiculous. On the contrary, our first standards in life are learned from our parents. It's therefore inevitable that we would return to them at times of stress. You will strengthen the emotional power of your story by understanding these dynamics and handling them with respect. Belittling the issues will lose the audience, for it won't ring true for them.

Whether you have the Father Figure in your story take the forefront (as in *The Equalizer*) or the background (as in *The Silence of the Lambs*), never forget the emotional power such a figure can bring to the tale. If your character reacts against the qualities the Father Figure represents, or must cope with the effects of a poorly done job by his own father, there's plenty for the audience to connect with. But again, never shortchange the Father Figure in your story. Even if you are dealing with a very flawed Father Figure, be sure you know exactly how the figure *is* flawed or fails. The audience very quickly spots hollow handling of Father Figures.

Let's now consider the counterpart to the Father Figure.

THE MOTHER FIGURE

Without a doubt, the most commonly used aspect of the Mother Figure is that of Nurturer. And yet, that element does not convey the entirety of what a Mother Figure can be.

Most certainly, the first element of a Mother Figure *is* that of being a Nurturer. A mother is the first source of nourishment for a newborn child, and that connection is hard to break. The expectation holds that just as a Father Figure would protect the child, so too would the Mother Figure provide nourishment and sustenance.

This leads into the second aspect of a Mother Figure, that of Encourager. Once the basic needs of the child are met, the Mother Figure encourages the child to venture forth. The Mother Figure conveys belief in the child's capability to meet the challenges of the world. Indeed, an ideal Mother Figure would be the Ultimate Fan of the child – win, lose or draw. Where the Father Figure as Mentor may instruct the child on *how* to achieve a goal, the Mother Figure as Encourager emphasizes a belief that the child *can* and *will* achieve that goal.

The third mode of the Mother Figure is that of Relator. The Mother Figure guides the child in building relationships and dealing with interpersonal interactions. This aspect is the fountain of all advice, and often (especially in stories) that fountain overflows. It's also the source of matchmaking mothers and interfering mothers-in-law.

Where in the Father Figure we have the Judge, in the Mother Figure we have the Comforter. The Mother Figure provides that warm, unconditional assurance of love and attention that the child craves regardless of whether or not a goal has been achieved, *and* regardless of how grown up the child is.

Like the Father Figure, the Mother Figure also has a Ruler aspect. She too lays out standards of behavior, expectations and obligations. This Rulership provides both parental figures with their power of Authority. That mantle of Authority is part of the job description. Your Hero may resist it, or submit to it, but either way, the Hero *reacts* to it.

We can find mythic models of Mother Figures in Thetis and Ceres.

> **Mother Figure – Thetis.** The sea nymph Thetis was very protective of her mortal son Achilles. She lavished care and attention on him. She would rush to his aid, and share in his sorrows. She dipped him in the River Styx to give him bodily protection (invulnerability – except for his heel). And when he finally did choose to go off to war, she made sure he had the best armor possible (it was forged by the gods).

Thetis certainly fills the role of Number One Fan of her son Achilles. Ceres, likewise, displays a passion for her child.

> **Mother Figure – Ceres.** Ceres was the Roman equivalent of Demeter. When her daughter Proserpina (whom the Greeks called Persephone) was snatched by the lord of the underworld, Ceres

gave up everything to hunt for the girl. And included in that everything was her job of teaching agriculture (thus socializing mortals and teaching them to grow relationships). And of course, her role as Nurturer shows up on your breakfast table every day – with your cereal (which gets its name from her).

The loyalty to the Hero which a Mother Figure displays need not be as blatant as the examples of Thetis or Ceres. A small amount of that unconditional concern can go a long way in a story.

A prime example of a Mother Figure appears in the character of Jessica Fletcher in the series *Murder, She Wrote*.[2] When the series began, there was concern that Jessica not appear matronly. Judging by the 12 seasons that followed, it would seem that by matronly, the storytellers (actress, writers and producers) meant someone who had completed her life's job and had settled into a background existence. Jessica comes to us as a vivacious and curiosity-filled personality, always appealing. Although she was widowed (and thus, experienced in life), she had never had children. Yet she ably displays all the traits of a Mother Figure. The fact that she *is* widowed without children allows Jessica to always be emotionally available to those she encounters.

The powerful draw of the Mother Figure leads to many stories where Jessica is actually *related* to a character she interacts with. Over time, the impulse to enforce the familial connection eased, because it became evident that Jessica as Mother Figure worked just as well with totally unrelated characters as she did with those with whom she shared a family tree.

In "Corned Beef and Carnage", Jessica's niece Victoria gets entangled in a murder in the advertising business, and becomes a suspect. On top of this concern, Victoria's marriage to struggling actor Howard has some problems – mainly because the newlyweds aren't communicating well. In this case, Jessica's involvement in solving the murder mystery connects directly to her unconditional support of and comfort for her niece. She also gives gentle advice to the pair about their relationship, but never as ultimatums and always in a supportive and encouraging mode.

In "Showdown in Saskatchewan", Jessica visits Jill on the rodeo circuit. Although Jill is called Jessica's niece, the relationship between them is less direct. Additionally, Jessica visits Jill in part at the urging of Jill's mother. Jill has been traveling the rodeo circuit with her boyfriend, rider Marty Reed. Although it's obvious that Jessica doesn't approve of Jill's choice to live with her boyfriend, she doesn't openly criticize it. She sticks by Jill, being supportive of *Jill*, and is present to be comforting when it turns out that Marty is already married. This loyalty plays to the Relator aspect of the Mother Figure. Jill learns from Jessica's discernment about relationships.

In "Threshold of Fear", in New York, Jessica becomes involved with her agoraphobic neighbor Alice Morgan. Alice suffers from emotional/psychological traumas induced when her mother was killed five years earlier. In addition to helping solve that mystery, Jessica gives Alice unwavering emotional support and encouragement. This support enables the young woman to confront her fears and to begin a relationship with Henry Phelps, a concerned young man who is also a neighbor.

If Jessica Fletcher is unequivocally a positive Mother Figure, what can we expect from her opposite, the negative version? Take a look at the film *Ever After* (1998)[3]. In her dealings with Danielle, Baroness Rodmilla definitely demonstrates a negative Mother Figure. The evil stepmother may be a cliché, but only because such women do exist, natural parents or not. Rodmilla gives Danielle no nurturing, but instead forces Danielle to be a servant. Rodmilla gives Danielle no encouragement and no protection. Additionally, she takes over Danielle's home, eventually selling Danielle herself to remove the girl from the place. When all Danielle's hopes seem dashed, she tells the Baroness, "I have done everything you ever asked me to and still you deny me the only thing I ever wanted." That is, a mother's love. Rodmilla coolly responds, "How can one love a pebble in their shoe?" Rodmilla's flat coldness shows how the negative version of a Mother Figure even denies the existence of a relationship with the Hero.

Before we consider a couple of other issues related to parental figures, there's another matter to address. You may have noticed that when either a Father Figure or a Mother Figure exerts an important influence in a story, the counter figure seems to be absent. There is a storytelling logic to this occurrence. The purpose of having a parental figure in the story is to enhance the *Hero*. Thus, the important relationship lies between the Hero and the Mother (or Father) Figure. If the second parental figure appears in the story, the relationship of the two parents *to each other* can distract from what we want to learn about the Hero. Now, I'm not saying that you cannot have both figures in a story. But if they *are* both present, you as the storyteller need to keep the audience's attention focused on the relationships those Figures have with the Hero, rather than focused on their relationship to each other.

BOTH PARENTAL FIGURES

Balancing the presence of both Parental Figures in a story requires that the storyteller be conscious of the elements involved in the relationships. Does the audience see that the Mentor aspect of the Father Figure gets balanced by the Encourager aspect of the Mother Figure? Or do they see the Father-as-Judge balanced by the Mother-as-Comforter? I'm not saying that the qualities of the two Figures are necessarily in conflict with each other. In the ideal situation, the qualities complement each other. Of course, few storytellers tell tales about *ideal* relationships. Where's the drama in that? So if you are going to have both Parental Figures present in your story, consider how you can mismatch their aspects.

In Disney's *Tarzan*, the ape Kala demonstrates the unconditional love of the ideal Mother Figure. After a leopard ills Kala's own baby, she hears the sound of a crying infant and finds her way to the orphaned human baby. She only sees a baby in need and responds with unconditional love. She raises this child with constant care and attention. When the youthful Tarzan finally confronts his difference from the gorillas (because Kerchak has said in his presence that Tarzan does *not* belong with the group), Kala consoles the child by demonstrating that love doesn't depend on appearance.

Later, when Tarzan's feelings for Jane confuse him, Kala finally shows him the treehouse where his human parents died. She is, in effect, opening the door to allow him to claim the heritage (as a human) that he has a right to. She tells him, "I only want you to be happy." Again, the unconditional love of the ideal mother is at work in the story. Whatever the child chooses or becomes, the mother continues to love.

Kerchak plays the Father Figure to Tarzan, a negative Father Figure. He rejects the inclusion of the human child in the gorilla family, although not to the degree of insisting that Kala abandon the baby. Throughout the story, Kerchak looms over Tarzan's activities, disapproving and chastising when the boy's activities endanger the family group. Yet, when Tarzan comes to the rescue of the group, finally acting as an adult, Kerchak realizes his own error. As he dies, he accepts Tarzan as belonging to the family and gives the young man his blessing as leader of the group.

THE CHILDREN

The last matter to consider in relation to Parental Figures is that of the Children.

At the simplest level, Children love their parents with adoration, giving them complete trust. Children need protection, hence their impulse to run back to parents at any sign that disturbs them. These basic impulses, because they're grounded on the early biological, physical experiences, remain strong. And storytellers need to understand that the impulse has nothing to do with whether or not the Parents are any *good* at their job. It's the imprinting and bonding which occurs in infancy that drives Children to give complete loyalty to patently unfit parents. The flip side of that situation appears in Children who are very conscious of the incompetence of their own Parents and so go seeking substitutes.

The possibilities that lie in the drive for Children to keep the security of Parents can generate many stories. A lot of variety is possible. Don't overlook an opportunity to explore the options.

The film *House Arrest* (1996)[4], captures this longing of the Child for the presence of Parents. In it, 14 year old Grover Beindorf is an ordinary youngster, who thinks his world is secure. To celebrate his parents' anniversary, he has a video tape made of film from their wedding and early happy days of marriage. But when he and his sister present the tape, Janet and Ned tell the children they are separating.

Grover tries simple means of getting his parents to talk to each other, but the adults fall into arguing. So, partly inspired by a friend's comment, Grover locks his parents in the basement. In the morning, when Grover asks if they've talked things out, the parents lie, saying yes, but again quickly lose their united front by squabbling. So Grover refuses to let them out. Janet pleads with her son, asking "What is *wrong* with you?" Grover snaps back, "You guys are splitting up, that's what's wrong with me!"

Grover's little project of forced therapy snowballs when classmates bring in their parents as well. The desire of each of the kids is for a secure home, where the relationships between the parents are stable and responsible, and thus healthy and nurturing for the children.

House Arrest deals with the desire of some juveniles for a home life where the parents are in balance with each other, thus giving the children a happy and secure home. And although that desire seems an obvious one in youthful characters, like the need for the individual Parental figures throughout life, the desire for the secure family background does not diminish with age. Even an adult can carry on that desire.

For all its mix of the trappings of science fiction time warping and the methods of a cop thriller, the emotional core of the film *Frequency* (2000)[5], is about the desire of 36 year old John Sullivan to have *both* his parents, Frank and Julia, in his life. The initial focus of the story deals with the adult John's freakish radio contact with his father in the past, just before Frank was about to be killed in a fire. John's warning to his father changes his personal history in several ways. The main change is that his mother, who had been a part of John's life all along, suddenly, in the past, becomes a victim of a serial killer. Abruptly, John lives in a present with *neither* of his parents, for although he saved Frank from death in a fire, John still lost him to lung cancer (Frank being a heavy smoker). Father and son, in separate time frames, labor to catch the killer and save Julia. The desire of the Child to have both Parents in his life drives this story forward. Because it's such a basic desire (to have loving and supportive parents) the audience can easily identify with John, and so they are willing to go along with the rest of the ride.

As we've seen, the interactions between a character and the Parental Figures in her life can be filled with highly charged drama. Whether dealing with the character's actual parents or surrogates, you should know what elements of the relationship are most crucial. Family issues in a story can be some of the most powerful elements you can use. Always be clear about the needs and desires that you put into the story.

MUSINGS

If you want to stop the audience in their tracks, the emotional power inherent in Mother and Father Figures can do the job. The universal nature of parent-child relations can entangle almost anyone. Don't let it fall short by being feeble in your use of these motifs. Knock 'em flat.

Think about it:

* Are you using a Father Figure in your story?

Is it your Hero's actual father or a surrogate? What aspect of the Father Figure is most important in relation to your Hero? Does your Hero have positive or negative feelings for (or issues with) the Father Figure?

* If the Protector aspect is most important, what does your Hero need protection from? Does the Father Figure do the job well, or does he fail? How does your Hero feel about this?

* If the Mentor quality matters most in your story, what does the Father Figure need to teach? Is he good at it, or does he have gaps in his knowledge? How does this affect the Hero?

* If Father Figure-as-Priest has the most weight in your tale, how is this manifested? What blessing does your Hero crave? Does the Father Figure give the blessing or does he withhold it? How does your Hero react to this?

* If the Father Figure appears mostly as the Judge, what actions or personality traits of the Hero's is he evaluating? Does he do it gently or harshly? Does the Hero accept the judgment of the Father Figure or reject it?

* If the Ruler aspect of the Father Figure is most important in your story, how does it appear? What standards and rules has the Father Figure laid out for the Hero? Are those rules reasonable or excessive? Does the Hero submit to the Father Figure's authority?

* Do you have a Mother Figure in your tale?

Is it the Hero's actual mother or a substitute? Which quality of the Mother Figure has the most power over your Hero? Does your Hero have negative or positive feelings for (or issues with) the Mother Figure?

* If the Nurturing side of the Mother Figure is most important in your story, how is this shown in relation to your Hero? What nourishment is your Hero lacking, and how does the Mother Figure provide it? What does this mean (emotionally or intellectually) to your Hero?

* If the Mother Figure-as-Encourager is most important in the story, how is this demonstrated? What activity is the Hero engaged in that the Mother Figure cheers him on about? Does the Mother Figure stay within bounds or does she over-do the Number One Fan act? How does your Hero respond to this?

* If the Relator aspect of the Mother Figure is most important, how is this presented? What kind of relationships is the Mother Figure teaching the Hero about? Does the Hero need the instruction? How does your Hero react to this?

* If the Mother Figure is acting as the Comforter, how is this demonstrated? What wound or trauma precipitates the Hero's need for comfort? Does the Mother Figure succeed or fail in providing the comfort? How does the Hero feel about that?

* If the Ruler aspect of the Mother Figure has precedence, how do you show this in your story? What rules and standards does she communicate to the Hero? How will the audience perceive these rules? How does the Hero react to them? Does the Hero submit to her authority?

* Do both Parental Figures participate in our story? How does your Hero respond to them? Are the qualities of Mother and Father Figure balancing each other or are they in conflict?

Do characters in your story demonstrate a need for both parents? How is that desire expressed? What does your character do to fulfill that need? Does your character succeed or fail?

There are a couple of character Archetypes that don't easily fall into any of the previous categories. But they have to do with related characters, characters in relationship to each other. So I've called them Relatives. The first set has to deal with what I call the Fair and the Dark imagery. The second concerns Doubles of various sorts.

THE FAIR AND THE DARK

The Archetypes of the Fair and the Dark (usually associated with female characters) seems initially to be rooted in ethnic aspects of European culture. At the simplest contrast, it sets the blonde, blue-eyed looks of Northern Europe opposite the dark-haired, dark-eyed Mediterranean type. However, the paradigm of the Fair and the Dark actually plugs into more elemental aspects, some of which we'll deal with later.

The aspects that actually drive the Fair/Dark dichotomy are not racial, but rather the tendency to draw analogies (even subtle ones) between ourselves and the world around us. The physical aspects that drive this symbolism begin with light and dark. You'll remember some of the qualities associated with them. Light carries the connotations of reason and order and the intellect, while darkness has connotations of the irrational and chaos and the emotions. The next stage of symbolic implications grows from the first. Fairness in color becomes linked with air symbolism – clearness, openness. Darkness by contrast gets linked with earthy symbolism – heavy, confining. Even directional connotations can be attracted to this pair: Light - upward, Dark - downward.

Now, again, although some have connected these qualities to racial identity, that parallel doesn't hold up. Let's go back to my reference to the blonde Northern Europeans and the dark Mediterraneans. Simply looking at the cultures will show us the failure of racial application, for in the North we find the blonde berserker Vikings while around the Mediterranean we find the darker-haired intellects who gave birth to the Renaissance and the sciences. So, just to pound the nail down flush with the surface: the imagery of the Fair and the Dark is *not* about race.

Whew. Okay. Now, let me lay out a bit of a diagram of connotations. This diagram represents four quarters: the Fair and the Dark, with their positive and negative aspects.

POSITIVE - FAIR	NEGATIVE - FAIR
The intellect, control, perception, order, rationality; cool.	Openness, flighty, breezy, unanchored. Calculating, unemotional; Cold.
POSITIVE - DARK	NEGATIVE - DARK
The emotional, intuitive, rooted; warm	Chaotic, entrenched, irrational; hot.

When laid out like this, the contrast between Fair and Dark may seem obvious. But when it shows up in stories, it can be more subtle. Let's consider some examples.

For a very straight-forward version of the Fair and Dark Archetypes, we can look at "The Cloud Minders" episode of the original *Star Trek* series.[1] In the episode, two female characters present the sharp contrasts of the types. The blonde Droxine lives in the floating city of Stratos, living the life of a devotee of the arts and of cool intellectual pursuits. Dark-haired Vanna represents the surface dwellers (actually miners underground), and passionately fights and contrives to better the conditions of her people. Droxine's life in the cloud city has, up to this point, been untouched by violence or strong emotion. Although the cause of the separation of intellect and emotion in this world has a "scientific" origin, the two young women presented in the Archetypes dramatize the distinctions.

From that uncomplicated example, let's look at how the contrasting types are used in the film *Ever After*. Marguerite demonstrates the negative aspects of the Fair heroine. She is calculating, self-serving, and lacking in feeling for others (i.e., cold-hearted). Jacqueline demonstrates the warmer aspects of the Dark heroine. She gives Danielle some first aid after Danielle is beaten. Although helping Danielle could get her in trouble, Jacqueline slowly begins to show more empathy for Danielle and for others. Danielle, with coloring that falls between Marguerite's blondeness and Jacqueline's black hair, exhibits a combination of the intellectual aspects of the Fair and the emotional power of the Dark.

Further use of the iconography of Fair and Dark shows up in *Shane*. In this film, the good versus evil connotations are heightened by use of the paradigm. Shane's clothing is basically light-colored. Gunslinger Jack Wilson wears a black hat and a black vest. We couldn't look for a more straight-forward use.

Lawrence of Arabia makes a more subtle use of the paradigm. It rests on the presentation of the characters of Lawrence and Ali. Now, of course, the real T.E. Lawrence was indeed a person of very fair coloring. Yet, when Peter O'Toole got the role, even though his own coloring wasn't very dark, he dyed his hair almost white blond.[2] From the beginning of the film, Lawrence appears in light-colored clothes. This parallels his rather rational approach to the Arab problems. By contrast, when Ali first appears, he is all in black, and his passionate nature stands out from the beginning.

However, variation does come into play in this Fair/Dark imagery. After crossing the Nefud, after Lawrence has won Ali's respect and loyalty, Ali is almost always seen in garments that are black *and* white, indicating that he is adding rationality to his passion. The one exception to this pattern comes when the men go into the town of Deraa, when Ali appears all in dark clothes again. The mixed coloring in Ali's clothes indicates a positive change in the character. But when *Lawrence* changes his colors, it has a not-so-positive result.

Lawrence begins in light colored military khaki. The fair aspect gets emphasized when Ali gives Lawrence white Arab robes. But when things begin to get difficult for Lawrence in the winter, we can see him wrapped in a dark blanket. It is in this scene that Lawrence makes the decision to go into Deraa. And when he *does* enter the town, he wears a dark robe. He's cloaked in or wearing dark clothes while Ali nurses him, and when he decides to call it quits. After Lawrence is convinced to return to the Arab campaign for Damascus, he reappears in dazzling white. But his garments do not stay that way. After the slaughter of the Turkish troops, Lawrence's clothes are smirched with blood and dirt. By implication, so is his character. From that point on, we never see him in light clothes again, only these dirtied ones, or a military uniform that is shot in shadow.

With Ali, then, we can see the contrast as passion tempered by reason. With Lawrence, the implications are more complicated. Whether it is a matter of hiding his light or making choices no longer grounded on reason (he goes into Deraa simply to prove he *can* do it), the darkening of Lawrence's outfits does not carry the positive tone that Ali's changes do.

The subtle implications of rationality and emotion that get tied to the Fair and Dark imagery, show up in interesting ways in *The Silence of the Lambs*. Jodie Foster is noted for the fairness of her coloring. So it's interesting that for this film her hair is dark. Whatever the reason for this choice, the effect of it plays into the Fair versus Dark motifs. The dark hair gives substance to the character, countering Foster's petiteness (which is humorously pointed out when she gets into an elevator with a bunch of tall men) and the fragility of her appearance. As Clarice is an intellectual person, being a brunette keeps her out of the Fair-Ice Princess territory. It also takes her more toward the earthy, emotive type. We see in the film that Clarice has a comfortable access to her emotions, a willingness to be vulnerable.

As I said, the distinctions between the Fair and the Dark are *not* actually grounded in racial differences. If you thought the dichotomies of the Fair and the Dark appear only in stories of Caucasian characters, then look closely at the film *Soul Food* (1997)[3]. In this story, four black women (three sisters and a cousin) each exemplify one quarter of the Fair/Dark paradigm.

On the Dark side, we find Maxine and Faith. Maxine, happily married and very stable about her relationships, demonstrates the groundedness that goes with the Dark side of the paradigm. Additionally, as a maternal figure she also directly connects to the aspect of fertility. Faith presents a disruptive force in the family unit, bringing in some of the more negatively charged aspects of the Dark figure. She also pursues her passion for dancing – exemplifying the non-rational arts which are usually connected with the Dark patterns.

On the Fair side, we find Teri and Bird. Teri represents the strongest contrast to Faith. Where Faith engages in the emotional creativity of dance, Teri is committed to the static intellectual life of law. Cool and controlled, Teri clashes with Faith's go-with-the-flow personality. And in contrast to Maxine's groundedness, Bird's very name places her up-in-the-air. Bird lacks practical wisdom in her relationships, creating problems for herself.

This story successfully juggles each of the possibilities of the Fair and the Dark without pushing any of them too far into any sort of negative territory. It also demonstrates the cross-cultural aspects of the motif.

Usually the motifs of Fair and Dark are played against each other, making use of inherent contrasts. That duality leads to the next section.

DOUBLES

The motif of Doubles has a long tradition in folklore. One of the oldest uses is that of something antithetical to the self, to the main character. Thus, a Double can very easily also be a Shadow figure of the Hero. You should remember this when you start to use a Double in your story: the possibilities of having the second character be a Shadow of the Hero (whether openly or hidden) can add some surprising twists to your tale. Tied into the idea of the second figure being a Shadow is the folklore tradition that seeing your double is definitely *not* a good thing. It was supposed to be very bad luck to see your double, possibly even signifying your own impending death.

Out of such traditions spring that well-known story motif (cliché, almost) of the Evil Twin. Good Twin pitted against Evil Twin has been used through the ages, and it remains an appealing motif. It touches our fears of our own selves: "What would I be like *if...?*"

As you can see, the idea of a Double has a repellant side to it. But the concept also has a very attractive quality. All Buddy stories draw upon the positive aspects of the Double – a partner who does not need to have important things explained, who can work in sync with oneself. Buddy stories focus more on balancing characteristics of the two personalities. Buddy stories are about pulling together, rather than pushing apart.

Mythically, some tales of twins give us examples of this balancing in partnership at work.

> **Doubles – Castor and Pollux.** In spite of the fact that twin births were considered an evil omen, to the Greeks the twins Castor and Pollux became important in areas needing balance. The pair were the protecting deities of sailors and travelers. They oversaw the laws of hospitality and oaths. They went adventuring together, backing each other up, even though one was mortal while the other was immortal. But even in death they refused to be separated, and so they were put into the sky as the constellation of Gemini.

Just to show that this sense of twins (or Doubles) dealing with balance is not isolated to the Greeks' outlook, consider the Aztec Hero Twins.

Doubles – Aztec Hero Twins. Hunahpu and Xbalanque were very much a team when it came to confronting conflict and turmoil. They set out to correct the misrule of Earth that followed the destruction of the boys' father and uncle by the Lords of the Underworld. Their cunning, courage and perseverance, refreshed by their partnership, allowed them to succeed in the face of some dire opposition.

Using Doubles in stories runs the whole spectrum from positive to negative outlooks.

The 1961 version of *The Parent Trap*[4] makes use of the fearful aspect of meeting one's double. As the film opens, Sharon McKendrick arrives at camp for the first time. She settles in with her cabin-mates. But her first time through the food line in the dining hall brings her face to face with Susan Evers. The girls are both startled, looking at each other. They move off to different tables, but the unexpected encounter bothers both of them. It bothers their friends as well. One of Susan's friends comments, "The nerve of her! Coming here with *your* face!"

Although Sharon attempts a polite approach, by remarking that they look alike, Susan rejects the overture. She pushes the other away by comparing Sharon to Frankenstein. Sharon's cabin-mate retaliates by dumping Susan and her friends out of their canoe and into the water. The look-alike girls continue battling until the camp headmistress Miss Inch banishes the pair to the Isolation Cabin. Their forced proximity leads to the revelation that they are actually twins.

The 1998 remake of *The Parent Trap*[5] doesn't focus as much on the animosity of the unexpected Doubles. Although the girls Hallie Parker and Annie James contend with each other, the rivalry begins with the fencing match before either girl has seen the face of the other. They've already traded mild insults before they come face-to-face (as it were). Both girls attempt to brush off the resemblance, but they bristle at the idea of looking alike. Here, again, we have the effects of the negative encounter with the Double – conflict and hostility.

However, the battle between the two doesn't last as long in the remake as it does in the original film. The mutual exchange of pranks quickly leads to the girls being banished to the Isolation Cabin – where they piece together information and realize they are twins separated in infancy by their divorced parents. From that point on they are unified partners working for a common goal.

In the identical twins Hallie and Annie we can easily see the concept of Doubles (whether negative or positive) at work. A less obvious (because it does *not* involve identical twins) case shows up in *Lawrence of Arabia*. Ali and Lawrence begin their relationship somewhat at odds with each other. Lawrence's boldness in suggesting that the Arabs cross the Nefud desert to capture Aqaba challenges Ali. Yet Lawrence's persistence wins Ali's respect. In particular, when Lawrence goes back out onto the Anvil to rescue the missing Casim, it is Ali himself who carries water to the returned Lawrence. From this point on Ali is Lawrence's committed disciple. He gives Lawrence Arab robes. When Lawrence leaves Aqaba to inform the British in Cairo that the port has been taken, Ali watches him depart with the gaze of hero-worship. Auda warns Ali about Lawrence: "He is not perfect."

Ali may have swung from the hostile end of the Double spectrum to the other end. Yet, Ali remains the faithful friend throughout the rest of Lawrence's trials and adventures. He alone of Lawrence's followers goes into the Turkish-held town of Deraa with Lawrence. He alone remains at hand until Lawrence is released by the Turks who arrest him on the street. It is Ali who nurses Lawrence after his beating. Yet it's also Ali who openly criticizes Lawrence's choices on the campaign toward Damascus. And Ali is the last of the Arab leaders to leave Lawrence in the Damascus council chamber.

Throughout the film, the two are paired, and Ali appears as almost the only person close to Lawrence. Both are shown to be somewhat at a loss without the other. The balance exemplified by paired Doubles comes to define the nature of their relationship.

You can vary how you choose to present your Doubles. Setting up the audience for an expectation of opposition can enrich the final results, as the two characters draw closer together. In *Lethal Weapon*, the characters of Riggs and Murtaugh are introduced back to back, letting the audience know that these two dissimilar characters will be brought together. In spite of their initial irritation with each other at being stuck with the other as a partner, they quickly settle down. After Murtaugh confronts Riggs about his suicidal tendencies, and after Murtaugh apologizes and thanks his partner for saving his life, the growing bond between the two gets addition emphasis. Murtaugh brings his new partner home for dinner, and Riggs slides into the novel and pleasant experience of affectionate family life.

The portrait of this Buddy Team doesn't mean that everything is in sync between the two, however. Murtaugh retains a realistic amount of doubt about his partner. When Murtaugh's daughter Rianne gets snatched by the Bad Guys, the partners plan their next move. Now that his daughter's life is at stake, Murtaugh's doubt prompts him to ask, "Are you really crazy? Or are you as good as you say you are?" Riggs' answer can only be called ambiguous, "You're going to have to trust me."

Riggs and Murtaugh demonstrate the delicate kind of balance a good Buddy Team should have: camaraderie mixed with just a shade of doubt and danger. For without those elements, the audience might as well be watching a character talk to his or her own reflection.

Reflection or partner? These are considerations you the storyteller need to deal with if you work with the motif of the Double. Likewise, you need to consider the implications of whether the pairing is a good thing or bad thing.

The 1992 film *Single White Female*[6] actually brings us two different perspectives of the matter of Doubles in a story. On one side we have Hedra who was born a twin. Her sister died when the girls were only nine. As a result of this loss, Heddy seeks a relationship that could replace that lost one, or at least provide a substitute for it. Indeed, that search has become an all consuming need on Hedra's part. It leads her to transform herself into a copy of Allison, and then to begin intruding into Allison's life beyond the boundaries of roommates.

The other side of the Double matter gets played out in Allison's reactions to Hedra's growing intrusions into her life. As the story progresses, Hedra makes all the motions of being a caring, supportive friend – a partner. And yet, it's clear that Heddy's rather manipulative about it all. She spends nearly $400 purchasing a puppy, but tells Allison the puppy was being given away free. Heddy intended the puppy to appeal to Allison's feelings, and it does. But underneath all of Hedra's seemingly concerned actions lurks a darker purpose. When Hedra drags Allison to a hair salon to cheer her up, she also has her own hair cut and colored – to match Allison's. When Allison sees the change, her reaction is an irritated, "You've got to be kidding."

Allison's reaction echoes that of the traditional reaction to meeting a *doppelganger* (or Double). The possibilities of loss of self and of life spring up in Allie's concern. She soon learns that Hedra has purchased some clothes exactly like her own. She also discovers that Hedra has been intercepting calls and at least one letter from Allison's former fiancée Sam who's trying to reconcile with Allie. And, in this story, Allison's fear of her double is quite reasonable.

It makes for an interesting clash in this story. An excessive and obsessive fixation on the good aspects of Doubles meets the aversion of an independent individual seeing the negative aspect of Doubles.

The last extreme to consider is that of Double as Shadow. It certainly has some of the greatest emotional power. Although Hedra did function somewhat as a Shadow figure, a better example appears in Harlan Ellison's tale "Shatterday."[7] Adapted for television,[8] in the story, the protagonist accidently calls his own apartment from a bar where he waits for his girlfriend, and he answers his own phone. Or rather, a literal alter ego answers. Peter Novins calls this alter ego Jay, and the alter accepts the name – it's their middle name. As the pair try to sort things out over the phone, they quickly realize they are the same. There is a catch, however, as Jay observes: "There's only one question: which of us is me, and how does *me* get rid of *him*?" Jay also adds, "Face it, we can't *both* be Novins. One of us is going to get screwed."

As the story unfolds, it's clear that the originals Novins, Peter, is a rather unsavory character. He's quite willing to ditch his girlfriend, ignore his ailing mother, and avoid his financial commitments. In fact, Jay says of Peter that the original Novins "has the ethics of a weasel." While the story moves forward, the unpleasant original self fades as the newer, more positive Double becomes more active. The shadow aspect of the Double gets touched on in the story. As the pair discuss it, Peter (the original) says:

"I remember the archetypes from Jung. Are you my shadow, my persona, my anima or my animus?"

"What am I now, or what was I when I got loose?"

"Either way."

"I suppose I was your shadow. Now I'm the self."

"And I'm becoming the shadow."

"No, you're becoming a memory. A bad memory."

Here, Ellison plays off the folklore of the *doppleganger*. Remember that traditionally, an encounter with one's Double is deadly. By combining it with the Shadow-aspect of the Double (i.e., the Double as the negative or opposite version of the original), Ellison turns the terrible encounter into something else – a judgment tale, perhaps.

MUSINGS

When you select something for your story, you want to be sure it has the right balance. When you throw it out there into the field of the audience, you want your missive to cover the distance and reach the target you're aiming for.

Think about it:

* Are you using the Fair and Dark motifs with your characters? How is it being manifested in your story?

* Do you have a character showing any one of the qualities of the Fair persona?

If so, are other traits of the Fair motif showing up? If not, why not? Consider the added depth you can include in your story by using them.

* Do you have a character demonstrating any one of the aspects of the Dark motif?

If so, have you included other qualities belonging to the Dark persona? If not, why not?

* Do you have a Fair character contrasted by a Dark one? Remember, this sort of pairing is not *required* when using one or the other. But it can enrich the story. And remember – Fair and Dark is *not* about physical coloring or about race.

* Do you have Doubled characters in your story?

If you do have Doubles, are they a positive pair (i.e., working partners) or a negative pair (one good, one bad)?

How do your Doubles interact with each other?

SECTION EIGHT – COMMUNITY HEROES

We've looked at many aspects of the Hero along the way. From the simplest level of main character to the more complex matter of extraordinary model, the term hero does a lot of work. Yet, even so, up to this point we've just considered the Hero as an individual, someone not necessarily tied to a community.

In this section, we're going to look at some specialized types of Heroes that have very specific relationships to the communities they appear in. These are Heroes whose actions are directly related to the other characters in the story. You may discover that your Hero functions as one of this trio: the Outlaw Hero, the Divine Hero, or the Sacrifice. We're also going to get acquainted with what could be called a Group Hero, the Band of Companions.

THE OUTLAW HERO

When I use the term outlaw here, I'm not talking about *criminal* activity. Rather, I'm referring to a character who acts outside the usual accepted boundaries of the society he lives in. Additionally, the Outlaw Hero is not the same as an Anti-Hero. The Outlaw Hero usually appears as a positive figure, unlike the Anti-Hero. The Outlaw Hero just operates outside the usual rules. Now, your Hero may be in this state for quite a wide variety of reasons. What's important about it is that for some reason, your Hero still has some crucial connection to his community.

This key phrase helps define an Outlaw Hero: The Hero is *of* the community, but not *in* it.

These are the qualities that characterize an Outlaw Hero: (1) he is displaced from society; (2) his actions criticize or are directed against some particular flaw of society.

Displacement from society

The Hero gets displaced from society, usually as a result of his criticism of that society. But you can kick your Hero out of the community any way you want. The consequence of being put outside the boundaries of the social order is that the Hero is outside the law (hence, outlaw). This gives the Hero a certain degree of freedom in his choice of actions. Since the community has set him outside their usual rules, he may feel free to ignore the old rules he knew. However, a mere breaking all the rules is *not* what the Outlaw Hero is about. Which brings us to the second point.

Criticism of a social flaw or failure

The Outlaw Hero focuses on some sort of failure of society. This concern about that flaw in society (whatever it might be) keeps the Outlaw Hero connected to his community. Instead of shaking the dust of the community off his shoes and heading off into new territory, the Outlaw Hero sticks around on the fringes. His persistent presence irritates the community. He becomes the sticking point, interfering with the normal flow of life in the community. His continued pecking at the edges of society will force an interaction between the Hero and the community.

Coming to terms with Society

The irritation caused by the actions of the Outlaw Hero will eventually lead to a confrontation between the Hero and the Community he haunts. When the Hero succeeds in his attacks and criticisms of society, the flaw or failure in the community gets addressed and corrected, and the Hero gets re-admitted into the community, regaining his former position. When the Hero fails in his campaign against the social flaw, the flaw remains and the Hero himself frequently ends up dead, killed by the community. Of course, it's also possible to poise your Hero in an unresolved conflict with society (which we'll consider in the **THEME PARKS** section), which would allow for multiple stories.

There are mythic models for the Outlaw Hero.

Outlaw Hero – Odysseus. The return of Odysseus to his home in Ithaca puts him in the role of an Outlaw Hero. He is certainly *of* this community, as he is its rightful king. But his long exile has placed him outside it. When he returned to his island, Odysseus learned that his wife was besieged by suitors who were disrupting the community's life (plus consuming his fortune). So Odysseus returns to his house in disguise in order to evaluate the situation. Things are so bad that he decides that the only way to clean up the problem is to wipe out the suitors. He swings into action (helped by his son and Athena) and speedily dispatches the parasites (thus taking care of that social problem). Once that chore was done, and his identity confirmed, Odysseus returned to his proper position in the community.

Odysseus' tenure as an Outlaw Hero has limited duration. But there is another legendary example who doesn't get quite that same re-integration.

Outlaw Hero – Robin Hood. In the basic form of the legend, Robin became an outlaw because he contested the way Prince John was running things in England. But even after he was kicked off his own property, he hung around the area of Nottingham. Prince John was taxing the people heavily, so Robin often did what he could to help the poor. He'd rob the wealthy nobles who traveled through Sherwood Forest and give the money to the needy peasants. Although some stories tell of how the heavy taxation was stopped and Robin was returned to his rightful position, most leave him perpetually doing his thing, "robbing the rich to give to the poor."

As you can see in these examples, one of the notable things about an Outlaw Hero is his strong attachment to the community he's been kicked out of. He can't just go away and start over somewhere else. A love of place or a sense of belonging keep him connected to the society that has cast him out. This can generate a lot of emotional power in your story, if you use the Outlaw Hero motif. The audience will long to see the Hero reinstated to his proper place in the community.

The flaw or problem that the Outlaw Hero addresses can be almost anything. But you do need to be clear about it, and it does need to be connected to *why* your Hero *is* Outlaw. In Robin Hood's case, his opposition to the taxation (in the most developed forms of the legend) contributed to his being outlawed. In the case of Odysseus, his long absence left a vacuum which the predatory suitors wanted to fill – he'd have to clear them out before he could claim his place.

As I said, when the Hero successfully redresses the flaw or problem in her community, she wins back her place within it. But what can that look like – both the process of fighting the wrong, and the reclamation of position?

In *The Fugitive*, Richard Kimble easily fits the Outlaw Hero mold. Mistakenly accused and convicted of his wife's murder, when he makes his escape, he quickly sets out to right this particular wrong. In the course of his adventures, he sneaks into three different hospitals and one medical conference. When Gerard and his team reinvestigate the murder, in order to get a better understanding of Kimble, we see that almost uniformly Kimble's colleagues speak highly of him. So definitely, Kimble is *of* that medical world, but as an outlaw he's not presently *in* it. When he calls his lawyer after his escape, the lawyer tells him that running makes him look guilty. Kimble responds by simply saying, "I wasn't worried about appearances." As an outlaw, of course he will not be concerned about appearances: he's trying to address an *actual* flaw in his society (his conviction for murder). Once the flaw and error are made known, it's clear that Kimble will be welcomed back into the society from which he's been outlawed.

The film *The Mask of Zorro* plays with the outsider aspect of the successful Outlaw Hero in several ways. In the opening, Don Diego de la Vega acts as Zorro, a masked man who intervenes on behalf of the common people. Although Diego himself lives secure in his position in society, his alter-ego of Zorro comes from outside the context of the community. He's the champion of the people, but Zorro does not seem to be *among* them Of course, Diego *does* become displaced from his position when Don Rafael Montero has Diego thrown into prison. Another spin in this story on the outsider quality of this Hero shows up in the Murrieta brothers. Not only are they orphans (displaced in society), they become outlaws in the more common sense: they steal, and are literally outside the law.

Diego's Zorro definitely acts to address a flaw in society. The people are being crushed by Montero's oppression. Diego's Zorro sweeps in to rescue peasants about to be executed for no discernable reason. By contrast, Alejandro's first steps as the masked outlaw hero (stealing the black stallion from the Governor's Hacienda) are more self-serving. Diego chides Alejandro, "You're a thief, Alejandro. A pitiful clown. Zorro was a servant of the people. He was not a seeker of fame, like you.... Zorro did what was needed."

Although Alejandro says he wants to be as Diego was – the kind of hero, the kind of Zorro Diego had been – Alejandro also remains set on getting his revenge (for his brother's death) on Capt. Love. Not until Alejandro sees the harsh treatment of the mine laborers (prisoners, people who stood up to or opposed Montero in some fashion) does he truly begin to take on the mantle of Zorro. A serious flaw must be addressed (his brother's death being only a symptom of the flaw), and *he* is the one to deal with it.

In the end, this Outlaw Hero succeeds. Diego gets reunited with his daughter. Alejandro has his revenge on Capt. Love. And most importantly, the peasants are saved from destruction at the mine and oppression from Montero. Diego's success comes at the price of his life, but Alejandro and Elena reclaim Diego's place in society. And the Hero does not vanish, as Alejandro tells his infant son in the finale, "But don't worry, little Joaquin. Whenever great deeds are remembered, your grandfather will live on. For there must always, always be a Zorro. And someday, when he is needed, we will see him again...."

These two stories show us what a successful Outlaw Hero looks like. What about when the Hero fails? In that situation, remember, the society the Hero criticizes will quash him one way or another.

Fletcher Christian in *The Bounty* shows us a character who is actually a sort of *double* Outlaw Hero. On the more obvious level, he starts out as a well-off member of Bligh's social order. By responding to the attractive freedoms of Tahitian culture, he becomes displaced from British society. Yet that very displacement emphasizes the flaw he fights – an excessive rigidity, an inflexibility. And when Bligh forces Christian to conform and return to the ship, Christian ends up following a course of action that could lead to his death. By the laws of the Navy, mutiny is a hanging offense. And there is no doubt that Christian mutinied. Society will kill him if it gets its hands on him again.

But the second level of Christian's position as an Outlaw Hero comes from his standing among the sailors, especially the mutineers. His social status and his refusal to kill Blight put him outside the society of the other mutineers. Likewise, his attempts to bring order to the unruly mutineers highlights the flaw of disorder in *that* society. He manages to hold them together long enough to reach Pitcairn Island. But whether he was successful as an Outlaw Hero remains unknown. Success would have been social integration with the mutineers. Failure would lead to a premature death. But no one knows (or rather no one has told if they *do* know) what the final fate of Fletcher Christian was.

But before you start thinking that the story of a failed Outlaw Hero would be too depressing, give some thought to the impact an example can have. In fact, let's look at *Braveheart* in this light.

The first element in defining an Outlaw Hero rests on his displacement from his position in Society (remember: *of* the community, but not *in* it). In *Braveheart*, his uncle takes young William Wallace from the community after his father's death. In his time away from the village, he receives an education in various languages and in the experience gained from far travel. This sets him apart from the community when he returns. After his wife Murron is killed, Wallace's assault on the English troops makes him completely an outlaw. In the English eyes, no one doubts that Wallace is an outlaw. On the Scottish side, Wallace's utter commitment to his cause makes him unnervingly uncontrollable for the Scots nobles, not far removed from being an outlaw.

The second element defining our Outlaw Hero consists in his actions being directed against a flaw in his society. The most obvious flaw that Wallace acts against is, of course, the occupation of Scotland by the English. But a second flaw lurks in the Scottish society, and that's the disunity that plagues the traditional leaders, the nobles.

The final element, regarding the Hero's relationship with society, in this version, lies in the Hero's failure in removing the flaw. In *Braveheart*, both of the aspects that Wallace has stood against come together to put an end to him. Because of Wallace's uncompromising stance against the English, the Scots nobles abandon Wallace at the battle of Falkirk. Even though he escapes that field, Wallace has become doomed. The nobles draw him into a trap, capture him and turn him over to the English. The English, of course, kill him.

Thus ends the influence of the Outlaw Hero.

Or does it? The film ends at yet another battlefield: Robert the Bruce, now king of Scotland, is expected to do homage to the English king in front of all his troops. Instead, the inspiration Wallace has been to the young man comes into play, and he chooses to fight against the English and free Scotland from the English overlordship. "You bled with Wallace. Now bleed with me," he cries to the Scots. And the legacy of this Outlaw Hero, William Wallace, continues on after his death.

Like a virus, the attitudes of an Outlaw Hero can be passed on from one carrier to the next.

An example of the mantle of the Outlaw Hero being passed on to another also shows up in the film *Barbarosa* (1982)[1]. The heart of the story in *Barbarosa* lies in the conflict between the Outlaw Hero and his society. And it fills both plot threads – that of Barbarosa himself and of Karl Westover. Barbarosa had married Josephina, the daughter of Don Braulio Zavala, and longed to be a part of the Zavala family. But Don Braulio disapproved, and for 30 years Barbarosa lived outside the family. Yet, Don Braulio's obsession was such that he constantly sent the young men of the family out to hunt and kill Barbarosa. Barbarosa would defend himself, and the young men would die. And the flaw in the Zavala society (a refusal to accept any outsiders) continued. Karl's troubles echo those of Barbarosa. After accidently killing his brother-in-law, Karl became the target of an implacable vendetta.

In this story, the sense that the Outlaw Hero *can* fail hangs over the whole. Yet, Barbarosa remains tied to the Zavalas even though he could leave. It would not have been impossible for him to remove his wife and daughter, yet he never does. At one point, the reason why he stays (even on the fringes) gets illuminated. Having snuck into the Zavala compound to visit Josephina, he comes face to face with Don Braulio. "All I ever wanted is to be a part of this family," he says. And of course, Don Braulio's murderous obsession has made that to be so, in the worst way possible. The quest to kill Barbarosa has become the whole family's obsession, leading to the constantly evolving song they sing about the exploits of the outcast.

When the Outlaw Hero fails to correct the flaws of his society, that society will kill him. And such is Barbarosa's fate. Young Eduardo hunts the aging outlaw with passion and fervor. He even tells Karl at one point that Barbarosa is tired and ready for death. Karl denies this. But Karl is absent when Eduardo makes a desperate assault on Barbarosa and fatally wounds him. Eduardo flees for home, and Karl finds the dying outlaw in his last moments. It saddens Barbarosa that this could be the end of it all, but Karl promises to stop Eduardo before he reaches home. The idea that the Zavalas would go on forever wondering if Barbarosa were "out there" cheers the older man. "Barbarosa will live a long time in that family. A long time."

Unfortunately, Karl does not stop Eduardo from reaching home. Don Braulio calls for a fiesta to celebrate the death of Barbarosa. The Outlaw Hero has failed and the society can at last move on without the disturbance of the pest. Or can it? Just as Eduardo bows to receive a tribute wreath, a figure on Barbarosa's horse and dressed like Barbarosa, intervenes. He returns to Josephina a locket Barbarosa wore and he salutes Barbarosa's daughter Juanita who watches with shining eyes. It is Karl, and the story begins all over again as Eduardo's hatred for the interloper leads him to bestow the name *Barbarosa!* on Karl.

As long as the flaw remains in the society, the Outlaw Hero exercises a power over the imagination. The impact of the Outlaw Hero as an example can lie hidden beneath the surface.

When telling a story about the Outlaw Hero consider the inspirational quality he can have. Even when the Hero fails in his attempt to correct a flaw in society, he will make an impression on other characters. He doesn't act in a vacuum after all, so think about which of your characters will be most affected by your Outlaw Hero's actions.

Up to this point, we have considered stories that reach a degree of resolution. But is that the only possibility that storytellers have? No. Especially in this age, which loves serial storytelling. If you choose to tell multiple stories about an Outlaw Hero, be sure you know the nature of the flaw or problem in the community. It should not be so simple that your Hero will look like a fool for not solving it in the first story. Nor should it be so insurmountable that anyone would be crushed by challenging it time after time.

We'll look closer at the specific shaping of an ongoing context in **THEME PARKS**. But for the moment, let's look at the shape an Outlaw Hero may take in such conditions.

The Batman mythos gives us a good example of the Outlaw Hero in a continuing context. For over 60 years Batman has haunted the fringes of night on the pages of comic books and on film. Tim Burton's 1989 *Batman*[2] film captures the essentials, while also demonstrating the lack of complete resolution that goes along with a continuing franchise.

The film begins by establishing Batman in action. He disrupts a pair of muggers, announcing his presence as a crimefighter by fighting them. By appearing as a costumed figure, he non-verbally proclaims his status as outside the law. To reinforce that element in the story, the police deny knowledge of this figure. Batman is an outlaw. And the flaw in society he criticizes is crime.

But how displaced *is* Batman from his community? As the story moves forward, we learn that Batman is (under the mask) the wealthy citizen of Gotham, Bruce Wayne. When we are shown a major social event taking place in his mansion, we are inclined to say that he isn't displaced at all. Yet, he is a solitary personality. And when photographer Vicki Vale and reporter Alexander Knox investigate the millionaire, they discover that as a child Bruce Wayne witnessed the murder of his parents by a street thug. That murder provides both the incident which isolates him from his community and the motivation for his crusade.

Batman's crusade against crime, and in particular the extreme type of crime the Joker creates, provides a strong enough hook for multiple stories. This Outlaw Hero can win the individual battles, but not completely eliminate the flaw he fights. Thus, the film ends with Commissioner Gordon revealing the Bat Signal, with which the "law" can summon the help of the "outlaw" when the battle against crime gets overwhelming.

THE DIVINE HERO

By using the term divine here, I do not mean to imply that a Hero of this type actually *does* have to be divine or non-human. Rather, the focus rests on the special destiny that this type of Hero has. We considered some of these issues in the Journey section. But where that discussion dealt with the *actions* of the Hero (or at least the plot elements), here we want to consider the *character*. The primary aspect a storyteller deals with is that the Divine Hero is *not* ordinary.

There's a key phrase to help define the Divine Hero, and it's the counterpart of the one for the Outlaw Hero: The Hero is *in* the community, but not *of* it.

The particular qualities of a Divine Hero are (1) a special birth or childhood (or origin), and (2) that her career and abilities are devoted to healing Society, bettering it, or giving it some special boon.

The special birth or childhood

Whether or not the origins of your Hero actually figure in the story you tell, it's a good idea if you as the storyteller know how this Hero came into being. Usually, the Divine Hero faces challenges which will require extraordinary abilities. So, the question for the storyteller becomes: how did the Hero come by these abilities? Our egalitarian society sometimes feels uncomfortable with the concept of a person who is *born* to a great destiny. But that doesn't stop us from responding to the concept (consider, for instance, the expectations Society placed on John F. Kennedy, Jr.'s shoulders).

How you choose to present your Hero's distinctiveness depends on the type of tale you want to tell. The primary problem lies in how to depict the differentness your Hero will have. For the audience will want to know about that difference.

The career devoted to benefitting Society

Unlike the Outlaw Hero, the career of the Divine Hero may not necessarily be focused on a particular flaw in Society. In this, the Divine Hero has a slightly broader range of possibilities in her interactions with Society. She may indeed be intent on healing a major injury or flaw in the social fabric. But she may also be bringing a boon to an aspect of life that the community might not rate as high on the survival scale. Intellectual knowledge might *seem* less important than, say taxation relief. But that doesn't mean you can't tell a powerful story about the gaining of knowledge.

For the purpose of the story, then, you need to show that your Divine Hero is better equipped than anyone else to deal with the challenge before the community. And in this case, you also need to demonstrate that the community in the story views the meeting of the challenge as a good thing.

Relations with the community

The relationship the Divine Hero has with her community is, in general, far more congenial than that of the Outlaw Hero. This character is far more likely to be one drawn into the center of society, for she's admirable in the more obvious ways (no, no, I'm not talking about physical appearance, at least not in a primary sense). In the version where the Divine Hero succeeds in meeting the challenge, the Hero is regarded as needed in the community, she is admired by Society, and the boon she brings is accepted. When the Divine Hero fails, Society rejects the boon or healing the Hero brings, and the Hero may be killed or driven out of the community. (Yes, failure on the part of the Hero can carry a very high price indeed!) And, of course, you can also shape your material for ongoing adventures for your Hero.

A mythic example for the Divine Hero can be found in Hercules.

The Divine Hero – Hercules. Hercules, as a son of Zeus, definitely had a hard time being considered just one of the guys.

His exceptional strength was difficult to ignore. As for tackling beneficial chores, we can look at his cleaning of the Augean stables as an example. Now anyone who's been around even a single horse stall knows it takes a fair amount of work to keep the place clean. Aging dung and dirty straw is not healthy for animal or human. Well, the Augean stables were big, really big. In fact, they were a *mile* long. That's a *lot* of stable, and it was piled high from floor to ceiling with dung. Not exactly ideal working conditions. Hercules, however, was not merely strong – he'd also been well educated. So he applied some thought to the problem and found a solution. He diverted the flow of two rivers, and used their waters to flush out the stables.

An extraordinary challenge. An extraordinary Hero. Those are the elements that may draw you to telling a story about a Divine Hero. But let's look at some further examples, to explore the possibilities.

In *Excalibur* we find signs of the Divine Hero. Explicitly, Arthur is born to be king. And just as the Divine Hero's career is devoted to bettering Society, so too Arthur's is devoted to unifying the warring factions and bringing peace to the land. He *is* needed – that much becomes evident when he falls ill and cannot rule. But when he does function, Arthur achieves (for a time) the ideal of "One land, one king."

But remember, flexibility is our watchword. We can find a specialized variation of the pattern of the Divine Hero in *The Godfather* (1972)[3]. Michael Corleone plays this role in the story. In this case, the community that this Hero benefits is not Society at large, but rather the Corleone crime family.

One of the first aspects of the Divine Hero is that the Hero is *in* the community, but not *of* it. Although Michael is born into the Corleone family, from his earliest appearances in the film, he is set apart. He shows up at his sister's wedding in his military uniform (when everyone else wears tuxedos). And Michael himself, at this point, sees himself as an outsider. After telling his girlfriend Kay a story demonstrating his father's ruthlessness, he says to her, "That's my family, Kay. It's not me." Later, as Corleone soldiers discuss an action, they observe that their opponents know that Michael is a civilian, meaning that he's not a part of the criminal community.

As for the element of the Divine Hero's special childhood, in this story, that specialness appears in the little things that demonstrate that Michael is Don Vito's favorite son. Don Vito won't allow his daughter's wedding pictures to be taken until Michael shows up. Michael had been sent to college, when obviously neither of his older brothers received that benefit.

Then we have the matter of the special benefit the Divine Hero brings to the community. What does Michael bring? First off, he demonstrates his identity of Divine Hero in using his quick wits in rescuing his father in the hospital. After arranging things to keep Don Vito safe when he finds all protection removed, Michael tells his father, "I'm with you now. I'm with you." It's Michael who works out the means of achieving the family's revenge for the attack on Don Vito, and it is Michael who carries it out.

The mark of success of the Divine Hero and his mission comes in the acceptance by the community of the Hero and the benefits he brings. In *The Godfather*, this comes for Michael after Don Vito finally dies. Michael settles all the family business in one fell swoop. The film ends as Kay watches the men paying homage to Michael as the new Godfather, the new leading power in the Families.

As you can see, the community which your Divine Hero enters can vary greatly. It can be what the audience might consider ordinary or it can be a world onto itself. The important element to remember when telling a story of this type of Hero is that she comes from *outside* the community in some way. She may have been separated from the community by special circumstances, or she may be completely alien to it. Although in both *Excalibur* and *The Godfather* the boon the Hero brings happens to be leadership, other qualities can be used as well. However, to make the impact on the audience that you want to make, be sure to demonstrate that the community in your story *needs* what the Hero brings. Soft-pedal it, if you want (by including only a line or two on the benefit) or hard-pedal it. But don't forget it.

We've considered successful Divine Heroes. What about ones that fail? For that, consider the film *Contact*.

From the beginning of the film, the audience sees that Ellie is not ordinary. The film's opening pull-back sequence, from the earth farther and farther out through the cosmos, ends with the revelation of young Ellie's eye. A further sign of her specialness comes with the grown-up Ellie's announcement at Aricebo that she's listening for "little green men." The reaction of her colleagues indicates that although she is *amongst* them, she is not *of* them.

Special birth and childhood

The film opens showing young Ellie's curiosity and intelligence in action. She possessed an insatiable curiosity as a child, asking inopportune questions that many adults could not deal with. When early testing indicated a high predisposition toward science and mathematics, her father raised her in such a way as to encourage such interests.

Career devoted to benefitting or bettering society

Ellie devotes herself to her search for extraterrestrial intelligence. She abandons her relationship with Palmer Joss rather than be diverted from her quest. Ellie considers the possibility of contact with other life forms to be the most important discovery of the human race.

The Boon is rejected; the Hero driven out

Officially, the committee rejects Ellie's testimony about her contact with alien life. She leaves the hearing apparently in disgrace. The boon she has returned with is the assurance that humans are not alone in the universe. The committee doesn't accept the boon. The general public, however, does believe Ellie.[4]

Ellie doesn't get killed, but she does get relegated to something of an outsider position. And although unstated, it's implied that the benefit she extended to society remains available should people ever desire it. But, at the end of *Contact, Ellie's* story is done with. What about continuing adventures of a Divine Hero?

If ever there was a Hero who met the "*in* the community, but not *of* it" description, it would be Superman. The film adaptation of 1978[5], the Hero's Kryptonian parents Jor-El and Lara discuss sending their child to planet Earth. Jor-El says, "He'll look like one of them," while his wife responds, "He won't *be* one of them." Still, they send their infant out into space as Krypton explodes. The special childhood of our Hero falls both in the education he gets on the journey and the sheltered up-bringing he receives from his adoptive parents on Earth, the Kents.

In the course of the story, Jonathan Kent gives a basic definition of a Divine Hero. The teen-aged Clark feels restless in restraining himself from using his powers in his daily life, so Jonathan tells him, "One thing I do know – you are here for a reason. I do know one thing, it's not to score touchdowns." Later, our young Hero hears a message from Jor-El telling him that he was sent to Earth because of the Earthlings' capacity for good. The message implies that the Hero's job will be to support and encourage the people of Earth in fulfilling that capacity.

When the adult Clark begins his career as Superman, his actions demonstrate his readiness to protect those he lives among. When he saves Lois Lane, she asks, "Who are you?" and he answers, "A friend." Later, when she interviews him, Lois asks, "Why are you here?" "I'm here for truth, justice and the American way." Do we accept this offered boon? Well, in spite of laughing a bit at the corny nature of the response, we also acknowledge (at least) that truth and justice are very worthy causes. We do want them upheld.

The nature of this Hero and the service he aims to bring to society are obviously broad enough to carry the weight of many adventures. When constructing a context for the ongoing experiences of your Divine Hero, you need to have a wide enough focus to allow many visits without being so nebulously vague that the audience doesn't know what the character is *about*. We'll look at this more in **THEME PARKS**.

That brings us to our third Community Hero, the Sacrifice.

THE SACRIFICE

In the discussion of the **SAVIOR**, I observed that sometimes that Hero will die in order to save others. This archetype, the Sacrifice, will also do that. However, the Sacrifice may not necessarily be your main character. But whether or not your Sacrifice will be the main character, one of the crucial elements concerning the Sacrifice is that of value.

So, let's back up a step. Just what *is* a sacrifice?

The primary or starting definition involves the offering of something to a deity, as either propitiation (that is, appeasement or conciliation) or homage. This brings us back to the matter of holy or sacred things. After all, (aside from Prometheus' trick about what mortals should sacrifice to the Olympians) if the object is to appease or impress that higher power, you want to give them the best you have at hand. With that in mind, take a look at the value your Sacrifice has. The Sacrifice needs to have value to the audience in some way, usually through a character the audience identifies with.

A second definition indicates that a Sacrifice involves the surrender or destruction of a prized object for the sake of something considered as having a higher value or more pressing claim. This is where the community aspect of the Sacrifice usually comes into play. At the very least, there's the relationship between the Sacrifice and the person (or thing) given greater value. But it also raises the issue of *why* the second person (or object) does have more value.

To be blunt, this point is what the storyteller should remember: the Sacrifice should not be cheap. A throw-away Sacrifice lessens the drama of the story. If the characters don't really care about the Sacrifice, why should the audience? Thus, you need to indicate, in some fashion, that the Sacrifice has value to *someone* in the story. And the greatest impact will be if the character who benefits most from the Sacrifice is also the one who defines the value of the Sacrifice.

In the ultimate form, this Hero takes his action for the community he represents. And there are very few prerequisites for a Sacrifice, beyond the matter of being valued. An Outlaw Hero can be a Sacrifice. A Divine Hero can be a Sacrifice. Any one or any thing you the storyteller choose can be the Sacrifice, as long as the audience understands the value placed upon the Sacrifice.

For a model of a Sacrifice, consider Jesus.

The Sacrifice – Jesus.[6] The traditions that Jesus' followers grew up with indicated that no human could achieve the perfection needed to actually come into the presence of God. They believed that God's holiness was so intense that nothing imperfect – or sinful – could approach God. And they also believed that, at rock bottom, a human's greatest desire was exactly that: to come near to God. How was this to be resolved? A perfect sacrifice was needed, but where would they find that? Jesus became that sacrifice. In spite of the efforts of those who did not like him, no one actually leveled the charge of any sin against him. To his disciples, if ever there was a perfect human, Jesus was it. So, his followers viewed his death as the offering needed to propitiate the intense holiness of God. The sacrifice allowed them to follow behind it and come close to God. They gave up the teacher they most loved, in order to gain their deepest desire. And they believed that they *did* gain it. And on top of that they believed that Jesus willingly played the part of the Sacrifice.

This is why sacrificial characters in stories get called Christ-figures. The willingness to sacrifice himself for others can give a character in a story a strong emotional charge. It's hard to imagine a more intense action on the part of a character.

Because the matter can be so highly charged, the storyteller needs to be careful in how it gets handled. The values and purposes need to be clear. It's important, whether the Sacrifice is seemingly small or obviously large.

In *The Return of the Jedi*, the storytellers pull a very neat trick out of the climax. As Luke rages against Vader, the audience roots for him to succeed in striking down Vader. And yet, a few short moments later, when Vader throws the Emperor into the pit, the audience applauds his action – and not just because Luke is saved. Suddenly, the audience roots for a figure (who obviously dies as a consequence of this act, sacrificing himself) who has been the ultimate villain through three films. How did the storytellers bring us to this point?

The value of a Sacrifice must be upheld by someone. In *The Return of the Jedi*, from early in the story, Luke asserts that there is still good in Vader. When Obi-Wan explains the finer details of Luke's family history, Luke says that he can't kill his own father. Even though Ben makes it clear that Vader's death is necessary for the Rebellion's survival, Luke disagrees. When Luke surrenders himself to Vader, he tells the older man that there *is* still good in him, which is why he could not kill Luke in their earlier encounter. Vader denies this, and continues to deny it even during their fight before the Emperor. When Luke refuses to kill Vader at the climax, he does so because he values the Jedi his father *had* been. Luke tells the Emperor, "I am a Jedi, like my father before me." These affirmations from Luke, spread throughout the film, build up Vader's value for the audience. When Vader turns and sacrifices himself to save Luke, the accumulation of Luke's statements has an impact. It matters to us, because it has mattered greatly to Luke. As he dies, when Anakin tells Luke that the young man was right about the father's true feelings, the value of Anakin's sacrifice itself is affirmed. His action has value, as do the causes for which he sacrificed himself (Luke, whom the audience values, and the Rebellion, as a fight against tyranny).

The value of Vader for the audience gets determined by Luke, for the audience sees little in Vader's actions which would lead them to value him. But because the audience *does* value Luke, they'll go along with *his* expressions of worth. That's one way a storyteller can communicate the value of the Sacrifice to the audience. Another way would be to engage the audience's interest in (or even affection for) the character or characters to be sacrificed.

In the film *Predator*, Dutch has a brief clash with Dillon when he realizes that Dillon did not tell him the truth about the mission. Dillon tells Dutch that the team is an asset, an *expendable* asset. Since by this time, the audience has met the team as individuals, they're not going to agree that the team *is* expendable. However, the degree to which we, the audience, feel each successive death depends entirely on how much we've seen of the team member, how much we like them. The less we know of a character, especially in a positive way, the less we are affected by his death. We can be aided by knowing what one character means to another. Our sympathy for the better known character can allow us to feel *that* character's sense of loss for another. Thus in this film, we have two variations at work. When Billy takes a stand to meet the Predator, his sacrifice has some significance for the audience. First, there's Dutch's valuing of his team as a whole, plus his appreciation of Billy's skills. Secondly, the audience has seen Billy's sense of humor (always a good quality in gaining the emotional connection). Billy takes his stand not simply as an ultimate challenge to his skills, but also because he values Dutch and willingly does what he can to enable Dutch and the remaining survivors to escape.

The more the audience can see the value of a Sacrifice Hero in the story, the better. You, as the storyteller, cannot simply say, "This character is important." We must *see* the accumulation of incidents, gathered coin by coin into a rich purse. Both the audience's evaluation and the evaluation of other characters in the story help compile that worthiness.

In *Braveheart*, the value of Wallace grows for us through the eyes of several characters. The Bruce is inspired by the early reports of Wallace's rebellion. When Wallace gives the Scots victory at Stirling, the unexpected success fires Bruce's imagination about the possibilities before him. Bruce learns from his betrayal of Wallace at Falkirk the value of what he has betrayed, and as a consequence, he begins to take on Wallace's earnestness for the Scottish cause. This leads to Bruce's anger at the capture of Wallace engineered by the Bruce's own father. The Bruce ends the tale having placed a higher value on Wallace than on his father.

Additional value for Wallace in the audience's eyes accrues through the loyalty of Hamish and Stephen to the hero. Because we like these characters, we invest in their loyalty. Even the concern of the Princess for Wallace, that he not suffer in the torture to come, builds the evaluation set on him.

With all the value gathered together, the Sacrifice of Wallace carries great power for the audience. No sacrifice should be cheap. Because the audience has invested greatly in Wallace, both through direct appreciation of the character and through acceptance of the value placed on him by other figures in the story, his Sacrifice for the cause of (Scottish) freedom inspires as much as it moves the audience.

In *The Green Mile*, John Coffey obviously takes on aspects of the Sacrifice. He acquired great value in the tiny community of E Block. But he also brings us back to what was said about the Savior figure. Although John saves others, he cannot save himself. The prospect of executing a man he knows to be innocent upsets Paul, but John accepts the sentence. This increases John's value in the eyes of the guards. But to maintain balance in the order of their society, the guards must comply with the execution order.

So, the Outlaw Hero, the Divine Hero and the Sacrifice are the basic types of Community Heroes. But before you start thinking that one type excludes the other, take a look again at *The Matrix*. Neo sees himself as "just another guy." In this, he plays the role of an Outlaw Hero, one who has been taken out of his original community, one who, by his hacking activities, criticizes that community. To Morpheus and his team, Neo is a Divine Hero, one destined to bring them healing. And then there's the matter of the Sacrifice. The Oracle tells Neo that because Morpheus believes Neo is the One who will save humanity, Morpheus will sacrifice himself for Neo. But she also tells Neo what Morpheus means to the Resistance, that they all would have died without Morpheus. The Oracle's statements reemphasize the value of Morpheus, beyond what he means to Neo. Remember, the Sacrifice must have value. Neo decides that Morpheus has more value to the community than he does. He denies that he is the One and insists on rescuing Morpheus. He is willing to sacrifice himself for Morpheus. Yet, by choosing that route Neo ends up proving his Special Destiny as a Divine Hero.

The qualities of these Community Heroes tend toward big picture stories. But that does not·mean that a storyteller has to be restricted to such a use. The example of *The Matrix* shows us how we can flex and combine these archetypes.

One last aspect of Community Heroes needs to be considered. We have looked at specific Heroes, individuals taking certain types of actions or having a special relationship to the Community. This last motif differs.

THE BAND OF COMPANIONS

The Band of Companions shapes a story when those friendly to the central Hero are more than just the Helpers and Allies we met in the discussion of Journey motifs. Although the Band usually does have one core or primary character, each member of the team also has more plot weight than a simple Helper does. Indeed, in some ways, it is the Band as a unit which fills the role of Hero. As a result, various individual members of the Band may experience different events of the Journey. One character may perform the Approach to the Inmost Cave, while another encounters Temptation. One may acquire the Ultimate Boon, while another becomes the Sacrifice (or Price).

By using a group identity for the Journey, a storyteller can increase the emotional impact of the story. It's a way of eating your cake and having it too. You can have the emotional power of a moving death at the mid-point in the story without having the story end *at* that point. There's an additional advantage for the storyteller in this form: when the storyteller uses a single character as the focal point, as the Hero, the audience has an unconscious assurance that *that* character isn't likely to die or disappear in the middle of the story. But when the storyteller uses a Band of Companions, that assurance becomes undermined. When the first member of the group is lost in some fashion and the story goes on without that character, uncertainty invades the audience's outlook. Suspense becomes heightened, because you've changed the rules on them.

Another factor the storyteller should consider in putting together a Band of Companions is that of the personalities of the Companions. If you want the experiences of the Band to have significance for the audience, the Companions should have distinct personalities. If the characters are indistinguishable from each other, the audience will have less of a connection with them.

How big should your Band be? We'll consider that matter in more depth in the **THEME PARKS** section. But for the moment, let us just say that the number of Companions is limited only by your ability to make the Companions distinctive. That includes the matter of not losing your individual characters in the mass of the whole.

Let's consider some legendary examples of such Bands of Companions.

Band of Companions – The Argonauts. When Jason set off to find the Golden Fleece, he chose a company of heroes to go with him. Since his ship was named the *Argo,* the group was called the Argonauts (that is, the sailors of the *Argo*). Legends say he took 50 men with him (because that's a good number of rowers to have on a big ship). But only about eight of them are of major note. Each was a hero in his own right: the twins Castor and Pollux, Amphion, Hercules, Orpheus, Peleus (the father of Achilles), Theseus and Meleager (who won renown for killing the Calydonian boar). Amphion and Orpheus were both musicians, although Orpheus' abilities were such that nature would literally stop when he played his lyre. Castor and Pollux were well-known for being ready for any adventure. Hercules was the greatest of heroes. Theseus had also earned some fame for his killing of the Minotaur. Peleus may not have performed such high profile deeds, but he was impressive enough to succeed in marrying a goddess (Thetis). He and Meleager took part in the legendary hunt for the Calydonian boar, a fierce beast that Artemis had sent to ravage a countryside. Like I said, Meleager killed that boar with his bare hands. These were the companions of Jason.

The distance between our age and the adventures of the Argonauts has somewhat clouded our perceptions of what the various Companions brought to the Band. But even these eight hint at varying abilities. A nearer example can be found around the figure of Robin Hood.

Band of Companions – Robin Hood's Merry Men. Robin Hood acquired a number of followers in his life of an Outlaw Hero. Many of them were fellow outlaws who chose to follow him. Of first note, there was Little John, who was anything *but* little. Then in the company we could find Will Scarlet, known to be hot-headed but good-hearted. Allan 'a' Dale became the resident romantic and minstrel. Friar Tuck provided a touch of faith to events, besides being a character who unabashedly enjoyed life. Much, the Miller's son, usually appears as the youngest of the group, and hence the Band's Innocent. And then there's Maid Marian, an independent minded female thrown into the mix and certain to unbalance events.

The mixture of personalities in the core characters of Robin's Merry Men gives us an idea of what can go into a Band of Companions. As a storyteller, you don't really want to construct the *perfect* Band. After all, what sort of drama would you get out of characters that are ideally suited to each other? In the Argonauts, we find two musicians: even though Orpheus had great powers (being the son of Apollo), Amphion was no slouch (besides, *his* father was *Zeus*). We can easily imagine an undercurrent of competition between them. In the Merry Men, the mere presence of a female (no matter that Robin was in love with her) would be bound to create a few tensions. And then you would also have the contrasting personalities of fire-eater Will and mild-mannered Much.

When constructing a Band of Companions for your tale, you need to take into consideration both the needs of the Quest and the natural mis-match of personalities that occur in real life.

The needs of the Quest will dictate some of your choices. If your adventure heads into mountain ranges, an oceanographer might not be a practical choice. I'm not saying you can't *have* an oceanographer along, only that her presence ought to be for reasons other than that skill. Haphazard choices in Companions will only irritate the audience unless there's good cause for the unlikely group to come together. That's one reason why natural disasters are so favored by storytellers as trigger events. Disasters tend to throw very unlikely people together.

The mismatch of real life gets its importance because the audience doesn't want the Band to feel too artificial. A perfectly matched team reeks of the mechanical, and there's no drama in machines. But one element or two which are skewed off of perfect balance will give the Band the needed breath of life, and the promise of drama. But, like anything, even mismatching in the Band of Companions can be overdone. It can very easily turn into a pulling together a collection of *stereotypes*, who end up having no life as *characters*.

It must also be said that the influence of Role Playing Games has affected the construction of Bands of Companions in some genres. The collection of characters ends up sounding like it was selected from a Chinese menu. "One from Column A (magic-users); Two from Column B (fighters); One from Column C (healer or priest)." You're going to want your Band to feel more organic. After all, sometimes a character may join a Band for a reason that has nothing to do with the quest itself, but rather for some connection to one of the other characters. With all that in mind, let's take a look at an example.

A classic version of a story of a Band of Companions (and one that spawned many imitations) is the 1954 Japanese film *Seven Samurai*.[7] When bandits threaten an obscure village, the villagers desperately decide to hire some masterless samurai, even though they are almost as afraid of the samurai as they are of the bandits.

Assembling the Band begins when the villagers find Kambei, a seasoned warrior who sacrifices his top-knot in order to trick a thief holding a child hostage. Overcoming his reluctance to help the villagers, Kambei begins to collect some other samurai. The first to enter the picture are two very different young men: Katsushiro, an obviously naive samurai looking for a mentor, and Kikuchiyo, an inarticulate ruffian who *says* he is a samurai. Kambei dismisses Kikuchiyo but allows Katsushiro to remain. Kambei's continuing search finds him the wary Gorobei, who passes Kambei's alertness test and who remains because he's intrigued by Kambei. And while Kambei encounters Shichiroji, an old comrade-in-arms, Gorobei finds the good-humored Heihachi chopping wood to earn his keep. Master swordsman Kyuzo initially turns down the quest, but changes his mind and joins the group. And even though Kikuchiyo was originally rejected for the adventure, his persistence in hanging around causes him to become part of the group.

This diverse Band heads off to the farmers' village and prepares to battle the bandits. At this point, the advantage of using a Band of Companions as the Hero comes into play. The incidents that make up the Hero's Journey are parceled out to various members of the Band.

Problems and Complications arise when Kikuchiyo finds weapons and armor the villagers had hidden. The rest of the Band (being *real* samurai as Kikuchiyo is not) realize the villagers got the equipment from stray samurai they'd killed. The Complication is played out, as Kikuchiyo berates them for ignoring the fact that samurai arrogance has oppressed the farmers as much as bandits have.

Temptation crosses young Katsushiro's path when he discovers a supposed boy is actually Shino, the disguised daughter of one of the villagers. The pair become romantically attracted to each other.

A further element which engages the audience in the fate of the Band comes when some of the group make a quick assault on the bandits' headquarters. Heihachi is killed. The shock of finding that individual members of the Hero Band might be killed ups the dramatic tension in the story. From this point on, the audience knows that any one of the Band could die and the story will continue.

The care with which we are shown the assembling of the Band increases our connection (as the audience) with its individual members. Likewise, when we observe one or another character experiencing one of the steps of the Hero's Journey, we become more emotionally invested in the Band as a whole. The fact that one of the Heroes can die and the story will continue draws us even more into the story.

From the individual Heroes to the Band of Companions, the Community Heroes give the storyteller options in the placement of the main character. A journeying Hero need not be a character moving in isolation, completely disconnected from society. The Hero (or Band of Heroes) can also be in the midst of a community, serving it and possibly even dying for it. You, the storyteller, have many options.

MUSINGS

When you want to get your message to a large audience, expanding the sound volume tends to be the most used practice. But if *everything* is louder, does that help the situation? Amplifying a specific part of the message may be all you need. You don't want to shatter eardrums – you just want some things to come through clearly.

Think about it:

*   Do you have a Hero who has been displaced from his position in his community? If yes, you may have an Outlaw Hero.

How did he become displaced? *Why* did he become displaced? Is this Hero fighting some flaw in the community? What flaw?

*   Does your Outlaw Hero succeed in her fight against the problem in her community? How does she achieve this? How is she re-integrated into her community?

*   Does your Outlaw Hero fail in his campaign? What defeats him? What is the consequence of his failure?

*   Do you want your Outlaw Hero's crusade to be an ongoing one?

Have you made the shape of his crusade broad enough, that we'll believe more than one fight is necessary?

*   Is your Hero *in* the community, but not *of* it? If yes, you may have a Divine Hero.

Does your Hero have a special birth or childhood, or training? How does this separate her from her community, or make her different?

What is the special Boon your Divine Hero brings?

*   Does your Hero succeed in her quest? If so, what does that success look like?

*   Does your Hero fail in his crusade? How does he fail?

What opposition does he encounter? What is the consequence of the failure?

*   If you plan ongoing stories with your Divine Hero, is the Boon he brings broad enough to be used in multiple stories? Is the response of society to the Hero ambiguous enough to sustain many tales?

*   Does someone in your story give up his life to save others? You may have a Sacrifice Hero in your story.

* What is the value of your Sacrifice? Has the audience had a chance to build up a value for the Sacrifice?

* What is the greater good for the community that requires the Sacrifice? Have you convinced the audience that this *is* a greater good? Have you convinced the audience that the Sacrifice is required?

* Does your story mix qualities of the different types of Community Heroes? If yes, have you carefully presented the elements which define each type?

* Does your story use a Band of Companions? Do you show the assembling of the Companions or are they already collected together at the beginning?

* If you show the assembling of the group, have you selected a core or anchor character for the others to gather around?

Have you brought the various Companions into the group by different methods? (You don't want them all to arrive the same way.)

* If the Band has already been formed before the start of your story, have you chosen ways of demonstrating their different personalities?

* How distinct have you made the personalities in the Band? Do any of them share characteristics? If so, what still makes them different?

* Have you made your characters too perfectly chosen for the quest? Have you covered all the bases or have you left gaps between the collective abilities of the group and the needs of the quest? Remember, an omni-competent group could end up boring the audience, while one that has to improvise solutions will engage the audience.

* Have you considered which member of the Band will experience a specific step of the Hero's Journey? Is that character the *most* obvious choice for it, or the *least* obvious?

What does your story gain in dramatic tension by choosing the obvious one for the experience? What do you lose?

What would happen if you chose a different member of the Band for that experience?

Consider the mini-dramas of the individual members of the Band, and what you might be able to do with them. Do not overlook the nature of the various inter-relationships between each of the Companions.

PART FIVE

LANDSCAPE

LANDSCAPE

Now that we've thoroughly covered the **LOCAL RESIDENTS** of the Land of Myth, we can turn our attention to the landscape. As with the time of day, the seasons and the weather, the shape of the landscape, the physical space, of a story conveys meaning to the audience. Knowing the implications of *where* you send your characters can add more resonance to your story.

SECTION ONE – SKY VERSUS EARTH

The first distinction we make when we look around ourselves is the difference between the earth and the sky. Consider all the physical effects we associate with the two elements: gravity versus weightlessness leads us to meanings of confinement versus freedom. Yet, we also value the two elements in an opposite polarity as well, finding the meaning in terms like grounded (i.e., in touch with reality) and air-head. It's worth noting, though, that the two are usually presented in opposition to each other. If the air/sky imagery gets the positive treatment, the earth/ground imagery shows up with negative connotations. And vice versa.

Before we explore all the possible meanings of earth and sky, let's look at some mythic examples.

> **Sky Versus Earth – Gaia and Uranus.** Gaia is a very ancient Greek goddess. She's the personification of Mother Earth. The Romans called her Terra (the name many science fiction writers have applied to our planet). She was born at the beginning of time and became mother to the physical forms of the earth. The Greeks considered her a bountiful mother, and stories about her often involve her fierce protection of her children. In contrast to Gaia, Uranus personified heaven and the starlit sky. Rain from him made the earth fertile – manifested in children he fathered with Gaia. But Uranus was also distant and disinterested in his children. His disdain for his children had violent consequences, however, since he was overthrown and killed by one of his sons.

These figures show us some of the impact the imagery can have on the audience. Earth has an immediacy that we can touch. We tend to regard that quality favorably. We can feel connected to the earth. The sky, however, is physically remote, and we translate that into emotional inaccessibility. Also, when it comes to combative behavior, the earth-connection has a fiercer emotional drive, while the sky-connection seems colder and more arbitrary.

Fertility frequently plays a part in the earth/sky dichotomy.

Sky Versus Earth – Mixtec Gods. The Mixtecs viewed the cosmos (i.e., the whole of creation) as having two halves; the Earth and the Sky. For them, like the Greeks, the Earth was female, and the Sky was male. Most especially, the sky consisted of water. Since the Mixtecs lived in the arid conditions of southern Mexico, rain was essential for agriculture. That need of rain for agriculture translated into myth as the importance of good sexual relations between the Earth and Sky.

As this example shows, earth and sky can also be in balance with each other, or at least ideally so. This myth reminds us of the links between sky and earth. When using the imagery of one, the effects of the other should not be ignored.

However, to remind us once again of the flexibility of mythic language, let us consider the Egyptian handling of sky and earth.

Sky Versus Earth – Egyptian Reversal. In the Egyptian language, the word for sky is feminine. The ancient myths of that land reflect the language, for the divine manifestation of the sky is the goddess Nut. By contrast, the earth is masculine. The god Geb represents the physical foundation of the world. He's often represented as lying on the ground, resting raised on one elbow, with a knee bent – thus symbolizing mountains and the undulations of the earth. Nut arches over the world, touching the ground with her toes and fingertips. She maternally watches over her children (and all humans). And she's the mother of the sun.

As you can see, you can give the sky positive qualities (the attentive mother sky of Nut) or negative aspects (the remote and disinterested sky god Uranus). Earth can be the rugged and challenging features of the masculine Geb or the nurturing and fertile shelter of Gaia. Consider which direction best serves the nature of your story.

Take advantage of all the contexts you can wring out of the imagery of sky and earth.

The sky is open and broad, high reaching. We often equate it with freedom, thinking of how winds can blow wherever they will with little to confine them. "The sky's the limit," we say when we mean to indicate limitless possibilities. The sense of expansiveness that comes with sky images also brings a sense of power. That power comes from a lack of confinement. Yet along with those positive connotations, we also get some negative ones. The lack of gravity leads to the negative phrase light-weight, meaning lacking in substance. Likewise, air-head implies an empty space where mental faculties should be.

When we look at the earth, the same sort of dualities come to mind. For every use of grounded to indicate being in touch with reality, we can find things like earth-bound meaning lacking in imagination. The earth imagery reminds us of gravity, both positive in that it keeps us anchored in the face of chaotic winds, and negative in that it keeps us anchored and confined from flying free. Whichever way you choose to use this imagery in your story, however, keep it consistent.

The film *Top Gun* (1986)[1] plays Earth versus Sky in very simple ways. In terms of masculine/feminine differences, "Maverick" (the male pilot) rules the sky, while "Charlie" (the female instructor) has the authority on the ground. However, one traditional pairing of qualities with sky and earth gets changed in this tale. Usually the sky is the realm of the intellect, while the earth is that of emotion. Here, however, "Maverick" carries the emotional thrust of the story, while "Charlie" as an instructor conveys the intellectual threads (such as they are). Another way of putting it would be that while "Charlie" has a very grounded personality, "Maverick's" is very much up in the air.

Top Gun uses the physical space in a very literal way. Terry Gilliam uses the opposition imagery of sky versus earth in a more symbolic way in his 1985 film *Brazil*[2]. The opening vision of the film shows us sunlit clouds and freedom of movement. However, an earth-bound confining image of ducts in cramped apartment quarters quickly replaces the soaring sky image. As the story moves forward, we learn that the pictures of the open skies come from the dreams and imagination of Sam Lowry. Although Sam is content with his obscure job, his mother arranges a promotion for him. Between his becoming more engaged with the bureaucracy of the city because of his promotion and his pursuit of Jill Layton who resembles the girl of his dreams, the imagery of Sam's dreams changes. While at the beginning, he flies freely and unconfined, as Sam's real life adventures entangle him more and more, his dream imagery becomes more earth-bound and confined.

These two examples should give you a start on the possibilities you can find in sky versus earth imagery. *Top Gun* uses it in a physical fashion, while *Brazil* uses it very symbolically. Both have the benefit of the mythic meanings underpinning their stories.

SECTION TWO – TOWER VERSUS CAVE

As with the sky and earth, towers (or mountains) and caves are traditionally the domains of the masculine and feminine respectively. Those linkages were founded on physical attributes, comparing forms of the world with humanity's primary sexual features. The similarity of appearance creates a powerful fusion of gender on the shapes of the world. As a result of those identifications, the other connotations that go with towers and caves end up acquiring those same gender identifications. However much in our modernity we may disagree with the sexual connotations assigned to towers and caves, the symbolism remains. It remains because two different origins of meaning have been fused together.

Towers (and mountains), in addition to being masculine, are also the realm of reason and intellect. They are associated with light and order. Now, this set of meanings (reason, intellect, light and order) get grouped with the masculine aspect not because men are inherently more logical than women (most would find that an un-provable assertion), but because *towers* give their residents the ability to oversee the world around them. One gains a greater sense of order when looking at surroundings from a height. That's why we like to get an overview of a situation. Men just get the benefit of resembling, in part, towers.

Caves, in their turn, are the realm of darkness and the unknown. Those things that belong to the unknown also became associated with caves: chaos and things uncontrollable (like emotions). When you step into a cave, it becomes physically impossible to achieve an overview of the situation.

Again, I'm not saying that men and women are characterized this way - that is, men = logical, women = chaotic. No, I'm only observing that the two parts of humanity have become identified with certain physical aspects of the world because parts of their bodies resemble features of the earth.

Before we go further, let's consider some mythic models.

Towers Versus Caves – Olympus Versus the Underworld. For the Greeks, Olympus the home of the gods was an exalted place of order (never mind the disorderly conduct of some of its residents). It was perceived as a place of reason and light. The underworld, by contrast, was dark. Things were hidden in Hades. It was a place of secrets and mysterious knowledge.

As a special figure connected with caves, the Sibyl gave seekers guidance with special knowledge.

Caves – The Sibyl. In *The Aeneid*, Aeneas seeks knowledge from the Sibyl. She lives in a deep, enormous cave. It's even called her secret home. There, she tells Aeneas that to learn what he wants to know, he must go farther into the underworld, to the land of the dead. Finding her cave in the first place wasn't the easiest thing to do, so one had to be very determined to reach her to gain her mysterious, hidden knowledge.

The knowledge the Sibyl can give is powerful stuff, not casual information. Keep that in mind when you include cave-like images in your story.

When using both towers and caves, you don't need to beat the audience over their heads. Consider the implications. If a tower is a masculine domain, imprisoning a woman there takes her out of her realm. Likewise, if you imprison a man in a dungeon or cave, you are removing him from the realm where, by means of identification, he has power.

Look at Disney's *Beauty and the Beast*: Maurice is imprisoned in a tower, but is soon set free by Belle's intervention; Belle, in turn, is imprisoned in a cellar, but fairly quickly makes her escape. In *The Silence of the Lambs*, as long as Lecter is held in his underground cell he cannot escape, but as soon as he gets moved to a "tower," the upper floor of an old courthouse (emphasizing the masculine aspects of order and logic), he makes his escape.

Indeed, *The Silence of the Lambs* makes much use of the tower versus cave imagery. When Clarice makes her second visit to Lecter (this time on her own), she finds Lecter in the dark. This heightens the sense of being underground. The fact that his cell has been stripped down, revealing the hard, unpainted stone walls emphasizes the cave-like sensation. Clarice has come into this realm (the deepest reaches of an *insane asylum*, let us remember) seeking hidden knowledge. She gets more than she expected. She *rationally* intends to find out who the beheaded victim is and who killed him. What she learns is (1) the psychological – non-rational – key to the killer's motivation, transformation; and (2) that Lecter knows who the Buffalo Bill killer is. Although both of these pieces of information are useful, because of their non-rational origins they have to be worked over. They are not straightforward. This is consistent with cave experiences.

Another cave sequence appears in "Bill's", Jame Gumb's, hide-out. His basement world resembles a maze, a realm of chaos, and emotion without reason. When Clarice enters this realm, she labors to act with intellect and reason, but when the lights go out and she's literally in the dark, we see, through the killer's night-scope, that she shakes with fear. However, she doesn't give into the fear, but rather does her job.

By contrast to that cave, Clarice's visit to Lecter in Memphis occurs in a tower environment. Lecter is held in an open cage on an *upper* floor of the old courthouse (a place of order). In this setting, Lecter gives Clarice the lesson on the psychology of coveting. It's a rational presentation, rather than his more usual cryptic comments (again, logically, since he's now out of the crypt). And of course, being imprisoned in the masculine realm, he uses his intellect to make his escape.

Let's look at some other examples. In Zeffirelli's *Hamlet*, the director uses the tower/cave elements to good effect. When the Ghost (a possible irrational element) comes to Hamlet to reveal the truth about how he died, Zeffirelli sets the scene on the top platform of a high tower. This emphasizes the truth and rationality behind the supernatural presence of the Ghost. The tower, the domain of reason, is indeed the proper ground on which Hamlet should learn these facts. The Ghost gives Hamlet a straight-forward charge – avenge his death on Claudius.

The contrasting scene for this tower sequence is the "to be or not to be" soliloquy. Hamlet delivers this in the underground crypt. For all that the Prince is reasoning in his speech, the *subject* of the speech deals with suicide and death. Hardly rational subjects. To consider the Great Unknown, Hamlet has descended into the dark, hidden realm of the Unknown, a cave. But since the realm represented by caves isn't a rational one, all of Hamlet's musings there bring him no answer. Attempting to reason out an irrational subject (death and suicide) in the territory of the non-rational obstructs any insight that might be gained there.

Look around and consider all the places which might be viewed as either towers or caves. In the modern age, underground parking structures have become settings for surreptitious meetings: they are fairly common and, by and large, don't have a lot of people hanging around. So when two characters want to meet privately, unobserved, a parking garage isn't too strange a choice. Still, in *All the President's Men*, the ominous, mythic qualities of caves come into play. In the scenes set in such garages, Woodward's special source, Deep Throat, makes it clear he will meet Woodward only there. He provides the reporter with cryptic special knowledge, very much in the fashion of a mythic oracle. Deep Throat definitely conveys hidden knowledge, exposing things the Nixon White House wanted kept secret. Additionally, these garage scenes carry the unsettling atmosphere of the underworld, where mysterious, and possibly threatening powers lurk, where reason and logic may not provide as much protection as we would like.

Yet, let us not forget how we, as storytellers, can flex the use of these motifs. The television series *Beauty and the Beast* (in the late 1980s)[1] played against our usual expectations of the tower versus cave motif. Catherine Chandler, the Beauty, lives in a tower, works in the field of law, serving reason and intellect, and has (or at least begins with) a repressed emotional life molded by others. Vincent, the Beast, lives underground, surrounded by books and other representations of the arts, and lives in constant connection with his emotions. Our expectations of what the Upper and Lower worlds represent are also reversed: for all its apparent order, Catherine's Upper world is chaotic, violent and isolating, while Vincent's Lower world is peaceful, harmonious and communal. Indeed, the violence promised in Vincent's leonine appearance usually manifests itself only in the Upper world, when he rushes to Catherine's aid. To emphasize the separateness of the two worlds, Catherine and Vincent often discuss the possible direction of their relationship at threshold locations between the two worlds (an entrance to the tunnels in a park or an access to the basement of Catherine's apartment tower).

By playing against our expectations of what the tower and cave mean, the show sets up interesting resonances. The audience becomes interested in how Catherine will be able to integrate the feminine aspects of the Lower world into her nature. Likewise, we (the audience) wonder how the Upper world will affect Vincent: will its violence always draw out his dark side, or will its law and intellectual aspect balance his near-constant emotional flow?

If you think back, you'll notice that towers and caves share many of the paired aspects of light and dark. Again, similarities in how we experience these physical manifestations lead to parallel meanings. However, we do also need to look at one variation of towers and caves before we move on.

Open versus Closed Spaces

Open spaces, like towers, are usually viewed as safe spaces (after all, don't we prefer to have things out in the open?). Closed spaces traditionally seem threatening and undesirable. However, the film *North by Northwest* subtly plays against these associations.

Roger Thornhill from his first appearance is a master of closed spaces. He exits an elevator, walks through a crowded lobby, heads outside and immediately enters a cab. Even the outside sequence looks enclosed, for Roger and his secretary are completely surrounded by other people. Throughout the film, Roger has control and a degree of safety in enclosed spaces. It's when he is in more open space that he has less control and greater danger. There is, of course, the famous scene where a crop-dusting plane chases Roger. The images dwell on the openness, flatness and emptiness of the remote crossroads where Roger expects to meet the mysterious Mr. Kaplan. Roger escapes the plane by means of a confined space – the underside of a truck that almost hits him. The other major open space of the film, the top and face of Mount Rushmore, likewise proves unsafe for Roger. To emphasize that closed spaces are Roger's safe domain, the film's happy ending occurs in the train compartment. In fact, Roger and Eve are last seen on the upper bunk of the compartment, referring to Roger's earlier safe hiding in the closed upper bunk.

All our usual expectations of fear of confinement and safety in open spaces are reversed in *North by Northwest*. Hitchcock handles the elements so easily that we are not conscious of the reversal. Indeed, so effective was the crop-duster sequence, open fields and distant crop-dusting planes are now almost automatically *ominous* for audiences.

Upward, downward, outward, inward. Each direction takes your audience some place slightly different. Take the high view from the tower, or the mysterious secret from the cave, either one. But take advantage of the mythic underpinnings those locations can give your stories. For instance, we've said that towers are the realm of the intellect (hence the phrase ivory tower for academic life). But what if you place a madman in that tower? The tension between the expectation of reason and the presentation of insanity can keep the audience hooked for some time.

SECTION THREE – SEA VERSUS LAND

Once again we find the land with an important role in a pair of opposite images, this time set against the sea. The contrasts of sea and land imagery can be very strong. The ocean has always been a powerful, primordial image, even in the most ancient cultures. The vast stretches of seascape defy confinement and move in seeming chaos, unaffected by human action.

The turbulence of the sea becomes the mythic representation of the turbulence of human passion. Likewise, the solidity and constancy of the land becomes the representation of all that we consider removed from passion: reason, logic, order. And yet, as with most other mythic images, either of these two can be handled with negative connotations, or positive. It all depends on what you want to say to your audience.

Mythically, the contrasts show up in some members of the Greek pantheon.

Sea Versus Land – Aphrodite and Athena. Aphrodite, the Greek goddess of physical love certainly leaves a wake of turbulent passion behind her when she moves through a story. Rightly so, for she is called Foam-Born. The story goes that she was born of the foam of crashing waves. Passion is her bailiwick. By contrast, Athena, who was born full-grown from the head of Zeus, represents cool intellect. She's also very much associated with the land, in particular, the cultivation of olive trees.

But, lest you think that sea and land have only feminine representatives, consider the next pair.

Sea Versus Land – Poseidon and Zeus. Poseidon was the great god of the sea. He held all its changing modes in his hand.

He was also the god of earthquakes. Anyone who has stood at a rocky shore and watched the ocean waves crash against the land can understand the awesome power of Poseidon. Zeus stood as a contrast to Poseidon. Although primarily a sky-god, Zeus was also an agricultural god, which bound him to the land. And also, as the ruler of Olympus, Zeus had charge over all that happened on the earth. Indeed, the division of lordship between the three divine brothers was the Underworld to Hades, the seas to Poseidon, and all the rest to Zeus.

The imagery of sea and land sets off contrasting elements: passion and reason, chaos and stability, emotion and unmoving stance. Much can be made of the two different elements.

The 1975 film *Jaws*[1] gives us one such clash of the sea and the land. The opening underwater imagery lets us know that the sea will be the dominant force in the story. The symbolic power of the sea versus the land mainly circles around Police Chief Martin Brody. Brody, transplanted from New York City to Amity Island, hates water – ocean water, large bodies of water. His occupation already inclines him toward the rationalism of the land. When confronted with the first evidence of the shark attack, Brody reasonably moves to protect the populace by closing the beaches until they can kill the shark. But the mayor and the local businessmen, whose livelihoods depend upon public access to the ocean, talk him out of that action. How is the rational Brody convinced to follow this unreasonable course? He's persuaded while the group is on a ferry *on the water*.

However, Brody isn't the only character to demonstrate reason on land and something else on water. Another is the fishing captain Quint. At the town meeting after the second attack, Quint logically lays out what it will take to kill the shark. The town leaders choose not to follow Quint's suggestion. But when Brody later does hire Quint, we see the boat captain in an entirely different mode on the water. Being on the water brings out all Quint's cracked irrational aspects. He certainly *sounds* crazy. He mocks Matt Hooper's high technological and rational approach to shark-hunting. Part the way through the hunt, when Brody tries to use the radio to call the Coast Guard for help, Quint smashes the equipment.

Yet, for all his irrational behavior, Quint (along with the sea) brings a degree of passion and conviction to Brody's life. Quint has the relentlessness of the sea, where Brody had frequently been eroded like a wave-pounded shore. Through the fight with the shark, out of sheer survival necessity, Brody becomes transformed. He loses his fearfulness, refuses to be defeated in spite of all reasonable evidence that he can't beat the fish. The battle won, Brody and Hooper begin a long swim back to the shore, and the last lines convey the change in Brody: "I used to hate the water." Hooper replies ironically, "I can't imagine why."

Jaws uses the imagery of the sea and land as a serious underpinning for the adventure. The film *Splash* (1984)[2] gives us a gentler view of the symbolic clash of the two physical elements. Young businessman Allen Bauer shows all the signs of a man lacking real feeling. His girlfriend, who has been living with him, breaks up with him on the phone. And to emphasize how emotionally disconnected this landlubber is, he continues supervising work and business matters without breaking stride. Even so, he is concerned enough about this emotional vacuum in his life, and so decides to visit Cape Cod – even though he can't swim and fears being on the water. He makes the trip seeking some sort of emotional refreshment or connection to the wonder of childhood.

By contrast, Madison, the mermaid smitten with Allen, acts on her emotions without consideration. Creature of the sea that she is, each of her actions moves swiftly forward. Her first kiss to Allen, her appearance at the Statue of Liberty, her immediate embrace at meeting Allen again, all demonstrate the unconfined emotionalism that Allen himself lacks.

Rationality proves difficult to overcome. When Allen discovers that Madison is a mermaid, he withdraws. He's at a loss. "I don't understand," he says. "All my life, I've been waiting for someone, and when I find her ... she's a fish." His brother Freddie responds, "Nobody said love's perfect." Allen bursts out, "I don't expect it to be perfect, but for God's sake, it's usually *human!*" Allen still tries to make love rational. Freddie, however, points out that the kind of love Allen shared with Madison was exceptional and rare. Freddie's chastisement of his brother pushes Allen over the threshold. He finally lets love wash over him. He rescues Madison from the super-rational land-based scientists, and the lovers escape to the sea.

Lest we forget the variety that can be achieved with mythic motifs, let's look at one more example. *The Bounty* gives us a reversed dichotomy of the sea versus land discussion. The sea in this case represents structure and order, specifically the order of British Naval discipline. The land represents freedom, demonstrated by the relaxed, open society of Tahiti. And inevitably, the two clash. The powerful attraction of life on shore disrupts the order of the ship. Indeed, as Christian becomes more and more involved in the life on shore, not only does his personal discipline relax, he neither participates in the ship-board officers' dinners nor sleeps on board at night. Yet, likewise, the ship-board regulations disrupt the life on land: Bligh overlooks the fact that Christian's love happens to be the daughter of the Tahitian king. Forcing Christian to unceremoniously leave her creates an unpleasant ripple on the land.

Whether standing on solid ground or being all at sea, these two motifs can bring a great deal of power to the imagery of your story.

SECTION FOUR – THE WILDERNESS VERSUS THE CITY

Up to this point, we've looked at *natural* features of the landscape (if you'll allow towers to be classified with mountains and other high places of the land). But cities and towns are as much a part of the mythic landscape as anything else. So we do need to discover the issues involved with cities, and the opposite image of the wilderness.

The natural world can face off against the artifice of the city, or the order of civilization can be set against the chaos of the wilderness. It all depends on the effect you the storyteller want to create. For instance, the film *Brazil* plays a bit with setting nature imagery against that of the city. The city Sam Lowery lives in is so pervasive with its high-rise, close-built buildings, it creates a sense of perpetual indoors. The sky is rarely seen in the city, and the only vegetation in it consists of potted plants. Brief glimpses of open countryside, of rolling green hills, occur only in Sam's dreams. The one occasion Sam goes outside the city walls, to the refinery, the audience sees that the landscape around the city has become a ruined wasteland. In its absence, the positive aspect of Nature becomes heightened. Since only the dream imagery contrasts the grey, grim city, the negative connotations of the city overwhelm the story. Of course, that's obviously the intent of the storytellers.

As with other motifs, both the city and the wilderness have positive and negative connotations. With that in mind, we need to look at each element separately.

THE WILDERNESS

The Wilderness, the countryside outside the city walls, can be seen as either natural, pure Nature, or completely wild and chaotic.

Nature

Nature, particularly in vegetation, represents life growing properly, in balance with everything around. It brings a sense of being unforced, of being in harmony with other phenomena.

The Romans had a goddess who represented this sense of rightness of life.

Nature – Flora. The goddess Flora was presented as a springtime divinity. Budding flowers and other plants were her specialty. Of course, fertility was also part of her purview.

We have come to use the word flora for the vegetation that's native to a particular region. That should give you a sense of things that belong where they are, rather than something alien, imported and disruptive to the life already resident in a region. When you use Nature this way in a story, civilization becomes the negative counterpart.

Dances With Wolves uses the motif of Nature in this positive manner. The contrast between wild Nature and civilization begins with the opening sequences. A field surgery tent in the Civil War gives us a sense of the unpleasant consequences of civilization. And outside the tent, the two sides of the War face each other over a fenced field. Nothing here is part of what would be considered a *natural* order. In the midst of this chaos, Lt. Dunbar, delirious from a wound, rides between the lines in a passive suicide attempt. Ironically, he survives the shooting from the Rebel side, inspiring his fellow Union soldiers to take the field. Out of this chaos, Dunbar wins a reassignment to the prairie, because he wants "to see the frontier.... Before it's gone."

The beauty of the broad sweep of Nature, unmarred by the dubious civilization of the white man, charms Dunbar. Even the extremely remote small post he's assigned to appears as a scar on the landscape. The previous soldiers left it an unnatural trash heap. Dunbar sets about cleaning up the place, burying the residue of civilization and putting the spot back into harmony with the surroundings. This activity draws representatives of the natural life to him, a wolf he works to befriend and a local Sioux tribe that he *does* befriend.

The Indians, unlike the white men in the story, are presented as in tune with Nature. Their delights are uncomplicated and their fights are concerned with immediate survival. Dunbar accompanies the tribe on a buffalo hunt. In the process, the group comes upon a field where the carcasses of many buffalo lie rotting, only their skins and tongues taken. The blatant wastage of the meat appalls the Sioux – and Dunbar, who concludes that such an action could only be done by men "without values or soul" (i.e., "civilized" white men).

Gradually, Dunbar leaves behind the trappings of his civilized life and identifies with the Sioux. He acquires the Sioux name of Dances With Wolves and he joins the tribe. Kicking Bird tells him, "I was thinking that of all the trails in this life, there is one that matters most. It is the trail of a true human being. I think you are on this trail and it is good to see." Nature not civilization, it seems, has made a "true human being" of Dunbar.

Dances With Wolves plays the extremes of nature and civilization against each other. All we see of civilization is chaotic, violent, and even a bit insane. Life on the prairie by contrast appears beautiful and harmonious.

Viewing the wilderness in a positive light, as Nature, implies harmony and peace. But it's also possible to take the opposite approach.

Chaos

The wilderness in a negative mode tends to appear as chaotic and dangerous. Vegetation growing rampant and disordered, out of control. All imagery of that sort springs from a chaotic view of the wilderness.

There are mythic models for this motif.

Chaos – Pan. Pan served out in the wilderness as a shepherd god. Woods and pastures were his territory. He also made sure that the goats and ewes were prolific. Since he rarely came near communities, he would amuse himself by giving lonely travelers sudden frights (hence the term panic attack).

Although there is a certain playful aspect to Pan (not to mention his phallic/fertility quality), he was regarded with wariness. He did not respond to the structures of order. A less playful model comes from Africa.

Chaos – Musso Koroni. Musso Koroni was an African goddess of disorder. She was the daughter of the Voice of the Void (the void being frequently linked with chaos). She planted her husband Pemba in the soil, but his vegetation had many thorns. She disliked the thorns and so abandoned the god. She took to wandering the world, in the wilderness, causing sadness and disorder among humans.

Musso Koroni conveys none of the playful wildness of Pan. Instead, she carries a sense of the isolation possible in the wilderness.

The musical version of *Little Shop of Horrors* (1986)[1] gives us a bit of the wilderness gone rampant. Of course, Audrey II is actually an extraterrestrial plant. Even so, it remains an example of nature out of control. The plant comes into a barren situation (the failing flower shop), and its fecundity seems to improve conditions. After all, the plant brings Seymour and Audrey together. But Audrey II does not stay contained. It grows and grows, until it's completely out of Seymour's control, taking over his world and putting it in danger. Audrey II also makes Seymour more and more isolated from his fellow humans, as he hides the secret that the plant eats humans.

As you can see, the Wilderness can bring connotations of either nature and harmony to your story, or it can bring those of wildness and chaos and isolation. The City stands in contrast to the Wilderness.

THE CITY

Human beings are social creatures, and so we tend to draw together in communities. Likewise, because we also desire a sense of permanence and reliability, we build structures to house ourselves in those communities. Because these *are* natural impulses on our part, the City as a representative of communities becomes a recognizable mythic symbol.

We've looked at various mythic figures who represented the *process* of being civilized: teaching humans to live together, instructing people in agriculture or other crafts and skills. But those considerations dealt with *characters* who brought order. We're now focusing on a sense of *place*.

Cities are places where people gather together, conveying a sense of protection and order (ideally speaking). As with other motifs, the City has positive and negative modes, in this case the contrast being between order and artifice.

Order – Utopia

In 1516, Sir Thomas More published a book titled *Utopia*. In it he described a seemingly ideal society. The concept (and desire for) a perfect community was hardly a new idea. But his name for the place, Utopia (which can mean good place or no place), has taken on a life away from his book. It now gets used for *any* ideal society – in the positive sense. It has come to mean the place that is perfectly ordered, where the citizens live in harmony, abiding by reasonable laws. A dream perhaps (as in unattainable), but a persistent one that humans strive for.

As a model, we can look to the imagery of Jerusalem (or rather, the New Jerusalem, God's ideal city).

Utopia – Order – Jerusalem. Historically, the city of Jerusalem became religiously important for the Jews as the Holy City, where God chose to meet his people. That sense of holiness continued for the Christians, in that Jerusalem was the site of the sacrifice of Jesus. But more than that, the real, historical city became the model for a heavenly city. The New Jerusalem would be a place where the people communed with God, where all was beautiful and perfectly ordered, and harmony reigned in all relationships.

Very rarely do stories actually *show* a perfect society. After all, there's not much drama when things work well. More often, it's the *desire* for the perfect place which drives the use of this motif in a tale. You, the storyteller, want to convey to the audience the sense of the ideal that the characters dream of, in spite of the imperfection in front of them.

It might seem improbable to use the film *Tombstone* (1993)[2] as an example of the City as a symbol of order. Yet the story itself raises the symbols for consideration: it's a town of opportunity where anyone might prosper, and in spite of the chaos created by the outlaw gang, the Cowboys, there's a desire on the part of the residents for law and order. The Earp brothers arrive in Tombstone, having retired from law enforcement, intending to settle down and try to make a fortune. They are asked several times to take up the job of bringing law to the town, but Wyatt rejects these approaches. Yet, when Curly Bill kills the town Marshal, it's Wyatt who imposes order, by keeping the mob from lynching Curly Bill on the spot. However, it's actually Virgil Earp, disturbed by the devastation the outlaws cause, who takes up the job of town Marshal. His choice to respond to what the town represents (order and opportunity) ignites the waiting conflict between the Earps and the Cowboys.

If the law and order of a Utopia is a dream, what will we find in the nightmare of a Dystopia?

Artifice – Dystopia

In the late 1800s, the term dystopia gained currency. The intention behind the word conveys the opposite sort of city-scape from a Utopia. The Dystopia is seen as a place where human misery, squalor, oppression, disease and overcrowding characterize society. All these unpleasant things are rather obvious. As time passed since the introduction of the concept of the Dystopia, storytellers have added to the context: when the enforcement of order has developed into oppression, for instance. The artificial appearance of order has become almost a trademark of the Dystopia.

The most effective model for a Dystopia comes from literature.

Artifice – Dystopia – Pandemonium. In his *Paradise Lost*, the poet Milton created the city of Pandemonium. The name means all-demons, and has come to be an alternate name for Hell. A place of chaos and continual noise, of wild, lawless violence, confusion and uproar. The demons gather together, pretending their assembly actually rivals the order of heaven.

We live in an urbanized age, so the realities of city life are on our doorsteps. Few storytellers these days would see anything ideal in the city they live in. Even so, there are also few who would label their town a complete Dystopia or Pandemonium. Yet, the power of these symbols remains, and you should take advantage of them, if it suits your tale.

For all the chaos in the story, *Tombstone* hinted at the desire for an ideal city. By contrast, the city in *Logan's Run* (1976)[3] is an ecologically balanced world. In the perfectly ordered domed city, the people live only for their pleasure. Of course, this balance is maintained by the expedient of ending life at age thirty, "unless reborn in the fiery ritual of Carousel."

This domed city, for all the hedonism of the residents, seems well ordered and aesthetically pleasing. Yet Sandmen patrol the city, watching for Runners – people who want to get out of the city (and live beyond the age of thirty). This desire to escape exposes the reality that the city is, in fact, a Dystopia. It's *not* ideal.

When the Sandman Logan turns in some artifacts taken from a terminated Runner, the computer which controls the city identifies one of them as having special significance. An ankh (an ancient Egyptian symbol of life) has been connected to several Runners who were searching for a place called Sanctuary. The computer gives Logan the assignment to find Sanctuary, and to destroy it. In the course of this briefing, however, Logan learns that *no one* has ever reached renewal in Carousel. This shakes his perception of the city as an ordered Utopia.

When he finally reaches the outside, Logan and his companion Jessica find that Nature isn't soft. The sheltering artifice of the city contrasts with the unaccommodating aspect of Nature. Yet when the pair encounter an Old Man and learn concepts such as committed relationships and family, the city's computer-designed order loses its appeal. The city may have a pleasing artificial surface, but there's nothing under it.

The hollow order of the city of *Logan's Run* is only one variation of a Dystopia. In that city, the order seemed to function well (even if it ultimately had no purpose). Indeed, as we've discovered in considering Utopias, cities frequently represent ordered society. But they can also show us structure gone to extremes. The city in the film *Brazil* presents such a social structure gone insane. Bureaucracy rules everything, and yet the institutions are completely disconnected from the people they govern. Errors made by machines can set off a chain of events that kill people and disrupt lives. Physically, the city has become so overbuilt that sunlight rarely reaches the ground. Few things in this Dystopia function correctly. The insistence on the *forms* of order has led to the strangulation of the *reality* of order. *Brazil* pushes the dream of civilization into nightmare territory.

Whatever you decide to do with the motif of the city, consider the various contrasting outlooks which can enrich your story. The city can be a heaven or a hell, and can represent either ideal order or constricting oppression. As long as you are consistent in how you handle the imagery in the story you can emotionally carry your audience further into mythic meaning.

SECTION FIVE – OTHER FEATURES

There are a few remaining landscape motifs for us to consider. They don't quite fit in with anything else, so we're looking at them here.

GARDENS – VEGETATION

In some ways, Gardens and Vegetation in general fit with the Nature motif. However, there are a few things about Gardens and isolated Vegetation images that are more specific.

The primary mythic models will get us started on these more specific images.

Gardens – Garden of Eden. Eden was the ideal place, which God created in the midst of the world, to be the home of the Man and the Woman. All the trees were pleasant and laden with fruit. A river flowed through the garden, clear and sweet. It was peaceful, sheltered and protected, and set aside from the rest of the world.

Some aspects of the Garden of Eden may seem like Nature in a positive mode. However, the Garden can be placed in the midst of the wilderness and still mean something different. In that situation, the wilderness can represent an unrestricted life while the garden can be a sheltered, ordered haven. Or in the midst of an overbuilt city, the garden can be a spot of life and fertility.

Gardens – Ceres. As a goddess of agriculture, Ceres brought order. And of course, her plants were a source of nourishment.

Ceres reminds us of the intentional aspect of gardens. A garden is not merely Nature growing in balance with the rest of creation. It also represents Nature shaped in a particular way, usually to a certain effect. Whether it be simply for beauty (as in flower gardens) or for consumable plants (such as vegetable or herbal gardens), a garden also speaks of the human presence in the landscape. Gardens are about the *people* who interact with them.

In regard to the general matter of Vegetation, consider again Osiris.

Vegetation – Osiris. As a nature god, embodying vegetation, particularly in the cycle from budding sprouts through post-harvest decay, Osiris as a dying and resurrecting god was seen in each stage in the life of plants.

Vegetation, especially if it's one particular stage of the plant's life cycle, can symbolize that state in the broader context of your story. If you don't want to venture into the broader landscape of Nature, using a representative bit of vegetation can create a similar effect for the audience.

In *The Secret Garden*, young Mary finds the gardens of the manor covered in hoarfrost from winter. Even the Secret Garden appears dead, just as the house seems dead. Yet she finds a small green shoot in the wild dead growth of the abandoned and hidden garden. Later, when she shows Dickon the garden, he teaches her that what appears to be dead is actually wick, alive. He cuts some bark from the branch and shows her the green life underneath the bark. The shoot and the green branch represent the potential for life in the house – the lives of Mary and Colin. As the garden grows green, Colin grows strong. In this story, the connection between the garden and the humans in the story comes through clearly.

To remind ourselves that the story can play against the meaning of the imagery, look back to *American Beauty*. Gardens, after all, are supposed to be indicators of fertility and fruitfulness. In the film, Caroline Burnham's rose bushes are bursting with beautiful blossoms. Cut roses are seen in virtually every room of the Burnham house, filling bowls. However, in contrast, Caroline herself is a sterile, barren personality. She has emptied herself of fertility in pursuit of image maintenance. But it brings her no joy. Her one flight of passion is in a dead-end affair. At home, she responds more fully to possible damage to the upholstery than she does to her aroused husband. The story pushes against the mythic symbolism, heightening the contrast between what the garden should represent and what Caroline really is.

The Secret Garden uses a full-blown garden. *American Beauty* uses a bank of rose bushes and cut flowers. In *It's a Wonderful Life*, before George makes his fateful wish, he has a brief moment with his youngest child Zuzu. Little Zuzu had brought a flower home from school under her coat. The flower had dropped some petals, and Zuzu had asked her father to put them back. He'd pretended to do so while stuffing the petals into his pocket. One thing not dwelt on in the story is how unusual it is for there to be a *flower* in bloom just before Christmas. After George's encounter with his guardian angel, he discovers that the petals have disappeared from his pocket, forcing him to realize he has truly been removed from his own life.

Shocked by the grim vision of the world without him, George begs to return to his life. He knows he's back when he finds Zuzu's petals once again in his pocket. In this case, a mere portion of vegetation carries the reference to life.

The more focused aspect that a garden can bring to your story should not be overlooked. The narrowing of the aspects of Nature to its effect on human interaction can be carried by a single flower.

FIRE AND VOLCANOES

One of the most primal forces in our physical universe is that of fire. It conveys the implication of passion and purification. We speak of passion as heat and the indulgence of it steamy. And just as fire and heat are used to purify ores, burning away unwanted substances, the image of fire can be used to represent a similar transformation of a situation or character. Volcanoes, the fire of the earth itself, expand the mythic implications of flames. Power and force can be seen as the further explosion of passion. Given these implications, it's hardly surprising that fire and explosions are used so frequently in visual imagery.

Mythic models for this motif come bursting out of volcanoes.

> **Fire and Volcanoes – Pele.** Pele, the Hawaiian goddess of the fire of volcanoes, is an exceptionally passionate personality. She's the mother of eruptions, and the suddenness and force of eruptions reflects her own volatility. She's both intensely amorous and intensely destructive. Yet, in spite of the danger she brings, she's also powerfully attractive.

Pele reminds us that fire has the power to attract us, just as it has the power to destroy us. We speak of moths to the flame, referring to the attraction light has for moths. But fire draws humans to it for its light and heat.

Yet, fire isn't completely uncontrollable. The figure of Hephaestus gives us a model for a bit of fire management.

> **Fire and Volcanoes – Hephaestus.** Hephaestus is a very ancient personification of fire, especially the fires of volcanoes. As the smith of the Greek gods, he does not represent destruction

(the way Pele does). Instead, he conveys the beneficial element of controlled fire, which allows people to work metal, a constructive, civilizing activity.

Once again, we find a motif working in two directions – destructive or constructive.

However, storytellers need to be cautious about the use of fire motifs. A little can go a long way. And when the use is careless, it can be laughable, taking the audience right out of the story. Fire, in particular, is an element that can be used either as a symbol or as a natural phenomenon. As with other motifs, consistency in use becomes important.

An example of the clash between natural phenomenon and symbol shows up in the film *Volcano* (1997)[1]. In the story, which deals with the improbable circumstance of a volcano disrupting the city of Los Angeles, Emergency Management Director Mike Roark fights lava and the fires it starts. Although the course of the story brings Roark into contact with geologist Dr. Amy Barnes, the fast pace of events forces the pair to spend all their time dealing with the lava as a physical force. There isn't enough time to play with building much of a strong emotional connection between the two. Additionally, every time the audience sees the lava, it is *not* playing emotional backdrop. Rather, it's the active opponent of the main characters, a force of nature, not a symbol.

Because the lava has been presented in this straightforward manner, when we get near the film's end, we are jarred by a sudden symbolic use of the imagery. The lava has been diverted and makes its way to the ocean. Meanwhile, Barnes searches through rubble looking for Roark. As he rises heroically from behind debris, Barnes sees him at last and lets out a relieved and joyful sigh. But the filmmakers intercut the human sequence with the imagery of the hot lava meeting crashing waves and sending up clouds of steam.

The implication of the juxtaposition of the images is that the lava, waves and steam symbolically represent the emotional forces between Roark and Barnes. Unfortunately, it fails. It *laughably* fails. Not only has there not been any time for the characters to develop a relationship at that intense an emotional level, but prior to that moment the lava has not been used symbolically at all.

"Sometimes a cigar is just a cigar." That's a perfectly obvious aspect of storytelling. Sometimes natural phenomena are simply *natural* phenomena, not symbols. If your storytelling has been using elements of the physical world in a non-symbolic way, you cannot suddenly thrust a symbolic use at your audience and expect it to work. Symbols are a language, and if you haven't been talking to your audience in that language, you can't use it just to have a cool punch line to your story. The filmmakers of *Volcano* suddenly switched to a symbolic visual cliché without considering whether the audience would be prepared for it.

The use of visual symbolism went overboard in *Volcano*. But even in a case where the storytellers have been using fire symbolism effectively, it's still possible to use too much. In *Excalibur*, fire gets used to indicate passion. Usually, we see no more than it ought to be, as it is when Arthur tells Merlin of his love for Guenevere. A fire burns in a hearth behind Arthur as he watches Guenevere dance. But earlier, there's the (infamous) love scene between Uther and Igrayne, where she's naked and he's in full armor. There's a fire burning on that hearth as well, but on that occasion, it's a virtual blaze of dancing flames. Of course, it's meant to symbolize their passion. We're almost beat over the head with that symbolism.

A better use of fire as symbol turns up in *Braveheart*. After the battle of Falkirk, the Scottish nobles become uneasy about Wallace (with reason). After all, they basically betrayed him. As the noble Mornay dreams, his vision shows Wallace fiercely riding straight at the viewer, backed by flames. The flames emphasize the power inherent in Wallace's character. Powerful, untamable, alarming – the flames here are doing exactly the right job.

When it comes to using fire in your story, remember that a little of it can go a long way, symbolically speaking.

There remains one factor of our physical landscape to consider.

COLOR

Earlier we looked at the effect that **RAINBOWS** can have in stories. But *color* conveys additional things.

Humans respond to visual stimuli and the different colors are part of that. Inevitably, because we frequently think in analogies, specific colors gain specific connotations.

The colors of the spectrum move from red to orange to yellow. Green follows, blending into blue which slips through indigo to violet. Those are the basic colors. They can be strong and un-muted or shaded down to pastels.

Red	The color of blood, so it can certainly signify that. We associate heat with reds, and also passion - especially anger (seeing red means to be angry). It can be dangerous, or just intense. But whatever else it is, it isn't easy or comfortable.
Orange	Orange tends to be less intense than red. It also plugs easily into autumn connotations (leaves changing) and sunsets. In many ways, it's a more friendly color than red.
Yellow	Yellow's history of meaning has very mixed results. On the positive side, it's the color of sunshine and gold. On the negative side, it's associated with illness (jaundice, the medical condition, gets its name from Old French *for* yellow) and cowardice (having a yellow streak).
Green	The color of growing things, from new buds to lush growth. It can be used to describe the inexperienced. It somehow also came to be associated with jealousy (perhaps because bile has a greenish color). It's also cooler in tone than red, orange, or yellow. After all, we've moved away from colors that look

like flames and are moving into colors that have less heated associations –
like cool shaded forests.

Blue   The color we associate with the sky and with water. And with melancholy
            and colder temperatures. Our fingertips turn blue in cold, because the body
            conserves energy by sending less blood to the extremities. The shadows of
            packed ice and snow have blue tinges to them.

Violet   Belongs with the night and darkness. And yet there's a certain ambiguity to
            it. If we talk about light waves, those of violet are the most different from
            red. But if we're talking about mixing colors of paint, for instance, you
            get violet from combining blue with (of all things) red. Violet is a color a
            storyteller can play with.

This brief discussion of what colors can mean isn't meant to exhaust the subject, only
to give you some things to consider when throwing a spot of color into your story. I'll only
warn that of red especially, like fire, a little bit of it can go a long way. And, let us also not
forget the benefits of contrast.

The film *The Wizard of Oz* was released at a time when color films were the exception,
rather than the rule. Thus, the opening sequences in black and white conveyed not just the
sense of dullness in Dorothy's life in Kansas, but also a sense of the usual, the expected, the
ordinary. Although Dorothy speaks of blue skies and blue birds over the rainbow, *we* do
not see that color. The filmmakers wisely chose to hold off the introduction of color until
Dorothy steps out of the house and into a new land of wonder. Then *everything* is in color,
in rich intense tones.

Color, especially striking unexpected color, gets used for emphasis. The powerful green
skin color of the Wicked Witch of the West, the optimistic yellow of the Brick Road, and
the glittering richness of Dorothy's ruby slippers, each color adds an emotional effect to
the tale.

In the later part of the story, when Dorothy and her friends venture into the Haunted
Forest and into the Witch's castle, most all the colors are removed. Dark tones fill the
setting. This makes any spot of color stand out even more: for instance, the red sand in the
hourglass of Dorothy's doom becomes ominous. One interesting element in this sinister
sequence is that although the Witch's huge crystal ball swirls with color, when Dorothy sees
the image of her Aunt Em, Aunt Em is in black and white. That small moment reminds the
audience of how fantastical the realm of Oz is, even in this bleak castle.

In *Pleasantville*, the introduction of color to the black and white world of the make-
believe town is used to mark the growth of characters. David, for all that he loves the TV
series, does not see the people of Pleasantville as real. Jennifer, who does not even *want* to
be trapped in this unreal town, does see potential in the people around her. And accepting
that potential leads to changes.

The key to the changes lies in perception. Jennifer changes Skip's view of what life can
be like, and he later sees the first color change - a red rose. Bill, the soda shop owner with

the heart of an artist, voices the theme of perception. After looking through an art book, he mourns that he will not be able to paint such things. "Where am I going to see colors like that? They must be awful lucky to see colors like that. I'll bet they don't know how lucky they are." Life in Pleasantville takes on color when it is *perceived* with passion. That fact holds the hidden answer to Jennifer's question to David about why she's still in black and white. For all her greater sexual experience than the inhabitants of Pleasantville, she (and by implication, David also) does not view life with passion. For David, the moment of change comes when he sees Betty being tormented by the still black and white boys. She has become real enough to him that he intervenes and rescues her. In that moment, he stops being an observer and becomes a participant.

Color gets used in this film to build the language of perception. The more the characters *perceive* a fuller, more passionate life, the more color they respond to, to the point of becoming colored themselves. David's desire to hold onto at least a bit of the ordered, controlled black and white world springs from the lack of control and involvement he has with his real world life.

One last consideration of playing with color in storytelling.

The Sixth Sense very purposefully used color as a specific element in its storytelling. Writer/director M. Night Shyamalan said of the film, "We used the color red to indicate anything in the real world that has been tainted by the other world."[2] Red, of course, is one of the most intense colors to the eye, bringing with it passionate connotations. Therefore, what could be more appropriate for a story dealing with one of the most intense of human experiences – death? Yet, one of the things that should be noted in the film's use of color is that it does *not* work on a good/bad paradigm. The murdering mother that Cole exposes wears a red suit at the wake for her daughter. That's certainly a negative context. Yet the tent Cole builds for himself in his bedroom, as a shelter from the ghosts, *also* is red. Yet it mostly represents a positive context. The color is used to mark "emotionally explosive moments."

Make use of color in your storytelling. Paint the town red, sing the blues or follow the yellow brick road. But don't let yourself get locked in a world of greys unless that's exactly the effect you want.

MUSINGS

If you really want to dig into the mythic meaning of your story, don't overlook the landscape where you set the tale. You can mine the possibilities in many ways, if you take the time to examine your foundations. Turn over every stone.

Think about it:

*   Does your story involve any sky-borne elements?

What sort of contrasts do you have between the sky and the earth? Which element is more dominant in your tale? Which has the more positive context in your story?

Do you have a rational versus emotional clash going on in your story? How are you using the sky and earth imagery to convey that?

*   Does your story have any tower-like or cave-like images?

If you have towers (or mountain peaks) in your story, are you getting any symbolic mileage out of them? Are you playing to the rational associations, or against them?

If you have any cave-like places in your tale, are they adding any mythic impact to it? Can your caves be places of hidden knowledge, realms of emotion, or the fearsome unknown? Are you pushing against the audience's expectation of this location, or are you delivering the images along traditional lines?

*   Is the contrast between the sea and land important in your story? In what way? Which aspect do you want to be dominant? Do you want one to be more positive or favorable than the other? How do you want to express that?

Is the sea the dominant force? If so, what sort of connotations do you want from it? Do you have a character that is closely connected to the sea? If so, how do her actions reflect that?

Is the land the ruling aspect in your story? How is it more powerful or effective than the sea and *its* meanings? What is the clash between the land and the sea? Do you have a character associated with the land? What does he do or say that indicates this?

*   Do you have a contrast between the wilderness and the city going on in your story? How is it manifested?

*   If the wilderness is important to your story, does it appear in a positive or negative mode?

If positive, how do you convey the sense of the proper balance of Nature? Do you have a character that represents this aspect? Do you have a character fighting this aspect? Or do you have a character who is learning to see the balance of Nature? How are you presenting these connections?

If the wilderness in your story is appearing in a negative mode, how are you communicating that to the audience? How are you demonstrating the chaos of the dark wilderness? How is this landscape affecting the characters? Do you have a character who identifies with the chaos? Or do you have someone resisting it? Is there a character who changes his connection to/resistance of the chaos?

* If the City (or civilization in general) is important to your story, is it a good thing or a bad thing? A Utopia or Dystopia?

If your City is a Utopia, how is that presented? Is it a dream or an ideal that's being aimed at? Or is it actively functioning in the story? How does the order and structure of the Utopia affect your characters? Are they drawn to it, or do they resist it?

* If the City is a Dystopia, what sort is it? Is the dysfunction of society obvious to the characters and the audience? Or are the dystopic qualities hidden under an artificial surface? How do your characters react to the Dystopia? Are they overwhelmed by it or do they fight it?

* Is a garden important to your story?

If so, how is it contrasted to the broader scope of Nature? Which character is most connected to this garden, and why? Are there negative or positive implications from the presence of the garden? If so, what are they?

* Are you using fire to any degree in your story? Are you using it as a straight-forward natural phenomenon? Or do your fire images have symbolic impact? If you use fire (or volcanic) imagery symbolically, have you worked it throughout the story, or presented the context carefully?

Is color of special significance in your story? If so, how? Do you know how the symbolic aspects of various colors affect your story?

PART SIX

THEME PARKS

Although specific stories have beginnings, middles and ends, humans also respond to the idea of ongoing adventures. On one side of the fence, we like *endings* and closure. Yet on the other side of the fence, we have a compulsive "What happens next?" response. So, when you want to move into the territory of serial storytelling, what sort of things do you need to consider? Can you do any old thing?

Successful story franchises need to have a substantial core. There are many things which can *form* that core. But a franchise fares better if it's about something, rather than just being one adventure after another. An appealing character with a particular attitude or outlook can serve as that linchpin. Or a special social context that can move through changing events can provide the series anchor.

Strange things have happened: hire a detective. You want to explore the implications of historical artifacts? Find an archeologist. You intend to venture into strange and alien territory? Send in a team.

Serial storytelling has a long and established tradition. In the ancient Greek world, Hercules became the core of a whole collection of adventures. In the basics of his story, Hercules, a half-mortal son of Zeus was driven from place to place by the wrath of Hera. Yet, even though he was hounded by fate, he would try to help the people he was with for that time. All around the Greek world are places that could put up signs "Hercules slept here." Hercules was a good, special guy (a Divine Hero) who moved around a lot. So a string of stories trailed behind him.

By contrast, King Arthur and his court represented a special context that generated a lot of stories. In fact, for two centuries in the middle ages, Arthurian stories were just about the most popular ones going. Now, as the material developed over time, the Arthurian cycle developed a fairly consistent beginning, middle and end. But it was spread out over an extended – and imagined – span of time. And it also had a sizable cast of characters, with all sorts of personalities and attitudes. Arthur represented the ideal of leadership in the midst of a world of chaos. His Camelot was a dream of ordered civilization. And the Arthurian mythos didn't get left behind in the Middle Ages (the way a similar cycle of stories about Charlemagne and his court did). We're still mining tales from the vein of Arthurian ore.

Robin Hood (and his Merry Men) brought a contentious attitude to stories. The resistance to tyranny conveyed by that attitude continues to find responses in audiences. As with Arthur and his court, Robin and his followers with their broad range of personalities support many different tales.

These three selections only hint at the other clusters of serial stories that have existed. The adventures of Maui through Polynesia, the pranks of Loki in northern Europe, the wanderings of Odysseus, all also collected multiple tales.

In modern times, we still come up with frameworks for multiple stories. James Bond ventures out, a man and his wits against the evil forces that would disrupt civilization. Although his original stories took place against the backdrop of a specific ideological conflict (the democracy of the West versus Soviet communism), it shifted easily into the broader context of a Hero fighting the forces of chaos on behalf of an ordered society. As a result, he still saunters up to bars ordering his Martini ("Shaken, not stirred."), he still cracks witticisms in the face of megalomaniacs, long after the Soviet order has fallen by the wayside. Bond is about something more.

Superman has become an icon of pure-hearted heroism (combined with an immigrant's desire for a home). Even though society may have gotten much more cynical, Superman's unshaken honor continues to provoke and inspire. For instance, in the film *The Iron Giant*, a little bit of coloration gets added to the story by using references to the Superman mythos. Young Hogarth tells the Giant some stories – from comic books. The moment continues building the friendship between the boy and the robot, and helps define the values being put forward. Hogarth tells the Giant about Superman: "He started off just like you. Crash landed on earth .... He only uses his powers for good. Never for evil." When the Giant looks at another comic book character – a metal robot – Hogarth tells the Giant he's not like that villain. "You're a good guy. Like Superman."

When the Giant goes berserk (because he thinks Hogarth had been killed), Hogarth pulls him out of it. "You don't have to be a gun. You are what you choose to be. *You* choose." When Kent causes a missile to be launched, a missile which could destroy the town, the Giant flies up into space to meet the missile. He saves the town. As he flies, he recalls Hogarth's words: "You are who you choose to be," and he says to himself, "*Superman.*"

The use of the Superman mythos in *The Iron Giant* exemplifies how powerful the underlying meanings of a franchise can be. Sure, some franchises may just be light-hearted fun because we enjoy the character. But more durable are the constructions which have solid cores of meaning. The key goes back to the Hero as role model. And after more than 60 years, Superman still is one.

Like Arthur's court, the *Star Trek* franchises provide a group context moving through adventures. A select set of characters get sent out to face all sorts of challenges. They serve as avatars for the audience, demonstrating what we might be capable of in similar circumstances.

Even Robin Hood has echoes in the modern age. Batman functions as one version of the Outlaw Hero. He labors in a perpetual present in a grim urban landscape, pursuing a crusade of fighting crime and protecting victims. Like Superman, he's survived 60 years of changing social contexts. That adaptability tells us that something universal is at work in these stories. Another variation of the Outlaw Hero would be the characters of *The X-Files*. Mulder and Scully frequently step outside their place as F.B.I. agents. They investigate strange phenomena, and battle hidden conspiracies. Their willingness to think outside the box inspires the audience to do likewise – and there's always a new box that needs getting outside of.

Those are what some versions of serial storytelling look like. But how do you, the storyteller, get there?

SHAPING A FRANCHISE

Open and Closed Stories

One of the first things you need to decide when you start to build your Theme Park is whether you want it to be an open or closed story. "What do you mean by that?" you ask.

An Open Story is one for which you have no intended ending. There may be a specific *origin* for the story (the infant Kal-El's space rocket crashes in a Kansas field), but no finale planned (Superman will probably never die). Stories in this context can go on and on, most likely in a perpetual present where the characters do not age or change much. This works because the characters themselves are the ongoing context, and you want that to be consistent. Some franchises of this sort occasionally irritate our expectation of real life aging, but the fact remains that humans are contrary creatures, and both the passage of time and a perpetual present appeal to audiences.

A Closed Story is one where you do have a specific beginning, middle and end in mind. The middle and end can be stretched out for a considerable period, giving the residents of the story plenty of room for multiple adventures (the way Camelot has a beginning and ending). Using a Closed Story allows you to have the characters go through significant changes as they head toward your finale, much more so than can be done in an Open Story.

So, as you begin to shape your franchise, consider whether you want to head toward a grand finale. It's possible that elements of one of the Hero's Journeys may guide the path you want the franchise to take. One benefit of a Closed Story is that since you know where it's heading, you can drop in foreshadowing elements in otherwise incidental episodes of the bigger tale.

The next two matters to consider can have major effects on the overall tone of the franchise.

The Constant Jeopardy Syndrome

The Constant Jeopardy Syndrome can be a troublesome matter for a franchise. The basic description of this storytelling force is this:

If the premise of the franchise involves a major problem for your main character (or characters), and if the overall story ends when the character solves the problem, you are dealing with the Constant Jeopardy Syndrome.

Many science fiction television shows, for a long time, were constructed around a Constant Jeopardy. The Robinson family (and their pesky stowaway Dr. Smith) can neither reach their intended destination of Alpha Centauri nor return to Earth, so they remain *Lost in Space*. Dr. Kimble must evade law-enforcement officials while hunting for the one-armed man in *The Fugitive*. In the original series, the survivors on the *Battlestar Galactica* cannot defeat the Cylons or reach Earth (although the series did attempt to do both, unsuccessfully in the eyes of the audience).

The danger of the Constant Jeopardy Syndrome makes its impact on characterization. However fantastical the setting of your story, the audience will follow you anywhere if the characters behave honestly. By that, I mean that their emotional reactions to the events they experience ring true. This would qualify as realism of presentation. It gives the audience something understandable to identify with, to feel with.

However, when the premise of the franchise falls into the Constant Jeopardy mode, you the storyteller are giving the audience a cast of characters who (for the purposes of the ongoing story) *cannot solve* the *major* problem of their lives. If you keep the characters reacting in a psychologically real fashion, then the audience should see the characters start to crack from the stress. The sanity of the characters should become wobbly. The fact is, human beings rarely deal well with what they perceive to be an unconquerable, insurmountable problem. If you don't let your characters behave realistically, the audience ceases to take the drama realistically. The story devolves into camp because it has nowhere else to go. (After all, realistically, in *Lost in Space*, for the safety of the crew of the *Jupiter*, Dr. Smith should have either been put into suspended animation, or more finally, thrust out an air lock into deep space.) Either the characters will go bonkers, or your story context becomes bonkers in the eyes of the audience.

The television show *M.A.S.H.* frequently played to these conditions of the Constant Jeopardy Syndrome. In "Peace on Us,"[1] it comes to the forefront. In that episode, the camp learns that the Peace Talks have been stalled, and as a result, the rotation points needed to return home are raised. This hits a weary Hawkeye hardest. Strictly speaking, there's little Hawkeye himself can do to change the major problem they face (that is, the ongoing Korean War). However, on this occasion, he decides to try. He jumps in a Jeep and heads for the Talks, to tell them to put an end to the fighting. As he drives off, Margaret yells after him, "You can't do that! Are you crazy?" The answer is that, yes, he is, a little bit. But his response makes sense in the face of the insurmountable problem in front of them.

Because *M.A.S.H.* allowed the characters to respond realistically to the major problem in their lives, they remained credible humans in the eyes of the audience – even *admirable*, in their creative coping methods of controlled insanity.

Again, if you don't intend to have your characters respond realistically to their Constant Jeopardy, you have plenty of room for high camp. But be certain that that's the sort of story you want to tell.

The Incidental Jeopardy Context

In contrast to the Constant Jeopardy Syndrome, the Incidental Jeopardy Context allows you a wider range of possibilities for the outcome of any particular episode of your over-all story.

The Incidental Jeopardy Context appears when the characters have a moderately stable basic situation, and when they have a 50/50 chance of success or failure in the immediate conflict they face.

The possibility of failure is an important dramatic element in serial storytelling. Your characters have to have something to lose, and they need to behave as if they *know* they can lose. Whether they actually *do* lose this incidental battle is up to you. It's true that when an audience comes to something they know will be serial storytelling, their expectation is that the *main* characters will be continuing on throughout the over-all story. You can achieve high drama if you disrupt that expectation. If your characters *do* fail occasionally, if major characters die or otherwise fall by the wayside, the audience becomes very intrigued with what happens next.

The Rule of Seven

Seven is a very basic number when it comes to storytelling. In particular, it has to do with the number of characters the audience feels comfortable with. It doesn't mean that you can't have *more* than seven characters. Not by any means. But it does mean that the characters beyond the fringe of seven get less face time with the audience. Once you adjust to that aspect, and as long as each of your characters is a distinctive individual, you can increase the size of your cast.

However, of your basic seven characters, you are likely to have three principal characters and four supporting characters. One of your principal characters may even be the *main* and most important character.

One thing about the mixture of characters, though, is that the focus of importance is a matter between the characters and the audience, not between the characters and the plot. The tendency is, of course, to make your main character in the audience's eyes the most important character in the story context. Storytellers have done that for ages on end. But you also have the option of centering the story's point of view on a secondary character – a sidekick, perhaps, someone observing the most important character in action. Don't overlook any storytelling options.

Spectacle

Spectacle and pageantry can show up in *any* story whether ongoing or not. And there are occasions when you may want to make a splashy presentation of something, a parade or a ceremony or some other dazzling event. But there are some important things to remember when using spectacle.

Spectacle as sensory overload only works once – the first time. By that, I mean that the *first* time the audience comes to your spectacle they may indeed be awed or amazed. But any repeat visit to the story may end up a dull experience for the audience: they've seen it, they've "been there and done that."

To include spectacle in a story just for the sake of spectacle can slow down everything in the story. It's one thing for us to see a fabulous parade, or a spectacular exhibit of fireworks.

But to include these things in a story and to treat them just as we do in real life will invite a failure in storytelling. The opening shot in *Star Wars* of the big, bigger, *huge* spaceship was breathtaking the first time anyone saw it, for the simple reason that never before had a film so successfully conveyed a sense of something that big. It survives repeated viewings because it is (1) actually a very short visual, in the amount of time it takes to see the whole ship, and (2) it's in the middle of some dramatic action, a fight between two vessels. The audience remains engaged with what they are seeing.

The other end of the spectacle spectrum can be seen in the film of *Raise the Titanic*. When the sunken ship reaches the surface, we get a visual fly-over of it. Unfortunately, there's nothing much present to give us a sense of scale, at that moment. No people on it, nor other ships in the frame with it. The opening credit sequence of the film had included photos of the actual *Titanic*, with people in them to give a feeling for its size. But *inside* the story in the film, there were no such markers. There was also an insufficient amount of reaction on the part of the characters in the story. Earlier in the film, when the searchers found the fabled vessel, there were long sequences of looking over the ship under water. Unfortunately, these sequences are incredibly boring, because the audience has no character they can identify with who is ooohing and aaahing and being generally excited. There are very few character reactions given at this point. Now, this may be a failure in the directing. But if the storytellers (screenwriter, director, effects supervisors) don't have a sense of the *awesome* in their spectacular sequences, the audience won't have it either.

No matter the medium of your story, always remember to connect your characters to the spectacle. If the event really *is* that amazing, show the audience that your character *is* amazed, and *what* amazes them, and *how* that amazement gets expressed. Let the audience see through your characters' eyes, feel with your characters' emotions. And if you feel uncertain about conveying a character's enthusiasm for a spectacle, I suggest you read Dr. Seuss' "And To Think I Saw It On Mulberry Street."[2] The narrator becomes more and more excited about .... But I'll let you explore that on your own.

MUSINGS

After you've captured the mythic snapshots that suit your story, take some time to get a feel for them. If the images feel organic to you, run with them. There's plenty of room for variety.

Think about it:

* If you are planning to shape some serial storytelling, have you decided whether yours will be an Open Story or a Closed Story?

* If yours is an Open Story, what is the main context for it? Who is the main character?

Do you know how this story began? What the origins of your characters are?

* If you are planning on telling a Closed Story, do you know what its beginning is? How about its ending?

What events do you absolutely need, to get from the beginning to the end? Can you set up and foreshadow elements as the incidental episodes go by?

* Are you going to use the Constant Jeopardy Syndrome in your serial story? If yes, what is the major problem your characters face? What keeps your characters from solving this problem?

Will your characters behave realistically toward their major problem? How do they handle the stress of their failure to eliminate the problem?

If you go with the high camp option, how wacky will the situation get?

* If you use the Incidental Jeopardy Context, what sort of problems will your characters face? Have you considered allowing your characters to fail on occasion? How will they react to that? Will they be changed by the events?

* How many characters do you plan on using in your story? Who is your linchpin character? Is he the Hero of the story or a sidekick or observer? Who are the other principal characters? Who are the supporting characters?

* Do you have any spectacle in your story? If so, what is it and why is it there? What does it add to the story? How are your characters interacting with the spectacle? Does the audience see what the characters see, feel what the characters feel? How do you convey that to the audience?

UNPACK THE BAGGAGE

You don't need any excuses to tell stories. If you love storytelling, enjoy the experience. Your enthusiasm will enrich the story for your audience. And you can be sure there *is* an audience out there somewhere. Human beings love to be entertained. In fact, the word entertainment means something held together, by a group. Something special and meaningful. It's also something between people. It's not a solitary activity: there's the storyteller and the audience. If you've got a story to tell, there's probably someone who wants to hear it.

This book has been all about how to enrich the experience between those two parties. About what you may intend and what the audience might expect. I hope you have fun telling all your stories.

PART SEVEN

HANGERS ON (APPENDICES)

ENDNOTES

JOURNEY OUTLINES

HIERARCHIES

REFERENCES

END NOTES

PART ONE: SECTION ONE – SETTING OUT

1:   *Star Wars*; 1977, written by George Lucas.

2:   *Clueless*; 1995, written by Amy Hickerling, from the novel *Emma,* by Jane Austen.

3:   *His Girl Friday*;1940, screenplay by Charles Lederer, from the play *The Front Page* by Ben Hecht and Charles MacArthur.

4:   *Harry Potter and the Sorcerer's Stone*; 2001, screenplay by Steve Kloves, from the novel by J.K. Rowling.

5:   *The Fifth Element*; 1997, story by Luc Besson, screenplay by Luc Besson & Robert Mark Kamen.

6:   *The Lord of the Rings: The Fellowship of the Ring*; 2001, screenplay by Fran Walsh & Philippa Boyens & Peter Jackson, based on the novel by J.R.R. Tolkien.

7:   *Groundhog Day*; 1993, story by Danny Rubin, screenplay by Danny Rubin and Harold Ramis.

8:   Sir Thomas Malory, *Le Morte d'Arthur* (New York: Bramhall House, 1962), modern rendition by Keith Baines, p. 21–27. Also *The Arthurian Encyclopedia*, edited by Norris J. Lacy (New York, Garland Publishing , 1986), p. 291.

9:   Exodus Chapters 1 – 3.

10:   *Excalibur*; 1981, written by Rospo Pallenberg and John Boorman, adapted by R. Pallenberg from Malory's *Le Morte d'Arthur*.

11:   *The Matrix*; 1999, written by Andy Wachowski, Larry Wachowski.

12:     *Manhunter*; 1986, screenplay by Michael Mann, from the novel *Red Dragon* by Thomas Harris.

13:     *Indiana Jones and the Last Crusade*; 1989, story by George Lucas and Menno Meyjes, screenplay by Jeffrey Boam.

14:     *Braveheart*; 1995, written by Randall Wallace.

15:     Homer, *The Odyssey*, translated by Robert Fitzgerald (Garden City, NY: Anchor Books, 1963)

16:     *The Iron Giant*; 1999, screen story by Brad Bird, script by Tim McCanlies, based on the book *The Iron Man* by Ted Hughes.

17:     *The Mask of Zorro*; 1998, story by Ted Elliot & Terry Rossio and Randal Johnson, script by John Eskow and Ted Elliot & Terry Rossio.

18:     *Real Genius*; 1985, written by Neal Israel, Pat Proft, Peter Torokvei.

19:     Matthew 3: 13–17

20:     *Dances With Wolves*; 1990, written by Michael Blake, from his novel.

21:     Matthew 4: 1–11

22:     *Lawrence of Arabia*; 1962, screenplay by Robert Bold, from the book by T.E. Lawrence.

23:     *The Truman Show*; 1998, written by Andrew Niccol.

24:     *Monsters, Inc.;* 2001, written by Robert L. Baird, Jill Culton, Peter Docter, Ralph Eggleston, Dan Gerson, Jeff Pidgeon, Rhett Reese, Jonathan Roberts, Andrew Stanton.

25:     *All the President's Men*; 1976, written by Carl Bernstein & Bob Woodward, from their book, and William Goldman.

26:     *The Client*; 1994, written by Akiva Goldsman and Robert Getchell, from the novel by John Grisham.

27:     Disney's *The Beauty and the Beast*; 1991, story by Roger Allers, animation screenplay by Linda Woolverton.

PART ONE: SECTION TWO – QUEST AND CONFLICT

1:     Virgil, *The Aeneid*; a verse translated by Allen Mandelbaum (Berkeley: University of California Press, 1971).

2:     *Raiders of the Lost Ark*; 1981, story by George Lucas and Philip Kaufman, script by Lawrence Kasdan.

3:   *The Fugitive*; 1993, story by David Twohy, based on the TV series by Roy Huggins, screenplay by Jeb Stuart and David Twohy.

4:   *The Silence of the Lambs*; 1991, from the novel by Thomas Harris, screenplay by Ted Tally.

5:   Jonah 1: 1-ff.

6:   *Ladyhawke*; 1935, story by Edward Khmara, script by Edward Khmara and Michael Thomas and Tom Mankiewicz.

7:   *Terminator 2: Judgment Day*; 1991, written by James Cameron & William Wisher.

8:   *Contact*; 1997, written by Carl Sagan and Ann Druyan, from Sagan's novel.

9:   *Indian Summer*; 1993, written by Mike Binder.

10:   *The Empire Strikes Back*; 1980, story by George Lucas, screenplay by Leigh Brackett and Lawrence Kasdan.

11:   A similar hook and lack of resolution exists in *Star Wars* (Episode IV). I recall when I first saw the film (with no real expectation that there would be a sequel), I felt a lack in the fact that Luke and Vader had not met in *direct* confrontation. Vader was the ogre, and although the fighter battle over the Death Star fits the position of confronting the ogre, it does not completely fill it. At that time I could not have said *why* I felt the two needed to meet face to face, only *that* they needed to do so. I suppose it is worth noting: on such hooks are sequels built.

12:   *Star Trek: The Next Generation,* "Sins of the Father"; 1990, written by Ronald D. Moore and W. Reed Moran, story by Drew Deighan.

13:   *Babylon 5*, "There All the Honor Lies"; 1995, written by Peter David.

14:   *The Return of the Jedi*; 1983, story by George Lucas, screenplay by Lawrence Kasdan and George Lucas.

15:   *It's a Wonderful Life*; 1946, from the story "The Greatest Gift" by Philip Van Doren Stern, screenplay by Frances Goodrich & Albert Hackett and Frank Capra.

PART ONE: SECTION THREE – SIDE TRIPS

1:   Jessie L. Weston, *From Ritual to Romance* (Garden City, NY: Doubleday Anchor Books, 1957).

2:   *Funk & Wagnalls Standard Dictionary of Folklore, Mythology and Legend*, edited by Maria Leach (San Francisco: HarperSanFrancisco, HarperCollins, 1984).

3:   *My Favorite Year*; 1982, story by Dennis Palumbo, script by Dennis Palumbo and Norman Steinberg.

PART ONE: SECTION FOUR – COMING HOME

1: *North by Northwest*; 1959, written by Ernest Lehman.

2: Tony Allan, et al., *Gods of Sun and Sacrifice: Aztec & Maya Myth* (Myth and Mankind series) (New York: Time-Life Books, 1997).

3: *Singing in the Rain*; 1952, written by Betty Comden, Adolph Green.

4: *The Green Mile*; 1999, screenplay by Frank Darabont, from the novel by Stephen King.

5: *Star Trek: Generations*; 1994, story by Rick Berman & Ronald D. Moore & Brannon Braga, script by Ronald D. Moore & Brannon Braga.

6: *Babylon 5*, "Sleeping in Light"; 1998, written by J. Michael Straczynski.

PART ONE: SECTION FIVE – THE ANTI-HERO'S PATH

1: I highly recommend James Bonnet, *Stealing Fire From the Gods* (Studio City, CA: Michael Wiese Productions, 1999). He has developed a cyclic outlook on the Hero's Journey, which includes elements that address the matter of the Anti-Hero. It is one of the few books which does touch on the matter.

2: *Macbeth*; 1972, written by Roman Polanski, Kenneth Tynan and William Shakespeare, based on Shakespeare's play.

3: *Citizen Kane*; 1941, written by Herman J. Mankiewicz and Orson Welles.

PART TWO – TRANSPORTATION

1: Northrop Frye, *Fables of Identity* (New York: Harcourt, Brace and World, Inc., 1963).

2: *Grosse Pointe Blank*; 1997, story by Tom Jankiewicz, screenplay by Tom Jankiewicz and D.V. DeVincentis & Steve Pink & John Cusack.

3: *American Beauty*; 1999, written by Alan Ball.

4: *Hamlet*; 1990, screenplay by Christopher De Vore, Franco Zeffirelli, William Shakespeare, from Shakespeare's play.

5: *Chinatown*; 1974, written by Robert Towne.

PART THREE: SECTION ONE – 24 HOURS

1: Alexander Eliot, *The Universal Myths: Heroes, Gods, Tricksters and Others* (with contributions by Joseph Campbell and Mircea Eliade) (New York: Meridian Books, 1976, 1990).

2: Michael Jordan, *Encyclopedia of Gods* (New York: Facts on File, 1993); and *The Encyclopedia Mythica*, http://www.pantheon.org/mythica.html.

3:   *The Birds*; 1963, story by Daphne DuMaurier, script by Evan Hunter.

4:   Tony Allan, et al., *Spirits of the Snow: Arctic Myth* (Myth and Mankind series) (New York: Time-Life Books, 1999).

5:   *White Nights*; 1985, story by James Goldman, script by James Goldman, Eric Hughes.

6:   From http://stardate.utexas.edu/resources/faqs/011.html. Accessed 6/20/2001

7:   *Shane*; 1953, story by Jack Schaefer from his book, A.B. Guthrie, Jr.

8:   "The Dawn of the Day", traditional ballad arranged by Steeleye Span, recorded on *Tonight's the Night* (Shanachie 79080 (CD, US, 1991)). Lyrics from http://rzdspc77.informatik.uni-hamburg.de/~zierke/steeleyespan/songs/dawnoftheday.html.

PART THREE: SECTION TWO – THE SEASONS

1:   *The Secret Garden*; 1993, from the novel by Frances Hodgson Burnett, screenplay by Caroline Thompson.

2:   *American Graffiti*; 1973, written by George Lucas and Gloria Katz.

3:   *Field of Dreams*; 1989, written by Phil Alden Robinson, based on *Shoeless Joe*, by W.P. Kinsella.

4:   *Cat on a Hot Tin Roof*; 1958, written by Richard Brooks, James Poe, based on the play by Tennessee Williams.

5:   *Sleepy Hollow*; 1999, story by Washington Irving, screen story by Kevin Yagher & Andrew Kevin Walker, screenplay by Andrew Kevin Walker.

6:   *King Lear*; 1984, written by William Shakespeare.

7:   It is worth noting that when Akira Kurosawa adapted *King Lear* in 1985, he gave his film the title *Ran*. The title is the Japanese character for "chaos" or "rebellion." *Ran*; 1985, written by Masato Ide, Akira Kurosawa, Hideo Oguni, based on William Shakespeare's play *King Lear*.

8:   *You've Got Mail*; 1998, screenplay by Nora Ephron & Delia Ephron, based on the screenplay *The Shop Around the Corner* by Samson Raphaelson, based on the play *Parfumerie* by Miklos Laszlo.

PART THREE: SECTION THREE – HOLIDAYS

1:   You can find descriptions of holidays in books like *The Folklore of World Holidays*; edited by Robert H. Griffin and Ann H. Shurgin; 2nd edition (Detroit: Gale, 1999) or *The World Holiday Book: celebrations for every day of the year*; Anneli Rufas (San Francisco: HarperSanFrancisco, 1994), and *Holidays and Anniversaries of the World*; Jennifer Mossman, editor, 2nd edition (Detroit: Gale Research, 1990).

PART THREE: SECTION FOUR – WEATHER

1: Loren Auerbach, et al., *Sagas of the Norsemen: Viking and German Myth* (Myth and Mankind series) (New York: Time-Life Books, 1997).

2: *Phenomenon*; 1996, written by Gerald DiPego.

3: Karl Williams, in the review of *Phenomenon* at www.allmovie.com.

4: *Pleasantville*; 1998, written by Gary Ross.

5: *Smilla's Sense of Snow*; 1997, from the novel by Peter Hoeg, translated by Tiina Nunnally, script by Ann Biderman.

6: Genesis 9: 8–17.

7: *The Wizard of Oz;* 1939, screenplay by Noel Langley, Florence Ryerson and Edgar Allan Woolf, from the book by L. Frank Baum.

8: "Over the Rainbow"; words by E.Y. Harburg, music by Harold Arlen, sung by Judy Garland.

PART FOUR: SECTION ONE – SEX (OR GENDER)

1: Genesis 1: 26–27; Genesis 2: 18.

2: Robert Hicks, *The Masculine Journey: Understanding the Six Stages of Manhood* (Colorado Springs, CO: NavPress Publishing Group, 1993). Also, Robert and Cynthia Hicks, *The Feminine Journey: Understanding the Biblical Stages of a Woman's Life* (Colorado Springs, CO: NavPress Publishing Group, 1994)

3: Edgar Rice Burroughs' books about Tarzan have remained popular since their first publication. They are available in many editions, and in fact, several are freely accessible online on the Internet.

4: Disney's *Tarzan*; 1999, from the novel by Edgar Rice Burroughs, screenplay by Tab Murphy and Bob Tzudiker & Noni White.

5: *Greystoke*; 1984, written by P.H. Vazak and Michael Austin, from the novel by Edgar Rice Burroughs.

6: Disney's *Peter Pan*; 1953, from the play by J.M. Barrie, script by M.H. Banta, Bill Cottrell, Winston Hibler, Bill Peet, Erman Penner, Joe Rinaldi, Tod Sears, Ralph Wright.

7: *Peter Pan*; 1955, from the book and play by J.M. Barrie, adapted by Jerome Robbins.

8: Judges chapters 14–16.

9: *Goldfinger*; 1964, screenplay by Richard Maibaum & Paul Dehn, from the novel by Ian Fleming.

10: *Lethal Weapon*; 1987, written by Shane Black.

11: *Soldier*; 1998, written by David Webb Peoples.

12: *The Jackal*; 1997, written by Chuck Pfarere, based on Kenneth Ross's screenplay *The Day of the Jackal*, from the novel by Frederick Forsyth.

13: *The Fisher King*; 1991, written by Richard LaGravenese.

14: *The Quiet Man*; 1952, from the story "Green Rushes" by Maurice Walsh, screenplay by Frank Nugent.

15: *Hope Floats*; 1998, written by Steven Rogers.

16: *Baby Boom*; 1987, written by Nancy Meyers, Charles Shyer.

17: *Erin Brockovich*; 2000, written by Susannah Grant.

18: *The First Wives Club*; 1996, screenplay by Robert Harling, from the novel by Olivia Goldsmith.

19: *The X-Files;* "Pilot," originally aired September 10, 1993, written by Chris Carter; "Clyde Bruckman's Final Repose," October 13, 1995, by Darrin Morgan; "Chinga," February 8, 1998, by Stephen King and Chris Carter.

PART FOUR: SECTION TWO – NEEDS

1: *Psychology*, second edition; edited by Douglas A. Bernstein et al. (Boston: Houghton Mifflin, 1991) p. 462–463. Also discussed by William G. Huitt in "Maslow's Hierarchy of Needs" at http://chiron-valdosta.edu/whuitt/col/regsys/maslow.html.

2: *The Edge*; 1997, written by David Mamet.

3: *Gone With the Wind*; 1939, from the novel by Margaret Mitchell, screenplay by Sidney Howard.

4: *Notting Hill*; 1999, written by Richard Curtis.

5: *Thelma & Louise*; 1991, written by Callie Khouri.

6: *The Maltese Falcon*; 1941, written by John Huston, based on the novel by Dashiell Hammett.

7: *Changing Habits*; 1997, written by Scott Davis Jones.

PART FOUR: SECTION THREE – DAY LABORERS

1: *Dead Poets Society*; 1989, written by Tom Schulman.

2: *My Fair Lady*; 1964, written by Alan Jay Lerner, based on the play *Pygmalion* by George Bernard Shaw.

3: *An Officer and a Gentleman*; 1982, written by Douglas Day Stewart.

4: *The Hunt for Red October*; 1990, screenplay by Larry Ferguson and Donald Stewart, based on the novel by Tom Clancy.

5: *Entrapment*; 1999, story by Ron Bass and Michael Hertzberg, screenplay by Ron Bass and William Broyles.

6: *Black Widow*; 1986, written by Ronald Bass.

7: *Wall Street*; 1987, written by Stanley Weiser & Oliver Stone.

8: *The Mask*; 1994, story by Michael Fallon and Mark Verheiden, and script by Mike Werb.

PART FOUR: SECTION FOUR – PROFESSIONAL SPECIALISTS

1: *The Terminator*; 1984, written by James Cameron & Gale Anne Hurd, William Wisher, from material by Harlan Ellison.

2: *Patch Adams*; 1998, from the book *Gesundheit: Good Health is a Laughing Matter* by Hunter Doherty Adams & Maureen Mylander, screenplay by Steve Oedekerk.

3: *Outbreak*; 1995, written by Laurence Dwore & Robert Roy Pool.

4: *Norma Rae*; 1979, written by Harriet Frank Jr. and Irving Ravetch.

5: M. Scott Peck, *Further Along the Road Less Traveled* (New York: Simon & Schuster, 1993), p. 238.

6: *M.A.S.H.*; based on the film written by Ring Lardner Jr., from the novel by Richard Hooker; "Operation Noselift" originally aired January 19, 1974, written by Erik Tarloff; "House Arrest," February 4, 1975, written by Jim Fritzell & Everett Greenbaum; "The Novocain Mutiny," January 27, 1976, written by Burt Prelutsky.

7: *The Bounty*; 1984, written by Robert Bolt, based on the book *Captain Bligh and Mr. Christian* by Richard Hough.

8: *The Bridge on the River Kwai*; 1957, written by Carl Foreman and Michael Wilson, Calder Willingham, from the novel by Pierre Boulle.

9: *Ronin*; 1998, story by J.D. Zeik, screenplay by J.D. Zeik and Richard Weisz.

10: Clive Cussler, *Raise the Titanic* (New York: Bantam Books, Viking Press, 1976, 1980), p. 15, 147, 318.

11: *Raise the Titanic*; 1980, from the novel by Clive Cussler, screenplay by Eric Hughes, Adam Kennedy.

12: *Romeo and Juliet*; 1968, from the play by William Shakespeare, screenplay by Franco Brusati, Maestro D'Amico, Franco Zeffirelli.

13: *The Vikings*; 1958, from the novel by Edison Marshall, screenplay by Calder Willingham, adaptation by Dale Wasserman.

14: *The Sixth Sense*; 1999, written by M. Night Shyamalan.

15: Material on this subject can be found in Richard A. Kalish, *Death, Grief and Caring Relationships* (Monterey, CA: Brooks/Cole Publishing Company, 1981); and TLC Group, "Beware the 5 Stages of Grief," http://www.counselingforloss. com/clic/article8.htm; and University Counseling Services, "The Stages of Grief," http://www.saf.uwplatt.edu/counsel/depress/griefstg.htm. The innovative work of Elisabeth Kubler-Ross, published in 1969, (*On Death and Dying*), broke the ground for these considerations.

16: In Thomas Pope's *Good Scripts, Bad Scripts* (New York: Three Rivers Press, 1998), the author discusses the stages of grief and how they helped shape the structure of this film. I highly recommend the book.

PART FOUR: SECTION FIVE – GOOD VERSUS EVIL

1: *The Talented Mr. Ripley*; 1999, from the novel by Patricia Highsmith, screenplay by Anthony Minghella.

2: *Clear and Present Danger*; 1994, from the novel by Tom Clancy, screenplay by Donald Stewart and Steven Zaillian and John Milius.

3: *The War of the Roses*; 1989, from the novel by Warren Adler, screenplay by Michael Leeson.

4: *Pollyanna*; 1960, based on the novel by Eleanor H. Porter, screenplay by David Swift.

5: *Predator*; 1987, written by Jim Thomas & John Thomas.

6: *Absence of Malice*; 1981, screenplay by Kurt Luedtke.

PART FOUR: SECTION SIX – PARENTS

1: *The Equalizer*; created by Michael Sloan and Richard Lindheim; "Lady Cop," originally aired October 16, 1985, written by Joel Surnow and Maurice Hurley; "Reign of Terror," December 11, 1985, story by Steve Bello, teleplay by Steve Bello and Coleman Luck; "Prisoners of Conscience," April 27, 1989, written by Robert Eisele.

2: *Murder, She Wrote*; created by Richard Levinson, William Link and Peter S. Fischer; "Corned Beef and Carnage," originally aired November 2, 1986, teleplay by Robert E. Swanson; "Showdown in Saskatchewan," April 10, 1988, teleplay by Dick Nelson, "Threshold of Fear," February 28, 1993, teleplay by James L. Novack.

3:   *Ever After*; 1998, written by Susannah Grant and Andy Tennant & Rick Parks.

4:   *House Arrest*; 1996, written by Michael Hitchcock.

5:   *Frequency*; 2000, written by Toby Emmerich.

PART FOUR: SECTION SEVEN – RELATIVES

1:   *Star Trek*; created by Gene Roddenberry; "The Cloud Minders," originally aired February 28, 1969, teleplay by Margaret Armen, story by David Gerrold and Oliver Crawford.

2:   *Peter O'Toole: Acting Out Loud*; A&E Biography

3:   *Soul Food*; 1997, written by George Tillman Jr.

4:   *The Parent Trap*; 1961, from the book *Das Doppelte Lottchen* by Erich Kastner, screenplay by David Swift.

5:   *The Parent Trap*; 1998, from the book *Das Doppelte Lottchen* by Erich Kastner, based on the screenplay by David Swift, script by Nancy Meyers & Charles Shyer.

6:   *Single White Female*; 1992, from the novel *SWF Seeks Same* by John Lutz, script by Don Roos.

7:   "Shatterday", Harlan Ellison (in *Shatterday*), (Boston: Houghton Mifflin Company, 1980), collection of stories, p. 315–332.

8:   *The Twilight Zone* (revival), "Shatterday," teleplay by Alan Brennert, based on the story by Harlan Ellison; starring Bruce Willis as Peter Jay Novis.

PART FOUR: SECTION EIGHT – COMMUNITY HEROES

1:   *Barbarosa*; 1982, written by William D. Wittliff.

2:   *Batman*; 1989, written by Sam Hamm, based on material by Bob Kane.

3:   *The Godfather*; 1972, written by Mario Puzo and Francis Ford Coppola, from the novel by Mario Puzo.

4:   The story of *Contact* has a logic hole regarding what must be called "statements of faith or experience." In the early portion of the film, Ellie's stance is one which requires evidence, therefore statements about religious experience, like Palmer's, can only be met with doubt. And it is implied that statements of faith are naive. Also, all those in official positions (at least those who have power over Ellie's progress) by claiming belief in God imply an acceptance of testimony of experience unsupported by objective evidence. And yet, after Ellie's return, when *she* is now asserting the reality of an experience unsupported (apparently) by objective evidence, the officials now ridicule such a stance. The storytellers are evidently unsure as to which is the proper attitude. In the end, whichever approach *Ellie* holds to becomes the "appropriate" attitude. As long as Ellie believes that beliefs unsupported by objective evidence are dubious, statements of faith are treated as naive. When Ellie insists on the reality of an experience for which she has no physical evidence (and which is subjective), the demand for such evidence is presented by the storytellers as being unfair.

5:    *Superman*; 1978, created by Jerry Siegel & Joe Shuster, story by Mario Puzo, script by Mario Puzo and David Newman & Leslie Newman, Robert Benton.

6:    I realize that this example runs the risk of sounding like proselytizing. I only ask that those who profess a faith other than Christianity consider the example as *story*. The storytellers of Jesus' story gave a definition and value to the elements of this Sacrifice. You are not obliged to believe that this story is objectively true. I only ask that you pay attention to the value the storytellers placed on the example.

7:    *Seven Samurai*; 1954, scenario by Shinobu Hashimoto, Hideo Oguni and Akira Kurosawa.

PART FIVE: SECTION ONE – SKY VERSUS EARTH

1:    *Top Gun*; 1986, screenplay by Jim Cash & Jack Epps.

2:    *Brazil*; 1985, written by Terry Gilliam, Charles McKeown, Tom Stoppard.

PART FIVE: SECTION TWO – TOWER VERSUS CAVE

1:    *Beauty and the Beast* (TV); created by Ron Koslow, "Once Upon a Time in the City of New York," originally aired September 25, 1987, written by Ron Koslow; "A Happy Life," April 8, 1988, written by Ron Koslow.

PART FIVE: SECTION THREE – SEA VERSUS LAND

1:    *Jaws;* 1975, written by Carl Gottlieb and Peter Benchley, from Benchley's novel.

2:    *Splash*; 1984, screen story by Bruce Jay Friedman, screenplay by Lowell Ganz & Babaloo Mandel and Bruce Jay Friedman.

PART FIVE: SECTION FOUR – THE WILDERNESS VERSUS THE CITY

1:    *Little Shop of Horrors*; 1986, written by Howard Ashman, from his musical based on Charles B. Griffith's 1960 screenplay.

2:    *Tombstone*; 1993, written by Kevin Jarre.

3:    *Logan's Run*; 1976, screenplay by David Zelag Goodman.

PART FIVE: SECTION FIVE – OTHER FEATURES

1:    *Volcano*, 1997, story by Jerome Armstrong, screenplay by Jerome Armstrong and Billy Ray.

2:    "Rules and Clues", short feature on the Collector's Edition Series DVD of The Sixth Sense. It includes a fuller discussion of the filmmakers' intentions.

PART SIX: THEME PARKS

1:    *M.A.S.H.*; "Peace on Us," originally aired September 25, 1978, written by Ken Levine & David Isaacs.

2:    *Six by Seuss: A Treasury of Dr. Seuss Classics*; Dr. Seuss (New York: Random House, 1991), "And To think I Saw It On Mulberry Street." p. 10–42.

JOURNEY OUTLINES

CHRISTOPHER VOGLER

JOSEPH CAMPBELL

M.M. GOLDSTEIN

KATHY LINTNER

DAVID ADAMS LEEMING

VLADIMIR PROPP

SCRIBBLER'S

ANTI-HERO JOURNEY

GRAIL QUESTS

Gawain

Perceval

Galahad

CHRISTOPHER VOGLER

Chris Vogler's version of the Hero's Journey was developed from Joseph Campbell's. Initially developed as a tool for story analysis, it became popular with Hollywood screenwriters as a tool for story construction. The implications of Vogler's terminology lead to the internalized aspects of the Hero's Journey, to what happens inside the Hero as he makes his choices.

1:   Ordinary World

2:   Call to Adventure

3:   Refusal of the Call

4:   Meeting the Mentor

5:   Crossing the First Threshold

6:   Tests, Allies, Enemies

7:   Approach to the Inmost Cave

8:   Supreme Ordeal

9:   Reward

10:   The Road Back

11:   Resurrection

12:   Return with the Elixir

The Writer's Journey, Christopher Vogler (Studio City, CA: Michael Wiese Productions, 1992).

JOSEPH CAMPBELL

Joseph Campbell's Hero's Journey outline is the most famous one available. One aspect of this outline is that it focuses on the external actions of the Hero. By that, I mean that more often than not the inciting factors for the incidents are external to the Hero. Rather than being prompted by internal reflection by the Hero, the actions can come in reaction to outside influences.

1: World of the Common Day

2: Call to Adventure

3: Refusal of the Call

4: Supernatural Aid

5: Crossing the First Threshold

6: The Belly of the Whale

7: Road of Trials

8: Meeting the Goddess

9: Woman as Temptress

10: Atonement with the Father

11: Apotheosis

12: The Ultimate Boon

13: Refusal of the Return

14: Magic Flight

15: Rescue From Within

16: Crossing the Threshold

17: Return

18: Master of the Two Worlds

19: Freedom to Live

M.M. GOLDSTEIN

M.M. Goldstein's version of the Hero's Journey outline compacts the elements of the Journey. By grouping elements conceptually in one stage, this outline helps a writer evaluate whether the story is wandering off track, or if a particular event is taking up disproportionate time. The groupings also remind us that combinations of elements of the Journey can be covered by as many swift sentences. This outline can be useful as a reality check, or a quick sketch guideline.

1: The Set Up; The Hero is introduced in his ordinary world

2: The Point of Attack or Call to Adventure; The Hero may be reluctant at first; The Hero is encouraged by a wise elder

3: The Initial Struggle; The Hero crosses the First Threshold

4: Complications; The Hero Faces His First Real Enemy or Challenge; The Hero encounters tests, enemies, allies

5: Valiant Attempts; The Hero approaches the Heart of the Enemy's Fortress; The Hero endures the Supreme Ordeal

6: Major crisis; The Hero seizes the sword, the Reward; Hero begins the Road Back, often chased by the bad guys

7: Climax - conclusion; Resolution; Moment of Resurrection, Return with the Elixir

"The Hero's Journey in Seven Sequences: A Screenplay Structure," M.M. Goldstein; http://www.newenglandfilm.com/archives/98September/sevensteps.htm

KATHY LINTNER

Dean Kathy Lintner of the Culver Academy developed this outline for teaching purposes. This outline seemed to me to be best geared for the Hero of Destiny. Stories about that sort of Hero have specialized needs, aspects that the writer has to address which might not come into play in a more "ordinary" story.

1: Mysterious or Miraculous Birth

2: Sequestered Childhood

3: Hero's True Identity Known Only to One

4: Completes Education with Wise Teacher

5: Call to Adventure

6: Revelation of Identity or Special Duty

7: Discovery of Virtues

8: Development of Special Powers

9: Journey of Arduous Tasks

10: Journey to Higher Plane / Descent to Darkness & Return

11: Journey Leads to Transformation

12: Hero creates Something Important

13: Conquest of Death / Ascent to Immortal

"Thirteen Steps of the Hero's Journey," Kathy Linter. http://culver.pvt.k12.in.us/academics/mythandlit/step13.html

DAVID ADAMS LEEMING

Leeming's outline also covers matters of the Hero of Destiny. It was used to organize texts from original source material that exemplified the elements of the Hero's Journey. He also introduces elements not found in other outlines.

1: The Miraculous Conception and Birth and the Hiding of the Child

2: Childhood, Initiation, and Divine Signs

3: Preparation, Meditation, and Withdrawal

4: Trial and Quest

5: Death and the Scapegoat

6: Descent to the Underworld

7: Resurrection and Rebirth

8: Ascension, Apotheosis, and Atonement

Mythology: The Voyage of the Hero, David Adams Leeming (Philadelphia: J.B. Lippincott Company, 1973)

VLADIMIR PROPP

Vladimir Propp drew the elements of his Hero's Journey outline from a study of folklore, particularly Russian folklore. His outline gives more detail than others, a factor which can help a writer in fine-tuning the story. A notable thing about his outline is its focus on the interrelation of the Hero and his home community. The nature of the Hero's relationship to his family and friends can affect the shape of the story. This outline also introduces the Villain or Opponent earlier as an active force in the story.

1: Family Member (older generation) absents self from home.

2: Interdiction addressed to hero

3: Interdiction violated

4: Villain attempts reconnaissance

5: Villain receives information about victim

6: Villain attempts to deceive victim & posses him or his belongings.

7: Victim submits to deception, unwittingly helps enemy.

8: Villain causes harm to member of family.

(variant) One member of family lacks something or desires to have something.

9: Misfortune/lack made known; hero requested or commanded; allowed to go or is sent.

10: Seeker agrees to or decides on counteraction

11: Hero leaves home.

12: Hero tested, interrogated, attacked; preparing for magical agent or helper.

13: Hero reacts to actions of future donor; hero does a service.

14: Hero acquires use of magical agent.

15: Hero transferred, delivered, led to whereabouts of an object of search.

16: Hero and villain join in direct combat

17: Hero is branded or wounded.

18: Villain is defeated.

19: Initial misfortune or lack is liquidated.

20:   The Hero returns

21:   The Hero is pursued.

22:   Rescue of hero from pursuit.

23:   Unrecognized hero arrives home.

24:   False hero presents unfounded claims

25:   Difficult task proposed for hero.

26:   Task resolved

27:   Hero is recognized.

28:   False villain exposed.

29:   Hero given new appearance.

30:   Villain is punished.

31:   Hero married; ascends the throne.

The Morphology of the Folktale; Vladimir Propp, translated by Laurence Scott, 2nd edition (Austin: University of Texas Press, 1968).

SCRIBBLER'S

This version of the Hero's Journey is the one I adapted from Propp's (the way Vogler's springs from Campbell's). I generalized aspects of Propp's outline in order to broaden the applications.

1: The Old World

2: The Missing Relative

3: The Prohibition to the Hero

4: Breaking the Prohibition

5: Enemy Seeks & Receives Information

6: Enemy's Successful Deception

7: Injury to Family

8: Call to Adventure

9: The Hero Sets Forth

10: Tests

11: Performance of a Service

12: Gaining an Aid

13: Path to the Goal

14: The Battle

15: The Price

16: The Victory

17: Completion of the Quest

18: The Road Home

19: Hindrance

20: Help

21: Unrecognized Victor

22: The Usurper

23: Providing Proof

24: Recognition

25: Judgment of All

26: The New World

THE ANTI-HERO JOURNEY

*A: **Becoming an Anti-Hero***

    1: The beginning state of fortune

    2: Unpreparedness

    3: Losses and Hazards

    4: Resistance

    5: Hinderers

    6: Movement

*B: **The Anti-Hero's regression***

    1: The First Change

    2: The Anti-Hero is Challenged

    3: The Victims

The Anti-Hero is indifferent to them.

    4: Opposition

    5: Refusal to Sacrifice

    6: Separation

*C: **Becoming a Tyrant***

    1: Claiming a prize

    2: Indulgence of Lust

    3: Self-Aggrandizement

D: *Consequences for the Antihero*

1:    Impossibility of Return

2:    Fall

3:    Isolation

4:    Devastation

5:    No Home

GRAIL QUESTS

The Grail Quest variations come from the work of Jessie L. Weston. Her study of Arthurian literature gives us these specialized quests.

Gawain

1:   The Hero travels with an Unknown, who is on a quest

2:   The Unknown dies

3:   The Hero takes up the Unknown's quest

4:   The Land is wasted because of the Unknown's death

5:   The Hero fails to completely fulfill the task

6:   The Land is partially restored

Perceval

1:   The Hero knows the object of the quest

2:   The King ails, the Land ails

3:   The Hero must recognize what will heal the King

4:   If the King is not healed, the Land will be devastated

Galahad

1:   The Hero is on a quest, for fulfillment of self

2:   The Hero is destined to succeed in the difficult quest

3:   The Hero heals the ailing King before he completes the quest

4:   The Land is healed

5:   The Hero achieves the goal of his quest

From *Ritual to Romance*, Jessie L. Weston (Garden City, NY: Doubleday Anchor Books, 1957).

HIERARCHIES

STAGES OF LIFE

Male

Female

MASLOW'S HIERARCHY OF NEED

PECK'S LEVELS OF SPIRITUAL DEVELOPMENT

THE STAGES OF GRIEF, OR RECEIVING TRAUMATIC NEWS

THE SEVEN DEADLY SINS

THE SEVEN VIRTUES

PARENTAL FIGURES

Father Figure

Mother Figure

STAGES OF LIFE

Male

1:    Noble Savage

2:    Phallic Man

3:    Warrior

4:    Wounded Male

5:    Mature Ruler

6:    Sage

Female

1:    Flower Child

2:    Young Woman

3:    Nurturer

4:    Wounded Woman

5:    Relational Woman

6:    Woman of Strength

MASLOW'S HIERARCHY OF NEED

1:    Survival

2:    Safety and Security

3:    Love and Belonging

4:    Esteem and Self-Respect

5:    Need to Know and Understand

6:    Aesthetic

7:    Self-Actualization

PECK'S STATES OF SPIRITUAL DEVELOPMENT

1: *Bottom (Stage One)*

Chaotic/Antisocial: The People of the Lie. Self-esteem is the most important thing to them, they are without spirituality, and they are utterly unprincipled. They are capable of pretending to be loving; relationships are self serving and manipulative; there is no mechanism to govern them other than their own will; they are self disciplined in service of their ambition.

2: *Falling (Stage Two)*

Formal/Institutional: They are dependent on an institution for their governance, are upset if the forms and rituals of their life are changed on them; God is external

3: *Threshold (Stage Three)*

Skeptic/Individual: They are questioning of set forms, committed and loving; they are truth seekers, often involved in society

4: *Rising (Stage Four)*

Mystical/Communal: They see cohesion beneath the surface of things, they speak in terms of paradox, and love to solve mysteries, but they know they'll encounter more mystery; they are usually comfortable with mystery.

STAGES OF GRIEF OR RECEIVING TRAUMATIC NEWS

1:   Denial

2:   Anger

3:   Survival

4:   Awakening

5:   Bargaining

6:   Depression

7:   Acceptance

8:   Forgiveness

9:   Transformation

THE SEVEN DEADLY SINS

1:   Sloth or Laziness

2:   Gluttony

3:   Envy

4:   Covetousness or Greed

5:   Lust

6:   Anger

7:   Pride

THE SEVEN VIRTUES

1:   Love

2:   Faith

3:   Hope

4:   Strength or Fortitude

5:   Temperance

6:   Justice

7:   Judgment or Prudence

PARENTAL FIGURES

Father Figure

Protector

Mentor

Priest

Judge

Ruler

Mother Figure

Nurturer

Encourager

Relator

Comforter

Ruler

BIBLIOGRAPHY AND WEBOGRAPHY

BOOKS

Alighieri, Dante; *The Divine Comedy, Vol. 2, Purgatory*; translated by Dorothy L. Sayers (Harmondsworth, Middlesex, England: Penguin Books, 1974)

Allan, Tony, et al.; *Gods of Sun and Sacrifice: Aztec & Maya Myth* (Myth and Mankind series) (New York: Time-Life Books, 1997)

Allan, Tony, et al.; *Journeys Through Dreamtime: Oceanian Myth* (Myth and Mankind series) (New York: Time-Life Books, 1999)

Allan, Tony, et al.; *Spirits of the Snow: Arctic Myth* (Myth and Mankind series) (New York: Time-Life Books, 1999)

Auerbach, Loren, et al.; *Sagas of the Norsemen: Viking and German Myth* (Myth and Mankind series) (New York: Time-Life Books, 1997)

Bernstein, Douglas A., et al.; *Psychology*, second edition (Boston: Houghton Mifflin Company, 1991)

The Bible; various translations.

Bonnet, James; *Stealing Fire From the Gods* (Studio City, CA: Michael Wiese Productions, 1999)

Campbell, Joseph; *The Hero with a Thousand Faces,* 2nd edition (Princeton, NJ: Princeton University Press, 1968, 1973)

Cox, Marian Roalfe; *An Introduction to Folklore* (Detroit: Singing Tree Press, 1968)

Crisp, Tony; *Dream Dictionary* (New York: Wings Books, 1990, 1993)

Daly, Kathleen N.; *Greek and Roman Mythology A to Z* (New York: Facts on File, 1992)

"Dawn of the Day", Steeleye Span

D'Epiro, Peter and Mary Desmond Pinkowish; *What Are the Seven Wonders of the World? and 100 Other Great Cultural Lists – Fully Explained* (New York: Anchor Books, Doubleday, 1998)

Ebert, Roger, compiler; *Ebert's Bigger Little Movie Glossary* (Kansas City, Missouri: Andrews McMeel Publishing, 1999)

Eliade, Mircea; *Gods, Goddesses, and Myths of Creation: A Thematic Source Book of the History of Religions* (New York: Harper & Row, 1967, 1974)

Eliade, Mircea; *Myths, Dreams, and Mysteries: The Encounter between Contemporary Faiths and Archaic Realities*; translated by Philip Mairet (New York: Harper & Row, 1957, 1960)

Eliot, Alexander; *The Universal Myths: Heroes, Gods, Tricksters and Others* (with contributions by Joseph Campbell and Mircea Eliade) (New York: Meridian Books, 1976, 1999)

The Folklore of World Holidays; edited by Robert H. Griffin and Ann H. Shurgin; 2nd edition (Detroit: Gale, 1999)

Frye, Northrop; *Fables of Identity* (New York: Harcourt, Brace and World, Inc., 1963)

Frye, Northrop; *Anatomy of Criticism: Four Essays* (Princeton, NJ: Princeton University Press, 1957, 1973)

Funk & Wagnals Standard Dictionary of Folklore, Mythology and Legend; Maria Leach, editor (New York: Harper & Row, 1984, 1972, 1950, 1949)

Gordon, Stuart; *The Encyclopedia of Myths and Legends* (London: Headline Book Publishing, 1993)

Grimm brothers; *Tales of the Brothers Grimm*; edited, selected and introduced by Clarissa Pinkola Estes, Ph.D. (New York: Quality Paperback Book Club, 1999)

Hicks, Cynthia & Robert; *The Feminine Journey: Understanding the Biblical Stages of a Woman's Life* (Colorado Springs, CO: NavPress Publishing Group, 1994)

Hicks, Robert; *The Masculine Journey: Understanding the Six Stages of Mankind* (Colorado Springs, CO: NavPress Publishing Group, 1993)

Holidays and Anniversaries of the World; Jennifer Mossman, editor, 2nd edition (Detroit: Gale Research, 1990)

Homer; *The Odyssey*; translated by Robert Fitzgerald (Garden City, NY: Anchor Books, 1963)

Japan: An Illustrated Encyclopedia (Tokyo: Kondansha, 1993)

Jordan, Michael; *Encyclopedia of Gods* (New York: Facts of File, 1993)

Kalish, Richard A.; *Death, Grief and Caring Relationships* (Monterey, CA: Brooks/Cole Publishing Company, 1981)

Leach, Marjorie; *Guide to the Gods*, edited by Michael Owen Jones & Frances Cattermole-Tally (Santa Barbara, CA: ABC-CLIO, Inc., 1992)

Leeming, David Adams; *Mythology: The Voyage of the Hero* (Philadelphia: J.B. Lippincott Company, 1973)

Malory, Sir Thomas; *L'Morte d'Arthur* (New York: Bramhall House, 1962)

Milton, John; *Paradise Lost*

The New American Desk Encyclopedia, third edition (New York: Penguin Books, 1993)

The New Larousse Encyclopedia of Mythology; translated by Richard Aldington and Delano Adams, from *Larousse Mythologie General*, edited by Felix Guirand (London: Hamlyn Publishing Group Limited, 1970, 1968, 1959)

Peck, M. Scott; *Further Along the Road Less Traveled* (New York: Simon & Schuster, 1993)

Propp, Vladimir; *The Morphology of the Folktale*; translated by Laurence Scott, 2nd edition (Austin: University of Texas Press, 1968)

Rogers, Robert; *The Double in Literature* (Detroit: Wayne State University, 1970)

Rufus, Anneli; *The World Holiday Book: celebrations for every day of the year* (San Francisco: HarperSanFrancisco, 1994)

Spencer, John and Anne; *Mysteries and Magic* (New York: TV Books, L.L.C., 1999)

Virgil; *The Aeneid of Virgil*; verse translation by Allen Mandelbaum (New York: Bantam Books, 1972)

Vogler, Christopher; *The Writer's Journey* (Studio City, CA : Michael Wiese Productions, 1992)

Webber, Elizabeth and Mike Feinsilber; *Merriam Webster's Dictionary of Allusions* (Springfield, Mass.: Merriam-Webster, Inc., 1999)

Weston, Jessie L.; *From Ritual to Romance* (Garden City, N.Y.: Doubleday Anchor Books, 1957)

Youngsman, Robert; *Scientific Blunders: A Brief History of How Wrong Scientists Can Sometimes Be* (New York: Carroll & Graf Publishers, Inc., 1998)

INTERNET SITES

Encyclopedia Britannica Online; http://www.britannica.com

Encyclopedia Mythica; http://www.pantheon.org

Goldstein, M.M.; "The Hero's Journey in Seven Sequences: A Screenplay Structure"; http://www.newenglandfilm.com/archives/98September/sevensteps.htm.

Huitt, William G., "Maslow's Hierarchy of Needs"; http://chiron.valdosta.edu/whuitt/col/regsys/maslow.html

Lintner, Kathy; http://www.culver/pvt.k12.in.us/academics/mythandlit/step13.html

TLC Group; "Beware the Five Stages of 'Grief'"; http://www.counselingforloss.com/clic/article8.htm

University Counseling Services; "The Stages of Grief"; http://www.saf.uwplatt.edu/counsel/depress/griefstg.htm

FILMOGRAPHY

After each entry, there are included notations of what discussions in the text reference that the film or television show.

ABSENCE OF MALICE (1981, Columbia Pictures)

> screenplay by Kurt Luedtke; directed by Sydney Pollack; starring Paul Newman (Michael Gallagher), Sally Field (Megan Carter), Bob Balaban (Elliot Rosen), Wilford Brimley (James Wells), Don Hood (DA James Quinn)

> Judgment

ALL THE PRESIDENT'S MEN (1976, Warner Bros.)

> written by Carl Bernstein & Bob Woodward (from their book), and William Goldman; directed by Alan J. Pakula; starring Dustin Hoffman (Carl Bernstein), Robert Redford (Bob Woodward), Jason Robards (Ben Bradlee), Hal Holbrook (Deep Throat)

> Interdiction / Straight Drama / Ruler / Cave

AMERICAN BEAUTY (1999, DreamWorks SKG)

> written by Alan Ball; directed by Sam Mendes; starring Kevin Spacey (Lester Burnham), Annette Bening (Caroline Burnham), Thora Birch (Jane Burnham), Mena Suvari (Angela Hayes)

> Downturn Drama / Vegetation-Garden

AMERICAN GRAFFITI (1973, Universal Pictures)

> written by George Lucas and Gloria Katz; directed by George Lucas; starring Richard Dreyfuss (Curt Henderson), Ron Howard (Steve Bolander), Charles Martin Smith (Terry "The Toad" Fields), Paul Le Mat (John Milner), Cindy Williams (Laurie Henderson), Candy Clark (Debbie Dunham), Mackenzie Phillips (Carol), Bo Hopkins (Joe), Suzanne Somers (Blonde in T-Bird)

> Summer

BABY BOOM (1987, MGM-UA)

written by Nancy Meyers, Charles Shyer; directed by Charles Shyer; starring Diane Keaton (J.C. Wiatt)

> Nurturer

BABYLON 5 (TV) (Warner Bros.)

created by J. Michael Straczynski

starring Bruce Boxleitner (John Sheridan), Mira Furlan (Delenn), Jerry Doyle (Michael Garibaldi), Richard Biggs (Stephen Franklin), Stephen Furst (Vir Cotto), Claudia Christian (Susan Ivanova), Bill Mumy (Lennier)

"Sleeping in Light" (1998: original air date: November 25, 1998)

written by J. Michael Straczynski; directed by J. Michael Straczynski; guest starring Wayne Alexander (Lorien)

> Ascent, Apotheosis / Sunrise

"There All the Honor Lies" (1995: original air date: April 27, 1995)

written by Peter David; directed by Mike Vejar; guest starring Sean Gregory Sullivan (Ashan)

> Scapegoat

BARBAROSA (1982, Universal Pictures)

written by William D. Wittliff; directed by Fred Schepisi; starring Willie Nelson (Barbarosa), Gary Busey (Karl Westover), Gilbert Roland (Don Braulio), Isela Vega (Josephina), Alma Martinez (Juanita), Danny De La Paz (Eduardo)

> Outlaw Hero-Failure & Inspiration

BATMAN (1989, Warner Bros.)

written by Sam Hamm, based on material by Bob Kane; directed by Tim Burton; starring Michael Keaton (Batman/Bruce Wayne), Jack Nicholson (Joker/Jack Napier), Kim Basinger (Vicki Vale), Pat Hingle (Commissioner Gordon), Robert Wuhl (Alexander Knox)

> Outlaw Hero

BEAUTY AND THE BEAST (1991, DISNEY)

story by Roger Allers, animation screenplay by Linda Woolverton; directed by Gary Trousdale and Kirk Wise; starring the voices of Paige O'Hara (Belle), Robby Benson (the Beast), Richard White (Gaston), Rex Everhart (Maurice)

> Starting Out / Tower v. Cave

BEAUTY AND THE BEAST (TV) (Republic Pictures)

created by Ron Koslow

"Once Upon a Time in The City of New York" (1987: original air date Sept. 25, 1987); written by Ron Koslow; directed by Richard Franklin

"A Happy Life" (1988: original air date April 8, 1988); written by Ron Koslow; directed by Victor Lobl

starring Linda Hamilton (Catherine Chandler), Ron Perlman (Vincent).

> Tower v. Cave

THE BIRDS (1963, Universal Pictures)

story by Daphne DuMaurier, script by Evan Hunter; directed by Alfred Hitchcock; starring Rod Taylor (Mitch Brenner), Tippi Hedren (Melanie Daniels), Jessica Tandy (Lydia Brenner), Suzanne Pleshette (Annie Hayworth), Veronica Cartwright (Cathy Brenner)

> Day vs. Night

BLACK WIDOW (1986, 20ᵗʰ Century Fox)

written by Ronald Bass; directed by Bob Rafelson; starring Debra Winger (Alexandra Barnes), Theresa Russell (Catherine), Sami Frey (Paul), Nicol Williamson (William), Terry O'Quinn (Bruce)

> Shapeshifter

THE BOUNTY (1984, Orion Pictures)

written by Robert Bolt, based on the novel by Richard Hough; directed by Roger Donaldson; starring Mel Gibson (Fletcher Christian), Anthony Hopkins (Lt. William Bligh), Tevaite Vernette (Mauatua, the king's daughter)

> Spiritual Development-Falling / Outlaw Hero / Sea v. Land

BRAVEHEART (1995, 20ᵗʰ Century Fox & Paramount Pictures)

written by Randall Wallace; directed by Mel Gibson; starring Mel Gibson (William Wallace), Patrick McGoohan (Edward I Longshanks), Angus MacFadyen (Robert the Bruce), Catherine McCormack (Murron), Sophie Marceau (Princess Isabelle), Ian Bannen (The Leper), James Robinson (Young William), Brendan Gleeson (Hamish), David O'Hara (Stephen), Alun Armstrong (Mornay)

> Refusal of Call / Shapeshifter / Betrayal / Outlaw Hero-Failure / Sacrifice / Fire

BRAZIL (1985, Universal Pictures)

written by Terry Gilliam, Charles McKeown, Tom Stoppard; directed by Terry Gilliam; starring Jonathan Pryce (Sam Lowry), Robert De Niro (Harry Tuttle), Kim Greist (Jill Layton), Katherine Helmond (Mrs. Lowry)

Sky v. Earth / City v. Nature / City-Dystopia

BRIDGE ON THE RIVER KWAI (1957, Columbia Pictures)

written from the novel by Pierre Boulle, by Carl Foreman and Michael Wilson, Calder Willingham; directed by David Lean; starring William Holden (Shears), Alec Guinness (Colonel Nicholson), Jack Hawkins (Major Warden), Sessue Hayakawa (Colonel Saito), James Donald (Maj. Clipton, Medical Officer)

Spiritual Development-Falling

CAT ON A HOT TIN ROOF (1958, MGM-UA)

written by Richard Brooks, James Poe, based on the play by Tennessee Williams; directed by Richard Brooks; starring Elizabeth Taylor (Maggie "The Cat" Pollitt), Paul Newman (Brick Pollitt), Burl Ives (Big Daddy), Jack Carson (Gooper), Madeleine Sherwood (Mae)

Summer (thwarted)

CHANGING HABITS (1997, Teagarden Pictures Inc)

written by Scott Davis Jones; directed by Lynn Roth; starring Moira Kelly (Susan "Soosh" Teague), Dylan Walsh (Felix Shepherd), Christopher Lloyd (Theo Teagarden), Eileen Brennan (Mother Superior)

Needs-Self actualization

CHINATOWN (1974, Paramount Pictures)

written by Robert Towne; directed by Roman Polanski; starring Jack Nicholson (J.J. "Jake" Gads), Faye Runaway (Evelyn Cross Mulwray), John Houston (Noah Cross), Darrell Zeroing (Hollis Mulwray)

Straight Drama

CITIZEN KANE (1941, RAO Radio Pictures)

written by Herman J. Mankiewicz and Orson Welles; directed by Orson Welles; starring Orson Welles (Charles Foster Kane), Joseph Cotton (Jedediah Leland), Dorothy Comingore (Susan Alexander), Agnes Moorehead (Mrs. Kane), Ruth Warrick (Emily Norton Kane), Young Charles Kane (Buddy Swan), George Coulouris (Walter Parks Thatcher), Erskine Sanford (Herbert Carter)

Anti-Hero / Pride

CLEAR AND PRESENT DANGER (1994, Paramount Pictures)

from the novel by Tom Clancy, screenplay by Donald Stewart and Steven Zaillian and John Milius; directed by Philip Noyce; starring Harrison Ford (Jack Ryan), William Dafoe (Clark), Henry Czerny (Robert Ritter), Harris Yulin (James Cutter), Donald Moffat (President Bennett), James Earl Jones (Adm. James Greer), Joaquim de Almeida (Felix Cortez)

Anger-Righteous

THE CLIENT (1994, Warner Bros.)

written by Akiva Goldsman and Robert Getchell, from the novel by John Grisham; directed by Joel Schumacher; starring Susan Sarandon (Reggie Love), Tommy Lee Jones (Roy Foltrigg), Brad Renfro (Mark Sway), Mary-Louise Parker (Dianne Sway)

Opponent Seeks Information / Wounded Woman / Woman of Strength

CLUELESS (1995, Paramount Pictures)

written by Amy Hickerling, from the novel *Emma* by Jane Austen; directed by Amy Heckerling; starring Alicia Silverstone (Cher Horowitz), Paul Rudd (Josh), Dan Hedaya (Mel Horowitz), Stacey Dash (Dionne), Justin Walker (Christian)

Ordinary World / Young Woman

CONTACT (1997, Warner Bros.)

written by Carl Sagan and Ann Druyan, from the novel by Carl Sagan; directed by Robert Zemeckis; starring Jodie Foster (Dr. Eleanor Ann Arroway), Jena Malone (Young Ellie), David Morse (Theodore Arroway), John Hurt (S.R. Hadden), Matthew McConaughey (Palmer Joss), Tom Skerritt (David Drumlin), James Woods (Michael Kitz), Angela Bassett (Rachel Constantine)

Man as Tempter / Quest / Coming Home / Divine Hero-Failure

DANCES WITH WOLVES (1990, Orion Pictures)

written by Michael Blake, from his novel; directed by Kevin Costner; starring Kevin Costner (Lt. Dunbar / Dances With Wolves), Graham Greene (Kicking Bird), Mary McDonnell (Stands With a Fist)

Divine Sign / Wilderness-Nature

DEAD POETS SOCIETY (1989, Touchstone)

written by Tom Schulman; directed by Peter Weir; starring Robin Williams (John Keating), Ethan Hawke (Todd Anderson), Robert Sean Leonard (Neil Perry)

Mentor as Hero

THE EDGE (1997, 20th Century Fox)

written by David Mamet; directed by Lee Tamahori; starring Anthony Hopkins (Charles Morse), Alec Baldwin (Robert "Bob" Green), Elle Macpherson (Mickey Morse)

Needs-Survival

EMPIRE STRIKES BACK (1980, 20th Century Fox)

story by George Lucas, screenplay by Leigh Brackett and Lawrence Kasdan; directed by Irvin Kershner; starring Mark Hamill (Luke Skywalker), Harrison Ford (Han Solo), Carrie Fisher (Princess Leia), David Prowse (Darth Vader), James Earl Jones (voice of Darth Vader), Alec Guinness (Obi-Wan (Ben) Kenobi), Frank Oz (voice of Yoda), Billy Dee Williams (Lando Calrissian)

Atonement With Father (Anti) / Price-Wound / Resurrection & Rebirth

ENTRAPMENT (1999, 20th Century Fox)

story by Ron Bass and Michael Hertzberg, screenplay by Ron Bass and William Broyles; directed by Jon Amiel; starring Sean Connery (Robert "Mac" MacDougal), Catherine Zeta-Jones (Virginia "Gin" Baker), Ving Rhames (Aaron Thibadeaux), Will Patton (Hector Cruz)

Shapeshifter

THE EQUALIZER (TV) (Universal)

created by Michael Sloan and Richard Lindheim

starring Edward Woodward (Robert McCall)

"Lady Cop" (original air date October 16, 1985)

written by Joel Surnow and Maurice Hurley; directed by Russ Mayberry; starring Steven Williams (Lt. Jefferson Burnett), Karen Young (Officer Sandra Stahl), Will Patton (Officer Nick Braxton), Esai Morales (Officer Miguel Canterra), Bruce MacVittie (Officer Frank Sergei)

"Prisoners of Conscience" (original air date April 27, 1989)

written by Robert Eisele; directed by Marc Laub; starring Tony Plana (Antonio Cruz), Pat Hingle (Waldo Jerrell), Dan O'Herlihy (Randall Payne), Robert Lansing (Control), Tim Woodward (Capt. William McCall)

"Reign of Terror" (original air date December 11, 1985)

story by Steve Bello, teleplay by Steve Bello and Coleman Luck; directed by Richard Compton; starring Lonette McKee (Dr. Elly Watson), Joe Maruzzo (Head), Fred Williamson (Lt. Mason Warren)

Father Figure

ERIN BROCKOVICH (2000, Columbia Pictures & Universal Pictures)

written by Susannah Grant; directed by Steven Soderbergh; starring Julia Roberts (Erin Brockovich), Albert Finney (Ed Masry), Aaron Eckhart (George), Marg Helgenberger (Donna Jensen), Tracey Walter (Charles Embry), Peter Coyote (Kurt Potter), Veanne Cox (Theresa Dallavale)

Relational Woman / Transformer

EVER AFTER (1998, 20th Century Fox)

written by Susanna Grant and Andy Tennant & Rick Parks; directed by Andy Tennant; starring Drew Barrymore (Danielle), Anjelica Huston (Baroness Rodmilla), Megan Dodds (Marguerite), Melanie Lynskey (Jacqueline)

Mother Figure / Fair & Dark

EXCALIBUR (1981, Orion Pictures)

written by Rospo Pallenberg and John Boorman, adapted by Rospo Pallenberg from Malory's *Le Morte D'Arthur*; directed by John Boorman; starring Nigel Terry (Arthur), Nichol Williamson (Merlin), Helen Mirren (Morgana), Cherie Lunghi (Guenevere), Paul Geoffrey (Perceval), Corin Redgrave (Cornwall), Katrine Boorman (Igrayne), Niall O'Brien (Kay), Clive Swift (Ector), Gabriel Byrne (Uther)

Hero of Destiny-Start / Grail Quest-Perceval / Sunset / Sage / Spiritual Development-Rising / Special Objects-Sword / Special Objects-Grail / Divine Hero

FIELD OF DREAMS (1989, Universal)

written by Phil Alden Robinson, based on the book *Shoeless Joe* by W.P. Kinsella; directed by Phil Alden Robinson; starring Kevin Costner (Ray Kinsella), James Earl Jones (Terence Mann), Burt Lancaster ("Doc" Graham), Amy Madigan (Annie Kinsella), Timothy Busfield (Mark), Gaby Hoffmann (Karin Kinsella), Ray Liotta (Shoeless Joe), Frank Whaley (Archie Graham), Dwier Brown (John Kinsella)

Summer

THE FIFTH ELEMENT (1997, Columbia Pictures)

story by Luc Besson, screenplay by Luc Besson & Robert Mark Kamen; directed by Luc Besson; starring Bruce Willis (Korben Dallas), Milla Jovovich (Leeloo)

Ordinary World / Grail Quest-Gawain

THE FIRST WIVES CLUB (1996, Paramount Pictures)

screenplay by Robert Harling, from the novel by Olivia Goldsmith; directed by Hugh Wilson; starring Bette Midler (Brenda Morelli Cushman), Goldie Hawn (Elise Eliot Atchinson), Diane Keaton (Annie MacDuggan Paradis)

Relational Woman

THE FISHER KING (1991, Columbia Pictures)

written by Richard LaGravenese; directed by Terry Gilliam; starring Jeff Bridges (Jack Lucas), Robin Williams (Parry), Mercedes Ruehl (Anne Napolitano), Amanda Plummer (Lydia Sinclair)

Wounded Man / Special Objects-Grail

FREQUENCY (2000, New Line Cinema)

written by Toby Emmerich; directed by Gregory Hoblit; starring Dennis Quaid (Frank Sullivan), James Caviezel (John Sullivan), Elizabeth Mitchell (Julia Sullivan).

Parents

THE FUGITIVE (1993, Warner Bros.)

story by David Twohy, based on the TV series by Roy Huggins, screenplay by Jeb Stuart and David Twohy; directed by Andrew Davis; starring Harrison Ford (Dr. Richard Kimble), Tommy Lee Jones (Samuel Gerard), Jeroen Krabbe (Dr. Charles Nichols)

Inmost Cave / Whale Belly / Performance of a Service / Gaining an Aid / Justice / Outlaw Hero

THE GODFATHER (1972, Paramount Pictures)

written by Mario Puzo and Francis Ford Coppola, from the novel by Mario Puzo; directed by Francis Ford Coppola; starring Marlon Brando (Don Vito Corleone), Al Pacino (Michael Corleone), Dianne Keaton (Kay Adams Corleone)

Divine Hero

GOLDFINGER (1964, United Artists)

screenplay by Richard Maibaum & Paul Dehn, from the novel by Ian Fleming; directed by Guy Hamilton; starring Sean Connery (James Bond), Honor Blackman (Pussy Galore), Gert Frote (Auric Goldfinger), Shirley Eaton (Jill Masterson), Tania Mallet (Tilly Masterson)

Phallic Man

GONE WITH THE WIND (1939, Metro Goldwyn Mayer)

from the novel by Margaret Mitchell, screenplay by Sidney Howard; directed by Victor Fleming (uncredited), George Cukor, Sam Wood); starring Clark Gable (Rhett Butler), Vivien Leigh (Scarlett O'Hara), Leslie Howard (Ashley Wilkes), Olivia de Havilland (Melanie Wilkes), Carroll Nye (Frank Kennedy)

Needs-Safety

THE GREEN MILE (1999, Warner Bros.);

> screenplay by Frank Darabont, based on the novel by Stephen King; directed by Frank Darabont; starring Tom Hanks (Paul Edgecomb), Michael Clarke Duncan (John Coffey), David Morse (Brutus "Brutal" Howell), James Cromwell (Warden Hal Moores), Doug Hutchison (Percy Wetmore), Patricia Clarkson (Melinda Moores), Sam Rockwell ("Wild Bill" Wharton)

>> Conquest of Death-Immortality / Transformer / Holy Ones / Death / Strength / Sacrifice

GREYSTOKE: THE LEGEND OF TARZAN, LORD OF THE APES (1984, Warner Bros.)

> written by P.H. Vazak (Robert Towne) and Michael Austin, from the novel by Edgar Rice Burroughs; directed by Hugh Hudson; starring Christopher Lambert (Tarzan/ John Clayton), Ian Holm (Phillippe d'Arnot), Ralph Richardson (Earl of Greystoke), Andie MacDowell (Jane Porter)

>> Noble Savage

GROSSE POINTE BLANK (1997, Caravan Pictures & Hollywood Pictures)

> story by Tom Jankiewicz; screenplay by Tom Jankiewicz and D.V. DeVincentis & Steve Pink & John Cusack; directed by George Armitage; starring John Cusack (Martin Blank), Minnie Driver (Debi Newberry), Alan Arkin (Dr. Oatman), Dan Aykroyd (Grocer), Mitchell Ryan (Mr. Bert Newberry)

>> Upturn Drama

GROUNDHOG DAY (1993, Columbia Pictures)

> story by Danny Rubin, screenplay by Danny Rubin and Harold Ramis; directed by Harold Ramis; starring Bill Murray (Phil Connors), Andie MacDowell (Rita)

>> Old World / Winter / Holidays / Grief-Stages

HAMLET (1990, Warner Bros.)

> screenplay by Christopher De Vore, Franco Zeffirelli, William Shakespeare, from Shakespeare's play; directed by Franco Zeffirelli; starring Mel Gibson (Hamlet), Glenn Close (Gertrude), Alan Bates (Claudius), Paul Scofield (the Ghost), Ian Holm (Polonius), Helena Bonham Carter (Ophelia), Stephen Dillane (Horatio), Nathaniel Parker (Laertes)

>> Downturn Drama / Sloth / Temperance / Tower v. Cave

HARRY POTTER AND THE SORCERER'S STONE (2001, Warner Brothers)

screenplay by Steven Kloves, from the novel by J.K. Rowling; directed by Chris Columbus; starring Daniel Radcliffe (Harry Potter), Richard Harris (Dumbledore)

Ordinary World

HIS GIRL FRIDAY (1940, Columbia Pictures)

screenplay by Charles Lederer, from the play *The Front Page* by Ben Hecht and Charles MacArthur; directed by Howard Hawks; starring Cary Grant (Walter Burns), Rosalind Russell (Hildy Johnson), Ralph Bellamy (Bruce Baldwin), John Qualen (Earl Williams), Helen Mack (Molly Malloy)

Ordinary World / Call to Adventure / Man as Tempter / Relational Woman / Woman of Strength

HOPE FLOATS (1998, 20th Century Fox)

written by Steven Rogers; directed by Forest Whitaker; starring Sandra Bullock (Birdee Pruitt), Gena Rowlands (Ramona Calvert), Mae Whitman (Bernice Pruitt), Michael Pare (Bill Pruitt)

Flower Child

HOUSE ARREST (1996, MGM)

written by Michael Hitchcock; directed by Harry Winer; starring Jamie Lee Curtis (Janet Beindorf), Kevin Pollak (Ned Beindorf), Kyle Howard (Grover Beindorf)

Parents

THE HUNT FOR RED OCTOBER (1990, Paramount Pictures)

screenplay by Larry Ferguson and Donald Stewart, based on the novel by Tom Clancy; starring Sean Connery (Capt. Marko Ramius), Alec Baldwin (Jack Ryan), James Earl Jones (Adm. James Greer), Richard Jordan (National Security Advisor Jeffrey Pelt)

Herald

INDIAN SUMMER (1993, Touchstone)

written by Mike Binder; directed by Mike Binder; starring Alan Arkin (Uncle Lou Handler), Bill Paxton (Jack Belston), Matt Craven (Jamie Ross), Elizabeth Perkins (Jennifer Morton), Kevin Pollak (Brad Berman), Vincent Spano (Matt Berman), Julie Warner (Kelly Berman), Diane Lane (Beth Warden), Kimberly Williams (Gwen Daugherty)

Atonement With Father / Fall / Father Figure

INDIANA JONES AND THE LAST CRUSADE (1989, Paramount Pictures)

story by George Lucas and Menno Meyjes; screenplay by Jeffrey Boam (with Tom Stoppard, uncredited); directed by Steven Spielberg; starring Harrison Ford (Indiana Jones), Sean Connery (Professor Henry Jones), Alison Doody (Dr. Elsa Schneider), Denhold Elliott (Marcus Brody), Julian Glover (Walter Donovan), River Phoenix (Young Indy)

> Absent Relative / Opponent Seeks Information / Tests, Allies & Enemies / Temptress / Atonement With Father / The Boon / Sunset / Special Objects-Grail / Father Figure

THE IRON GIANT (1999, Warner Bros.)

screen story by Brad Bird, script by Tim McCanlies, based on the book *The Iron Man* by Ted Hughes; direct by Brad Bird; starring the voices of Eli Marienthal (Hogarth Hughes), Jennifer Aniston (Annie Hughes), Harry Connick Jr. (Dean McCappin), Vin Diesel (the Iron Giant), Christopher McDonald (Kent Mansley)

> Education / Special Objects / Theme Parks-Superman

IT'S A WONDERFUL LIFE (1946, RAO Radio Pictures)

story "The Greatest Gift" by Philip Van Doren Stern, screenplay by Frances Goodrich & Albert Hackett and Frank Capra, additional scenes by Jo Swerling; directed by Frank . Capra; starring James Stewart (George Bailey), Donna Reed (Mary Hatch Bailey), Lionel Barrymore (Mr. Henry F. Potter), Todd Karns (Harry Bailey), Henry Travers (Clarence), Thomas Mitchell (Uncle Billy)

> Supreme Ordeal / Reward / Winter / Holidays / Mature Ruler / Vegetation-Garden

THE JACKAL (1997, Universal Pictures)

written by Chuck Pfarere, based on Kenneth Ross's screenplay *The Day of the Jackal*, from the novel by Frederick Forsyth; directed by Michael Caton-Jones; starring Bruce Willis (the Jackal), Richard Gere (Declan Mulqueen), Sidney Poitier (Preston), Diane Venora (Valentina Koslova), Mathilda May (Isabella)

> Warrior

JAWS (1975, Universal Pictures)

written by Carl Gottlieb and Peter Benchley, from Benchley's novel; directed by Steven Spielberg; starring Roy Scheider (Martin Brody), Robert Shaw (Quint), Richard Dreyfuss (Matt Hooper)

> Sea v. Land

KING LEAR (1984, Granada Television)

written by William Shakespeare; directed by Michael Elliott; starring Laurence Olivier (King Lear), Diana Rigg (Regan), Dorothy Tutin (Goneril), Anna Calder-Marshall (Cordelia), Gloucester (Leo McKern), Robert Lindsay (Edmund), David Threlfall (Edgar)

Winter

LADYHAWKE (1985, 20ᵗʰ Century Fox & Warner Bros.)

story by Edward Khmara, script by Edward Khmara and Michael Thomas and Tom Mankiewicz; directed by Richard Donner; starring Matthew Broderick (Phillipe, the Mouse), Rutger Hauer (Etienne Navarre), Michelle Pfeiffer (Isabeau), Leo McKern (Imperius), John Wood (Bishop)

Meeting the Goddess / Day v. Night / Lovers

LAWRENCE OF ARABIA (1962, Columbia Pictures)

screenplay by Robert Bold, from the book by T.E. Lawrence; directed by David Lean; starring Peter O'Toole (Lawrence), Omar Sharif (Sherif Ali ibn el Kharish), Alec Guinness (Feisal), Jack Hawkins (General Allenby)

Meditation & Withdrawal / Day v. Night / Mentor / Fair & Dark / Doubles

LETHAL WEAPON (1987, Warner Bros.)

written by Shane Black; directed by Richard Donner; starring Mel Gibson (Martin Riggs), Danny Glover (Roger Murtaugh), Traci Wolfe (Rianne Murtaugh)

Warrior / Temperance / Doubles

LITTLE SHOP OF HORRORS (1986, The Geffen Company)

written by Howard Ashman, from his musical based on Charles B. Griffith's 1960 screenplay; directed by Frank Oz; starring Rick Moranis (Seymour Krelborn), Ellen Greene (Audrey), Vincent Gardenia (Mr. Mushnik), Levi Stubbs (voice of Audrey II)

Nature-Chaos

LOGAN'S RUN (1976, MGM-UA)

screenplay by David Zelag Goodman; directed by Michael Anderson; starring Michael York (Logan), Jenny Agutter (Jessica), Richard Jordan (Francis), Peter Ustinov (Old Man)

City-Dystopia

THE LORD OF THE RINGS: THE FELLOWSHIP OF THE RINGS (2001, New Line Cinema)

screenplay by Fran Walsh & Philippa Boyens & Peter Jackson, from the novel by J.R.R. Tolkien, directed by Peter Jackson; starring Elijah Wood (Frodo Baggins), Ian McKellen (Gandalf), Ian Holm (Bilbo Baggins)

Ordinary World / Absent Relative

MACBETH (1971, Caliban Films & Playboy Productions)

written by Roman Polanski, Kenneth Tynan, and William Shakespeare, based on Shakespeare's play; directed by Roman Polanski; starring Jon Finch (Macbeth), Francesca Annis (Lady Macbeth), Martin Shaw (Banquo), Terence Bayler (Macduff), Stephen Chase (Malcolm), Nicholas Selby (Duncan), Keith Chegwin (Fleance)

Anti-Hero

MALTESE FALCON (1941, Warner Bros.)

written by John Huston, based on the novel by Dashiell Hammett; directed by John Huston; starring Humphrey Bogart (Sam Spade), Mary Astor (Brigid O'Shaughnessy), Peter Lorre (Joel Cairo), Sydney Greenstreet (Kasper Gutman), Elisha Cook, Jr. (Wilmer Cook), Effie Perine (Lee Patrick), Ward Bond (Det. Sgt. Tom Polhaus), Jerome Cowan (Miles Archer)

Needs-To Know

MANHUNTER (1986, DeLaurentiis Entertainment Group)

screenplay by Michael Mann, from the novel *Red Dragon* by Thomas Harris; directed by Michael Mann; starring William Petersen (Will Graham), Dennis Farina (Jack Crawford), Brian Cox (Dr. Hannibal Lecter), Tom Noonan (Francis Dollarhyde)

Call to Adventure / Opponent Seeks Information

M.A.S.H. (TV)

based on the film *M.A.S.H.,* written by Ring Lardner Jr., from the novel by Richard Hooker, directed by Robert Altman.

series created by Larry Gelbart

starring Alan Alda (Hawkeye Pierce), Wayne Rogers (Trapper John MacIntire), Larry Linville (Maj. Frank Burns), Loretta Swit (Maj. Margaret "Hot Lips" Houlihan), Harry Morgan (Colonel Sherman T. Potter)

"House Arrest" (original air date February 4, 1975); written by Jim Fritzell & Everett Greenbaum; directed by Hy Averback; guest starring Mary Wickes (Colonel Rachel Reese)

"The Novocain Mutiny" (original air date January 27, 1976); written by Burt Prelutsky; directed by Harry Morgan

"Operation Noselift" (original air date January 19, 1974); written by Erik Tarloff; directed by Hy Averback; guest starring Todd Susman (Private Baker), Stuart Margolin (Maj. Stanley Robbins, E.N.T. Surgeon)

Spiritual Development-Falling

"Peace on Us" (original air date September 25, 1978); written by Ken Levine & David Isaacs; directed by George Tyne

Constant Jeopardy Syndrome

THE MASK (1994, New Line Cinema)

story by Michael Fallon and Mark Verheiden, and script by Mike Werb; directed by Chuck Russell; starring Jim Carrey (Stanley Ipkiss/The Mask), Amy Yasbeck (Peggy Brandt), Peter Riegert (Lt. Mitch Kellaway), Peter Greene (Dorian), Cameron Diaz (Tina Carlyle)

Trickster

THE MASK OF ZORRO (1998, TriStar Pictures and Amblin Entertainment)

story by Ted Elliot & Terry Rossio and Randal Jahnson, script by John Eskow and Ted Elliot & Terry Rossio; directed by Martin Campbell; starring Anthony Hopkins (Don Diego de la Vega/Zorro), Antonio Banderas (Alejandro Murrieta/Zorro), Catherine Zeta-Jones (Elena Montero), Stuart Wilson (Don Rafael Montero), Matt Letscher (Capt. Harrison Love)

Education / Initiation / Outlaw Hero

THE MATRIX (1999, Warner Bros.)

written by Andy Wachowski, Larry Wachowski; directed by Andy Wachowski, Larry Wachowski; starring Keanu Reeves (Neo), Laurence Fishburn (Morpheus), Carrie-Anne Moss (Trinity), Gloria Foster (Oracle)

Hero of Destiny-Start / Resurrection / Return With Elixir / Storms / Divine & Outlaw Hero

MONSTERS, INC. (2001, Walt Disney Pictures)

written by Robert L. Baird, Jill Culton, Peter Docter, Ralph Eggleston, Dan Gerson, Jeff Pidgeon, Rhett Reese, Jonathan Roberts, Andrew Stanton; directed by Peter Docter, David Silverman, Lee Onkrich; starring the voices of John Goodman (Sulley), Billy Crystal (Mike Wazowski), James Coburn (Henry J. Waternoose III).

Interdiction

MURDER, SHE WROTE

created by Richard Levinson, William Link and Peter S. Fischer; starring Angela Lansbury (Jessica Fletcher)

"Corned Beef and Carnage" (original air date November 2, 1986); teleplay by Robert E. Swanson; directed by John Llewellyn Moxey; starring Genie Francis (Victoria Brandon Griffin), Jeff Conaway (Howard Griffin)

"Showdown in Saskatchewan" (original air date April 10, 1988); teleplay by Dick Nelson; directed by Vincent McEveety; starring Kristy McNichol (Jill), Patrick Houser (Marty Reed), Larry Wilcox (Boone Talbot)

"Threshold of Fear" (original air date February 28, 1993); teleplay by James L. Novack; directed by Vincent McEveety; starring Cynthia Nixon (Alice Morgan), Michael Zelniker (Henry Phelps)

Mother Figure

MY FAIR LADY (1964, Warner Bros.)

written by Alan Jay Lerner, based on the play *Pygmalion* by George Bernard Shaw; directed by George Cukor; starring Audrey Hepburn (Eliza Doolittle), Rex Harrison (Professor Henry Higgins), Wilfrid Hyde-White (Colonel Hugh Pickering).

Mentor as Hero

MY FAVORITE YEAR (1982, MGM)

story by Dennis Palumbo, script by Dennis Palumbo and Norman Steinberg; directed by Richard Benjamin; starring Peter O'Toole (Alan Swann), Mark Linn-Baker (Benjy Stone), Joseph Bologna (King Kaiser)

Grail Quest-Galahad

NORMA RAE (1979, 20th Century Fox)

written by Harriet Frank Jr. and Irving Ravetch; directed by Martin Ritt; starring Sally Field (Norma Rae Wilson Webster), Beau Bridges (Sonny Webster), Ron Leibman (Reuben Warshowsky)

Transformer

NORTH BY NORTHWEST (1959, MGM)

written by Ernest Lehman; directed by Alfred Hitchcock; starring Cary Grant (Roger Thornhill), Eva Marie Saint (Eve Kendall), James Mason (Phillip Vandamm), Leo G. Carroll (The Professor), Martin Landau (Leonard)

Coming Home / McGuffin / Open vs. Closed

NOTTING HILL (1999, Universal Pictures)

written by Richard Curtis; directed by Roger Mitchell; starring Julia Roberts (Anna Scott), Hugh Grant (William Thacker), Rhys Ifans (Spike)

Needs-Love & Belonging

AN OFFICER AND A GENTLEMAN (1982, Paramount Pictures)

written by Douglas Day Stewart; directed by Taylor Hackford; starring Richard Gere (Zack Mayo), Debra Winger (Paula Pokrifki), David Keith (Sid Worley), Louis Gossett, Jr. (Sergeant Emil Foley)

Threshold Guardian

OUTBREAK (1995, Warner Bros.)

written by Laurence Dworet & Robert Roy Pool; directed by Wolfgang Peterson; starring Dustin Hoffman (Sam Daniels), Rene Russo (Robby Keough), Morgan Freeman (General Billy Ford), Donald Sutherland (General Donald McClintock), J.T. Walsh (White House advisor)

Transformer / Spiritual Development-Falling

THE PARENT TRAP (1961, Walt Disney Productions)

from the book *Das Doppelte Lottchen* by Erich Kastner, screenplay by David Swift; directed by David Swift; starring Hayley Mills (Sharon McKendrick/Susan Evers), Maureen O'Hara (Margaret "Maggie" McKendrick), Brian Keith (Mitch Evers), Ruth McDevitt (Miss Inch)

Double

THE PARENT TRAP (1998, Walt Disney Productions)

from the book *Das Doppelte Lottchen* by Erich Kastner, based on the screenplay by David Swift, script by Nancy Meyers & Charles Shyer; directed by Nancy Meyers; starring Lindsay Lohan (Hallie Parker/Annie James), Dennis Quaid (Nick Parker), Natasha Richardson (Elizabeth James)

Double

PATCH ADAMS (1998, Universal Pictures)

from the book *Gesundheit: Good Health Is a Laughing Matter* by Hunter Doherty Adams & Maureen Mylander, screenplay by Steve Oedekerk; starring Robin Williams (Hunter "Patch" Adams), Monica Potter (Carin Fisher), Daniel London (Truman Schiff)

Transformer

PETER PAN (1955, NBC)

from the book and play by J. M. Barrie, adapted by Jerome Robbins; directed by Dominic Dunne and Clark Jones; starring Mary Martin (Peter Pan); Cyril Richard (Mr. Darling/ Capt. Hook); Kathleen Nolan (Wendy/ Jane), Joe E. Marks (Smee)

Noble Savage

PETER PAN (1953, Walt Disney Productions)

from the play by J. M. Barrie, script by Milt Banta, Bill Cottrell, Winston Hibler, Bill Peet, Erman Penner, Joe Rinaldi, Ted Sears, Ralph Wright; directed by ; starring the voices of Bobby Driscoll (Peter Pan), Kathryn Beaumont (Wendy), Hans Conried (Mr. Darling/ Capt. Hook), Bill Thompson (Smee)

Noble Savage

PHENOMENON (1996, Touchstone Pictures)

written by Gerald DiPego; directed by Jon Turteltaub; starring John Travolta (George Malley), Kyra Sedgwick (Lace Pennamin), Forest Whitaker (Nate Pope), Robert Duvall (Doc), Jeffrey DeMunn (Professor John Ringold), Richard Kiley (Dr. Wellin), Brent Spiner (Dr. Bob Niedorf)

Lightning

PLEASANTVILLE (1998, New Line Cinema)

written by Gary Ross; directed by Gary Ross; starring Tobey Maguire (David/ Bud Parker), Jeff Daniels (Bill Johnson), Joan Allen (Betty Parker), William H. Macy (George Parker), J.T. Walsh (Big Bob), Reese Witherspoon (Jennifer/ Mary Sue Parker), Marley Shelton (Margaret), Paul Walker (Skip Martin)

Rain / Rainbow / Color

POLLYANNA (1960, Walt Disney Pictures)

from the novel by Eleanor H. Porter, screenplay by David Swift; directed by David Swift; starring Hayley Mills (Pollyanna Whittier), Jane Wyman (Aunt Polly Harrington), Richard Egan (Dr. Edmond "Ed" Chilton), Agnes Moorehead (Mrs. Snow), Mary Grace Canfield (Angelica "Angey")

Hope

PREDATOR (1987, 20th Century Fox)

written by Jim Thomas & John Thomas; directed by John McTiernan; starring Arnold Schwarzenegger (Major Dutch Schaeffer), Carl Weathers (Dillon); Bill Duke (Sergeant Mac Elliot), Jesse Ventura (Blain), Sonny Landham (Billy Sole), Shane Black (Hawkins), Kevin Peter Hall (the Predator)

Strength / Sacrifice

THE QUIET MAN (1952, Republic Pictures)

from the story "Green Rushes" by Maurice Walsh, screenplay by Frank Nugent; directed by John Ford; starring John Wayne (Sean Thornton), Maureen O'Hara (Mary Kate Danaher), Barry Fitzgerald (Michaleen Flynn), Victor McLaglen (Red Will Danaher), Ward Bond (Father Peter Lonergan)

Wounded Man

RAIDERS OF THE LOST ARK (1981, Paramount Pictures)

story by George Lucas and Philip Kaufman, script by Lawrence Kasdan; directed by Steven Spielberg; starring Harrison Ford (Indiana Jones), Karen Allen (Marion Ravenwood), Paul Freeman (Rene Belloq), Denhold Elliot (Marcus Brody)

Inmost Cave

RAISE THE TITANIC (1980, ITC)

from the novel by Clive Cussler, screenplay by Eric Hughes, Adam Kennedy; directed by Jerry Jameson; starring Jason Robards (Adm. James Sandecker), Richard Jordan (Dirk Pitt), David Selby (Dr. Gene Seagram)

Grail & Sword / Spectacle

RAN (1985, Nippon Herald Films & Orion Pictures)

written by Masato Ide, Akira Kurosawa, Hideo Oguni, based on William Shakespeare's play *King Lear*; directed by Akira Kurosawa; starring Tatsuya Nakadai (Lord Hidetora Ichimonji)

Winter

REAL GENIUS (1985, RCA)

written by Neal Israel, Pat Proft, Peter Torokvei; directed by Martha Coolidge; starring Val Kilmer (Chris Knight), William Atherton (Professor Jerry Hathaway), Jon Gries (Lazlo Hollyfeld), Gabriel Jarret (Mitch Taylor), Robert Prescott (Kent Torokvei)

Initiation / Spiritual Development-Threshold / Hermit

RETURN OF THE JEDI (1983, 20th Century Fox)

story by George Lucas, screenplay by Lawrence Kasdan and George Lucas; directed by Richard Marquand; starring Mark Hamill (Luke Skywalker), Harrison Ford (Han Solo), Carrie Fisher (Princess Leia Organa), Billy Dee Williams (Lando Calrissian), David Prowse (Darth Vader), James Earl Jones (voice of Darth Vader), Alec Guinness (Ben Kenobi), Sebastian Shaw (Anakin Skywalker), Ian McDiarmid (Emperor Cos Palpatine)

Apotheosis / Price-Wound / Temptation / Faith / Sacrifice

ROMEO AND JULIET (1968, Paramount Pictures)

from the play by William Shakespeare, screenplay by Franco Brusati, Maestro D'Amico, Franco Zeffirelli; directed by Franco Zeffirelli; starring Leonard Whiting (Romeo Montague), Olivia Hussey (Juliet Capulet), John McEnery (Mercutio), Milo O'Shea (Friar Laurence), Michael York (Tybalt), Pat Heywood (Nurse)

Lovers

RONIN (1998, MGM)

story by J.D. Zeik; screenplay by J.D. Zeik and Richard Weisz (David Mamet); directed by John Frankenheimer; starring Robert De Niro (Sam), Jean Reno (Vincent), Natascha McElhone (Deirdre), Stellan Skarsgard (Gregor), Jonathan Pryce (Seamus)

McGuffin

THE SECRET GARDEN (1993, Warner Bros.)

from the novel by Frances Hodgson Burnett; screenplay by Caroline Thompson; starring Kate Maberly (Mary Lennox), Heydon Prowse (Colin Craven), Andrew Knott (Dickon), Maggie Smith (Mrs. Medlock), John Lynch (Lord Craven)

Spring / Vegetation-Garden

SEVEN SAMURAI (*Shichinin no samurai*) (1954, Toho Production)

scenario by Shinobu Hashimoto, Hideo Oguni and Akira Kurosawa; directed by Akira Kurosawa; starring Takashi Shimura (Kambei), Toshiro Mifune (Kikuchiyo), Yoshio Inaba (Gorobei), Seiji Miyaguchi (Kyuzo), Minoru Chiaki (Heihachi), Daisuke Kato (Shichiroji), Isao Kimura (Katsushiro), Keiko Tsushima (Shino)

Band of Companions

SHANE (1953, Paramount)

story by Jack Schaefer from his book, A.B. Guthrie, Jr.; directed by George Stevens; starring Alan Ladd (Shane), Jean Arthur (Marian Starrett), Van Heflin (Joe Starrett), Jack Palance (Wilson), Brandon De Wilde (Joey Starrett), Elisha Cook Jr. (Frank "Stonewall" Torrey)

Sunset / Thunder / Warrior / Fair & Dark

THE SILENCE OF THE LAMBS (1991, Orion Pictures)

from the novel by Thomas Harris, screenplay by Ted Tally; directed by Jonathan Demme; starring Jodie Foster (Clarice Starling), Anthony Hopkins (Dr. Hannibal Lecter), Scott

Glenn (Jack Crawford), Ted Levine (Jame "Buffalo Bill" Gumb), Anthony Heald (Dr. Frederick Chilton), Kasi Lemmons (Ardelia Mapp)

Inmost Cave / Whale Belly / Day v. Night / Sunset / Shadow / Holy Ones / Spiritual Development-Bottom / Spiritual Development-Threshold / Corrupter-Devil / Father Figure / Fair & Dark / Tower v. Cave

SINGING IN THE RAIN (1952, MGM)

written by Betty Comden, Adolph Green; directed by Stanley Donen, Gene Kelly; starring Gene Kelly (Don Lockwood), Donald O'Connor (Cosmo Brown), Debbie Reynolds (Kathy Selden), Jean Hagen (Lina Lamont)

Usurper

SINGLE WHITE FEMALE (1992, Columbia Pictures)

from the novel *SWF Seeks Same* by John Lutz, script by Don Roos; directed by Barbet Schroeder; starring Bridget Fonda (Allison Jones), Jennifer Jason Leigh (Hedra Carlson), Steven Weber (Sam Rawson)

Doubles

THE SIXTH SENSE (1999, Hollywood Pictures)

written and directed by M. Night Shyamalan; starring Bruce Willis (Malcolm Crowe), Haley Joel Osment (Cole Sear), Toni Collette (Lynn Sear), Olivia Williams (Anna Crowe)

Death-Threshold / Color

SLEEPY HOLLOW (1999, Paramount Pictures)

story by Washington Irving, screen story by Kevin Yagher & Andrew Kevin Walker, screenplay by Andrew Kevin Walker; directed by Tim Burton; starring Johnny Depp (Constable Ichabod Crane), Christina Ricci (Katrina Anne Van Tassel), Christopher Walken (the Hessian Horseman)

Autumn / Wild Hunt

SMILLA'S SENSE OF SNOW (1997, 20th Century Fox)

from the novel by Peter Hoeg, translated by Tiina Nunnally, script by Ann Biderman; directed by Bille August; starring Julia Ormond (Smilla Jasperson), Gabriel Byrne (the Mechanic), Richard Harris (Tork Hviid), Clipper Miano (Isaiah), Robert Loggia (Moritz Jasperson), Emma Croft (Benja)

Ice & Snow

SOLDIER (1998, Warner Bros.)

written by David Webb Peoples; directed by Paul Anderson; starring Kurt Russell (Sergeant Todd), Jason Scott Lee (Caine 607), Connie Nielsen (Sandra), Jason Isaacs (Colonel Mekum), Gary Busey (Captain Church)

Warrior

SOUL FOOD (1997, Fox 2000 Pictures)

written by George Tillman Jr.; directed by George Tillman Jr.; starring Vanessa L. Williams (Teri), Vivica A. Fox (Maxine), Nia Long (Bird), Michael Beach (Miles), Mekhi Phifer (Lem), Gina Ravera (Faith)

Fair & Dark

SPLASH (1984, Touchstone)

screen story by Bruce Jay Friedman, screenplay by Lowell Ganz & Babaloo Mandel and Bruce Jay Friedman; directed by Ron Howard; starring Tom Hanks (Allen Bauer), Daryl Hannah (Madison), John Candy (Freddie Bauer)

Sea v. Land

STAR TREK (TV) (Paramount)

created by Gene Roddenberry

"The Cloud Minders" (original air date, February 28, 1969); teleplay by Margaret Armen, story by David Gerrold and Oliver Crawford; directed by Jud Taylor; starring William Shatner (James T. Kirk), Leonard Nimoy (Spock), Diana Ewing (Droxine), Charlene Polite (Vanna)

Fair v. Dark

STAR TREK: GENERATIONS (1994, Paramount Pictures)

story by Rick Berman & Ronald D. Moore & Brannon Braga, script by Ronald D. Moore & Brannon Braga; directed by David Carson; starring Patrick Stewart (Capt. Jean-Luc Picard), William Shatner (Capt. James T. Kirk), Malcolm McDowell (Dr. Tolian Soran), Scott (James Doohan), Walter Koenig (Chekov)

Apotheosis

STAR TREK: THE NEXT GENERATION (TV) (Paramount Studios)

created by Gene Roddenberry

"Sins of the Father" (1990: original air date: March 19, 1990) written by Ronald D. Moore and W. Reed Moran, story by Drew Deighan; directed by Les Landau; starring Patrick Steward (Jean-Luc Picard), Michael Dorn (Worf), Tony Todd (Kurn), Charles Cooper (K'Mpec), Patrick Massett (Duras)

Scapegoat

STAR WARS (A NEW HOPE) (1977, 20th Century Fox)

written by George Lucas; directed by George Lucas; starring Mark Hamill (Luke), Harrison Ford (Han Solo), Carrie Fisher (Leia), Alec Guinness (Obi-Wan Kenobi), Phil Brown (Uncle Owen)

Ordinary World / Meeting the Mentor / Sage / Mentor / Herald

SUPERMAN (1978, Warner Bros.)

created by Jerry Siegel & Joe Shuster, story by Mario Puzo, script by Mario Puzo and David Newman & Leslie Newman, Robert Benton; directed by Richard Donner; starring Christopher Reeve (Clark Kent/Superman), Jeff East (young Clark), Glenn Ford (Jonathan Kent), Phyllis Thaxtor (Ma Kent), Margot Kidder (Lois Lane), Gene Hackman (Lex Luthor), Marlon Brando (Jor-El), Susannah York (Lara)

Divine Hero-Success

THE TALENTED MR. RIPLEY (1999, Miramax Films, Paramount Pictures)

from the novel by Patricia Highsmith, screenplay by Anthony Minghella; directed by Anthony Minghella; starring Matt Damon (Tom Ripley), Gwyneth Paltrow (Marge Sherwood), Jude Law (Dickie Greenleaf), James Rebhorn (Mr. Herbert Greenleaf)

Envy / Covetousness

TARZAN (1999, Walt Disney Productions)

from the novel by Edgar Rice Burroughs, screenplay by Tab Murphy and Bob Tzudiker & Noni White; directed by Chris Buck, Kevin Lima; starring the voices of Tony Goldwyn (Tarzan), Alex D. Linz (young Tarzan), Glenn Close (Kala), Lance Henriksen (Kerchak), Minnie Driver (Jane), Brian Blessed (Clayton)

Noble Savage / Parents

THE TERMINATOR (1984, Hemdale Film)

written by James Cameron & Gale Anne Hurd, William Wisher, from material by Harlan Ellison; directed by James Cameron; starring Arnold Schwarzenegger (the Terminator), Michael Biehn (Kyle Reese), Linda Hamilton (Sarah Connor)

Innocent-Fool / Savior

TERMINATOR 2: JUDGMENT DAY (1991, Carolco Pictures)

written by James Cameron & William Wisher; directed by James Cameron; starring Arnold Schwarzenegger (the Terminator), Linda Hamilton (Sarah Connor), Edward Furlong (John Connor), Robert Patrick (T-1000), Earl Boen (Dr. Silberman), Joe Morton (Miles Dyson)

Meeting the Goddess / Temptress / Wounded Woman

THELMA & LOUISE (1991, MGM-UA)

written by Callie Khouri; directed by Ridley Scott; starring Susan Sarandon (Louise Sawyer), Geena Davis (Thelma Dickinson), Harvey Keitel (Hal Slocumb), Christopher McDonald (Darryl), Michael Madsen (Jimmy), Brad Pitt (J.D.)

Needs-Self-respect

TOMBSTONE (1993, Hollywood Pictures)

written by Kevin Jarre; directed by George P. Cosmatos; starring Kurt Russell (Wyatt Earp), Val Kilmer (Doc Holliday), Sam Elliot (Virgil Earp), Powers Boothe (Curly Bill)

City-Order

TOP GUN (1986, Paramount Pictures)

screenplay by Jim Cash & Jack Epps; directed by Tony Scott; starring Tom Cruise (Lt. Pete "Maverick" Mitchell), Kelly McGillis (Charlotte "Charlie" Blackwood), Val Kilmer (Tom "Iceman" Kasnasky), Anthony Edwards (Lt. Nick "Goose" Bradshaw), Tom Skerritt (Comdr. Mike "Viper" Metcalf)

Sky v. Earth

THE TRUMAN SHOW (1998, Paramount Pictures)

written by Andrew Niccol; directed by Peter Weir; starring Jim Carrey (Truman Burbank), Ed Harris (Christof), Laura Linney ("Meryl"), Natascha McElhone (Sylvia)

Prohibition / Innocent-Fool / Corrupter-Devil

TWILIGHT ZONE (REVIVAL) (TV)

"Shatterday"(original air date Sept. 27, 1985);

teleplay by Alan Brennert, based on a story by Harlan Ellison; directed by Wes Craven; starring Bruce Willis (Peter Jay Novins)

Doubles

THE VIKINGS (1958, United Artists)

screenplay by Calder Willingham, adaption by Dale Wasserman, based on the novel by Edison Marshall; directed by Richard Fleischer; starring Kirk Douglas (Einar), Tony Curtis (Eric), Ernest Borgnine (Ragnar), Frank Thring (Aella)

Hanged Man

VOLCANO (1997, 20th Century Fox)

story by Jerome Armstrong, screenplay by Jerome Armstrong and Billy Ray; directed by Mick Jackson; starring Tommy Lee Jones (Mike Roark), Anne Heche (Dr. Amy Barnes), Gaby Hoffman (Kelly Roark)

Fire-Volcano

WALL STREET (1987, 20th Century Fox)

written by Stanley Weiser & Oliver Stone; directed by Oliver Stone; starring Michael Douglas (Gordon Gekko), Charlie Sheen (Bud Fox), Martin Sheen (Carl Fox), Daryl Hannah (Darien Taylor), Terence Stamp (Sir Larry Wildman), Hal Holbrook (Lou Mannheim), Tamara Tunie (Carolyn)

Shadow / Corrupter-Devil

THE WAR OF THE ROSES (1989, 20th Century Fox)

from the novel by Warren Adler, screenplay by Michael Leeson; directed by Danny DeVito; starring Michael Douglas (Oliver Rose), Kathleen Turner (Barbara Rose)

Anger-To Hate

WHITE NIGHTS (1985, Columbia Pictures)

story by James Goldman, script by James Goldman, Eric Hughes; directed by Taylor Hackford; starring Mikhail Baryshnikov (Nikolai Rodchenko), Gregory Hines (Raymond Greenwood), Isabella Rossellini (Darya Greenwood), Jerzy Skolimowski (Colonel Chaiko), Helen Mirren (Galina Ivanova)

Sun v. Moon / Needs-Aesthetic

WIZARD OF OZ (1939, Metro-Goldwyn-Mayer Pictures)

screenplay by Noel Langley, Florence Ryerson and Edgar Allan Woolf, from the book by L. Frank Baum; directed by Victor Fleming; starring Judy Garland (Dorothy), Margaret Hamilton (Wicked Witch of the West/Miss Gulch), Clara Blandick (Aunt Em)

Rainbow / Color

THE X-FILES

created by Chris Carter; starring David Duchovny (Fox Mulder), Gillian Anderson (Dana Scully)

"Chinga" (original air date February 8, 1998); written by Stephen King and Chris Carter; directed by Kim Manners; guest starring Susannah Hoffman (Melissa Turner), Jenny-Lynn Hutcheson (Polly Turner)

"Clyde Bruckman's Final Repose" (original air date October 13, 1995); written by Darin Morgan; directed by David Nutter; guest starring Peter Boyle (Clyde Bruckman), Stu Charno (the Puppet)

"Pilot" (original air date September 10, 1993); written by Chris Carter; directed by Robert Mandel; guest starring Charles Cioffi (Section Chief Scott Blevins)

Woman of Strength

YOU'VE GOT MAIL (1998, Warner Bros.)

screenplay by Nora Ephron & Delia Ephron, based on the screenplay *The Shop Around the Corner* by Samson Raphaelson, based on the play *Parfumerie* by Miklos Laszlo; directed by Nora Ephron; starring Tom Hanks (Joe Fox), Meg Ryan (Kathleen Kelly), Greg Kinnear (Frank Vavasky), Parker Posey (Patricia Eden)

Seasons-Winter

INDEX

Made in the USA
Columbia, SC
09 August 2018